Mélusine

Mélusine

Sarah Monette

ACE BOOKS, NEW YORK

THE BERKLEY PUBLISHING GROUP
Published by the Penguin Group
Penguin Group (USA) Inc.
375 Hudson Street, New York, New York 10014, USA
Penguin Group (Canada), 90 Eglinton Avenue East, Suite 700, Toronto, Ontario M4P 2Y3, Canada
(a division of Pearson Penguin Canada Inc.)
Penguin Books Ltd., 80 Strand, London WC2R 0RL, England
Penguin Group Ireland, 25 St. Stephen's Green, Dublin 2, Ireland (a division of Penguin Books Ltd.)
Penguin Group (Australia), 250 Camberwell Road, Camberwell, Victoria 3124, Australia
(a division of Pearson Australia Group Pty. Ltd.)
Penguin Books India Pvt. Ltd., 11 Community Centre, Panchsheel Park, New Delhi—110 017, India
Penguin Group (NZ), Cnr. Airborne and Rosedale Roads, Albany, Auckland 1310, New Zealand
(a division of Pearson New Zealand Ltd.)
Penguin Books (South Africa) (Pty.) Ltd., 24 Sturdee Avenue, Rosebank, Johannesburg 2196,
South Africa

Penguin Books Ltd., Registered Offices: 80 Strand, London WC2R 0RL, England

This book is an original publication of The Berkley Publishing Group.

Text design by Stacy Irwin.

First edition: August 2005

Library of Congress Cataloging-in-Publication Data

Monette, Sarah.
Mélusine / Sara Monette.— 1st ed.
p. cm.
ISBN 0-441-01286-8
1. Wizards—Fiction. 2. Fugitives from justice—Fiction. I. Title.

PS3613.O5246M46 2005
813'.6—dc22

2005045753

PRINTED IN THE UNITED STATES OF AMERICA

10 9 8 7 6 5 4 3 2 1

For A.L.M.

Mélusine

Introduction

Mildmay

This is the worst story I know about hocuses. And it's true.

Four Great Septads ago, back in the reign of Claudius Cordelius, there was a hocus named Porphyria Levant. The hocuses back then had this thing they could do, called the binding-by-forms, the obligation d'âme. It happened between a hocus and an annemer, an ordinary person, and it was like an oath of loyalty, only a septad times more. The hocus promised to protect the annemer from *everything,* including kings and other hocuses and basically anybody else who had an interest. The annemer promised to be the hocus's servant and do what they said and no backchat, neither. And they renounced their family and all their other connections, so it was like the only thing in the world that mattered to them was the hocus. And then there was a spell to stick it in place and make sure, you know, that nobody tried to back out after it was too late.

You can see the problem, right? Most half-bright folks can. But some hocuses were so powerful and so nasty that I guess it seemed like it was better to go ahead and do the obligation d'âme with a hocus you sort of trusted than to go wandering around waiting for a different hocus to get the drop on you.

So there was Porphyria Levant. And there was Silas Altamont. Silas Altamont was annemer, a guy who'd been the favorite of Lord Creon Malvinius, and then when Lord Creon got married, Silas Altamont was out on his ear, and scared shitless of Lord Creon's wife, who was way better connected than him, and was rumored to have three or four hocuses on her string to boot. And she was poison-green with jealousy, because she loved Lord Creon like a mad thing, and everybody knew he didn't give a rat's ass about her. So Silas Altamont goes to Porphyria Levant—who was powerful enough to protect him from Lisette Malvinia, no matter *who* she had running her errands—and begs Porphyria Levant to do the obligation d'âme. And Porphyria Levant smiles and says okay.

Now, the thing about the binding-by-forms, the way my friend Zephyr explained it to me, is that it lets the hocus *make* you do what they want. Except for kill yourself. They can't make you do that. But what Porphyria Levant tells Silas Altamont to do is fuck her. I've heard it different ways. Some people say Silas Altamont was beautiful as daylight, and Porphyria Levant had been hot for him for indictions. Some say Porphyria Levant didn't know he was molly, thought he was janus and wouldn't mind. And some say—and I got to admit, this is what I think—that she knew he was molly and that was why she did it. There are other stories about Porphyria Levant, and it's the kind of thing she *would* do.

Anyway, there's Silas Altamont. He's molly, and he's still in love with Creon Malvinius, but he has to do what the obligation d'âme says, and it says, You got to fuck Porphyria Levant and make her happy. And after a while he goes to her and says, "I can't stand this no more, please, let me stop or I'm going to go out and slit my wrists."

And Porphyria Levant says, "Silas," and smiles her little smile, "I forbid you to kill yourself."

That's what hocuses are like, and that's why, if you live in the Lower City of Mélusine, you keep one eye on the Mirador all the time, same way you would with a swamp adder. It's just common sense.

Part One

Chapter 1

Felix

The Hall of the Chimeras, having no windows, was lit by seven massive candelabra hanging above the mosaic floor like monstrous birds of prey. Their fledglings, twisted iron stands crowned with candles, rose up at intervals along the floor, interspersed with the busts of dead and ancient kings. At the east end of the hall—not that east and west mattered in the great, labyrinthine bulk of the Mirador—the Virtu of the Mirador on its obsidian plinth cast its own strange, underwater light, which reached down to touch the steel spearheads of the Lord Protector's throne, but reached no farther.

The Lords and Ladies Protector traditionally had a penchant for being painted in Lord Michael's Chair, as the throne had been called for one hundred seventy-seven years. Lord Stephen Teverius, Lord Protector these past nine years, had not yet commissioned the portrait to commemorate his reign, but I doubted that Stephen, who hated pomp, would choose that particularly iconic and self-important pose.

Pomp was not the only thing Stephen hated. "Darling," I murmured in Shannon's ear, "your brother is scowling at me again."

Shannon glanced over his shoulder. "Nonsense. Stephen always looks like that at soirées."

"I made allowances for that. Trust me. He's scowling."

Shannon's smile lit his entire face. "You are incorrigible."

"I try," I said, smiling back.

"Besides, how do you know he's scowling at *you?* He might be scowling at Vicky."

I did not look at Stephen and Shannon's sister, dancing with my former master, Malkar Gennadion. "I wouldn't blame him for scowling at that. Do you think she really loves him?"

"I wouldn't even hazard a guess. Why?"

"No reason," I lied.

"I know you don't like him, but she's a grown woman."

"Of course she is." And if she could not or would not see Malkar for what he was, even the sacrifice of my pride to the truth would not make her believe me. She did not like me. Moreover, she was a daughter of the House of Teverius, a house notorious for its obstinacy. And in any event, whatever game Malkar was playing, I knew he was too clever to cause any harm to Victoria Teveria.

Behind us, a voice said, "I am surprised at you, Shannon."

Shannon rolled his eyes at me before we turned. It was Robert of Hermione, Agnes Bellarmyn just behind him. Robert was smirking. Agnes did not smirk—it was beneath her dignity—but I recognized the exalted look on her face from more Curia meetings than I cared to count. The two of them meant trouble.

"Are you, Robert?" Shannon said quellingly.

"*I* wouldn't care to be seen in public with Felix Harrowgate."

As if I weren't there. "The feeling is mutual, I assure you," I said.

Agnes said, "I'm surprised you aren't ashamed to go out in decent company."

"Oh, you know me, Agnes. I have no shame."

Shannon said, "Robert, I collect that you have some slander you wish to air regarding Felix. Would you, for the love of all the powers, just *do* it and go away?"

"But it isn't slander," Robert said, with a fine air of injured innocence.

"It's true. Your lover was a common prostitute in Pharaohlight before Lord Malkar found him."

I saw Shannon blanch, but that was peripheral to the satisfaction on Robert's face. I said, "*Where did you hear that?*"

"Are you denying that it's true?" Robert's grin had too many teeth in it.

"Oh, don't be stupid," Shannon said bravely. "Felix lived in Arabel until he was seventeen. You know that."

"Well, Felix?" Robert said.

"Where did you hear it, you verminous weasel?"

"Then you don't deny it?"

"I hardly think, Lord Felix," Agnes said, "that you are in a position to be insulting your betters."

"I hardly think, Lady Agnes," I said, "that anything other than a sewage-eating rat could consider Robert of Hermione its 'better.' And if he's going to spread rumors about me, I think I have the right to know what his sources are."

"But I'm not spreading a rumor," Robert said, lying, lying, through his hideous smile. "I'm warning Shannon."

"I could stand you better," I said, "if you were honest about your hatred. But the hypocrisy is wearing. You like Shannon no better than you like me."

"I know my duty to the House of Teverius. And you haven't answered my question, Lord Felix. Do you deny that you were a prostitute?"

"I deny your account of your motives. If your true concern were Shannon, or the House of Teverius, or anything but petty malevolence, you would hardly have opened the discussion in a public place." I waved a hand at the people around us, some of whom were staring, some of whom were not, but all of whom were listening. "I deny that you are anything but a carrion-eating jackal, a—"

"Lord Felix."

Stephen's voice, like a black rock. I spun around.

"I don't care," he said, his deep-set gray eyes going from me to Robert to Shannon, "to have the wizards of my court brawling like dockhands in the Hall of the Chimeras. What is going on?"

There was a dreadful silence, deep and cold, in which Robert failed to repeat his claim, Shannon failed to come to my defense, and I failed, abysmally, to think of anything I could say. I was struggling to control my temper, to resist the black urge to say, *Robert has discovered I used to be a whore.* Stephen's gaze made the circuit again, Robert to Shannon to me, and then remained on my face, waiting, patient as stone and as hard.

Finally, I said, "Robert and I had a difference of opinion."

"Indeed," Stephen said. "I know you don't think highly of my brains, but you might give me more credit than that."

Robert, I realized, had no need to say anything. Stephen would not embarrass him without greater provocation than he had yet been offered—the last, poisonous legacy of Emily Teveria, Stephen's dead wife, Robert's dead sister. All Robert had to do was stand still and let Stephen drag it out of me.

I could not look at Shannon, afraid of what I would see on his face. And the blackness was getting worse, boiling around the edges of my thoughts. I took a deep breath and said, "Robert has discovered—I don't know how and I wish you would ask him—that I was a"—I thought for a moment I wasn't going to be able to say it, that the word was going to stick in my throat like a fishbone and choke me to death—"a . . . prostitute when I was fourteen."

The silence was merciless, and I could no longer count the number of people listening. Stephen's eyebrows rose slowly. "And that's why you called him a carrion-eating jackal? I think, Lord Felix, that you need to control your . . . temper."

Behind me, Robert hissed, too low for anyone but me to hear, "You should go back to Pharaohlight where you belong."

I could stand the humiliation no longer. Stephen was about to turn to Robert and ask for the details; Robert, I knew, would tell him, lavishly. And the news would spread throughout the Mirador of the truth beneath the lies I had built my life on, the degradation I thought I had escaped.

"My lord, I shall remove my . . . temper from your vicinity." Stephen gave me an infinitesimal nod, not so much permission as acknowledgment that he did not want to keep me. I bowed and left. Although I listened, all the way down the Hall of the Chimeras and out its massive bronze doors, Shannon neither followed me nor tried to call me back.

Mildmay

I met Ginevra Thomson in the ordinary way of business. She was looking for a cat burglar. I was looking for a client. Meet at the Glorious Deed in

Ramecrow, second hour of the night, 10 Pluviôse. Ain't where I'd choose, but I said okay. The Glorious is tacky, but it is a real bar, not like in Dragonteeth, where you feel like you're stuck in the theater scenery for all the slumming flashies and the demimondaine. And I ain't good scenery for that kind of play.

I got there early. It's a habit, like always knowing how to find the back door of anywhere you walk into. It don't mean nothing in particular, just, you know, she *could* be fronting for the Dogs, even though I didn't think she was. No, since you ask, it ain't a nice way to live, but it sure beats the fuck out of dying.

The Glorious is about the most fashionable bar in Ramecrow. It opens its doors at sundown, and halfway through the first hour of the night it was already too loud and too smoky, and it seemed like everybody in there had about five elbows apiece. The bouncer gave me the hairy eyeball with mustard, but he let me by.

After an ugly quarter hour, a table opened up along the wall. I got there just before a slumming flashie who didn't have the sense to wash off his decagorgon-a-flask perfume before he came down to the city. He thought he was going to argue about it—looked at my face and thought again—and by then the two gals at the next table had agreed they wanted to move in on this one, and they got him to sit down with them instead. When he wasn't looking, the taller one winked at me.

I sat down with my back to the wall and waited. Watched the crowd, looking for the gal who thought she needed a cat burglar. I was hoping she had something good for me, because this was starting off to be one shitty night.

She was a tall girl in green taffeta, and she recognized me by the scar on my face. Good as a fucking carny barker. I watched her come through the crowd like she was dancing. She wasn't coy. Came straight up to me and said, "You're Dennis?"

I ain't, of course, but I don't go around using my real name all the time neither. Too many people it would make too fucking happy if they knew where Mildmay the Fox was hanging out. "Yeah," I said.

She sat down. "My name's Ginevra Thomson. I believe we have business together."

"You want to talk about it *here?*"

She looked around, puzzled, and I thought, Oh, powers, a flat. She said, "But I thought . . . I don't know anyone in Ramecrow."

"Don't mean they won't listen in, sweetheart. Come on."

It wasn't raining, for a change, and after the inside of the Glorious, the air tasted practically clean. Miss Thomson followed me okay, but she was frowning, and when we got about a block away, she said, "I don't see how anybody could have eavesdropped on us. It's so *loud* in there."

"I ain't taking chances. 'Less you want to get hauled off to the Kennel, you better follow suit."

"Oh," she said, in a tiny voice.

She came with me then, no more fuss, and it was only after we'd crossed from Ramecrow into Pharaohlight that she said, "Where are we going?"

"Min-Terris's."

"What? Are you *mad?* It'll be *crawling* with people."

"Not the roof."

"Oh. Is that safe?"

"Safe enough." I stopped and turned and looked at her. "You don't got to come if you don't want."

She thought about it for a moment, then her chin came up, and she said, "I'm coming."

"Okay," I said and went on.

Min-Terris-of-Pharaohlight is the Pharaohlight district's biggest cathedral. It ain't a patch on the cathedral of Phi-Kethetin in Spicewell, and it ain't got that big bronze dome that makes Ver-Istenna's the best landmark in the Lower City. But for my money, it's the prettiest cathedral in Mélusine, like one of them fancy cakes that the bakers in Breadoven do for flashie weddings and the Mayor's birthday and shit like that. And the roof of Min-Terris's—they let tours go up there every Cinquième, but otherwise it's as deserted as anybody could ask, and if you climb up one of the minarets, you can see people coming from miles off.

So that's where I took Miss Thomson. We worked our way through the crowd in the courtyard—whores and pickpockets and jugglers and candy sellers and all the rest of them—and into the cathedral itself.

"Dennis," Miss Thomson said. "Where are we going?"

She sounded nervous, like she was thinking of bolting.

"It's okay," I said. The stairs to the roof are in the corner of the foyer—I know that ain't the right word, but you know what I mean. They lock the door, but it ain't much of a lock, and I'd jiggered it so many times that I didn't even have to think about it.

We climbed the stairs, up and around a spiral so tight I was practically stepping on my own heels, and then up and around again through purely brilliant moonlight, up to the top of the minaret, where there wasn't room for but two people, and anybody tried anything clever and you'd *both* be human custard on the flagstones. Another reason I like Min-Terris's.

"Okay," I said. "What's the deal?"

"Finally," she said with a sniff. "I used to be the lover of Lord . . . of a nobleman with a house in Lighthill. We, um, parted ways about a month ago." She didn't sound sorry. She looked up, caught me full force with her big blue eyes, and said, "I want my jewelry."

"He kept it?"

"Yes."

"Bad manners."

"I'm sorry. What?"

I said it again.

"He was a pig," she said. "And I want a couple other things, a clock and a figurine."

"How much jewelry?"

"It's a blue velvet box, about so big—" Her hands shaped it in the air.

"Okay. I can do that. Now, payment—"

"You can take your commission out of what you recover."

"You sure?"

"Oh yes. I was worth it."

I believed her. Tall, stacked, with those big blue eyes—her flashie wouldn't have gotten to see how hard her eyes were, or how smart. I wondered how many guys she had on her string.

She asked, "How long will it take you?"

I shrugged. "Maybe a decad."

"A *decad?*"

"What, you got a deadline?"

She tilted her chin away from me, like she didn't give a rat's ass. "Of course not."

"I *could* go after 'em sooner, but I got other business . . ." Which was a lie, but she didn't need to know that.

She thought about it. "If I ask you to go tonight, what's your price?"

"Four septas."

"Four septas," she said, like she thought she hadn't heard me right. "You must think I'm a cretin. Sixteen gorgons."

"Three septas and four."

"Eighteen."

"Lower'n three septas and you go get 'em yourself."

For a second, she thought she was going to turn on her heel and march right back down all them stairs. But she didn't do it. "Oh, all right. Three septas. But you don't get your commission 'til I've seen them." She gave me a smile as fake as the paste diamonds in her ears. "Some of those pieces have sentimental value."

"Uh-huh. Now. What can you tell me about the lay?"

"The what?"

Kethe, spare me from flats. "The layout, the deal. Where'm I going and what'm I doing when I get there?"

"Oh." She opened her reticule—a ladylike little job with some not half-bad crewelwork—and pulled out a folded piece of paper. "I drew a map."

"Easier if you tell me whose house I'm after."

"Oh!" The gasp was about as ladylike as her reticule. "But I can't—"

"D'you think I'm not gonna know when I get there?"

"You won't . . ."

"Won't what?"

"I heard . . . things."

Well, you must've heard *something* to have found me in the first place. "I don't do nothing I ain't paid for. So cough it up."

"Oh, all right. Lord Ellis Otanius."

"Thanks. And whereabouts in the house?"

Her hand paused on the clasp of her reticule. "I did . . . I drew a map."

All at once I liked her. She was a flat, sure, and she was spoiled, for damn sure, but she'd done her best to think things through, and she was trying hard not to make the same mistake twice. Some days you got to accept that's all you can do, and it takes guts to admit that's the kind of day you're up against.

"Hand it over," I said, and she smiled and gave me the map.

Couldn't get no good look at it by moonlight, but I could tell she'd drawn it big enough to read.

"It's a wall safe," she said. "And I'm really sorry, but I don't know the combination. I know that makes it harder . . ."

I shrugged that off. "Anybody likely to be up?"

"Oh, they're all off in St. Millefleur for the winter. They won't be back 'til Ger—Endes, I mean."

"Smart."

"I try," she said, and even by moonlight I could see the corners of her mouth tuck up in a little smile.

"Okay. Meet tomorrow, same time. Where?"

"Where do you suggest?"

And she was a fast learner. I said, "Worried about your virtue?"

"What?"

"If I hire us a room, you gonna come over all coy and tell me you can't be alone with me or something?"

"Oh." She looked around. I had to agree, she was about as alone with me as she was going to get. "No, I don't think I mind that."

"If you bring a knife," I said carefully, "I won't get mad."

"Thank you." She met my eyes, and I liked her for that, too.

"Okay. Then we'll meet at the Spinning Goblin on Rue Celadon, Engmond's Tor. You gonna be able to find that okay?"

"I think so."

"It's on the maps." There are streets in the Lower City that ain't, but they ain't places I'd take a flat.

"Then I'll be fine," she said, her chin coming up.

"Good girl," I said. I hadn't meant to. It just got out, 'cause it's the sort of thing you say to somebody you're training when they do something right—or just show willing, the way Miss Thomson had done. I expected to get my ears boxed for it—and I would've stood still and let her do it—but instead she gave me another knockout smile.

All the way down the stairs, following the rustle and swish of her dress, the smell of her perfume, I was saying to myself, Watch it, Milly-Fox. Watch your stupid self. Don't get involved with the demimonde. You fucking well know better.

But I wasn't listening, and I knew it.

Felix

I stood on the battlements for an hour, my hands clenched around the edge of the parapet, barely feeling the cold. The stars shone heartlessly against the vast indigo drape of the sky. Below me, the lights of the Lower City were warmer, smaller—the sordid markers of the things that happened in Mélusine after dark. I did not look toward Pharaohlight.

I had hoped that I might replace the burning blackness in my mind with the simple, remote darkness of the night sky. Sometimes I could calm myself that way, but tonight the longer I stared at the sky, at its untouchable beauty, the more I wanted to hurt someone.

When I opened my pocket watch and saw, by the light of the lantern I had brought up with me, that it was ten-thirty, I knew I could find a victim. I knew Shannon would have returned to our suite by now, no matter what he and Stephen had said to each other.

I stalked through the halls of the Mirador. The servants I encountered murmured, "Lord Wizard," and backed hastily against the walls. They were tempting targets, but they wouldn't give me any real satisfaction, and I passed them by. I came to our suite without meeting a single other wizard, and even through the blackness I knew that was for the best.

I slammed the door behind me.

Shannon turned. His blue eyes were as cold and distant as the stars. "Is it true?"

"Of course it's true. You knew that as soon as Robert said it."

"Why didn't you tell me?"

"Why do you *think*, my lord?"

"Don't call me that."

"Then don't ask stupid questions."

"It's not a stupid question! Why didn't you tell me? Didn't you think I had a right to know? Or didn't you trust me? Did you think it would change how I felt?"

"Clearly it has," I said. I crossed to the sideboard, splashed bourbon into a glass, swallowed smoke and bitterness.

"Damn it, Felix, you *lied* to me!" His face was bleak, white as bone. "Are you even from Caloxa?"

"I don't know. I might be."

"*Might* be? And what else *might* you be? What else are you that I don't know about? Who are you, really?"

"You know who I am."

"How can I? You've been lying to me for five years about your past. What else have you been lying about? How do I know that any of it was real?"

"You think . . ." I slammed my glass down and crossed the room to where he was standing against the emerald-green drapes. "Go ahead and say it. Call me a whore. *Say it!*"

"Felix, I—"

I hit him, an open-handed blow across his right cheek. He staggered back against the wall, his hand going up to his face.

"Is that how they do it in Pharaohlight?" He was panting, his face blotchy, his eyes like fire and ice. "Does that settle the argument? Or is it just supposed to make me shut up?"

I wanted to hit him again, harder, to backhand him and let my rings tear fierce gouges in his alabaster skin. I wanted to hurt him, as I had been hurt. I wanted to show him "how they do it in Pharaohlight," to beat him bloody and drag him down on the floor and rape him. I wanted to show him what I had protected him from, all the five years that we had been lovers, the blackness, the rage that festered in me like power.

I slammed back out of the suite instead, flung myself out into the night-infested fortress to find a whore.

Once through the Mortisgate, where the guards eyed me sidelong but did not speak, it did not take long. The Arcane was home to a great many people of whom the Lord Protector did not admit awareness, knowing that with awareness came the onus of responsibility: procurers and drug dealers, prostitutes and thieves. I had been down there many times before in my black moods, and I knew exactly where to find what I sought.

The procurer was a burly, swarthy, hirsute man with one eye; he and his prostitutes catered to tarquins, the men and women who could only reach sexual release through another person's pain. He was happy to oblige me when I told him what I wanted. The boy he produced was fifteen or so—the age Shannon had been when we first met—blond and blue-eyed, although the hair was dyed and the boy rat-faced and half-starved. I assured the procurer that I would not kill the boy—"I can give you the name of a man in Simside if that's what you're after, m'lord," he said, scratching his chest, but I just smiled and shook my head and paid him—and he waved us into a dingy box of a room with a filthy mattress on the floor.

The boy stood in the middle of the room, with neither fear nor life in his eyes, and waited to discover what I would do to him.

My hand rose, as if of its own volition, and then, all at once, my howling rage burned itself out, so that I was left standing in an ashy bewilderment, unable to think, unable to move. I felt filthy, beslimed, and the worst part was knowing that the cause of my contamination was myself. I had paid a man for a boy's body, and I was about to . . . was I? I looked inside myself, at the fury, the snarling monster, and I knew that it was true.

I shut my eyes, putting one hand out to brace myself against the wall.

The blackness within me rose up, closing over my head like the black water of the Sim. I must be damned, I thought, though I wasn't sure there was any god who would be willing to claim me long enough to pronounce sentence. If no god would do it, I would willingly damn myself, and if I knew one thing in all the world, it was where to find the man who would help me.

I left the boy standing where he was, fled him as if he were my enemy, the undead specter of my childhood, fled back into the Mirador to find my damnation.

Malkar's suite was in the part of the Mirador called the Fia Barbarossa, still lavish with the tastes of long-dead Ophidian kings. The walls were faced with white marble and hung with gold brocade. Statues of ancient heroes stood in niches, watching me with painted eyes. I knew all their names, all their histories, and their very indifference woke me, alarmed me, and I was caught frozen, able neither to walk forward into Hell nor to turn and walk away.

I stood in that white and gold hall, the last approach to Malkar's door, my hands clenching and my nails digging into the skin of my palms, fighting myself, so intent that I didn't realize anyone was there until a voice purred in my ear, every word an obscure mockery, "Why, Felix! Fancy seeing you here! What a . . . *pleasant* surprise."

I turned. It was Malkar, smiling a horrible, complacent smile. He knew why I was in his hall. He had not changed, in the six years since last we had . . . had been intimate. His mahogany-dark hair was untouched by gray, his broad, harsh-featured face still unwrinkled. His light brown eyes were clear and open and as false as glass.

"Come along," he said, sliding his arm through mine with easy, poisonous familiarity and assailing me with the scent of musk. "Let me help you."

The damnation I sought had come to find me. If I closed my eyes, I could see Shannon's face, the mark of my hand on his cheek, the tears standing in his eyes like diamonds. And I could see that poor, hopeless boy, waiting to be beaten, waiting to be raped, waiting to be hurt. I went with Malkar.

He locked the door of his suite behind us and bade me sit down. I accepted the wineglass he offered, knowing without needing to taste it that the wine, a heavy southern red, was laced with phoenix. I had been addicted to phoenix six years ago, just as I had been addicted to Malkar. I had beaten the addiction and not taken phoenix since. I was horrified by how comforting the taste was. I had known people, in Pharaohlight, who had insisted that phoenix was tasteless, but they were wrong. It tasted like tears.

This is what you wanted, isn't it? a voice said mockingly in the back of my mind. I downed half the wine in one gulp, shamefully aware of Malkar sitting opposite and watching with his abominable smile.

He said something I didn't catch, my pulse pounding in my ears; I said, "I beg your pardon?"

"I said it's been a long time, Felix." He came to stand beside me. I took a nervous swallow of wine and felt his fingers teasing themselves through my hair, flicking gently against the rings in my ears. He had always had that habit; it was as comfortable and vile as the taste of phoenix. "Six years." I could hear the smile in his voice when he added, "Almost a septad."

Malkar was not from Mélusine; he used the old-style reckoning only to taunt me, to remind me of the months it had taken him to teach me to use weeks and years and decades instead of decads, indictions, and septads, to remind me of the punishments he had inflicted when my tongue had slipped.

My hands were shaking. I put the glass down.

Malkar crouched down beside the chair, one hand still cradling my skull, making it impossible for me to turn my head. He knew—the only person in the Mirador who knew—how close to blind my right eye was. He knew how much I hated having anyone on my right, just as he knew how much I hated being touched. "I was beginning to think," he said, "that I'd lost you for good."

"I haven't—"

"Haven't what, my dearest?"

But the words wouldn't come. I couldn't find them in the blackness and morass. Malkar laughed, the low, purring chuckle that I had once thought wonderful, and leaned over to kiss me, pressing his mouth against mine. The familiarity of his mouth, of the situation, was itself erotic, a groove worn by the patterns of the past; I could feel my body wanting to respond and fought it.

"Coy?" Malkar said, raising his head, though he did not loosen his grip on my hair. "Well, that will pass."

I flinched back, though the movement hurt my scalp. His look was predatory, gloating. All the power in this room was his, and he knew it. "Malkar, please," I said, hating the weak, fearful breathlessness of my own voice, "let me go. You know you don't really want me—"

"On the contrary, my darling," he said, using his free hand to caress the side of my face. "I know no such thing." He lowered his lips to mine again, forcing his tongue into my mouth. And my body was responding, drugged on phoenix, drugged on the past, drugged on my own self-hate. His smile curved against my mouth.

"No!" I gasped, bringing my hands up and pushing him away, a few strands of my hair torn free in his fingers. "No!"

But he had moved around so that his bulk was blocking me in the chair, and he could see me shaking, knew how thin and pathetic my defiance was. "Felix," he said, catching my jaw with one hand, so that I could not look away from him, "why are you fighting? Do you think it's going to do you any good?"

We had played this scene again and again, in every possible variation. Malkar knew how it ended; I knew how it ended. I had known what I was doing to myself when I chose to come to him. There were no words left to me. I shook my head; Malkar's fingers relaxed to let me do it.

"Then why play the shrinking violet, dearest? We both know what you are." His smile added, *The whole Mirador knows what you are.* "Come along."

His hands, his blunt, brutal, powerful hands, closed around my wrists, dragged me out of the chair. It was getting harder to remember why I was frightened, why I was angry, why I wasn't doing what Malkar told me. That was what phoenix was good for; that was why procurers loved it. Probably the boy in the Arcane had been flying on phoenix himself.

Malkar led me to his bedroom, helped me undress, his fingers lingering on my back. I made a choked, whimpering noise, but that was my last crumbling resistance. The phoenix was making everything blurred and soft, like fog. It was all right, the phoenix told me. There was nothing to be frightened of, no need for concern. Let go, it said. Just let go.

I was aware of hands on my body, touching and teasing, aware of a mouth pressing against mine, of the scent of lavender oil everywhere around me. I felt softness against my chest and stomach and legs; I felt Malkar's weight pinning me down. "If you scream," he said in my ear, "I will gag you."

"Malkar, *please,*" I said. I couldn't move, except to shut my eyes against the tears in them.

"Don't be silly, my darling," he said and caressed my face.

And then, as they said on the streets of the Lower City, the phoenix screamed.

I could not see, and I could barely hear, save for my own harsh breathing. But I could feel. I could feel Malkar's hands like silk, running up and down my back, tracing the scars, the old palimpsest of pain. I could feel his body against me, his bulk, his heat. I felt his hands slide under my hips, stroking, exciting, felt the stiffness of him against my thigh.

Pain, then, but not too much.

Pain and phoenix and arousal all woven together like a tapestry. I was moaning, gasping; the only words I could form were "Please, Malkar, please, please," and I didn't know if I was begging him to stop or to continue. Not that it would have made the slightest difference either way. Pain and phoenix and frenzied arousal, and when the scream finally tore free, though I fought it until I drew blood from my lower lip, it was a scream of climax, of pain, of release, of loathing for what I was, for what Malkar made me.

He drew away from me; I rolled over and lay gasping, spread-eagled on his bed, and fell into a thin, uneasy dream.

❧

I am lost in an enormous maze, made of great carved stone blocks. I can't find the heart of the maze; I can't find the way out. Maybe it has neither; maybe it is like the great serpent Yrob, who has neither beginning nor end.

It's dark and cold, and the stone is wet beneath my hands. I can hear rats and other, bigger creatures in the darkness, and I know that if I stop moving, they will find me. I'm bitterly cold, and my entire body aches with exhaustion, but I have to keep moving. I daren't stop. And I think I know—or maybe I only believe—that if I can find the heart of the maze, Shannon will be waiting there, and he won't hate me.

I keep moving, although there's almost no light. I fall and pick myself up, fall and pick myself up. I hurt, and it's endlessly dark, and the padding creatures are getting closer, and I—

❧

Someone slapped me.

"Felix!" Malkar's voice.

I opened my eyes and saw Malkar's dark, blurry shape looming over me. "Get up, slut. I won't have *you* in my bed."

I remembered him dancing with Vicky, the candlelight making prisms of their intertwined hands.

I crawled to my feet, shaking with phoenix and fear and weakness. He shoved my clothes at me, and I managed to put them on, more or less straight. I was afraid that he would make me stay, but he seemed to have lost interest in me, merely watching like a bored cat while I stumbled across his sitting room and out into the hall. I shut his door behind me and leaned against it, almost sobbing with relief. I knew Malkar; this wasn't over, but at least, for now, he had let me go.

I started away from his door. I didn't know where I was going to go, only that I could not stay there, so close to Malkar. I was trying to think of someone I trusted, someone I could go to as I was, with my hair hanging around me like a lunatic's and my pupils contracted to pinpoints, someone who would let me in and not ask questions and not spread gossip.

I couldn't think of anyone. Friends, colleagues, former lovers—no one in the Mirador would accept me now. I could not go to Shannon, not like this, not with Malkar's reeking miasma still surrounding me.

I heard footsteps, coming toward me from around the next corner, and I knew, because this was the Mirador, that it would be Shannon, Shannon with some adoring young nobleman, talking and laughing. Or Shannon alone, his eyes red with weeping. I dove into an unfamiliar side hall and fled.

And then my dream came back to me, or maybe the Mirador simply became strange. I was lost again. The floors were cold beneath my feet, the walls slick and hostile against my hands. I felt like a ghost, the ghost of someone dead for centuries, condemned now to wander forever in darkness, among familiar things turned strange and vague.

I remembered that I had been seeking damnation, and I knew that I had found it.

Mildmay

I waited for the septad-night before I started up to Lighthill.

The Otanius town house was one of them big houses from the Protectorate of Deborah that line up along Cherubim Street like they're getting ready to make some poor bastard run the gauntlet. I'd had business on Cherubim Street before.

I got there across the roofs. If you know what you're doing, you can get all the way from the Plaza del'Archimago to the Launderers' Guild in Lyonesse without ever once having to set foot on the ground. And the cits never think to look up. People live on the roofs, too, them as have reason to. It's a good way to travel if you're leaving the Lower City and don't want to run into the Dogs. Which, not being in the mood for suicide, I didn't.

Felix

Dizzily, as I try to find a way through a series of rooms interconnected like honeycombs, I remember Shannon telling me that there are whole sections of the Mirador that no one has been into since his grandmother's time, some that aren't even marked on the thick roll of maps Stephen keeps in his study. Maybe I have wandered into one such deserted wing, or maybe the Mirador has become a ghost. Instead of me haunting it, maybe it is haunting me. Or maybe we are haunting each other, trapped in a chain of mirrors that cannot be broken.

The thought scares me, and I run from it.

Sometimes I think I am a child again, wandering the dark streets of the Lower City, looking for someone to steal from or someone to sell myself to. Sometimes I hear the roaring of the Fire behind me, and I know I have to keep moving; if I stop, the Fire will catch me, as it has already caught Joline and Eva and Jean-Croix and Keeper and Freddy and Sulla and . . .

I trip over something and fall, hurting my hands. But I realize that these rough stones are not the cobbles of the Lower City, that I am not a child any longer, and I am almost grateful for my stinging palms.

After a moment, I pick myself up and move on. I don't want the Fire to catch me.

Mildmay

Kethe's the patron saint—if he is a saint, which some folks take leave to doubt—of thieves and secrets and things done at the septad-night. He's also a practical joker, as all the stories will tell you, and so I shouldn't—I mean, really—I *shouldn't* have been surprised at what he had waiting for me three blocks down from the Otanius town house.

The job itself had been a piece of cake. Let myself in through the attic of the house on Cherubim Street, found Miss Thomson's things. She'd been worried about the safe, but she shouldn't have been. The lock was gorgeous, the work of Selenfer and Kidmarsh, who'd been the hot boys in locks back in the Protectorate of Helen. I ain't much of a cracksman, not for the fancy stuff, but I could handle an old S-and-K combo. I was glad there was nobody standing behind me with their pocket watch, the way Keeper used to, but it wasn't no trouble. Blue velvet box, ugly gilded porcelain clock you couldn't have paid me to keep, and there was the figurine, a little bronze dancer, up on pointe and so perfectly balanced she looked alive. Kethe, she was gorgeous. I guessed her for a Tolmattin, and off the top of my head I could think of two guys in the Lower City who'd commit cold-blooded murder to get their hands on a genuine Tolmattin and a double septad more who'd pay through the nose for it. Miss Thomson hadn't been kidding about the value of the commission.

And it had been easy, the kind of job a guy like me prays for. Got myself back out of the house and started home across the roofs like I owned the whole city.

There's only four packs that run the rooftops. I was on pretty good terms with three of them, but the guy who led the fourth wasn't going to be happy until he had my balls on his watch chain. So—you can see it coming, can't you?—there ain't nobody I can meet, coming home across the Corandina's roof in the dark, excepting only Rindleshin and a septadworth of his pack. It's the way things work.

We stared at each other, Rindleshin and me, like we couldn't neither of us believe our luck. Then I took off running like an alley cat. If Rindleshin caught me—well, I might not be dead before the sun cleared the city walls, but I sure would *wish* I was dead by then.

Rindleshin hated me because of something stupid—a knife fight, almost a septad ago, where I'd made him look really fucking dumb. It's easy to do if you're good and the other guy only thinks he is. And I was too young and too dumb myself to see that it's better to leave the other guy some face. I thought I was quite something back then, like I was another Charlett Redding and they were going to have my hands plated with gold when I died.

Anyway, Rindleshin's hatred of me was pure poison-green, and his pack hated me right along with him. That's what you got a pack leader for, I guess, to tell you what to think. I knew, the same instant I bolted, that I had to make it to the Badgers' territory. Rindleshin would follow me into the streets, but he wouldn't follow me there. Badgers and Rindleshin's pack were about half an inch this side of war, and Margot was a friend of mine. She'd render him into lard if he took me down on her turf.

Rindleshin's Pack ran mostly in Simside and Queensdock and almost never came up farther than Engmond's Tor. Kethe only knows what they'd been doing in Lighthill. They didn't know the ground, and I thought, running, to be glad for small favors. On their turf they would've had me cold in a septad-minute, tops.

They couldn't catch me, but I couldn't fucking ditch them, either. I was lucky to get across the Corandina ahead of them, and I just about killed myself vaulting down into the maze of tenement roofs. It bought me a little time, though, because you got to have training to do it that way, and not all of them did. They were smart enough to know they didn't want to split up.

I dragged in a breath, got my bearings against Ver-Istenna's bronze dome, and then I put my head down and ran. Ver-Istenna's marked the north side of the Badgers' territory. I could hear Rindleshin's pack yelling behind me, like I was cheating or something. I wanted to turn around and tell them to go fuck themselves sideways with a barge pole, but my lead wasn't long enough. I just ran, and they didn't quite catch me.

Up the fire escape on Lornless's sweatshop like a madman, praying the rungs wouldn't break under me. Rindleshin's pack was shouting ideas about what they wanted to do with me. I ran full tilt across Lornless's roof and didn't even stop at the edge. I just jumped, like a squirrel in Richard's Park, and caught hold of one of Ver-Istenna's gargoyles, the ones that watch all the time, in all directions, to tell her where balance is slipping out of true.

I glanced over my shoulder then. I couldn't help it, because I was a big fat target, spread out there with my fingers digging into the gargoyle's neck like I was trying to strangle it and about half a foot braced on the cornice of a window. Anybody in Rindleshin's pack fancied themself a knife-thrower, and my life was going to get even nastier than a three-and-a-half-story drop under me and a gargoyle covered in pigeon shit.

The pack came to a screeching halt at the edge of Lornless's roof. Then they stood there and watched me like owls. After a moment, Rindleshin shouted, "You're going to break your fucking neck, Mildmay!"

"Don't you wish," I said between my teeth. But he wasn't telling the kids with him to break out their throwing knives, so I figured I was at least safe from that direction.

I took stock of my situation, real quick-like. The gargoyle was steady—nobody cut corners when they were doing stuff for Ver-Istenna. I edged my left foot a little farther onto the cornice, then braced my right foot against the wall and used the leverage to hook my right elbow over the gargoyle.

The fuckers on the roof gave me this snarky round of applause.

But I was in a better position, and it wasn't no big thing to go from leaning against the gargoyle to getting one hip up on it. It didn't stick out quite far enough for anything super-fancy, but I could just reach, by bracing my right foot as high up as I could get it and pushing sideways, a crevice in the frieze of eyes and balancing scales, and once I had a handhold up there, I could get my right foot on the gargoyle, and it was plenty big enough to stand on.

And from there—well, I'm a cat burglar. And cathedrals are easy. There was a bad moment with the overhang around the dome, but I'd gotten into my rhythm by then and hooked my knee over before I'd really even had time to think, I'm fucked if this don't work.

And then I was standing on the walkway around Ver-Istenna's dome. Her priests do tours, too, like Min-Terris's. I turned around. Rindleshin and his pack were still standing on Lornless's roof, staring up at me round-eyed as owls.

I gave 'em the finger, like I'd been itching to do for, I don't know, a good half hour—ever since they gave me that snarky applause for not turning myself into pâté on the pavement. Then I walked widdershins around Ver-Istenna's dome and started for Midwinter.

Felix

The fog burned away at last, and I knew where I was: a tiny, circular antechamber off the Stoa Errata, hung with the sand-colored velvet that had been in fashion when Shannon's grandmother had been Lady Protector. My watch, miraculously still in my pocket, told me that it was five-thirty. I snapped it shut without letting myself read the inscription Shannon had had engraved on the inside of the case.

I didn't want to think about Shannon.

I sat down on one of the spindly chairs. My hands were shaking. *I* was shaking, as if with cold. I knotted my hands together, pressing them between my knees, and tried to work out what to do.

I remembered my revelation of the evening before, that there was no one in the Mirador I trusted. If Thaddeus de Lalage had been here, things might have been different, but Thaddeus was in Aurelias, had been for five years, and even Thaddeus . . . no, I could not have gone to Thaddeus. There was too much truth in the air around me. I was not sure I could look anyone in the face. I remembered Shannon saying, *Didn't you trust me?*

I had trusted no one since Joline, and Joline had been dead for sixteen years.

"I cannot stay," I said aloud, and flinched at the sound of my own voice.

I got up again, beginning to pace, seeing myself caught between two impossibilities. For I *could* not stay, could not bear the thought of meeting Shannon again. Even worse was the thought of looking across the Hall of the Chimeras and seeing Malkar smile at me. But I could not go, for where would I go *to?* I tried to imagine myself, like Thaddeus, going to a faraway town to help the townsfolk, to teach the children, to send the gifted ones back to the Mirador—Lord Gareth's gentle inspiration, after a century's worth of thaumaturgic war, a way to be sure that blood-magic and its vile offshoots were not being practiced. But first I had to imagine myself asking Stephen to let me go, and that I could not do.

And if I were just to leave . . . with the tattoos on my hands and forearms, crimson and azure, emerald and gold, gaudy, blazing, like a fanfare of trumpets or a cavalcade of banners, I could not hide what I was. The guards at the city gates would not hinder my passage, but they would remember me, and they would tell anyone who came riding after me just when I'd passed the gates and which direction I'd been going when they lost sight of me.

I wondered, with a convulsive shiver, if I could hide in the Lower City. The Lower City had always been a haven for apostate wizards, heretics, dissidents of all stripes. Would my tattoos make them leave me alone, or would they turn them against me? I tried to remember what I had thought of wizards as a child, before Malkar had found me, but all I could remember were the times I'd had them as clients. I'd asked one about the tattoos, I remembered: *Don't it hurt, having that done?* And he'd laughed and said, *Everything worthwhile hurts. Surely you know that.*

But the thought of the Lower City gave me the answer. The Arcane. I went down there often enough; if the denizens were not used to me per se, they did not look on me as anything peculiar. They might give me space. And the court wouldn't know to look for me in the Arcane. The court barely knew the Arcane existed.

I almost bolted out of that antechamber, despairingly glad to have a direction, a purpose. I realized only then, as I crossed from the straw-colored carpet to the smooth parquet of the Stoa Errata, that my feet were bare. I must have left my stockings and boots in Malkar's suite, and of course it would have amused him to let me do so, to let me walk out with my feet bare, my hair unbraided. I ran a panicky glance over my person, but the only other thing missing was my gold wizard's sash, and I wouldn't need that where I was going.

"I can buy shoes," I muttered to myself. "I can buy shoes in the Arcane." And then I gave a sort of strangled howl and plunged my hands into my pockets. No money, of course. I'd used the last of it the night before, buying . . . I flinched away from completing that thought.

But my fingers found my watch, the watch that Shannon had given to me for my birthday last year. I didn't know when my birthday was, of course, but Shannon had asked and I had made up an answer, and I could still remember the delight on his face when I opened the box he gave me. My hand clenched around the watch's cool, hard smoothness, and I thought, It's perfectly possible to redeem things from a pawnbroker. Once I'm making money again, I can get it back. I did not ask myself how I was going to make money in the Arcane, but there were always ways. My childhood had taught me that.

I descended through the levels of the Mirador as quickly as I could, avoiding the legions of servants who were preparing the fortress and the court to face another day. I had a vague, uneasy feeling, too gossamer-thin even to be called a hunch, that I had only a limited amount of time, as if I were caught in one of the fairy tales that Belinda had liked to tell. This muddled, superstitious instinct told me that if I was not out of the Mirador by dawn, I would find all its gates locked against me, and I would be trapped. I was all but running by the time I reached the Rose Arbor, already mentally tracing my course through the Warren to the Mortisgate, where the guards would be coming off duty, and even if they noticed me, would not be curious.

Once again I was unaware of Malkar until he spoke.

"Felix!" he said, one hand, as powerful as a lion's paw, catching my arm before I could get by him. I could tell from his expression that he had decided to ignore the events of the night, ignore them in his own peculiar way that meant I would never be allowed to forget them.

"Malkar," I said; I could hear the strain and fear in my voice and hated myself for giving him the satisfaction. "Guh-good morning."

"Indeed it is," he said with an expansive smile. I recognized the smile; it was the one he wore almost constantly around Stephen and Vicky. I wondered distractedly if either of them ever saw in it the fanged snarl that I saw. "Where are you off to in such a hurry?"

I froze, and no plausible lie came to mind.

"Nowhere?" he said. "That's what I thought." His paw tightened, and he turned me around with him. "Someone who didn't know better might imagine that you were planning to skip court."

I made a faint, inarticulate noise, but he took no notice. "I'm surprised at you, Felix. You left your sash in my room, and you need to bathe and change." He gave me a sidelong, glittering smile that made me feel like a rabbit who sees the shadow of an owl. "We certainly don't want to be late."

"We?"

He couldn't have heard me; it wasn't even a whisper. But he knew, and he was gloating. "Absolutely. You don't think I'd *desert* my protégé just when he needs me, do you, Felix?"

"No," I said, and as he pulled me past the Harriers' Gate, I saw the sun rising over the walls of the city.

Mildmay

I made it back to Midwinter about the second hour of the morning. Scabious was on the front stoop, pretending like he wasn't waiting for me.

"Morning, Scabious," I said.

"Hi, Gilroi." He shuffled his feet and said, "You're home early. Late, I mean."

"Yeah."

"Um. Is everything okay?"

"Sure."

"Were you out all night?" His eyes were wide.

"Yeah." He would've been thrilled to death if I'd told him even a quarter of what I'd been up to. I said, "I got to get some sleep. Later, okay?"

"Sure! I mean, you know . . . sleep well, Gilroi." He went red as a brick.

"Thanks, Scabious."

I went inside. Scabious's mother was waiting for me, arms folded, at the foot of the stairs.

"Rent ain't due for a half decad," I said.

She looked me up and down, making me realize that the knee was out of my right trouser leg and the front of my shirt was covered with muck. And I was out without a coat. But Mrs. Pickering never had thought I was a gentleman. "What nonsense are you filling my boy's head with now?"

I was too tired even to be pissed off. "Mrs. Pickering, I—"

"*I* know. Pure as rainwater, you are. Never broken the law in your life."

"Whatever I done, I ain't gonna hurt Scabious."

"Not if you know what's good for you," she said and finally quit blocking the damn stairs.

"Yeah," I said and dragged myself up to my room to get some sleep.

Felix

We waited in Malkar's preferred antechamber, the Crimson, for court to convene. It had been six years since I had been in the Crimson Antechamber, and I had forgotten how much I hated it, hated that particular crowd of hungry, ambitious wizards who cultivated Malkar like fanatical gardeners with a hothouse flower. And Malkar smiled and let them. They had all hated me, and there was some tiny, mean part of me, the part that was still a whore, that enjoyed the looks on their faces when I followed Malkar into the room: those huge, horrified eyes, those hasty, fake smiles—for of course I had hated them, too, insane with jealousy that Malkar might decide he wanted one of them instead of me.

A pinch-faced spidery little man, whose name I could not remember, said, "Lord Malkar, is it true? Is he really . . ."

The water torture would have been nothing compared to the silence that followed his question; I could feel Malkar wondering if it would be amusing to force me to answer. But this time the knowledge that he could have done so was enough. He said, "From Pharaohlight? Yes, of course."

"But you never . . . Why?"

"Because he asked me not to," Malkar said, shrugging, and I cringed at the warm generosity in his voice. The Mirador knew how vain I was; they would not judge Malkar's explanation implausible or incomplete in the slightest.

No one had an answer to that. I could feel Malkar's malicious enjoyment. I locked my throat against the keening noise building in my chest, looked carefully, neutrally, at an empty chair, and waited.

The doors to the Hall of the Chimeras cried their opening like brazen lions. "Come, Felix," Malkar said, and the entire Crimson Antechamber was a silent seethe of hatred as I followed him out. As far as they were concerned, the last six years might not have happened at all.

The atmosphere in the Hall of the Chimeras was scarcely any better. The scandal had spread like plague; I could feel the word *whore* following me down the hall. My eyes went automatically to Lord Michael's Chair. Stephen slumped there, bearlike as always, with Vicky standing beside him. I could see Robert's blandly good-looking face just behind her. I looked to Stephen's other side before I could stop myself.

Shannon had covered the bruise on his cheek with court maquillage, but I knew it was there. Only the rituals of the Mirador, ingrained by years of repetition, kept me upright and moving, and my face was surely as stark white as the shirt Malkar had given me.

Shannon did not look at me, and the cursory glance Stephen gave me said that Shannon had not told his brother about the evening farce's second act. Vicky was harder to read, but I thought the pin-scratch frown between her eyebrows was for Malkar—and the very fact that I couldn't be sure suggested that she didn't know what I had done, either.

Like a clockwork dog on a short leash, I followed Malkar to his favorite place, beside the bust of a haggard, vulpine king. I wanted to break away, to go back to my habitual place on the opposite side of the hall, where Sherbourne and Vida were standing, their hurt and concern plain on their faces; I wanted to scream out the truth about Malkar, about myself. But Malkar had defeated me, and I could only stand beside him, my eyes fixed on the mosaic chimera's tail beneath my feet, and try to outwait my pain.

I heard very little of what happened in court that morning, my mind in some dark, faraway desolation of stone and water. Voices eddied and swirled around me without penetrating. I didn't need to know; Malkar wouldn't let me care.

Eventually, I realized that the boots and skirt hems around me were moving. I looked up and saw that Stephen had risen, dismissing the court; he was leading Vicky and Shannon, with Robert in solicitous, inevitable attendance, through the family's personal door behind the Virtu's plinth. I followed Malkar toward the bronze doors at the other end of the hall.

Halfway there, a hand caught at my sleeve. I turned, aware of Malkar nearby, and saw Sherbourne, scared but determined; Vida was making her way toward us through the crowd.

"Felix," he said, "what's going on? Are the things they're saying about you true? What are you doing with *him?*"

"I hardly think that's any concern of yours," I said in a hard, flippant tone—the tone I used on Shannon's multitudinous admirers—as my heart tore itself into shreds. I knew what I had to say to make Sherbourne leave me alone. "But if you want the truth"—and I smiled at him, a deliberately brilliant, horrible, mocking smile—"you bore me, darling."

Sherbourne's crush on me had been an open secret for a year and a half. I had never breathed a word about it, never indicated by so much as a glance that I was aware of his feelings. I couldn't have chosen anything crueler to do if I'd had a week to plan in advance.

But it worked, and by working it would protect him from Malkar's poison. Sherbourne jerked back as if I had slapped him; as Vida came up to us, I could see the storm clouds already gathering in her face. But Malkar, adroit as always at heading off potential aggravations, interrupted.

"Come, Felix," he said. "We have much to accomplish." And he pulled me away.

I followed him like a child going obediently to be punished.

Mildmay

That afternoon, out of pure, cussed curiosity, I used my lock picks to take a look inside Miss Thomson's jewelry box.

It was a nice collection of stuff, and somebody'd picked it pretty careful with her in mind. Either Lord Ellis Otanius had taste, or he knew somebody who did. Lots of blue stones, sapphire and lapis lazuli, set in rings and earrings. Strings of pearls, varying quality. Some nice amber. And a choker necklace of cabochon rubies that could have fed all Lyonesse for a decad and a half.

I picked them up. They were real. They were old. I could take a guess at how much they were worth, and it made my mouth go dry. I was willing to bet that these were what Miss Thomson particularly wanted. The rest of it was just window dressing. And I wondered—I couldn't help wondering—what they were doing in a box of her jewelry when you'd have to be blind not to see they flat didn't suit her. And then I thought, He gives 'em to each gal in turn. Every time he takes a new lover, out come the rubies. I was glad Miss Thomson had taken them away from him, no matter what she wanted them for.

Felix

Malkar gave me some more of his phoenix-laced wine as soon as he had locked the door of his suite behind us. He thoughtfully left the decanter within reach, and I spent the afternoon lost in phoenix's soft, obscuring fog. It was better than thinking about the stricken look on Sherbourne's face, the contempt and anger in Vida's eyes, the bruise I knew was underneath Shannon's maquillage.

I longed for the oblivion that excessive consumption of phoenix would bring, the fugue state in which the consciousness could release itself, leaving the body to do as it was told, leaving no memories, no shame, no fear. But, ironically, I was too frightened of Malkar for that surrender; I could not bear to leave him where I could not watch him. It would be too much like turning one's back on a starving, sadistic lion.

He left me alone for hours; I was grateful. Even through the cloud of phoenix, every muscle in my body knotted when he finally came back and dragged me out of the chair.

"You're awake," he said; he sounded disappointed.

I couldn't answer him, numbed and fogged with phoenix as I was.

He snorted. "Well, at least it means I don't have to carry you. Come on, then."

"Wh . . ." I licked my lips, tried again. "Where?"

"We have work to do, dearest." He put his hand under my elbow and started toward the door.

It was half formula, half code, and I had not forgotten what it meant, no matter how much I wished I could have. "What are you going to do?"

"An experiment," Malkar said, with his wide, feral smile.

I made a noise—a moan, a whimper, the sob of a small animal caught by the predator it most fears—but had neither the courage nor the strength to pull away.

"Really, darling, pull yourself together." Contempt in his voice, contempt in his face. "Don't make an exhibition of yourself in the halls."

"Yes, Malkar," I said, by reflex alone.

He opened the door and led me out into the Mirador.

Mildmay

The Spinning Goblin is about halfway between a hotel and a whorehouse. The guy at the desk don't ask what you want the room for, but if you come in too often, he starts wanting a cut of your action. I didn't go there much—not enough for his fingers to get itchy. But the rooms were clean, and I like people who don't ask questions.

I waited for Miss Thomson outside. Stood in a tenement doorway and watched the traffic on Rue Celadon. The Engmond's Tor Cheaps mostly shut down at sunset, 'least for the perishables, so the road was full of wagons, the drivers keeping to their same slow amble no matter what the hansom and fiacre drivers shouted at them. You want a real feud, just look at the state of affairs between the Wagoners' Guild and the Handsome Men.

I saw Miss Thomson coming just as the bells started ringing the second hour of the night. The dress she was wearing was nothing like the green number she'd worn yesterday. It was a dull, smoky blue, with the high neck and the little fichu, like bourgeoises wear. When she got closer, I saw she'd pinned her hair in a big coil on the back of her head, so her neck looked long, like a swan's. She was wearing pearls in her ears, boring little things as genteel as that fichu, and she looked like she belonged in an old story, the sort of gal that heroes rescue from dragons and shit like that.

I stepped out of the doorway as she passed, and said, "What's with the dress?"

"Oh!" She jumped a little, and her cheeks colored. "Dennis. I . . . I work in a shop on the Road of Carnelian. I didn't have time to change."

"What kind of shop?"

"Oh, you know. Perfume and maquillage and lingerie—ladies' goods."

She had long-fingered, delicate, lily-white hands. I could imagine them among the silks and the cut-glass bottles.

"It's boring," she said, "but it pays the rent."

"Yeah." We were at the door of the Spinning Goblin, and I said, "Let the clerk think whatever he wants. Okay?"

Her blush got redder. She wasn't real demimondaine, just a bourgeoise trying hard to make it. "All right," she said, and I thought again that she had guts. She wasn't flinching from what she'd started.

We went in. I gave the clerk a half-gorgon. That got us a room for an hour. He pushed a key across the desk. "Room six."

I jerked my head at Miss Thomson, and we climbed the stairs. Two flights up and down at the end of the hall, there was Room 6. I unlocked the door, waved her in like a gent, locked the door behind us.

Miss Thomson looked around, at the bed, at the table and two chairs, at the fashion plate somebody'd cut out and pinned to the wall two septads ago. I saw the way her hands tightened on her reticule, and I knew what she was thinking.

"I ain't gonna," I said.

She jumped again, and blushed, and lied, "I didn't think you were."

If she really hadn't thought so, she would have said, *Going to do what?*

I shrugged out of my topcoat, the one I didn't hock unless I was really a half-centime this side of starving. It had been tailored careful, so you could carry a fair amount of stuff under it and it would still hang all right. I'd balanced the dancer on one side with the clock and the box on the other. I put them on the table.

Miss Thomson gave a little squeak of excitement and brushed past me—I felt the soft weight of her dress and breathed in her perfume. She touched the clock and the dancer—just little pats, like she had to prove to herself they were really there—and then pressed her hands down on the box. That wasn't only greed, and I wondered just how nasty Ellis Otanius had been.

I said, "Is the dancer Tolmattin?"

Her laugh was half a gasp. "Oh, yes. El—Lord Ellis's mother wrested it from her older sister at their father's funeral. It is the family's great pride."

"Nice people. You got a key for that box?"

"Oh! I didn't even think—"

"Hang on." I had my lock picks in my inside waistcoat pocket, where nobody was going to find 'em unless they were specially looking for trouble. I got them out and forced the lock again. I didn't fuck up in front of Miss Thomson, either, and it didn't take but a second longer than a normal key would have.

I glanced up into a narrow-eyed look of interest. "Is that a particularly easy lock?" she said.

" 'Bout average for jewelry boxes."

"Could you tea—I mean, could one learn to do that?"

"I guess. It ain't all that hard."

"It looks like a useful skill."

She reached to open the box. Our hands touched for a second, and then I backed up out of the way. I won my bet with myself. The first thing she went for was the rubies.

I said, "Know a good fence?"

"And what makes you think I won't wear them myself?"

"Ain't your color."

"True," she said, with a cute little grimace that it looked like she'd practiced. It was the sort of face to get a guy to kiss her on the tip of her upturned nose and give her anything she wanted. "Actually, I have a buyer. They're supposed to be off Corundum Gate."

"Oh pull the other one!" I said, and she laughed.

"No, I promise. Is provenance the right word?"

"Yeah. If you mean where they came from and everything."

"Well, I've heard their provenance. Three times. It might even be true."

"Yeah, and dogs got wings." I meant to leave it there—she wasn't none of my business once I had my cut—but I couldn't help asking, "Your buyer got a name?"

She looked at me sidelong, her eyebrows raised. "Do you have a better price?"

"Don't I wish. Some people waving gorgons around for bits of Corundum Gate . . . well, let's say they ain't safe." And fire's hot and plague's a bad time. Calling Vey Coruscant "not safe" was like saying arsenic would give you a stomachache.

"I know that. I'm not stupid."

"Yeah, but do you know why?"

"What are you talking about?"

"Look, dammit, there's people out there might be planning to buy *you* right along with them fucking stones!"

"I didn't understand a word of that," she said, and I took a quick chokehold on my temper before I boxed her ears. She'd said it on purpose to be nasty—and, yeah, I had got going too fast—but that was only because she didn't yet know what she'd walked into.

"Look. It ain't none of my business. But if your buyer is Vey Coruscant—or Desirée Vaumond or Christine Cooper, 'cause she uses those names, too—you could be in deep trouble."

Her eyes went wide. "How . . . how did you know?"

"I didn't. It's what you call an educated guess."

"Who's . . ." She licked her lips. "Who's Vey Coruscant?"

"Dassament boss. Blood-witch. You *do* know about blood-witches, don't you?"

She shook her head. But she was listening now, not mad.

"It's nasty shit. People that get tangled up in it mostly don't come out the other side alive—or in one piece."

She thought that over. "I don't suppose I can call it off."

"Nope."

"Can I hire you again?"

I had my mouth open to say, *Fuck, no,* when she said, "Double your cut."

"What d'you want me to do?"

"Just come with me."

"Bodyguarding ain't my thing."

She gave me a look. And behind those raised eyebrows, saying as how I looked nasty enough for her purposes, I could see that she was scared. But she wasn't going to beg, and I admired her for that.

"Okay, fine. What's the lay?"

"We, um, we're meeting at nine o'clock tomorrow night in Adrian's Park."

Of course they were. And that told me what Vey Coruscant really wanted. Gems from Corundum Gate, that had belonged to Sharon Thestonaria, were supposed to be extra good for blood-magic. "You ever been in Adrian's Park?"

"No. Why?"

"You know about it, right?"

"About what? It's a park, like Richard's, isn't it?"

Powers and saints, if she was any flatter, they'd be using her to pave the roads. "No. It's a cemetery." Adrian's Park was a cemetery the same way Vey Coruscant wasn't safe, but I didn't think Miss Thomson would believe me about that until she'd seen it for herself.

"Are you saying you won't go?" She wouldn't let me see she was scared, so it was all prickle and a mulish tilt of the chin.

"No, I ain't saying that." Though Kethe knows I should've been. "We're gonna have to be careful. Who d'you follow?"

"Phi-Kethetin."

"Good."

"Why?"

"He don't like blood-witches."

"Okay, but, Dennis, I don't think he's particularly interested in me."

She was in over her head and knew it, but she was brave enough to try a joke. The gal had guts. "Don't matter," I said. "You're consecrated, right?"

"Of course I am." She even sounded a little offended, like I'd asked whether she bathed regularly.

"Then we're okay. Get one of them little sun necklaces—"

"Like this, you mean?" She pulled a long chain up over her collar. It was as fine as spider silk, and hanging on it was Phi-Kethetin's sun, the circle with the five spiky rays. The circle and the tips of the rays were set with tiny diamond chips. That had set somebody back, and not to a gorgon and change, neither.

I had my mouth open to ask why she hadn't been wearing it last night when I realized the answer. Flat she might be, but not stupid. You don't go meet a thief wearing your good jewelry. I started wondering what it meant that she'd worn it tonight and stopped myself in a hurry. I said, "Good. You'll give her a bad moment with that."

She was frowning. "How do you know all this?"

"Don't matter. You'll wear it?"

"If it will make you feel better."

"Yeah. And don't let her touch you if you can help it. Can you use a knife?"

Her hand moved toward her reticule again. But she stopped it and, blushing, said, "Not for fighting."

"It ain't that hard. Point the sharp end at the other guy."

"Very funny," she said, but her mouth twitched a little.

"Other'n that . . . where d'you want to meet?"

"Oh. Min-Terris's. Is that all right?"

"Sure." Min-Terris's courtyard is always crowded, and one more gal meeting one more guy—nobody's going to give a fuck. "How quick can you get there?"

"We close at sundown, and I can take a hansom. Give me half an hour?"

"Okay. We want to be early 'stead of late."

"I understand."

Looking at her, I thought maybe she did, and that was the best news I'd had since my stupid mouth had agreed to go with her to meet Vey Coruscant, the woman folks in the Lower City, when they had to talk about her at all, called Queen Blood.

Felix

We met no one in the halls—the one time when I was begging the Mirador to send me a vile coincidence, none came. Malkar moved without hindrance down through the snarl of half staircases and spiraling, slanted rooms called the Nautilus, debouching in an old, old servants' passageway in the heart of the Warren. Perforce, I moved with him. The fog of phoenix around me made it difficult to remember from one moment to the next what was happening, where we were going, why I should not go there. It made it even more difficult to remember that I was twenty-six instead of twenty, that Malkar was no longer my master.

A second's unwelcome clarity: Malkar had never quit being my master. He had just let me run on a remarkably long leash.

"Could you have called me back anytime you wanted?" I said, as we turned into a long hallway, louring with soot and cobwebs and the ominous, intrinsic darkness of its stones.

"Of course I could, my dear. But I *didn't* call you back. You came to me of your own accord."

I opened my mouth to protest, saw Malkar's eyebrows raised in polite disbelief, and looked away, the words withering on my tongue.

"You can't deny what you are." He sounded amused. "And you're useful, my dearest, but about as stable and resolute as an aspic. Can you deny it?"

"No, Malkar," I said, thinking of the boy in the Arcane.

"At least you are honest . . . for a whore."

I couldn't help the way my muscles tensed with revulsion—for him, for myself—and he roared with laughter. "What, dearest, no devastating riposte? Can this truly be Lord Felix Harrowgate, whose deadly wit is the terror of the court?"

No, I thought. No, that was someone else. That was someone who wasn't afraid of Malkar. But I was as terrified as I had been in Arabel, so terrified that I could not even answer him. That pleased him—Malkar was always annoyed by defiance—and he forbore to taunt me further.

We came in silence to the door, *his* door—ironbound, worm-eaten, it looked no different than any of the doors along that hall. But I knew what lay behind it. He unlocked it and, with abrupt violence, shoved me through.

I almost kept from falling, ending up on one knee, with my left hand braced against the floor. Behind me, Malkar locked the door again, calling witchlights as he did. The phoenix was lifting, faster and faster, as I looked around, seeing the familiar threadbare hangings, the familiar ugly braziers, the familiar red mosaic pentagram . . . the completely *unfamiliar* shackles anchored to four of the pentagram's five corners.

After a second, the implications sank in, and I made a noise that was too thin, too paralyzed to be a scream.

"None of that," Malkar said. He dragged me upright again. "Really, Felix, *why* couldn't you have drunk yourself into a stupor and saved us both the bother?"

I was staring at him, both hands pressed against my mouth, thinking in an idiot babble, The door is locked, I can't get out, the door is locked, I can't get out. Only Malkar could open that door from the inside; I'd helped him cast the spells that ensured it.

"Never mind," he said, with a little, impatient sigh. "A compulsion will work just as well."

"But you can't . . ." I said, my voice barely more than a squeak.

He laughed. "I'm not a Cabaline, remember? I can do anything I damn well please. If I had more time, I'd reinvoke the obligation de sang—and *then* you'd tell me how you'd broken it, wouldn't you, dearest?—but this will do for now."

Malkar's compulsion cracked across my mind like a whip. I knew ways to avert compulsions, break compulsions—most of them, Malkar had taught me himself—but even as I tried to cast them, he swatted them aside. "Don't be silly, darling. You've never been able to beat me. You never will. Now take your clothes off. And hurry. I have to get this done before midnight."

I did as he said, shivering with cold and fear and the pain of my futile struggle against his spell. When I was naked, he scooped my clothes up negligently and tossed them aside. "And one other precaution," he said, "for I will need all my concentration, and I know how . . . loud you can be." I forced myself to look at him; he was smiling. He produced two lengths of silk from his pocket.

If you scream, I will gag you.

"No, Malkar, please, I won't—"

"Shut up, Felix," he said and gagged me. Then he left me there, like a marionette, while he made his preparations: lighting the braziers, changing into a white, open-fronted silk robe that confirmed my fears about what he intended, for he wore nothing beneath it.

And all the while, as I stood there shivering, I was fighting the compulsion, searching for cracks and leverage, telling myself over and over again that my magic was stronger than his, that I could beat his spell. And the spells of the Virtu were on my side. I knew that, that the Virtu's defenses extended to a ward against compulsions—although Malkar seemed to have walked past that ward as if it weren't there—that somewhere that strength was waiting, too.

But I could not find it. At first I thought I had to be looking past it; I'd grown so used to the Virtu's spells and wards and power over the past six years that I frequently forgot about them for days on end. But the harder I looked, the more the ward wasn't there.

What has Malkar done to me?

Panic closing my throat, I struggled, wedging my power into the places where Malkar's compulsion was weakest. As he'd said, he was in a hurry, and it showed in his casting. And no compulsion could ever hold for long against a determined wizard. When he turned to me and said, "Lie down," I was able to keep standing, although the effort had me panting, almost choking for breath around his gag.

"Lie *down*!" He knocked me sprawling, facedown in the pentagram. I rolled back to my feet and lurched away from him. I had one thing I could try on the door, if I could just reach it.

"You little bitch!" One paw caught my shoulder, spinning me around;

the other knocked my head against the wall, but the only star I saw was the one in the floor. He knotted his hand in my hair and dragged me to the pentagram, dragged me down to the floor. He leaned his knee between my shoulder blades and forced first one arm and then the other out straight, to where he could snap his shackles closed around my wrists. I could feel the pull against my joints—even worse when he had done the same to my ankles—and since I was one of the tallest men in the Mirador, that meant both that Malkar had designed these shackles expressly for me and that he had meant them to be uncomfortable. The latter was no surprise; the former . . .

"Now," he said, a growl in my ear that made my skin crawl, "be still!"

As if I had a choice.

He began his ritual standing over me. The spell he was casting seemed to be a bastard compilation of Cabaline ideas and blood-magic and even some things from the Bastion. But he had taught me, and I probably understood the way his mind worked better than anyone else in the world. I was able, not to follow what he was doing, exactly, but to get the gist of it, as if I were listening to a play in a foreign language, a language with which I was familiar, but not fluent. Long before Malkar touched me, I had gone cold with horror down to the marrow of my bones.

To be a wizard of the Mirador implied a certain understanding of how magic worked and how it was to be used, different from the understandings of the Eusebians in the Bastion or the other schools of magic that flourished in Norvena Magna and Ervenzia and faraway Corambis. Cabaline magic worked with the material world, channeling power through material objects, such as the rings that every Cabaline wizard wore, or the Virtu itself. And, of course, Cabaline dogma said that the worst possible thing a wizard could do was to touch a person with their magic in any way. Even benevolent magics such as healing were anathema to the Mirador, and old Iosephinus Pompey had only taught me how to ward dreams after making me swear a variety of bloodcurdling oaths that I would not betray the source of my knowledge to any other wizard.

What Malkar was doing—and I wanted to shriek and giggle and weep, all at once—was creating a spell that would allow him to use me in the same way that Cabaline wizards used their rings. It was a brilliantly evil parody of Cabaline magic; even if I'd had all my wits about me, even if I hadn't still been mind-numbed by phoenix, I didn't think I would even have been able to find a place to start a counterspell. No wonder, though, that he'd gagged me; no wonder that he'd chained me flat to the floor. I could work magic without either voice or motion, but it was always harder—and he'd known I wouldn't be able to do it tonight. I had no doubt he'd been watching the level of wine in the decanter with great and expert interest.

He knelt between my legs, tracing patterns on my back and thighs. I could feel him using the lines of my scars to guide his patterning, just as a Cabaline wizard might use the grain in a piece of wood or the flaws in a gemstone. My head was canted to the left; I had a shatteringly clear view of the rings on my left hand as the stones began to glow in answer, a sullen, brooding, blood-tinged light that I had never seen in them before. Malkar's spell was working. My eyes began to blur and burn with tears as his hands moved lower, his thick fingers pressing in, cruel invaders, preparing me for the next step.

I tried to breathe through my fear, through the gag. It wasn't as if this would be the first time Malkar had used my body sexually as part of a spell-casting, just as it wasn't the first time he'd laid compulsions on me. And I knew how to cope with violent intercourse. I'd even been good at it, once upon a time. Some of the tarquins who came to the Shining Tiger had asked for me particularly. Relax, I said to myself. You can't fight him, so don't try.

Malkar pulled back. There was a moment of stillness, in which I could not hear him, could not feel him, could not see him. Then he entered me, brutally, throwing my weight forward against the shackles.

He lunged again, and I felt him working his spell, using his penetration of my body to penetrate my mind, using the material to work upon the spiritual. And with his presence came understanding of what he was going to do. I screamed against the gag, screamed my throat raw. Screamed uselessly and far, far too late. I'd thought I'd understood the rules of the game we were playing, Malkar and I, a particularly vicious and twisted version of cat and mouse, the same game we'd been playing since I was fourteen and his eye lit on me amid all the shabby gaudery of the Shining Tiger's parlor. But Malkar had changed the game, changed the stakes, changed the rules, and how stupid I had been to think I understood him, to think I knew what I was letting myself in for. I'd known he would hurt me, and I'd known it would be bad. That playlet the night before had only been practice; I'd known that as soon as he let me go. But I had thought that the catastrophe would be mine alone—and, after all, no more than I deserved. I had been wrong, so terribly wrong that the knowledge of my stupidity and blindness was like a separate pain all to itself.

I felt him in my mind, even more vividly than I felt him in my body, a hurtful, hateful, rending presence, like the color of blood, like the taste of iron, like the scent of burning, destroying everything in his path until he reached the core of my power and seized it.

There were no words for the agony that stabbed through me, from head to heart to hands, enveloping my entire body in the molten blackness of cramp and spasm. No words. No strength. Nothing.

I can't breathe; I can't see; my heart is beating itself to death against the sides of an iron box.

And then Malkar's hand comes down, just at the base of my neck; I feel the pull, as he siphons power through me, just as I was accustomed to siphon power through my rings. And my body responds to this new guidance, this new understanding of what it is supposed to do with its magic. I can breathe again; I can see. I can see blood on my left wrist.

"Now," says Malkar, his voice rough with triumph, with the power he holds. And he begins to use our magic, to wield it like a sledgehammer against the one thing in the Mirador that should be proof against him.

For a moment, I am not in his workroom. I am in the Hall of the Chimeras. It is dark, all the candles snuffed. The Virtu stands by itself, alone on the granite plinth at the east end of the hall, its serene radiance bathing the air around it. I have never seen the Virtu in the dark before, have never seen it this beautiful.

Then I am back in the workroom, in the smell of sweat and blood and magic, Malkar's weight on me like a curse.

He thrusts, and I am in the Hall of the Chimeras again. The Virtu, which no one guards because it needs no guarding, seems to dim for a moment, then responds in a pulse of brilliant viridian. I flinch back, but Malkar's weight shoves me forward. I can feel the Virtu's surface beneath my palms, smooth and astonishingly cold. I see Malkar's attack, like a wave of blackness, traveling from my palms inward toward the globe's puissant tourmaline heart.

I am bathed in the pain of cobalt as the Virtu responds, and fall back into the workroom, where Malkar is snarling curses, even as his power is building, building in him, in me, in the hollow vastness where my magic once was.

He thrusts; the blackness roars down into the Virtu, deeper, stronger. The Virtu's answering flash lights the entire Hall of the Chimeras, but is a pale dream of blue. It is weakening. Malkar thrusts again, harder. And again and again, using the rhythm of his attacks on my body to augment the power of his attacks on the Virtu, as the Virtu's responses weaken, as blood begins to drip from my wrists and ankles. I am crushed between them, asphyxiated; I wonder if I will break before the Virtu does.

And then I am in the Hall of the Chimeras, staring into the heart of the Virtu, and I see the crack, hairline thin, deep within the stone. And through me, Malkar sees it, too. He drives our power down through the stone, hitting the crack again and again. I see the crack widen, see other cracks begin to radiate out. I feel Malkar gather himself.

He climaxes in a terrible explosion of power, a massive surge that roars along the path of the ritual, hurling itself into those cracks, combusting itself in the heart of the Virtu's blue-green purity as Malkar's orgasm combusts itself in my mind and body.

The Virtu shatters like glass.

Malkar collapses on top of me, and I am so deafened by the sound of the Virtu's shards smashing against the plinth, against Lord Michael's Chair, against the dais, against the mosaic chimeras, that I only gradually realize he is speaking.

"Wonderful," he murmurs in my ear, as if he were truly my lover, while he works out the knot of his gag. My hair is caught in the knot; I feel the pull, but as if from miles away. "Magnificent. You have met my expectations, my dearest, and I will take you with me." He removes the gag. I draw a deep, shuddering breath that comes out in painful sobs. He makes no threats this time; I am beyond being able to make enough noise to bother or imperil him, and he knows it.

He lifts himself off me, kneeling over me while he opens the shackles that bind me to the floor. I cannot move, even to flinch from his touch. The light in my rings is gone; there is nothing in my head where my magic was, nothing except hurt. I shut my eyes. Tears run down my cheekbone, down my nose.

I feel Malkar get to his feet. The only thing he can do to me now, the only thing that could hurt me more, is kill me, and I hope he will. I lie and wait. At some point I realize my eyes are open, staring at my dead rings.

Malkar returns. "Come on, Felix, get up. We don't have time for this nonsense."

"Just kill me," I say, half into the floor, and shut my eyes again. I don't recognize my own voice, that harsh, hoarse croak with the Lower City vowels.

"Kill you?" He laughs. "Don't be trite, dearest. I have promised General Mercator the chance to meet you, and I don't like to go back on my promises."

That is a lie. Malkar loves breaking promises. Then the sense of what he said hits me, and my eyes open again. "General Mercator?"

"Well, of course, darling. You didn't imagine I was going to stay here, did you?" But teasing me is no lasting pleasure this evening. His voice changes. "Now, get up, slut, and if you love your tongue, *mind it.* I don't want you talking like a cheap whore."

I remember the lengths he went to, in order to teach me to talk like the Marathine nobility. He does not intend to kill me, and my fear of him wraps back around me like a coat made of chains and shards of glass.

"Ye . . . yes, Malkar," I say, jerking my vowels under control. I manage to roll over, manage to sit up, although my head is spinning. I look at Malkar, purely from reflex, and do not scream only because I am too frightened. The thing standing there, wearing Malkar's clothes, is vast, the color of the Sim, the terrible black river of Mélusine. It has the broad, cruel head of a bull-baiting dog; its eyes are red, glowing like cinders, and the drool hanging from its jaws is flecked with blood.

"Better," it says in Malkar's voice. "Clean yourself up and get those clothes on. *Hurry,* curse you."

Numbly, my hands shaking, I do as it tells me. I have plenty of experience in dealing with the aftereffects of what Malkar has done to my body, know all too well how to ensure that there will be no bloodstains on my clothes. Once I am dressed, the dog comes back and bandages my wrists. It has Malkar's hands, Malkar's rings. The air around it shivers with red and copper.

It ties back my hair, although I know that nothing now can hide the fact that I am mad. "Come along," it says.

"Wh . . . where are we going?"

"I told you. The Bastion. Now, come on, Felix, or I'll leave you for Stephen."

I do not want to be left for Stephen.

I follow the dog.

Chapter 2

Felix

I had a moment of clarity, a moment when the world snapped into place like a dislocated joint back into its socket. We were in the yard of a livery stable, not far off the Plaza del'Archimago. Malkar was bargaining with a lanky, squinting individual. And he was Malkar again, not a dog-headed monster. The lanky man with the squint was suddenly free of the wash of purple that had half obscured him from me. I could hear them arguing, and their voices were voices, and their words made sense.

I thought, Malkar has driven me mad. And the thought was a comfort, because it meant the dog-headed monster was not real, that the colors I had seen around the guards at the Harriers' Gate, the colors around the ostler, were not real, either. It was only madness, not that I had fallen into Hell.

Then I thought, And what, pray tell, is the difference?

Looking at the ground, I saw that Malkar's shadow had a dog's head.

I ride behind the dog out of the city, the city of shadows, the city of burning, the city of ghosts. When the gatemouth has shrunk behind us, the dog stops and comes back and ties my hands to the saddle. Then we ride again. I don't know how long we ride. Everything hurts, and the city is screaming behind me.

We stop. The dog drags me off the horse. There is a fire. Later, the dog makes me eat; everything tastes like soot. I am afraid the dog will make me do other things, but it leaves me alone. I am so grateful I start crying, and it snarls at me to keep still.

I must have slept, for I woke from a nightmare in pitch-blackness, with the stars above me like cold eyes. The Virtu still shattering in my head, I realized that I could hear myself screaming.

Malkar's paw caught me across the face with bone-rattling force. "Quit that noise!"

I had nothing left but obedience to Malkar; I did as he said. He kicked me and then, satisfied, went back to the other side of the fire. I sobbed, half strangling myself in my efforts not to make a sound, and eventually fell back asleep because I was too exhausted even for grief.

My dreams were chaotic and confused, full of fire and stone.

Shannon weeps in endless silence, and the Virtu shatters like a child's toy. Malkar chains me in his stone pentagram. Keeper smiles at me, fingering the haft of his whip, and I take off my shirt obediently. Robert's poisonous malice drips from his smile, and Stephen looks at me and looks away.

Malkar shook me awake at dawn. He was himself; I did not look at his shadow.

He tied my hands to the saddle again before we started; I wondered if he was afraid that I would bolt or that I would faint.

Last night it had all been darkness and dizziness. This morning, I recognized that we were in the Grasslands, in the vast, empty land that neither the Protectorate of Marathat nor the Empire of Kekropia valued enough to start a war over. We were, of course, heading toward the Bastion, where Malkar would doubtless be greeted as a hero and I as his catamite.

As his catamite. For a second, I couldn't breathe.

I could feel the damage done to my mind as vividly as I saw the wreckage of the Virtu every time I closed my eyes. I could not touch my power, sundered from it by a chasm of pain as dark as the Sim. My last possible weapon against Malkar was gone; now that I was desperate enough, mad enough, to turn my magic against him, I could not. He had taken it away from me, as he had taken everything else.

Mildmay

Mrs. Pickering pounded on the door.

I came bolt awake, out of a dream—something about the Boneprince, and Rindleshin, I don't know—and shoved my fingers through my hair on the way to the door. More for me than her.

I was expecting a fight—about the rent, about Scabious, about Kethe knows what—but when I opened the door, her face said otherwise.

"What?" I said.

"I've been hearing things all morning. Something happened up there. Something bad. You know anything?"

In the Lower City, "up there" means the Mirador. People don't like to say the name. It's bad luck.

"Not me," I said. But bad news from the Mirador is bad news for everybody, one way or another. "I can go ask around."

"That's good of you, Gilroi." She stood there a second, like she was going to say something else, and then went away.

I dragged my boots on and went out.

I knew where I was going. I mean, if you're just out to shoot the shit, that's one thing, and I could have gone a septad different places for that. But that would only get me the same rumors Mrs. Pickering had been hearing. For real information, you have to go deeper.

I spent a lot of time in the Arcane. The tunnels run under most of the Lower City—except in Simside and Queensdock, where the ground's only barely fit to build on—all the way out to Carnelian Gate on the east. About two blocks south of the Road of Ivory, to the west of the Lower City, somebody bricked 'em off. Perfectly straight line, perfectly regular brickwork, all the way from Ivory Gate to the Plaza del'Archimago. There's spells there, too, or so the hocuses say, and if anybody's ever been crazy enough to try and see what the mason and the hocus were hiding—well, they ain't come back to brag about it, that's for sure.

Can't get to the Arcane from Simside. Can't get to the Arcane from

Queensdock. Breadoven don't have a way into the Arcane, neither, but I don't know why. Other'n that, you got your pick. The big, official entrance is in Scaffelgreen, with the fancy carving over the doors that says CATACOMBES DES ARCANES. That's where the tours go in, but what they don't tell you on the tours is that what you see ain't even the *beginning* of what's down there. They take your half-gorgon and show you the Executioners' Ossuary and the buried church of St. Flossian and probably a couple miles of crypts, but that ain't the Arcane. That entrance ain't much good for nobody but the flats.

There's three entrances in Midwinter that I know about—probably more—but two of them are hard to get at. One's under the altar in the church of St. Griphene, and the other's in the root cellar of a house on Excalibur Street, and the family that lives there now don't know about it. I went in through the trapdoor in the basement of the Hornet and Spindle and started for Havelock, where the lady I wanted to talk to ran her business.

Her name's Elvire. She's the madam of the Goosegirl's Palace. Her and her girls cater to the hocuses and flashies along with the thieves and pushers, so the Palace is about as much about gossip as it is about fucking. Elvire'd passed her Great Septad, but she hid it with corsets and rice powder and this enormous black wig like her own private cathedral. She talked flash—rumor said she'd been Lord Gareth's mistress for an indiction or three. Her information was always good, and worth its weight in gold.

The Palace is way, way under the Butchers' Guild. I never went there without wondering how many butchers knew that. The guy at the door today was Philippe Wall-Eye—so as not to get him confused with Philippe le Coupé, the eunuch who ran the Palace's bar. Philippe Wall-Eye knew me, and he let me past without any fuss. Me and Elvire had done deals before, and I'd played fair by her.

She had two offices. I found her in the one that wasn't meant to impress the clients. She looked up when I knocked and gave me a smile. Elvire had been a madam for three septads and a whore for at least two before that—her smile didn't mean nothing about how she felt.

"Hey, Elvire," I said. "What's going on?"

"You mean Upstairs." The Arcane don't like the word "Mirador" neither.

"Yeah."

"Sit down."

My stomach muscles clenched up, 'cause she hadn't said that like it was just to be sociable. I sat.

Elvire took a deep breath and came out with it. "The Virtu was broken last night."

"*What?*" I was glad I was sitting down, 'cause that was a nasty kick in the teeth, no two ways about it.

The Virtu of the Mirador was created by the Cabal back in 16.5.1. It was a big blue globe, as tall as a man. They kept it in the Hall of the Chimeras, smack in the middle of the Mirador, and what it was supposed to do depended on who you asked. The Mirador talked a lot of mystic bullshit about purity and strength—the name "Virtu" was some kind of cleverdick Marathine-Midlander pun. The hocuses in the Lower City talked about focusing and matrices, and made even less sense than the official line. All I knew for sure was that all the hocuses in the Mirador swore oaths on the Virtu every single day, and that was what kept the Mirador from tearing itself apart. No matter how you felt about the hocuses sitting on top of the city like a pack of vultures, you didn't want the Virtu broken.

Elvire just sat there and let me grapple with it, and finally I said, "I thought . . . I mean, that's impossible, right?"

She spread her hands in a sort of helpless I-only-know-what-I'm-told way. "Well, they seem to know who did it, and if *that*'s true, then I believe it. Do you know about Felix Harrowgate?"

"Elvire, you know me. I stay *away* from hocuses."

"He's Caloxan," she said, like it should mean something to me.

"He's what?"

"From Caloxa. Blessed saints, don't you ever look at a map? North. Past the Perblanches."

"So?"

"They had a *king*."

"Oh boy."

"Yes. Exactly. And when their king was deposed, Lord Felix's mother took her child and ran south. I've heard that she was related to him."

"To the king?"

"Yes. In any event, she got as far as Arabel and was taken in by a wealthy landowner. She died, the landowner raised Lord Felix, and when he had two septads and three, he came to the Mirador."

"And he's related to a king."

"A dead king."

"Fuck."

"And he's very powerful. My clients are scared witless of him." She paused, gave me this look from under her eyelashes. "Nobody can find him this morning."

"Fuck."

"Lord Stephen left at dawn, riding east. That's all I know."

"We're all fucked sideways, ain't we?" East toward the Empire. East toward the Bastion. East was a bad direction. "Thanks, Elvire."

I did a little fishing for other things—you got to keep your ear to the ground in my line of work—but the news from the Mirador was really all there was, and I was out of Elvire's office before long. Philippe Wall-Eye said he had a hot tip for the dog races next Deuxième, but I told him to give it to somebody who cared.

I made Mrs. Pickering one popular lady that morning. Seemed like half Midwinter was jammed into her kitchen, wondering what that hocus had been thinking of and what they'd do with him when they caught him. I sat in my front room and stared out the window, imagining the news traveling through the Lower City like a fire.

And you know fear would be traveling right along with it.

Felix

They caught us a little after midday, as Malkar must have known they would. He made no attempt to outrun them, instead stopping at the top of a rise, dismounting, making me dismount, too. We stood and watched the riders approach.

Stephen led them—although sometimes when I looked at him, he had a bear's head—and I saw faces that I knew among the riders: Luke and Esmond and Vida looking as if she had been carved out of stone. Stephen was black and lurid scarlet with fury; I was frightened to look at him.

"My lord," said the dog, with a slight nod.

"Lord Malkar," said the bear. "I expect you know why I have come."

"I do, and I am prepared to offer you a bargain."

"A *bargain!*" Red and yellow incredulity washed across the whole company.

The dog nodded again, its jaws parting in a slavering grin. "Felix for my freedom."

I thought I was going to faint, with the shock and panic and horror slamming through my skull. I knew Malkar did not keep his promises, but this I had not expected. The only thing at this point that seemed worse than staying with Malkar was being given to Stephen. Malkar's cruelty was at least a known quantity, and I had the protection of being useful. Or, rather, I had thought I did. Never trust Malkar. Never, never, never.

"You want the man who broke the Virtu," Malkar said. "You must know—Victoria surely has told you—that it was not I. I do not have the power."

Stephen nodded grudgingly, but his eyes were suspicious. I wanted to scream at him, tell him not to listen—*never* listen to Malkar—but I could not speak. I knew all that would come out were the whining howls of a coyote.

"Felix is the only wizard in the Mirador with the power to break the Virtu," Malkar said, so reasonably, so truthfully. "I will give him to you; in return, you will let me go on my way."

"You are going to the Bastion."

"Yes. I had been going there anyway. Felix begged me to take him with me. I do not know why. I refused. But after he broke the Virtu, I . . . reconsidered."

Those sparks of blackness in the raging red corona around Stephen told me that Shannon had admitted our fight, confessed to the bruise. And Stephen had loathed me for years. He would believe any evil of me, and gladly.

"I could take both of you," the bear growled. "You are as much a traitor as he."

"Please, Lord Stephen, be reasonable. I am not a Cabaline. I have not sworn your ridiculous panoply of oaths. I am not even a citizen of Marathat. If I wish to visit the Empire, it is no one's business but my own. And I do not care to have my business interfered with. Take Felix, who is too far gone on phoenix to cause you any trouble, and let us part without further . . . unpleasantness."

I could see that Stephen believed him about the phoenix, just as he seemed to believe that I would have broken the Virtu in consequence of a nasty piece of gossip and a lovers' quarrel. He sat and thought. I could see, too, that his fury was almost too great for him to think at all; it washed off him in great scarlet waves, splashing the riders and lapping against my feet. I wanted to move back, but Malkar's grip on my arm was too strong.

"Malkar, please," I said, "please don't—"

"Hush, Felix," the dog said. "Lord Stephen is thinking."

The mockery in Malkar's voice acted on Stephen like spurs. "Very well," he said. "Give me Felix, and you can go. But do not think this is the end of it."

"Not at all," Malkar said. "Thank you, my lord." He turned and caught me in a kiss that probably looked passionate, but was nothing more than a brutal, numbing intrusion, a blind for the compulsion he cast, winding me about in a shroud of briars, ensnaring me and silencing me, so that I could tell no one the truth, tell no one what he had done and how.

He murmured, just loud enough for the riders to hear, "Good-bye, my darling," and pushed me suddenly toward Stephen. I stumbled halfway down the hill and dropped to my knees, drowning in a pool of bloody hate. Malkar had already swung onto his horse and spurred it away, over the top of the rise, the second horse running after.

The bear dismounted, his movements deliberate with fury as he waded through the bloody surge of his own hatred, and grabbed me by my coat lapels, hauling me to my feet.

"Do you know what you've done?" he said, his voice low, his eyes red and black and horrible. "Do you even care? The Curia managed to contain the damage, which I'm sure disappoints you, but *every single spell* has been weakened. Victoria says they may begin to unravel at any moment."

He paused, waiting for me to make some response, but the briars and the abyss were all that were in my head, and they gave no answers. Stephen's grip tightened on my coat, and he went on, his hatred staining both of us with carmine guilt. "We haven't been this vulnerable since the days of Lucien Kingdom-Breaker. Every wizard in the Mirador has been working desperately to shore up our defenses since we realized what you had done. I shouldn't have taken Lady Vida away from that, but I *thought* her services as a member of the Curia would be required to hold you. I *thought* you'd put up a fight." He stopped, staring at me; the red blackness of his eyes was making me dizzy. "Why did you do it?" He shook me, a sharp, hard snap like a terrier killing a rat. I wished it had killed me. "Damn you, *why?*"

I could not answer him; he shoved me away in disgust, sending me sprawling, and said, "Get this vermin away from me. And make sure you tie his hands."

The riders surrounded me, tying my hands, pulling the ribbon out of my hair, shoving me roughly up onto a horse.

"Do you have him, Vida?" the bear demanded.

The lady is an obsidian statue with eyes of green stone. "He's taken phoenix. He won't be able to concentrate to work magic until—"

"Do you have him?"

The obsidian statue bowed her head. "Yes, my lord. I can hold him until we return to the Mirador."

"Then, by the powers and saints, let us ride."

I could feel their revulsion, Stephen's and Vida's and Luke's and Esmond's and everyone's, and I swallowed hard against the lump in my throat. I did not want Stephen's excoriating mockery, and that was all he would have for my tears. Hate splashed around the horse's hooves in oily pools. I shut my eyes and wished I knew how to pray.

They ride all day. They stop sometimes to let the horses drink, but never for long. No one looks at me. I try to pretend I am not here.

I can tell that time is passing because the city gets louder in my head. I can hear it screaming. And I can see it, getting bigger and bigger, like a tower of thunderclouds.

They stop at sunset. I am glad. I don't want to ride into the screaming city in the dark. They drag me off the horse. They are all monsters, with the heads of owls and cats. They are all drenched in blood; they leave trails of it behind them when they move. I wonder what they have killed.

They speak to each other; their voices are like breaking glass. Then they are around me again, their hands on my arms. The bear-headed monster is not with them. I can't see him, or the woman made of obsidian. I try to cry out, but I have no voice. They are pushing me and dragging me, and I don't know where we are going, or why. All I can see is blood and broken glass.

Then the ground is gone, and the air. It is all water. Water and hands. Hands gripping my shoulders, my arms, hands knotted in my hair. The hands hold me under the water, until my lungs are burning and blackness is swallowing the world. Then they pull me up. Mud under my hands. I am gasping for air; I can't see anything.

I hear a voice, as cruel as glass, "Can he swim?"

"Nah."

"Then throw him in."

Hands haul me upright. There are too many of them. The ground is gone; everything is gone. The water is cold, black, like hatred. I fight it desperately, screaming, and I know the monsters are laughing at me. Then there are hands again, holding me under, dragging me down. I am screaming and screaming. And then the ground is under me again, and the hands are pushing me down, like Malkar, and I fight them, clawing and biting. They hit me until I can't breathe and can't scream and can't fight, and they hit me and hit me.

And then the hands are gone, and a monster is roaring. Different hands come and drag me upright. For a moment I hear Stephen's voice, ". . . think I want to try any of you idiots for *his* murder?" And then we are going in a direction I know is away from the river, and I am shaking and can't stop.

Then the bear tells me to sit down, and they tie my hands and feet and drop a blanket over me.

The obsidian woman gives me one flat, indifferent glance and looks away.

After a time, I sleep.

My dreams are all of broken glass and deathly water.

Mildmay

Min-Terris's courtyard was packed when I got there, even more so than normal, which was saying something. People were talking about the Mirador and the Virtu and the hocus along with all the usual talk about getting laid and calling people out and where to score good spiderweb. I said " 'Scuse me" a lot, working through the crowd, looking for Miss Thomson. It was half an hour after we'd agreed to meet that I finally spotted her. She was still in her shop dress, like she'd been the day before.

I got over to her. She said, "Oh thank goodness! I was beginning to think I'd have to go all by myself."

"Let's get out of the crowd," I said. "C'mon."

We started back toward Rue St. Bonamy. About halfway there, between a little gang of hookers in black velvet and a couple of muscle-men who were probably there with a pusher, Miss Thomson caught at my arm. "Sorry," she said, "but I'm afraid if I lose track of you now, I really *will* have to go by myself."

"It's okay." Her perfume smelled like summer. "C'mon," I said again.

Out on the street, she let go of my arm. We started for Ruthven and the Boneprince. After a block or two, Miss Thomson said, "Do you mind if I talk?"

"Mind?"

"I know I chatter too much. But I'm nervous. And I'd feel better if I . . . if, you know . . ."

"Kethe, I don't mind. If you need to shut up, I'll say so."

"Thanks," she said, only a little snarky. She talked the rest of the way to the Boneprince, not minding that I didn't say nothing back. And I could see that she glanced at me, like we were really having a conversation, and like my face didn't bother her.

She talked about her job. It was boring, she said, and she'd quit as soon as she'd found "something better." I knew what she meant, but I didn't say so. And she told me more about the hocus that broke the Virtu. She knew a woman who'd seen him once, in one of them flash jewelry stores so far up the Road of Carnelian they're practically in the Plaza del'Archimago. "He came in with *Lord Shannon*," Miss Thomson said, in a kind of awed whisper. "Minna says he dyes his hair bright red."

Powers, who'd want to? I thought. But I didn't say that, neither.

"And she says his eyes don't match. One's blue and the other's *yellow*. She says she was scared to death the whole time that he'd hex her."

"Did he?"

"I don't think so. But they were there for an hour and a half, and Lord Shannon was looking at stickpins while this wizard, Lord Felix, was sort of wandering around. You know, the way people do in stores when they don't want to buy anything. And then finally, Lord Shannon says, 'Felix, what do you think of this one?' And Lord Felix says, 'Darling, I think they're all hideous, but buy whichever one you like.' And then they left without buying anything. Minna said that was hex enough."

"Oh," I said. I knew Lord Shannon was molly—he wasn't at no pains to hide it and hadn't been since he finished his second septad—and I'd heard rumors he was sleeping with a hocus. Mostly, people look the other way from the Teverii's love affairs. It's polite—and it's less likely to get you sent to the sanguette. After the Golden Bitch, the whole city is pretty damn twitchy about that kind of thing. And I guessed that explained why the Lord Protector was always fighting with this Lord Felix. The Lord Protector didn't like molls.

I told Miss Thomson when we crossed into Ruthven that we'd be reaching the Boneprince in another couple blocks. She fished in her reticule and brought out a pair of them sunflower-yellow kidskin gloves that were all the rage this season. If I'd chucked a stone just right in Min-Terris's courtyard, I could've bounced it off five women wearing gloves that exact color.

"Smart," I said.

"No matter what you think, I'm not a *total* flat," she said and smiled at me in a way that made my stomach turn over.

"There's the Boneprince," I said, pointing up ahead where the spikes on the gate stuck up over the buildings. There was a ring of vacant lots around the Boneprince, like a moat—or the mange—and it was easy to see.

"Why is it called that?" Miss Thomson said. " 'The Boneprince'?"

"Where're you *from?*" I said without meaning to.

"Wraith," she said, like she was daring me to make something of it.

"Oh. Well, okay. It's Adrian's Park, right?"

"Right."

"Well, what Adrian's famous for, in Mélusine, is fucking up his chance to murder his brother."

"Excuse me?"

"Him and Richard were twins. Mathurin the Open-Handed's sons. Richard was older by like a quarter hour. So, when he finished his third septad, Adrian had a pretty good go at getting rid of Richard—him standing between Adrian and the throne and all. Only some people, when they tell the story, they say Adrian didn't care about being king. He wanted to kill Richard because Richard was telling lies about him to Mathurin. Richard was called the Visionary, when *he* was king."

"Oh," said Miss Thomson.

We were at the gates now, black and awful like dragon's wings. I stopped where I was, to finish the story.

"So, anyway, Adrian tries and fails, and they arrest him. They got to, you know, but you got to pity the guys who drew the short straw on that one. And he manages to kill himself before they figure out what to do with him, or who's got the right to try him, or anything. Richard brought him poison."

"Why?"

"Dunno. Some people say it was to show he forgave Adrian, and some people say it was an apology, and there's some people say it's 'cause Richard knew which side his bread was buttered on, and wanted Adrian's mouth shut permanent-like."

"That's horrible."

"Some people got nasty minds." I shrugged. "But Mathurin didn't care. He'd had the parks built to celebrate their second septad, and now he said Adrian's Park was going to be a cemetery for murderers and heretics. Adrian was the first burial. That's why it's the Boneprince."

She signed herself, a religious gal's reflex, and I decided I wouldn't tell her about the ghosts.

Everybody knows the Boneprince is haunted, and I got like a triple septad of stories about the ghosts, and the people they've appeared to, and the things they've said. I ain't seen no ghosts myself, but, Kethe, I've felt 'em. Felt 'em watching. I've walked in at the septad-day, when ghosts are weakest, and after a minute or two, I was looking over my shoulders and up into the trees. Never saw so much as a bird.

It was way worse at night.

And then there were the kids' graves. Not even in the gates yet, and I was already tensing up. About a Great Septad ago, Lady Jane had decided to clean up the Lower City and get rid of all the kept-thieves. Kethe only knows what put that into her head, since you didn't need but a thimble-worth of common sense to see it wasn't going to work. But the Dogs rounded up a bunch of kept-thieves—even a keeper or two—and gave them all to Madame Sanguette. Don't know what happened to the keepers' bodies, but the kept-thieves were buried in the Boneprince. Their graves lined the way from the one and only gate to the statue of Prince Adrian in the middle of everything, like the Boneprince was still a park. No gravestones or nothing. Nobody remembered their names. Nobody'd thought to ask before they whacked their heads off. There were never flowers on the kept-thieves' graves, although sometimes there'd be flowers left for Marius Leeth, an assassin who'd been in the Boneprince for ten septads, or even the poisoner Quinquill, who'd died in the days of the last Ophidian king.

Everywhere else in the Boneprince, they'd tore up the marble that had paved the paths. They left it there, though, on the path from the gate to the statue, between the kept-thieves' graves. People called it the Road of Marble, as a sort of nasty joke. Didn't matter where you went in the Boneprince, you'd feel yourself being watched, but it was always worst along there, and that night, powers and saints preserve me, it was like getting hit with a sandbag. We were wrong and stupid to be here, and if it hadn't been Vey Coruscant we were meeting—and we were even stupider to be doing that—I would have said, *Let's ditch this and go get drunk someplace, okay?* But no matter what you thought she was up to, you didn't break a date with Queen Blood.

"Dennis?" Miss Thomson said. "Do you feel something . . . odd?"

"Ghosts," I said, too nervous to lie. "Watching."

"*Ghosts?* For real?"

"Yeah. If we're lucky, they won't do nothing but watch." The kind of luck I was talking about was the kind of luck that lets one cat escape from a septad dogs, and that kind of luck don't happen to people very often. I mean, Vey Coruscant had a reason to be here, and I didn't think it was a reason me and Miss Thomson were going to like. And I couldn't help thinking, us walking down the Road of Marble like two stupid kids in a fairy tale, that Brinvillier Strych was buried somewhere in the Boneprince. And, alive or dead, Brinvillier Strych—him the Lower City called Lord Bonfire—was bad news. Even worse news if that had anything to do with Vey Coruscant wanting to meet here. Fuck me for a half-wit dog, I thought, how the fuck did I get into this?

But I knew the answer to that. I'd fallen for Ginevra Thomson's big blue eyes, and the way she brought her chin up when she was facing something she was scared of. Stupid, Milly-Fox. Very stupid.

We got to the statue at last—even two minutes walking through the Boneprince at night was like one of them Great-Septad-long journeys in the stories about Mark Polaris. The statue was bronze, life-size, bolted to a big square piece of granite. Originally, it'd been gilded, but thief-keepers liked to send in their best kids to scrape the gilding off, mostly right around the septad-night. That separated the sheep from the wolves in a hurry. If you didn't come screaming out of the Boneprince within a septad-minute of being sent in, you had the nerves for cat burglary—and worse things, too, if your keeper was into those, like mine was.

There was precious little gilt left on Prince Adrian now—a few fragments in his curls, a few more maybe in his fancy belt buckle. His eyes were gone, too. Somebody'd probably made off with them as soon as the news came down that he'd died. Story was that they were matched sapphires, but I checked out Prince Richard one day, when I didn't have nothing better to do, and his eyes were lapis lazuli. I'd've bet, both that Adrian's were the same, and that they sold for the price of diamonds. People will pay through the nose for a good story.

It was too dark to see the statue's empty eye sockets, and I was perfectly okay with that.

"Now what?" Miss Thomson whispered.

"We wait," I said and put my lantern down carefully where neither of us would be liable to kick it. "Dunno how long. 'Til your buyer shows up, I guess."

"Wonderful," she said. We were standing close enough that I could feel her shiver.

"Shit," I said, suddenly thinking of something I should've remembered a long time ago. "She know your name?"

"No. The, um, fence I went to first said not to use my real name, though he didn't say why."

"Be glad he told you that. It's important. Don't give her your real name."

"All right. Don't give her my name. Don't let her touch me. Anything else?"

I took a deep breath and tried to pretend it helped my nerves. "If I tell you to run, *run*. Whether you got the gorgons or not. Whether you think I got a reason or not. Okay?"

"Yes. I'll do what you say. I'd be a fool not to."

I caught myself just short of saying, *It's what you hired me for, darlin'*. That was just nerves, and me getting snarky wasn't going to help us nohow.

There wasn't nothing to say after that, and I think we were both scared of what we wouldn't be able to hear if we were talking. So we stood there, not saying nothing, and after, I don't know, maybe a quarter hour, the lantern went out, quick as winking and not on its own. A voice said out of the darkness to our right—*not* from the Road of Marble—"You are early, and you are not alone."

It was a woman's voice, deep and smooth with an edge on it like a knife. Vey Coruscant, Her Majesty of Blood.

Miss Thomson said, her voice steady as a rock, "I was not aware that either is a crime."

"Neither is," Vey said. She moved to stand in front of Miss Thomson, about a septad-foot back. "I was merely . . . surprised. I had not understood either to be a condition in the arrangements. Or was my messenger at fault?"

"No. I didn't think it necessary to mention that I was taking sensible precautions. Perhaps it was. I beg your pardon." All stiff and icy and prickly, like she wasn't scared half out of her mind.

Vey laughed. I wished she hadn't. It wasn't a nice noise. "Lay your hackles, foolish girl. Do you have the rubies?"

"Yes," said Miss Thomson. "Do you have the gorgons?"

"Jean-Lundy!" Vey called.

Something rustled in the ornamental hedges, back of where Vey's voice was coming from. I hoped her Jean-Lundy was getting himself stuck full of thorns. Vey said, "Jean-Lundy has them." It wasn't the most graceful I'd ever seen that done, but it worked. Like I was even thinking about trying to jump Vey Coruscant anyway.

"Who is your silent companion?" Vey asked, lightly—oh so fucking lightly—but with something thin and cold somewhere away beneath it, like the Sim beneath the city.

"Local muscle," Miss Thomson said, and I thought if we got out of here, I should tell her to go audition at the Cockatrice, 'cause she was wasted on the lordlings from up the city.

"Indeed." Vey didn't quite sound like she was buying it, and I was glad Miss Thomson had been dumb enough to agree to a night meet, because Vey couldn't see my face, and that was about the only good thing in this whole fucking mess. "No matter. The rubies, please."

"Gorgons first."

There was a pause, like the pause when you get in a knife fight and the other guy waits just a second, because he knows how much better he is than you, and you know it, too. I heard thunder, way off in the distance, like a giant grumbling, and thought, Oh Kethe, not now!

Miss Thomson said, "You don't really think I'm stupid enough to try running off with your money when the bushes are crawling with your servants, do you? On the other hand, how do I know you'll pay me once you have the rubies? Gorgons first."

"Very well. Jean-Lundy!"

It took Jean-Lundy like fucking *hours* to come thrashing out of the bushes to give Vey the money. I knew she was stalling, drawing this out just as far as she could before she sprang the trap, letting the rain come toward the city, toward whatever nasty thing it was she'd got planned. There was another rumble of thunder. I would have sold my soul for the hour of clear weather me and Vey both knew we didn't have. If I'd dared, I would've told Miss Thomson to hurry up, but that would be telling Vey I'd caught on to what she was doing.

"Here is the money," Vey said then. "Where are the rubies?"

"I have them," Miss Thomson said. I felt her shift her weight, and she stepped forward. "Let us trade."

I moved forward, too. Not much, just enough to keep more or less in range. The wind picked up, whispering and rustling through the leaves. We had maybe a quarter hour—probably less—before the rain hit. I heard the trade in the dark, heard the click of Miss Thomson's heels as she stepped back, heard Vey say something in a curt undertone. Then, all at once and with no noise at all, two fucking enormous hands grabbed me, one around my upper arm, the other over my mouth. I was twisting as I felt their heat, part of my mind howling, Where'd he *come* from? But even as my elbow went backwards for his floating ribs, he was moving away again. He was only there to keep me busy while the others attended to their real business.

Miss Thomson shrieked, "Dennis! Hel—" And bang went that safe name. I hoped I was going to live long enough to worry about it.

"If you move, whoever you are," Vey's voice came out of the darkness. She wasn't where she'd been standing, but now I wasn't sure where she was. "If you move, she will be dead some moments before you reach her. Do you believe me?"

"Yeah," I said, not adding that we all knew Miss Thomson was going to be dead in an hour whether I moved or not. Good going, Milly-Fox. Some bodyguard you are.

"Good," Vey said. "Claudio, if he so much as twitches, kill him."

"Yes, madame," a deep, rough voice said from somewhere behind my left shoulder. And he could do it, too. It wasn't that he was faster than me from a standing start, but he knew right where I was, and I was having a fuck of a time getting him placed. Way too late, I remembered the stories about hocuses and the spells they could cast to make people think that left was right and down was up and shit like that. You never know how much to believe about hocuses in stories, but my feeling about Vey Coruscant was that she could probably do anything she damn well pleased.

"Brandon," Vey said, "bring me the girl."

Sounds of movement, a grunt of pain. "She bit me, the bitch." At least Miss Thomson was still conscious.

"Take her gloves off," Vey said. "And hold her!"

"Yes, madame," Brandon said, just like Claudio.

"Now, girl, what is your name?"

"Lucy," Miss Thomson said. Her breath caught in a sharp gasp of pain. I didn't need the light to know that Vey had cut her across her palm.

Now, I don't know shit about blood-magic, and I don't want to. And besides, it was pitch-black. So I can't explain what Vey did. I don't know if the words I heard her saying, in some weird language like an iron box falling down a flight of stairs, were a spell or instructions to her goons or her recipe for ginger cookies. I know that she hadn't been going long before I felt the rain start, little cold finger touches on my face and arms, and she wasn't done before I was soaked to the skin. And I could feel the ghosts around us, crowding close. I could feel them watching, the same way I could feel the lightning up in the clouds, just biding its time. Whatever she was doing, they were interested.

When she stopped, about a decad after the end of the world from the way I felt, there was this weird, flat pause, like when you ask somebody a question who's not in the room. I knew something was fucked then, fucked bad.

Vey shrieked—and I mean that, it was like the noise tomcats make when they fight, not nothing human at all—"*Where is he?*"

There was a voice. I thought it was coming from the statue, but I couldn't swear to it or nothing, although I still hear it sometimes, in those dreams you get where you wake up sweating and scared to move. It said, "I am afraid, madame, that he is not among us. You bound your search with the iron fence of the . . . Boneprince"—and, Kethe, the disgust in the voice when it said that word, like it was talking about somebody eating their own shit—"and within those bounds . . . within those bounds, madame, your nets have come up empty."

Vey was whispering frantically under her breath, more words in that ugly language I didn't know. Behind me, somebody really really big was being laid, really really quiet, on the ground. Shit, I thought, 'cause I couldn't get nothing more useful through my head, 'cause I suddenly had a pretty good guess about what happens when you call up a dead guy who ain't there. And then it felt like my heart slammed into my ribs, and I could breathe again, and I yelled, "Lucy, run!"

And then I bolted.

I cut back behind the statue, crashing through them damn bushes with their brambles like grappling hooks, staggering across the graves of murderers and heretics, tearing both knees out of my trousers on some fucking wicked tombstone like this big granite bed—it had spikes, too, like the bushes—and I had a fucking *putrid* moment, thinking it had me, that I was never going to get free, and when the dead people were done with Vey and Brandon and Jean-Lundy and Claudio, they'd come find me. But then I tore loose, and staggered upright, and kept running, toward the only section of fence around the Boneprince that you could climb from the inside.

Then I heard her calling, "Dennis! Dennis, please!"

I had about half a second where I wondered if it was really her, or if one of the dead people was smarter than I wanted them to be, but then she got closer, and I could hear her breathing and the wet weight of her dress dragging across the ground.

"Here!" I called back.

"Oh! Oh, thank the powers! Oh, Dennis, please!" I caught her, her heat and weight, and I could feel the life in her like it was a fire.

"Got to run," I said, my breath sawing. "Got to get out."

"Oh, *can* we?"

"Yeah, *now*." I kept hold of her hand, and we ran.

We ran like kids in a story, like I'd been thinking earlier, only this was a different story and we had the Iron-black Wolves on our heels. I couldn't hear nothing behind us—though I wasn't sure I would—and nothing caught us before we got to the fence. Maybe nothing was chasing us. Maybe they were all busy with Vey and her goons. But I wasn't gambling on it. "Fence!" I warned, caught Miss Thomson by the waist, and tossed her upward. I heard her dress tear as she grabbed the top rail and pulled herself over, but I didn't give a fuck, and she didn't, neither. I swung over after her, drew this huge, hoarse, gasping breath, said, "Pennycup." And we were off and running again.

It was pouring rain. By the time we reached my rooms in Persimmony Street—the rooms I used when I was looking particularly not to be found—water was running out of our clothes and hair in rivers, and we were both starting to shake with the cold. We kind of dragged each other up the stairs, and I picked my own damn lock.

"I knew it was a useful skill," Miss Thomson said. She sounded punch-drunk, and I didn't blame her.

"I could teach you. Sometime." Then I pulled myself together. It was like trying to collect water in a fucking sieve. "Wood. For a fire. Powers." I pushed my hands through my hair, hard, feeling the water squish out and run down my back. "Fire should be laid. You light it, and I'll find the blankets."

"Please." She went dripping across the floor and settled in this kind of puddle, mixed cloth and water and mud, by the hearth. The skirt of her dress was torn practically into streamers.

I went into the back room, opened the cedar chest. There were the blankets, plus some dry clothing. I was just about drooling at the thought. I gathered it all up together and went back into the main room. She'd got the fire lit and was feeding it kindling with a look on her face like it was the most important thing she'd ever done.

"Oughta get out of them wet clothes," I said. I sorted out the blankets and the clothes on the daybed I'd kited when Anna Margolya and all her girls were evicted from the Hourglass just down the street. "Think I've got some things should fit."

"That would be marvelous. I'd like to burn this damn dress."

"Okay by me. Won't your boss be upset?"

She laughed. "Maybe I'll quit my job. I could. I didn't lose the gorgons."

"Fuck," I said, and I was staring at her like she was a lion with two heads. "For real?"

"Yes," and her smile was pure sunshine. "Her lackey didn't grab me until after I'd got them safe." She pulled the little wash-leather bag out of her skirt pocket. Then her face fell. "Or do you think . . . I mean, could they be counterfeit?"

"Dunno. But my understanding is if you don't want to fuck up your witchery, you don't get Ver-Istenna mad at you right before you start."

"Oh. Oh, of course. Then I really *could* quit."

"Think about it tomorrow. Here." I handed her one of my older shirts and a pair of secondhand trousers I'd been meaning to take in for a half indiction or more. "Change in the other room if you want."

"Thanks." She dragged herself up. I could almost feel how heavy her dress and layers of petticoats were, just watching her plod across the floor. I'd thought she'd take the other room, good little bourgeoise that she was.

I stripped my clothes off as soon as the door closed behind her. Each piece of clothing landed on the floor with a squishing noise. By the time Miss Thomson came out, I was decent again, my stuff by the fire where there was at least a chance it'd dry out, and I'd worked out an arrangement of blankets on the floor that I thought would be okay. I put a stack for her on the daybed. Then I just sat there on the daybed, being glad I was still breathing.

Miss Thomson came back looking like the lead in a trouser farce, and I said, "There's no bed." I'd had to sell the bed the winter before. "You can have this. 'Less you *want* to go back out there."

"No, thank you. Dennis . . ." And then her face changed, going white and slack. I thought she was going to faint. "Oh, *Dennis!* I did, didn't I?"

"Did what?"

"I said your name! I know I did. I am so terribly sorry." Her eyes were huge.

"No, it's okay."

"But you *said*—you said I shouldn't tell her mine, and surely . . ."

"No." I could feel my face going red, and that made me feel even stupider. "I mean, that ain't my name."

"What?"

" 'Dennis' ain't my name. It's a whatchamacallit."

"An alias?" she said doubtfully.

"Maybe, if that means a name you use when you don't want nobody to know yours. I got a septad or so of 'em."

"Really." She thought it over, the color coming back into her face. "Then what should I call you?"

"Oh, Kethe, I don't know." I was tired of it. I'd been tired of it for indictions, since I'd left Keeper and didn't have her to keep me safe. I was tired and lonely, not to mention wet and cold. I said, "My name's Mildmay. That's for real."

She was from Wraith. She didn't know the baggage that name had. "Mildmay," she said. "That's nice. You can call me Ginevra. If you like."

"It's a real pretty name."

Her lips twitched. "My aunt found it in a romance and talked my mother into it. But thank you."

"Here," I said and got off the daybed. "You must be tired."

Her face flooded with color. It was like watching a sunrise.

"What?" I said. I couldn't help checking, but I'd put my trousers on, and they were buttoned. "What is it?"

"I'm sorry. This sounds so horrible, and I'm sure you wouldn't, but . . ." She took a deep breath, and I did my level best not to stare at her chest. "You won't try anything, will you?"

"If I do, kick me in the balls."

"I'm serious."

"So'm I. I don't like rape, and I ain't in the mood besides." That made her laugh. I'd hoped it would. "Vey scares the living daylights outa me."

"Me, too," she said, and we both sat down on the daybed. "What . . . what was she *doing*?"

"Dunno. I mean, I can guess, but that's about it."

"Well, what's your guess?"

"My guess is she was looking to raise Brinvillier Strych."

"Brinvillier Strych? You mean Lord Bonfire? In the stories? He's *real?*"

I wondered who was the patron saint of little provincial girls who came to Mélusine without no more brains on 'em than a chickadee. "Fuck, yes," I said. "Porphyria Levant was real, too. I know people who knew Strych."

She opened her mouth and shut it again.

"And I know a guy"—a crazy old resurrectionist so crippled up with arthritis he could hardly move—"who swears he saw them taking Strych's body into the Boneprince."

Her breath hitched in, and she signed herself, that quick five-point circle to ward off hexes and bad luck and Phi-Kethetin's especial dislike.

"Vey Coruscant was his student. Like I said, my guess is she was trying to raise him."

"But he wasn't there. I mean, that voice—"

"I know."

"Do you think he's still . . . alive?"

"Dunno. I don't think so, though. I mean, if he was—where the fuck is he? He wasn't the sort to lay low, even with the Mirador on his ass. I think they lied about where they put him."

"Oh," she said, like the idea was a relief. "Really?"

"They're hocuses. It's what they do."

She yawned. Not one of them polite, ladylike little yawns to tell the guy he's being a bore, but a real jaw-stretcher.

"Go on and sleep," I said. I got up and went to my own blankets. "It's okay. Whatever was going on in the Boneprince tonight, nobody's gonna have the space to come looking for us for, oh, at least a decad."

She gave a sleepy little chuckle and rolled herself up in the blankets. Far as I could tell, she was asleep as soon as she got settled. As for me, I heard the Nero Street Clock chime the tenth hour that night before I finally fell asleep.

Felix

The rain started sometime later, sometime in the dark. I felt it in my dreams and dreamed of drowning the rest of the night. At dawn, when one of the cat-headed monsters kicked me awake, I was almost glad.

The guards got me down in the mud again when Stephen and Vida walked away from the camp to argue, but they had no higher purpose this time than degradation and filth. When Stephen came back, one of them said blandly, "He tried to escape." Stephen knew it for a lie; he did not pursue it. They shoved me up onto the horse again and started for the walls of Mélusine.

By noon, we were in sight of Chalcedony Gate. Stephen reined in at the end of the causeway through the St. Grandin swamp, held up a hand. "He walks from here," he said, and Esmond dragged me off the horse.

Stephen intended me to walk to the Mirador.

I wondered if I could, and I was still wondering when we passed beneath the arch of Chalcedony Gate.

Mildmay

In the dream, I'm a kid again, like maybe a septad and two, septad and three. Keeper and me are standing outside the Boneprince's gates. It's past the septad-night.

In you go, Keeper says and shoves me forward, so that I'm in the Boneprince before I'm ready for it. I'm scared out of my mind, but proud. We all know what the Boneprince test means.

I start walking, not too fast, not like I'm scared or nothing, along the Road of Marble. Behind me, the gates swing shut with this horrible noise, like screaming and laughing and puking all at once. Even in the dream, I know them gates were welded open back in the reign of Laurence Cordelius, 'cause he was sick to death of people breaking the lock or being found in the morning hung up on the spikes.

And that's kind of worrisome, you know, them gates closing when I know they can't. I turn around. Keeper's still there, on the other side of the gates. She smiles at me. Things are okay, then. This is just part of the test, and I can take anything she throws at me.

I turn back and keep walking. I can hear my footsteps and my heart beating. It's dark, not just like the night being dark when the moon's gone in, but dark like being shut in a room with black walls. I can see the Road of Marble, and that's about it.

And then there's a voice beside the path, and it whispers my name.

I stop in my tracks, looking from side to side, even though it won't do me no good. There's nothing to see. Just blackness and more blackness. *Is . . . is somebody there?*

Mildmay, another voice calls, from someplace else.

I spin around, but I can't see nothing. There's just the path, gleaming white, and all that blackness.

Mildmay, Mildmay, Mildmay. Lots of voices now, and I know who they are. They're the kept-thieves, the kids that got the sanguette 'cause Lady Jane didn't know no better way to deal with her city.

Come play with us, Mildmay, they call. *We're lonely. You're one of us.*

No! I say, too scared to keep my mouth shut.

It's true. It's true. You belong *to us, Mildmay. You know it.*

I'd run if I knew which way to go, but the voices are all around me. I can see things on the path, like shadows.

Then something tugs my hair. I yelp and try to dodge, but I'm fenced in now, with bone, all their skeletons, some of 'em still hung about with bits of rotting cloth and bits of rotting flesh. They catch hold of me with their fingers like brambles, crowding around me, and I know they can feel my body heat. The eye sockets of their skulls are dark, like they've got all the night inside their heads.

You are ours, one says, close enough to kiss me. I pull back, fighting their grip and the things they say, and wake up.

❧

It was near the septad-day. Ginevra was still asleep on the daybed. I was tangled up in my blankets like they had a new career coming as an octopus.

"Powers," I muttered under my breath and unwrapped myself. Standing up was hard—I ached all over from that crazy run through the Boneprince—but I did it anyway and went to the window. There ain't much happens on Persimmony Street in the daytime. I saw two cats fighting over a fish head and a girl scrubbing the steps of the Hourglass. The sky was dark and kind of far-off-looking. There'd be more rain soon.

I couldn't settle. The dream was in my head. So I pulled on my boots, still damp from last night, and left. Persimmony Street's only four blocks from the Road of Chalcedony, and across the Road and up three stories, there's a roof market. Stuff there was cheaper than what you could buy on the Road itself—and fresher, too, half the time.

The air was cold enough to bite, and I could smell the rain coming. I walked fast, not needing to get soaked again, thanks all the same. But when I came to the Road, I couldn't go no farther. Couldn't even get near it.

"What the fuck is going on?" I said.

A scissors-grinder said, "It's the hocus. Lord Stephen caught the son of a bitch, and they're bringing him back to the Mirador." It's the Mirador's way with hocuses they're pissed at. They drag 'em the length of the Road of Chalcedony, and the people of the Lower City, who ain't got them nice bourgeois manners, line the sidewalks and yell and throw things.

I wasn't annoyed no more. Now all I wanted was a better view. Don't get me wrong, I don't like the Mirador, and they don't like me—but I ain't no fool, neither. The guy who broke the Virtu was nobody's friend. I started edging closer.

You could track their progress by the way the shouting got louder, and I knew I wouldn't have to wait long. The Mirador don't do that sort of thing very often, but I could remember the last one. They'd found out that one of the younger hocuses was fucking around with "forbidden magics"—if you put a knife to my throat, I'd guess that meant blood-magic, but it could've been most anything. They marched her up through the streets to the Plaza del'Archimago and burned her in front of Livergate. She was young and pretty, and half her body was most of the way to charcoal before she finally died.

Everybody around me started yelling their stupid heads off when the Lord Protector and the Protectorate Guard came into view. The hocus was walking behind Lord Stephen's horse. I couldn't get close enough to see good without doing somebody some serious damage, but I could see how tall he was, and Ginevra'd been right. He *did* dye his hair bright red. I couldn't think why anybody would want to. That was all I could see of him.

I saw when the rock came out of the crowd, though, somewhere near me. I'd've thrown one myself, if I could've got a clear line of sight. The people around me were yelling insults. The stone hit the hocus—you could tell by the way the crowd screamed—and that's when I left. I hoped they stoned him to death right there in the middle of the Road of Chalcedony.

Felix

Pain explodes in my head, and I fall to my knees, blood trickling into my good eye and down my face. The Road of Chalcedony blurs and doubles around me. With my good eye half-gummed shut, I am nearly blind. Malkar is somewhere, waiting to hurt me.

There is a terrible howling, shrieking noise assaulting me from all sides. Monsters line the street, baying like hounds. I have been trying not to look at their gaping maws, their red, glaring eyes, ever since we came through Chalcedony Gate. The bear-headed man keeps his horse moving forward at the same deliberate pace. He does not care whether I walk or am dragged.

I stagger to my feet and walk, stumbling over the cobbles, flinching from the howls of the monsters, which only makes them howl louder.

I am coming apart, on the verge of howling back at them. I lock my throat, keep moving. I can see nothing now but blurred shadows, terrifying bursts of movement that my bad eye cannot track. I fall a second time, tripped by a pothole. I can hear myself whimpering, and I hope that no one else can hear. I get up again, cringing from the noise, from the monsters I can no longer see. I fall the third time because I can't go on walking. There is too much pain, too much fear. My legs can no longer bear me through this maelstrom of shrieking glass.

Stephen does not look back; the crowd, sensing blood, redoubles its baying in anticipation. The noise is a whip; I am back on my feet, though I am shaking from head to foot, fighting to keep from falling again.

Mildmay

When I got back to Persimmony Street, Ginevra was sitting on the daybed, combing her hair.

"Want to go to the Tunny?" I said as I came in.

"The *what?*"

"The Tunny Street Baths. Over in Gilgamesh."

"Aren't there baths in Pennycup?"

"Oh, sure, but the Tunny's better."

She was looking at me weird. "Are you all right?"

"Yeah. I'm fine." I sat down beside her. "Lord Stephen caught the hocus. I saw them taking him along the Road of Chalcedony."

"Good," she said.

Our gazes locked for a second, and then we looked away from each other, Ginevra and me. She cleared her throat. "Mildmay?"

"Right here."

"Last night . . . I was . . . there was a minute or two where I thought I wouldn't be alive this time today."

"Only *two?*" I asked, and she laughed. It was a beautiful sound. "We're lucky—I mean, *really* lucky—just to be here, sitting and talking to each other." One cat and a Great Septad dogs.

There was a little silence. My heart was thumping in my chest like it wanted out. She touched my wrist, light as a butterfly, and said, "Don't you think we should celebrate our good luck?"

I couldn't believe my ears. I mean, just could not fucking believe she'd said it. I looked up, and she was leaning toward me. Her eyes were as blue as the sky, no clouds, no smoke—just a blue you could die for. Kethe, maybe she meant it. I leaned in and kissed her, real careful in case she changed her mind—it had happened before. Her hand moved up my arm and tightened around my biceps. She knew what she wanted, and I wasn't anywhere near stupid enough to start asking questions.

"Kethe," I said, "the Tunny can wait," and she laughed like a cat purring.

My shirt hung loose on her. I slid my free hand underneath it. Her skin was warm and smooth. I started to lift the shirt off her, and then it was like we got caught in a cyclone or something, both of us pulling clothes off as fast as we could.

When we were naked, we lay down together on the daybed. Kethe, she was beautiful, beautiful like a queen. I kissed her breasts, and she made a noise way back in her throat, like a growl. Her fingers were tracing patterns across my back.

"No scars," she said.

"Just my face."

"I don't care."

I wouldn't start wondering 'til later whether she meant she didn't care that my face was scarred, or she didn't care that my body wasn't. Right then, *I* didn't care, and that was a fucking miracle all by itself.

Felix

Somehow, I did not fall again. I was still on my feet when we passed under the grim lintel of Livergate. I stood, shivering, my breath coming in sobs, while the monsters dismounted, and other, meeker monsters came and led the horses away. They did not look at me at all. I raised my bound hands to my face and managed to wipe the blood out of my left eye.

The guards on duty at Livergate had swung the doors closed behind us; the silence was gray and terrible and absolute. I could feel it encasing me, hardening like layers of ice. No one said anything; the guards stood around Stephen and Vida and me like statues. Stephen took his gloves off, tucked them carefully behind his belt, all his attention on the task as if it were the answer to some vital question.

I could see the bear around Stephen like a mantle, its jaws dark with old blood. "Bring him," he said, with a curt jerk of his head, and strode across the courtyard, letting the arched brick mouth of the passway swallow him back into the Mirador. Vida followed him without a backward glance; she was cloaked and crowned with shadows.

Two of the monsters with the heads of owls took my arms, one cold claw above my left elbow, one cold claw above my right. They took me into the Mirador after the bear and the black lady.

The Mirador was closed against me. I saw that in the blurred, hostile faces of the people who watched us pass; I saw it in the texture of the floor, slick like glass, impervious. I felt it in the silence, like the silence in a mausoleum after the doors have been riveted shut. I had no sense of life, no sense of power, no sense of warmth. I was cast out. I walked across the Mirador's surfaces, denied entry to its heart.

The bronze doors of the Hall of the Chimeras were standing open. I could see the crowds within, their eyes glittering like jewels. I would have tried to stop, not to go in, but I knew the owls would drag me. We passed through the doors, and I saw the Virtu. I did stop walking, and they did drag me, but I no longer cared.

I stared at the Virtu all the way from the bronze doors to the place before the dais where the accused traditionally stood. Great shards rose on its plinth still, like the teeth of a wounded animal, but they were twisted, petrified bones where once had glowed beauty and strength and power. I had never seen anything so annihilated. The great poison tide of madness, ebbing away across the black sand, left exposed the wreckage of my guilt.

Stephen said, his voice like a clap of thunder, "Felix Harrowgate!"

I looked away from the Virtu, down to where Stephen sat beneath it. They must have cleared the glass off the dais and the throne. "Yes, my lord?"

"You stand accused of breaking the Virtu of the Mirador. Do you understand?"

"Yes, my lord."

"Do you deny the charges?"

"No, my lord."

"Do you have anything to say in your defense?"

The silence stretched out, like wool spun of grief. The briars of Malkar's compulsion twisted round and round me, gouging me, mocking the truth I could not speak, mocking my pain.

"Well?"

"No, my lord," I said.

"So. He admits his guilt. Does anyone speak in defense of this person?"

Behind me I heard a rustle, a murmur, like tree branches in the wind. But no one spoke.

"For the second time of asking, does anyone speak in defense of this person?"

And then someone said, "Not in defense, but the Curia petitions that execution be stayed until we understand how it is that he has done what he has done."

"Haven't you figured that out yet, Lord Giancarlo?" Stephen sounded annoyed, and I wanted to tell him it was unfair to expect miracles from anyone. Only Malkar could make miracles happen on demand, and Malkar's were all miracles of evil, miracles of madness, miracles of hate.

I lost the rest of the debate between Lord Giancarlo and Lord Stephen; my hearing shredded away from me again, and all I could hear was the roaring of beasts. And beneath it, a thin strand of threnody, the song that the broken Virtu was singing to itself. I listened to that song, quiet and hurt-filled, and the Hall of the Chimeras faded away, becoming as distant and unimportant as the vanities and schemes of the person I had been.

"FELIX!"

The voice hit me, like a bar of iron between the eyes. I flinched back, my hands going up reflexively, uselessly. The bear sat enthroned beneath the Virtu. I thought for a moment I saw dead kings standing around him, their faces white and proud and desolate, but I shook my head, and they went away.

"My . . . my lord?"

"You are on trial for your life," the bear said, dry as salt. "I suggest you pay attention."

I looked down. Beneath my feet, a chimera's paw curled around a globe of the heavens. "Yes, my lord."

"Can you explain, Felix Harrowgate, how you broke the Virtu?"

I opened my mouth, and the compulsion whip-cracked across me. ". . . no, my lord."

"No?"

"I cannot."

"Your point carries, Lord Giancarlo," the bear said. "And I admit that I agree with you. If we're going to keep this from happening again, we'd better understand how it happened to begin with."

"More than that, my lord," Giancarlo said, "much though I hate to say it. If we are to mend the Virtu, we must understand how it was broken."

The bear made no response for a moment, then said, "Very well. Here is my judgment. Felix Harrowgate!"

I looked up, because the bear demanded it. It regarded me, its mad red eyes unfathomable. "You are to be stripped of your powers, title, and privileges as a wizard of the Mirador. You will be kept under guard and ward, subject to the examinations of the Curia, until such time as the destruction of the Virtu is fully understood. At that time, your fate will be decided. Do you understand?"

"Yes, my lord."

"Victoria," Stephen said. "If you would."

She rose and came down from the dais. She stopped in front of me. Her face was like granite. "Extend your hands," she said. I wondered if she had asked for this duty, wondered how much Malkar's decampment hurt her. I remembered his parting gift—the kiss, the compulsion, the terrible lie—and knew that someone had told her. Malkar breaks whatever he touches, and laughs.

I lifted my hands, and she stripped the dead rings off my fingers. I looked over her shoulder, avoiding her face, and my eyes met Shannon's. They were sapphires set in the living flesh of his face, faceted and brilliant and soulless. I shut my eyes. I felt Vicky's fingers brush across my forehead. I knew she was binding my powers, subjecting me to the will and whim of the Curia, but I felt nothing.

I listened for the song of the Virtu, but I could no longer hear it.

Chapter 3

Felix

The darkness is solid. It presses in around me; the weight makes it hard to breathe. I have to get up sometimes, touch the walls, touch the angry iron of the bars, to be sure that they have not moved, that there is still space for me.

They have taken my earrings, my watch, my boots, my sash, my coat and waistcoat, my rings. I have nothing but my trousers and shirt, and the darkness is cold. There is one blanket, and I wrap myself in it, but I still shiver. I am afraid to ask for another blanket. I already know they will not let me have light.

I can feel the Virtu, like a distant ache; I can feel it when they try to mend it or to work with it, and then I curl up on the narrow cot and try not to make any noise as I cry.

Mildmay

That Neuvième, I went to see my friend Cardenio. Cardenio's a cade-skiff, and I spent a while cooling my heels on the Fishmarket's long marble porch before he could get away. Neuvième's supposed to be his half day, but the master cade-skiffs always seem like they got to squeeze it down to a quarter. But then he came out, grinning all over his shy, mousy face at seeing me, and we walked over to Richard's Park, where we could sit and talk.

Cardenio'd made journeyman not long before, and he still wore the big black hat and the long coat like they were about the greatest things since they started minting gorgons. I don't think he really believed, even then, that they'd really let him in, that he'd really passed the ordeal and sworn the oaths and gotten a master to teach him their mysteries. Cardenio'd never had much use for himself, and it was weird for him that somebody else did.

He said while we were walking, "I hear you got a new ladyfriend."

Cade-skiffs know everything. Ain't nothing to be done about it. "Powers, ain't nothing sacred? Yeah, I got a new 'ladyfriend.' She's a shopgirl over on the Road of Carnelian."

"You're moving up in the world," he said. I looked sideways at him, but he was smiling, and his face had gone red, so I knew he was just teasing.

"Yeah," I said, "pretty soon I won't know you to spit on you no more, so you better watch your step."

"I can just see you cutting me dead, all lah-di-dah with your lace and expensive perfume."

"Shit, Cardenio, d'you mind? I got *some* pride."

He giggled for the next block and a half after that.

We had our bench in Richard's Park that we specially liked, and that afternoon it was free. So we sat in the middle of the formal garden, where nobody could sneak up on us, and I said, "I, um, I got you something. For making journeyman."

His eyes got big. "Do you mean it?"

"No, numbnuts, I'm just being a prick. *'Course* I mean it. Here."

It was a little box, but the shop assistant had wrapped it up pretty. Cardenio held it and stared at it, but didn't open it. "Mildmay, really, you shouldn't—"

"I'm flash this decad," I said. Me and Ginevra hadn't got round to figuring out my cut, but I knew what kind of money I was looking at. "And I wanted to. Go on and open it."

He worked real careful, like the paper was precious. I sat and watched, feeling kind of shy myself. He opened it, and his eyes got big as bell-wheels. "Powers. Mildmay, you *really* shouldn't—"

"Put 'em on," I said. I would've been grinning, except I don't do that. Not ever. "Anna Christina at The Sphinx Was A Lady says they're old. Maybe even Cymellunar work."

"Powers." He untied the loops of silk ribbon in his ears and slid them out. Then, so carefully I could tell he was holding his breath, he put the earrings in. Gold rings with jade beads carved like dragons. Then he turned his head gently to feel them move.

"Okay?" I said.

"Yeah. Really okay. I mean, nobody's ever given me this good a present before. Thanks."

"Hey, you're the only person I know's ever made it to journeyman cade-skiff. That's gotta be worth something."

He blushed like a girl, and I let him off the hook by asking him to tell me what kind of thing he was learning this decad. We talked the way we always did, about everything under the sun. Cardenio was maybe the best listener I'd ever met. With him I didn't feel like I had to worry about my scar. We had an early dinner at the Wheat-Dancer and then started back toward Havelock, where he'd disappear back into his guildhall and I'd see if I could flag down a hansom to get me to the Blue Cat in Dragonteeth, where Ginevra wanted me to meet her.

After a few blocks, I said, "Cardenio?"

"Yeah?"

"You know anything 'bout Brinvillier Strych?"

"What kind of anything?"

"Dunno. Just, you know, like what happened to his body."

He gave me a look. Cardenio was shy, but he wasn't stupid. You don't make journeyman with the cade-skiffs if you don't got some fucking grand machinery up top. "This got anything to do with what happened in the Boneprince on Deuxième?"

And he *still* sandbagged me, even though I knew better. "What happened in the Boneprince on Deuxième?" I said, just like I should, only I said it a beat too late, and Cardenio knew it.

But he was a friend. He let it go. "Nobody knows for sure. The necromancers in Scaffelgreen say it was something big, and as far as we can tell, nobody's seen Vey Coruscant since."

"Fuck," I said, not faking. "What do y'all think?"

He shrugged. "We don't know, either. We're cade-skiffs, not gods. But you were asking about Brinvillier Strych."

"Yeah," I said, and I knew that Cardenio was putting stuff together, even if he didn't say nothing about it. But it was okay. Whatever he said to his masters, he wouldn't tell 'em I was part of their headache.

"Well," he said, "the Mirador said they buried him in the Boneprince."

"Yeah. The Mirador also says Crenna of Verith is a sinner and a heretic."

"For shame, Mildmay." He was grinning. "Are you saying they lied?"

"Dunno. I'm just wondering. That's all."

"Okay. You're just wondering. I don't really know. I mean, there's all sorts of places I can *imagine* they'd put him—there's crypts in the Mirador, you know."

"Powers. For real?"

"Yeah. Master Auberon says *his* master, Master Rosamund, when she was a girl, she actually saw the crypt of the Thestonarii once—her dad was a butler, and he snuck her into the Mirador and showed her—but she could never remember how she got there. And Master Auberon says they figured writing a letter to ask the Lord Protector to let them look wouldn't go over so good."

"No, guess not. But you think—"

"If the Mirador was gonna say they buried him one place and really bury him somewhere else, then that's where I think they'd do it."

"Makes sense. Thanks."

"Dunno for what. But you're welcome."

We came to the Fishmarket and stopped on the porch, under one of the big iron-caged lamps. I said, "Next Neuvième the same?"

"Yeah, I think so. I mean, unless you got something better to do?"

"Well, the Lord Protector asked me to dinner, but I told him I was busy."

Cardenio grinned. "Next Neuvième, then." He sort of paused a second, said, "Thanks. I mean . . . thanks." He turned bright red and all but ran off.

I shouted after him, "You're welcome!" and I think he heard me before the Fishmarket's doors slammed shut behind him.

Ginevra had shitty taste in bars. I'd never been in the Blue Cat before, but it was pure Dragonteeth swank, with blue velvet on the walls and brass filigree inlay on the bar. I was dressed decent, at least, in my bottle-green coat where the darn on the elbow didn't show, but I wore my hair too short to be a gentleman, and with the scar on my face, nobody was going to believe I thought I could land a flashie. Which I couldn't, and didn't want to. But that's the sort of bar the Blue Cat was. I wished I wasn't wondering if Ginevra had met Ellis Otanius here.

Ginevra waved at me from a back corner. I started toward her. About halfway there I realized there was somebody at the table with her, a big, dark girl in blood-red silk. I stopped short.

"Gil!" Ginevra shouted. Since I'd been fool enough to tell her my real name, I'd had to give her something else to call me. "Gilroi Felter" was safe enough. The only thing that name was connected to was Mrs. Pickering's house. Ginevra'd promised she wouldn't forget, and I was glad she hadn't, but I wished she would've warned me before she went inventing nicknames. And I particularly wished she would've warned me before she dragged her friends along.

But I couldn't very well turn around and walk back out, although it was what I was wanting to do. Manners, manners, Milly-Fox, Keeper said in my head, laughing, and I walked up to the table.

"Gil, this is my friend Estella Velvet. Estella, this is Gil."

"So," said the dark girl, drawling, "you're Ginevra's new flame."

Fuck, I thought. Estella Velvet was tall, stacked, dark and rich like chocolate. Her hair was black and thick and curly. Her skin was golden bronze, and there was a lot of it on display. I mean, I ain't no prude, but I wasn't sure her neckline was legal. Her eyes were heavy-lidded and sort of sleepy and sharp-looking at the same time. She might as well have called herself Sex on the Hoof.

"If she says so," I said. Estella Velvet burst out laughing. The sound was as dark and rich as her hair, and I didn't have to wonder how she'd afforded the dress she was wearing or the rings on her fingers.

"Sit down, Gil," Ginevra said.

"Okay," I said. I hooked a chair out and sat down.

"Is Faith coming?" Ginevra said to Estella.

"She'll be here. She has no sense of time. You know that."

"Estella's girlfriend works at the Hospice of St. Cecily," Ginevra said to me.

I kept my eyebrows from going up, but it took some doing. St. Cecily's in Candlewick Mews is the biggest hospice in the Lower City—not the best, mind you, just the biggest. St. Latimer's in Gilgamesh is better, or St. Gailan's in Spicewell. What makes St. Cecily's different is that it's where the nature-witches hang out, the ones that think they should be using their magic to heal people. Nobody said nothing, along of how the Mirador said it was heresy and evil to boot, but everybody in the Lower City knew. The Mirador knew, too, but mostly it wasn't worth their while to fuck around with it. So Estella's girlfriend was either stupid or crazy.

I'd've bet on stupid and lost my money. Faith Cowry turned out to be little, dark, skinny, bright-eyed as a wren, and not the least bit stupid. And despite what Estella'd said, she didn't strike me as absentminded either, just somebody who knew what mattered, and it didn't include showing up on time to meet Estella's lowlife friends. She was sort of just barely tolerating Ginevra, from what I could see, and she sure wasn't cutting me no slack. The look she gave me said she about half expected me to eat with my fingers, and three-quarters expected me to get drunk and start brawling. I couldn't blame her. I know what I look like.

So socially speaking, the evening was pretty much sunk from the start. Ginevra and Estella did most of the talking—gossiping, I guess would be a better word. They were all into who was sleeping with who and who wasn't speaking to who and all the rest of it—which I suppose ain't bad if you know everybody involved, but I didn't, and from the look on her face Faith Cowry didn't, either. I think it was somewhere around the third or fourth hour of the night that our eyes met by accident, and I saw that she felt just like I did: she didn't want to know *none* of these people, and wished to fuck Estella and Ginevra didn't, either.

I raised an eyebrow, to let her know that was how I felt, too, and she cracked up.

"What?" Estella said.

"Nothing," Faith said. "Did you bring your cards, Estella?"

"They go everywhere with me. Why?"

"I thought Gil and I might play a hand of Long Tiffany while you and Ginevra . . . catch up." Faith raised her eyebrows at me, and I nodded.

"I don't know why you want to play such a vulgar game," Estella said, but she got the cards out. "What's the matter with Griffin and Pegasus?"

"It's too bourgeois," Faith said, very sweetly, and that cracked Estella up, and everything was okay.

So me and Faith played Long Tiffany until the septad-night, while Estella and Ginevra bickered and gossiped and giggled together. Estella was on the prowl, and I lost count of the number of flashies who came over and asked if they could buy her drinks.

"Don't that bother you?" I asked Faith, under cover of a burst of laughter.

She shrugged. "I can't change Estella. I can live with her how she is, or I can break up with her. And mostly we get along okay."

She dealt out the next hand, and I shut up.

Faith played pretty good Long Tiffany. We played five hands. I won three, and she only won on points on a fourth.

"It's a good thing we weren't playing for money," she said when we'd finished the fifth hand and were getting ready to go.

"I don't play for money," I said. And I didn't. I'd spent too many indictions sharping.

She gave me a kind of funny look, but then Estella said, "Let's *go*, Faith," and we followed her and Ginevra out of the Blue Cat.

Estella and Ginevra made their plans to meet again, and this time to meet up with another friend, some guy named Austin, and then Estella and Faith grabbed a hansom to take them back to Candlewick Mews, and me and Ginevra started for Spicewell, where she had a room.

It was a nice night for the middle of Pluviôse, and Dragonteeth is good for walking. Always lots of shit going on. So we walked for a while, not saying nothing, looking at the guy juggling torches, and the three women doing acrobatics in Godwell Square, and then Ginevra said, "Gil, do you like me?"

"Um, sure," I said.

"Gil! You know what I mean!"

"Um, no. Not really."

We walked by a streetlamp, and I saw she was blushing. "Estella called you my new flame."

"Yeah. So?"

"Well . . . I mean . . . do you want to? You looked kind of mad at Estella."

Powers. I was slipping. Mind your ugly face, Milly-Fox. I said, "I didn't much take to Estella. I like you fine. But I thought you was looking for a fancy boy from up the city."

"Gil!"

"Well, ain't you?"

"You make it sound so . . . so *crass.*"

I almost said, *Being a whore is,* but I grabbed it back before it got out of my mouth.

She said, "And anyway, I'm not *looking*. Not exactly."

You just don't mind getting found, I thought. I knew how it worked. I said, "What is it you're wanting from me, Ginevra?"

"I don't know." She sounded mad. "I wanted to know how you feel about me, I guess."

"I ain't known you but a decad."

"Do you want to know me better?"

"Sure," I said. "I mean . . . I guess so."

"Powers! Don't do me any favors, will you?"

"I'm sorry. I don't know what you want me to say."

"Maybe I don't know either! Maybe that's what I'm trying to find out!"

"Shit," I said. I'd really pissed her off. "I ain't . . . I ain't real good with words. I didn't mean to make you mad."

"It's okay." We walked another block and a half, and she said, "I guess all I really wanted to know was if you wanted to . . . to sleep with me again."

"Kethe, why didn't you ask that to start with? 'Course I do."

"Oh," she said, and gave me a smile as bright as all the streetlamps in Dragonteeth. "Then that's all right, then."

Felix

Light.

"You want one of us to stay, m'lord?"

"No, not necessary. I believe I can cope with the, er, threat he poses. But thank you."

"We'll be right outside. You just shout, and we'll come in."

"Thank you."

I have my hands over my face, trying to protect my eyes. I hear the armored monsters leave.

"Well, Felix. Are you ready to tell us how you did it?"

The words make no sense. I squint, my eyes watering, at the shape, dark against the light of the torch. I can't remember how to speak. I put my hands over my eyes again, hunch my shoulders against the light.

"This stubborn silence will do you no good, you know. If you cooperate, I promise I will do everything I can at least to make your execution painless. You'll be burned, you know, if no one intercedes."

I can't answer.

After a long time, the person on the other side of the bars sighs and says, "I'll come back."

I hear him leave.

Darkness.

Mildmay

So me and Ginevra were seeing each other pretty regular, and it got to the point in about a month where it didn't seem like there was any point in her keeping her room in Spicewell, when she was spending all her time at my place in Midwinter. Kethe, I was happy. I mean, she was gorgeous and smart, and my face didn't bother her or nothing. So things for us were really good. Things in the city were getting kind of hairy, with the Lord Protector calling up a new Witchfinder Extraordinary and nobody knowing just how that crazy hocus had broken the Virtu. And people were worrying about the Obscurantists again, along of the bad magic in the Boneprince and some other shit that I never did get the right of. Cardenio tried to explain it to me, but it got all tangled up in what different kinds of necromancers believed and what the nature-witches thought was going on, and I finally had to ask him to stop before my brains froze solid and died.

But there wasn't much of that kind of gossip in Midwinter, and anyways Ginevra wasn't interested. She was sure the Witchfinder Extraordinary—Erasmus Spalding was his name—would get everything sorted out, and it would all be okay. I could have told her otherwise, could've told her horror stories about the last Witchfinder Extraordinary for days on end, but then I would've had to explain how come I knew so fucking much about Cerberus Cresset and the round of witch-hunts from three indictions back, and I didn't particularly want to explain that to Ginevra. Not yet.

So I kept my mouth shut and didn't bore her with city politics. I didn't introduce her to my friends—Cardenio and Margot and Lollymeg—because I knew from meeting her friends that it wouldn't work out. And if there was anything I wanted—anything that could've made things better—it was for Ginevra to see her friends for what they were and give them up.

Faith wasn't so bad, but Faith wasn't Ginevra's friend. I got to see that real plain after a while. Faith was like me. She was in love with Estella, and she came along to the Blue Cat because it made Estella happy. Faith didn't give a shit about Ginevra. I wished she had. Because Faith was the only one of them I liked.

There were a bunch of girls I never did get straightened out. They only came when their protectors didn't want their company, or when one guy'd gotten tired of them and they hadn't picked up a new one yet. They were giggly, and they flirted with everything in sight. Except me. I frightened them, and it didn't even bother me. Although it did make me wonder if Ginevra was showing off, bringing me with her, trying to get them to take her seriously. She was the youngest of them, and one of only two or three who hadn't been born in the Lower City. They thought she was a lightweight. I wanted to tell her it was okay to be a lightweight, that she didn't owe these gals nothing and didn't need to make them think she was tough. But I found out real early on that she wouldn't listen to me about her friends.

I found that out because of Austin. Austin Lefevre, who thought he was a poet. I hated him on sight. He was tall, with gray eyes and black, black hair. I thought he was probably dyeing his hair—believe me, I know the signs—but it didn't matter none. He was one of those bastards who'd be handsome if they were mud-brown and fishbelly-white, and he didn't have to do no more than raise an eyebrow to have all them gals twitching on his string. That kind of handsome. And his voice was deep and smooth, and he'd got the Lower City out of his vowels somehow, so he sounded flash, and he knew how to talk pretty and pay compliments and shit like that.

Austin came with a musician in tow, a rabbity little middle-aged man even more out of place than me. His name was Hugo Chandler. He came from the music school in Nill, where he was teaching and angling for a court appointment, like every other musician in Mélusine. He nursed one weak sherry all evening and jumped a foot when anybody spoke to him. The girls all teased him something fierce, batting their eyelashes at him and cooing, like they did to the flashies. Hugo Chandler went red as a beet, but you knew he was always looking at Austin, even when his eyes were pointed somewhere else. And it seemed to me like Austin was always looking at Ginevra.

I told myself I was being stupid, that it was because I hated Austin Lefevre's beautiful guts and nothing more, but then one night Estella said to me, "They used to have a thing going, you know."

"Sorry?" I said. Estella didn't talk to me much. She couldn't get a rise out of me the way she could out of Hugo, and I knew I bored her.

"Austin and Ginevra. Before she took up with Lord Codface. He was expecting her to come back to him when she came back down the city."

"Well, she didn't."

"No. There's no accounting for taste."

She waited a moment, but I knew better than to try any kind of comeback. She snorted and turned to say something to one of the other girls—Dulcie or Danielle or something like that. I sat and watched Austin watching Ginevra and tried to convince myself she wasn't watching him back. I didn't do a very good job.

Felix

Light.

The voices in my head—babbling, excoriating, mocking, whining—fall silent as if slain. I sit up. Sometimes the monsters get angry if I don't. But I keep my face turned away from the light. It hurts too much.

A voice says, "Blessed saints. Can't you even leave him a light?"

"Not 'til he talks. That's our orders. You want us to stay?"

"No, thank you."

The clash and cacophony of armored monsters. They slam the door behind them.

The first voice says, "Lord Felix."

I shake my head. "Not a lord."

A silence. I can hear, all through it, the labored arrhythmia of the Mirador's magic. Even when the voices in my head are silent, I have to listen to that.

"Do you know me at all? My name is Erasmus Spalding."

I squint in his direction, but all I can see is a blurry shape, blue and deep violet with circling sparks of gold. "Yes," I lie.

"Good. That is, Lord Stephen and the Curia have appointed me Witchfinder Extraordinary. I need to ask you some questions. Not about the Virtu. It's all right."

I wonder what they think of me, in their world of light, deaf to the broken patterns around them. I wonder what stories they have invented, to explain me when I cannot explain myself. "All right," I echo him.

"The night after . . . after the Virtu was broken, something strange happened in Adrian's Park. Do you know anything about it?"

"No."

"Was it something to do with you? With Malkar Gennadion?"

"I don't know. I don't think so."

"But it *can't* be coincidence. Are you sure?"

Pushing the limits of what the compulsion will allow, I whisper, "Malkar didn't say anything."

"What about your contacts in the Lower City?"

"What?" I think I must have misheard him. My hearing is erratic; I know that. But he repeats his question, and it sounds the same the second time.

"I don't have contacts in the Lower City."

"Very well," he says. The colors around him flex into darkness for a moment, and I know he thinks I am a liar. He is frightened of me. "What about Malkar?"

"I don't know! I really don't. I'm sorry."

"It would not hurt you to cooperate."

"I'm sorry," I say. He says something else, but I can't understand him. Sounds are blurring, booming. The monsters are coming out. I knot my hands together in my lap and try not to shake, try not to cry.

After a while, the monster leaves.

Darkness.

Mildmay

The political situation was getting hotter and hotter, and I started spending more time with Lollymeg and Cardenio and Elvire, listening to news, trying to figure out which way to jump. The Lord Protector had learned his lesson from last time. *This* time the Witchfinder Extraordinary wasn't coming down the city with the Protectorate Guard, arresting everybody who looked like maybe they could hex a teapot. *This* time, the Lord Protector and the Witchfinder Extraordinary were talking to the Mayor and giving the Dogs money to hire extra people and trying to keep everything from exploding the way it had when Cerberus Cresset was in charge. There'd been rioting, the summer of 20.2.1, and shops and houses got smashed up, and people had died who weren't heretics or sympathetic to heretics or nothing like that—just in the wrong place at the wrong fucking time. Erasmus Spalding was trying to keep that from happening again, and I kind of liked him for it.

Even so, he was going at it all the wrong way round. He was being all cautious and methodical, and telling the Mayor about what he was doing, and what was happening was he was giving people more time to get frightened. Especially because people were getting confused. What the Witchfinder Extraordinary was after was people who were helping the Bastion, and what people in the Lower City were frightened of was Obscurantists. And it was no good people saying that the Obscurantists weren't nothing to do with the Virtu getting broken or the bad magic on 12 Pluviôse that now it seemed like everybody knew about. Because the Lower City's been frightened of Obscurantists since the days of King Jasper, and everybody knows that the Obscurantists would sell us all to the Kekropians in a minute flat if it meant they could do what they liked and not get burned for it. And, I mean, they're all heretics anyway, according to the Mirador, so when the Mayor says that heresy will not be tolerated, that don't exactly help straighten things out. But nothing the Mayor did helped the Lower City anyway. We all knew he would have been crying just buckets if the Great Fire of 19.7.2 had burned the whole Lower City flat.

Lollymeg was a fence in Ruthven. She wasn't as good a source for news as Elvire, but she didn't mind me sitting in her store all afternoon—not that anybody in Ruthven was stupid enough to fuck with Lollymeg. I could sit and look at people's faces and hear them saying as how they weren't letting their kids out after dark no more and how they were going to church and they'd asked their priest to come bless their doorstep, so nobody who meant evil could cross it, and I could feel for myself that the Lower City was getting frightened.

And Lollymeg, who listened to people all day long, like pawnshop owners got to—Lollymeg told me all the things she was hearing and weird stuff, like that last Quatrième, it seemed like half the Resurrectionists' Guild had been in looking for saints' medals.

"Anybody special?" I said.

"Anybody they thought would look out for them. I mean, ain't no good them asking St. Carmen for favors, you know?" And she tapped the little gold medal with one fingernail, so it swung back and forth above her head. Lollymeg kept all the cheap jewelry like that, hanging off this kind of trellis over the counter that divided the store in half.

"Yeah," I said. St. Carmen is the patron saint of dutiful children, and ain't going to have no kindness for resurrectionists.

"They was just spooked," Lollymeg said. "All of 'em. They said as how they weren't doing no business in the Boneprince no more, they didn't care who asked and they didn't care how much they'd pay."

"Think it'll last?"

"Nah. *I* know how much some people will pay for a murderer's finger-bone. But they mean it for now. They ain't happy."

"Who is?"

"I hear you," Lollymeg said glumly, and the bells in the door jangled as a new customer came in.

Not all of Lollymeg's news was bad, though. I'd taken Ginevra's jewelry and the clock and the dancer to her, and she'd come back right away with a good price on the jewelry and the clock—the stuff that was easy to shift. It took her longer on the dancer, because with genuine Tolmattins you got to find somebody who's rich enough to afford it and crazy enough to buy it. But Lollymeg was a good fence, and she tracked somebody down around the middle of Germinal. I didn't ask too many questions, along of not really wanting to know, but the dancer's new home was someplace in Roy-Verlant, where rich is where people *start*. I was just glad of the money.

Ginevra was happy, too, but it got us into a fight, because she wanted to spend it. She might not care about politics, but she got all the scandal sheets and the fashion books—and she worked in that flash store. She knew who the best modistes were, and the best parfumiers, and who you went to for really top-notch hats, and those were the places she wanted to go. I didn't mind that so much—except for wishing she'd go through our money a little slower—but what she'd got in her head that Germinal was that she wanted a miniature of me, and she wanted it from Stavis Macawnbrey, who painted people like Lord Shannon Teverius and Araminta Packer, the Mayor's third wife, and Susan Dravanya, the lead actress at the Empyrean.

"You got to be kidding," I said.

"Why?" She leaned up on one elbow to look at me in the candlelight. We'd just finished fucking, and she was flushed and bright-eyed and so gorgeous it hurt to look at her.

"What makes you think . . . I mean, Stavis Macawnbrey ain't gonna paint *me*."

"We can afford it."

"That don't change things."

"What things?"

"I ain't exactly the type of person gets painted by Stavis Macawnbrey. Besides"— I looked away from her, up at the ceiling where the plaster was starting to crack—"you don't want a picture of me."

"Of course I do. Why wouldn't I?"

I gave her the hairy eyeball and hard. "Fuck, Ginevra, you ain't blind, so don't pretend like you are."

"Oh. You mean the scar."

"Of *course* I mean the scar. Kethe!"

"But I don't . . . I mean, you could be painted in profile if you wanted, but it doesn't matter to me."

"I don't want to be painted at all."

"You don't? Why not?"

"I got reasons."

"Mildmay, this is silly," she said, stroking my hair. "It's not like you've got two noses or anything."

"It ain't that."

"Then what is it? What's the matter with you?"

"Ain't you been paying attention? Ain't you caught on yet? I'm a *thief*."

She pulled her hand back, like I'd threatened to bite. "Yes, but—"

"I done things they'd send me to the sanguette for if they caught me."

"But surely no one in the Mirador—"

"I ain't going to the Mirador."

She stared at me. I didn't blame her. It'd come out halfway to a shout, and it wasn't no use pretending she hadn't caught me on the raw.

"What's wrong with the Mirador?" she said finally.

"Nothing. I just ain't going there. You want a miniature, you go get one of yourself."

"But I don't understand—"

"There's nothing to understand. I just ain't going nowhere near the Mirador, and I don't want my picture done anyways, so it don't matter."

"You're scared," she said.

"I ain't scared. I just don't do stupid things, okay?"

"Fine," she said, like arsenic over ice, and rolled over to put her back to me. But she didn't bring the idea up again.

Felix

Light.

I sit up.

The darkness has been full of pain and screaming; I am still shaking, and I cannot hide it. Monsters booming at each other. I hope they are not angry at me, but I know they are. They always are.

They open the cell door. I scramble backwards on the cot, pressing myself against the wall. If I could become part of the wall, I would be safe. One monster comes nearer. I am shaking. I put my hands over my ears, but I cannot block out the assault of noise.

It stands in front of me. I think there are fragments of words in its roaring, but they make no sense: "here . . . feel . . . use . . . in." I dare to glance up, but the monster looks back at me with the gleaming eyes of a hawk.

It reaches out, takes my arm, drags me to my feet. I am too scared to try to fight it. It pulls me out of the cell. The light hurts my eyes; I keep my head down.

I follow where the monster leads. More light. I cannot help crying out; I twist, trying to hide my eyes, trying to retreat into the darkness, but the monster will not let me go.

More monsters, roaring and crashing. I see a confused blur of colors, red and black and orange and green. They are all angry. I have my hands over my face; I am trying not to cry.

The monster holding my arm keeps dragging me. The other monsters follow us. There is light everywhere. The stones beneath my feet are cold. I don't know where I am. I can only follow the monster and hope that it will lead me out of the maze.

We walk for a long time. The floor changes from stone to wood to blue and violet tiles. The monsters are silent, but I can feel their anger, like water in the air. I do not look at them. Their colors frighten me, and their eyes glow red. I can hear broken edges, failures, a great emptiness where there should be beauty. I can hear a faint, sobbing thread of song, running through the desolation like a trickle of tainted water through a battlefield strewn with corpses. It is all my fault. I cannot remember how or why, but I can feel my guilt in everything I touch.

Now there are carpets. They are the colors of old blood and bone. The monsters begin booming again. Their anger stabs through me like knives. I cross my arms, cup my elbows in my hands, try not to shake. Feet approach me. I hunch my shoulders. A hand catches at my chin; I flinch away. It is a statue: white marble with gilded hair and sapphire eyes. Behind it, I see a bear, and a lioness made of granite. They are all surrounded by black and red, streaked with orange, striated with a terrible drowning green.

For a moment, my hearing clears. The monster beside me, hawk-headed, says, "Don't you see? It's too late for that." And then sense is swallowed up again by terrible noise.

I lose, I think, a fragment of time. A new monster appears. It is small and dark and quick, like a cat. Its colors are different; they don't hurt. The bear roars at it; it answers. Then it comes and takes my arm, its touch as soft as a cat's paw. It leads me out of the room. I am glad. Wherever it takes me will be better than that room, with all the anger in it.

I walked through the spiked, gaping maw of the Harriers' Gate, and it was as if I'd taken off a topcoat forged of iron and lead. My mind cleared; my eyes cleared. I recognized the man with me: Stephen's steward Leveque. There were still colors clouding him, but they did not make him monstrous. I saw that he did not care for the task Stephen had assigned him.

I could no longer hear the Virtu. I could no longer feel the Mirador's broken magic.

I said, "Where are you taking me, Leveque?"

He shrank together, startled. "L-Lord Felix," he said.

"I'm not a lord," I said. Had I said that recently, or was it just that it echoed in my head like a leaden death knell, a requiem for the person I had been?

"Beg your pardon. We're . . ." He broke off to flag down a hansom. The Plaza del'Archimago was, as always, full of them.

I got in obediently, and did not hear what Leveque said to the driver. When Leveque climbed in next to me, I said, "Where are we going?"

"Oh, blessed saints," said Leveque. "I'm sorry, my lord, truly."

"Don't be, please. I just want to know."

I caught the twitch of Leveque's fingers, as he restrained his impulse to sign himself. He said, quite clearly but without meeting my eyes, "St. Crellifer's, my lord."

"Oh," I said. I thought about that as the hansom rattled through its turn out of the plaza. "Am I mad then?"

"Saints and powers," said Leveque, in a kind of strangled moan, but did not otherwise answer me. The colors around him showed me I was frightening him; I did not repeat my question.

We traveled in silence to St. Crellifer's. I looked at the sunshine and tried to believe in it. But behind every sunbeam I saw darkness, and I knew that the darkness was true.

St. Crellifer's was a massive presence of soot-stained brick, with barred windows like blind eyes. I stood in the courtyard, craning my neck at its façade while Leveque pattered up the steps and rang the bell.

A spy-hole in the left-hand door slid open. I did not hear what Leveque said to the person on the other side, nor what they said in answer. After a minute, the spy-hole slid shut again. Leveque came back down the steps. He approached me cautiously, like a half-feral cat. I looked away from the sullen windows of St. Crellifer's; his eyes were dark and bright. He said hastily, whispering, "Lord Felix, it was that Malkar, wasn't it?"

Malkar's compulsion slammed down on me. The world convulsed; for a moment I was standing before a great bank of lightning-lit clouds, black as ink, and there was a monster touching my wrist, a monster with the sleek fur and luminous yellow eyes of a cat. Then I was in the courtyard of St. Crellifer's, brick and glass and iron, and Leveque's eyes were brown again. But I could not answer him; I could barely keep my knees from buckling.

Before Leveque could even begin to look puzzled at my silence, the front doors of St. Crellifer's swung open. I flinched back as a wave of boiling, rioting colors poured down the stairs. They were dark and violent, angry and fearful and insane, a turmoil of violet and crimson and green with great terrible streaks of darkness through everything. Leveque's fingers tightened on my wrist.

"Please," I said, knowing it was useless, knowing my fate had been decided in the Mirador and that Leveque could do nothing other than what he was ordered. "Please, don't—"

A great booming voice came rolling out of the open doors like the seething colors. "So this is our new guest. Splendid!" The voice's owner followed it out of St. Crellifer's, a massive figure, as tall as I but at least three times as wide, the sparse brown hair on its scalp looking like nothing more than an ill-advised joke or a desultory attempt at camouflage, at pretending that this monstrous creature was human. It wore the robes of a friar of Phi-Kethetin; I wondered in dizzy panic if St. Crellifer had his own separate order, or if this hospice was maintained by the brothers of St. Gailan. I was still trying to break Leveque's grip and had actually succeeded in dragging him backwards a pace or two.

"Now, no need to fear," said the monster, coming down the steps. "No one here wishes to harm you." But the colors of madness and pain were still swirling around us, and I knew it lied. It reached us in two huge strides and caught my other wrist. Leveque let go of me in palpable relief.

"I am Brother Orphelin, Warder of St. Crellifer's." His eyes were small, gray, like tiny chips of polished stone set deep into the swollen dough of his face. I could see the gloat in them as he said, "I understand that this guest is consigned to our care by the Mirador—by the Lord Protector himself?"

"Yes," said Leveque.

Brother Orphelin lifted my arm; his hand was like a pillow wrapped around a set of iron rods. "And a wizard," he said. The little gray eyes took in my hair, my mismatched eyes; he knew who I was.

"His . . . his powers are bound," Leveque said.

"Of course they are," said Brother Orphelin. He knew I was frightened of him. I looked at Leveque, but he avoided my eyes. He was backing away, eager to be gone. The colors around him spoke of embarrassment and dread.

"What's your name?" said Brother Orphelin, booming with fake bonhomie. By mistake, I met his eyes; I had to look away quickly from their gray malice.

I wanted to say, angrily, that he already knew and that I did not appreciate being toyed with. But I was too scared; he reminded me too much of Keeper. "Felix," I said and was pathetically grateful that my voice did not squeak or shake.

"Then, Felix, why don't you come with me? I'm sure Mr. Leveque has duties to attend to."

Leveque mumbled something—gratitude and urgency and I thought I caught Stephen's name—and bolted. He might not believe that I was guilty of the crimes laid at my feet, but he surely did believe that I was mad.

Am I mad? I wondered. But before I found an answer, Brother Orphelin said, "Come, Felix," and started toward the doors of St. Crellifer's, my wrist still enveloped in his hand. His size and strength were terrifying; I did not even have a chance to brace my feet before I was off-balance, stumbling after him, desperately trying to keep from falling on the stairs.

My first impression of St. Crellifer's was the smell. It stank of urine and sweat, with an underlying tang of excrement and rotting garbage and death. When the doors slammed shut behind us, it was nearly as dark as the Mirador; only dim smears of daylight made it through the barred and filthy windows. Somewhere, distantly, I could hear someone sobbing, and as Brother Orphelin turned to speak to the porter, dragging me after him like a stick tied to his tail, there was a shriek that sounded only dubiously human. Brother Orphelin and the porter both laughed at the way I jumped.

"You'll grow accustomed soon enough, Felix," Brother Orphelin said.

He and the porter had a brief, lazy argument about who was on shift, and when the porter's relief might show up. Then Brother Orphelin said, looking at me, "I'll be downstairs." The evil omen of the porter's yellow-toothed smirk followed me as I perforce followed Brother Orphelin, who had not yet let go of my wrist.

The staircase was immediately off the vestibule, a narrow dank shaft whose wooden treads quickly shifted to stone, slick and treacherous. "Fall on me and I'll break your thumb," said Brother Orphelin. I concentrated on my footing and wished that the lanterns were hung at more regular intervals. The darkness was crowding up around me, and, while I couldn't hear the Virtu any longer, I was becoming fretfully aware of something else, a noise like some vast heartbeat, only with too many pulses. Mélusine, breathing.

Then Brother Orphelin towed me out of the stairwell, down a short corridor, and into a broad, stone-flagged room with a drain set in the center of the floor and a cistern tap on the wall opposite the door, with a bucket set beneath it. He let me go with a shove, so that I staggered a couple of steps into the room, ending up far closer than I wished to the gaping mouth of the drain.

"We believe in hygiene," said Brother Orphelin. "Take off your clothes."

I turned, hoping futilely that I had misheard; the air around him was seething with violet and red, orange streaks shooting through the mass like greedy fire.

"You heard me," he said, crossing the room with his rolling stride to open the cistern tap. "Get rid of those disgusting rags you're wearing."

The water poured into the bucket. My breathing was getting faster and shallower. I had no thought of defiance, but I could not remove my clothes in front of this gelid giant.

He snorted. "Do you think I won't make you?"

I shook my head, but I couldn't move. I couldn't make my hands betray the last shreds of my dignity, my privacy, my pride.

Brother Orphelin turned off the tap and started toward me. I stood, blank with panic, watching him approach. He took a good long look at me and said, "You aren't going to give me any trouble."

It wasn't a question. I couldn't have answered if it had been.

Clearly he'd had practice; he had my clothes off with ruthless efficiency, heedless of the tearing fabric, nearly dumping me off my feet onto the floor. His gaze didn't linger on my genitals; that wasn't what interested him. He walked slowly around me; I could feel him staring at my back. He whistled, long and low.

"*That*'s not ornamentation you see on a Cabaline wizard every day in a decad. Who'd you aggravate, and how often?"

I shook my head again. I couldn't answer; I didn't have the words.

"You'll tell me soon enough," he said with gruesome cheerfulness. His thick fingers brushed across my back, and I shuddered. But his attention was on my hair. He took a handful of it, tugged—not gently—and said, "This has to go."

"What?" I said, shrill and shaky, my voice mostly breath.

"There's no point trying to get this mess clean. Stay here while I get the shears." It was his idea of a joke; his volcanic chuckle told me that.

He waddled out. I stood, shivering, feeling my hair with both hands, feeling the mats and the dirt and the terrible dead heaviness of it. I began reckoning back frantically, but I could not remember the last time I had bathed—or for that matter, the last time I had eaten or laughed or picked a fight with someone just because I felt like it. Then I realized I did not know what the date was. I was still trying to remember if it had seemed like summer or winter in the courtyard of St. Crellifer's when Brother Orphelin returned with a pair of shears that looked more like a murder weapon than a household tool.

"Hold still," he said, "and you won't get cut."

I held still; he hacked my hair off, long snakelike mats, no color but dirt, falling to the floor around my feet. He cropped it ruthlessly short, and I was grateful that there was no mirror. I felt now not merely naked, but vulnerable, exposed.

"Better," he said and lumbered away to get the bucket.

I watched his return toward me like the commander of a battered fortress watching the approach of the siege engines. He lifted the bucket off his shoulder with a grunt and tipped it forward.

For a moment, as fast and brutal as a lightning strike, I was a child again, drowning with Keeper's hand clamped on the back of my neck. The bitter taste of metal was in my mouth and nose, and the cold was eating its way in toward my bones. Then I blinked the water out of my eyes, gasped for breath, and was back in St. Crellifer's basement. Brother Orphelin was rolling back toward the cistern tap. I would have fled, dripping and naked as I was, except that I knew the outer doors were guarded. And this swollen, sullen building was Brother Orphelin's domain. There would be no inch of it, no crevice, no crawl space, that he did not know.

He refilled and emptied his bucket twice more before he was satisfied. By then, no matter how I shook my head or rubbed at my eyes, I saw the whole room underwater, full of darkness. Brother Orphelin became a sea monster, vast as the whales I had read about in books from Lunness Point, vast as a cloud. I stood and shivered and did not scream.

"Come on, then," he said, setting the bucket back under the tap and starting for the door. He turned, saw my face, and burst out laughing. "Your eyes are as big as bell-wheels. We're going next door, to get you some clothes."

"Oh," I said, a bare whisper.

"Don't worry. I won't parade you bare-ass naked through St. Crellifer's unless you aggravate *me*. Now come on."

I followed him, shivering convulsively and leaving a trail of footprints, black as murder, black as guilt, behind me.

The storeroom was musty and dark, its shelves heaped with piles of rough smocks and trousers. Brother Orphelin shoved a set at me. I put them on as fast as I could. The clothes St. Crellifer's provided were coarse, baggy, made of undyed cloth, but they were clean. In some small way I was glad to be rid of those ragged, stained, dirt-stiffened garments that had once been a white cambric shirt and my best court trousers. And even these clothes—too short, too loose, scratchy and ugly and not warm enough—were protection.

"And now no one can tell you've got those wicked scars on your back," Brother Orphelin said. He had echoed my thoughts uncannily, and I could not help staring at him. "Only you know, and I know, and it can be our secret, can't it?"

I understood him then, as tendrils of the violet-red miasma that surrounded him reached out hungrily toward me. He was not interested in my body, as I'd already realized; for Brother Orphelin, celibacy was not a difficult discipline. His lust was for secrets, for shame and guilt, for petty darknesses. More and worse, he was a sophisticate; his pleasure was not in the secret itself, but in the power it gave him over me, in his knowledge of what it did to me to know that he knew.

I lowered my eyes, not wanting him to see my revulsion.

"We'll talk later," he said and led me out of the storeroom and back to the ground floor again. We left the water behind in the basement. This time, he held open the vestibule's inner door; still aware of the porter's smirk like a knife between my shoulder blades, I walked into St. Crellifer's.

"Come then," Brother Orphelin said as I passed him in the doorway, smelling the bloated reek of his sweat. I could not help looking at him as his face widened in a hideous smile. "Let me show you your new home."

Mildmay

The Blue Cat again. Kethe. I had to be out of my fucking mind. I hated it more every time we came here. Cardenio'd asked me this afternoon, "So why do you go?" and I hadn't been able to tell him. Not like I didn't know, mind you, but I couldn't tell Cardenio. Couldn't tell nobody.

See, the thing was, I was jealous. Austin Lefevre, him and his poems and his long black hair that he wore queued like a gentleman—which I'm here to say he wasn't. And the way he looked at Ginevra, and the way he'd say when he came in, "I wrote a new poem for you," and hand it over. He used the best-quality stationery—three gorgons for four septad sheets—and violet ink. And Ginevra'd read his fucking poems, and her eyes would go all wide and her face would go pink. I couldn't write poems for her. I could barely even write my own damn name.

And, powers, he could talk. He told stories about the guy he worked for, this crazy old historian who lived in Nill and was trying to write a history about the Raphenii, along of how he thought he might be a descendent of theirs. He'd hired Austin to keep track of his notes and his letters and shit like that, and to hear Austin tell it, it was a full-time job for three or four guys, so it was lucky the old historian was crazy and didn't care that he could never find nothing.

And Austin told stories about the other poets he knew—seemed like there was quite a rookery of them over in Nill and the north end of Havelock—and about things he said he did at night, wandering around in Gilgamesh and Britomart. I knew those were all lies, but I didn't say nothing. Nobody'd believe me, and it'd just piss Ginevra off. She didn't like nobody saying catty things about Austin.

But that night he was telling stories about hocuses. Faith wasn't there, or maybe he wouldn't've. Estella just sat and watched him like he wasn't even worth her while getting mad at. And, I mean, *everybody* was telling hocus stories. The mood was getting worse and worse in the city. People weren't thinking about the nature-witches at St. Cecily's—and, I mean, they might be about as much use as garters to a cat, but at least they was trying—they were thinking about the necromancers and the blood-witches and the Obscurantists. Powers, it seemed like every damn story I'd ever heard about the Obscurantists I'd heard again in the past decad and a half. And most of the shit Austin was talking was just them same old rehashed stories, about kids disappearing from orphan houses and which guilds were hiding secret cults—and if you believed everything you heard, that was like three-quarters of the guilds in Mélusine that were really Obscurantists and only fronting as coopers or chandlers or whatever. But then he started talking about the Mirador's witch-hunts and about all the good Cerberus Cresset had done and all the blood-witches he'd found and how the Lower City had been safe when he was in charge, and I just couldn't stand it no more.

I hadn't meant to say nothing. I didn't want to talk to Austin, and I didn't want to make Ginevra mad, and I didn't want to get going on the witch-hunts anyway, but it was like he just trotted out one too many of them old tired lies that the Mirador's been living on for septads, and I said, "That's bullshit."

Everybody looked at me like I'd turned bright, coal-tar purple. "I *beg* your pardon?" Austin said, in this snotty sort of voice.

Shit, Milly-Fox, I thought. You and your big fucking mouth. But I couldn't back off it now. "I don't mind you telling lies," I said, " 'long as they ain't hurting nobody else."

"A liar, am I?" he said, his eyebrows going up.

"Gilroi," Hugo Chandler said, all nervous and squeaky, "don't—"

I said to Austin, "If you don't know you're lying, you got no right to talk about Cerberus Cresset."

"And what do *you* know about Cerberus Cresset?" he said.

Too fucking much, I thought. "Lemme tell you a story," I said.

"A *story*." Austin got this look on his face, like a kid seeing somebody'd left the candy shop unlocked. "Well, go on then, Gil. Tell your story."

"Austin," said Hugo, still trying to make peace.

"Shut up, Hugo," Austin said.

I hated him. I hated him so much I went ahead and told them about Zephyr Wolsey, even though I knew Zephyr deserved better than having what happened to him pawed over by this mangy bunch of weasels. "Okay," I said. "I knew this guy, Zephyr Wolsey. He was a hocus, a pretty good one from what I understand. He was a nature-witch. He lived down in Gilgamesh, and he did some healing and some good-luck charms—just shit like that, nothing big, nothing scary. He had an apprentice, and he was teaching him right, warning him off of blood-magic and the hard-core necromancy. Not hurting nobody. And then Cerberus Cresset comes down the city with his goons and he starts asking people to name nature-witches, and he says, 'If'n you don't give me names, I'll know it's 'cause you're hiding 'em, and you know that's treason, don't you?' And people got scared, and they started naming folks off, and somebody told him about Zephyr. And they came and trashed his shop and dragged him off. But we all figured Zephyr'd be okay, 'cause he wasn't doing nothing wrong, wasn't hurting nobody, wasn't doing no necromancy or that shit blood-witches get up to. And he was tried and convicted, and then he was burned. So don't tell me what a hero Cerberus Cresset was."

There was this silence. I was remembering Zephyr, how he'd been tall and heavyset and had a face like the full moon, round and all scarred from smallpox, and it didn't matter what you'd come in for, he'd tell you all about his latest experiments with growing roses and the weird thing he'd found in the Library of Heth-Eskaladen last Neuvième, and, oh yeah, that thing you were asking about the other month, I think I got an answer for you. He never said a mean word about nobody, and about the only thing Zephyr wouldn't help you with was hexes. He'd never done nothing wrong in his life—except not playing by the Mirador's rules. And they burned him for it.

Ginevra said, loud and fake, "I think we'd better be going. Come on, Gil."

I didn't want to hear what Austin was going to say about Zephyr. I got up and followed Ginevra out.

She walked for a block and a half without saying nothing, just staring straight ahead. She had her lips pressed together, and I knew she'd have little lines between her eyebrows. We'd had enough fights I knew what she looked like when she got mad.

Finally, she said, "Thank you very much for embarrassing me like that."

"Ginevra, I didn't mean—"

"Of course you did. You told that horrible story on purpose to make Austin look stupid."

"Well, yeah, but what's that got to do with you?"

"He'll think I put you up to it!"

"So?"

There was this long silence. "You think he's handsome, don't you?" I said. It wasn't what I meant, but I couldn't say, *Do you love him?* any more than I could say, *Do you love me?*

"Powers!" She turned. We'd gotten into the north end of Ramecrow by then, the part people always joke about making its own district called Losthope. Nobody lives there no more, and nobody wants to. Nothing wants it. Even the Fire didn't touch it. "Let's get this over with," she said and stalked into one of the courtyards—weeds growing between the paving stones, empty, broken windows staring down on all sides.

"Ginevra, we—"

"What if I *do* think he's handsome? What then?" she said. She was too well launched to listen to me. "What does it matter? Is that why you dye your hair, because you think you'll look more handsome?"

"I don't—"

"Yes, you do, you liar!"

"So does Austin," I said.

"He does not!"

" 'Course he does."

"You just don't like him, that's all. You don't like any of my friends. Aren't they good enough for you?"

Kethe knows what I would have said to that, and Kethe knows where the fight would have gone, except that a voice said in my ear, "Tell the lady to keep her trap shut, and maybe nobody gets hurt."

That's the trouble with Losthope and why it ain't such a good place to thrash things out. You got the jackals. But this one, by somebody's mercy, was stupid, stupid enough to start yapping before he had either mark where he wanted them. I said, "Ginevra, get back!" even as I was ducking down for the knife I kept in my boot, and coming back up at him from where he wasn't expecting me.

I didn't want to kill him—not worth anybody's blood, this stupid little fuck-up—so I slammed the knife out of his hand and got him pressed up against the wall before he knew where he was or where I was or what he should be doing about it.

"Kethe, mister," he said in this shaky little voice, "don't kill me."

Fuck me sideways 'til I cry, I thought. He was a kid—two septads, two septads and one, no older than that. "I ain't gonna kill you," I said. "You fond of that knife?"

It took him a second to understand what I'd said. Then he said, "Oh. No! No, I ain't!"

"Good. Then I'm gonna let you go, and you're gonna leave. Okay?"

"Okay! Sure! I'm sorry, mister, really I am. I thought you was—"

He stopped short.

"You thought I was a flat," I said. "I ain't. Now scram."

I let him go, and he bailed.

I turned to Ginevra. "You okay?"

"Um. Yeah." Her voice sounded shaky. "What just happened?"

"There was a kid thought he was gonna get your jewelry."

"Oh. And you just—"

"I been there myself," I said. "Come on. Let's go home."

She took my arm, and she held on to it all the way through Ramecrow and home to Midwinter, like we hadn't been fighting or nothing. But I could still feel it there like an alligator, sunk back under the water and just biding its time.

Chapter 4

Mildmay

The Dogs started raiding on 19 Prairial. They were supposed to be rounding up heretics and spies, but you noticed how they were starting in Queensdock and Simside, and you had to wonder. Erasmus Spalding had one idea about what was going on, and Mayor Elvenner Packer had another. The Dogs didn't touch Scaffelgreen, and they didn't touch Dassament, a sure sign that Vey Coruscant was alive and well and looking out for her own. And those smug, stupid fucks in the Mirador didn't know enough about their own city to know that the Mayor and the Dogs were lying to them. For the Mirador, I guess it was all just the Lower City, and Breadoven no different from Ruthven. And the Dogs didn't believe in Obscurantists and Kekropian spies. They wanted to clean out the packs and the kept-thieves and the pushers. And the Mirador had handed 'em an excuse on a stick.

The Dogs did raid in Candlewick Mews. Even the Mirador knows there are hocuses there. And the Dogs don't like the nature-witches. They ain't like ordinary cits, but you can't rightly say they're doing anything wrong, trying to heal folks and shit like that—'til the Mirador wakes up and notices all over again that it's got heretics in its backyard.

I was gladder and gladder I hadn't let Ginevra spend the money from the dancer, because it didn't take no genius to see we were going to need it. The whole Lower City was scared and thinking mainly about keeping their heads down. Nobody was going to want to hire a cat burglar, and even Lollymeg couldn't promise me good prices if I brought anything in.

Which is how come I was home *and* awake on 23 Prairial when Estella Velvet came looking for Ginevra.

"She's at work," I said before I took in how Estella was looking. I'd never seen her scared before. "What's the matter?"

"It's sweet of you to pretend you care," she said. But I guess she'd got to the point where she had to tell *somebody,* because she said, "They arrested Faith."

"Shit," I said.

"That's not a bad way of putting it." She closed her eyes and pushed her fingers against her eyelids—carefully, so she wouldn't smudge her maquillage. "I don't even know why I came here. Ginevra's no help with stuff like this."

"What d'you mean?"

She looked at me, her eyes mocking and mean and sad all at the same time. "Oh, poor Gilly. Haven't you figured it out yet?"

"Don't call me that."

"But Gilroi doesn't suit you at all. Let me give you some free advice, Gilly. Keep Ginevra happy, because she'll leave you flat if you don't."

She turned and started down the stairs.

She was almost to the bottom before I could get the words out. "I'm sorry . . . I mean, about Faith."

"Don't worry," she said and gave me a look like she was daring me to notice that she was crying. "I'll figure something out."

❧

My dreams that night were fucking terrible. I dreamed that there was something I had to tell Zephyr, something he could tell the witchfinders and then they wouldn't kill him and everything'd be okay. So I'm looking for him everywhere in Gilgamesh, but his shop's been burned to the ground and all the bars and teahouses he liked are closed, and I can't think of nowhere else to look. And it's getting dark—it's one of *those* dreams—and once it's dark, I know it'll be too late, that then Zephyr will be dead and *he*'ll come looking for *me*. And I keep meeting other people, like Christobel and Nikah and Letty, and if I could tell them the right thing, then *they* wouldn't be dead. But the thing I know, it'll only work for Zephyr, and I can't help them.

I woke up to Ginevra saying, "Powers, Mildmay, you've got all the blankets again." And I did, tangled around me in this kind of knot.

"Sorry," I said. Ginevra didn't ask about my dreams, and I didn't tell her. It seemed fair.

We kind of wrangled all the time she was getting ready for work. I mean, we weren't fighting or nothing, just going back and forth over the same dreary half acre of land we'd been going over since she'd come home the night before and I'd told her Faith was in the Kennel.

She didn't want to believe it. She said Estella liked to tell elaborate lies to get people worried about her. I said Estella hadn't been lying. She said nobody would want to hurt Faith, that she was a healer. I said that didn't matter when the Mirador was witch-hunting. She said I was horrible, and besides I couldn't've understood Estella right.

I knew what she wanted. She wanted me to say, yeah, Estella lied, or, yeah, I didn't hear her right, or even I guess, yeah, I'm lying to you just to be mean. She wanted me to tell her everything was okay. And I couldn't do it. Because everything *wasn't* okay. The whole Lower City was fucked, and I just couldn't tell lies about it, even though I knew that was what Estella'd been getting at when she told me to keep Ginevra happy.

I thought when she was going out the door, I bet Austin would have told her what she wanted to hear. Austin would have made her feel safe and like he'd take care of her. And I didn't know whether that made me or him the better person.

Felix

The Hospice of St. Crellifer was run by the order of St. Gailan, and the order of St. Gailan believed that work was the best cure for all ills. Most of them also believed that lunacy was nothing more than weakness of will. Brother Orphelin did not subscribe to that philosophy, but seen through Brother Orphelin's stonelike eyes, the world was a madhouse, a leperhouse, and a reservoir of the damned. He did not care if we were sane or not.

Every patient in St. Crellifer's who could understand Marathine and be trusted not to bite anyone was put to work. I had suffered through a humiliating interview with Brother Orphelin and Brother Lilburn, the subwarder, my first morning there, in which they had determined I had no skills at all. I had wanted to protest, but realized in time that my skills were limited to sex and magic, and kept my mouth shut.

They set me to scrubbing floors. There was nothing else I could be trusted with, and it was certainly the case that the floors needed scrubbing. A brother came by occasionally to see if I was working. If I wasn't, he'd box my ears or knock my head against the wall, more or less in passing. The casual violence reminded me inescapably of Lorenzo, the owner of the Shining Tiger, who had sold me to Malkar when I was fourteen; I found it harder and harder to remember where I was and what had happened to me. Once, I came back to myself with a jolt to discover I'd spent some unknown length of time searching for Joline.

Joline's dead, I told myself firmly. You saw her die.

And I had—I had dragged her out of the burning tenement, only to have her die, choking and gagging, in the street. But if I could just *find* her . . .

But even that wasn't as bad as when I did.

I was scrubbing a hallway on the third floor. Every door along the hallway was locked, and I did not want to know what lay behind them. I kept finding blood on my hands—caked under my fingernails, smeared and sticky across my palms—and I couldn't touch anything with blood on my hands. Then Brother Dillard would come by and clip me over the ear, and the blood would be gone.

And then I would look down and my hands would be bloody again.

I didn't hear her, but I felt something behind me and turned, and there she was, skinny and dark in that cut-down dress she'd begged from the madam of the Black Swan's Promise, the gap in her front teeth showing when she smiled at me.

She didn't say anything—I couldn't have answered her if she had—merely watched me for a while and then walked away. I saw her vanish just as she began to turn the corner.

I never, after that, saw anyone I knew; that brief, unhappy vision of Joline was merely a transition, a bridge away from normal sight and into the world of ghosts. Like the colors I saw surrounding people, filling even empty rooms in St. Crellifer's with a red-purple tinge like spectral blood, the ghosts were clearly manifestations of my madness, but I was never comfortably sure that was all they were. One of Lorenzo's other prostitutes, a tired boy named Vincent, had been able to see ghosts; he had never gotten any joy out of the ability that I could observe, but that made the thing more rather than less credible.

Mostly, I saw the ghosts of the mad. They clustered in the corners, weeping and shrieking as they had when they had been alive. I saw that even in death they were frightened of Brother Lilburn, that female ghosts followed Brother Clayton from room to room, their nakedness an accusation and an imprecation. I tried not to watch them. Brother Clayton would hit me for staring at nothing; Brother Lilburn's attention was infinitely worse, those perfectly cold, perfectly righteous eyes like a burning brand against my face. Brother Lilburn led us madmen in prayers every day, and if anyone disrupted prayers, he would not eat until Brother Lilburn was satisfied that he had "repented." What repentance looked like in a madman was anybody's guess; in Brother Lilburn's lexicon, it looked like fear and weeping. Brother Lilburn frightened me even more than Brother Orphelin did.

I also saw ghosts of former friars, still walking their rounds. And there were other ghosts, from even longer ago, when St. Crellifer's had been some nobleman's town house: two little children playing tag through the halls; servants on cryptic errands; a woman in cloth of gold who sat by a window on the second floor, weeping as if her heart had broken and was still breaking, into smaller and smaller pieces, into a pile of fine dust, like the dust on the windowsill that did not register the pressure of her elbows. I wondered who she was, but I knew nothing of the history of the city; I did not even know which family had donated their sprawling house to the Order of St. Gailan. All I knew of her tragedy was what I saw: her dress, her jewels, her endless weeping.

Mildmay

I had to get out of there. I mean, if I stayed sitting in my front room all day, with things going 'round in my head like they were, I was going to end up barking, and they'd have to come and take me away to St. Crellifer's Hospice in Spicewell, where they take all the crazy people. And the dream

I'd had, it made me remember something I'd had sort of crawling around at the bottom of my mind for months. And today was a good day for it.

24 Prairial is St. Vivien's day, and St. Vivien is one of the Witnesses, the septad of saints who petition Phi-Kethetin on behalf of the dead. So, round about the septad-day, I went out and bought flowers from a street vendor on Rue Rachevin. The flower-seller was an old lady, and her forehead was tattooed with the blue aversion-signs people had used to try to protect their kids with during the plague nine septads ago. It had worked, for her anyway.

I asked for trumps.

"Wouldn't your young lady like the roses better?"

"They ain't for a lady."

Her eyebrows went up, wrinkling the aversion-signs into nonsense, but she tied up my trumps for me without no more lip. I gave her a quarter-gorgon I didn't have to spare and took my trumps. Ginevra would be pissed if she found out, but I wasn't planning on telling her.

Trumps are big bright flowers. They grow in the St. Grandin Swamp, south of Queensdock and the Septad Gate, and they bloom all summer and on into fall. During the Trials of Heth-Eskaladen, Lower City mothers pick them or buy them and weave them into crowns for their kids. The first Trials after the Fire, Keeper bought trumps and made crowns for all of us. I only had five indictions then, but I've never forgot it.

I walked through Pennycup and Ruthven, trying not to think about the last time I'd been over in the east end of Ruthven. Nobody'd heard nothing for certain from Vey Coruscant since 12 Pluviôse, which I thought was a bad sign. You couldn't get no sense from the stories coming out of Dassament, but, powers, that was nothing new. People in Dassament are all liars. And you should've heard the people who thought it was Obscurantists trying to get all the pieces to make sense. Claudio Draper—the Claudio who'd been supposed to kill me if I moved—was dead for sure. The cade-skiffs had dragged him out of the Sim near the end of Ventôse, and if they knew what he'd died of . . . well, anyway, Cardenio wasn't saying. And that all by itself didn't mean nothing. There were all sorts of ways to end up dead in the river that weren't nothing to do with Vey Coruscant. Only thing I knew for sure was I was staying the fuck out of Dassament.

There was nobody in the Boneprince. There almost never is. But I could feel the dead people, like water in the air.

"I brought you flowers," I said to the unmarked graves along the Road of Marble. "Trumps." I sat down on the path and untied my trumps. I started weaving them into a crown. I could feel the kept-thieves, little ghosts hiding behind the tombstones, watching. I didn't look up, just sat there working with the flowers and thinking, Why didn't they ask their names? Didn't nobody care? Didn't nobody see that they were just kids, that the stuff they were trained to do wasn't their fault?

But nobody'd seen that. If they'd seen it, the kept-thieves wouldn't be buried here with the grown-up monsters.

She might've thought I was crazy, but the old lady had been generous. When I'd finished, the crown was too big for a kid to wear, but, Kethe, it was bright and gorgeous, and it made me remember how I'd felt when Keeper had put her trumps on my head. I hoped the little ghosts had something like that they could remember.

I put the crown beside the path, where I knew their graves were. I said, "It's for all y'all. I hope you like it. And I hope St. Vivien prays for you."

I turned and left. I didn't look back. I knew better.

I walked around a while after that. Not doing nothing, not thinking nothing, either. Just walking. Trying to get my head on straight, get rid of the dreams and that dark, prickly feeling I'd been having for days, like being watched by gators. It must've been near the eleventh hour of the day when I sort of woke up, took a look around, and figured out that I'd got myself into Havelock, up near Nill.

"Kethe," I said. I found Ver-Istenna's dome, south of me and some east, and started home again. I thought about flagging down a hansom—you could, in this part of the Lower City—but the cabbies wouldn't like where I wanted to go, and they wouldn't like my face. And my feet would get me there just as good. So I walked, and when I thought about it later, I figured that walking might have saved my life. I don't know. You never *can* know with the luck Kethe throws at you, whether you got it 'cause you did the right thing, or whether he was looking out for your ass anyways.

But what happened was, I turned the corner onto Madrigal Lane, and Scabious came running up. He'd been watching for me, like he did, only this time his face was white as paper, and he grabbed my arm and said, "There's Dogs in your rooms. Gilroi, what—"

"Fuck," I said. "Scabious, d'you know where Ginevra works?"

"Yeah, I think, but Gilroi—"

"Will you go and tell her not to come home tonight? Please?"

"Oh. Yeah. Yeah, I'll go right now!" He took off running, but he was smart enough to loop the block, starting back the way I'd come from and hanging a left, so if the Dogs waiting in my front room happened to glance out the window, they wouldn't see my landlady's kid running like a racing dog along the street.

Me, I was gone before he'd turned the corner.

I headed for the Arcane first, pure stupid instinct, like a fox booking it for his den when he hears dogs. But I caught myself, remembered that the door under the Hornet and Spindle was pretty common knowledge, and if the Dogs wanted me bad enough to be laying in wait like this in my rooms, they might want me bad enough to have a guy in the Hornet and Spindle.

You got to understand, my life in the Lower City was pretty precarious. "Precarious" was Zephyr's word, what he'd said when I asked what it was like being a hocus in Gilgamesh. And I'd asked him what it meant—you could with Zephyr, he wouldn't get snotty about being smarter than you or nothing—and he'd told me, and I'd thought it was a damn good word for a lot of things. Like the way I lived.

The Dogs wanted me. The Mirador wanted me. What was standing between me and them was that the Mirador didn't know it was me they wanted, and the Dogs knew it was me, but didn't have the first clue where the fuck I was, and they didn't have the money to go knocking door to door through the Lower City. And they couldn't arrest every guy five-foot-eight with a scar on his face—there's a lot of guys like that, and maybe some of 'em deserve a visit to the Kennel, but most of 'em don't, and anyways, none of 'em but me deserve it on the strength of being Mildmay the Fox. But me staying out of the Kennel depended on the people who knew I was Mildmay the Fox not saying anything about where I was to the Dogs. That's why I used all the fake names—Gilroi Felter and Dennis and Jean-Thermidor and Esteban Ross and Umberto and the rest of them. And mostly the people who knew what Mildmay the Fox looked like, and knew where I was—and there weren't many of 'em—were people on just as bad terms with the Dogs as me, and they weren't going to say nothing to nobody.

Except that somebody had. I ducked down an alley, monkeyed my way up onto the fire escape, and started for the roof, wondering all the time if it was Ginevra. I knew she hadn't turned me in—*she* didn't have a clue about Mildmay the Fox, even though I'd been fuckheaded enough to tell her my real name, and if she'd figured it out, I knew she couldn't have hid it from me. But I didn't know what she might have said. That was another reason for going to the Blue Cat, along with being poison-sick jealous. I didn't trust Ginevra to keep her mouth shut, not to drop hints about the exciting, secret life her boyfriend led. And all it would take was a couple of those hints getting to somebody who'd grown up in the Lower City and could use the money the Dogs gave their snitches. I'd tried to tell her it was dangerous, not exciting, but standing on the roof, sighting on Ver-Istenna's dome and starting that way, I could admit that I knew she hadn't listened. She thought she was in a romance, like the one she said her aunt got her name out of. She thought nothing bad could ever really happen to her or anybody she knew. She hadn't been in the Lower City long enough to learn better.

And there was fuck-all I could do about that now. If I could keep out of the Dogs' paws another couple days, if somebody in Margot's pack could write, I could send her a message. And maybe, if I got super-lucky and Kethe didn't feel like dropping another load of shit on my head, I could get back to her and try to talk to her. Maybe tell her *why* things weren't as safe and easy as she thought. Maybe tell her about the shit I'd done before I left Keeper.

That was a bad thought. I didn't talk about that stuff with nobody, tried not to think about it as best I could. But if you love her, this voice said in my head, you got to trust her. Either that, or you got to say you *can't* trust her, and then you got to let her go.

That was a bad thought, too. I brought myself up short. I was fucking with my concentration, and I wasn't safe yet, and nowhere close, neither. Shut it down, Milly-Fox, I said to myself, thought about my breathing while I counted a septad, and then started again toward Ver-Istenna's and the Badgers' territory.

I'd never called it in, but Margot wouldn't've forgotten the favor she owed me.

Felix

Brother Orphelin appeared in the doorway of the ward, as vast and improbable as the moon. "Felix," he said, "you have a visitor."

Everyone stared at me. No one in St. Crellifer's had visitors; it wasn't that kind of hospice. I floundered up through layers of darkness, obedient to Brother Orphelin's beckoning gesture, as I obeyed Brother Orphelin in all things. He had the whip hand, and we both knew it.

He had bided his time, an expert in his own peculiar game of cat and mouse. Every day for that first week, I had expected to be called to his office, a round room on the third floor with yellow, cracking plaster and an ineradicable stink of sweat. Every day for the second week, I flinched at the sound of his footsteps, kept my eyes lowered when he was in the room, hoping—as a child hopes—that if I did not make eye contact, he would forget about me.

Then, although I neither forgot nor ceased to fear, I began to drift, to sink. My madness, the colors and ghosts, the terrible intangibility of time, made it first difficult and then impossible to keep track of the calendar. So I had no way of telling how long it truly was before Brother Orphelin made his move.

I was in a hallway on the second floor, at the very back of the building. It was another hallway the uses of which I did not know and did not want to. The ghosts who thronged the corners and window bays were all shaven-headed, with terrible scars on their scalps. Many of them could not even weep or scream; they simply stared straight ahead with dull, burnt-out eyes. I had never been so glad that the ghosts of St. Crellifer's did not see me.

I had been having trouble that day with the echoes of an argument. I knew this hallway was deserted except for the dead; I had checked every room. But still the voices argued, just out of sight around a corner, or just behind the half-ajar door of one of the deserted rooms, or even somehow seeming to belong to men standing outside the window, arguing violently on empty air.

The argument made it hard to work; the voices hovered just on the edge of comprehensibility, so that I could never understand them but kept being drawn into futile attempts to make the words resolve into sense, only coming back to myself when the duty brother hit me. The third time he'd boxed my ears, he'd warned me that if he caught me shirking again, he would be obligated to tell Brother Lilburn, and I had grimly set myself to concentrate on the floorboards, the scrub brush, and the pail of water.

For some time I was able to stay focused, but then I caught a word: "reprehensible." My head came up, and I strained to hear more; the argument would be easier to bear if I just knew what it was *about*. But it remained maddeningly muffled, as if the original sound had carried into the hallway from behind a closed door. I could hear their anger, their loathing for each other, the vituperative poison of their exchanges, but no other words, only a stray syllable here and there, rendered meaningless by lack of context.

I began to get up, turning to go back down the corridor one more time, to see if I could find the room in which the argument had first taken place, and found myself staring at the broad expanse of Brother Orphelin's robes.

I startled back, more horrified than I would have been to find the arguers behind me, tripped over the water pail, and came down hard on my back in a spreading lake of soapy, grimy water.

"Clumsy," Brother Orphelin said chidingly.

"I'm sorry," I said, scrambling to my feet. "I'm sorry, I didn't mean . . ." Malkar had punished me for clumsiness with an ever-fertile imagination.

"And you've gotten your clothes all dirty," Brother Orphelin said, as if I had not spoken. "We'll have to find you fresh. Come along."

I could feel the future before me, laid out with the strict unchanging formality of a minuet; what Keeper hadn't taught me about power games of this sort, Malkar had. I followed Brother Orphelin, misery a stone in my throat, and watched the violet and red and orange swirl around him like a cloud of carrion-feeding butterflies.

He took a different staircase down, this one even narrower and steeper, but we ended up in the same place: the storeroom in the basement.

"Now strip out of those wet things," he said, with a mocking parody of concern. I could feel his smirk, although I could not look him in the face.

My hands were shaking; I knew he could see that as I obediently took off my shirt and trousers to stand hunched and naked before his tiny, gleaming eyes. I realized I was running my hands across my scalp, the hedgehog prickle of hair against my palms, a parody of my own old habit, developed when I was a prostitute and my hair one of my great assets. I dragged my hands back down to my side and deliberately straightened. I had stood naked before men I loathed, men I despised, men who disgusted me. I told myself this was no different.

Brother Orphelin picked up a clean shirt and clean trousers from one of the shelves, but he did not give them to me. He walked slowly around me, like a potential buyer inspecting a horse. He stood behind me for a long time, staring. There had been a particular set among the Shining Tiger's clientele who always asked for me; I felt now the ghosts of their hot fingers and their repulsive breath and their hot, wet eyes, tracing the white web of scars across my shoulder blades. The scars continued down across my buttocks and thighs, hateful, ugly, shameful.

When he had looked his fill, he came back around to face me and said, "How did you get those scars?"

When Shannon had asked that question, I had lied. He was a scion of the House of Teverius, privileged, protected; he had never seen whip scars up close, did not recognize them for what they were. I had told him that they were the result of a rare Caloxan plague that caused tremendous welts radiating outward from the spine. The only treatment was to lay them open, I said, although it caused dreadful scarring. I was careful that he never saw my back in good light—easy enough in the Mirador's perpetual gloom—and I told him the scars were painful to the touch, which was another lie. He never got any clear idea of the extent or the severity of the damage to my back. And he believed me, because he was younger than I, because he was annemer, because he loved me. And I'd never even felt guilty about it until now.

I kept my chin up, my shoulders straight, my eyes focused somewhere past Brother Orphelin's left shoulder, and did not answer.

He found that amusing. "Come now, Felix. You don't think you can hold out against me, do you? You have no idea of what I can do to you."

It can't be worse than Malkar, I thought. I said nothing.

"I should perhaps warn you," he said meditatively, "that my word is law in St. Crellifer's. No one will defend you."

I said nothing.

"And you realize, of course, if you don't tell *me,* I will have to commend you to the attention of Brother Lilburn."

Maybe, before the Virtu had been broken, I would have been able to hold out even then, but I was terrified of Brother Lilburn, and I knew that once he had noticed me there was nothing in the world that could save me, in the same way that as children Joline and I had known the Tallowman was waiting for us on the landing outside the dormitory door. It was the same black, unreasoning fear, and my eyes flicked to Brother Orphelin's face before I could stop them.

"Oho, Brother Lilburn makes you nervous, does he? I can't say I blame you, Felix. He's a spooky bastard and no mistake. Do you know what Brother Lilburn does with sinners who resist confession?"

He told me, slowly, with a wealth of detail, his tiny, porcine eyes fixed gloatingly on my face. By the time he was done, my eyes were closed, and I was swallowing hard, trying to keep from crying. I didn't have the strength for this; I couldn't stand against Brother Orphelin's smothering weight.

I said in a choked whisper, not opening my eyes. "I was a kept-thief. My keeper beat me."

"There, see? That wasn't so hard. Look at me, Felix."

I did, staring at his round, pallid face, those tiny, cynical, glinting eyes. I felt like a mouse or a shrew—some small, stupid creature being mesmerized by a snake.

"I think you'll find," he said, "that you feel better for having told me this of your own free will. Don't you?"

Another of Malkar's favorite games, forcing me to thank him for hurting me. "Yes, Brother Orphelin," I said.

"Good," he said and, unbelievably, smiled at me, a smirk like a round of rotted cheese. "What did your keeper use on you? A bullwhip?"

I felt the blood mounting to my face; even Malkar had never been quite so brutal in describing my back. I couldn't meet Brother Orphelin's eyes any longer. "A nun's scourge," I said. "It's not . . . it's not as bad as it looks." I had been lucky; Lorenzo, seeing my potential, had paid for a chirurgeon to treat my adhesions and Malkar had continued those treatments—mostly, I believed, because they were excruciatingly painful, and that had amused him—so that I reached adulthood still able to straighten to my full six-foot-two, still with a complete range of motion in my shoulders. Only the ugliness remained.

Brother Orphelin said nothing, staring at me until I looked at him again. Then he gave me another hideous smile and said, "You may put your clothes on now."

He handed them to me. I wanted to dress slowly, deliberately, to show him he hadn't affected me, but the scarred skin of my back was crawling with the weight of remembered stares, and I scrambled into my clothes as quickly as I could.

"Very good, Felix," said Brother Orphelin. "Your truthfulness pleases me." And with that cruelly ironic joke, my torture was over. Brother Orphelin had opened the door, and I had followed him back up to the second floor, my scrub brush, and my pail.

And here I was, following Brother Orphelin again, to meet a visitor I had not expected and truthfully did not want.

"You may talk with your visitor in here," he said, waving me into a parlor that was normally reserved for the brothers themselves. It had a carpet, and chairs that weren't broken or missing half their upholstery, and someone had cleaned the window within living memory. I was already in the room, Brother Orphelin's bulk blocking the door, when I saw my visitor clearly.

I stopped in my tracks, even went back about half a step. The person waiting for me had the gray-brown, scaly head of a snake. Its eyes were lurid yellow, and they fixed on me instantly, identifying me as prey. I remembered the legends of the basilisk, and looked down.

"Felix," said the snake. "It is good to see you . . . well again."

Robert's voice. I dared a glance at the monster's hands: Robert's rings, gold set with emeralds. "What do you want?" I said.

The snake must have shifted the flat malevolence of its gaze to Brother Orphelin, who said, "I'll leave you to your visit," and closed the door.

"Giancarlo sent me," Robert said.

"Why?"

"Come sit down. Let's discuss this like reasonable men."

"I'm not reasonable," I said, not moving. "That's why I'm here."

The snake chuckled; I knew the expression that would have been on Robert's face if I had been able to see it. "You don't have any bargaining power here, you know. Nothing you say is going to get you out of St. Crellifer's."

"What do you want?" I said again, despairingly.

"Just to talk," the monster said in Robert's voice, and I knew it lied.

I said nothing, and the silence stretched out. The snake was staring at me. I kept my gaze on the toes of its boots, glossy black and pointed. I told myself that I had once worn boots like those, but I could no longer believe it.

"Sit down, Felix," Robert said, and if I didn't look up, I could pretend that it really was Robert, whom I had always hated but never feared, not a monster with a snake's head and Robert's rings. I sat down.

"That's better," the monster said. I felt those yellow eyes evaluating me. "Giancarlo still wants to know how you did it."

"I can't tell you," I said, barely whispering, skirting the edge of the truth as closely as I could.

"There are other ways to find out." The monster leaned forward suddenly, too fast for me to avoid, and caught my wrists. "I wanted to do this all along, but Giancarlo wouldn't let me, the pompous old fool."

"Let me go!" My head was full of Malkar; I broke away, knocked the chair over, and retreated as far as the door, where I stood, trembling.

"Don't be stupid, Felix," the snake said. "It won't hurt if you cooperate."

But that was what Malkar always said. I clawed the door open and ran.

Mildmay

Me and Margot had been friends for more than two septads. She'd been one of Keeper's kids, too, an indiction to one side or the other of my age. She'd been the first of us to get out. I thought she still steered clear of Britomart, and I didn't blame her. Keeper had been pissed.

Margot'd gotten herself into a pack, where the stuff she'd learned from Keeper was useful, and she didn't have to start turning tricks. And she'd stayed with the pack, and then somehow she'd ended up leading the pack, and that was when I'd done her a favor, just before I left Keeper myself, getting somebody off her back who Margot said was going to get her and all her pack killed. I hadn't had to kill him, just done what Margot called "heavy leaning." A couple of broken fingers and the kind of reputation I'd had back then had been enough. He hadn't given Margot no more trouble.

So Margot owed me. I hate calling in favors, and I hadn't ever wanted to use this one, just stayed friends with Margot and swapped news with her every month or so. But I was in a hole now, and if the Dogs were sweeping, and if they knew to look for me anyway . . . I could at least be safe with Margot for a day or two, until I'd figured out where to go. I had that bad, shaking feeling that said any decision I tried to make right now was going to go wrong. I was too scared and too mad. I needed to get somewhere I could hold still and think things out. And the Dogs didn't come up on the roofs, any more than they went down in the Arcane. All they ever found were booby traps and broken legs.

I went up the city through Engmond's Tor and into Dragonteeth, sticking to the roofs and being real open and real careful. Margot'd given me a couple of signals to use to say I wanted to talk to her and it was urgent, and I used them both. My body wasn't shaking, but my mind was—Kethe, that ain't no good way to put it, but I can't say it better than that. Things were fucked up, and I knew they were getting worse, and I didn't know how to stop it. I was afraid for Ginevra, afraid she wouldn't listen to Scabious, and she'd come home and the Dogs would want to know where I was, and there was no way in Hell they were going to believe her when she said she didn't know. I was trying hard not to think about Ginevra in the Kennel.

It wasn't long after I crossed into Dragonteeth that I knew the Badgers had found me. I could feel 'em watching. I stopped where I was and waited, keeping my hands out so they'd know I wasn't planning to get cute.

One of Margot's lieutenants, this flabby kid named Carmody, jumped down from a higher roof, and said, "Whatcha want?"

"Need to talk to Margot."

He gave me this scowl.

"Your name's Carmody," I said. "You know who I am. Get Margot for me."

"She don't got to come when you call."

"Fuck, kid, that ain't what I said. I need to *talk* to her."

"What about?"

That didn't rate an answer, so I didn't give it one. I just waited.

He wanted to tell me to go away, but Margot'd tear strips out of him, and he knew it. Finally, he said, "I'll get her," like he was doing me this big favor instead of exactly what he was supposed to, and scrambled back the way he'd come.

I didn't have to wait long before she came over the roof, still wearing that damn ugly motley coat that she'd kited off some barrow in the Cheaps when she'd had a septad and three or so. She still hadn't grown into it, and it didn't look like she was going to.

"You," she said. Margot'd never in her life admitted to being glad to see anybody. "What's up?"

"Dogs," I said.

"You and the rest of the Lower City."

"No, I mean, they *found* me."

"Oh," she said. "Shit. How close?"

"Prob'ly they're still in my front room, waiting."

"Okay. So they ain't on your tail or nothing."

"Nah. I'm clean. I just . . . I got to hide."

"Okay. We can do that. Just don't give my kids any crap, okay?"

"Okay."

"Come on, then." I followed her into the maze of rooftops over Dragonteeth, heading for the Judiciary, where the Badgers made their home.

Felix

I went to a place the ghosts had shown me.

I had noticed that the older ghosts still paced the rooms and hallways of the building they had known, not the building as it was now. Sometimes, when no one was around to see me, I tried to follow them. Mostly, this habit led me into dead ends, walled-up doorways, and rooms partitioned without grace or kindness. But once I followed an anxious ghost into a broom closet and discovered a partly boarded-up staircase. The ghost walked through the shelves; I crawled under them. Three-quarters of the way up the stairs, the ghost disappeared. I kept going and found myself in a long, narrow attic, a triangular wedge just beneath the main gable of the roof. I wondered what business the ghost had had up here and why he had been so nervous, but the ghosts did not speak to me, and I had no way to find out.

I had not stayed long that first day, afraid that my absence would be noticed. But now all I wanted was to get away from Robert; as long as they did not find me, I did not care if they knew I was hiding. I was lucky; I met no one on the stairs, no one in the grim corridors of the third floor. I shut the broom closet door behind me and wished I could call witchlights. But I could not do magic; I could not even remember what it felt like, only pain and Malkar's voice.

I felt my way to the back of the closet, ducked under the shelves, squeezing through a gap barely wide enough for me, and climbed the stairs, still feeling my way with my hands.

There was a little light in the attic from louvers at either end. I curled up on the floor just to the left of the stairwell. It was stuffy up here and smelled terrifically of dust, but it was safe. Robert could not find me; Brother Orphelin was too fat to follow me. I fell asleep.

Since I had come to St. Crellifer's, I had begun to dream of gardens—when I was not dreaming of Malkar or Keeper or the Virtu, or of Shannon. In these fragmentary, fleeting dreams, I found myself walking in a garden I had never seen before, through stands of dark, twisted trees with small white flowers whose scent was as sweet as remembered joy; through rose gardens laid out in elaborate knots; through simple plots of herbs, whose names and properties I could, in my dreams, still remember. And everywhere the grass was dense and soft and heartbreakingly green. Sometimes I saw people—dim and vague like memories or ghosts—on the garden paths, but they were always far ahead of me, and I could never catch up with them.

This time, I find myself among the trees again. I step off the path to touch one; the trunk is hard and ridged beneath my fingers. The scent of the flowers seems to surround me like a cloud of peace. I wish that I could stay here forever.

Even as I think it, the dream begins to break apart around me. I turn, thinking confusedly that perhaps I can hold the dream together if I get back on the path, and find myself face-to-face with a man, tall, redheaded, yellow-eyed, a Sunling out of a child's story. He is vividly and vibrantly present, clearly real, clearly alive; I am so shocked that I back into the tree. My head strikes one of the gnarled branches, and I wake.

My head ached where I had banged it on the attic wall. The light seeping through the louvers was purple with dusk. I waited for my heartbeat to calm, then crept back down the stairs. I made it back to the ward just in time for dinner. No one commented on my disappearance. Brother Lilburn's intolerant eyes scourged me in passing, but did not linger. Of course, I realized, Robert would never admit to anyone that he couldn't control a weak, whimpering, broken madman. I felt as giddy as I had when I had evaded some richly deserved punishment from Keeper. For a moment, St. Crellifer's felt like sanctuary.

Mildmay

Margot put me in with the younger members of her pack. She said it was the only free bed she had. I think it was a kind of joke, maybe a little revenge for me bringing her trouble she hadn't asked for. Her little Badgers—maybe a septad old, a septad and two at the most—didn't think it was funny. I made them tongue-tied, and they watched me with their eyes as big as bell-wheels. I would've smiled, except that would've scared 'em worse. But when the last candle was blown out, when we were all laying in bed in the dark, one of them got up the gumption to ask if I knew any stories. Another voice said as how they'd told all the ones they knew. "Three times," said somebody else, sadly.

"Okay," I said. "You know the one about Jenico Sun-Eyes and the Clockman?"

"No," said somebody.

"That sounds exciting," said somebody else.

"Who's Jenico Sun-Eyes?" said another voice, I thought the one who'd asked me first if I knew any stories.

"Well, lemme tell you," I said, and I lay there, staring up into the dark, and instead of thinking about Ginevra or the Dogs or the witchfinders, I told Margot's little Badgers all about Jenico Sun-Eyes and his terrible journey to get back the heart of the Princess of Keys from the Clockman. They didn't care that my words came out funny and slurred. They loved my story and made me promise to tell it again the next night. We all went to sleep happy.

I guess it ain't no surprise I had nightmares. I kept waking up and having to think where I was, and then I'd fall back asleep and right back into that horrible gray version of Gilgamesh, where there was nobody alive but me. It was like being caught in a maze, like the curtain-mazes at the Trials, only I get a kick out of them, and this was like being buried alive. In the dream I was trying to get to Britomart and find Keeper, except that I didn't want to, the way you do sometimes in dreams, so that I was trying to get out of Gilgamesh and at the same time hoping I wouldn't. When the little Badgers woke up, I dragged out of bed feeling worse than I had the night before.

The Badgers mostly slept in the attics of the Judiciary, behind doors that nobody'd tried to open for a Great Septad or better. They'd rigged a stove in the longest attic, with a kind of half-assed patch into a chimney flue that gave me the crawling horrors just looking at it. But Margot swore it worked, and it let her be sure that her littlest kids had a hot breakfast before they went out to the pickpocketing and begging and petty thievery that was what pack kids did before they got old enough to cardsharp and stuff like that. Margot's two best lieutenants, Io and Ramon, did the cooking. Everybody else was on their own, to go steal fruit off the costermongers' stalls in the Cheaps or to scrounge up a septad-centime for a bakery bun. Me and Margot drank tea and had the last of the oatmeal when everybody else was gone.

We'd swapped gossip the whole time—what the Dogs were doing, what the witchfinders were doing, what people in Scaffelgreen and Ramecrow said about the Obscurantists now. But when everybody else was gone, Margot got up and wandered around, putting things away, damping the stove out. That was Margot. She had a tidy mind. And I thought it was why she'd kept the Badgers as long as she had, and why she'd kept them safe.

After a while she came back and sat down and said—gently, for Margot—"D'you want to talk about it?"

"About what?"

"If I knew that, I wouldn't have to ask. About what's got you so upset."

"I ain't upset."

"Mildmay." She gave me a look. "I know you better than that. Something's got your tail in a knot, and it ain't the Dogs. Now would you put that fucking knife down and *talk* to me?"

Startled, I looked down. Sure enough, there was the butterfly knife from my boot, dancing like it used to when I had a septad and five and thought I was some kind of fucking hero. "Sorry," I said, closed it, put it back. "Thought I broke that habit." She still looked worried, and I added, "Not nobody here."

"You could knife Yapper, and I'd kiss you for it. But if it ain't us, then who is it?"

"Dunno."

"Well, who are you mad at?"

"Dunno who tipped the Dogs."

"That ain't quite what I asked."

"It's my business, ain't it?"

"'Course it is. I'm just wondering if it's something I can help with."

"Dunno," I said. "Don't think I'm mad at anybody."

Her eyebrows went up. "And the knife?"

"Dunno. I'm sorry, Margot, but I don't."

"Well, if you don't, you don't. I got shit to do, but if you figure it out enough to talk, you let me know. Okay?"

"Okay." I watched her leave, and then, because I didn't have nothing better to do, I followed her out, closing the door like she'd showed me, and went to try to walk off my twitchiness across the roofs.

I couldn't do it, couldn't shake whatever black dog had my scent. I was scared of the Dogs and worried about Ginevra and even worried about Faith Cowry—I mean, she'd never done me no harm. And I was scared of what I felt building. I remembered the mood that had got people rioting three summers ago, and I was feeling something like it now. Not the same. It wasn't that people were angry now, like they'd been angry at the Mirador, but they were scared. And one thing I knew was if you got scared enough, you ended up acting just like you were angry. It was the Obscurantists had people scared, and the fact that nobody—not the Dogs, not the Mayor, not the Mirador—was doing nothing about them. Of course, looked at right ways on, that's because there was nothing *to* do. There'd been no actual Obscurantists in the Lower City for near on two Great Septads, and I had Cardenio's word on it that there weren't now. Cade-skiffs know that kind of thing. But most people just had rumors to go on, and the rumors said the Obscurantists had done something big in the Boneprince back in Pluviôse—so big it had Vey Coruscant hiding—and that they'd paid off the Mirador to ignore them, and they were planning something more, something worse. People wanted the Obscurantists locked down, and what were the Dogs doing about that? Zip, zero, and zilch.

Powers and saints, it was no wonder the mood was getting ugly.

I went round and round with it all fucking day, but I still hadn't figured nothing out by sunset, when the Badgers all came back to the Judiciary, to pool the day's taking and sort out who was doing what in the night. They were in the middle of it, arguing and laughing, when one of the kids Margot had on sentry came charging onto the Judiciary roof from the north, heading straight for Margot and her motley coat.

"Laurie?" Margot said. "What—"

"Dogs!" the girl yelled, waving back the way she'd come with one arm. "They're coming, upside *and* down! Run! RUN!"

Margot bellowed, *"RAID!"* at the top of her lungs. The Badgers were just starting to scatter, Margot was just turning to grab the little kids near her, when there was this wave of armored men from the *south*—Kethe, from the *south,* the fucking opposite direction and nobody apparently there to think it was worth singing out—and the Dogs were on us.

Felix

I looked for the gardens all day. I couldn't find them, though I knew they were close to me. Every time I opened a door, I expected to meet the scent of those beautiful, twisted trees. But I never did.

Brother Torquil, who never hit anyone, found me in empty rooms, at the wrong end of hallways, once struggling with the catches of a window that hadn't been opened in more than a century. Each time, he led me back to my pail and scrub brush; each time, he said a prayer over me. I would have preferred him to hit me. And each time, I told myself there were no gardens in St. Crellifer's and tried to concentrate on my task.

But it was no good. No matter how I fought it, the conviction would grow on me that I could find the gardens if I looked in the right place, and I would put my scrub brush down and start looking. Trying to ignore that feeling was almost physically painful, and even though I knew it was a lie, it seemed as true as the stones and plaster of St. Crellifer's.

Brother Torquil finally gave up and sent me back to the ward, with a warning that he would "have to speak to Brother Lilburn about this." Even that didn't bother me; if I could find the way into the gardens, I could escape Brother Lilburn entirely.

The ward was all but deserted at that hour of the day. Elias was lying on his cot, staring at the bars on the window. No one knew how old Elias was—least of all Elias himself—but he had to be over eighty. He was too frail to do any work, but since his madness consisted mostly of a terrible fear of going outside, he was allowed to stay in what Brother Torquil, freshly imbued with the ideals of St. Gailan, persisted in referring to as the "Helping Ward."

"What's up with you?" Elias said when I came in.

"I can't find the gardens," I said, crossing the room to look out the window. But they weren't out there, either.

"The what?"

"Something I dreamed." I rested my forehead briefly against the cool glass.

"You must have drawn Torquil," Elias said. Elias had been in St. Crellifer for twenty years or more, and he had been a brother of St. Gailan before that. He knew St. Crellifer's inside out. "He'll tell Lilburn, you know."

"Yes. He said he would." I glanced sideways and saw Elias's grimace of sympathy.

"What's it like out there?" he asked presently, as he asked anyone who was near a window.

"Sunny," I said. "There's a scissors-grinder across the street, and two merchants' daughters taking the air. One of them is dressed in green muslin and the other in white organdy. The girl in green has a parasol painted with violets."

"Lovely," Elias said. "Like a beautiful dream."

I realized then that I did know how to reach the gardens, even from St. Crellifer's. And maybe if I just dreamed *hard* enough . . .

I lay down, turning my back on Elias's fearful longing, and pushed my way down into sleep.

*

Even in sleep, it is hard to find the gardens. My dreams are jumbled and dark. I remember the voice of the old man who taught me to understand my dreams; although I haven't used it in years, I remember the way he taught me to map my dreaming. I call that map into being now; it is not magic, or so the old man told me, simply a mental structure, like the memory houses that traders' clerks use.

I stand in the middle of a compass rose; for a moment, I am not part of any dream. The gates of Mélusine rise around the compass, Corundum to the north, Horn to the northeast, then Carnelian, Chalcedony, Ivory, Porphyry. In my dream map, the Sim does not exist, and the northwest and south are blank, without gates or gaps.

My mind feels clearer, stronger, than it has for a long time. I begin to organize my dreams as the old man taught me. Dreams of the future lie beyond Corundum Gate, and that gate is closed. I do not want to know the future. Porphyry, to the west, rules dreams that answer questions; I leave it open. Ivory is the gate of nightmares, and I swing that shut. My imagining of my dream city is more vivid than it has ever been; Ivory Gate closes with an audible thud, and I feel the jar in my shoulders. I know with terrible relief that it will stay closed.

I was taught that south is the direction of dreams of the past, but I will not use the Sim. I give the past to Chalcedony Gate and close it. Carnelian Gate is the gate for dreams of revelation; I leave it open. And Horn Gate rules true dreams, dreams that are more than just dreams. I hope that the gardens lie beyond Horn Gate; it, too, stands open.

I look at the city and realize that there is a gate I did not imagine. To the south, there is a dark, ragged hole in the city wall, where the so-called Septad Gate exists in the real city. Keeper had a vile, obscene song about the Septad Gate, which he sang when he was drunk. I am afraid that if I think about it any longer, I will remember the words. I see that there is no way to close the Septad Gate, no way to block out the poisoned swamp that lies beyond it. The Septad Gate is the gate of madness.

I stand in the middle of the city, where the Mirador is. For a moment, I imagine I am standing on the battlements again, looking out across the squalid patchwork of the Lower City. I turn to face north, shut my eyes, and count slowly to seven. Then, thinking fixedly of the gnarled trees and their white flowers, I look at what the gates have to tell me.

I look at Porphyry Gate; through it, I see water, great heaving dark masses of it. That is not what I seek; I turn, wrenching my attention past the Septad Gate and its morbid seeping. Through Carnelian Gate, I see a fox, sitting in a gray place full of cruel stones. That means nothing to me, and I turn to Horn Gate. Through Horn Gate, I see trees, twisted and black, their spreading arms full of flowers.

My breath catches in something that is almost a sob. I step through Horn Gate. I would close the gates behind me, but they will not budge. I walk into the stand of trees, quickly, wanting to get away from Horn Gate, wanting to find the Sunling.

I follow the path as it twists and meanders; though I am anxious, I find that I cannot hurry. The beauty of the place drags at my feet; I stop and stare as wide-eyed as a child at yellow-flowering bushes taller than I am, at dense beds of delicate purple flowers, at the black trees with their wide, white-clothed branches. Although my knowledge of herbs is extensive, I know almost nothing about ornamental flowers—Malkar scoffed at them as toys for the bourgeoisie—and my ignorance hurts me here, where I want to call all the myriad beauties by name.

And when the Sunling finds me, lost in contemplation of a bed of rioting trumpet-shaped, flounced flowers—brilliantly magenta and scarlet and flame-red, and no more than two inches long—I ask him before I can think, "What are they called?"

His eyes crinkle at the corners with his smile, and he says, "Snapdragons."

He is as tall as I am; his hair is brilliant golden red, graying at the temples. His eyes are yellow, just as one of my eyes is yellow, and the only signs of age in his face are the crow's-feet around his eyes. I realize I am staring and look away, my face heating.

"Who are you?" he asks; his voice is gentle, and I know he is afraid that he will scare me away. "Why are you walking in this dream of our garden? What has happened to you?"

I cannot answer any of those questions. I say, in a strangled, unhappy whisper, "My name is Felix."

"You are a wizard," he says, coming near. "And our blood must run in your veins, or you would never have found this dream at all."

"Keeper always said I was a changeling child."

"A what?"

I do not know how to explain. I look up, and he says quickly, "It doesn't matter."

He touches my forehead lightly; I cannot help flinching. He steps back at once. He says, "You have been grievously hurt. How has this happened?"

Even in my dreams, the compulsion sinks its iron claws into me. I feel the gardens starting to shred around me and drop to my knees, digging my fingers into the cool, moist heft of the grass. The dream steadies.

"I am sorry," the Sunling says. "I did not mean to upset you. I would like to help."

"No one can help me. I am . . . I am mad."

"You are damaged," he corrects me briskly. "Damage can be mended."

"Damaged."

"We are healers. We could help you. Where are you?"

But before I can answer him, Horn Gate rears up in the middle of the snapdragons and swallows me. I am back in the dream city, but it has tilted, heaving me up in a parody of its real geography, and I am sliding south, being dragged through the Septad Gate, falling into the swamp, falling into the real world.

I woke with my cheek stinging and knew I had been slapped awake. I blinked my eyes frantically into focus and saw Brother Lilburn leaning over me. Brother Lilburn never smiled, and his cold pale eyes never lit, but we all knew he enjoyed his work.

I saw his eyes record the fact that I was awake. He said, his voice calm and level and too rational to be human, "Brother Torquil tells me that you have been shirking."

I stared at him, my heart already pounding nastily, and knew I had forgotten the name of the burning flowers.

Mildmay

I'd hated the Dogs for indictions, been brought up hating them, and come to hate them on my own account, but I'd never hated them like I did that night, the way they came down on Margot's Badgers like they were full-grown men instead of just kids. They were after me—I could hear them shouting my name—but they weren't giving the Badgers no time to give me up. I was just an excuse, a reason they could give if anybody asked 'em why they were killing kids. We had to get Mildmay the Fox, they could say. Those damn kids were harboring him. And nobody'd ask. Nobody cared about kids in packs. Nobody was going to ask ugly questions about how they ended up dead. If I'd thought it would have helped, I would've given myself up. But that wasn't going to stop them, and I knew, I could feel it all the way down, that I was dead the instant any of them could catch me long enough to cut my throat. Three or four of them tried. At least one of them ended up dead for it. Considering I'd seen him brain a little girl with his sword hilt—and she was dead, no question about it—I couldn't be sorry.

Kids ran. Kids got arrested. Kids got killed. I got out of the fighting entirely, got up on the rainwater cistern and just laid low. And these Dogs—I got glimpses of their uniforms, here and there—these weren't the smart ones, the inspectors, the guys who'd been sitting in my front room sneering at my furniture. These were the rank and file, the flatfeet. All they wanted was to be pointed at a target and told they could do anything they liked to get it. They didn't have the brains to *look* for anybody. So when there was nobody in sight but them and the kids they'd arrested and the kids they'd killed . . . they left. Back to the Kennel with those frightened, sobbing, angry kids.

I came down off the cistern. Slowly. Half the reason they hadn't thought to look there was because it didn't seem like the sort of place a person could get himself. And if you ain't been a cat burglar, you don't ever look at things with the right kind of eyes. But it was a tricky bastard. By the time I got down and could look around again, there were two more people on the roof: Carmody and Margot.

They were yelling at each other.

"You *what?*"

"He wasn't one of us," Carmody said. "And we *need* the gorgons, Margot. You know how the roof's leaking."

Oh, Kethe, I thought, and stopped where I was. I didn't want to get any closer to this.

"What the fuck does that matter? Even you ain't stupid enough to think this was worth it."

"They weren't supposed to raid," he said, sort of sullen and puzzled at once, like he didn't see how his clever plan had got away from him, and he didn't see why she was pissed at *him* when it wasn't his fuck-up.

"Fuck me, Carmody, did you really think they'd just come knock and say, 'Pretty-please will you hand over Mildmay the Fox now?' "

His face said, yeah, that was about what he'd thought.

"You told them how to find us."

"I couldn't take him alone. They said they'd be backup."

"Get away from me," she said through her teeth. She actually took a step back, like she thought he might be contagious.

"Margot—"

"Get *away* from me!" She looked away from him and said, her voice tight with what might've been tears or fury or fear or, Kethe knows, all three, "If you go right now and you *run,* you might make it out of the city before the other packs catch up with you."

"But, Margot, you don't—"

"Didn't you hear me? I can't kill you myself, though all the saints know you deserve it, but right now, Carmody, I'm probably the only person in the Lower City who'd even think twice. Run, you stupid son of a bitch!"

Finally, finally, he got it. His face changed. For the first time, it wasn't sullen, wasn't scowling. He looked around, saw me. He went a dirty green color with fear, backed away two steps, then turned and bolted. He was running like Cade-Cholera's hounds were on his heels, but I knew he'd be lucky if that was the worst that found him.

Margot folded up slowly, until she was sitting on her heels. Stiffly, like she was run by clockwork, she reached over to the nearest of the dead bodies, checking for a pulse, for the heat of breath against her fingers. There weren't none to find, not with a great gaping slash all through the chest like that. One of her hands kind of wandered up to touch the dead child's forehead.

I came closer. I couldn't help it. I said, "He won't make it out of Dragonteeth."

"I know that," she said. She was staring at the dead body beside her. It was terrible, but I was glad I'd only talked to her little Badgers in the dark, that I'd never got their names put with their faces. I didn't have to know if this was the little kid who'd said last night, half-asleep, "That was a *good* story."

But I knew anyway, because the truth was it didn't matter. It didn't fucking matter at all. The Dogs didn't care.

Margot said, "He didn't used to be like that. I remember when he first came up here. He was so amazed that nobody was *hitting* him, he went around for days just being *happy*. I remember him like that."

" 'Course you do," I said.

There was a long silence. I didn't know what to say. I didn't think she'd hear me if I said anything anyways. She didn't look up, but finally she said, "When I go to the Kennel . . ." She stopped. I knew she had to go to the Kennel, had to try to get her kids out, try to patch things up and get on with something. Those kids needed her, and these dead ones didn't, not no more. I wondered if the Dogs would believe she was old enough to stand surety. Not that standing surety was anything but a lie on both sides anyway, since the people standing surety for the kids in the Kennel were all thief-keepers and pimps.

Margot took a deep breath, still didn't look up, tried again: "When I go to the Kennel, I'll tell them you're dead. I'll tell 'em one of these dead fucking Dogs killed you. They'll like that. Maybe they'll even believe it. But that's it." She looked at me. I backed up without even meaning to, because the thing in her eyes was screaming and sick with blood. I'd always kind of wondered, when I told stories with them in it, what the Eumenides looked like. But I wasn't wondering no more. "If I ever see you again, I may have a go at killing you myself."

"Thank you, Margot," I said. I didn't say she'd never get near me. She knew that.

"I don't want your fucking thanks!" She started crying, big racking sobs that looked more like somebody was beating her with invisible sticks. She pulled the dead child into her lap and bowed over it, sobbing and sobbing.

She wouldn't take comfort from me, and I couldn't stay on this rooftop no more. I just couldn't. I left, starting back for Midwinter because I couldn't think of no place else to go. It didn't matter. The Dogs knew I'd been here, on the Judiciary roofs, and before long they were going to think

I was dead. I was as safe as I'd been in a full septad, and I hoped Kethe was enjoying the joke, because I wasn't.

Felix

Brother Lilburn and I were alone in the Chapel of St. Crellifer, which jutted awkwardly out from the back of the hospice like a wart. It was a dank stone hemisphere with narrow-slitted windows, and gory renditions of the martyrdom of St. Crellifer were frescoed around the walls. It was too small for all the patients to be crammed in at once, and so was not in regular use, except for the morning devotions of the brothers. Otherwise, it belonged to Brother Lilburn, and everyone in St. Crellifer's knew it.

There was a ghost kneeling at the end of the first pew, praying. She had clearly been a patient in St. Crellifer's before her death; her hair hung in ragged strands around her face, and she was wearing an ugly, shapeless dress like the ones the women wore.

"What are you looking at?" Brother Lilburn said.

"N-nothing," I said, wrenching my gaze back to my hands.

"You weren't praying."

It wasn't a question, and there would have been no right answer even if it had been. The sun was rising somewhere outside these merciless stone walls; Brother Lilburn had kept me here all night, to do penance and to pray that the saint would offer me guidance and strength. My hands were freezing; my knees felt as if I were kneeling on knives; I could not feel my feet.

He said, his voice soft but not in the slightest gentle, "Are you praying, Felix?"

"I'm trying, Brother Lilburn." I had learned that that was a better answer than a straight "yes," although both were equally lies.

"Good. Prayer will help you more than anything, but you must learn to submit your spirit to the saint."

"Yes, Brother Lilburn." I did not confess that I found the idea spiritually, morally—almost physically—repugnant. Instead of my knees and aching hips, I tried to think about the gardens, about the flowers and the grass, the faint breeze that had ruffled my hair. I thought about the Sunling, who had been kind, who had said I could be helped. I did not think about St. Crellifer at all, but I watched Brother Lilburn as best I could out of the corners of my eyes. He wore gray around him like a shroud. Although I could not see his face, I knew he was watching me, his eyes as remote and indifferent as the cold stones beneath me.

It came to me, half fancy and half conviction, that Brother Lilburn was dead, that he had died years ago but had held off corruption, decay, the helplessness of death, with the force of his will alone, that I was kneeling here in the cold darkness being stared at by a corpse. I shut my eyes, gripping my hands together tightly, and sank my teeth into my lower lip to keep from screaming.

"Good," said Brother Lilburn. "*Now* you are praying."

Mildmay

I went to unlock the door, and it swung open. I stood staring at it. The Dogs *couldn't* still be waiting for me. I'd just died in Dragonteeth. But if they were there, they knew I was out here, and somehow the only thing that seemed important at all was not waking Mrs. Pickering and particularly not waking Scabious. It was nearly dawn. They'd be stirring in another half hour. But maybe the Dogs would be nice and arrest me quick, and we could be out of here by then.

I went in. Ginevra turned around with a gasp that was almost a shriek. Not the Dogs.

"What're you doing here?" I said.

It came out bad, in this sludgy kind of mumble, but either she understood it, or it was just the only thing anybody was going to ask, because she said, "I came . . . I came to get my things. Austin says the Dogs wouldn't arrest me if they knew . . . I mean, I haven't done anything wrong."

"Yeah, right."

"I *haven't!* I don't have any idea what the Dogs want you for or . . . or anything!"

"I told you they was after me." I could've said something about Ellis Otanius and whether he might think Ginevra'd done "something wrong," but I didn't. That wasn't the point here anyway.

"I didn't know . . ." I think she figured there was no good way to get out of that sentence, because she said, "I'm really sorry."

"Sorry?"

"I . . . oh, damn." Her chin came up, and she said, "I'm moving in with Austin."

"Austin."

"He loves me. He always has."

I love you. But I couldn't say that. I never had said it, so maybe she didn't think I felt it. And it was too fucking late now. I said, "Go on, then. Take whatever you want and go."

But I went first. I turned around right then and left. There was nothing for me in Midwinter.

Felix

I did not look for the gardens anymore. In my dreams, I could not get to the city, could not find Horn Gate; I could only catch bare glimpses of the gardens, and I never saw the Sunling at all. Brother Lilburn's dead gaze followed me everywhere; even in dreams of Shannon, or dreams of my childhood, he would be there, in one corner or another, his hands folded, white as bone against his black robe, watching.

In the waking world, I was desperately careful, focused so intently on my scrubbing that at night my hands would stay cramped around the absent shape of the brush. I could not think about anything else, could not let myself raise my head. I did not look at the ghosts, even when I had to move through them; when I thought I smelled the trees of the garden, I leaned over the bucket beside me and inhaled the bitter reality of the Sim.

I was good, as I had tried to be good as a child. But I had never been good enough for Keeper, and so, in some terrible way, I was not surprised when it turned out I wasn't good enough for St. Crellifer either.

It was morning, after breakfast. I was scrubbing halls on the second floor, outside the women's intractable ward. I could hear Jeanne-Chatte singing, as she always sang when she was not trying to kill herself or one of the brothers. I was cleaning flagstones, listening to Jeanne-Chatte's beautiful voice, ignoring the ghostly madwomen rocking back and forth along the outside wall.

Brother Orphelin's voice said behind me, "You have a visitor."

The scrub brush dropped out of my fingers. I turned. Brother Orphelin, beaming, and Brother Lilburn, expressionless as always, advanced; they took my arms, one on each side, and dragged me upright.

"Your visitor was very disappointed, last time he came," Brother Orphelin said as they marched me toward the stairs. "He says you were very rude to him."

"No," I said, but it was a strengthless half whisper. Robert again, Robert after something that was more important to him than his vanity.

"Don't lie," Brother Lilburn said.

They started down the stairs, dragging me between them.

"Your visitor has asked us to be sure you aren't rude to him again," Brother Orphelin said.

"No," I said again, but this time so weakly that not even Brother Lilburn heard me.

Behind us, in the women's intractable ward, Jeanne-Chatte began to scream.

They took me to the basement, as Brother Orphelin had taken me on the first day. But this time, we penetrated farther into the maze of stone, down sloping corridors into greater and greater darkness, until at last we came to a room crudely squared out of the rock, rank with the breath of the Sim. It was lit by torches; I tried to count them to keep the panic back, but I couldn't make the number come out the same twice.

Robert was waiting among the torches—himself, although his eyes were the snake's, sulfurous yellow and staring—standing beside a wooden table fitted out with straps and buckles. I was distracted by the torches, and it took me a moment to realize what that table was, to realize what Brother Orphelin had meant, to realize what Robert planned to do. Then I dug in my heels, wrenched free of Brother Lilburn and Brother Orphelin—they had not expected resistance—turned, and bolted. I didn't care if I got lost; in that moment, I didn't care if I never found my way to the surface of the city again. I just ran.

I had known the first day that it was useless to run from Brother Orphelin, and now the truth of that was proved to me. He and Brother Lilburn trapped me in a dead end, as neatly as wolves work together to bring down a deer. I tried to dodge past them, but Brother Orphelin used his great weight to pin me against the wall, and Brother Lilburn caught my hands and tied them, bound my ankles together. They carried me back to the room where Robert waited, sleek and self-pleased.

I fought them like a feral cat, but they fastened the straps around my wrists, around my ankles; a strap across my neck threatened to strangle me, and I was forced to lie still. I cursed them, cursed Robert, my voice shrill and hard, the vowels thick as molasses, the voice of the whore I had been. I tried to bite Robert's fingers when he brought them near my head, but the strap cut into my jaw, and I could not keep him from touching my temples.

"Now," he said triumphantly, and I felt his fingers tense.

❧

Pain explodes through my head like a swarm of iron hornets. A snake and a corpse and a terrible monstrous pig with tiny red eyes are staring down at me and laughing. I scream for help, but the Sunling is not there, and Joline is not there, and the ghosts in the corners are screaming, too. No one will help me.

The darkness swallows me alive.

Mildmay

On 11 Messidor, Cardenio found me.

I'd dumped everything—the rooms I rented, the fake names, the cat burglary on commission like I was some kind of flash merchant—and gone down into the Arcane, where nobody cared what you did and nobody'd go to the Dogs, no matter who you were. Nobody'd even tell the daylight world you existed. That's what the Arcane is for. I played cards for money—and every time I got up to go out to another bar and find another sheep, I hated myself for it—and sat in a shabby rented room and stared at the cheap lithograph of St. Suphrysa on the wall. I didn't get drunk. I didn't pick fights. I just sat there and waited for time to pass.

And on 11 Messidor, when I got up to go out, there was Cardenio in the lobby of the boardinghouse, clutching his black guild-hat like he was thinking of maybe tearing it in two.

"Nice earrings," I said.

"There's . . ." He stopped and swallowed. "There's some bodies. Out of the Sim. Master Auberon told me to come get you."

I knew it right then, I think, but I followed him anyway. Sometimes there's traps laid for you, and sometimes you deserve to walk into 'em.

I'd been down in the Dead Gallery before. It's this long natural gallery along the Sim, where it oxbows sideways under Havelock. They dug the Undercanal, sometime way back when, so that people using the river, like people always have, don't have to take a tour of the corpses—and there's a grating mesh, so the cade-skiffs don't got the river garbage coming through their guildhall—but the Sim's a big river, and it don't mind filling two channels.

The river keeps the bodies at least kind of cool, and that seems to be worth the damp as far as the cade-skiffs are concerned. Or maybe they got some way of keeping the damp off. I don't know. There's torches every two septad-feet or so, and Cardenio grabbed an extra off the wall when we came in. They lay the corpses out on marble-topped tables that are probably worth more than Queensdock and Simside put together, and they cover 'em with whitework percale sheets. The sheets come from the convent of St. Lycoris in Britomart, where the nuns sew them as penance.

About halfway down the gallery, Cardenio stopped. He gave me a look that said he really didn't want to do this and he was sorry as a sick horse about it. Then he put the torch in an empty bracket, walked between two tables to the river end, and stripped the sheets back on both of 'em.

She hadn't been in the water long, and she'd been dead before they dumped her. Her throat had been cut. There was no color in her face, but it was perfectly calm, and somebody'd combed her hair out. She'd had her pick of heroes, but nobody'd saved her from the dragon, not when it mattered.

I looked away. Austin had drowned. I wished I couldn't tell, but I could. Probably he didn't know how to swim. Most people in the Lower City don't. And some of the guys in Mélusine who'll kill people for money—the ones that ain't no brighter than bull-baiting dogs that'll bite anything they're pointed at—they think it's funny to throw the mark in the Sim, someplace where there ain't much current, and bet on how long it takes him to drown.

I wondered if the crazy historian in Nill would ever know what'd happened to his secretary, and something tightened in my chest.

I couldn't look at her, at her perfect body that should've been loved by a king, not some no-good thief like me, at her lips, her nose, the arch of her eyebrows. I turned away, put my hand on the wall beneath Cardenio's torch, bent my head.

"Mildmay?" Cardenio said. I could see his hands if I looked sideways, and he was still mauling his damn hat. "You okay?"

I'd never told her I loved her. I swallowed the hard lump in my throat and said, "Yeah, I'm fine."

He didn't call me a liar to my face, which was nice of him. "You wanna come upstairs and have some tea?"

I swallowed again, although it wasn't like it was doing any good, and said, "No, thanks, I don't want tea." I couldn't look at Cardenio, couldn't look at the torches or the tables or the bodies laying there, waiting for whatever the cade-skiffs were going to do with them.

"C'mon, Mildmay," Cardenio said. "I think tea might do you some good."

I couldn't keep arguing with him. It was too much work. And if I did what he wanted, I'd be able to get away from her dead, empty face. "Okay," I said. "Tea."

I looked up. Cardenio's face was stricken, even though he tried to smile at me. He came out from between the tables and started back the way we'd come. I covered Ginevra with the sheet before I followed him.

I thought about simple things. Follow Cardenio. Hold the mug. Sit where he tells you. I didn't meet anybody's eyes. We ended up in a place that was like some kind of cade-skiff bar, with little groups of them at tables and standing along the walls, all with their black hats and long black coats. I hated them for being alive when Ginevra was dead. I hated me, too.

Cardenio said urgently, "Stay put," and went darting away.

It was still too much work to argue with him. I stayed put. I stared at the tea in my mug, at the ugly patterns the tea leaves made at the bottom. People read the future in tea leaves sometimes. I wondered what they'd see in mine and then thought, Why the fuck do you care? The future's dead.

Cardenio came back with an older cade-skiff in tow. I looked up long enough to see who it was, that, for instance, Vey Coruscant hadn't gotten in here somehow to finish the job, and then looked back at my tea. They sat down opposite me. Cardenio said, "Mildmay, this is Master Auberon. My master."

"Nice to meet you," I said. After all Cardenio'd said about his master, I'd expected him to be a septad-foot tall and gilded to boot, but he was just a square, white-haired old party who looked like a pretty decent sort of guy.

He had a dark, rich voice, like plum cake. "The young woman's name is Ginevra?"

"Ginevra Thomson," I said.

"And the young man is Austin Lefevre?"

"Yeah." I didn't ask how he knew. You don't ask cade-skiffs that kind of question, because either they won't answer you, or they will—and then you wish they hadn't.

"We are a little puzzled as to why they were killed, and we were wondering if you had any ideas."

"What's the mystery? They got murdered. It happens a lot."

"They went into the Sim," said Master Auberon, steepling his fingers, "under St. Kirban's."

I shut my eyes, but it didn't help none.

"You see why we are troubled."

"She crossed Vey Coruscant," I said. Phoskis Terrapin, the fat bastard who controls St. Kirban's flooded crypts—and the smuggling and other nasty shit that gets run through there—had been in with Vey for septads. "In Pluviôse."

"I see," Master Auberon said. "Thank you."

"Thanks for the tea," I answered and got up. I hadn't touched it, any more than I'd looked either of them in the eye.

"Mildmay," Cardenio said, reaching across the table. "Don't you—"

"Keep your fucking hands off me," I said and knocked his hand aside. Then I turned and left, and pretended I couldn't hear Cardenio's voice calling me back.

Chapter 5

Felix

The corpse stands in the doorway of the intractable ward like the shadow of winter. I can feel all the monsters looking at him. Everyone has gone extremely still, holding their breath, praying that if they do not make a sound, the corpse will not notice them. Even intractables are frightened of the corpse.

I turn around. I know that the corpse has come for me, that the others have no reason to be afraid. He gives me that little come-along jerk of the head. He knows I don't understand him when he speaks. I follow him. At first, I tried to defy him, but all that happened was that he got other brother-monsters to come and drag me. I would rather walk into the darkness on my own feet.

This time I swear, as I have sworn before, that I will not forget what happens, that I will find a way to hold it in my memory. I push my fingers through my hair; my hands are already starting to shake. And I remember now, following the corpse down the stairs, that my hands *always* shake; my body remembers what is coming.

I follow the corpse beneath the earth; I wonder if he is taking me to Hell. I know that Hell must lie beneath St. Crellifer's. But we do not come to a river. Instead, we come to a room.

I remember the table and the straps; I remember the monsters who are waiting: the yellow-eyed snake and the enormous gray piglike thing with its tiny, glowing, red eyes. I remember the sobbing ghosts. I remember that it is useless to run, useless to struggle.

The pig grabs my arm, envelops me in its grayness, the weight of its flesh; it forces me down on the table. The corpse and the snake buckle the straps. I lie and stare at the damp and cracking plaster of the ceiling and tell myself that this time I will not scream, will not cry, although I know already—I remember—that I am lying to myself.

I feel the snake's fingers in my hair. It hisses and rasps instead of roaring, but I still cannot make out any words in what it says. Pain begins to stitch through my head; the cracks in the ceiling begin to blur with the tears in my eyes.

A globe of orange light spins into being above the table; the darkness opens its mouth like a trap, and I am gone.

Mildmay

Around about 27 Vendémiaire, it started raining like the end of the world was coming, and it had to get all this water cleared out of the way first. It was early for the winter rains. Folks said as how it was balancing out for having been late last indiction. I remembered Ginevra and me, soaking wet in my rooms in Pennycup, and tried to think about something else, but every time I turned around, there was *more* rain.

The damp got into everything. Every room you went into smelled like mildew and rot. Every time I went out, I got soaked to the skin. I wasn't going out much—I had an ugly little room above a bar in Engmond's Tor, and the bartender'd hired me as a bouncer and a second-string bartender, and if anybody needed a fourth for Grimoire, well, there I was. But even staying in, the damp crawled up and wrapped its clammy little fingers around my joints and my head and my chest. The Winter Fever—it always shows up in Mélusine along with the rains, you can set your watch by it, and it was working its way through the Lower City with a butcher's knife and a nasty snigger. It'd get me sooner or later, and then I'd lie here in this ugly little room and nobody in the Circle of Lions would even wonder where the fuck I was. Not 'til I died and started to stink, anyway.

I needed money. Gilles at the Circle was paying me, sure, but he was paying me about half of what I could've made as a bouncer in Dragonteeth, never mind all the other shit I did. He knew he had me where he wanted me. You don't take a job like that one unless you're too fucking desperate to complain. So I was living hand to mouth, and I knew the first day I couldn't make it downstairs on time, he'd fire my ass and not think about it twice. And I didn't have nothing to fall back on, no other job I could go to, no money saved up, no place that would take me in, except St. Cecily's, and taking yourself there with the Winter Fever is just the same as walking out in the street and letting a brewer's dray run you down. Except slower.

I had to do something, but I knew I couldn't swing a better job, not now, and I've always been nervous about doing cat burglary in the rain. You may make it in and out, no trouble in the world, two times, three times, but sooner or later, the shingles are going to be just a hair more slippery than you thought they were, and there you are, smashed to pieces three stories down. And it might be the first time just as easy as the fourth.

They say that when you dream you're falling, you got to wake up before you hit the ground. I felt like I was at a septad-foot and falling fast. Nobody in Mélusine gave a rat's ass about me. Nobody was going to pay good money just to keep me alive. I mean, that had been true anytime the past three indictions, ever since I'd walked away from Keeper, but it had never bothered me none. I'd never thought I'd need anybody to care. I'd been so sure I was careful and reasonable and not cocky—I'd learned my lesson about that and carried it around on my face with me—that I'd backed myself into another kind of cocky and not seen it until the rug was already out from under my feet.

When I was awake, it seemed like I was always thinking about Ginevra. I didn't have to close my eyes to see her face—cold and dead and empty as a broken pot. It was always right there. But at night, I dreamed about Keeper, the way I hadn't for indictions, dreamed about her mist-gray eyes and her pale skin and her long nails that she lacquered the same color as her eyes. I dreamed about her long, snaky body and about her deep, drawling voice. The voice was the worst. I'd wake up at the ninth or tenth hour of the night, my heart banging in my chest, and I'd lie there holding my breath in case she called my name again.

I felt like an old bone being worried by three dogs, like sooner or later one of them was going to pull too hard, and I was just going to snap in half. The Money Dog, the Fever Dog, and the Dreams Dog I called them, and I didn't know which one of them I should be scared of most. They all three had teeth like alligators.

Felix

I come back, and I don't know where I am. This isn't the ward. Then I see the cracks in the ceiling, feel the wooden table beneath me. I come upright with a panicked scrambling jerk and only then realize that the straps are unbuckled.

The monsters are staring at me, yellow eyes and red eyes and the corpse's blank, fish-white eyes. They are speaking to each other. I bring my knees up to my chest, wrap my arms around them, try to stop shaking. My head hurts, and I cannot hear the off-kilter rhythm of the city because my own heartbeat echoes in my ears.

The corpse jerks his head at me. I get off the table. The snake looks me up and down, and I know by the colors around it that it is pleased. I don't know why. Then the snake turns and leaves the room. The corpse flaps his hand at me, and I follow the snake. The corpse and the gray pig bring up the rear.

We do not go back to the intractables' ward. Instead, we are in the vestibule, and the porter is opening the doors. I stop, sure that this is wrong, but the corpse pushes me, his hands like black, jagged ice even through my shirt, and I realize that I am supposed to follow the snake out of St. Crellifer's. I can't remember how to move across that black threshold, but the corpse takes my elbow and drags me through the door with him.

It is raining. There is a fiacre in the courtyard; the horses hitched to it look like horses, which is a relief, because the driver looks like a man-sized rat, huddled into a shabby shapeless overcoat as if it will help him pass for human. The corpse does not release my arm until we are in the fiacre—the corpse and the snake and I—and then he slams the door shut, and the fiacre moves off.

Out of the gates of St. Crellifer's, it turns uphill. At first I cannot think why I should find this frightening, although I know that I do, and then I begin to feel the terrible, black brokenness in front of us, coming closer; I remember the Mirador, the laboring arrhythmia of its broken magic.

"No," I say, in barely a whisper. It is the first time I have spoken since . . . I have to shake my head to clear it of the effort to remember how long it has been. The snake and the corpse ignore me.

We make the turn into the Plaza del'Archimago. I have my eyes shut, but I know what that feels like. "No!" I say again, more loudly. Someone catches at my wrists, and I strike their hands away. It hurts to open my eyes, but I have to so that I can find the latch of the fiacre door; I reach for it, but then the corpse grabs me, pinning my arms to my side, and drags me back onto the seat. I struggle, but there is no room in the fiacre, and the snake catches my ankles.

The fiacre turns in through Livergate, and the weight of the Mirador drops on me. I can't fight any longer. It's too late. The monsters have won.

Mildmay

You know how if you sit and think about something stupid long enough, it starts looking like a good idea? That's what happened to me.

See, robbing hotels ain't something I was ever into. Keeper kind of sneered at it, like it wasn't no decent way to make a living, and I guess the hardest habit in the world to break was that habit of wanting Keeper to be proud of me. So I'd never done it. I knew people who swore by it, and mostly they were the kind of stupid pig-lazy people you'd expect, and most of them had got caught by the Dogs. But I couldn't help remembering what one of them had told me, how he'd cleared two great-septad gorgons in one night. I kept thinking about that and about how long I could stay comfortable on that kind of money and about how fast I was sinking, here in this nasty room in Engmond's Tor, with the Money Dog and the Dreams Dog and the Fever Dog growling at each other, and pretty soon it started looking like the right thing to do.

I knew I was wrong—that's the bitch of it. I *knew* I was being stupid, but I was also feeling like I'd run out of smart options. And then Gilles's cousin Claude showed up needing a job, and Gilles didn't like me anyway. I expect I could have hung on if I'd tried, but the dreams and the aches and the worries were getting to me, and I didn't feel like sucking up to Gilles for a shitty job like that one. So I left with half a gorgon in my pocket and the clothes on my back and nothing else. I'd lost the rest of it somehow—I can't even tell you how anymore.

I went up into Havelock, where they got nice hotels and lots of out-of-town custom. I walked around in the rain for I don't know, an hour or two, and finally picked a hotel called the Anchorite's Knitting. I liked the sign.

I got up onto the roofs, about three blocks away from the Anchorite's Knitting, and worked my way back. The bells were just tolling the septad-night when I dropped onto the roof. We'd turned the corner of the night and were starting back uphill toward day—not that it made all that much difference, what with the rain and all. You got just as wet regardless.

I listened at the roof door for as long as it took me to do all of "Jeniard's Lover" in my head. It was something Keeper'd taught me. I was scared to death I'd lose my place and end up standing out there all night in the rain while the first half of "Jeniard's Lover" went round and round in my head like a broken music box. But I did get to the end, although it seemed to take forever and a half, and by the time I did, I hadn't heard a sound from the other side of the door. So it was about as safe as you could ask for to go picking a lock.

I was shivering, but the lock opened practically just for breathing on it. I got through and closed the door again, and then I had to sit down and catch my breath. That took a while, and I was still sort of panting, and I could hear my breath rasping in my chest. Kethe, that's a nasty noise. The Fever Dog had a lock on his end of the bone. I got up again and went downstairs, hanging on to a banister that was wobbling about as bad as I was.

I felt better once I made it to the third floor and so wasn't going to go pitching down the stairs on my head. I prowled down the corridor a little ways, but all the rooms were dark, and there wasn't no sound like people talking or fucking or even snoring. So I picked a door. It wasn't locked, and I went in wondering, even though I knew better, if this was going to be as boring as it looked like.

Kethe always gives you what you ask for.

There was a guy in the chair by the window. He had a dark lantern by him, open just a little, and he was watching me with a sort of bright, perky look, like I was his entertainment for the evening and he'd been looking forward to me for hours. He was a spare sort of guy, wearing a half beard that said he wasn't Marathine, and dressed in clothes that were clean, neat, and secondhand. His eyes were this amazing deep blue, clear as water.

"Good gracious," he said. "I don't think *you* were what I was expecting."

I'd never been caught so flat-footed in all my life. If I'd been well, I'd've been back out the door in a hot second, before he'd even got his mouth open, but I was still standing there, gaping at him like a half-wit dog, when the door swung shut and locked behind me. I heard the bolt go over.

I must've jumped a foot. It made him laugh. "Now," he said. "Who are you? A common thief?"

That "common" stung, but there wasn't no point pretending I was a chambermaid, so I nodded.

He was frowning. "Come here," he said.

The door was locked, and the way it'd happened said this guy was a hocus. If there was anything in my head at all, it was this kind of panicky prayer that he wouldn't turn out to be a close personal friend of Vey Coruscant's. So I went over to the table. There was some kind of diagram drawn on it in chalk and a big silver watch fob laying in the middle on top of a piece of pasteboard that looked like a playing card. Shit. Hocus-stuff.

"What's your name?" he said.

"Mildmay." I don't know if he levered it out of me somehow, or if I was just too stupid and sick to give him one of the others.

His eyebrows went up. "How . . . unusual."

"I can't help that," I said. The indiction before I was born, my mother converted into one of them faddy little cults that come and go in the Lower City like mayflies. This particular one died in the Fire, along with all its members, so all I know about it is my jawbreaking name: Mild-may-your-sufferings-be-at-the-hands-of-the-wicked. I don't even know if she meant it for me or for her. Keeper axed it right off, which I've always been glad about. I knew a gal in Pharaohlight once named Fly-from-fornication-and-blasphemy. She went by Butterfly, which went down a whole bunch better with her tricks.

The hocus had that look on his face like he was going to ask, so I said in a hurry, "What's yours?"

He gave me this kind of bow, like a joke, without getting up. "Mavortian von Heber, at your service."

Well, that was obviously a lie, but I didn't say nothing.

He was still frowning at his chalk lines and his watch fob and his playing card. "I know it worked," he said, and looked at me, "but why on earth are you here?"

"Sorry?" I said and coughed.

"Here. Sit down." I sat in the table's other chair, because it beat ending up on the floor. He opened the lantern wider and looked at me. "You are quite phenomenally wet. I would offer you a towel if I had one to hand."

"I'm okay," I said. This time I didn't cough. "What's the chalk for?"

"Well, that's just it. It seems to have brought you to me, but I'll be damned if I know why."

"It did what?"

"Here," he said and handed me a handkerchief. "At least dry your hair. This"—and he pointed at his chalk lines—"is a calling charm. I set it up to call the person who would be most helpful to me in solving a particular problem, and that person seems to be you. Any ideas why?"

"Not without you tell me what your problem is." I used his handkerchief on my hair, and at least it quit dripping down my neck.

"Come now. What do you do besides petty larceny?"

"I'm a cat burglar."

"A cat burglar," he said, like he thought he hadn't heard me right.

"Petty larceny," I said.

There was a pause. He was looking at me funny. I sat and dripped into the hotel chair and tried not to cough.

Then his face changed, all at once, like he'd been hit by lightning or something. He said, in this kind of awed, hurried voice, like he had to get it said before anything happened, "Can I *hire* you?"

"Sure. I mean, depending on what you want."

He brought his hand down on the table, hard enough to make me twitch, and shoved it sideways across his chalk lines, like he figured he didn't need *them* no more. He stopped just short of knocking his watch fob off the table. He tucked it and the playing card away in his waistcoat pocket and said, "I'll tell you. I'll tell you *exactly* what I want."

I waited while he got his thoughts organized. It was kind of comfortable, in a weird sort of way, watching a client's face while he decided how he was going to lie to me. He said, "I want to get a man out of St. Crellifer's. Can you do it?"

"St. Crellifer's? You mean the bat-house?"

"If you like to put it that way. Can you do it?"

I was beginning to wonder if he didn't belong in St. Crellifer's himself, hocus or no hocus. He had this light in his eyes that was spooking me out.

"Why can't you do it yourself? Last I heard, St. Crellifer's don't look too hard at anybody offering to take a crazy off their hands."

"I'm sorry. I didn't quite . . ."

Kethe, I thought, and this time the cough got past my guard. When I could talk again, I said, "Why don't you go get him yourself?"

"I can't. I can't go myself for various reasons, and they won't talk to my . . . colleague."

Shit, I thought. Looks like you've walked into another prize mess, Milly-Fox. "Why not?"

He took his watch fob out and gave it a look like it had said something he was thinking was a lie. Then he looked up at me and said, "The man I want to talk to is Felix Harrowgate."

After a while, I said, "I didn't know he was in St. Crellifer's."

"He's apparently quite mad, from what I hear," Mr. von Heber said, tilting his watch fob so the light from the lantern showed up the lines of engraving—some kind of pattern, I couldn't quite make it out—and staring at it now like it could tell him something he really wanted to know.

"Then what good . . ."

"That, I think"—and he looked up and caught me just with the force of his bright blue eyes—"is my business rather than yours. I will pay you to get him out of St. Crellifer's. What more do you need to know?"

"Well. I mean, he broke the Virtu. And I don't know nothing about you. I mean . . ."

"I assure you," he said, with this snarky little quirk at the corner of his mouth, "I do not seek to topple the Mirador."

Which was what he'd say anyway. But my head was starting to pound, and it had sort of occurred to me that if I said I'd do what he wanted, he might not throw me back out into the rain.

"Okay," I said, "but—"

That's when the other guy came in. He was a big guy, blond, dripping wet just like I was. His eyes were the same blue as Mr. von Heber's, but he wasn't no hocus. He was a for-hire bruiser. I didn't need the leather jacket or the braided mustaches to tell me that. It was in his eyes and the way he carried himself and the way his nose had been broken at least once. Like mine.

I was on my feet before I'd even got a good look at him. He stopped dead where he was, kicked the door shut behind him, and said in Norvenan, "Who the fuck is this?"

"This your 'colleague'?" I said—in Marathine because I didn't feel, all at once, like I wanted to let them know I understood Norvenan.

"Yes," Mr. von Heber said. He said, also in Marathine, "Bernard, this is Mildmay. He's going to help us with our, er, problem. He's a cat burglar."

Bernard snorted. He wasn't no more impressed with me than I was with him. "It's a novel approach," he said, "recruiting riffraff."

"I haven't noticed you coming up with any bright ideas."

That's when I started coughing again. It felt like the Fever had filled my lungs up with dry grass. I ended up leaning over the chair, gasping for breath, with the room going round and round like a waltz I couldn't hear.

"Sit down, you fool," Mr. von Heber said in a voice I hadn't heard out of him before.

It was smart advice. I would've taken it, except I was too dizzy and I couldn't let go of the chair. And then I couldn't feel the chair no more, and I fainted. The last thing I heard was the hocus swearing.

Felix

Darkness.

I'm alone.

I know I'm in the Mirador because I can feel it. It feels like people beating me with hammers, except that the blows come from everywhere, and more from inside my head than anywhere else. But nothing about this room, this darkness, feels familiar, and I have no idea how I got here. I get up and feel my way around the room. It's a small room, and there isn't anything in it except the cot and a washstand. But I find the door, and it isn't locked.

The snake and the corpse must be somewhere. I remember that they hurt me, and I don't want them to find me again. I open the door. I don't recognize this hallway, either, but there's no one here, only a lantern on a bracket.

I take the lantern and start down the hall. I move quickly, afraid that the snake and the corpse will come back. I come to a staircase leading down and take it, almost running. At the bottom I turn left, still away from the room I woke up in. For a long time I walk without any greater pattern than that—taking every staircase I can find that will lead me deeper into the Mirador and always, as best I can, getting farther away from that lightless room. The farther I go, the clearer my head becomes. I can still feel the broken magic of the Mirador pounding in my temples, but it is no longer overwhelming; it is as if these older, deeper levels are not beholden to the magic of the Virtu and resist its influence.

There are ghosts everywhere, in every imaginable style of clothing: ghosts fighting duels, ghosts kissing, ghosts dancing, one ghost kneeling in the middle of the hallway, striking over and over at one particular flagstone. Like the mad ghosts in St. Crellifer's, they do not seem to notice me. As I pass through an ancient, dust-swagged ballroom, I notice one ghost—a boy, tall, dark, beaky-nosed, wearing strange, stiffly padded clothing—who is standing in a corner, apart from the other ghosts. Our eyes meet. I am jolted so badly I almost drop the lantern, and the boy disappears, as quick as snuffed candlelight, into the wall.

After a minute, shaken, I go on. He saw me. No ghost since Joline has actually seen me, but he did. It makes no sense. But then, I do not know very much about ghosts. The Mirador does not believe in them, and even the old man who taught me about dreams would not discuss ghosts. Maybe there are rules and patterns that I simply don't know.

A few hallways later, I look over my shoulder, mostly because I am still afraid the corpse will find me. The boy is there, following me. His eyes are pale and patient and sad.

I know the boy means no harm, but fright closes over my head like the dark waters of the Sim. I am running without meaning to, chased by my panic and nightmares, running and running. When my strength gives out, I slump against the wall, end up sitting in a sort of huddle, the lantern beside me on the floor. My breath is coming in great tearing gasps; I am not quite sobbing, and I am working hard to keep it that way. Gradually my breathing slows and quiets, and my hands relax from their tight fists against my chest.

I am sorry. I did not mean to frighten you.

I jerk around, my shoulders slamming flat against the wall. The boy is there, maybe five feet away, standing straight and grave and quiet.

Please. I do not wish to hurt you. I do not think I could in any event.

"I . . . I know." My voice sounds strange, thin and full of breath. "Who are you?"

He looks at me for a moment, almost as if he is disappointed that I have to ask. Then he says, *Come with me.*

I get up and follow him, gripping the lantern handle so tightly that it starts to cut into my fingers, and I have to switch hands.

The ghost leads me unhurriedly, but without hesitation. I don't know enough about clothes to guess at how long he has been dead, but I am sure it must be more than a hundred years. He has had a very long time to become familiar with the labyrinths of the Mirador.

He brings me to another staircase; it begins at an arch in a corridor wall, faced with white marble. The staircase is white marble, too, and the pilasters and banisters are carved with the Cordelius roses. I have a bad feeling that I know where we are going. I can remember someone telling me once that the crypt of the Cordelii was somewhere in the depths of the Mirador.

The ghost pauses, four steps down, and glances back.

"I'm coming," I croak.

The door at the bottom is made of iron, fronted with a wrought-iron grille of twining roses and flanked by grotesquely skeletal caryatids crowned with roses.

I do not believe the door is locked, the ghost says.

I try the knob; the door swings open. I step inside.

It is all white marble and black iron, with three rows of sarcophagi, and wall tombs all the way around. The center row of sarcophagi are the largest; approaching, I see the name of Paul Cordelius, the first of his line, and succumbing to the silent weight of history, I follow the names down the hall: after Paul comes Matthias, then Sebastian, Edmund, Laurence, Charles, Claudius, Jasper, and the ill-fated John. I wonder who risked a charge of treason to be sure that John's remains were properly interred here with those of his forebears.

I look up and see the boy standing by another sarcophagus, this one in the row nearest the door, the last but one from the end. I make my way through the cold immensity to join him.

This is, er . . . that is to say, when I was alive . . .

I look at the engraving on the sarcophagus:

SILVESTER LUDOVIC MAGNUS
CORDELIUS
13.1.2–13.3.2

The dates are in the old-style reckoning and mean nothing to me.

I look up at him.

The boy sighs, a little line of worry pinching between his brows. *Does no one remember me at all?*

"I don't know," I say. "I'm not . . . I'm not very well educated." I remember suddenly, too clearly, Shannon teasing me about my "patchy" knowledge of history. It seems so separate from me now that it might have happened to someone else. I look down at my hands.

It does not matter, the boy says; I can tell from his voice that he knows he has upset me, although he does not know how. *It is only, I suppose, the last of my mortal vanity, and it is in that case well served.*

"Would you like . . ." My voice breaks, and I have to try again. "If you wish to tell me, I will listen."

You are very kind. I look up in time to see him smile, and although he is ever so slightly translucent, and although his eyes are pale and strange, it is a charming smile, full of kindness and warmth. *But there is nothing to tell. I died of plague, and it is only by the great mercy of the gods that my brother Edmund did not die as well.*

I say, stupidly, "I'm sorry, Prince Silvester."

Oh, please, call me Magnus.

"Magnus. And my name is Felix."

For a moment, the brightness of his smile makes him look almost alive. *You must be wondering what I want—why I have frightened you half to death.*

"You didn't." We both know I am lying. "What I want," I say hastily, "is to know why you can see me. Why you can talk to me."

Your question is the obverse of mine, then. I was wondering if, because you can see me, you might be able to help me.

"Help you?"

I can talk to you, he says very carefully, *because I was, er . . . is "raised" the correct term?*

"Um. You mean necromancy?"

Yes.

"I think so. I'm not a necromancer."

Neither were the wizards who raised me, he says, a sharp flick of contempt in his long-dead voice, and I remember that the court wizards of the Cordelii were all necromancers. *And they were fools. They were seeking to raise Loël Fairweather.*

I recognize the name Loël Fairweather, and then I realize that I know what happened to Magnus. "They thought that since he had defeated Porphyria Levant, he could show them how to defeat Brinvillier Strych."

Was that *their reasoning?* He sounds disgusted.

"They didn't know any better," I say, feeling obscurely guilty and ignorant on their behalf. "They were desperate."

Which does not excuse them. He sighs, and the fire goes out of him. *They did not disperse me before, er . . .*

"Before they were successful," I say, and there is a moment's grim silence as we contemplate the rewards of their success.

I want to be dispersed, Magnus says. *This existence is unnatural and painful.*

"But I . . . you don't think . . . surely you aren't imagining *I* can help you?"

You can talk to me. I know you said you weren't a necromancer, but—

"There are no necromancers in the Mirador. And I can talk to you because I'm crazy."

Oh. It is a tiny noise, barely more than a gasp. *But you* are *a wizard. Isn't that what those tattoos mean?*

I look at the staring blue eyes on my palms. "Yes. But . . ."

But?

It is too much. I cannot explain. "I cannot help you. I am sorry. I can't even help myself, or I would . . ." But I don't know what I would do if I were not crazy, if Malkar had not broken me, if I still had my magic. "If I ever can help you, I will. I promise."

But you do not think it likely. His expression is uncompromising, bleak, and I see that he does not want to be lied to.

"No. I am sorry."

Please. Do not be, he says and reaches out, as if he would touch me. *Felix. And I can do even less for you than you can do for me. Do you wish me to take you back to . . . to the part of the Mirador that is still alive?*

"No," I say. "I don't want to go back there."

But—

"It makes me worse," I say, and suddenly, brilliantly, I see the truth. It is the weight of magic that keeps me mad. I *was* better in St. Crellifer's, before Robert came. And this part of the Mirador, where no magic has been worked for hundreds of years, is better for me. There is a headache throbbing behind my eyes, from the effort of holding myself together, but I *can* hold myself together, I *can* talk to Magnus like a normal person. I haven't been able to do that since . . . since Robert came to St. Crellifer's. I remember the yellow-eyed man in the garden; I wonder if I could find him again.

Magnus says, obstinately worried, *But there is nothing for you to eat down here. It does no good to be sane if you starve to death.*

"I'm not so sure of that."

You cannot be cured of death.

And the yellow-eyed man had said he thought my madness could be cured.

"Very well." I cannot help sighing. "But if I start to become . . . odd, please leave me."

As you wish, he says, although his gaze is troubled. He leads me out of the crypt; I close the door behind us. We start back toward, as Magnus put it, the part of the Mirador that is still alive.

Mildmay

In the dream, I'm lost in the curtain-mazes at the Trials. This is a stupid dream, and I know it. I didn't go to the Trials this indiction. I couldn't stand being around that many people having a good time when Ginevra was dead and cold and was never going to laugh again. And anyway, I've never been lost in the curtain-mazes in my life. Even when I hadn't finished my first septad yet, and some of the older kids thought it would be funny to ditch me, I didn't get lost. I still remember them staring when I came out, and that was the first I'd known they'd done it on purpose.

So it's a stupid dream. But I can't get free of it, and I can't find my way out, and sometimes I think there's something behind me, although there never is when I look. And even though I feel like shit, I keep walking.

Even in the dream, I had the Fever in my lungs, and what finally woke me up was a coughing fit that could've waked the dead. About all you could say for it was I didn't cough up blood and I didn't quite puke.

When I was okay again—at least, I wasn't coughing, and that was good enough to get by on—I lay there and looked around. I didn't know where I was, and I knew that should have scared me, but it didn't. I couldn't seem to care enough to be scared. The light coming in the window was sort of morning-colored, even with the rain, and there was nobody in the room. And then I saw the table by the window, and the chairs, and the dark lantern still sitting there, and I knew I was in the hocus's room. He hadn't pitched me out to die in the street, and that was nice, but he hadn't had his bruiser drag me to St. Cecily's either, and that was worrisome. Would have been worrisome, I mean, except then I fell asleep again, and I was right back in that fucking maze.

Felix

The first sign is the blood on the floor. At first it is just occasional drips, then pools, then streams running down the corridors, and then the floor disappears entirely beneath a river of blood.

What's wrong? Magnus says.

"Nothing," I say, and wrench my eyes away from the tide of blood rising above my ankles. I cannot feel it, but that makes it worse, because I do not know whether I should mistrust my sense of sight or my sense of touch. And I think I can smell it faintly, a faraway stench of copper.

Are you sure? You look ill.

"Don't worry about me." My voice is shaking.

Felix, are you—

"It might be better if you left me." The blood is up to my thighs, and I can feel the Virtu distinctly, the black, rotten core of my throbbing headache.

But we—

"Please!"

Very well. He gives me a slight bow and returns down the corridor the way we came. I cannot watch him go; the effect of the blood washing through him is more than I can bear. I am afraid I have offended him, but I truly don't know how much longer I can keep from screaming. After a moment, I continue walking; the blood is up to my waist, and darkness is rising off it, like fog off the Sim. I glance over my shoulder; Magnus is gone. I fold up where I am. If the blood is real, it will drown me; if it isn't real, it doesn't matter, because the darkness will drown me anyway. My knees hit the floor; blood fills my eyes.

Darkness.

ꟹ

The small monsters find me. They get me on my feet; their paws are gentle. They take me to a larger monster; my vision wavers for a moment, and I see Master Architrave, who is the Second Steward of the Vielle Roche, the oldest part of the Mirador. Then Architrave is gone again, and I am surrounded by monsters. In time, they bring me to the snake and the corpse.

The snake is furiously angry; the corpse is not angry, but the corpse is *never* angry, and that means nothing. I expect to be beaten, but they only make me wash my hands and face, and then drag me after them, out into the hallways. The blood is gone, and I am grateful.

The Virtu is getting louder in my head, but every time I try to stop, the corpse grabs my arm and drags me farther. I don't want the corpse to touch me, so I keep walking, even though my vision has started pulsing with the Virtu's brokenness, and sometimes I cannot see where I am going through the darkness. I only fall once; the corpse jerks me to my feet, and we go on.

Then we are in front of the great bronze doors of the Hall of the Chimeras. They are open. I don't want to go in, but now the snake takes my other arm, and it and the corpse march me through the doors.

The shards of the Virtu streak the darkness in my eyes with strident blue. My magic is bound and broken; I have no defenses against the throbbing wrongness that fills the Hall of the Chimeras. I clench my teeth to be sure that I don't start keening.

We come to a halt somewhere in front of the Virtu. My eyes won't work, and all I can hear is the Virtu's frail song. I know there are other monsters here; I see them in fragmentary glimpses: a bear, a granite lioness, an alabaster statue with eyes as blue as the Virtu's shards, a thing like a silver wolf, a hawk-headed monster in a blue coat.

The corpse forces me to kneel. The snake's fingers touch my temples.

I am screaming. I can't see; I can't hear; everything is black and terrible, and the pain is like being turned inside out. If I could see my hands, I know the bones would be splintering through my skin. I can feel the black, howling thing in my chest ripping itself free of my ribs.

Suddenly, the pain is gone. I fall forward, catching myself on my hands, retching, although there is nothing in my stomach to bring up.

The mosaics bite into my palms. Slowly, I fold backwards, bringing my hands up to cover my face. I can feel tears on my cheeks, and I am still shaking. I can't see, and my ears are full of a roaring noise.

Something touches my shoulder; my hands go up, reflexively, to ward off the blow that must be coming, and I touch the stiff elaboration of brocade. But my eyes will not work; there is nothing here except darkness and the terrible blue shards of the Virtu. Then the monster—it must be a monster, for I have seen no people since the boy left me—is gone, and I curl up on myself again and wish my head would just split open and end this horror.

But all that happens is the corpse grabs me and drags me upright. I know it's the corpse, even though my eyes won't work, because my arms start going numb where he has touched me. And he turns me around and drags me out of the Hall of the Chimeras, and I am sobbing now with gratitude and relief.

As we leave the Virtu behind, back in the hallways of the Mirador, my vision starts to return, in patches and smears. I can see the snake's anger in front of me. I glance at the corpse, looking away before he can notice. He is as gray and indifferent as ever. Even this is a relief.

We walk to Livergate, where the snake shouts at the small monsters until one of them darts out to flag down a hansom. The snake comes over to me, far too close, and stares up into my eyes. I look back, almost mesmerized by its vile yellow eyes, until finally it turns away with a gesture of disgust. Then the corpse opens the hansom door and waves me in.

The hansom rattles out Livergate; again, I feel the Mirador leaving me like a burden finally set down. The release is like joy, but I remember the corpse beside me and do not move. And my head is still jangling. I remember the boy; his name was Magnus, and he needed help. It seems to me terribly important that I remember him, and I sit and think about him, about the crypt of the Cordelii, until the hansom turns through the gates of St. Crellifer's, and the corpse prods me to make me get out.

The pig is waiting for us on the steps.

Mildmay

It was probably a decad and a half—maybe more—before I could sit up and take notice again. It used to drive Keeper crazy, the way the other kids could have a sniffle, and I'd have a cough and a fever and a throat you could use to scour pots. And the Winter Fever is bad news. People die of it, and I probably would have died if I hadn't happened to be useful to Mavortian von Heber.

They fought about it, him and Bernard. When I was really sick and supposed to be asleep—Mr. von Heber had this syrup that I think was probably half laudanum—they'd fight in the room with me, in whispers, and I'd hear them even in my dreams. When I was getting better, they'd try to do all their fighting in their other room, the one they were sharing now that they had a sick cat burglar in the room that had been the hocus's, but sometimes they'd forget. And sometimes I'd hear them through the wall anyway.

Bernard didn't like me. No skin off my nose—I didn't like him, either. I don't know whether Mr. von Heber *liked* me or not, but he sure was convinced I was useful to him. I couldn't figure out why at first—once I was better enough to even care about it, I mean—but then I heard them going at it in the hall.

I didn't catch the beginning—though I'd bet money Bernard said something nasty. And Mr. von Heber said, "I read the cards again last night, because I'm getting tired of this. They were clear as daylight. He's the key to it."

"You don't always trust your cards like this."

"Do you want to go out and bring me back a sheep so I can read the entrails? It'd be worth it to watch you trying to get it up the stairs."

"Mavortian . . . Look. I don't know about your fortune-telling, but I *do* know he's bad news. I don't want to come back some afternoon and find he's slit your throat for you."

"In his current condition? I think that's rather insulting."

"I don't argue with you about magic, do I? You know what you're doing. Why don't you believe that I know what I'm doing?"

"I do. Bernard, I'm not doubting for a moment that he is what you say he is. I'm trying to tell you it doesn't matter. He's *still* the key, and I have been looking for a key for a very long time."

"And what good does it do you to find one if it gets you killed?"

"It won't. I'm not nearly as naïve—or as careless—as you think me. Now, if you'll excuse me . . ."

Bernard muttered something I couldn't hear and stomped off toward the stairs. The door opened, and Mr. von Heber came in.

He was a cripple. I didn't know what had happened—an accident or an illness or what—but his legs were just about useless to him. They'd hold him up, sort of, if he was mostly leaning on something else, but they'd barely move at all. He had a pair of them canes with the handgrips and the elbow braces, and he got around okay, but he was slow and it looked like awful hard work.

He shut the door behind him and started toward the chair by the bed. "You heard that, didn't you?"

"Yeah." No point in lying about it.

He sighed. "I hope you don't think . . ."

"It's okay. I mean, I don't care if Bernard—"

"Bernard is an idiot," he said, with some heat in it. "And he does not like Mélusine."

"Can't blame him."

Mr. von Heber got to the chair, and we didn't say nothing while he was getting settled. Then he looked at me and said, perfectly pleasant, "Your roots are showing."

"Fuck," I said, one hand going up out of pure stupid reflex, like I could hide something Mr. von Heber had already seen.

"What color is it naturally?"

"Red. Oh sacred bleeding *fuck*."

"What's the matter with that? Many people rather like red hair."

"How many redheads you seen since you been here?"

He opened his mouth, then closed it again, frowning. "Now that you mention it . . . people here don't even use henna, do they? It's quite the rage in Ervenzia."

"Unlucky," I said. You go waltzing around with red hair in Mélusine, and people are liable to think you're a spy for the Empire or a blood-witch or something. And it's fucking conspicuous, which I always figured was why people like Felix Harrowgate and Madeleine Scott used henna. They didn't have to worry about what people said about them.

Keeper didn't care about the stories. She just didn't want me walking around with my damn head like a torch. People tend to remember things like that. You can guess, maybe, how pissed off she was when I got my face laid open. But she made me keep dyeing my hair anyway. I'd been going to a guy in the Arcane since I hit my fourth indiction. The dye stank, and it cost the earth, but Purvis did it right every single time.

"I thought black didn't suit you," Mr. von Heber said.

"Thanks."

He gave a kind of sigh and said, "How are you feeling?"

"Some better. Got all the way to the water closet without leaning on Bernard." I didn't think I'd tell him how near I'd come to crawling back.

"Good."

"You're still wanting me to go get the hocus for you."

It took him a moment to understand what I'd said—I think I mumble the word "hocus" because it makes me nervous—and then he said, "Yes."

"Gonna be another decad at least. I can't do nothing until I quit with the cough some."

He nodded, so I didn't have to tell him how bad it upsets your plans when you have a coughing fit in the middle of somebody's upstairs hall. A hospice would be worse, because there'd be people awake at all hours. And I wasn't real happy about walking into a nest of crazies anyway, but it wasn't like I had anything better I was doing with my life.

"There isn't any great hurry," he said. "Felix Harrowgate isn't going anywhere."

"Yeah," I said. "Don't s'pose he is."

Kethe must've been laughing his ass off.

Felix

This time, the Sunling comes into my dreams. He is a thin, cloudy presence, like a ghost, but he is there, and his eyes shine like lamps.

"Felix," he says, his voice cutting through the great murmuring throng that surrounds me in this dream. They fade away, like fog before the sun, and leave me standing alone.

Slowly, I lower my hands, which were protecting my head from the stones the crowd threw, stones that were also bones. The Sunling comes toward me through my dream, which is now just a great, cloudy, echoing space. "You found me," I say.

"It wasn't easy," he says. "And this will not last long. What is that?" He points to something I hadn't noticed, a black, jagged spike skewering through the layers of my dream like a sword. But I recognize it when I see it.

"The Mirador."

"The *Mirador*? Are you a wizard of the Mirador?"

"I was."

"No wonder. I have read of the Mirador; the little oneiromancy I have can do nothing with it. Were you inside it, this meeting would not be possible at all."

"But why are you here?"

"I want to help you."

He says it as if it should have been obvious to me; I cannot think of anyone else in the world who wants to help me. Because I do not know how to tell him so, or to thank him, I say, "What is your name?"

"Diokletian. But—"

And then the dream surges and heaves and dumps me out into the waking world, where my feet are cold because the blanket I have is not long enough, and the monsters prowl restlessly around the ward.

❧

Later—the next day, the day after? I don't know—the dove-headed monster takes me downstairs. I do not want to go, for I am afraid of the snake and the terrible things I can almost remember happening to me, but the monster booms at me and boxes my ears, and I follow it obediently.

We do not go to the stairs that lead down to the basement, and I feel marginally less frightened. Instead, the monster leads me to the parlor where once I talked with the snake, back when I could understand the monsters' speech. I don't want to go in there, but I know the monster will merely box my ears again if I try to balk. And I have a vague feeling that the snake isn't as dangerous up here, that maybe things will be all right.

But it isn't the snake waiting for me. This monster has the black, shiny head and bead-bright eyes of a raven. I stop just inside the door, bewildered. It stands up, booming something. I cannot back up; the dove-headed monster is just behind me, and behind it the door is closed.

The raven advances. It wears rings, as the snake does, and the rings look familiar: gold set with tiger's eyes. It stops in front of me, its hands extended, palms up. I do not know what it wants, and can only stand and stare at it.

The dove and the raven are booming at each other around me. The raven is angry, I think, and drop my gaze; perhaps it does not want to be stared at.

The dove grabs my right wrist, hard enough to bruise, and shoves my hand toward the raven. Before I can twist away, the raven has taken my hand; the dove lets go.

There is a crack like thunder, only silent, all through my head. For a moment, I hear a man's voice, swearing vilely in Midlander; then I wrench free of the raven's grip. I cannot get out the door, but I can at least get out from between the two monsters, get my back against the wall. I crouch in the corner, so that my right side is against the wall, too, and then I just wait. My head hurts, and even my good eye is blurred.

The dove and the raven boom back and forth some more; then the raven leaves, slamming the door behind it. After a moment, the dove turns toward me, and I feel my fingernails digging into my palms. But I can bear any punishment it chooses, so long as it does not tell the corpse. The dove does not like the corpse—I see the colors around it when the corpse is nearby—and I think maybe it will not tell him. It is the only thing I can hope for.

The dove comes to fetch me from the ward again sometime later. I don't know if it's day or night; light is untrustworthy. The dove did not tell the corpse; it did not even punish me, beyond boxing my ears again. I think it is trying to be kind. I follow it back to the parlor. The raven is waiting, and there is another monster with it: a statue made out of obsidian, who wears silver rings set with dark amethysts.

The dove herds me into the room and stands with its back against the door. The raven and the statue stare at me; I hear the roaring of their voices. Then the raven approaches me; I back up, bump into the unyielding solidity of the dove, duck sideways—and the obsidian hand of the statue closes around my upper arm. Her other hand touches my temple.

Thunder echoes through me; I can't pull away, because the raven has come up on my other side and is holding my other arm. And a woman's voice says, "Powers and saints, what *is* that?"

"It looks like a compulsion to me." A man's voice, a Kekropian accent. "Didn't anyone notice?"

I recognize the voices; these are people I used to know. But I can't remember their names, any more than I can see their faces.

"I don't think anyone looked," the woman says. "But if that's a compulsion . . ."

"Exactly. Makes you wonder what might happen if we took it off, doesn't it?"

"But this is terrible! This isn't madness, most of it."

"What do you mean?"

"It's like being told someone's been crippled by disease and finding that their legs have been broken in five places. I don't think . . ." Something prods at the broken places in my mind, and I gasp with the pain. "Blessed saints. He didn't *go* mad—he was *sent* mad."

"Malkar. I can guess at some of what must be behind that compulsion then."

"I can't do this on my own. We have to take him to the Curia."

"What?"

"He's under the Curia's interdict. I don't have the authority to . . . to meddle. Come on."

"But we can't—"

"Robert could, the weasel. And Giancarlo will want to see this."

"Well, I . . . Brother Ferien?"

"Yes, m'lord?"

"We need to take your patient to the Mirador. Is that all right?"

"Well, I guess so, m'lord. I ain't been told otherwise."

"Good," says the woman in a low voice. "*Now,* Thaddeus, before that vile warder comes back."

They are still holding my arms; they turn me and march me out the door. I would like to tell them that they don't have to, that I understand what they say and I want the compulsion taken off me so badly . . . but I can't. I can't seem to make any sound at all.

Out of the parlor, down the hall, through the vestibule, where the porter, who is Brother Orphelin's creature, stares and does not help, but is too frightened of my escort to hinder. Pieces of the world are coming into place around me. The rings the raven and the statue wear are wizards' rings; their voices are agonizingly familiar. They have a fiacre waiting on the street. I climb in; without their touch, I lose their voices as well, but I hold on to the knowledge that they want to help me, that they have seen the compulsion and are going to do something about it.

Outside St. Crellifer's, the world glows with midmorning sunshine. It occurs to me dimly that the monsters must have ducked out of court to come get me, but I cannot get the thought to have any deeper meaning. I'm not even sure I know what I mean by "court." It meant something to me once.

Coming into the Mirador hurts, like being shut in an iron maiden. But I remember that the monsters with me are kind. The raven disappears; the statue leads me through the Mirador to a small room hung with canary-yellow silk. I don't know how long we wait. I have no time sense; clocks have become a bewilderment and a misery. I don't think it can be too long, because the statue does not seem impatient.

The door opens, and more monsters come into the room, the raven with them. One of them has a hawk's head. The others are a dark jumble; I try not to look at them. They are booming back and forth, and the colors show they are angry. The statue joins the argument. Finally, she takes my arm, dragging me forward; I am almost used to the thunderclap by now.

"Look for yourself!" she says, not quite shouting. "Dammit, Giancarlo, just look!"

"Oh, very well," the hawk says, exasperated; its voice is deep and strong and rough. It touches my forehead. It takes all my courage, but I do not flinch.

After a moment, its hand drops again; it says, "Powers."

"It's a compulsion," the raven says. "And that's not Cabaline working, either."

"It's Malkar," the hawk says, dry with distaste. "I recognize the style."

"We have to get it off him!" says the raven.

"Gently, Lord Thaddeus," says the hawk. "I agree. This may change . . . many things. But for that reason, Lord Stephen and the Witchfinder Extraordinary had best be present. I'll call an emergency Curia meeting for this afternoon. I fancy that the wait could be put to good use."

His voice is loaded with meaning.

"Oh," says the raven. "Rather. We'll, er, clean him up."

"And find him something decent to wear. He *is* a wizard of the Mirador, after all."

"Yes, my lord," the raven and the statue say in chorus.

The hawk and the jumbled entourage of others leave the room. I can feel the raven and the statue looking at each other.

"Well," says the raven, "your place or mine?"

The statue snorts with laughter. "Yours."

She keeps her hand just behind my elbow as we walk. I should know where we are going; I should be able to understand the maze around me, but I cannot. I can't hold the sense of the world together long enough.

The rooms we come to are deep in the Mirador; I feel the weight of stone and wood and plaster above us like a curse. They are low, rectangular rooms, austere with whitewash. The rugs on the floors are dark and thick, and the few pieces of furniture are likewise dark and heavy. As we come in, a green shape rises from one of the chairs. I can't see it clearly, as if it moves in a trailing cloud of fog, just the greenness and a sense of ferocity carefully held in check.

It and the raven and the statue roar back and forth at each other for a while, and then there are small monsters in the room with a big copper tub. They pour water into the tub and bow to everyone nervously and scurry out.

"Oh powers," says the statue, her hand on my arm, "here we go."

"Come on, Felix," says the raven. "Gideon, will you go get the soap?"

The green shape leaves the room; I watch it, anxiously, because it is strange.

"It's just Gideon," the raven says. "Come on, Felix. You need a bath."

The raven and the statue are both gently, uneasily, urging me toward the tub. It is not the Sim; I remember I saw the small monsters pouring the water. It is safe. And I am filthy. I take off my clothes and climb into the tub.

The green monster returns with the soap, which I accept gratefully. The three monsters stand close together at the other end of the room. I know that they are whispering, but the roar and boom of it still hurt my ears. I would tell them that they don't have to whisper, that I can't understand them, but I still can't find any language in my head.

I wash thoroughly, scrubbing my fingers through the ugly short curls of my hair. When I am done, the water is brown. But there are towels laid out, left by the small monsters, and the raven brings me clothes. They don't fit very well—two inches of wrist protrude from the cuffs of the shirt, and the trousers threaten to fall off my hips until the green shape offers a belt—but they are clean, and I am grateful.

The monsters are all watching me, the colors around them purple and smoky green. They are troubled, upset. But they don't seem angry, and I am glad enough to sit quietly in a chair. The green monster sits near me, and I can feel its brilliant gaze on me. I stare at my hands, and I suppose time passes, although I cannot tell.

The green monster touches my arm, gently; I wish I could explain my flinch was for the thunderclap, not for him. But I get up and follow the raven and the statue. The green shape does not come with us. It is one fewer monster to worry about; it is bad enough that the raven is walking on my right side.

We come to a room, high-ceilinged and light; it almost seems as if the windows painted on the walls are real, although I know they are only frescoes. There are monsters around the table that dominates the room: the hawk-headed monster, a bear, a silver wolf, others and others. I look at the floor. They roar and howl; the room is full of red. Finally, the bear booms out a phrase that cuts through the din. There is a moment in which I can feel something rising, swelling, advancing, and then the thunder cracks across me. My knees buckle, and I feel the inside of my head tearing, spinning, burning.

I was on my knees in the Lesser Coricopat, and the entire Curia was staring at me, as was Lord Stephen Teverius and a wizard I didn't know, who a moment before had been a silver wolf. Vida Eoline was standing on my left; I turned my head to the right, almost before I realized that the clouds had cleared from my mind, and saw Thaddeus de Lalage, whom I had last seen five years previously, when he was sent to the wizard's tower in far northern Aurelias.

I got to my feet, all of them staring at me like a taxidermist's gallery, pushed my fingers through my hair. I opened my mouth in a spirit of academic curiosity, and the words "Thank you," emerged as if there had never been any reason that they could not. The colors in the room were throbbing with disbelief and distrust.

"*Was* that a compulsion laid by Malkar Gennadion?" said Giancarlo; he was glaring at me horribly beneath his eyebrows, but that was no different than Giancarlo had ever been.

"Yes," I said. "He laid it on me so that I could not tell anyone what he had done."

"And what *had* he done?" said Stephen, smoldering like a charcoal-maker's fire. Stephen hated histrionics. I was so deeply relieved to know that, to be able to look at him and recognize him, even with the bear hanging around him like a pall of smoke, that his tone did not bother me.

"He broke the Virtu," I said. "He used me."

"How could he?" said one of the other Curia members. "You are a wizard of the Mirador. No one can lay compulsions on you."

Except the interdict, I thought, but did not say. "I don't know. He got past the Virtu's wards somehow, but I don't know how."

"Interesting," Giancarlo said, his eyebrows pulling together in an alarming frown. "So if we ask you again all those questions we asked you back in Théoc, will you now answer them truthfully?"

"I'll try," I said. "I'll do my best."

Hours later, after the Curia released me and after a particularly excoriating interview with Stephen, Thaddeus and Vida took me back to Thaddeus's suite. I felt as if I'd been run through a mangle. My memory was not good enough to please them, and we found, Giancarlo and I snarling at each other in a duet of frustration, that the intervening months of madness had rather violently colored and reinterpreted what I did remember of what Malkar had done. They had all been shouting questions at me by the end, and I had waited and waited, shaking with tension, for someone to ask about the physical aspects of Malkar's ritual, but no one did. They were Cabalines; the right questions simply did not occur to them, and although the truth beat at the inside of my skull, I could not say it. I didn't know why: shame, fear, some twisted kind of pride . . . a last poisonous legacy from Malkar. In Arabel, even before he began teaching me to do magic, he had forbidden me to tell anyone that we were lovers, just as he had later forbidden me to tell anyone of the magics he worked with my help in that workroom in the Warren. That later injunction I had found myself able to defy, but the older one was stronger. If I let myself think about it, I knew I would be able to remember exactly what Malkar had said he would do to me if I ever told anyone, and even the thought of the memory was enough to make me shudder. If someone had asked, point-blank, maybe I would have been able to say it, but I could no more volunteer the information than I could fly to the moon.

In the halls, trying not to watch the courtiers and servants and wizards as they saw me, recognized me, and tried to pretend they weren't staring—too conscious of my ill-fitting clothes and my ragged hair to enjoy their confusion—I said to Thaddeus, "So, how long have you been back in Mélusine?"

"A couple of weeks. They called us all back when the Virtu was broken." He had not changed in the five years he had been gone; he was still Thaddeus, his eyes dark and bright in his swarthy pirate's face. His hair stayed in a queue more tidily than mine had, even before Brother Orphelin hacked it off. I realized I had a headache, a slow dull pounding that had been there for hours.

"And he wasted no time in finding a new crusade," Vida said. "You should be grateful to him, Felix. First he wouldn't rest until *he*'d seen you, and then he wouldn't rest until *I*'d seen you."

Thaddeus waved this away. "The story didn't make any sense. You'd broken the Virtu and then gone to Malkar of all people for protection? It sounded backward, and I couldn't help noticing who'd gotten all the benefit."

"Malkar," I said. "Do they know . . . ?"

"He's in the Bastion," Vida said. "General Mercator seems to think highly of him."

"Wonderful," I said.

"That would have made me suspicious, if nothing else," Thaddeus said. He said it lightly, as if it were a joke, but I knew it wasn't. Thaddeus hated the Bastion, hated it with a raw, pure fury that itself bordered on madness. One reason the Curia had sent him to Aurelias was to get him away from the Bastion, in the hopes that time might erode the sharp edges of that passion. I wondered if it had.

"The other person in your suite," I said. "Who . . . ?"

"Oh," said Thaddeus. "Gideon."

"Gideon?"

"Gideon Thraxios. I knew him in the Bastion."

"Another defector?"

"Yes. He won't bother you."

I wanted to say that wasn't what worried me, but my head hurt, and the colors spiking around Thaddeus told me that this was not a subject he wanted to discuss. Unless and until the Curia decided to revoke their interdict, I was dependent on Thaddeus's goodwill; I knew that at this stage in the proceedings it would take no more than a word from him to send me back to St. Crellifer's, or back to the crushing darkness in the Verpine.

"You know what Robert said when Giancarlo asked him why he hadn't noticed Malkar's compulsion?" Thaddeus said, breaking in on the downward, anxious spiral of my thoughts. That must have been what Thaddeus and Giancarlo had been talking about after the meeting was officially dismissed, while Stephen was forbidding me to see Shannon again, *at least until this matter is satisfactorily cleared up*.

"When did Giancarlo ask him?" Vida said.

"This morning, after he'd seen it for himself. And Robert said he thought it was the interdict."

Vida said, "Surely even *Robert* isn't that stupid!"

"Maybe," said Thaddeus, "maybe not. But nobody's going to be able to prove it."

"And Robert weasels free again," I said dully.

"Felix?" said Vida. "Are you all right?"

"I'm just very tired." I didn't want to talk about the headache or the colors surrounding them both, or the way that Vida, walking on my right, was a blur to begin with, and then kept dissolving into shadows. I was not cured, I realized; I was coherent now, but not necessarily sane.

The stranger, Gideon Thraxios, was sitting by the fireplace in Thaddeus's main room, curled up in one of the big chairs like a cat and reading a treatise on water magic from Imar Eiren. He stood up when we came in; either his manners were naturally very good or Thaddeus made him nervous. Or I did.

Now that he wasn't just a green shape in a cloud of fog, he proved to be a man of medium height, slenderly built, with the bronze tone to his skin that indicated he came from the eastern end of the Kekropian Empire. His hair was dark and curly, escaping from his queue in wild tendrils; his eyes were dark and startlingly intelligent, shining like beacons out of an otherwise undistinguished, snub-nosed face. He was older than I, but I wasn't sure by how much.

The colors between him and Thaddeus were a brooding brownish red shot through with lightning-white, belying the seeming friendliness of the way Thaddeus told Gideon about the Curia meeting and introduced him to me. Reintroduced, I corrected myself, but Gideon and I shook hands anyway. I decided his manners were just naturally good.

I could feel the conversation moving, like a boat tugged by a strong current, toward the subject of Malkar and my madness—things I did not want to talk about any more today. The knock at the door was a reprieve, and I welcomed it.

The crimp in Thaddeus's eyebrows suggested he was not so pleased, but he opened the door.

"My lord?" he said. "What—"

"Felix? I'm sorry, Lord Thaddeus, but I must—"

"Shannon?" A moment's ice-locked paralysis, and then I was at the doorway with no memory of the intervening yards of carpet, and his arms were around me. *"Shannon!"*

"Oh, powers, Felix!"

Dimly, I heard Thaddeus say, "By all means, my lord, please come in," but though I flinched at the sarcasm in his voice, there was no room in my thoughts for it to make more than a momentary impression.

Somehow we got ourselves sorted out, got inside Thaddeus's sitting room, the door closed, standing a little apart from each other, although our hands were clasped tightly. Without my rings, there was no need for caution in that touch, no need to fear that I would hurt Shannon. Thaddeus, Vida, and Gideon had tactfully withdrawn to the other side of the room, where the periphery of my attention observed that they were having an undervoiced but heated discussion of their own.

Shannon's eyes, brilliant as sapphires, were fixed on my face. For a dizzying moment, I saw the alabaster statue, and then the world fell into place again.

Shannon was saying breathlessly, "Felix, I'm so sorry, I should have known, I shouldn't have let them, I didn't know, I never wanted—"

"Shannon," I said gently.

He stopped speaking at once, as if I'd . . . I remembered that I *had* hit him, that horrible night when I let Malkar get his claws into me again.

"Shannon," I said again, because I did not know what else to say. Slowly, clumsily, I said, "I'm not angry. You aren't . . . you have nothing to blame yourself for."

"But I—"

"You could not have kept me from destroying myself," I said, and then winced at the truth of what I'd said.

"Can we, do you think . . ."

"I don't know. I am . . . I am not the same." Even to Shannon I could not say, I am still mad.

"Can we *try?*"

"Yes," I said; the force in him was too much for me to stand against. "We can try."

Chapter 6

Mildmay

It was the third decad of Brumaire and I was more or less on my feet again, when Bernard brought the news that Felix Harrowgate was back in the Mirador. Mr. von Heber just about hit the roof, and he was mad enough to spit nails for two days. Me and Bernard kept our mouths shut. It was like they'd moved the hocus as a personal insult, aimed just at him.

But anyway, there wasn't nothing for him to hire me to do no more, and after dinner on 25 Brumaire, I said so.

Bernard looked up, like he'd been praying and praying I'd say it and now couldn't believe I had. I'd figured out, especially by listening when they were talking in Norvenan and didn't know I could understand them, that they were half brothers or stepbrothers or something. Norvenan don't distinguish so as you can tell. But I was betting half brothers, and I was betting Bernard's mother had been a laundrymaid. That was how they acted toward each other. And one of the things it meant was that Bernard would grumble and argue and bitch from one end of time to the other, but he wouldn't ever go against Mr. von Heber, not straight out. So when Mr. von Heber had told him to quit hinting as how they should chuck me out on my ear, he did what he was told. But he didn't stop giving me the hairy eyeball, and I got to say I was tired of it.

Mr. von Heber looked up, too, from this book Bernard had brought him from the Cheaps a couple days ago. "What?"

"If he ain't in St. Crellifer's, then I ain't no good to you."

"But we know where he is. I don't see—"

"I ain't going in the Mirador."

For a second, they had the same look on their faces, like they thought maybe I was going to start biting. "All right," Mr. von Heber said. "But that doesn't necessarily mean that you are useless to us."

"Mavortian!" Bernard said. He'd thought they were rid of me, free and clear, and here was Mr. von Heber making up some shit to keep me around.

I got to admit, I kind of agreed with Bernard. "How?" I said.

"I don't know," Mr. von Heber said, perfectly cheerfully. "I'll think of something. Why won't you go near the Mirador?"

Fuck. " 'Cause I ain't crazy," I said.

He gave me a look—he knew I was hiding something, same as Ginevra had—then looked at Bernard and let it drop. Smart of him to figure out that I'd let him pull my toenails out one by one before I'd say anything in front of Bernard.

After a minute, I said, "Well, if you got any jobs that ain't in the Mirador, I'll do 'em. I think I'm okay to work again."

"You're still coughing," Mr. von Heber said.

"It's okay." I was going nuts with nothing to do but lay around and stare at the walls.

"I'll think of something," Mr. von Heber said, and grinned at Bernard.

Felix

It took several days, but we ended up where we had both known we would: Shannon's bedroom, in the sprawling territory of the Teverius apartments. Shannon had made a brave statement when he had moved out of these apartments to live with me, and I was not surprised to discover that he had moved back when I had . . . when I had fallen.

His suite in the Teverius wing was familiar to me from the early days of our relationship; I noticed that he had redecorated since then, and that his taste had improved. But the furnishings were the same, and especially the massive curtained bed that had belonged to his great-grandmother Helen Teveria.

We had been to see a play; Thaddeus had protested, but Shannon had said airily that Thaddeus didn't own me, and I would be the better for not moping around his suite all the time. And I did not want to make any attempt to insert myself back into the society of the Mirador. Those of my former friends whom I had seen in the halls had either hastened away in embarrassment or driven me to flight by their extravagant concern. I blamed neither camp, but it was not comfortable.

And thus Shannon had taken me to the Cockatrice, to see Madeleine Scott in *The Singer's Tragedy*. I had not enjoyed the play—Madame Scott's notorious flame-red hair had seemed a mockery, and the play itself a farrago of doleful nonsense—but I had not told Shannon so. I was afraid of displeasing him.

He was sitting on the bed, taking off his boots and dissecting the performance of one of the secondary characters, whose role in the convoluted plot I could no longer remember. Shannon had always favored candlelight in the bedroom—as did I, for different reasons; it lit his hair like a dragon's treasure and made the planes of his face remote and abstractly exquisite. His eyes were shadowed, and without their light, his face seemed like a cruel stranger's. I had never been awed by his beauty before, though I had reveled in it endlessly, but now I thought, Why does he want me?

"Felix, are you even listening?"

"Yes, of course," I said. Malkar had trained me well. "You said Vitellian could have been played with more conviction by a cross-dressed twelve-year-old girl and added a disparaging remark about Edwin Croyland that I prefer not to repeat."

"Prude." He smiled and tossed his boots across the room for his valet to deal with. "Have you *ever* been caught nodding?"

"Not for a long time," I said, forcing myself to smile back.

He held out a hand, half-inviting, half-commanding, and I crossed the room to stand beside the bed. "You've gotten so shy," he said. "Not even a kiss?"

"I'm sorry. What . . ." My mouth was dry; I swallowed hard and tried again. "What would you like me to do?"

His eyebrows went up. "The ingenue doesn't suit you, you know. Sit down, for the love of the saints! I'm getting a crick in my neck."

I sat, obediently. The colors around him were the colors of fire, orange and gold and red. He would not tell me so, but he was angry. Probably he was angry at me; probably I had done something wrong.

"I know," he said, "that we did not . . . part well, and I am sorry for that. But you said you weren't angry at me."

"I'm not."

"Then why are you so standoffish?"

No one, not the Curia, not Thaddeus, had demanded the details of Malkar's ritual, and I had not been forced to tell anyone that he had physically raped me. The devastation his spell had wrought was enough that I supposed no one saw any need to look further for explanations. And without the relentless hammer of questions, I could not say it. I could not confess that sordid, bitter truth, any more than I could bring myself to describe the table in the basement of St. Crellifer's. And because I could not say that touch was pain and disaster, I could not tell Shannon that I was afraid.

"I don't know," I said, tried a shrug, a smile. "You try being crazy for eight months and see if *you* can explain yourself afterward."

The color mounted into his face. "Oh, Felix, I'm sorry. I didn't mean it like that. I just wondered if it . . . if it was *me*."

"No! No, it isn't that. It isn't that at all." And because I did not want to hurt him, and I did not know how else to make him believe me, I leaned forward and let him kiss me.

I had been a prostitute; I had learned how to have sex with men who repelled me. To submit to Shannon was easier by far. I let him run his fingers through my hair; short as it was, it seemed to please him. Remembering fragments of our old routine, our old love, I reciprocated by untying his hair ribbon and unbraiding his queue; unbraided, his hair fell nearly to his waist, running like sunlight through my hands.

He remembered my preferences and snuffed the candles before we began to undress. I was doubly grateful tonight, not merely that he would not be able to see my back, but that he would not be able to see my face. My body could lie; Malkar had often told me that my face was transparent as glass.

Shannon's voice murmured in the darkness, words of love, of passion. I could not think of anything to say in return, but he did not seem to mind.

I lay down on my back, as he wanted me to. His hands touched my face, my neck and chest, stroked across my stomach and thighs. I lay still; I told myself that this was Shannon, who did not want to hurt me, with whom I had made love hundreds of times. His hand caressed the arc of my hip; his lips met mine.

And I couldn't do it. I couldn't respond, couldn't soften my lips to meet his, couldn't raise my hands to touch his body. Shannon liked languorous foreplay, liked to spend a long time in soft, teasing, mounting excitement before the often savage release of our coupling. And all I could think tonight was how long I would have to wait, in cold anticipation, before . . .

I choked back a sob, wrenched free of his hands, scrambled off the bed, already searching desperately for my clothes. I had to get out of here before I started crying, before Shannon realized just how damaged, how broken, I was.

"Felix? What are you doing?"

I said nothing. I dragged on my trousers, wrestled my arms into my shirt, and grabbed my waistcoat and coat off the floor. My cravat, my boots, my underthings and stockings were somewhere, but I didn't want them now. I was shaking in violent all-over tremors, in a way I hadn't since Thaddeus had brought me before the Curia.

"You're not *leaving?*" Shannon said. I could hear him moving. I couldn't bear the thought that he might touch me and fled for the door.

"You bastard!" cried Shannon, who was never vulgar. I wrenched the door open and bolted, overwhelmingly grateful that Shannon's servants were all somewhere else, not witnessing this shameful debacle. And as I fled, Shannon's voice echoed after me: "Don't come back! Don't you dare come back!"

Out in the hall—knowing that my luck was not going to hold more than a few minutes longer, and knowing, too, that Shannon would not follow me—I stopped and fastened the buttons of my shirt and trousers, my hands jittering so badly that the task was almost impossible. I put on my waistcoat and coat, but I couldn't cope with the buttons. I was decent; at this point, surely the Mirador expected nothing more of me. I set off as swiftly as I could for Thaddeus's suite, a rabbit fleeing from a fox.

Around the next corner—and I must have known it was inevitable, for why else waste time on buttoning my shirt straight?—I all but ran into Lord Stephen Teverius.

"Felix," he said, his voice grating.

"My lord," I said and essayed a sketchy, wobbly bow that would have made Shannon laugh.

"You're out late," he said. He eyed my clothes with disfavor and added, "Prowling."

"My lord, I beg your pardon. I will not . . . trouble you further."

"I sincerely hope not. Did I not tell you to stay away from my brother?"

I knew now, I thought, how the pebble felt when it was dropped into a deep well. "I will not trouble you further, my lord."

His eyebrows went up. But although Stephen hated me, he was not as insensitive as his stone façade made him seem. "Pleased to hear it. Good night, Felix."

"Good night, my lord." I could feel him watching me all the way down the corridor, until I turned the corner and was mercifully out of his sight.

Thaddeus and Vida were sitting by the fire when I came in. Gideon had dragged a chair over to the sideboard and was engrossed, with pen, ink, and a dog-eared sheaf of papers, in something that looked like a diagram for a warding spell. They all three looked up when I came in, but none of them commented on my deshabille.

I crossed to the fireplace and stood, hoping that the palpable heat would counteract the ice within me. Thaddeus, Vida, and Gideon continued to watch me silently.

"Have you talked to Sherbourne?" I said abruptly.

"Sherbourne?" Thaddeus's eyebrows went up. "Yes. Why?"

"Would you tell him . . . would you tell him I'm sorry about what I said that day in court? That I didn't mean it? He'll know what you're talking about."

"Can't you tell him yourself?"

"No. I can't." My voice threatened to crack; I stopped, swallowed hard. "If he believes you . . . tell him I'd like to see him again."

"Just out of curiosity, what *did* you say?"

I looked at Vida.

She shook her head. "I didn't hear it, and he won't tell me."

"I don't remember it exactly. But it was monstrous."

"You could have said it was none of my business," Thaddeus said.

I did not tell him that Malkar had once used a spell to make me deaf, dumb, and blind for over an hour because I had refused to answer one of his questions. "What would be the point? I'm sure Sherbourne remembers it word for word."

Thaddeus and Vida glanced at each other, a conversational glance, the sort that lovers who are also friends can share. I turned away, memories of Shannon digging into me like shards of glass. And Gideon said, "Felix?"

I looked at him. He had put his pen down. He said, in his perfect, though heavily accented, Marathine, "I fancy a walk. Would you care to come? I have a pair of slippers you can borrow."

I felt my face redden. But I wanted very badly to get away from Thaddeus and Vida and the things they thought they knew about me, and he was offering me an excuse. So I said, "Thank you," more or less to the floor, and Gideon went and fetched me a pair of scuffed carpet slippers.

"Have fun," Thaddeus said, very dryly, as we left, and I caught Gideon in a grimace of exasperation.

We walked in silence for a while. Gideon was a stranger to the Mirador, and I knew I should be exerting myself to identify landmarks and important rooms, to share the odd bits of history that I could remember. But my throat felt like it was full of ashes, and my eyes were burning, and it was all I could do to keep from the even greater rudeness of forcing Gideon to pretend not to notice that I was crying.

We came to an intersection, where a hallway hung with enameled scales, like the sides of a sea serpent or a dragon, met the Wooden Hallway, and Gideon said, "Where do you like to go?"

"I beg your pardon?"

"You are an inhabitant of the Mirador. Which parts of it do you *like?*"

"Oh," I said. "The battlements."

"Then let us go there."

"All right." I hadn't gone up to the battlements since I had been returned to the Mirador.

There were staircases to the battlements scattered throughout the fabric of the Mirador, though most of them were in the Vielle Roche, leading to the Crown of Nails, the highest ring of merlons. We climbed up, around and around in a dizzying corkscrew, until we came out the narrow door at the top into a night cold and clear. I only then remembered that it was Petrop and should have been raining.

I looked at the stars sailing serene and distant above my head, and for the first time since the beginning of *The Singer's Tragedy,* felt my heart unclench just slightly.

Gideon said, "I have never been much of an astronomer. Where is the Minotaur?"

"There." I pointed. "That red star is Oculus, and see? There's his horns, and his shoulders."

"And his feet. Thank you." I could just make out Gideon's profile; he, too, gazed up at the stars.

After a while, he laughed. "Consider the stars. Among them are no passions, no wars. They know neither love nor hatred. Did man but emulate the stars, would not his soul become clear and radiant, as they are? But man's spirit draws him like a moth to the ephemera of this world, and in their heat he is consumed entire."

"Is that a quotation from something?"

"The *Inquiries into the World's Heart* of Nahum Westerley. An atheist philosopher from Lunness Point."

"Oh. Do you read much philosophy?"

"I read everything," he said, perhaps a shade ruefully. "Since I have come here, I feel like I am drowning in a wealth of books. But the *Inquiries into the World's Heart* is an old friend. I had to leave my copy in the Bastion, where it has doubtless been burned, but I am told there are shops here—in the 'Cheaps' if I understood correctly—where I can buy another."

"You can buy almost anything in the Cheaps. You must have left the Bastion in a dreadful hurry."

"Oh yes. One doesn't sit on a decision like that. Secrets in the Bastion do not stay so for long."

"Why did you leave?"

"Because I had to."

It was gently delivered, but a rebuff nonetheless. I wanted to ask him why he and Thaddeus hated each other and why—that being so—he had not yet left Thaddeus's suite, but I did not have the courage, and he would not have answered me anyway.

I said, "I don't know much about philosophy. My education was almost entirely . . . pragmatic."

"It is either a consolation or the heaviest possible curse. I have never been able to decide which."

We watched the stars in silence for a few minutes longer before Gideon remarked that it was cold, and we went back in.

All night long, I dreamed that Malkar was searching for me, and all night long, I hid from him.

Mildmay

Mr. von Heber was dealing out his cards again.

I'd got used to watching him do it while I was sick, same way I got used to listening to him and Bernard fight. At first, I'd thought he was playing solitaire, like I did when I didn't have nothing better to do with my hands, but when I got so as I could sit up and see the cards, they weren't ordinary playing cards, and the layout he used was really weird.

So after a while—long enough that I figured if he was a blood-witch or a friend of Vey Coruscant's, I'd already know and most likely be dead—I asked him.

He was sitting at the table, like he'd been when I met him, and the sunlight showed up the lines on his face and the gray starting in his hair. I was guessing he was in his seventh septad, but that was only a guess. He said, "I suppose you would call it fortune-telling."

"Okay. For real fortune-telling or to gull the flats?"

"What?"

"Is it for real?"

"Yes, of course," he said, like I shouldn't've had to ask, and that was all the conversation I could handle right then, and I went back to sleep.

But I'd had plenty of chances to watch him since then. His deck of cards was old, old enough that most of them were missing their corners, and some were creased down the middle, and there was one looked like a dog'd been chewing on it. They were about the right size for playing cards, and I recognized the suits—grails, swords, staves, pentacles—but then there were the other cards, the ones with pictures on them, and there was the fucked-up spiral he laid them out in, and there was the way he'd sit and mutter at them for upwards of an hour with his silver watch fob that didn't have no watch gripped in one hand. He seriously spooked me out sometimes.

I would've liked to ask Bernard about it, but there was no point. He'd get too big a kick out of not telling me. So I just watched, and I wondered what Mr. von Heber's cards said about me that made him so sure he had to have me around. Whatever it was, it was the closest thing I'd had to a future since 11 Messidor, and I was even kind of getting to the point that I was glad of it.

He said now, sweeping the cards together, "I've done fortune-telling for money in other cities, but Bernard thinks it would be a bad idea in Mélusine right now."

"Bernard's right," I said.

"Would I get arrested?"

"Dunno. You might."

"That makes things rather unpleasant. You see, that's half our income gone."

"Oh. And I been a drain, ain't I?"

"I don't begrudge it, but it does mean that we don't have the money to hire you."

"That's okay. I mean, I owe you. You got stuff you want done, I'll do it."

"Well," he said, "that's the trouble. I don't."

"You want me to stay, but you got nothing for me to do."

"I will! I just don't yet."

"Then why don't you come find me when you need me?"

"It's not that easy. We don't know this city well, and I may need you . . . without much warning."

He hadn't acted like he was looking for a mollytoy, but it'd been worrying me some, and now was worrying me more. I said, "If'n you're thinking of making a pass, spare your breath. I ain't a whore."

I think it took him a minute to understand me. I saw when he got it, though. His face flushed brick-red, and he said, "Nothing of the sort, I assure you."

"Then what d'you *want?*" In some ways, me and Bernard were an awful lot alike, and it was driving me nuts just as much as him that Mr. von Heber wouldn't say what it was he wanted me to do.

"I don't know yet."

"Why the fuck not? You said you do fortune-telling."

"No form of divination provides precise instructions. I can't read the future in my cards the way I can read about history in a book."

"Why not?" I realized as I said it how it sounded and went on in a hurry, "I mean, I believe you and everything, I just . . ."

"Want to know," he said. He was giving me a weird look. Then he shook his head like a man trying to get rid of a fly, and said, "Well, there's no reason you shouldn't be told. Sit down."

I'd been standing near the door, half-thinking about walking out and not coming back. The only thing stopping me was I knew I didn't have nowhere better to go. So I went over to the table and sat down.

He'd been shuffling his cards while he talked to me—it was a habit he had, like some people crack their knuckles, and he had a flashy box shuffle to go with it—and now he swept his hand across the table and let the cards spread themselves out in a fan, facedown.

"Nice trick," I said, and he grinned.

"Don't pretend you couldn't do it."

"Still a nice trick."

"Oh, I'm good at card tricks," he said, kind of gloomy, like he wished he wasn't. "But here. These are the Sibylline." He swept his hand back the other way, and now the fan of cards was faceup.

"And they tell you the future."

"Yes and no." He folded his hands on the table behind the fan of cards. "They show me the patterns the future is likely to take. They are symbols, not facts. For instance, turning up the Death card—" He edged it out of the fan with one finger, a card painted black with Cade-Cholera's sigil picked out in gold. "The Death card literally means death, but in a reading it may mean stagnation or destruction or the necessity of speaking to a dead person. You see?"

"Sort of," I said. "I mean, I guess so."

"They show the pattern of the future, not the events. And therefore, they show me that you are important to my plans, but they do not show me how."

"They do? How do you find me in them cards?"

"When we arrived in Mélusine, I did readings searching for the patterns that I could trace to reach my goal. And this card"—he slid it out of the fan to lie next to Cade-Cholera's card—"kept showing up. Over and over."

It was one of the picture cards, showing a youngish guy surrounded by swords, all pointing in at him.

"The Knight of Swords," Mr. von Heber said. "He kept showing up, and in ways that indicated he was a person and not one of the more symbolic meanings. So I did a calling, using that card, and you walked through my door. I did clarifications every way I could think of while you were sick, and they all agreed: you were the Knight of Swords, and my plans depended on you." He smiled at me, but it wasn't no nice smile. "You tell me why."

"Fuck. I don't know. But . . . I mean, can't your cards make mistakes?"

"No," he said, so flatly that I jumped. He gave me maybe a quarter smile's worth of apology. "I can make mistakes in reading them, although that doesn't happen very often anymore, but I assure you, this is not a mistake."

"Kethe," I said and rubbed at the back of my neck. "That ain't a nice feeling."

"No, I suppose it isn't."

"It don't bother you?"

He shrugged a little, swept up the cards, and started shuffling them again. "It's my magic," he said. "I trust it."

I don't trust magic. But I didn't say it. I sat and watched him lay out his cards. He didn't talk to me while he did it, but I saw them two cards over and over again, until Bernard came back and Mr. von Heber put the cards away: Death and the Knight of Swords.

Felix

The yellow-eyed man stands in Thaddeus's sitting room, at the edge of the candlelight.

"Hello, Felix. Do you still need my help?"

"Yes. But I thought you couldn't reach me here in the Mirador."

"I found a way around that," he says carelessly. "Will you trust me?"

"Yes," I say, because I have no choice, because I know I am still mad. "What will you do?"

He starts toward me, where I am standing in the doorway of the room I sleep in, moving out of the light entirely. "You must trust me," he says, "and let me do what I need to. Do you understand?"

"Yes," I say, noting uncertainly that he seems to be larger than he was when I dreamed about him before. And I remember him saying that he could do nothing with the Mirador, although now it seems to have become no more than a trivial problem.

"Give me your hands," he says.

I extend my hands and realize, just as it becomes too late to evade his grasp, that he is wearing Malkar's gold and ruby rings.

I try to jerk away, but he is fast, as Malkar is fast, and he traps my fingers.

"Come now, my dearest," Malkar's voice says out of the darkness, mocking and brutal, "don't you trust me?"

I make a convulsive effort to pull free of him, to get out of this dream, to break the spell Malkar has already ensnared me in. From what little I know of it—most of that learned from Malkar himself—oneiromancy, even more so than ordinary magic, is predicated on symbolism, and Malkar has centered his symbolic working on our hands: my tattooed hands, symbols of the Mirador as much as of my own sundered magic; his heavy, clever hands, with their rings glowing like blood and fire. His grip hurts me, and I cannot break free.

Hopelessly, I ask, "What are you going to do?"

"I'm so glad you asked, darling." I feel him in my mind, oily and monstrous and laughing. "You see, I assured the General that, using you as a conduit, I could destroy the Mirador. I do not think he has entirely believed me, and it has been very frustrating these past few months, not being able to find you. Where have you *been*?"

"St. Crellifer's," I say in a gasp of pain, as he wrenches my hands over so that the tattooed eyes on my palms stare blindly upward.

"The lunatic asylum." He snorts, amused. "I am glad they had the sense to bring you back where I could reach you."

"You can't . . ." I say weakly, not even finishing the sentence, as it becomes apparent that he *can*.

He takes my magic, as he has before, as Robert has, as well. The pain is like a flensing knife along my nerves, but I am cushioned by the dream in which we stand; this time I am not ripped free of myself.

The broken Virtu does not interest him; he goes after the spells weakened by its destruction and only imperfectly repaired, the spells of ward and guard that have protected the Mirador for close to two hundred years. He sweeps them aside like a housekeeper attacking cobwebs. In a flourish of malice he kindles fire across the roofs of the Vielle Roche; the Crown of Nails gains its own crown, a halo of fire against the night. I am tugging fruitlessly against his grip, but his hands are like stone.

He is working deeper, searching for the spells of binding that were the first and best of the Cabal's reforms; they created spells that hold the wizards of the Mirador—the magic of the Mirador—together without any conscious effort on any one wizard's part. Those spells make the Mirador formidable, make it more than just a collection of squabbling academics and self-dazzled show-offs. With those spells, we are the Mirador; without them, we are a group of individuals of varying levels of ability and training, and we become, as the old saying has it, only as strong as our weakest link. If he finds those spells, we are doomed; the Empire will overrun us before summer.

He has my magic; I cannot touch it. I have nothing but the madness and damage Malkar himself has given me. But this is my dream, and I do not have to be able to do magic in order to use my dreams. I found the yellow-eyed man, the real one, through dreaming, not through magic.

I change the dream. Instead of Thaddeus's sitting room, we are now standing in the chapel of St. Crellifer. The darkness around us is full of ghosts, and on the walls, St. Crellifer writhes in the seven stages of his martyrdom. His blood drips down the walls to puddle on the floor.

I don't know if I truly believed this alteration would do anything, but it does. Malkar falters, the rhythm of his magic-working broken. I have shifted the symbolism of his spell-casting, and for this one precious instant, his spells will not work.

He forces the dream back into the Mirador—not into Thaddeus's sitting room, which he has never seen in waking life, but into his workroom; my counter to that is reflexive, a frantic gesture of revulsion and fear. We are standing now in the Hall of the Chimeras, on the first step of the dais, but he has lost his perfect mastery of the situation. My right hand is free, and by the terms of his own spell, he cannot proceed until he has caught it again. I put my hand behind my back.

It is a ludicrous situation in the midst of this horror, and Malkar hates to look ludicrous. "Damn you, Felix." His grip tightens on my left hand, grinding the bones together. "Why did you do that?" His hand catches me across the face with blinding force.

But it isn't his hand. I blink, shake my head, realize Malkar's hands haven't moved. His entire attention is focused on the struggle to salvage his spell, and I can feel a ghostly pressure against my right hand, as he tries to reformulate the dream to meet the conditions of his working.

But the strange, invisible hand hits me again, and for a moment the dream doesn't even exist, only blackness and Malkar's desperate grip on my left hand. I can hear someone cursing—not Malkar—and I realize that the waking world is close.

I am slapped again, hard enough that my head rocks and slams against a wall that is not there. Malkar's grip wavers. I jerk back as hard as I can. Malkar's fingers tighten as my fingers slide out of his grip, and I hear three distinct cracking sounds, as the bones of my fingers break. A long, rolling moment later the pain wakes me.

Mildmay

I woke up, and there was Bernard halfway through my door.

"What?" I said.

"The Mirador's burning."

"Motherfuck."

"Mavortian says we have to leave."

"Okay," I said, rolling out of bed, grabbing for my clothes.

"We'll be in the other room when you're ready," Bernard said. He put the candle he was carrying down on the table and left, moving like a man getting back to the important stuff. Hadn't been his idea to come wake me up—that much I was sure of.

I dragged my clothes on fast as I could, and only stopped long enough to stuff my clean shirt and clean linen in a bag—and all of 'em things Mr. von Heber had insisted on buying for me—because I knew I'd be sorry in a couple days if I didn't. Even the Great Fire of 19.7.2 hadn't been able to touch the Mirador. Not so much as a scorch mark.

In the other room, Bernard was cramming things into packs while Mr. von Heber sat and watched, holding his canes awkwardly across his lap. "Good," he said when I came in. "I want a native guide. Which gate should we make for?"

"Which *gate?*"

"I want to get out of the city before the fire spreads. Which gate will be easiest to get to?"

"You're nuts," I said.

I caught the look on Bernard's face, like he wanted to smack me one for lipping off to Mr. von Heber, but Mr. von Heber just said, "What makes you say that?"

"The Mirador don't burn."

"I assure you, it is."

"Not that. I mean, it *don't* burn. Not ever."

"Are you trying to tell me that the city is in a state of panic? I know that already. It's why I want to get out."

"You and everybody else."

"Oh. You mean . . ."

"We won't get near the gates. Prob'ly, I mean, if we just stay up here—"

"No."

"No?"

"Let's just say this is going to be a very bad city to be a wizard in for the next several days. Things are coming loose."

"Oh," I said. "Okay. I believe you. You're saying you gotta leave town."

"Yes. If we can."

"There's ways," I said. But from Havelock, there was really only one way, because everybody in town would be doing the same figuring I was, and everybody who knew about the Arcane—and the half septad ways them tunnels offered to get under the city walls—was going to be down there already. Fuck, I thought, but there wasn't no force to it, because I'd known something like this would happen sooner or later. I'd felt it coming for decads, months . . . since 11 Messidor. "But I got to know how much money you got."

You could have chipped splinters off the silence in the room. I said, "Look. I don't care, okay? It don't make no difference. But the way I know about you got to pay for."

"I see," said Mr. von Heber. Him and Bernard gave each other a kind of look I couldn't rightly figure out, and he said, "About seventy-five gorgons. I have no idea how to translate that into this benighted city's arithmetical system."

Ten septagorgons and five. I wondered, just for a second, how much else he was lying about. "That oughta do. But we'd better hurry."

"We're ready to go," said Bernard. He'd got their packs slung across his shoulders, and now he knelt down in front of Mr. von Heber's chair, so Mr. von Heber could grab him around the neck.

"Can I carry something?" I said. Because, I mean, I was pretty much stuck with the two of them anyway—the slower they went, the slower I went.

"These damn canes," said Bernard, who was getting smacked across the ribs with one and poked in the eye with the other.

"If you lose them," Mr. von Heber said, "I will string your intestines out through your eye sockets."

"I won't lose 'em," I said. "Promise." And he let me take them.

We made it down the stairs okay. The lobby was full of people yelling at the desk clerk, and the streets were Hell. It was a good thing both Bernard and me knew all about getting through crowds and how you make people give you room even when they weren't planning on it, because otherwise we'd never have got off the square foot of sidewalk in front of the Anchorite's Knitting. The Mirador was burning like the world's biggest torch, and you could feel people panicking and feel it spreading like another kind of fire. The noise was like having somebody bash you in the head with a hammer, only it just went on and on and on without even a backswing to have half a thought in.

But finding Phoskis didn't need thinking. He hadn't left the church of St. Kirban in septads, not since he'd run the priests out and settled in. I couldn't recall offhand which god Kirban had gotten himself martyred for, but Phoskis didn't give a shit anyway. The only god he worshipped was the gold standard—Zephyr'd said that once and it'd stuck in my head like it was glued there.

Rue Courante was practically deserted compared with the rest of Havelock, and nobody got in my way up the steps to the church porch. I stopped there, so Bernard could catch up, and offered Mr. von Heber his canes back.

"You think?" he said.

"Yeah. This guy don't like me." Which was so much an understatement as to be most of the way to a lie, but I really didn't want to explain about Phoskis Terrapin and why we hated each other.

"Put me down, Bernard," said Mr. von Heber, and I knew he'd followed enough of what I hadn't said to get the picture.

Bernard didn't argue, for a wonder. Once Mr. von Heber had himself organized again, I pushed open the door. It wasn't locked. Phoskis never locked it, and I'd never figured out if he was making fun of the priests he'd chased out or if he was just too fucking lazy to bother. He knew nobody in Mélusine was stupid enough to make a try at him.

It was dark and quiet and musty in St. Kirban's, and you could smell the river. No panic, no ruckus. The walls were two septad-feet thick, and the world didn't bother Phoskis. There was one branch of candles lit, and I stopped under them.

"Phoskis?" I called.

"Will wonders never cease," said Phoskis, thick and deep, like a giant chewing on gravel, and way too close. Sacred fuck, what was the matter with me that I couldn't smell Phoskis coming? "It's Mildmay the Fox. What are you after, Foxy dear?"

"Passage for three out of the city. What's your price?"

A rumbling, wheezing chuckle. Kethe, I hated him. "Five septagorgons a head."

"You're nuts," I said, and I wasn't just haggling, either. "Ten gorgons."

"I have what they call a monopoly on the market, but I've always liked you, Foxy my boy. Four septagorgons."

"Two septas," I said, because Phoskis was hoping I'd beg and I wasn't about to.

"Three septas. Take it or leave it."

And that was damn near all of Mr. von Heber's money. I glanced at him.

"We'll take it," he said.

"Got a new keeper, Foxy?" Phoskis said, and then to Mr. von Heber, "Stack the gorgons on the hexagonal table to your right."

Mr. von Heber counted them out like we had all the time in the world, and even if he was lying to me about everything including the color of the sky, I loved him for it. No matter what Phoskis said, he hated me just as much as I hated him, and we both knew it. But paying customers were paying customers, and he was too greedy to turn nine septas away, even on account of me.

"Very well," Phoskis said. "Foxy knows the drill." Something skittered out of the darkness and fetched up against my foot. It was a key. I picked it up and said, "Come on," to the other two. I knew the drill, sure, and that was why Phoskis hated me. I led Bernard and Mr. von Heber into the darkness, pretending everything was okay, everything was normal, pretending I couldn't feel Phoskis hating me out there somewhere in the dark. Kethe, he made my skin crawl.

We came to a little, ironbound wooden door, sunk back in the wall like Phoskis's piggy eyes in his ugly face. I unlocked it, and waved Bernard and Mr. von Heber through. You could have curdled milk with the look Bernard gave me.

I stepped through the doorway, took hold of the door handle to pull it shut. "Here," I said and tossed the key toward the sound of Phoskis breathing. I heard him miss the catch just before I slammed the door shut.

Bernard said, "Where in the name of all the powers are we going?"

"The river," I said. There was a shelf of cheap lanterns just to the left of the door. I took one and dug the lucifers out of my pocket to light it.

"The river," Bernard said, like he was sure he'd misunderstood me.

"You just paid Phoskis for a boat. Come on."

Mr. von Heber couldn't manage the stairs—they were too narrow and too slick. So we loaded him up on Bernard again, and I took his canes, and we started down.

I was wondering all the way down—without wanting to, you know how that goes—if Ginevra had still been alive at this point, if she'd heard the scary echoes of her own footsteps, if she'd still thought she was going to get away. Or had they killed her first, wherever they jumped her, and carried her down here like a load of dirty laundry? Stop fucking *thinking* about it, I said to myself, but I couldn't.

The stairs went down a great-septad foot, and you were pressed up against St. Kirban's foundation wall on one side and had nothing but air to hold you up on the other. I could hear Bernard behind me, cursing just under his breath—not panicked or nothing, just muttering. And the farther down the stairs we got, the smaller my lantern looked, because we could see more and more of St. Kirban's huge flooded vaults opening up around us. St. Kirban's ain't the only place where you can hire a boat and not get asked a lot of questions you ain't in the mood to answer, but it's the only one you can get to without going down in the Arcane first. And sometimes that's worth the price Phoskis charges.

Normally, when you go down in the vaults of St. Kirban, you come to a kind of half-assed dock built off the stairs, with Phoskis's little boats tied to it. What with all the rain, you couldn't even tell the dock was there tonight, and the boats—all two of 'em that were left—were bobbing around well past the spot where them dark, narrow, nasty stairs disappeared under the water.

"Good thing we weren't no slower," I said and gave the lantern to Mr. von Heber.

"What are you going to do?" he asked.

"Get a boat," I said and sat down to take off my boots and socks and coat and waistcoat. I got my knife out of my boot while I was at it, because I wasn't in a mood to do Phoskis no favors, particularly not favors that involved me holding my breath while I tried to untie a knot underwater in the dark.

"You can swim?"

"Yeah." Keeper made me learn. She was frightened to death of the Sim—most people in the Lower City are, and most of them can't swim a stroke. She knew a guy who knew how to swim, and every summer she'd drag all of us that had hit our first septad down into the Arcane, where there was another flooded vault—this one had belonged to a chandler's warehouse—and her friend Michin taught us how to swim.

So I ain't afraid of the Sim. I don't like it, though. The smell of it—that nasty, metallic smell like a dead foundry—gets basically painted onto anything it touches. And it's fucking cold. But there was no way back from here. The door up top was locked, and Phoskis wouldn't open it no matter how hard we pounded. He didn't give refunds.

I plunged in, swam out to the nearest boat, cut the rope. I braced my feet against the wall, pushed off, and started towing the boat back to where Bernard and Mr. von Heber were waiting.

That's when something grabbed my ankle.

"SHIT!" I said and got a mouthful of water as it pulled me under. I had my knife. I was just starting to double over, to hack down into the murk and pray I hit it instead of my own damn foot—and it let go.

I thrashed back up—I ain't no graceful swimmer, even when I ain't in a panic—gasping for air. I made it back to the steps in about a half a second, and never mind the fucking boat.

"What the hell?" said Bernard.

"The Kalliphorne. That fat fuck let out the Kalliphorne."

After a moment, Mr. von Heber said, "And what, pray tell, is a . . . did you say 'Kalliphorne'?"

"Take a look at my ankle."

Bernard bent down with the lantern. The Kalliphorne's handprint was clear as daylight, red marks already starting to swell and turn purple. And where its fingers had met, just above the knob of my anklebone, you could see where its claws had torn my skin. And it hadn't even been trying.

"Powers," said Bernard.

"I ain't never seen it. Nobody does and lives to talk about it. It lives down here, and Phoskis lets it out to eat people he don't like. It's why he's got a whatchamacallit."

"Monopoly," Mr. von Heber said. "We have to go back."

"Can't. Door's locked."

"Then we have to go on," Bernard said. "It'll get us for sure if we just sit here."

"Yeah. Fuck." The boat had floated close enough that I didn't actually have to swim for it, just waded down three steps and leaned out—and then splashed back up so fast I damn near tripped myself.

Then I sat down and put my socks on and shoved my feet back into my boots before my ankle could puff up any further. While I got the rest of my clothes on, Bernard got Mr. von Heber and all our stuff in the boat. Then he got in, and I got in. I took the stern, since I knew where we were going and they didn't. I used one of the oars to give us a shove off the steps, and then handed them both forward to Bernard. He started rowing.

"Is it going to attack?" Mr. von Heber asked from the bow.

"Fucked if I know," I said. I thought about it and added, "If it was hungry, I'd be dead."

"How comforting. Is it frightened of anything? Fire? Sunlight? Silver?"

"Not that I ever heard. Phoskis feeds it." Mostly his whores when he was done with them, but I didn't think Mr. von Heber would want to know that.

Somebody, a long time ago, had painted marks on the pillars to show the way. I followed them. The only sound was the splash of Bernard's oars. We didn't say nothing. I was watching the water for anything that looked like trouble, but I wasn't even sure I'd recognize trouble if I saw it. And from the stories I'd heard, it was more likely the Kalliphorne would just come straight up through the bottom of the damn boat.

But nothing happened and nothing happened, and I was beginning to think, even though I knew better, that maybe we were going to get out okay, that it had gotten bored and gone off to kill something else. Then a voice said, "I smelling magic."

It wasn't a person. I mean, it was speaking Marathine and everything, but there were too many teeth in the words and the sound of it was more like a cat crying than anything else. I can't explain it no better than that. The voice was too high-pitched and too low-pitched at once, and it just sounded *wrong*.

Bernard and Mr. von Heber were both looking around, trying to figure out where it was coming from. I pointed—couldn't've said nothing, not even if they'd paid me, the way my mouth had all turned to cotton—and they turned that way, and Mr. von Heber conjured up a witchlight, a blue globe about as big as my fist.

I don't think it would've looked better in real light. It was hanging on to one of the pillars, about three septad-feet from our boat, this black thing like a shadow only half out of the water. It had long, tangled weedy hair. Its eyes caught the light and flung it back—like a cat's again, only they weren't set in no cat's head. It was kind of like a person's head, except for the angle of the nose and the fucking horrible teeth. I could see the way it was gripping the pillar, its claws flexing into the stone like a cat's do into a tree. Kethe, it could have taken my foot off and not even noticed.

After a moment, Mr. von Heber took a deep breath and said, "It is I you smell."

It showed more of its teeth. I wondered if it thought it was smiling. "The Fat One wishing you all dead—most the young foxlike one."

It paused. I said, "That ain't news."

The Kalliphorne looked at us, tilting its head like a cat does just before it pounces. "Trade."

Mr. von Heber said, "What did you have in mind?"

"Not wishing to be eaten, you?"

"No, we would rather not be eaten."

I think it laughed. I can't think of nothing else that weird, ratchety, hissing noise could have been. Then it was serious again, like snuffing a candle. "My mate. Husband." It pronounced the word slowly and real careful, like me trying to get one of Zephyr's words right. "He being sick."

Me and Bernard goggled at each other like frogs.

But Mr. von Heber sounded almost happy. "What kind of illness?"

She hissed. "Sick from magic. Magic curing, nothing else. You curing, I not eating. You going away in silly little boat. Everything okay."

"And if I cannot cure him?"

She bared her teeth again, and this time it wasn't no smile. "I eating young foxlike one. Not eating magic one. Terrible bad luck."

"I don't see that we have any choice," Mr. von Heber said to me and Bernard.

"You could just chuck me overboard," I said.

"No," he said—just like that, flat as a paving stone. Then he called to the Kalliphorne, "We accept your bargain."

She said, "Okay. Following now," and slid off the pillar. Bernard started rowing, and I swung the rudder to follow her.

Bernard didn't have to row for long. The Kalliphorne's den was maybe six septad-feet from where she'd stopped us. I don't know what it was originally, just like I don't know what the cellars of St. Kirban were for, but now it was a shelf of rock sticking out into the water. I wondered how far down it was to the cellar floor.

The boat got closer, and I could see the pits in the floor, a straight row of them about a foot back from the water's edge. I looked up and could just see the glint of metal—the caps on the teeth of the portcullis that, Phoskis said, kept the Kalliphorne from eating his customers. I'd seen the wheel that ran it, in the same half-level basement that housed the furnace. I'd never touched it—Phoskis wouldn't stand for other people near that wheel—but I'd seen him use it, and I knew how light the balance was. Even a fat old man like Phoskis could crank the gate up in the time it took someone to come down the cellar stairs. I hoped someday soon he'd give himself a heart attack doing it.

The Kalliphorne didn't so much as give the portcullis a glance, like it wasn't there. I was getting spooked worse and worse, and I had to ask: "Lady? What if the, um, fat one drops his gate while we're . . . ?"

She made her ratchety, hissing noise again, so I guess she thought I was funny. "Worrying about the Fat One's toy, you?"

"A little," I said. The boat chunked against the ledge.

"Not being. Okay."

After a second, I realized that was all I was going to get. "Oh. Um. Thanks."

She gripped the ledge and hauled herself out of the water. Below the hips, she stopped looking human at all. She had a tail, long and thick and finished with trailing fins, like a burgher's goldfish. As she moved, I saw that her hair grew from a kind of crest that started halfway back on her skull and didn't stop until a good handspan past her hips. She rocked up on one hip and turned to look at the boat, and I saw that while she didn't exactly have tits, she had six nipples. Cat-fish, I thought and had to cough to keep from giggling. Yeah, since you ask, I was spooked bad.

"All coming," she said. It wasn't a question, not even close.

"Give us a minute," Bernard said.

It took some doing, getting all three of us out of the boat without nobody having to take another plunge into the water. The Kalliphorne watched. At least she didn't laugh. When we were out, and me and Bernard had heaved the boat up so it wouldn't go floating off without us, the Kalliphorne said, "Come now."

She dragged herself along the floor—her shoulders and arms were like a blacksmith's. If you looked at her wrong, it was like looking at a baby not quite old enough to crawl, and I was chewing on the insides of my mouth to keep the giggles from getting out.

She kept craning her neck up and back to look at Mr. von Heber, and finally she said, "Not walking, you?"

The canes were back laying in the boat. Mr. von Heber didn't say nothing for a minute, then said, "Like your husband, I have been made ill by magic. Crippled."

She hissed. I guess it might have been sympathy, but I wouldn't bet on it. Maybe it was just that it would've made it even worse luck to eat him. And I wondered how you got yourself crippled by magic and how bad you had to piss off a hocus for it to be worth their while.

The Kalliphorne and her husband had made their den in an old storeroom. It still smelled just a little like cedar chips, under the smell of dead things and water and a weird scent, sort of sharp and smoky and green, like sage, that I was guessing was the monsters themselves. The Kalliphorne's husband was in a kind of nest of water-stained quilts and ragged blankets. He looked just like her, the same dark, greenish skin, the crest of hair, the eyes and teeth and claws, and the tail—which was whipping around like a snake in a death agony. Me and Bernard stopped where we were, half the room away from him.

"Being *very* sick," said the Kalliphorne, and you couldn't miss the worry in her voice.

"Saints and powers," Mr. von Heber said under his breath. Then he said, "Put me down, Bernard." I could see by Bernard's face that it was the last thing in the world he wanted to do, but he did it, leaving Mr. von Heber face-to-face with the Kalliphorne.

Mr. von Heber glanced sideways, and I can't think that thrashing tail looked any nicer from where he was. "I'll need someone to help hold him down."

"I'll do it," I said.

Bernard said, "Do you suppose your fat friend has a way to get down here?"

Me and the Kalliphorne looked at each other.

"Dunno," I said.

"He not coming before," she said, but she didn't sound no more sure about it than I did.

"Then I think I'll keep an eye out." Bernard went back over to the doorway and settled in.

The Kalliphorne crawled over by her husband and caught his hands. She was talking to him, in this language that sounded like a teakettle coming to the boil, and after a little, I could see the tail calming down. And her husband hissed back at her.

"He willing," she said over her shoulder. "Not biting. Coming now, you."

"You still want me?" I asked Mr. von Heber. And that was me *not* thinking about what it would be like to get bit by something with teeth like that.

"I may," he said, making his own way over to the Kalliphorne's husband. "Without knowing what's wrong with him, I don't know what I may have to do to cure him."

"Okay." I went over and crouched down by the Kalliphorne and took a look at her husband. He was maybe a little smaller than her, but not enough to be helpful or anything. I just had to hope the stuff I knew for making guys bigger than me lay quiet would work on him. The bony armor they had across their foreheads and down their noses made it really hard to read their faces. About all I could tell was that he was looking at me. I said, "I, um . . . If it gets bad and I got to hold him still, I ain't sure I can do it so as it don't hurt. Can you tell him I'm sorry now? Just in case?"

"Okay," she said and hissed at her husband. He looked at her while she was talking, then looked back at me and nodded.

"Okay," I said. Fuck, I thought.

Mr. von Heber came up on the other side. He bowed politely to the Kalliphorne's husband, and said to her, "I need to know his symptoms."

The Kalliphorne tilted her head, same way somebody with eyebrows would've raised them. Mr. von Heber said, "The signs of his illness."

"Yes," she said. "Symptoms. He being very hot." Mr. von Heber's hands were moving over her husband's body, testing pulse and temperature and Kethe knows what else. "But also very cold. Needing many blankets." And where the fuck was she getting blankets from? Did Phoskis give them to her? Trying to picture that was enough to make my head hurt. "Sicking up food. Drinking much water. Sometimes sicking that, too. Cramping bad. Being very sick. You fixing?"

"How long has he been ill?"

"Four hours. Never being sick like this. Not him. Not me."

"Four hours. That's strange. Why should he become ill when the Mirador began to burn?"

I said, "I, um."

Mr. von Heber, the Kalliphorne, and the Kalliphorne's husband all looked at me.

"Yes?" said Mr. von Heber.

"The Mirador got warding spells. I mean, like, spells to kill you if you get where you shouldn't."

"Indeed," said Mr. von Heber. "You think those might have something to do with this?

"Dunno. I ain't no hocus. But, I mean, we know *something*'s gone wrong with the Mirador's spells."

"And the timing is uncomfortably precise. I will keep your hypothesis in mind." Zephyr'd liked the word "hypothesis." I remembered him saying "Fancy word for 'idea,'" and grinning like the Man in the Moon. Mr. von Heber shifted around so he was sort of propped up with the quilts and where he could get a good grip on the Kalliphorne's husband's hands. "This may take some time. You will not disturb me if you wish to talk, but I must ask you to move as little as possible. Oh, and Bernard!"

"Yeah?"

"Put out the light. We haven't another, and I don't trust my witchlights tonight."

"All right," Bernard said, like he wasn't sure it was. But he did what Mr. von Heber said to.

It got really dark. I mean, sure, dark is dark, but there's times, like when you're in your own room and you know where everything is, where it don't seem as dark as all that. And then there's times where it's like the dark is breathing down the back of your neck and wrapping itself around you, and you can feel it deciding whether it should eat you starting with the feet or with the head. This was that kind of dark. I was sitting next to the Kalliphorne, both of us next to her husband, and I could smell them, and after a while I could hear her husband breathing, too hard and too fast.

I'm sure she could hear it, too, and maybe it was to get away from that noise that she said, "Young foxlike one?"

"Yes, lady?"

She made her laughing noise and said, "The Fat One hating you very much?"

"Yeah."

"Why this being? He shouting down, telling me about you. Not doing this before. Not telling single prey."

Prey, I thought, and swallowed hard. She'd probably eat me if Mr. von Heber couldn't cure her husband. She might eat me if I didn't answer her question, just for crossing her. But given a choice between her and Phoskis, I'd pick her seven times in a septad. I told her the story.

It started with Lord Stephen's cousin Cornell, who might or might not have had a claim to the Protectorate. Big ugly catfight in the Mirador. Didn't seem like nothing on earth was going to make Lord Cornell Teverius shut up, and what happened in 20.1.7 was somebody decided to find something that would. It was a plot, a big one, and there were people in on it from the Mirador as well as from the Lower City. I don't know how Keeper got connected with those people. If I'd asked, she would've laughed at me and told me to leave the thinking to those that could. And back then, I didn't want to know things like that about Keeper. I was happy to have her doing my thinking for me.

The part I knew about was Phoskis. Keeper got me into St. Kirban's, telling Phoskis I'd "lost my edge" and she wanted me settled with some safe job. It wasn't no secret that Keeper was sleeping with me. So what neither of them said, but they both knew they were talking about, was that I'd be standing surety for Keeper's good behavior, just like going to get a kid out of the Kennel, only the other way round. Phoskis had been leaning on Keeper for months, and this had been made up careful to look like the offer of a truce. And Phoskis took the bait.

I moved into St. Kirban's the next decad. Learned the routine. Hated Phoskis. And hated him more with every passing day. I started praying to Kethe, daily, that this wouldn't last much longer, that I could just kill this guy like Keeper wanted and go home.

It took months, though. It wasn't until a night in the middle of Floréal that Lord Cornell showed up, started banging on St. Kirban's doors like he was set to break them down with his bare hands. Phoskis grunted at me to stop standing around like a fuckwit and open the damn door.

There were two of them outside, a flashie in a panic and a dark guy in livery with one of them smooth faces that don't change whether they've got love or murder going on behind them. The guy in livery gave me the tiniest flicker of a wink, and the flashie panted, "Is this St. Kirban's?"

I stepped aside and let them in.

It didn't take long. Phoskis took his money and waddled away. I took them down to the river, dragged in a boat for them, grabbed Lord Cornell by the hair just as he was off-balance between the boat and the dock, and cut his throat. I gave the body a shove, and it tumbled across the boat's middle seat.

Me and the guy in livery looked at each other a second, and he said, "That went about as well as could be expected. You know the rest?"

"Yeah. You just be sure you say it was a guy in a black boat that ambushed you, and it'll be okay. Phoskis is the only one uses black boats."

"How many of them does he have?"

"Used to have six. It'll be five in a minute."

"Good. I can manage the rest. Lord Cornell Teverius is dead, and everyone will know Phoskis Terrapin had a hand in it."

"That's the plan," I said.

He rowed off. I took one of the boats out a ways, sank it, and swam back. I'd probably have gone a lot faster if I'd known the Kalliphorne didn't give a rat's ass about Phoskis's portcullis.

Cleaned up, tidied away the evidence, and settled in to wait. For preference, I'd've been out the door and halfway to Britomart already, but Keeper'd said no. Wait, she said. Don't let him think it was you. Wait and pick a fight. Let *him* throw you out. And I was still an indiction and a half away from learning not to jump when Keeper said frog.

The news of the murder got to us the next day. The cade-skiffs had found the body, and the boat, and the guy in livery, who was half out of his head with grief and shock—and some damn good acting—and swearing revenge on the man who'd murdered his master, and on the fat bastard who'd led him into the trap. Even the goon who brought the news thought Phoskis had been bought—I could see it in the way he was standing and the shifty look in his eyes. All at once, I saw how I could confuse things even more, and I made like I believed it, too.

Of course Phoskis suspected me, but he saw the way I was watching him, and he thought I was stupid, so I don't think it crossed his mind that I might be acting. Leastways, when the Dogs came calling, he let me hide in the back and didn't say nothing. Of course, he was also lying his face black about not ever having seen Lord Cornell Teverius and most particularly not on the night in question, and he didn't know nothing about boats or rivers or nothing of the sort, officers, so you can see where it might have been kind of hard for him to say he thought he knew who'd done it.

We stared at each other sidelong for two decads, while the Dogs sniffed around the Lower City in this hopeless kind of way—they knew they weren't going to find nothing, but they couldn't say so—and the Mirador made these big speeches about what they were going to do to the murderer when they got their hands on him. Sounded good and didn't hurt nobody. And then finally Keeper sent word that I could come home again. She'd been paid, and half the Lower City believed Phoskis Terrapin had let himself be bought by the Mirador, and just that morning some poor scullery maid in Tamerlane had fallen over a headless body in her employers' areaway, and her employers were the daughter of a cadet branch of the Vesperii and the second son of the President of the Dyers' Guild, so the Dogs had a new flea in their ear. The truth would get out eventually—secrets don't keep in the Lower City—and Phoskis would hate me twice as much, but right then I was so glad I could've sung.

Picking a fight with Phoskis was the easiest part of the whole fucking job. Took about five minutes to get him mad enough to throw me out. And because it was a real fight—between him and me, I mean, and not just a proxy thing for him and Keeper like it was supposed to be—I dragged his poor little whore with me when I went. He was too scared of me to try and stop me, and it hurt him right in his vanity, the way nothing else I could have done would have touched him. Keeper was mad enough to spit nails, but I didn't back down—I think it was the only time I ever got my own way against Keeper, and she fucking well made me pay for it—and in the end she got the girl a job as a 'tween maid in a flash house in Lighthill. A cadet branch of the Gardenii, I think, but I ain't rightly sure no more. Far as I know, she's still there, and that's the one good thing that came out of the whole stupid mess.

Felix

The Hall of the Chimeras. I don't know how I got here. I don't know why my hands hurt.

There are monsters holding me, green and sharp and cloudy and thorny black. "You traitor," says one in Thaddeus's voice, and his hatred washes over me, red and staining.

"Then it wasn't just a dream," I say hopelessly.

"A dream! The Mirador is burning! How in the seven names of God did you do it?"

"I didn't. It was Malkar. He tricked me."

"Malkar! Is that your answer to everything? *Oh, it wasn't me, it was Malkar.*"

His mockery hurts; I say, "But it *was* Malkar. Thaddeus, you don't think I'd do this, do you? Really?" I know there is something I can say, something that will make him believe me, but I don't know what it is.

"I don't know what to think any longer. I don't understand you."

"But, Thaddeus—"

The other monster, the green one, says, "I thought you told me the Curia had him under interdict."

Gideon's voice, the blessed voice of reason—the thing I hadn't been able to think of.

Thaddeus curses in Midlander. "Malkar?" he says to me, but his tone has changed. "Really?"

"I swear," I say, and make some foolish, unguarded movement with my hands. The pain—the fingers on both hands, crushed by Malkar's grip—makes my vision go black; through it, I hear them both cursing, Thaddeus's Midlander oaths of his strange, unnameable god, Gideon cursing in Kekropian, which I don't understand.

"Did Malkar do this?" Thaddeus says. "My God, Felix, I'm sorry. I had no idea—"

"I have never been trustworthy," I say, my own voice distant and dreamy in my ears; the darkness is thickening, swirling around me like cream stirred into tea.

It is too heavy for me. I sink under it and hear nothing more.

Mildmay

After I finished my damn bedtime story, everybody was quiet for a while. I'd almost forgotten about Bernard and Mr. von Heber—I get like that when I'm telling stories, and the dark made it easier—and I wondered what they thought. I'd just proved Bernard right about me five times over, and he was probably thinking now that if he hit me quick and dumped me in the river, it'd be too late for Mr. von Heber to complain.

But before anybody came up with anything polite to say—and before I got too nervous and said something myself—Mr. von Heber's breath hissed in, and the Kalliphorne's husband let out a terrible screech, and before I even thought about it, I'd thrown myself forward to try and pin him down.

The next five minutes, minute for minute, were about the nastiest five minutes I'd ever spent. It was pitch-black, and the Kalliphorne's husband, sick or not, was strong as a fucking ox, and I was scared to death I was going to hurt him *and* that he was going to knock me flying *and* that one or the other of us was going to hurt Mr. von Heber. And the Kalliphorne's husband was still making that terrible noise, and I could hear Mr. von Heber cursing, and he was shouting, "Mildmay, I've got to get his hands! His *hands!*" And I was thinking, Well, fine, just as soon as you can tell me where the fuck they are. And then the tail whacked me upside the head, and I was seeing great blue and purple and red stars, but at the same time I'd got myself oriented as to where I was and where that fucking tail was, and where that meant the rest of *him* was.

And then I'd got him pinned down okay, although he was bucking underneath me in a way that meant it wouldn't be for long, and I said, "Quick, grab his hands if you want 'em!"

I felt what happened next, just through the monster's body. Even though we didn't move, it felt like we dropped about a septad-inch, slam onto the floor.

"There," said Mr. von Heber, and he sounded dog-tired.

"Can I let go now?" I said, and realized the monster wasn't screaming no more.

Right next to my ear, somebody said something in the teakettle language. The Kalliphorne said, "He saying, you moving please. Not comfortable."

"Oh, powers, I'm sorry," I said and got off him—and fell straight over Mr. von Heber.

He yelped, and I said, "FUCK!" because I should've known he was there before I moved, and he said, "Bernard, where the hell is the light?"

"Oh, do you want it now?" Bernard said, all snarky. "I dropped the damn lucifers when you started your hullabaloo, if you want to know, so you're going to have to give me a second."

"Fine," said Mr. von Heber. "Madame, will you ask your husband please if he is feeling better?"

A long bout of teakettles while I picked myself up and moved a little farther away, where I wasn't going to go falling over people without no warning. Then the Kalliphorne said, "He saying, cramps being gone. Fever being gone. Feeling not so sick."

"Excellent," said Mr. von Heber, and Bernard finally lit the fucking lantern.

The Kalliphorne and her husband were holding hands like any courting couple, and you could see they were happy, even if it didn't show up on their faces. Mr. von Heber was looking about as tired as he sounded. I looked at myself. My hands were bleeding from where I'd grabbed hold of the wrong part of the tail. I checked the side of my head. A little blood there, too, nothing too bad.

"I'm not quite sure what that was, but I've lifted it from him. I do not think you will be troubled again."

"Being very kind," said the Kalliphorne. "We thanking very much."

"Thanking," said her husband. He sounded even weirder than she did, even less like a person, and I could see it took him more effort to get the word to come out.

"Then I think we should leave. Working that magic was quite remarkably uncomfortable, and I do not think things in the city are going to improve for some time to come."

"You rowing away."

"Yes," said Mr. von Heber.

"I guiding," she said, in a no-nonsense tone, like she wasn't going to take no lip from us. She said something to her husband in Teakettle, and started out of the room. We followed her meek as anybody could ask for. I saw her go into the water, headfirst and without barely a ripple. Bernard set the lantern, and we got ourselves in the boat and shoved back off the ledge.

The Kalliphorne led us back to the pillar where we'd met her. She caught herself against it and said, "Following painted marks, you?"

"Yes, lady," I said. "I know the way."

"Wishing you good luck."

"Thank you, lady. Good luck to you, too."

"We will all need it," Mr. von Heber said.

"Good-bye," said the Kalliphorne and dropped off the pillar.

"Good-bye, lady," I said, then shouted after her, even though she'd already disappeared, "You want out, go to the cade-skiffs—tell Cardenio I sent you!" And I don't got no fucking idea why I said it neither, except how much I hated Phoskis, and I knew Cardenio would help her if anybody would, and maybe I was a little dizzy with not being eaten. And I was betting she heard me, even if I couldn't see her.

"Start rowing," I said to Bernard.

He rowed and I steered, and we followed the marks without saying nothing for a long time.

Finally, like it was against his better judgment, Bernard said, "Is that story you told true?"

"Yeah," I said.

"You murdered a member of the House of Teverius?"

"Yeah."

"*Why?*"

"For shame, Bernard," said Mr. von Heber. "Weren't you listening?"

"Dammit, that's not what I mean!"

"You ever been a kept-thief?" I said. I should've had the sense to keep my mouth shut, but I didn't like Bernard, and my head hurt and my hands hurt, and sometimes you get off your own leash, you know?

"No, of course not."

"Then don't be so fucking quick to judge."

Mr. von Heber said, and maybe it was half an apology, "We don't have kept-thieves in Norvena Magna."

I said what Zephyr'd always said about kept-thieves: "It's a southern perversion."

And maybe they heard something funny in my voice, because after that they left me alone.

It was almost dawn when we came out through the Hellmouth. I glanced back north and saw the Mirador still sort of smoldering, like its own damn funeral pyre. The smell of fire was everywhere, and if anybody'd cared to lay odds, I would have bet that the tenements in Gilgamesh were burning, and probably there were fires in Simside and Queensdock, too. Fire runs through the Lower City about the same way the Winter Fever does, and once it starts, it's fucking hard to stop.

"What now?" Bernard said.

"Keep to the middle of the river," I said. "The cade-skiffs won't bother us, and most everybody else should be too busy to pay attention." Rindleshin was out there somewhere, and we were going to go sailing right through the middle of his territory, but Rindleshin was scared of the river, like the rest of the Lower City, and I didn't think he'd be near it. The Sim's bad luck, and you stay clear of it when things go wrong.

A couple times, people shouted at us from the banks, but they were just people looking for a way out of town, and we didn't pay them no mind. Couldn't've fit another person in that boat even if we'd wanted to. Bernard found the current—the Sim runs faster once it gets back out in the daylight—and shipped the oars. It carried us through Simside and Queensdock, past the big wharves and warehouses from the days of the Ophidii, when there was more trade than farmers and fishermen up and down the river. And near the city wall, we went past Mad Elinor's Palace, where King Faramond's daughter spent the last indictions of her life, watching the river go past. The ballads say she wept into it, but them windows are awful high up, and even if you hung your head over the sill, I don't think you could be sure your tears got in the river. The ballads also say her son was never told her name—but he knew who she was, and he knew who his father was, and I don't think it's any wonder that King Henry Ophidius was noted for being a little peculiar.

The sun cleared the clouds to the east. The city walls rose over us, like a black bank of clouds themselves, and the river carried us out through the Septad Gate into the St. Grandin Swamp.

Part Two

Chapter 7

Felix

We leave Mélusine underground, like the dead. And the dead are behind us, in the halls of the Mirador beneath its burning crown, rising from their crypts and confines, released at last from the magic that forced them down. No one alive knows the spells that the Cabal used in that, the first decisive strike of the Wizards' Coup; no one in the Mirador has been taught how to work with the magic of the dead. I know a little—what little Malkar would teach me—but I cannot work magic, and I cannot explain what I know, and I do not think anyone would listen to me anyway.

The anger and despair and terror of the necromancers has not abated in all these years, and the creatures of their bidding remember still what they were meant to do. And the warding spells of the Mirador, even those which are not broken, do not work on the dead. Many wizards were killed in the first onslaught, before anyone knew what was happening; among them were Erasmus Spalding, the Witchfinder Extraordinary, and Sherbourne Foss, who had been my friend. The last thing I ever said to him was designed to hurt, and despite what I said to Thaddeus, I find now that I remember my words perfectly: If you want the truth, you bore me, darling. He never even knew I didn't mean it.

It will not be safe to work magic in Mélusine for days, perhaps for months. It took all Gideon's strength of will to perform a minor healing on my broken fingers, and even that slipped and went awry in the working. I can feel the stiffness in my aching, swollen-jointed fingers, and I know that they will never fully recover from what Malkar did.

My vision is warping and splintering again; I can feel the darkness waiting for me, feel myself sliding inch by inch, fingertip by fingertip, back into the world of monsters and ghosts out of which the Curia lifted me. Sometimes when I look at him, Thaddeus has the head of a raven.

I know that I missed huge swatches of the emergency Curia meeting that has led to us being, now, in this ancient tunnel beneath the Road of Ivory. We are going to Hermione, I know that much, where there is a long-disused, long-decayed wizard's tower, which the other wizards intend to wake and to use to work with the sundered and twisted magics of the Mirador. I, of course, will be no help; I have been brought along because it seems to be the point from which I can do the least damage. I am dangerous baggage, and the flatly hostile looks the guardsmen give me show that they know it.

There are six of them; none of them are men I know, and I am grateful for that. They are in this tunnel with us because of Shannon. However problematical, he is the closest thing Stephen has to an heir. Moreover, Shannon's famous—or infamous—charm will be useful in dealing with the Mayor of Hermione. The Mayor's distant kinship to Stephen's dead wife is unlikely, everyone says, to be sufficient to reconcile him to our presence, but Shannon's flattering attentions and the threat of force discreetly symbolized by the Protectorate Guard are hoped to do the trick.

Shannon walks at the head of the column, with Vicky. Neither by glance nor by word has he betrayed any awareness of my existence.

The wizards in the company are mostly the shy, inoffensive scholars who study thaumaturgical architecture, the only ones who have any hope of making sense of the ruins. Vicky also demanded the presence of Gideon Thraxios, who has the most recent information available on the Bastion's intentions and abilities. And Thaddeus is here as the baggage handler, my keeper. I did not miss the acrimonious arguments over that; Thaddeus did not want to come.

The tunnel is straight, level, and dry, and smells only faintly of sewers.

The guards, taking their duty seriously, have arranged themselves in the front and rear of the party. Their lieutenant is young, tall, hatchet-faced and eager, and (I think) already half in love with Shannon. I keep my head down and try not to force anyone to notice me.

But Thaddeus is not satisfied by my silence. He keeps asking questions, about my dreams, about Malkar, about the catastrophe for which I have been the conduit. I am painfully aware of the guards and the other wizards listening, but I cannot tell Thaddeus I don't want to talk about it. I have no right to refuse him information—not now, not after this latest disaster—and if the colors around him suggest that he is aware of my discomfiture and enjoys it . . . I am mad, I tell myself, and shut my eyes against the colors.

But still, I am grateful when Gideon drops back to walk on Thaddeus's other side and starts a low-voiced argument in Kekropian. I catch my own name once or twice, and I can guess the general thrust of their debate. I wish, miserably and without force, to be dead.

It is seven miles from the Mirador to Ivory Gate, a mile beyond that to the end of the tunnel. We walk steadily, though not very fast; the horrors of the night are visible in gray, haggard faces and staring eyes. It is an hour past dawn when we finally reach the spiraling ramp that takes us up into the daylight world, revenants ourselves.

The egress from the tunnel is concealed within a courier's way station. Courier horses are not stabled within Mélusine, where at certain times of day and in certain directions, a man on foot can make his way more swiftly and more safely through the congested traffic than a man on horseback. The station officer does not seem surprised to see us, whether because a messenger has reached him from the Mirador or because he has been watching the Mirador's roofs burn all night and is smart enough to draw the correct conclusion, I do not know. Obedient to the letter of authorization from Stephen that Vicky carries, he empties his stables for us and gives careful and precise directions to the lieutenant for finding the courier station between here and Hermione.

Most wizards, being sedentary creatures, ride with the grace of so many sacks of potatoes. Malkar taught me to ride, long ago in Arabel, and at least I do not disgrace myself in the confusion of the stableyard. My hands hurt, but Gideon's healing, warped though it is, has done its work, and they are usable. I am glad that in the chaos no one thought to accuse him of heresy. I hope that it will not occur to Thaddeus later.

I hope that later I will still understand why it is important.

Mildmay

What you're supposed to do when you hire a boat from Phoskis is take it all the way down to Gracile, where he's got a goon who bags it and brings it back to Mélusine. The more I thought about it, though, the more that looked like a really bad idea. The goon in Gracile knew me, and he knew Phoskis hated me, and I didn't have no way to know if Phoskis had ever said, Oh, by the way, if Mildmay the Fox shows up, wring his neck for me, okay?

I said as much to Mr. von Heber, and I guess he'd been thinking about how lucky we'd been that the Kalliphorne had happened to have a use for us—besides being lunch, I mean—because he said, no fuss, "What do you suggest?"

"We ditch the boat and walk."

"Can we? The ground looks none too stable."

"Quicksand ain't gonna be our problem."

"No?" said Mr. von Heber, and Bernard was giving me the hairy eyeball again.

"Shit," I said. "There's things in the swamp."

"What kind of things?"

"You know. Gators. Ghouls."

"Charming," said Mr. von Heber. "And you think ghouls are better than a 'goon' in Gracile?"

"Yeah. We can maybe avoid the ghouls."

"Oh," said Mr. von Heber. "Yes, I see."

" 'Sides, you're a hocus, ain't you? You must got spells for this sort of thing."

"I might, but there's no guarantee just at the moment that they will work. The magic of the Mirador is thrashing around like a snake in its death convulsions."

"I still think we got a better chance. We can make for Alchemic—there's a hotel there that ain't too bad." I waved a hand westward and south. I'd been to Alchemic on Keeper's business a time or two, and the dead-eyed woman who ran the Long Time Coming would take your custom if you were dead yourself and rotting to boot. She didn't give a fuck so long as your money was good and you didn't cause no ruckus.

"Well, Bernard?" said Mr. von Heber.

Bernard didn't like none of it, and the look he was giving me said he knew who to blame. "You're the boss," he said, sullen as an overloaded mule.

"Yes," said Mr. von Heber, "I am. Mildmay, if you can find a suitable place for us to disembark, I think you should."

"Fine," said Bernard.

"Okay," I said.

There wasn't nothing real "suitable" anywhere in the marshes, so I just picked the next piece of bank that looked like it was more or less solid and swung the rudder. The boat dug its nose into the mud like it was looking for something, so it turned out to be a good thing we wanted to ditch it, because we would've had a fuck of a time getting it free again.

Bernard made real heavy weather of getting Mr. von Heber out of the boat, and the packs out of the boat, and how were we going to carry all this shit halfway to Vusantine. And finally Mr. von Heber said, "The longer you stand there complaining, the farther your boots are going to sink into the mud, and the more likely you are to lose one. At which point, I assure you, I will start laughing and probably not stop."

Bernard gave him a look like black tar and said to me, "You'd better help carry."

"Sure," I said, and he loaded me down with as much as he thought he could get away with. But he had to carry Mr. von Heber—no way could he use his canes on stuff like this—so I actually figure I didn't come off too bad.

Now, you've got to understand, I've always hated the St. Grandin Swamp. St. Grandin is this guy who got harrowed to death, and I don't know if it's his swamp because he got harrowed out there, or because it's the sort of land nobody can use a harrow on, or some other reason, but it suits anyway. You can't build nothing in the swamp—every once in a while somebody comes up with some wild idea about drainage and shit like that, but people just laugh at them—and I think half the plants that grow there are poisonous. The trees are these nasty swoony kind of things and the wood ain't good for nothing. And people dump things there that they don't want nobody finding. You know, like bodies. And there's been ghouls in the swamp since at least the days of King Mark Ophidius, and nobody's ever figured out what to do about them, neither. All them great necromancers, like Bathsheba Dunning and Fortinbras Allison and Loël Fairweather, and they never did nothing about the ghouls in the St. Grandin

Swamp. And the Mirador now just says as how they're folktales, and there ain't no ghouls, and ain't them suckers in the Lower City a bunch of superstitious flats?

No ghouls my ass.

I'd been hearing stories about the St. Grandin Swamp since I was old enough to pay attention, and if I tried to tell you I wasn't the least little bit nervous when we started away from the boat, I'd be a liar. Truth is, I was scared half to death. Most of what I knew about dealing with ghouls was what Keeper said: stay the fuck away from them. I'd picked up little bits and pieces of stuff from Lollymeg and Zephyr and the crazy guy in the Arcane who made his living scavenging in the swamp, but mostly I did what Keeper said. I wondered how much Mr. von Heber knew about ghouls, but I didn't feel like making a noise loud enough to find out.

We headed for Alchemic, me and Bernard picking our way as best we could, and nobody saying nothing. I was listening so hard I was giving myself a headache—half for ghouls and half for gators, 'cause you don't want to fuck around with them, neither, although mostly they don't go after people on land along of how mostly it don't work. Pretty soon—like within a septad-foot—me and Bernard were muddy up to the knee, and by the time the sun said it was the septad-day, we were all three of us covered in mud from head to toe, mostly because of this one bad patch where Bernard had got snarled up in some kind of bramble and taken this tremendous header, him and Mr. von Heber both. It had taken a really loud quarter hour to get them both free again, and I was worried about what might've heard us. But Bernard had been so scared he might have hurt Mr. von Heber that he forgot he was pissed off at him, and I guess that was something.

At the septad-day, we stopped and rested. We didn't have no food, but Mr. von Heber had this little spell he could do to make the water okay, and he even got it to work, although it took him four tries, and I could see what he meant about the Mirador's fucked-up magic fucking him up. But it did work in the end, so at least we didn't have to be thirsty on top of everything else.

When we went on, I started really hearing things, not just listening so hard everything sounded bad. When you actually hear something, you know the difference. I was walking ahead of Bernard, because I knew where Alchemic was and more or less how to get us there, but I started walking slower and slower, trying to pinpoint where the thing was that I heard, and Bernard caught up to me.

"What is it?" Mr. von Heber said, quiet-like.

"Dunno," I said. "I hear something, but I ain't sure—"

And then I was sure, and I wished I wasn't.

The thing about ghouls is, they're fast. They ain't like the Walking Dead in stories, where the hero can always outrun 'em even if he can't do nothing else. You can't outrun a ghoul.

It came barreling at us out of nowhere, and my reflexes sent me one way and Bernard's sent him the other, and it missed us both. I don't know if it had been male or female when it was alive. It was smallish, and a kind of blackish red all over. The only thing I really remember is its eyes. They were the color of blood, and they were angry. Oh, and the teeth. I'd like to forget the teeth, but I don't suppose I ever will.

It made this horrible kind of yowling sound when it figured out we'd both dodged, and it swung round. And then it just stood, looking at me, then looking at Bernard and Mr. von Heber, then looking back at me. That's why I remember the eyes so good, the way its head came round and those eyes were glaring at me like pure distilled bottled hate. It wasn't just hungry. It was pissed off that it was dead and we were still alive.

The only knife I had was the butterfly knife I kept in my boot, and right then it seemed about as much good as a toothpick. But if Bernard was going to get his sword out without getting his arm bitten in half, he needed a distraction, and that had to be me, because there was no way I could kill that thing with a butterfly knife. And, I mean, there wasn't nobody else.

"You gotta cut its head off," I said, not looking at Bernard because I didn't dare take my eyes off the ghoul. Its head was swinging faster now, like it was trying to make up its mind.

"I hear you," said Bernard.

"Okay," I said, and came up out of my crouch with my knife ready.

And even then I was very damn nearly too slow. It seemed like the fucking thing was moving before I was, and my knife came up straight into its stomach—which if it had been anything normal, would've been the end of the argument right there. But the ghoul just yowled again and tried to get its teeth into my throat. I couldn't swear that there was anything going on in my head at all, but if there was, it ran, oh, Kethe, don't let it bite me. Ghouls got the filthiest mouths this side of cottonmouths, and anything it bit I knew for a fact I was going to lose. I got my other hand under its chin and pushed straight back, with my fingers tucked down against my palm so it couldn't bite *them,* and it yowled and spat, and its fingers were sinking into my shoulders like I was made of butter. I would've broke its neck, except it wouldn't've done me no good. The ghoul wouldn't care.

And then Bernard said, "Let go!"

I wasted about half a second hoping that he knew what he was doing, then let go of the ghoul's head. It was already aiming for my throat again when Bernard's sword came around in a flat sweep and buried itself in the ghoul's neck. The ghoul shrieked, and its head fell over to its left shoulder—Bernard had got through about half the stuff in its neck, including its spine—and this black gunk that wasn't really very much like blood started spurting everywhere. Bernard was cursing steadily, and the ghoul was still trying to figure out how to bite me—and it hadn't let go of me neither.

"The angle's bad," Bernard shouted over the noise the ghoul was making.

"Fuck," I said. But I saw what he meant. To take its head off now was going to take a chop straight down, and he didn't have no way to get no power behind it from here. I had this horrible flash of a thought of me standing there while Bernard sawed the thing's head off like it was a loaf of bread, and then I did the only thing I could think to do. I dropped to my knees, figuring either it would go down with me and Bernard could get his angle, or it'd let go of me and then we'd all be better off.

Ghouls are fast, but they ain't bright. It still wanted my throat and hadn't figured out yet that it couldn't get there. It bent its knees right along with me, and its head lolled forward, the teeth still snapping and grinding, trying to get close enough to bite me.

I didn't like him none, but Bernard did know what he was doing. We'd barely touched the ground when his sword came crashing down like a judgment, went through the rest of the ghoul's neck and buried itself somewhere around the collarbone. The head fell forward off the body. I lurched back, but the hands were still clamped down on my shoulders, and the body came with me, and I fell over.

Bernard had to break the thing's fingers, one by one, to get me free of it, and I had these black and purple bruises that lasted a decad and a half. We were both covered in its black, swampy blood before I could stand up again, and when he kicked the body over on its back, we saw that the ghoul's head had buried its teeth in its own thigh.

"Kethe," I said and just about sat down again without meaning to.

"You all right?" Bernard said.

"Yeah. Sure. I mean, it's just that . . . that was aiming for me."

Bernard cussed up one side and down the other in Norvenan, then said, "Thanks for drawing it off."

"Thanks for taking its head off."

"Are there likely to be more of them?" said Mr. von Heber.

"Fuck," I said, "I don't know."

"Well, they must not hunt in packs, or more of them would've shown up by now," he said, and Bernard went over to start collecting their stuff.

I picked up the things I'd dropped, including my knife. It was still the only knife I had, even if it was covered in black gunk I didn't even want to think about. I cleaned it off as best I could before I closed it, and stuck it back in my boot.

And then we went on—mud and mosquitoes and every once in a while we'd hit a clear patch and I'd look back and there'd be this nasty gray smudge over the Mirador and I knew they hadn't got the fires out yet. But we didn't have to fight off no more ghouls. Maybe they saw what happened to the first one. Or maybe there were better pickings somewhere else. The Road of Chalcedony—and once I'd remembered this I couldn't stop thinking about it, even though I was trying to—for part of its length it runs along a causeway through the eastern edge of the St. Grandin Swamp, and if I was a ghoul and I was hungry, that's sure where I'd be.

We made it to Alchemic about the tenth hour of the day. The Long Time Coming was full up with people out of Mélusine. "No room," Jeanne-Phalene said. But she recognized me—people do, I can't help it, it's the fucking scar—and said, "You want work?"

"What kind of work?"

"Ricko in the bar—" She jerked her head sideways at the wall where somebody a long time ago had knocked a doorway between the hotel and its next-door neighbor, The Mule's Daughter. "He's run off his feet, and Lev the bouncer's gone haring off to the city to see if his boyfriend's okay. You wanted to do him a favor, I imagine he'd find you and your friends a place to sleep."

"Thanks, Jeanne-Phalene," I said, and we went next door, where the bartender fell on us like long-lost cousins. I can tend bar okay, and Bernard admitted as how he'd done his share of bouncing, and there was this kind of pause, and I could see Ricko thinking that Mr. von Heber wasn't no use to him and could maybe be used to bargain us down, and I said in a hurry, "He can tell fortunes."

"Fortune-telling, huh?" Ricko said, giving Mr. von Heber the hairy eyeball. "What kind?"

"No magic," I said. "Just cards."

"Oh, cards are okay. And, powers, anything to keep the fuckers quiet. Lemme see if I got a place you can lay up."

He went into the back, and Mr. von Heber said, not nicely, "Mildmay."

"What?"

"You know perfectly well—"

"You don't *got* to use magic, do you? And you said you did it for money sometimes."

"It's not that," he started, but Ricko came back, and he never did explain what'd set him off. I could guess, though. He never liked things that weren't his idea first.

Felix

We come to the courier station hours after sunset, and it is only by the indefatigable efforts of the lieutenant that we find it at all. He sometimes has the head of a hunting hound; more and more often as the shadows lengthen and Thaddeus and Vicky begin a snarling, acrimonious interchange that is not even an argument, merely a festering growl, I cannot see him at all. The world is disappearing, piece by piece; the darkness has closed in around me long before the sun sets.

The courier station is full of shadows; some of them move. I find a chair as close to the hearth as I can get. The heat and the light help—or at least I can pretend they help—and I am not in anyone's way. I hope that they will leave me alone.

But I cannot have that. I have never had that.

"Felix!" It is Thaddeus's voice. I wish I could pretend not to hear him, but I turn. The raven-headed monster is beckoning to me, and I still remember that that is Thaddeus, that the raven's glittering black eyes and the storm cloud of red and purple surrounding it are only my madness.

I get up, leave the fire. I can see the darkness winding around me like silk ribbons, streaming and flapping in a wind that is not there.

The raven is sitting at the broad, scarred common table. The stone lioness is sitting across from him; she wears Vicky's rings. They both watch my approach, with eyes unblinking and pitiless.

"Sit down, Felix," the raven says, but I no longer believe the friendliness in his voice. Once, I know, Thaddeus and I were friends, but the colors tell me he does not like me now. He does not want to be here, and it is my fault he is.

I understand wizards; if I do not cooperate, I will be coerced. I sit.

The lioness says, brisk, no-nonsense, Vicky dealing with a distasteful subject, "How did Malkar do it?"

"Do it?" I say. My own voice, a tenor as light and fragile as half-rotted gossamer, sounds not merely mad, but half-witted.

"How did he reach you?" the lioness says. "How could he put a compulsion on you? How did he *do* it?"

"I don't know."

"Come now," says the raven. "You must have *some* idea. You were his student."

"I don't know! I really don't."

"We have to find out," the lioness says. "What if he does it again?"

"It will kill me," I say, the truth emerging unexpectedly from the darkness. "It has already driven me mad."

They eye me suspiciously and with distaste.

"You have the head of a raven," I tell the monster who I hope is really Thaddeus. "You are a lion made out of granite," I say to the other. "The colors around you are red and purple, streaked with black, shot through with green. You are angry, and you dislike each other, and you would rather drown me in the river and be done with it."

"Really, Felix, these histrionics are pointless," the lioness says.

"I don't think he's lying about being crazy," the raven says, and his callous tone cuts through me like knives.

"Will you let us look?" the lioness says. Vicky has ever been single-minded.

"I cannot stop you," I say and lay my hands, palms up, on the table.

"Powers, Felix, must you be such a bastard about it?"

"But I *can't* stop you. I'm still under interdict."

"I was being polite," she says, her voice a growl like millstones grinding.

"Oh, leave it be," the raven says. "Let's just get this over with."

Their examination is excruciating. I do not faint, although there is a long, slow space of time when I think I may; I emerge from the thunderous red-shot blackness to find my hands pressing palms down on the table, as if it can anchor me, and the lioness and the raven arguing across me. Their voices keep dissolving into howls and roars, so that I cannot follow their debate clearly, but I understand that they have found something strange in the Cabaline spells, something small, something the Curia overlooked—something, the raven says, that no one would find without already knowing it was there. They call one of the other wizards over, a badger, round and amiable with small, blinking eyes. There is more debate, but I am hearing fewer and fewer words in the dreadful booming that reverberates through me as if I were the clapper of a bell.

The raven catches my shoulder, shaking me, and his voice comes clear: "Felix!"

I stare at him. I want his hand off my shoulder, but I cannot move. I am no longer sure that it is safe.

"Did Malkar ever cast any spells on you?" I wince at the exaggerated patience in his voice; he must be repeating himself for at least the third time.

"Yes," I say, because it is true.

The lioness and the badger mutter like the dying echoes of thunder. The raven lets go of me. I want to leave the table, but I am afraid they will drag me back. And no one else cares.

The truth coalesces around me like a layer of ice. No one cares. I have no friends among the monsters and shadows. Even if I could get someone to believe me, believe in the colors and monsters and darkness and pain, they would think it is no more than I deserve.

And maybe that is true.

Mildmay

It was well past the septad-night when me and Bernard and Ricko got the last pissed-off drunk shoved out the door and we could go to bed. Ricko'd cleaned out a space in one of the storerooms, and Jeanne-Phalene had chipped in blankets and stuff. She got some kind of kickback from Ricko, but I ain't exactly sure what their deal was.

Mr. von Heber'd done okay. I think people are crazy, myself, but since the cards weren't magic, they were falling over themselves to find out what they said. If we'd said they were magic, or been dumb enough to admit Mr. von Heber was a hocus, the best we could've hoped for was to get run out of town on a rail.

Mr. von Heber looked up from counting his take when me and Bernard came in, and said, "We've got to do something about your hair."

I was getting punchy with lack of sleep, and it took me a minute even to understand what he'd said. I said, "What?"

"It's looking very . . . peculiar."

Bernard gave me this look and said, "I can think of some other words."

"I think you should strip the dye out of it," Mr. von Heber said before I could get my act together to tell Bernard what he could do with his words.

"You're nuts," I said.

"Whatever it is that you use, it's not going to be easy to come by outside of Mélusine."

"How long you planning on being gone?"

"Who says we're coming back?"

I looked at him for a while, thinking things through. "You gonna start paying me?"

"I thought you admitted yourself to be in my debt."

"You just upped the stakes—and don't try and act like you don't know it."

"What does it matter to you? You have nothing holding you in Mélusine."

That hurt because it was true. "It's still my home. I mean, I wasn't ever thinking . . ." But I couldn't find no good way to say what I meant.

"I will reward you for your service," Mr. von Heber said.

"Them's weasel words." That sort of thing sounds great in stories, but when somebody trots it out in real life, you'd better watch 'em close, because they're fixing to pull a fast one.

"I can't offer you a salary," he said, sharp enough that I knew I'd called him on something he'd thought he could get away with.

"You want me to leave Mélusine, you'd better offer me something more than 'The cards say you're important.' "

"Can't this wait?" Bernard said. "I don't know about the two of you, but I'm tired. Fight it out tomorrow."

"Whatever," I said.

"I am crushed by the rebuke of your common sense," Mr. von Heber said to Bernard, which I thought was snarkier than it needed to be, but at least it meant we could get some sleep.

I had this weird dream that night. I dreamed about my mother.

You got to understand, I don't really remember her. I got sold to Keeper when I didn't have no more than three indictions, and most of what I knew about my mother is what Keeper told me, and that ain't much. So I knew she was a whore, and she had red hair and yellow eyes, like Jenico Sun-Eyes in the stories, and I knew the weird fucking thing she gave me for a name. And I knew her name was Methony. Keeper said she had a funny accent, but I never had a clue about where she was from.

So I don't remember her, but every once in a while, I'll have a dream, and she'll be in it. I had nightmares for indictions after Keeper told me how my mother died, that were just dreams of her burning. Not screaming or nothing, just burning and burning and staring at me out of the fire with eyes like a wolf's. And I'll have dreams where I'm in some flash house and I'm supposed to be stealing something, only I know my mother's somewhere in the house, and I can't do nothing until I find her. Mostly I don't find her in those dreams, though every once in a while, I'll open a door and there'll be a red-haired woman staring out a window. And that's when I wake up.

This dream, I was in the Cheaps, outside the leather-workers' shop. I was waiting for Ginevra, but I knew she wouldn't come. But it wasn't no big deal, and anyway she *might* show up, so I was leaned against the wall watching people go by. I saw Margot and Lollymeg and Crenna. Anna Christina and Elvire walked by, talking like they were old friends. I saw Zephyr across the way, but he didn't notice me waving at him—nose in a book like always. Cardenio was there for a while, waiting with me, but he didn't say nothing. I lost the thread of the dream there for a while because I was trying to say I was sorry for being such a prick, but he didn't seem to hear me, and after a while Scabious darted out of the crowd and tugged on his sleeve, and they both waved at me and left. I remember thinking, It's okay, he don't seem mad, and I'll apologize next time.

I saw some more people go by, most of them dead, and then the door of the leather-workers' shop opened, and my mother came out.

I can't tell you what she looked like—I couldn't really see her, even when I was staring straight at her—but she stood next to me and said as how she was sorry she'd let me be sold to Keeper.

"It's okay," I said. "I mean, it could've been worse."

That made her even sadder, but I didn't know why. She was trying to explain to me what had happened, only she was a ghost and couldn't use real words, and I was still looking for Ginevra, so I wasn't paying attention and kept missing what she wanted me to understand. Even in the dream I wanted to smack myself for it, except there was something important I had to tell Ginevra, something really important, and it was hard to see people in the crowd.

Finally, my mother sighed and started to walk away toward the flower market. But she stopped and came back and stood in front of me, and all I can tell you is how yellow her eyes were. She reached out and touched my scar, and her fingers were so cold they woke me up.

❧

It was nearly the septad-day. Looked at in daylight, there wasn't nothing I could do about the mud and stains on my coat and trousers. I was wondering where Mr. von Heber and Bernard were—I'd heard 'em get up and go out, about the time Cardenio went off with Scabious—and whether I could talk Jeanne-Phalene into giving me some breakfast, when they came back. They had breakfast with them, and secondhand clothing from the store run by Jeanne-Phalene's head housekeeper's second cousin. It was all clean, and it didn't fit too bad.

We changed clothes and ate, and while we were eating, Mr. von Heber said, "This town has more apothecaries and alchemists than any town I've ever been in."

"Poisoners' town," I said.

"I beg your pardon?"

"Didn't you know that?"

"Know *what?*"

"All the court poisoners—back when they had 'em—came from Alchemic. All the good ones, anyway. Quinquill and Godiva Frethwarren and Merleon the Halt. All from Alchemic."

"Powers," Mr. von Heber said.

"It's the swamp," I said. I think my dream had made me nervous. "Stuff grows there that don't grow nowhere else 'til you get south of St. Millefleur. And I heard there's stuff there that don't grow nowhere else at all."

"Interesting. That certainly explains why I didn't have any trouble getting a powder that should deal with your hair."

"We didn't decide we *were* 'dealing' with my hair," I said. I try not to lose my temper with people, because it's too easy to hurt somebody you're mad at, but Mr. von Heber was really starting to piss me off.

They both looked sort of taken aback, and I thought, I been letting these guys walk all over me like they own me.

"I have come up with an arrangement," Mr. von Heber said, almost nervously.

"Let's hear it."

"One-third of whatever money we make is yours. When we don't have any money, of course, this means you don't get paid, but that doesn't seem egregiously unfair."

I wanted to ask what "egregiously" meant, but I didn't say nothing.

"What more do you want?" And I was glad to hear how pissed off he sounded.

"I want to know what you're doing. What you want Felix Harrowgate for. I ain't leaving Mélusine for a pig in a poke."

"Your gratitude doesn't stretch very damn far at all," Bernard said.

"Shut up, Bernard," said Mr. von Heber. "He has a right to be curious." But he didn't look no happier than Bernard did.

I'd reached the end of where I gave a rat's ass what either of them thought. All my choices looked basically shitty from here, and I wanted to know if going back to Mélusine on my own—probably to starve to death in a gutter in Ruthven or something—was really going to be worse than whatever the fuck it was Mr. von Heber wanted me for.

He heaved this big sigh, like I was asking him to start yanking his own toenails out, and pulled the locket he wore out of his shirt. I'd seen it before, but I'd figured it for some hocus thing like his watch fob, and I hadn't wanted to know no more. But now he pulled it off over his head and opened it and handed it to me.

It was a miniature, a nice one, of a Norvenan-looking girl. She had that white-blond hair, all in curls around her face, and her eyes were a kind of gray-blue color. She was pretty. I priced the locket at maybe a septagorgon and handed it back.

"Anna Gloria Pietrin," Mr. von Heber said.

I raised my eyebrows and waited.

"She died twenty-five years ago. We were engaged to be married."

"Sorry," I said.

"She committed suicide in Myro. She was abandoned there by the man who did this," and he waved a hand at his near-useless legs. "He seduced and betrayed her. His name is Beaumont Livy, and my purpose is his death."

Fuck, I thought. He really does think he's in a story. "How you gonna do that?" I said.

"I don't know," he said, and he gave me a nasty, nasty smile. "The strong divination I performed at the turn of the year gave me the name of Felix Harrowgate, and the cards have brought me you. There. Now you know as much as I do."

Yeah, right. But I hadn't lost sight of him being a hocus, and I knew I couldn't push much further without getting myself in some serious trouble. "Okay. So you're looking for this Livy guy to kill him. And you don't know where he is?"

"Felix Harrowgate can lead me to him," he said. Whatever a strong divination was, it sure seemed to work just the way he said divination didn't. But I didn't want to get into that, either, and at least now I knew that he had a goal, that there was going to be a point where he said, "Okay, we're done," and I could go home.

"Okay," I said.

"Okay?"

"You want to hire me to help you kill this Beaumont Livy. You're offering a third of whatever money you've got by the time we're done. Okay. I'll do it."

"You sound like you've done this kind of thing before," said Mr. von Heber.

I shrugged. "You think Cornell Teverius was the only one?"

"Oh," said Mr. von Heber, and it took him a second to get past it. "In any event, here is your third of my take from last night." He dug in his pocket and handed me two half-gorgons and a septacentime piece. "And will you now, for the love of all the powers, let me get that foul dye out of your hair?"

"You're the boss," I said.

Felix

We reached Hermione near dusk. The hotel they chose was called the Chimera Among the Roses, a defiantly royalist sentiment that had probably gotten someone nearly hanged 150 years ago. Not even the lioness cared now, and it was clear that the hotel manager had no idea of what his sign meant. I thought of Magnus.

The wizards commandeered half the hotel, including the private parlor and all the best bedrooms. I observed that Thaddeus was still stuck with the baggage, sharing a room with Gideon and me, the volatile and undesirable elements of the party. I wondered if he had been asked to stand surety for our good behavior, like a thief-keeper retrieving a child from the Ebastine.

Thaddeus was angry enough. He and Gideon argued in Kekropian half the evening, and the colors around them showed me the depths of loathing underneath their sparring. They hated each other, and still I did not know why. I sat on the bed I was sharing with Thaddeus and rubbed at my aching hands. Thaddeus and Gideon ignored me; Thaddeus knew that I was as stupid as an owl about languages, and that there was thus no need to fear that I would understand their quarrel.

I caught occasional words—the Bastion, my name, Malkar's name, the Kekropian word for necromancy—enough to understand that they were still arguing about what Malkar had done and how, about his purpose and the Bastion's purpose behind him. But I was still completely unprepared when Gideon turned and demanded, "Felix! What do you think?"

Thaddeus snorted. "You'll get more sense out of the hotel cat. Besides, Lady Victoria and I already tried."

"Yes, I heard you. Felix, what do you think Malkar hopes to accomplish?"

"I . . . I don't know. Not what you think."

"What do you mean by that?" Thaddeus said, dark with suspicion.

"That he's Malkar. That he never wants what you think."

"Madness," Thaddeus said.

"Do you think so?" said Gideon. "I am inclined to think otherwise."

"Yes, well, it's not news that *your* mind is twisted." And he added viciously, "You always were a little sneak."

Gideon said, "Is this really the time to bring up the past?"

"Why not? Why in the name of God should we *not* talk about it? We were boys together." And Thaddeus smiled, although there was nothing good-humored or friendly about it. "Come, Gideon, let us reminisce."

"Thaddeus—"

"Yes, let's. I can tell Felix about being beaten for daring to ask questions, and you can tell him about being Louis Goliath's favorite minion. Don't you think?"

"Thaddeus—"

"Or are there other stories you'd like to tell? Perhaps you could tell him about the mystery cults of the Bastion. I'm sure he'd be fascinated. Perhaps he'll write a monograph."

"Thaddeus, *enough*." The colors around Gideon were terrible with rage and old pain and fear. "Baiting me accomplishes nothing, and baiting Felix . . ." I shrank back under the look he gave me. But all the passion seemed to go out of him, and he said tiredly, "Baiting Felix should be beneath you."

"Aren't we the gentleman?" Thaddeus said.

"No. I'm a docker's brat from Thrax. As you know and have known any time these past fifteen years. But at least I know what's decent behavior and what's not. I had imagined a man of your ideals would be able to distinguish that as well, but clearly I was mistaken."

"Are you quite finished being pompous?"

"Probably not. If you mean, shall we let our disagreement rest until tomorrow—by all means. Good night, Thaddeus."

Thaddeus gave him a savage parody of a bow. "Good night, Gideon." And snarled at me, "Good night, Felix."

He stalked out. The silence he left behind him seemed almost too thick to breathe. After a moment, Gideon pushed his hair off his face with both hands, then turned to me and said, gently, "You need to sleep."

"Yes, Gideon," I said and lay down obediently, huddled around my aching hands. But I did not sleep, could not sleep. I was still awake when Thaddeus came back in some hours later, and went to sleep finally with his stiff, angry presence like a sword beside me in the bed.

Mildmay

You got no idea how weird it was to look in the palm-size mirror that Mr. von Heber had. I hadn't been a redhead since my fourth indiction, and I barely even knew how to look at myself. I don't like mirrors anyway, and I looked fucked up. I mean, just plain wrong.

"Powers, I look like a freak," I said.

Mr. von Heber didn't even look up from his cards. "You looked even more peculiar with a half-grown-out dye job, I assure you. Why on earth does it bother you so much?"

"No reason."

"Oh, come now." He did look up, then, and his eyes were like skewers. "Really. Why?"

I put the mirror down. I didn't smash it, although I felt like it. " 'Cause I don't like people looking at my face, okay?"

"Oh. Oh, I'm sorry." Something in his eyes changed, and I had the funny feeling that he was seeing *me* now, instead of just the guy on his stupid card, the Knight of Swords. "How did it happen?"

"A knife fight. I had a septad and six, and I was stupid with it. I knew the other guy was no good, and *he* knew he was no good. If he'd been good, I'd've lost an eye. Or part of my nose. Or, you know, I'd be dead. So I guess I'm lucky."

"It is sometimes difficult to be grateful for luck," he said, real slow and careful, like now *he* wanted to break something, and I knew what he meant.

"Yeah," I said. "Sometimes it is."

Mr. von Heber laid his cards out over and over again all day, and then after we closed up The Mule's Daughter, fuck me if he didn't start laying 'em out again. Bernard rolled his eyes at me, and I took his meaning. No point arguing. Me and Bernard went to sleep, but we were woken up a couple hours later by Mr. von Heber cursing something terrible. I sat up and saw he'd dropped his cards. But it didn't seem like that was what he was pissed off about. "What's west of Mélusine?" he said when he saw I was awake. "West and south."

"Um," I said. "Dunno. What kind of thing you after?"

"I don't know! The Spire card keeps coming up, but I'll be damned if I can figure out why."

I thought, while Bernard got down on the floor and started picking up the cards. "There's a river. The Linlowing. It runs into the Sim about three septad-miles south of here. There's some decent-sized towns. Lotta farmland."

"Towns. Anything like a tower, or a cathedral—anything like that?"

Bernard said, "Couldn't this wait until morning?"

"No," Mr. von Heber said, and he was still staring at me like he was going to open up my skull to look for the answers here in a minute.

"I don't know," I said. "I'm sorry, but I really don't. You could ask Jeanne-Phalene."

"Ha!" said Mr. von Heber. He grabbed his canes and was off. Bernard barely got up in time to hold the door for him.

And my stupid fucking curiosity got the better of me, and I went after them.

Jeanne-Phalene always took the night shift at the front desk of the Long Time Coming. She liked to deal with the nighttime weirdness herself. "Nice hair," she said to me when I followed Bernard into the lobby.

"Thanks." I caught the look Mr. von Heber was giving me and said, "Jeanne-Phalene, you know about any towers or anything southwest of here?"

"Towers? I think there's an old wizard's tower or something in Hermione, but—"

"Hermione?" said Mr. von Heber. "How far away is Hermione?"

"Two days if you got a fast horse. Half a decad if you don't. Or you can catch the diligence to Sharcross. It takes about three days."

"Thank you," said Mr. von Heber, with a look on his face that said as how the diligence could go right on without us, and that'd be okay. "We'll leave tomorrow then."

"Okay," said Jeanne-Phalene, "but you know Ricko's going to be sobbing into his beer barrels."

Mr. von Heber waved that away—him and Ricko didn't like each other one little bit—and said, "Come on," to Bernard and me. "We'd better get some sleep."

"Good night," said Jeanne-Phalene, and you could've used the irony in her voice to load a catapult. But she didn't ask questions. It was all the same to Jeanne-Phalene.

Felix

I wanted to find the yellow-eyed man, the *true* yellow-eyed man. But my dreams were full of murk and evil, and I could not raise myself clear of Hermione, of the wizard's tower at its center like the hub of a wheel.

In the daylight, I told myself I was being stupid. The wizard's tower wasn't anywhere near the center of the town, and it was certainly nothing like a hub; it was a stubby thing like a half-melted candle, two blocks from the river that formed Hermione's southern boundary. But at night, the tower was black and terrible, and my dreams revolved helplessly around it.

On the third day, I tried to tell Thaddeus that there was something wrong with the tower, but he just laughed at me. That night, my dreams were worse than ever; there was something in the tower watching me, watching all of us. Its eyes were dark and hungry, and it was not alive.

It was late morning when I woke up, for when the dream had let me go, I had fallen into a sodden, heavy blackness that contained neither dreams nor rest. The others were gone—I could feel their absence—except Gideon, who was sitting in a chair by the window, making notes in the endpapers of a book called *A Treatise upon Spirit.* He said, without looking up, "They've gone to frighten the Mayor."

"Oh," I said. The colors around him were blue with concentration, luminous as the sky. I was afraid I would disturb him.

He said, "Breakfast is still laid out in the parlor."

"Thank you," I said. I got up, washed my face and hands, and went downstairs, where I breakfasted on soggy toast and congealed eggs and cold tea as strong as iron. It was better than nothing. I knew that a year ago I would have rung the bell, or shouted for the maid, and demanded fresh tea and new toast, but the knowledge was dim and distant and useless.

I stayed downstairs as long as I could, but I was anxious about the maids wanting to clear the room, and the thought of having to speak to one of them, even to say, I beg your pardon, was more than I could bear. I went back to the bedroom. Gideon looked up at my entrance and did not say, Oh, it's you, although I saw it around him. Instead, after a moment's contemplation, he put his book down and said, "Let's go out."

"Where?"

"I don't know. Surely there must be something in Hermione worth seeing besides that damned tower. Old fortifications or gardens or *something.*"

"But won't Thaddeus—"

"Damn Thaddeus. Put your shoes on, and I'll ask the desk clerk about sites of interest."

Thaddeus would be angry if he found out. But I put my shoes on, because Gideon said to and because I had been stuck in that room for three days, and I did not love it. I was standing by the door, wondering if I should go downstairs to find Gideon or if I should wait, when he came back in.

"*There* you are. Are you ready?"

"Yes."

"Come on, then. The desk clerk says the Municipal Gardens across the river are worth a look."

"In the middle of Petrop?"

"There's a hedge maze. Hedge mazes are interesting year-round."

He was treating me like a person instead of an inconvenience or a disgrace. I could no more refuse to go with him than someone freezing to death could refuse the offer of a blanket. I put my coat on and followed him out of the Chimera Among the Roses.

It was a beautiful day for Petrop, the sun only half-obscured by clouds and the air no more than chilly. We walked briskly but without hurry, at first without speaking, but then Gideon began to tell me stories of his childhood in Thrax before he had been conscripted by the Bastion—in Kekropia, wizards could be pressed into service as young as thirteen—and I was able to respond with a few harmless, amusing things that I remembered from my early days in the Mirador. My mind was clear; although most of the people who passed us had the heads of animals, I knew that these were merely hallucinations, neither true nor necessary, and they did not frighten me.

As we descended a set of stairs toward the river, Gideon said, "I have been wondering since I first saw you: how did you come to Mélusine?"

"I beg your pardon?"

"I did not think Troians ventured away from the coast."

"Who?"

He was a stair ahead of me; he turned to look up and back, frowning. "You *must* be Troian. Your hair, your height, your eyes and skin."

"I . . . I thought maybe I was Caloxan," I said timidly, skirting around the snarl of lies and truth, Malkar and Pharaohlight, that comprised my past.

"Caloxan!" He snorted. "You're Troian. You can't be anything else."

"Who are Troians?"

"Troians are the people who once ruled half this continent."

"Oh."

We had reached the path leading to the Linlowing Bridge; Gideon dropped back to walk beside me.

"They are tall, red-haired, pale-skinned. They have yellow eyes."

Like one of mine, the good one. "Oh," I said again.

"The Empire still trades with them, but, as I said, I thought they never went inland. There are still, er, folk-beliefs."

"Rather," I said. I could imagine what kind of folk-beliefs he was talking about. Keeper always said my hair was unlucky, and beat me for it. Lorenzo scoffed at superstition; he saw my hair as a draw and he made it be one. But the men who chose me were the men who wanted the illusion of danger in their cheap transactions with a cheap teenage whore. Malkar, too, had traded on my hair with his story about Caloxan nobility, although apparently that was as much a lie as everything else.

Gideon broke in urgently on my thoughts: "When was this bridge built? Do you know?"

"No."

The Linlowing River was a tributary of the Sim; as it flowed through Hermione it was wider than the Sim, but slower. The Linlowing Bridge stood on five pairs of pylons; each pylon was carved in the shape of a man kneeling in the river, so that the bridge appeared to be supported on their shoulders. They stared out with blank, solemn faces, softened by time and water and wind, five looking east and five looking west. Gideon was entranced.

"It looks like Cymellunar work." As we reached the first pair of kneeling men, he leaned out over the parapet in a way that made me nervous. "Which would mean it's ruinously old. Do you know anything about it at all?"

"No."

"There will be someone to ask," he said cheerfully and, much to my relief, straightened up. Then he frowned at me. "You've gone white as a sheet. Are you all right?"

"I'm fine."

He looked at the statue's head, then back at me. "Heights?"

"No. Really, I'm fine." I started walking, because it wasn't the height that frightened me, it was the water underneath. Obligingly, he followed me; even more obligingly, he didn't press for an answer.

Hermione no longer extended to the south bank of the Linlowing, if ever it had. The great bridge served primarily as an awe-inspiring entrance to the town for traders from the south, and as the town's connection to the farmlands that supported it. The only land south of the Linlowing that belonged to the city was the expanse of the Municipal Gardens. They were vast, rigidly landscaped and bleak with winter. The entrance price was two centimes; Gideon paid, and we went through the gate. Gideon struck up a conversation about the Linlowing Bridge with the gatekeeper, who must have been both lonely and bored at this time of year, and because no one forbade me, I wandered away along the carefully tended path.

Everything was laid out in a strict geometry, exactingly and mercilessly pruned. The fountains were all dry and silent, prisoners of winter. I walked through a topiary—where the woven, leafless shapes made my eyes hurt—climbed a narrow staircase and found myself in a gazebo, looking north at Hermione proper. Clearly the gardens' designers had intended this as a splendid vista, evoking civic pride in the garden-strolling burghers. I remembered standing on the Crown of Nails, looking out across Mélusine, and to me Hermione seemed petty and dull.

But from here, I could see the wizard's tower. It looked as I knew it did, short, squat, the windows boarded up, and empty patches in its red-tile roof. The tower in my dreams was the creation of my madness, the black looming shape of my fear—nothing to do with the real world.

"You are mad, Felix Harrowgate," I said to myself and turned to go.

Out of the corner of my eye, I saw the black shadow of the tower stretching across the river, reaching for me. I spun back, and there were no shadows at all. It was almost noon, and in any event, a three-story tower two blocks in from the Linlowing's northern bank could not cast a shadow that could reach me here. I knew that. But now I was afraid to take my eyes off the tower. And the longer I looked at it, the more it seemed to me that the real tower *was* the one in my dreams, that this dilapidated structure was only a façade. And if that was true, then the rest of my dream was true, and there was something in that tower, something terrible. I had to make Thaddeus believe me; I knew that, and at the same time, I knew he never would.

"Felix?" Gideon's voice, and I almost broke my neck getting down the stairs again. Whether I could make anyone believe me or not, I knew I could never be convincing with the tower where I could see it. And only then, back down on the path and trotting toward Gideon, did I think to wonder if maybe Gideon would believe me.

"Thaddeus would flay me if I lost you," he said. "Let's go look at the hedge maze."

"Do you like mazes?" I said, more or less at random. I was wondering how I could tell him about my dreams without sounding like . . . well, like a madman.

Gideon started talking about the theory and practice of mazes—mazes made of hedges, mazes made of stones, mazes inlaid in the floors of temples in the Myrian Mountains, a maze made of mirrors that was said to have stood in Cymellune before it sank. He mentioned the string mazes of the wizards of Lunness Point and the dance-made mazes of the far north. He told me about the *De Doctrina Labyrinthorum* written by Ephreal Sand, who had gone mad and spent his last years drawing insoluble mazes, first with pen and paper, then with a stick in the dirt, then with his finger in the dust, and finally in his own blood on the walls and floors and windows.

At that point, Gideon broke off abruptly and said, "I beg your pardon."

"Why?"

"I have a tendency—I've been told about it before, I assure you—to, well, to go on rather about things that interest me. I must be boring you to tears."

"I'm not bored," I said, because I wasn't.

"Then you are unique." His momentary smile lit up his face like a flash of sunlight through clouds. "But I really have done about three people's share of the talking, and I ought to let you get a word in edgewise."

"There's the maze," I said.

"Oh good. The gatekeeper's description has not led me to hope for great things, but perhaps I shall be pleasantly surprised."

The hedges of the maze were only about shoulder high on Gideon, which was some comfort. At least we could not become permanently lost. "That tower marks the center," Gideon said. I followed the direction of his pointing finger rather wildly, but the wizard's tower was not lying in wait for me. The center of the maze had a square wooden openwork tower, with a roofed platform at the top. "If we climb up there, we'll be able to see our way back."

We started into the maze. Gideon led me confidently, muttering things under his breath about various books he'd read, and within ten minutes we had come to the wooden tower.

"As I expected," he said. "Shall we climb up?"

"All right," I said.

Five short flights of stairs brought us to the platform. Gideon leaned on the railing, looking out. "It's a nice maze," he said, "but child-simple."

I leaned beside him, looking at the neat square symmetry of the lines of the hedge. And I said, before I was fully sure I was going to, "Do you believe in dreams?"

"How do you mean?" he said, tilting his head to look at me.

"Do you think they can . . . that they can tell the truth?"

After a meditative silence, Gideon said, "As I recall, the Mirador teaches that they cannot."

"Yes. I mean, no. I . . ." I trailed off in confusion.

Gideon said mildly, "I've never liked Cabaline dogma."

"But you . . . that is . . ."

"Yes, I hate the Bastion, but that's more personal than doctrinal. I *admire* the Cabal quite dreadfully, mind you, but I think they were, in some ways, misguided. It is foolish to say, simply because one does not wish to have any truck with necromancers, that the magic that makes necromancy possible is evil."

"But dreams don't—"

"Have anything to do with necromancy? You say so only because you have not been properly taught. What do *you* believe about dreams?"

"I don't know. I know my dreams are strange. They always have been. There was an old man—he's dead now, so I guess it can't hurt to tell you about him. He taught me how to control my dreams a little, to keep the nightmares away, and I didn't think about them much for a long time. But they've gotten worse, since . . . since the Curia put me under interdict. More . . . more true, somehow."

"Well, with your magic out of the way," Gideon said, but he wasn't talking to me, not really; the look in his eyes was one I'd come to recognize, that distant but not at all dreamy expression that meant he was on the track of an errant splinter of thaumaturgical theory.

"But I thought you said my dreams were like necromancy."

"Good gracious, no. I said they were related to necromancy, and so they are. True dreams of the sort you're talking about exist in the same world of the spirit as ghosts and revenants—and the forces of divination, for that matter. But dreaming isn't magic, although for some people it can come close."

"You mean like what Malkar did?"

"No!" Gideon said, vehemently enough to make me flinch. "What Malkar did is something completely different. It's called a sending, and it is one of the nastiest pieces of magic the Bastion has failed to outlaw. Sendings use *other* people's dreams, not the caster's own. But that's not what you're talking about, if I'm understanding you correctly."

"I don't think I've ever used anyone else's dreams."

"You'd know if you had. Do you dream about the future?"

"Iosephinus—that was the old man's name, the one who helped me, Iosephinus Pompey—he said I could, but it was better not to. He said it never helped. I just . . . I dream about real things. I think."

"What do you mean?"

It was the opening I had been both hoping for and dreading. "The tower," I said, all in a rush. "There's something awful in the tower, and I tried to tell Thaddeus, but he won't listen. Gideon, can you talk to him?"

I saw the refusal before Gideon said anything; the colors around him darkened and furled like wings. "Felix, I'm sorry. I can't. He won't listen to me, and—I know it's hard to believe, but truly—I would only make things worse."

"It's all right. I didn't mean . . ."

"No, I am sorry. But it probably isn't as bad as you think. I don't know very much about the history of this wizard's tower, but probably you're just feeling . . . echoes of the past."

"It's there. It's there now. It's watching us."

"Are you sure," Gideon said very gently, "that it isn't just a nightmare?"

Yes, I thought. "No," I said aloud. "Maybe you're right."

An uncomfortable pause, and he said, "We'd better be getting back."

"Yes," I said hopelessly and followed him back through the maze.

The others didn't return to the Chimera Among the Roses until nearly sundown, and they were tremendously pleased with themselves. They had extracted the keys from the Mayor, and a promise that repairs to the tower would be undertaken as soon as the wizards told him what they needed. I was almost sorry for the Mayor of Hermione.

But the longer I sat and listened to the wizards making plans, the worse the feeling got, the residue of my dreams, the knowledge that the thing in the tower was hungry and waiting and powerful. And finally, although I knew it would do no good, although Thaddeus had already laughed at me, I said, "Thaddeus, can I talk to you?" I knew no one else would listen to me; the other wizards all avoided me as if I were a leper—except for Vicky, whose mind was as inflexible as an iron rod—and Shannon was still looking through me as if I were not there. The guard lieutenant was faithfully following Shannon's lead, and the guards were all copying their lieutenant. If Gideon would not help me, there was only Thaddeus left.

His eyebrows went up, a slow, deliberate display of incredulity, a pause long enough to attract the others' attention and make them aware of the burdens he labored under. Then he said, "Very well. I assume you mean privately?"

I nodded, embarrassment choking me, and followed him up to the bedroom we shared with Gideon. It was already going wrong; the situation was already twisting out of true. But the only way out was to go forward.

"Well?"

"The tower," I said. "Thaddeus, there's something there. I can feel it, and it's dangerous. You have to—"

"Oh, for the love of God. *This* again? Felix, it's a building. It's been deserted for two centuries. There's nothing there but pigeons and spiders and rats."

"Can't you feel it at all?" I said, although I knew it was the wrong thing even as I said it. Thaddeus was only a middling-powerful wizard, and it had always been a sore point with him.

"No," he said, and I saw red sparking around him. "Because there's nothing there. Look. I'll prove it to you. We'll go there tomorrow, you and I. Lady Victoria wants someone to have a look at the roof, and you can see that there's nothing there but cobwebs. All right?"

"Yes."

"And don't flinch like that!"

"Yes, Thaddeus," I said, but he was already halfway back down the stairs.

I followed him as far as the doorway, where I heard him say, "Felix thinks there's a bogeyman in the tower," and I turned and fled back up to the bedroom. No one would come to look for me; no one cared. I shut my eyes, so that I could pretend I wasn't crying, and eventually I fell asleep.

❧

The thing in the tower watched me all night long.

❧

Thaddeus was in a dangerously good mood in the morning, the sort that was bright and sparkling because it was made of shards of glass. I said nothing, even when he made all the guards laugh by saying we were off to hunt my nightmares. He could still change his mind if I gave him a reason.

Thaddeus and I did not speak on our way through the streets of

Hermione. The tower was squat, decrepit, wearing its deceitful face of neglect. But I could feel the truth; as we approached, I began to see the darkness spreading out like a pool from the door. Thaddeus waded into it without even noticing. I stopped with the darkness coiling around my ankles and watched, unable either to force myself to follow him or to call him back. The darkness rose to his calves, his thighs, his ribs. He was neck deep in it when he reached the door and turned to look back.

"Well? Are you coming?"

I almost said, *Don't talk! You'll swallow darkness*. But I could hear in my own head how mad that sounded. I stepped forward.

The darkness was dry and cold and heavy without having any weight. I felt it on my skin; my clothing was no protection. Thaddeus said, "The ground isn't going to open up and swallow you, so you can quit walking like a cat on eggshells." He took the key to the tower out of his coat pocket and fitted it in the lock.

Everything became very still, as if the tower were holding its breath. It had been deserted for two hundred years, left to its shadows and cobwebs and dust—and the thing that watched me in my dreams. I realized, as Thaddeus muttered in Midlander and applied magic to the corroded mechanism of the lock, that the tower had been influenced by its inhabitant, as any object was influenced by the magic that moved through it. The stones of the tower partook of that watching spirit and shared of its darkness.

A bright blue spark arced out from the key, and it revolved obediently in the lock.

"Ha!" said Thaddeus and pulled the door open. The hinges howled with rust, and the door juddered to a halt only half-open. Darkness poured out, engulfing us both, and on the instant it disappeared, although I could still feel it whispering against my skin.

"Come on," Thaddeus said, calling witchlight, and stepped through the door. I understood suddenly why he had agreed to bring me here; it meant that he was the first person into the tower. Vicky would be asking his opinion on the repairs needed, the tower's suitability for what they meant to do. I remembered how greatly it had chafed at Thaddeus not to be appointed to the Curia, how bitter he had been in the months before he had gotten the position in Aurelias, that Vida and I had been chosen—and not only was I the youngest member of the Curia by nearly ten years, but everyone in the Mirador knew how much Stephen hated me—and he, Thaddeus de Lalage, had been rejected. I knew how close it had come to poisoning his love for Vida. He needed to feel important, needed to have power. All wizards were like that to some extent, but in few of them was it the parched craving that it was in Thaddeus.

I followed him into the tower and found myself in a narrow staircase between the stones of the outer wall on my right and a wooden interior wall on my left. The wood was in better shape than I had expected—no sign of termites or worms—and, I thought, there won't be any spiders, either. Nothing living. I followed the dim blue glow of Thaddeus's witch-lights up and around, past doors in the inner wall that he did not stop to try. The wizard's workroom, the room the Cabalines needed, would be at the top of the tower, where there was the cleanest meeting of the stones raised from the earth and the vast power of the sky.

The staircase ended in a trapdoor. It wasn't bolted, and Thaddeus did not need magic to shove it open. We climbed into the workroom.

There wasn't any dust.

I stayed by the trapdoor as Thaddeus prowled around. The room was circular, bare, strewn with bits of glass from the broken windows. The floor was marked in places, where heavy furniture had once stood, and there was a red circle still visible under the apex of the roof, as if it had been drawn so many times that it could not be erased. My gaze kept returning to it; even if the floor caved in, I thought, that circle would still be there, drawn on nothing but the air.

Thaddeus was examining the windows. I was drawn, step by step, across the floor to the circle. I could not tell, now, if it was my need for knowledge that drove me or the hunger of the thing that infected this tower.

The circle was six feet in diameter; the dim, blurry line that marked it was two inches wide. I could not tell what it had been drawn with, chalk or paint or something else; there was only redness left, ingrained in the ancient gray boards of the floor, dustless, waiting.

I stepped into the circle.

With the suddenness of a blink, the room changed. The marks on the floor were concealed by the furniture that had made them. There was a long table to the right of the trapdoor and an enormous, looming cabinet, my height or better, fitted with an array of small drawers, its clawed feet tensing into the floor. And there was a long, low chest, under the window where Thaddeus had been standing a moment ago, with cushions on it so that it could be used as a couch. Right now, there was a woman sitting there, dressed like a man. She had a solemn, horsey face and wore her coarse brown hair braided around her head. She seemed to be staring at me, but after a panic-stricken moment, I realized she was looking at something behind me, and I turned around.

The man standing there, gems flashing on his fingers as his hands moved, was clearly explaining something to the woman: teaching. Unlike her baggy laborer's clothing, his clothes were silk and velvet. His black hair, streaked with silver, hung in lovelocks to his shoulders; his eyes were dark and very bright. Despite the silver in his hair, he was very young, maybe no more than two or three years older than I, very little older than the woman. She was his student, she was a stronger wizard than he, and she would not sleep with him. I could see all these things in the way he looked at her.

I knew that in this one scene I was witnessing months of interactions, months of the woman's self-evident excellence, months of her sublime indifference to any aspect of her teacher's personality save his ability to tell her what she wanted to know. Months—or perhaps years—of his knowing that she would be leaving, that she would find a better master who could teach her more, that he himself would be stuck in this squat, ugly tower in this backwater town until his brains rotted and dribbled out his ears. Most wizards would insist, sincerely and desperately, that they were above the feelings that such reflections stirred in the human breast. Probably the black-haired wizard would once have said so himself.

The scene changed. Now it was night in the tower; lit candles stood on every flat surface. The black-haired wizard was alone. There were books open on the table, diagrams scrawled on scraps of paper, chalked on the plaster of the walls. Although his school of magic was largely foreign to me, I could tell that the spell was too big for him, that his resentment and anger and bitterness had driven him to magics better left alone, that his gnawing sense of inferiority was pushing him to attempt a working he knew he could not control.

He spoke a word, which penetrated the circle and the barriers of time; I heard it with an awful clarity, and I knew it was the name of the thing he summoned, the thing that still watched in the tower, the thing that was not alive: *fantôme*.

I did not know the word *fantôme,* although it was Marathine. Much of the study of necromancy had been lost when the Cabal declared necromancy a heresy and started burning books. But I did not need to know what a fantôme was to know that the black-haired wizard was making a terrible mistake. No, I said, although I knew he couldn't hear me; I couldn't hear myself. Don't do it.

The black-haired wizard stepped into the circle. I edged aside, even though he could not feel me. He was chanting, and I could see the light in his rings. I felt the thing, the fantôme, coming into being; it was like a miasma in the circle. It stank of rotting lilacs, and I no longer wondered that spiders and rats would flee it. The wizard extended his hands, palms up, and the dim, shining sludge of the fantôme flowed into them. He shut his eyes for a moment, staggering; when he opened them again, I saw the fantôme like a sheen of oil on his irises. Together, wizard and fantôme, they stepped out of the circle. I watched as they crossed the room to the trapdoor, descended out of sight. I knew where they were going, and when they reappeared with the woman slung over their shoulder, I was not surprised.

They threw her down in the circle. I tried to move out of the way, but found I could not cross the boundary and was forced to stand with my feet in hers. The wizard was giggling to himself—or perhaps it was the fantôme, since I could hear it, just at the edges of my hearing, a faint, whispering, grating sound. He got a knife and a stick of chalk; I watched as he chalked signs around the woman, and then on her forehead and on her palms. She woke up before he was done and tried to move, but the fantôme's power held her, and she could do no more than twitch. She spoke to him, I thought, but I did not know what she said. All I could hear was that terrible chittering, the fantôme bubbling over with delight.

And when his preparations were made, the wizard butchered his student, and the fantôme fed on her pain and fear, fed on her death and her magic. I watched her blood as it spread across the floor; when it encountered the chalked sigils around the circle, it flowed into their shapes. From them, it flowed into the circle itself, until I was standing inside a ring of blood, and now I knew why that circle could not be eradicated. Even the teachings of the Cabal admitted that workings with blood were powerful beyond the strength of the caster. That was one reason they were forbidden.

I could feel the fantôme's power growing; when the ritual was done, the woman dead, the wizard no longer controlled what he had called, if ever he had. He could not banish it, and the shine in the wizard's eyes was the shine of madness and death and blackest despair.

I watched helplessly as he gathered her body together and left the room, watched helplessly as he returned. I could feel the struggle between them, fantôme and wizard; it made the air thick, viscous. I thought I would choke on the stench of rotted lilacs. The wizard crossed the room, one stiff step at a time; he stopped in front of the chest where I had first seen the woman sitting. He climbed up on it, although the power of the fantôme nearly dragged him off backwards. But there was a difference between magic and will, and the fantôme had no magic of its own with which to compel him; it only had the thunderous, beating force of its will. And I had seen in his eyes when he came back up the stairs that there was nothing it could offer him, no power, no glory, that would mean anything.

He shoved both hands through the window glass. There was a terrible moment when he wobbled on the chest, and the fantôme nearly succeeded in forcing him back down into the room, and then he threw himself through the window, headfirst.

There was an endless howling moment of blackness, and then I was snapped back into the present day, where Thaddeus was turning from the window—the window the black-haired wizard had just thrown himself out of—and I was standing in a faded, innocuous circle.

. . . *fantôme* . . . said the breeze through the broken window, and I smelled rotting lilacs.

I screamed, and bolted out of the circle.

"What in the seven names of God?" said Thaddeus, but I could feel the fantôme in the air of the room, could feel its hunger, and the unerring eye of a predator for weak prey. And I could no more shut it out than that broken window could shut out the wind. The fantôme was gathering itself out of the dustless air, marshaling its strength, and then it would walk in and claim whatever there was to be found.

I would have screamed again, but I couldn't catch my breath. I flung myself, scrambling, scrabbling, at the stairs, and did not fall headfirst down them only by luck, an outflung hand that caught the far edge of the opening and steadied me long enough that my feet got under me. Thaddeus was shouting behind me as I ran down the stairs, but I did not heed him. The fantôme was bounded by the same working that gave it strength. That ring of blood held it in that room, confined it to the tower; it could not follow me out the door and into the deserted square, where I slumped to my knees, panting, almost sobbing for breath, my heart beating in my chest like a terrified bird.

I heard Thaddeus slam the door of the tower. The tide of his contempt and disgust swept ahead of him; I understood that he found my madness revolting, as if I were masturbating in public. The color was a sullen, lurid yellow, the color of bile.

I wanted to cry out, *I'm not doing it on purpose!* but I choked the words back. Instead, I got to my feet again, so that by the time Thaddeus reached me and had come around to stand in front of me, I was at least not on my knees like a penitent slave.

"God, Felix, what is *wrong* with you?" Thaddeus demanded, his words like hammers. He wanted an apology, an admission of weakness and wrongdoing.

"It's a fantôme," I said. "The thing . . . in the workroom—it was called up by the last wizard who used the tower, and when he couldn't get rid of it he threw himself out the window, and it's still—"

Thaddeus hit me.

It was an open-handed blow, but hard enough to stagger me. When I touched my mouth, my fingers came away bloody; I had bitten my lip.

"Shut up," Thaddeus said.

"But, Thaddeus—"

"I said, shut up!" I flinched, dropping my gaze, and I felt his disgusted satisfaction as clearly as if he'd hit me again. "I've had enough of these pathetic efforts at sabotage—you leave me no choice but to tell Lady Victoria."

"Sabotage? Why would I . . ."

The look in his eyes was all the answer I needed, but he said, "I have wondered if you were as unwilling to be Malkar's tool as you claim. And this farrago about a monster in the tower . . . You haven't done much damage to our mission yet, and I intend to see you don't get the chance."

"You think I . . . you think Malkar . . . you're crazier than I am!"

He gave me a thin-lipped, furious smile. "We will see if Lady Victoria agrees with you."

He turned and strode out of the square with the brisk arrogance of a man who had never imagined the possibility of his being in the wrong. I followed him, because his theory would only look more convincing if I did not. Behind us the fantôme waited in its dustless room, watching with the patience of a predator who always hungered yet could never starve.

Mildmay

We ended up buying tickets on the Sharcross diligence, although me and Bernard had to take seats on the roof. Mr. von Heber was mad as a wet cat about the whole thing. But the diligence would get us to Hermione in three days, and I hadn't been able to see us doing it in less than a decad, considering Mr. von Heber's normal walking speed.

The second night, in the one tiny hotel room that was all we could afford—and I'd voted for sleeping on the floor instead of sharing the bed with either of them—Mr. von Heber got his cards and his watch fob out again. Bernard rolled his eyes and went down to the bar. I stayed put. I didn't want to go drinking with Bernard, I didn't want to wander down there and find out whether I could get myself into a game of Long Tiffany, even though the money would've been nice, and I was getting interested in Mr. von Heber's cards. I can't help it sometimes.

"Whatcha looking for tonight?" I said.

He shrugged a little, shuffling. "Information. The Spire is a bad card." He flipped it out of the deck so I could see, a big black shiny needlelike thing, with this guy . . .

I gave the card back to Mr. von Heber. "What's with the guy?"

"The impaled man, you mean?" he said, shuffling it back into the deck.

"The guy with the spike through his guts, yeah. What's he mean?"

"I told you. The Spire is a bad card. It can mean a literal tower, but it also means a fall from a height, whether literal or figurative, the destruction of something old and valuable. It means isolation, abandonment. It is the card of the scapegoat."

"*All* them things?"

He raised an eyebrow at me. "The card also means falling prey to your own self-confidence."

"Oh. Yeah. I'm with you. But how do you know which thing it means?"

"Well, you don't exactly. That's why reading the Sibylline is an art." He started laying the cards out, and I shut up.

I recognized the Death card when it came up, and there was the Spire again. And there was a whole bunch of other cards I didn't know, but they didn't look pretty. Mr. von Heber's frown got darker and darker, and after a while he said, "Either I'm asking the wrong question, or there's something extremely peculiar about the tower in Hermione."

He swept the cards up again, shuffled, flipped the Spire card out. Then he shuffled again, and again—I lost count, but I think he did a septad, like the really superstitious cardplayers do when their luck's out. Then he cut the deck and flipped a card out. It landed across the Spire card.

"Shit," I said.

"Yes," he said.

The Death card, black and gold, laid there and laughed at us.

"What's *that* mean?" I said.

"The tower is death. The tower contains death. The tower is a place of stagnation, or a place where the dead can be talked to. I don't think it means anything good, but I don't know what the cards are trying to tell me."

"D'you got some other method? I mean, I knew people who did tea leaves and shit like that."

"Tea leaves are even more obscure than the cards. Most forms of divination are." But I noticed he didn't say nothing like, *Oh, never mind, I'll try again tomorrow*. And I sure wasn't saying, *Cut this shit out so I can get some sleep*. We'd get to Hermione tomorrow.

"I wish I knew more about this tower," Mr. von Heber said. "You've never heard *anything*?"

"Nope. Sorry."

"Why doesn't it have a wizard in it? The Mirador sends wizards out all over the place—why not one to Hermione?"

"I really don't know."

"I'm sorry. I wasn't asking you. I was just *asking*. What's the *matter* with this tower?"

I almost didn't say it, but he looked like he was really racking his brains. "Could it be a ghost or something?"

"I beg your pardon?"

My face was getting hot. "Nothing. I was just . . . I mean . . ."

"The Sibylline is certainly trying to tell me about something dead. But even a haunting wouldn't give readings like this."

"But, I mean, what else is there?"

"All kinds of things," he said, and I could tell by the way he said it that they weren't none of them nice things. "But"—he sighed all the way up from his boots—"there's another kind of divination I can try."

"You don't sound happy about it."

"I don't like automatic writing. It's a necromantic technique to start with, and my teacher always said it was better left to the necromancers."

"What is it, exactly?"

"If you'll ask at the desk if I can borrow pen, ink, and paper, I'll show you."

So I went back downstairs. The gal at the desk wasn't real crazy about the whole idea, but she was even less crazy about having me hanging around all night, and she caved pretty quick. I came away with a bill of lading from last indiction, a half-full jar of rusty ink, and a seriously mangy quill. Bernard was still in the bar and not likely to be much help anyway. I went back upstairs alone.

"Mr. von Heber?"

He was laying out his cards again, and said without looking up, "You *can* call me Mavortian, you know. I shan't be offended."

"Okay. I, um . . ."

He looked at what I'd got and pushed his cards out of the way. "It'll do. If this is going to work, it won't take long."

"So what're you gonna do?"

"Automatic writing is one of the most direct forms of divination. The diviner goes into a trance and writes."

"Writes what?"

"That's the interesting part. If it works—and oftentimes it doesn't—one writes the answer to a question or the words closest to the shape of the pattern. Frequently, one merely writes gibberish. But it is the only form of divination I know of that produces simple words." He found a clear space on the paper and dipped the quill in the ink. "I'd appreciate it if you'd guard the door."

"Um, okay. Sure." I was just as glad to be nowhere near him. I braced my back against the door and waited.

Mavortian raised the pen and set it down on the paper. I saw him close his eyes. Then nothing happened for a really long time. I was just starting to wonder if maybe he'd missed the trance or something and just gone to sleep, when the pen jerked.

It wasn't him moving it. I can't explain how I could tell, but I could. It started scrawling across the paper, fast and hard, and my heart was up in my throat, and I was thinking he should've told me how you *stopped* doing this automatic writing shit, when his eyes came open, and the pen made this long jagged shriek across the page, tearing right through it, and then he threw the pen across the room.

And then he sat there, staring at the paper and cursing under his breath in Norvenan, until I finally figured it was okay to move and came across to look at what the pen had written.

I don't read so good, but I could see this was the same word, over and over and over again.

"What is it?" I said.

Mavortian looked at me. His face was white as white. "Fantôme," he said.

Felix

Vicky believed Thaddeus. They all did. They called me saboteur and malcontent and running dog, said they should have known all along, said they had never trusted me, said I was Malkar's creature through and through. They called me deranged, delusional, hysterical, untruthful, craven, sneaking. They would not listen to me. I stared at my hands and did not let myself cry, but when Thaddeus banished me to the bedroom, I fled their hatred and their anger, lay on the bed and still did not cry, staring with hot, dry eyes at the cracks in the ceiling and listening to the fantôme in my head. It could not invade me at this distance, could not possess me as it had possessed that poor, stupid wizard, but it could feel me, it could call to me, and I knew that before long I would answer it, whether I wanted to or not.

It knew my name.

"I can't fight it alone," I said to the ceiling. And the wizards did not believe me and would not help me. They gave the fantôme more fuel, for it whispered to me that it could make them sorry. I could use its power to hurt them, and it would help me willingly. It would protect me, it said, and no one would be able to hurt me ever again. All I had to do was come to it, step back into the circle, and let it in.

"No," I said, but I heard the weakness in my own voice.

"I cannot fight it," I said again. I got up, opened the window, and climbed out onto the roof of the veranda. The fantôme exulted; inside, cold and small and wretched, I wept.

I climbed down from the veranda. The fantôme pulled at me like true north to a compass needle, but I still had enough strength to resist. I started toward the Linlowing Bridge.

The streets were deserted, abandoned to the darkness. I did not make swift progress, for the fantôme was dragging at me with all the strength it had. But I remembered the look in the black-haired wizard's eyes, and I kept going. Even the cold death of water would be better than becoming that.

No, screamed the fantôme, he was a fool! He didn't understand! Things would be different. *I* was different, more worthy, better able to appreciate the gifts the fantôme could offer.

"I am not," I said. "I am *not*."

The fantôme told me it was the envy and hatred of those around me that made me think so. It could see their small, petty minds. It knew differently, it said. It saw my worth, my beauty. It would love me, it promised, love me and protect me and allow nothing to hurt me.

"You will devour me," I said. And I almost sobbed with gratitude to discover myself at the top of the steps. The river was near, and the end of pain.

But I will end your pain! the fantôme protested. Trust me, Felix. Trust my love.

"No," I said, descending the stairs with both hands on the rail. And I kept saying it, under my breath, a prayer, a mantra, swinging my denial like a sword at every promise, every seeming kindness the fantôme offered.

I came to the bridge and began to climb. I passed the first pair of supporting giants, then the second. As the great, patient heads of the third pair emerged from the darkness, I knew I was at the highest point of the bridge. If I jumped from here, the river would kill me even if the fall did not. I climbed onto the parapet and then, on hands and knees, edged out onto the giant's head.

I could hear the river, although I could not see it. The fantôme's entreaties in my head were replaced by the memory of Keeper's hard, booming voice, his hard hand on the back of my neck. I remembered what it was like to be held down underwater, fighting not to breathe, not to struggle, because he wouldn't let you up until he felt you'd submitted to him. I remembered the children he had drowned, maybe by accident, maybe not: Rhais, Marco, Ursy, Paulie, Leo, Belinda . . . Keeper didn't care. There were always more.

I forced myself forward another few inches, until my fingers felt the slope of the giant's forehead. And then I froze, crouched on this great stone head in the dark, listening to the terrible river somewhere beneath me. It is not the Sim, I said to myself. It will not be black and bitter. It will be kind. But I did not believe myself. I could not move, neither back toward the fantôme nor forward toward the memory of Keeper's hand and the black reek of the Sim. I cursed myself for a craven fool, but I could not move.

I saw the light approaching from the north end of the bridge; I knew it was too much to hope that this might be some late-night wanderer who would not notice me, and so I was not surprised when the light stopped, a few feet shy of the giant, and a voice said, "Felix?"

But I had not expected it would be Gideon's voice.

"Gideon?" I said, my own voice shaking and shrill.

"Felix, please don't."

"Why not? You heard them—I'm traitorous, murderous, evil. Why shouldn't I jump?"

"They're wrong. I know they're wrong. You were trying to tell them something important, and they would not listen. What was it?"

"You said you wouldn't help!"

"I'm sorry. I didn't . . . I think I didn't understand." The light came a little closer. "Felix, *please*."

I could not answer him.

"Let me make amends for not believing you. Let me listen. Please."

"It . . ." My voice choked off into nothing, and I had to try again. "It's called a fantôme. It—"

But Gideon said something violent in Kekropian that sounded like it was both obscene and blasphemous, and then in Marathine, perfectly calmly, "I will flay Thaddeus with a dull knife."

"You believe me?"

"Yes. I certainly don't believe that if you were sowing dissension, *that* is the story you would pick. You're a Cabaline. Do you even know what a fantôme is?"

"It's evil. I felt it. I still feel it. It talks to me. It wants me to come to it."

"Oh, I'm sure it does. I can ward you from it, if you'll come back on the bridge."

"You can?"

"Yes. I promise. It will take no more than a minute. Please, Felix, let me help you."

"Will you talk to Thaddeus?"

"Oh, I'll do better than that. I'll talk to Lady Victoria."

"Vicky won't listen."

"Unlike Thaddeus, she isn't a fool. And she does not . . . never mind. Felix, I *believe* you. Trust me."

"I can't," I said, my fingers throbbing with their pressure against the stone giant's head. "I can't."

Gideon cursed in Kekropian, then said quietly, "The White-Eyed Lady must want you very badly. But she lies to you, Felix. She is not a kind lover, and her embrace will not dull the pain you suffer. And her betrayal will never end. I realize that I betrayed you yesterday, although I did not mean to, and I am sorry. But that doesn't have to be the end between us. Do you understand me?" He stopped and then said, even more quietly, "Felix, you don't have to be alone."

"I . . ." But the words were gone. I had to lower myself flat onto the giant's head before I could move, and then I edged backwards, one horrible inch at a time, until my toes touched the parapet. I all but fell back onto the sidewalk. Gideon was there, warm and green and smelling slightly of cloves but not at all of bitterness and death, and I could hear no voices in my head at all.

Chapter 8

Mildmay

"What's a fantôme?"

"It's a type of ghost," Mavortian said. "At least, as most people understand the word. Necromancers would classify it as a spirit."

"What's the difference?"

"As I understand it—and I am not a necromancer—a ghost is more like a memory. A spirit is . . . aware."

"Oh. Kethe. That's bad, ain't it?"

"It doesn't have to be. But a fantôme is a spirit that has been invited to partake of materiality."

"Come again?"

"Some appalling imbecile let it possess him."

"So there's some guy wandering around Hermione—"

"No. The cards say something *dead*. Some guy, as you put it, died while possessed by a fantôme."

"But it's still there? I mean, when he died, wouldn't it . . ."

"Unfortunately, no. Fantômes are raised with a spell, and they must be laid with a spell. Balance. With its vehicle dead, it would simply haunt its place of conjuration until . . ."

The look on his face was like a guy who's opened a door and found a pack of ghouls on the other side. "What?" I said.

"Until it found a suitable . . . host."

"I ain't following."

"It will want a wizard."

"Well, you ain't gonna go offer yourself or nothing, are you?"

"I'm not worried about me. But remember that we are chasing Felix Harrowgate."

"Yeah, I got that."

"The cards and the other divinations I've done say that he is in Hermione. Where there is a tower. Where, I would bet large sums of money I do not currently possess, the fantôme was conjured."

"Yeah. But still. I mean, nobody's using the tower or nothing—"

"If Felix Harrowgate, who we know is crazy and possibly a traitor, is in Hermione, I would be shocked to discover he is alone."

"You think there's hocuses in Hermione?"

"More than that. I think I know what they're doing there."

I waited, and he said, "The tower. They're planning to use the tower."

"Why?"

"Not being a Cabaline wizard, I really couldn't say. But they have a fondness for towers, and this must be the only tower within a week's ride of Mélusine. And clearly they don't know there's a spirit trapped in it."

"Won't they feel it or something?"

"They're Cabaline," he said and laughed, although not like there was anything funny. "They don't believe in ghosts."

We got to Hermione about the tenth hour of the day. We spent the rest of the afternoon hunting around for hocuses. I could think of things I'd've rather been doing, starting with getting a pair of pliers and pulling my own toenails out, but I'd hired on to Mavortian's crusade, and something that scared him as bad as this thing he said was in the tower wasn't nothing to wish on nobody.

The second hotel we tried, the desk clerk had heard there were hocuses in Hermione and was willing to say so. He said they were staying in a place called the Crimson Ape. The Crimson Ape was a fleabag, and the gal there said as how she'd heard the hocuses were staying at the Dragon's Hoard, what passed in Hermione for a flash hotel. So we hiked back across half Hermione—we saw the wizard's tower over the roofs, and Mavortian made us go the long way round, to be sure we didn't get nowhere near it—and at the Dragon's Hoard, they said there weren't no hocuses on the books, but we could try at the Chimera Among the Roses for our friends.

"Sun'll be down soon," Bernard said when we came out on the sidewalk.

"So it will," Mavortian said.

"I'm just wondering how much longer this is going to take."

"I don't know, Bernard. Until we find them."

They both looked at me. "What?" I said.

"Nothing," said Mavortian. "Which way?"

"This way," I said, although I wanted to point out that I was just as much a stranger here as them and why didn't somebody else play guide. But I'd listened to the desk clerk's directions, and I knew where to go, and I wasn't going to help Bernard pick a fight.

The Chimera Among the Roses was only another four blocks east. It was two stories tall and sprawly—you could see the way the city had kind of snuck up behind it while it wasn't looking. I liked it.

This time the desk clerk got this sort of awed, nervous, unhappy look on his face and said, "Oh, yes. Is it Lady Victoria you wish to speak to, or Lord Shannon?"

Mavortian's eyebrows shot up, but he covered like a champ, saying, "I didn't know Lord Shannon was with them," in this way that said as how somebody—somebody stupid like maybe Bernard or me—must have forgot to tell him. "I believe my business is with Lady Victoria."

"Yes, sir," said the desk clerk. "If you'll step into the parlor, I'll send somebody to fe . . . to ask if she is available." And the way he looked around told me a couple things. Firstly, that he didn't have nobody to send except himself, and secondly that the Chimera Among the Roses had never had flash types staying with them before and the desk clerk, for one, was praying hard they never would again.

So we went into the parlor, and Mavortian sat down with a sigh of relief, and Bernard sat down next to him, and I went and looked out the window and tried to think of a good excuse for leaving suddenly—something that Mavortian wouldn't see through like it was window glass I mean, so that I wouldn't get him asking me what was really wrong. Not to mention something that wouldn't make Bernard laugh himself sick.

I hadn't thought of nothing by the time a voice said, "I believe you wished to speak to me?" and I turned around and got my first close-up look at Victoria Teveria. She was tall, square-shouldered, dark-complected. She had the Teverius jaw, which was square and heavy, and heavy eyebrows besides. She wasn't bad-looking, but she just naturally looked like a fairly low-grade goddess fixing to smite somebody. And it didn't make me feel better to realize the blond with her—the guy about twice as pretty as her and not quite as tall—had to be Shannon Teverius, only child of the Golden Bitch.

Fuck, I thought, because there wasn't nothing else I could do, and waited to see how Mavortian was going to play it.

He hauled himself up out of the chair and made the best bow he could with the canes and all. He said, "My lady, thank you for seeing us."

"I am rather busy," she said, and I realized that some of the thundercloud on her face was left over from something else, "so if you could be quick, Mr. er . . . ?"

"Mavortian von Heber," said Mavortian. "I am a wizard of the Fressandran school."

"Diviners," Lady Victoria said, her eyebrows going up a little.

"Yes, my lady. Do you, as a good Cabaline, deny utterly the validity of my methods?"

She thought about that, and I noticed the way she didn't mind no more about how much of her time he took up, now that she knew he was a hocus, too. "The Fressandran school, so far as I know, does not promulgate heresy." Something that maybe she thought was a smile jerked at one corner of her mouth. "Is that the safe-conduct you desire?"

"It will do. Lady Victoria, I have come to warn you."

"To warn me? Of what?"

"There is," Mavortian started, but he didn't get no farther, because right then Lord Shannon looked at me—not only noticing I was in the room, I mean, but actually looked at my face—and just about passed out.

"Vicky!" he said and clutched at her arm.

"What?"

"That, that—who *are* you?"

"Me?" I said, and now Lady Victoria was staring at me, and I saw her sign herself.

"Is there a problem?" Mavortian said.

"No," said Lady Victoria, although she was lying and we all knew it. "There is . . . the resemblance is . . . Shannon, do you think it can possibly be a coincidence?"

"No," said Lord Shannon. "Is your hair dyed?"

"I wish it was," I said. Mavortian got it, and gave me half a grin.

"Is this some kind of trick?" Lady Victoria said, her voice like a carving knife.

Mavortian said, "I am afraid that none of us has the slightest idea of what you mean."

"Let's have this out right now," Lady Victoria said. "Go get Felix."

Lord Shannon went. Mavortian said, "Felix Harrowgate?"

"As if you didn't know," she said, and you could have withered ripe corn with the look she gave him. "I was frankly prepared to dismiss Thaddeus's theories as paranoia and hysteria, but this is really more than I can stomach. How much is Malkar paying you?"

"Malkar?" said Mavortian, and I'd never heard him sound quite so much like he'd had a fast frying pan upside the head.

She heard it, too, and she must have known how hard it is to fake total what-the-fuck-are-you-talking-about confusion, because now *she* was looking confused. She said, "But it *can't* be coincidence, you showing up with someone . . . and what was it you wanted to see me about?"

In Mavortian's place I would've been tempted to try a lie and known better, and he did, too. He said, perfectly straightforward, "There is a fantôme in the wizard's tower."

"And you ask me to believe this isn't a trick!"

"I assure you, there is no trick involved," Mavortian said, and that's when Lord Shannon got back.

He wasn't alone. There were two medium-sized Kekropian guys with him, and, powers, if looks could kill, them two would've taken each other out in a heartbeat. There was somebody taller behind them, and then one of the Kekropians—the one who looked like the brother of all the smugglers I'd done business with for Keeper—he grabbed the guy behind and dragged him forward, and I understood why Lady Victoria and Lord Shannon looked like they'd been seeing ghosts.

It wasn't my face. I mean, it *was*—same corpse-white skin, same slanted eyebrows, same mouth, even with my scar—but his cheekbones weren't as sharp as mine, and nobody'd ever broken his nose. And his eyes . . . I'd made a hex sign before I even realized what my hands were doing, because he was skew-eyed. His left eye was yellow, like an owl's, like a Sunling's out of the stories. His right eye was pale, cloudy blue, and it didn't even look human. And that was how I knew this guy that looked like me was Felix Harrowgate.

After a second, I started taking in the other details. He was half a foot taller than me, and his hands—long-fingered like mine—well, the Mirador's tattoos are gaudy. They start at the knuckles and go all the way to the elbows. He was a hocus, all right. You couldn't miss that a mile away in the rain. And his hair, wild and curly and way badly cut, was even darker red than mine.

I didn't quite know what to make of the way he was staring at me, and I was even less sure of what to make of *him*. I mean, here he was, the monster who broke the Virtu, and he didn't look like a monster. He looked scared half to death, to be honest, and I thought it was the other hocuses he was scared of. And that made me think maybe the Lower City hadn't got the whole story. Like always.

"I don't s'pose you dye your hair," I said.

He flinched at the sound of my voice.

"Hey," I said. "It's okay." I'd finally placed the way he was looking at me. He looked like a little kid who'd just been bought by a thief-keeper, like there was nothing familiar in what he saw and probably somebody was going to hit him soon. I'd seen that look a lot, but never on the face of a grown man, and I didn't care what he'd done, nobody should have to have that look on their face. "I mean, I hope it's okay."

"Felix," said Lady Victoria, "who is this man?"

He moved his flinch-look from me to her, then back to me. "I don't know," he said. His voice was higher than mine, which I totally hadn't expected, and he talked way flash, vowels and all. Kethe, I thought, because I could see how scared he was of them, and I hadn't thought hocuses got scared of each other. I mean, except for people like Porphyria Levant and Brinvillier Strych, but it's only common sense to be scared of people like them.

"What about this wizard?" Lady Victoria said, with a gesture at Mavortian.

Felix Harrowgate's weird eyes turned to Mavortian, but I don't think he saw him. I don't know what he was seeing, but I bet it looked like nightmares. "I don't know," he said again.

"He also says that there is a fantôme in the tower," said Lady Victoria. "I congratulate you on the coordination of your stories."

"Did you see a fantôme in the tower?" Mavortian said, pouncing like a cat on the first thing in the whole conversation that made any sense.

Felix nodded, but I saw the way his shoulders hunched, and I knew he was expecting to get hit.

Lady Victoria snorted, and the other Kekropian, the one who looked like a cross between a bank clerk and a choirboy, said, "My lady, I beg your pardon, but when do you imagine this 'story' was hatched?"

"What?" Lady Victoria said.

"When has Felix had time to talk to anyone long enough to invent a story like this one? And why do you persist in calling it a story when we have done spells to prove the thing's existence?"

"Eusebian spells," she said darkly.

"My lady," the Kekropian said, like he was getting ready to say something with knives in it, and Mavortian said quickly, "I assure you—and I will swear any oath you like—that I have never met Felix Harrowgate before, and I do not know the other person you mentioned."

"Then what about . . . what *is* his name?"

"Mildmay," Mavortian said.

She waited a moment. "Just 'Mildmay'?"

"Yes, m'lady," I said. I don't care to be talked about like a piece of furniture.

"And what is your explanation of this?"

"Don't got one," I said. "He hired me."

"Why?" she said to Mavortian.

He'd seen it coming, because he didn't hesitate or nothing. "He has certain skills that I believed would be useful. I'm afraid it is just a coincidence."

He lied well, now that I could watch him doing it where I knew that was what was going on, and I thought I'd better remember that. I didn't blame him, mind. The Mirador might not call divination heresy, but they'd feel different about the calling spell he'd done on me, and there was something in the air like people looking for somebody to throw stones at. I looked at Felix again, and I remembered Mavortian saying the Spire card meant a scapegoat.

I can't explain quite why I said what I did next. I mean, I figure I would've said it sooner or later, 'cause the curiosity would've killed me otherwise, but I don't know why I was in such a fucking hurry about it.

Except maybe that feeling like the hocuses were getting ready to throw stones—or maybe start biting. I said, "Felix, was your mother's name Methony?"

He looked at me, and this time I didn't make a hex sign, although my fingers twitched. It ain't so bad, I told myself, even though I was lying. Because it wasn't just the skew-eyed thing. You could see in his eyes that he was crazy, and that ain't nothing to have looking you in the face.

"Methony?" he said. He wasn't sure he'd understood me.

"Yeah. Your mother's name. Was it Methony?"

There was this long, long silence. He went white, then red, and finally said in almost a whisper, "Yes."

"Shit. Then we're brothers. Half brothers, I mean." Because no respectable bookie would have given you odds on the chance we had the same father.

"Half brothers," he said, and I really did think for a second he was going to pass out. Which—I mean, I know I'm no prize, but I hadn't thought I was as bad as all that.

"Fascinating," said the smuggler-looking Kekropian, not meaning it even a little, and made Felix jump. "But can we return to more important matters, such as—"

"The fantôme in your tower," Mavortian said, quite nicely, but with just enough edge that I knew he didn't like the smuggler-type either.

"There is no fantôme!" the smuggler shouted. "They're fairy tales, bogeymen to scare children!"

"You know better than that," the choirboy-clerk said and then switched into Kekropian. I knew a little Kekropian, but I couldn't follow much of the fight they had then, because it was all hocus-talk, and I ain't ever been into that end of the dictionary. But when I noticed that the smuggler had the Mirador's tattoos and the choirboy-clerk didn't, I figured I could get the gist of it anyway. And I was more interested in the way Felix had got himself behind a chair and was gripping the back with both hands, like he was afraid it was going to buck him off.

Then Lady Victoria said, "Gentlemen."

Both Kekropians stopped and looked at her.

She said, slowly and carefully, like somebody picking her way across a river on wobbly stepping-stones, "We have recently had a demonstration of some of the ways in which the Cabal's teachings may be . . . inadequate. I no longer know what to believe in this case, and therefore I wish to know: is there some spell, some test, that we can perform in order to determine once and for all whether there is something in the tower or not?"

"There is noth—" the smuggler began, and Mavortian said loudly, "Yes."

Lady Victoria looked at him. The smuggler might as well have been a snuffed candle for all the attention she was giving him.

"I know of three spells that would do what you ask. I imagine that the Kekropian gentleman—" He nodded at the choirboy-clerk, who bowed back and said, "Gideon Thraxios."

"That Messire Thraxios," Mavortian went on, "knows several others just as efficacious. Since I understand that you are in some doubt concerning my truthfulness, I would suggest that we both perform such spells as we know, and you may judge the results."

There was this pause, where none of the hocuses were quite looking at each other.

"What?" Mavortian said.

"I have already done as you suggest," Gideon Thraxios said. "This morning."

"And your results?"

"Unambiguous," he said, and that thin little smile made him look for a second like somebody who wasn't a choirboy and wasn't a clerk. "We have been having doctrinal differences since then."

"I see," Mavortian said. "Lady Victoria?"

"Mr. von Heber," she said, "I would appreciate it if you would perform the spell you know, once I have summoned the other wizards of our party to observe. I believe Chloë knows something of Fressandran theory, and will be able to judge whether the spell does what you say or is an illusion."

"Gladly."

She gave him a little nod and said, "Please, come with me."

So we followed, Bernard sticking close to Mavortian, and me behind them. I noticed the way Felix hung back, the way his hands were shaking when he pushed his hair off his face, and so I kind of hung back myself to walk with him.

I didn't mean for it to unnerve him, but I could see that it did, and after a moment he burst out with, "What do you want?"

He didn't mean it in a nasty way. He just honestly didn't know, and was frightened. I was getting the idea he'd been frightened for a really long time. I said, "I didn't mean to scare you."

"Oh. No, it isn't . . . I just . . ."

"I swear I ain't as mean as I look. I don't bite or nothing."

"I didn't . . . I can't . . ."

"Can't what?"

"The past," he said. Then he shut his eyes, took a deep breath, and said, "Do you really think we're brothers?"

"Two red-haired whores named Methony? 'Less you know something I don't, I'm thinking, yeah, we are."

He went red as a lobster and said in a hurry, "No. No, I'm sure . . . but, but how old were you when she died?"

"Kethe. Four or five, I think. But I got sold in my third indiction, so it wasn't like . . ." I wasn't sure what it wasn't like, and the sentence didn't get finished.

He stopped where we were, at the foot of the stairs and still a good distance from the door the others were going through. His eyes focused on my face, and for a second I saw what he would've been like when he was on top of the Mirador's food chain instead of at the bottom, and I went back a step without meaning to. "How old *are* you?"

"Third septad almost." I stopped and did the math. "Twenty, I guess, by the flash calendar. How old are you?"

The sharpness went, all at once. "I . . . I don't know. What's the date?"

"Nine Frimaire, twenty-two-five," I said. "But that don't help you none."

"No," he said, and managed something that was almost a smile. "I suppose I must be nearly twenty-seven by now. I'll have to ask Gideon . . . later." He shook his head, like he was trying to jar something into place, and some of the sharpness came back. This time he did smile, but there wasn't nothing nice about it. It was the smile of somebody about to spring a trap. "Tell me, little brother, what are you, by profession?"

"Running dog for a hocus, right now."

"And what were you the summer Cerberus Cresset died?"

He nailed me with that one. I couldn't even think of a lie, not that I would have fooled him for a second. He knew. Hocuses always know things like that.

He said, like it was normal and made sense and everything, "You are circled about with thorns."

And before I could get on top of it, ask him what he meant, shit like that, the smuggler-type hocus stuck his head out and said, "Felix, are you coming?"

I saw it give way in his face. The sharpness wasn't just gone. It was crushed flat. He'd been baiting me, sure, but I saw why, all at once, saw how he'd been fencing off this . . . this . . . I don't know the word I want. Zephyr would've had one, I guess, but all I can say is that I saw how bad he was hurt, and how it was worse than just being hurt, it was more like somebody being tortured with the red-hot pokers and the rack and everything, only it was all inside, and there wasn't no torturer that you could kill or reason with or nothing. It was just there.

His shoulders slumped, and suddenly he wasn't making eye contact no more. He moved past me without nothing but a kind of tightening-up, but I was right behind him, so the smuggler-type couldn't shut me out. Whatever I'd walked into here, I wasn't letting go of it yet.

Felix

Another fragment of the wall barricading my past had fallen away. I could not have denied my kinship to this man, not when our common blood was stamped so plainly on our features. I could not deny, either, what he was, the worst kind of Lower City tough. His stance, his feral eyes, his drawling, hard-edged vowels: he was the avatar of all the men I had feared and hated as a child.

And at the same time, he reminded me in some distant aching way of Joline, and so I could not repudiate him, denounce him as the murderer of Cerberus Cresset and let the Mirador's justice sever the bond between us.

I could not pretend that I did not know. I saw the spells of the Mirador ringing him about with black thorns, and the only person who could have such a curse laid on him and still be at large was the one who had murdered the Witchfinder Extraordinary three years ago.

But my own experiences of being accused of treason and heresy were raw and throbbing, and I could not help thinking that, just as Thaddeus had been wrong about me, so might I be wrong about this man. The colors surrounding him, although bleak and dark, were not the colors of a man bent on evil, and his wariness, the way he watched the men with whom he had arrived just as carefully as he watched the Cabalines, suggested that his story was more complicated than it appeared at first glance.

And I, in turn, watched him, trying to make sense of who he was, searching for clues that would tell me whether he was Keeper or Joline. But he was remarkably hard to read. I would never have guessed he was as young as he said, and I was sure the wizard who had hired him would be equally shocked. His face was like something carved out of stone, expressing nothing except watchfulness. And the scar made everything worse. It ran from the left side of his mouth up across his left cheekbone to scrawl jaggedly into his hair at his temple. The scar tissue had twisted his upper lip, giving that side of his face a slight snarl, even in repose. He was like a fox who has learned about traps the hard way, who knows that the world is dangerous.

The wizards had clustered together by the window, where the Fressandran seemed to be using the last of the sunlight to work his spell. Shannon had vanished quietly. Doubtless he was telling the guards about these newest developments, but even that thought was better than having him here, looking past me as if I did not exist. I sat down at one end of the settle and rested my forehead against one hand. The argument between Gideon and Thaddeus—which had begun when Gideon had brought me back to the Chimera Among the Roses the night before—had been both protracted and vicious, and between that and my own state of nerves I had gotten almost no sleep before the equally protracted scene this morning as the wizards began to debate in earnest the existence of the fantôme. I had never hated my own school so much, or been so ashamed of our belief in tradition, our reliance on doctrine. It seemed to me now that the Cabal's teachings produced nothing but closed-minded and ineffectual parochialism; if this was the best the Mirador had to offer, I was not sorry to have been thrown out.

"You okay?"

I recognized his voice before I looked up—those terrible vowels. "I'm fine," I said.

He nodded, but I couldn't tell if it was because he believed me or because he wasn't going to argue with me. He glanced at the wizards; at the blond man who'd come in with him and the Fressandran; at the door; and then sat down beside me. I felt myself tense, but he made no conversational gambits, simply sat and watched, leaning forward a little, his long-fingered hands hanging quietly between his knees. His eyes were green, an unusual color in Marathat, although not as unusual—meaning unique—as my own unnatural combination. The colors around him were dark with death and grief and guilt, with the briars of the curse tangled through them. I wondered if he could feel it at all, if he even knew it was there. I wondered why he had killed Cerberus Cresset and how he had escaped, even provisionally. But I was too aware of the wizards' proximity to ask.

I hoped the crippled Fressandran wizard knew what he was doing; I hoped he could convince Vicky of the fantôme's reality, because everything that Gideon and I between us had tried had crashed into the wall of Thaddeus's antagonism and Vicky's orthodoxy and, like weak siege engines, had shattered. There was fear now in the colors around her, fear and real uncertainty; she was wise enough to recognize that there was trouble somewhere, wise enough to see that it was larger than I was. The Fressandran's uncomfortably serendipitous appearance had at least accomplished that much.

There was a murmur around the table, and Peter Jessamyn backed away a step, so that I had a clear line of sight. There was a bright blurry spinning shape in the middle of the table. I could see it throwing skeins of light off, splashing the table and the window and the faces of the wizards.

"That mean anything to you?" Mildmay said quietly.

"Not a great deal, no," I said. "I think it worked." The wizards pulled into a tight cluster again. They were probably arguing, but I was losing their voices in the bright singing of the Fressandran's spell. I looked at Mildmay, and for a moment he had a fox's head.

"I have to go," I said. I got up, hoping desperately that my shaking wasn't visible. Mildmay tilted his head back to watch me, his face still completely unreadable.

"You ain't okay," he said. It wasn't really a question.

"I'm fine. I just need . . ." But what I needed wasn't anything I could explain. I turned and left. I felt his gaze on me all the way to the door, but he did not come after me.

❧

I lay in the darkness of that miserable bedroom, and the air was full of a thin, whispering noise, like the slither of silk on flesh. Gideon had warded me from the fantôme, but he could not ward me from the darkness in my head.

The door opened; I sat up quickly.

"Felix?"

Thaddeus's voice.

"Yes?"

"*There* you are. You shouldn't run off like that."

"I'm sorry . . . I had to—"

"Did that man say something to you?"

"Who?"

"Your alleged brother."

"Oh. No. No, it wasn't him. It—"

"Do you really think he's your brother?"

He came in, bringing a candle with him; I could see a blurry sphere of light, but everything else stayed dark, murky. The shadows had swallowed the world. I turned away from the light so that Thaddeus wouldn't see anything wrong in my eyes.

"I don't know," I said. "He . . . he looks like me." When he doesn't have a fox's head.

"Yes. Quite remarkably so. Is he Caloxan, too?"

I didn't have to see Thaddeus to sense the malice in that question. "I don't know what you mean."

"I'm just puzzled, is all." I heard him shut the door. "See, I remember you telling me you grew up in Arabel, and if that gutter rat's ever been out of sight of the Mirador before in his life, I'll eat my rings. All ten of them."

I said nothing. Thaddeus continued, "And really, Felix, you *can't* expect me to believe *he*'s the son of a Caloxan noblewoman." His voice came closer. I steeled myself not to flinch. "So what I'm wondering is just how much you've been lying about."

He knew about Pharaohlight; I could hear it.

"Where are you from?" He barked the question at me, and I did jump. But Malkar had trained me by just such methods, and I responded by reflex.

"Caloxa."

"Don't give me that. The story doesn't wash, Felix. You must see that. How did you get from Arabel to Pharaohlight?"

You've got it backwards. But the mere thought of saying that made my throat lock up.

"I'm waiting," Thaddeus said, much as Malkar might have.

"I cuh . . . I can't tell you."

"You can't *tell* me?" Gloating incredulity in his voice, and I shut my eyes against the sting of tears. "You mean there is no answer, don't you? You can't tell me because it never happened. You're as much a gutter rat as your brother, aren't you? *Aren't* you?"

I tried to get up, to get away from him, but he grabbed my arms and slammed me down on my back on the bed. "We aren't done here. You've been lying to all of us for years, putting on your airs and graces, laughing at the *fools* who believed you."

"Please let me go," I said, but my voice was barely a whisper, and Thaddeus wasn't listening.

"My God, when I think of you, claiming equal standing with the Lemerii and the Bercromii, taking advantage of Lord Stephen's good nature, of Lord Shannon . . . !"

"Let me go!"

"How'd you do it, Felix?" he said, leaning in so close to me that I could smell the mint he always chewed on his breath. "Where'd you learn the manners? Who taught you to talk like a gentleman? Who gave you that perfect, perfect story?"

"Let me *go!*" I struggled halfway up, but he caught my shoulder and pinned me flat again. "Tell me!" he was shouting. "Tell me!"

I was sobbing, and I hated myself for it, but I couldn't get away, couldn't get away from his weight pinning me down, couldn't *breathe* . . .

A voice. Gideon's voice. Words I couldn't understand. The weight gone, the cruel hands gone. I rolled over, away from the light, from the harsh voices, and wept into the quilt, disgusted by the noises I was making, but powerless to stop.

The door slammed.

A hand touched my shoulder, and I spasmed away from it, making a dreadful, humiliating animal-like noise. And then the hand was gone, and I was sobbing again, so hard that the only noise I could make was a rasping struggle for breath.

Stop it! I said to myself. Stop it! But I couldn't. It only died down when my body was simply too exhausted to support it any longer. I lay there then and wished Gideon had left me on the Linlowing Bridge.

A voice said quietly, "Felix, I am sorry."

And there was Gideon. Again. I said, not moving, my voice thick and rasped halfway to nothing, "Why didn't you leave?"

"I couldn't. You are hurting."

I started laughing.

"What?"

"I'm sorry. It just . . . I couldn't . . ."

"Thaddeus will leave you alone," he said after a moment.

"He's afraid of you."

"A little. But that doesn't matter. Are you all right?"

"Yes, thank you. I'm fine."

His voice was suddenly hard. "Sit up. Look at me."

I sat up, looked as near as I could judge in his direction. I still couldn't see anything clearly, only the globe of candlelight near the door.

"Now say it again. Tell me you are well and happy."

"Really, Gideon, I promise, I'm . . ." And I realized I had been about to say "okay," that ubiquitous piece of Lower City idiom that Malkar had beaten out of me before I was fifteen. I did a quick, panicky review of everything I'd said since Gideon first spoke to me, but I was fairly sure my Marathine had been standard and my vowels clean. "I'm really fine," I said lamely.

I wouldn't have been convinced either. Out of the murky jumble of darkness, Gideon's voice said, "Indeed? And that's why your eyes appear to be focused two inches to the left of my left ear? Can you even *see* me?"

"It's . . . it's very dark in here," I faltered, the blood mounting painfully to my face.

"I heard you describe your hallucinations to Thaddeus and Lady Victoria. Is that what's happening now?"

"Oh. Oh damn."

"I wish you would trust me."

"I . . . I'm sorry."

"Failing that," Gideon said, as if I had not spoken, "I wish you would tell me the truth." Everything in my chest congealed into a block of ice. Gideon continued: "For instance, when did your vision begin to . . . become peculiar? You seemed all right earlier."

He was after a different hare than Thaddeus had been. My relief made it possible to say, quite reasonably, "Why do you care?"

"Call it intellectual curiosity. When?"

"The spell," I said, remembering. "It was right after that Fressandran wizard cast his spell that . . ."

"Yes?"

I lay down again, staring up at the dark cloud that was the ceiling. "That the monsters came out," I said in a bare whisper.

"Interesting," said Gideon. I felt him sit down on the bed, but he did not touch me, and I was able to hold myself still. "Do you think there's a causal connection?"

"Between the Fressandran's spell and me being crazy?" I had my voice back under control now; I sounded almost sane.

"Let's clarify this," he said, almost snapped. "I'm tired of people calling you crazy, and I'm even more tired of you accepting the label."

"But I *am* crazy. Gideon, I appreciate your support, but you can't—"

"You have been profoundly damaged by a spell, in ways that no wizard in Marathat or Kekropia is competent to assess, much less mend. I grant that the end results look like madness, but it is not the same thing."

"The distinction fails to comfort me."

"That's because you're not thinking. This is the effect of a *spell,* Felix, not anything intrinsic to your mind. It may be possible to *do* something about it. Now, do you think the abrupt deterioration in your condition is or could be related to the fact that an act of magic was being worked near you?"

"Maybe. Magic . . . I could feel it, in the Mirador, whenever they were trying something else to mend the Virtu. It hurt."

"Aha."

"You have a theory," I said to the ceiling and wished Gideon would go away.

"I am investigating a theory. I think you may have developed a . . . a morbid sensitivity to magic."

"That sounds very impressive. What does it mean?"

He was silent for a moment. "You've said that Malkar separated you from your ability to do magic. Thaddeus thinks you're using that excuse to pretend that the Curia's interdict doesn't bother you—"

"Then Thaddeus is even stupider than I thought him."

"Point taken. I'm afraid I can't think of any way to explain this without resorting to a florid metaphor."

"I think," I said wearily, "that at this juncture your rhetorical style is the least of my problems."

"It's a wound that isn't healing. It's like raw flesh."

"And magic would be like salt, is that your thinking?"

"Crude but accurate."

"I'm not a poet. And I don't see what good it does us to know that."

"You don't find any shred of hope in the thought that it isn't some random and senseless plague that strikes you without warning or reason?"

"No."

"Then you are as stupid as Thaddeus." I felt him get up, heard him cross the room and go out. He shut the door firmly, but without slamming it.

"I trusted Thaddeus once," I said to the ceiling when I was sure he was gone.

Mildmay

When we were back out on the sidewalk, Mavortian said, "Well, *that* was interesting," like it was only good manners keeping him from actually biting me. "Why didn't you tell me he was your brother?"

"Because I didn't know, okay?"

"You didn't *know*? How could you not *know*?"

"Oh fuck me sideways 'til I cry. Let's make this fast. My mother was a whore. That good enough for you? And anyway, why didn't *you* tell *me*?"

"What?"

"*You*'re the hocus. *You* got the cards that see patterns in everything. How come they didn't see this one?"

"If you'll excuse the interruption," Bernard said, at his nastiest, "are the two of you planning to sleep out here tonight?"

"Powers, Bernard," Mavortian said, "must you be so plebeian?"

"Somebody's got to be. We need a place to stay, since your new friends weren't exactly welcoming us with open arms."

"Cabaline wizards are not my 'friends,' " Mavortian said.

"I meant him," Bernard said, jerking his head at me.

"I ain't friends with hocuses."

"Even when one of them is your brother?" Mavortian asked.

"Yeah, and us so close and all. Bernard's right. Let's find a hotel."

"Suggestions?"

"Yeah, let's go back to the Crimson Ape," I said, and maybe it was more of a snarl than anything else, and maybe I had reasons.

Mavortian gave me a look, but didn't bother with actually saying nothing. Bernard said, "That first place we tried for news looked all right. And it's not far, since we spent the afternoon walking in a great big circle."

"Your reasoning is impeccable," Mavortian said, and you could have sliced bread with the edge in his voice. "Let's go."

I was also getting really tired of walking at Mavortian's pace, but I'd seen what happened the one time Bernard had tried to suggest hiring a mule or a sedan chair or something, and since it was Mavortian paying me instead of the other way around—at least, if he did pay me, which could still happen—I didn't figure I had the leeway to tell him to stop being an asshole about it.

The hotel was called the River Horse. It was clean and cheap, and since most of the building was a bar, not real quiet. I practically cheered when they finally bounced the last drunk at the ninth hour of the night and I could get to sleep.

Where I dreamed about Keeper. Which figures. In the dream we're laying in her bed, with the huge teak bedframe carved with dragons and knights and all kinds of weird shit. We've just fucked, and she's still laying half on top of me, propped up on her left elbow so she can see my face. She's tracing the scar on my face with her index finger. She knows that bugs me. I move my head, but she just laughs, and her right hand is still there. I'd move again—I don't like Keeper's mind games—except that her left hand has got itself clenched in my hair, just behind my right ear.

"You weren't going to leave, were you, Milly-Fox?" she says. "Because you know I don't like you leaving before I'm done."

"You ain't done?"

She laughs, like a tiger growling. Her right hand leaves my face—and Kethe I'm grateful—and slides down my neck, my chest and stomach, curls around my cock. "I don't think you're done either. Or are you going to tell me you're just being polite?"

"Keeper, I can't. I got a girl."

"Do you, Milly-Fox?" she says, and her right hand comes back up my body until her fingers are against my cheek again.

"Yeah. Her name's Ginevra."

"Sweetheart, I'm sorry to be the one to tell you this," and she ain't sorry at all, I can hear it in her voice, "but she's dead."

I woke up with a start. It was nearly dawn, and the voice I was hearing wasn't Keeper's. It was Mavortian, chewing Bernard out like the end of the world. Powers, what *now?* I thought. A lifetime in the Lower City suggested pounding on the wall and yelling at him to shut the fuck up, but I was grateful enough to be out of that dream to let it slide. And besides, right about then Bernard started yelling back, and they wouldn't have heard me anyway.

"Another great morning," I said to the ceiling, and rolled out of bed.

Mavortian had convinced the hocuses that there really was something nasty in the tower, and him and the clerky-looking Kekropian even seemed to know what to do about it. So we were all supposed to go there today and do whatever it was you did to nasty shit like that to make it go away. I didn't see what good us annemer types were going to be, but when I caught Mavortian and said so, he said, "No, you have to come."

"Why?"

"Would you believe moral support?"

"No."

"Pity, since it would even be true, more or less. I'm outnumbered, to put it bluntly, and that can be bad news with Cabalines. They tend to think in packs."

"And what good are me and Bernard gonna be if they get ugly?"

"No, no, you've missed the point. You're there to *keep* them from getting ugly."

"I don't get it."

"Don't worry. Just believe me when I say that the possibilities for unpleasantness will become drastically reduced if there are a few annemer in the room."

"Okay. You're the boss."

"How right you are. Shall we?"

"Sure," I said and followed him out of his and Bernard's room and down the stairs and out, to where Bernard had decided to skip the whole argument and just hire a mule.

"Bernard," Mavortian said, like he was going to go on and have the argument anyway, and I just couldn't put up with it no more.

"It's a mule," I said. "What's the big deal?"

"Bernard knows how I feel about this sort of thing," he said, and he was glaring at Bernard like he was making notes for the dissection later.

"What sort of thing? Not having blisters on your hands the size of St. Millefleur? Being on time in front of them other hocuses? What?"

Now he'd turned the glare on me. "Look," I said, "you want to pretend you ain't a crip, it's fine with me. But I don't get it."

"Ah, the refreshing directness of street filth," Mavortian said, as nastily as he could. "Fine. I'll ride the damn mule."

Bernard didn't say nothing while he was getting Mavortian settled on the mule, but he did give me kind of a wink where Mavortian couldn't see, and I followed them and the mule through Hermione mostly thinking how weird it was that me and Bernard had ended up on the same side of anything.

This tower that everybody was so excited over wasn't much to look at. The guys from the Mirador were already there, standing around the door and looking like a funeral. Felix and Mr. Thraxios were standing a little apart from everybody else, and the other Kekropian looked like he was trying to put a hex on both of them. Lord Shannon Teverius looked like a fairy-tale prince who'd got himself in the wrong story. I wondered if they'd brought him for the same reason Mavortian had insisted on bringing Bernard and me. Lady Victoria was arguing with one of the other lady hocuses, and the rest of them looked like they were waiting for the sangerman. And from the way they looked at Mavortian when he got down off the mule, they thought he was it.

Powers and saints, I thought, today's just going to go on getting better and better, ain't it?

And that's when the little squad of soldiers came out from behind the tower.

I realized in time they were heading for Lord Shannon, not for me, and I didn't bolt. Maybe Felix hadn't betrayed me after all. I looked at him, and he was staring at Mavortian, and I thought maybe I was okay. But you'll understand that I was hanging back a little.

I was specially not-happy when the hocuses decided that the guards should stay down here, outside, and Mavortian wouldn't let me stay, too. But he only knew half of why the Mirador made me twitchy, and the half he knew wasn't the *really* bad half. And all my instincts were against picking a fight in front of people who weren't friends and couldn't be trusted. So I followed the hocuses into the tower.

It was spooky. Not spooky like the Boneprince, not exactly, but I got some of the same feel. And there was no dust and no cobwebs, and even with the broken window, there weren't no birds' nests or nothing. And it didn't smell like an old building. That hit me about halfway up the stairs, and I almost did turn around and bail, even if it meant I had to sit and dice with the Protectorate Guard the rest of the day. 'Cause, see, I'd spent a lot of time in old buildings, and I knew how they smelled. Dust and water, and air that ain't nobody been breathing for a septad or six. And this tower didn't smell like that at all. It didn't smell like anything. When I came up into the room at the top of the stairs, I caught like a hint of something sweet, but it was gone before I was even sure it was really there.

The hocuses went over to the broken window, dragging Felix with them, although he was looking really white around the eyes, like *he* was wanting to bail in the worst possible way. Me and Bernard stayed right by the stairs, and Lord Shannon sort of wandered off, so he wasn't getting in his sister's way, but he wasn't hanging out with us street filth either.

"So," Bernard said, "are you enjoying the shit out of this or what?"

"Oh yeah."

"Yeah. Me too."

Lord Shannon gave us this look like he'd found a dead rat under his bed, and moved farther away.

Me and Bernard were both looking around like we expected something to jump out at us, even though I ain't never been in a room with less hiding places. But it felt like a trap. I kept thinking about them doors we'd passed on the way up and how we didn't know what was behind them, and any monster or anything with the sense to just lay low had us caught like rats, since the only other way out from here was straight down to the paving stones. I mean, I knew that wasn't the kind of monster we were dealing with, but it was how the room *felt,* like we'd just walked into a trap like a bunch of trusting sheep.

The hocuses were arguing now—and I wished I'd thought to make book with Bernard on how long *that* would take—and Lord Shannon was still sort of exploring, looking at the walls and the holes in the roof. He went across to examine this big red circle in the middle of the floor. He crouched down and touched it, straightened up again looking at his fingers—there wasn't no red on them, I could see that from where I was—and started to step into the circle.

"Shannon, don't!"

I know everybody in the room didn't really stop breathing at once, but that was what it felt like. Felix was absolutely as white as chalk, and I didn't know how good an actor you'd have to be to fake that note of panic, but I didn't think he was that good. I couldn't see the look Lord Shannon was giving him, but I guess he didn't think Felix was acting either, 'cause after a moment he nodded and stepped back.

He was real stiff about it, like it pissed him off to be doing anything Felix said. I remembered all at once, out of nowhere, that they'd been lovers before the Virtu got broken. Looked like that was over and then some.

"The longer we argue," Mavortian said loudly, over one of the hocuses whose name I didn't know, "the more pointless our presence here becomes. Let us perform the spell and argue about the theory later."

"Hear, hear," said one of the lady hocuses, the sensible-looking one, like you could have a conversation with her—if you were crazy enough to be talking to a hocus in the first place.

"I agree," said Lady Victoria. "Bickering is futile. Come."

The hocuses moved over to the red circle. Felix came across the room to stand by me and Bernard, though I didn't think it was because he wanted our company. He looked scared and kind of sick.

"You okay?" I said.

"Fine," he said, but not like he meant it. I was starting to think it would be a good idea for somebody to pin him down and find out what it was he really meant when he said "fine," but this wasn't the time for it, and I wasn't sure I was the right person anyway. I was still wondering how I felt about having a brother who was a hocus and crazy with it and maybe not a very nice guy besides.

The hocuses made a circle around the red circle—and I noticed they were all being real careful not to step inside it—and then they started chanting in this language I didn't know and didn't want to. It sounded like the same shit Vey Coruscant had been rattling off in the Boneprince, and that wasn't making me feel no better about the whole thing.

They went on for a while—I don't know how long exactly, but it felt like forever—and just when I had decided nothing was going to happen, something did. It wasn't nothing big, but I realized that the smell I'd noticed when we came in was getting stronger and ranker. I could see in between two of the hocuses that there was something clouding up in the circle, like somebody'd breathed on a windowpane. It wasn't an actual shape or nothing, but it was there, and it was watching. I knew that feeling from the Boneprince. The thing in the circle, the fantôme, was watching and hating, and I could feel it looking for an opening, like a guy in a knife fight waiting for the other guy to let his guard down.

Me and Bernard and Felix and Lord Shannon were all clumped by the stairs now, and the hocuses were chanting louder. I hoped whatever it was they were doing was working, because if that thing got free, I didn't think there was anything short of flying that could get us down the stairs fast enough to get away from it.

Then, over the hocuses' chanting, Mavortian shouted something, five words like the hammer of doom. The thing in the circle seemed to pull in on itself. The hocuses kept chanting, and Mavortian shouted his words again. I could feel the fantôme screaming in the bones of my skull. Mavortian shouted a third time, my ears popped, and the fantôme was gone.

It really was. You could tell by the way the room felt. It was just a room again. I could feel the breeze from the broken window.

I glanced at the others. Lord Shannon was already heading for Lady Victoria. Bernard was staring at Mavortian, looking grumpy like always. Felix's face had gone all stiff, like there was something he was trying real hard to keep from showing on it.

One of the hocuses said, "Is it gone?"

"Yes," said Mr. Thraxios. "We should do something about this circle, but the fantôme is gone."

"I know a number of good ritual cleansings," said the plump lady hocus. "What do you think will be most effective?"

They were just getting into it when I heard the door open at the bottom of the stairs. Me and Bernard looked at each other and moved away from the stairs. Felix came with us, but he still had that funny look on his face, and I didn't feel like it was a good time to try talking to him.

There was more than one person coming up the stairs—three or four from the sound of it, but the echoes were weird. I wondered if I should say anything, but whoever it was had got past all them guards with no fuss so probably wasn't a big threat—or was the sort of thing a warning wouldn't help with. And the hocuses were arguing so that I figured they wouldn't pay me no mind anyways.

Out of the blue, Felix said to the hocuses, "Don't use garlic. It'll only make your eyes water."

Everybody got real quiet for a second, all of us staring at him, and the people on the stairs rounded the last turn and came up into the room.

And that's when every bone in my body started trying to twist into a different shape, and my blood started burning, and my brain tried to crawl out my eyes and ears and nose. It was purely on instinct that I got past the guy standing at the head of the stairs and a personal miracle that I didn't fall down the entire staircase from top to bottom. But I knew what was happening, and I wasn't going to die with all them hocuses watching.

Felix

"Who was that?" said Stephen Teverius.

A moment's frozen silence. Vicky said, "Stephen?"

"Yes, yes, of course it's me. I need to talk to you. And what are you doing up here anyway?"

"Powers," said Vicky. "Stephen, it's . . . it's delightful to see you, but what . . ."

"Don't blither, Vicky," Stephen said, crossing the room. "I have news, and we need to make decisions that can't wait, so . . ."

I lost the rest of it in the realization of what I'd just witnessed. The thorns around Mildmay lashing into life, the lurching, clumsy way he'd started down the steps—it made no sense, but I knew what I'd seen.

Gideon was standing by the window, watching the other wizards, the expression in his eyes thoughtful but otherwise unreadable. I was amazed, peripherally, that I could see him so clearly, since Stephen was shrouded with the mantle of the bear, and I saw other, stranger things out of the corners of my eyes. But Gideon was clear to me, and I was as grateful as I was surprised.

I went up to him. "Gideon?"

"Felix," he said, politely but without warmth.

"I don't want . . . it's not about me. Do you think you can tell the Fressandran wizard—"

"Von Heber."

"Von Heber. Do you think you can tell him he should go and find Mildmay right now?"

Gideon's eyebrows went up. "Why?"

"Because . . . because I think he's in trouble. And I don't think the others should know. Please?"

He gave me a narrow, green look.

"It may be extremely urgent," I said. "Gideon, *please*."

"All right," he said. I watched as he went over to the Fressandran wizard, touched his sleeve, said something in his ear. They had a quick, almost silent exchange, and then Gideon came back to me, the Fressandran limping behind him.

"Messire von Heber would appreciate it if you would explain what's going on," Gideon said.

"I can't," I said. "But . . . but Mildmay may be dying."

"Of *what?*" said the Fressandran.

"A curse. *The* curse. The Mirador's curse. But I don't know. I don't know how—"

"No *wonder* he said he wouldn't go anywhere near the Mirador. Are you sure?"

"No. Not really. But I think—"

"No, you're right. Find him first, work out the details later. Messire Thraxios, do you think you can spin a story . . ."

"To cover our hasty departure?" Gideon thought a moment. "Yes. We're going to consult about cleansing spells. I don't think they'll ask why Felix is tagging along."

Resentment flared and died at the contempt in the verb. I deserved nothing better. Gideon went and caught Chloë Wicker, who was the best of his limited range of options. Von Heber crossed to the stairs, where his blond hireling was waiting, arms folded and eyebrows up. I followed him.

"Let's start down the stairs," von Heber said. "No haste, but no loitering."

"Something's going on," the hireling said.

"Brilliant, Bernard. *He*"—with a jerk of the head in my direction—"says Mildmay may be in trouble."

"How shocking," said Bernard.

We'd made one full circuit of the tower when Gideon caught up with us. "We'd better be quick," he said. "Thaddeus knows something strange is going on. And I must admit, that's all *I* know. Felix?"

"I'm not sure. I may be wrong. I hope I'm wrong."

"Wrong about what?" said von Heber.

"I don't see why it would have been activated," I said. "The Cabal cast that warding curse on the Mirador itself, and it shouldn't—"

And then we heard the noise. It wasn't a scream, but it was more than just the harsh breathing of someone in pain.

"What's that?" said Bernard.

"I think you weren't wrong," von Heber said to me. "Where is he?"

Like a hurt animal, Mildmay had sought out a hiding place. We found that one of the doors off the stairwell was ajar. We went through it, von Heber and Gideon calling witchlights. For a moment, the shadows seemed to be watching us with tiny glowing eyes, but I said the words *morbid sensitivity* to myself like a talisman, and the hallucinations receded.

We found ourselves in a warren of tiny rooms; I knew the configuration of walls had to have some thaumaturgic significance, although I could not read it myself. Mildmay was curled in the far corner of the second room we came to, shaking as if he had an ague.

"What's wrong with him?" Bernard said.

"It's a curse," I said. "But I don't understand—"

"Bernard, shut the door," von Heber said. "We'd better not move him, and I don't think we want anyone else walking in. Now. Explain this curse to me."

I took a deep breath, hoping that I could stay lucid, hoping that they could understand what I could not. "Mildmay murdered the Witchfinder Extraordinary three years ago. I saw the Mirador's curse on him, and since that curse is designed to kill and Cerberus's killer is the only person who has ever escaped it . . ."

"Yes, I see," von Heber said. "But then what is this?"

"I don't know. I mean, I *do* know. It's the curse. But I don't understand what set it off, and I don't understand why it isn't working."

"What do you mean, it isn't working?" Bernard said. "It looks pretty effective to me."

"He's still alive."

There was an uncomfortable, unsettled pause before Gideon said, "Since most of the Mirador's spells are either broken or monstrously weakened at this point, I don't find that beyond explanation. My question is, what are we going to do?"

"We have to help him," I said.

Gideon gave me a politely disbelieving look. "Did I misunderstand you when you said he murdered a wizard?"

"No, but—"

"I have need of him," von Heber said.

"Gideon, please," I said. "I can't let him die."

"Why not?" Gideon said. "What is this farouche murderer to you?"

"My brother."

"Whose existence you were not aware of two days ago. Your fraternal concern is touching but overdone."

"Damn it, Gideon, are you saying we should stand here and watch him die?"

"Kethe! Just kill me and get it over with!"

We all jumped; none of us had imagined Mildmay was still coherent. But he raised his head, his eyes the lurid green of absinthe against his chalk-white face. He said, "I did for Cerberus Cresset, sure enough, so if you want me dead for it, go ahead and—" He broke off, bowing his head, and I saw the spasm tear through him. When he could speak again, he said weakly, "This is gonna take hours."

"I think you have a choice, Messire Thraxios," von Heber said. "Either help us, or go inform the Cabalines upstairs—"

"You can't!" I said. "Gideon, *please*. You said you'd help me."

The look he gave me was like being stabbed. "I did not realize what your definition of 'help' would entail."

"Then go on," I said, looking away from Gideon. "Go tell Stephen that you've found Cerberus Cresset's murderer. He will doubtless greet you like a long-lost brother, and I imagine you will be able to name any reward you like."

There was a long moment in which the only noise was Mildmay's rasping, panting breath. Then Gideon said, "No."

We all stared at him; even Mildmay's head came up a little. Gideon looked embarrassed but unbudging. "I didn't listen to you once, and that turned out to be a nearly fatal mistake. I don't feel inclined to make *that* mistake a second time. I shall make a new one instead. What do you intend to do?"

I discovered von Heber was looking at me, too. "I don't know," I said.

"You're the only Cabaline in the room," von Heber said.

"But we've never understood what happened."

Gideon shrugged. "So ask."

"Ask?"

"He's right here. Ask him."

"Oh." I could feel my face heat. I went down on one knee. "Mildmay, do you know why the curse didn't kill you when you . . . that is, when Cerberus died?"

"Miriam had a thing," he said, his words harsh and slurred and barely comprehensible.

"A 'thing'?"

"Yeah. Little wooden box. She said, don't open it, and I didn't."

"And what did it do?"

"Dunno. She said, keep it in your pocket. 'Til you're out of the Mirador.

And I did. And the curse didn't get me. 'Til now." He stopped, going rigid against another convulsion.

"Oh," I said, straightening up again. "That's brilliant."

"What's brilliant?" Gideon said.

"I didn't think there was anyone in the Lower City capable of working that kind of magic. This wizard—Miriam—she constructed a decoy."

"Explain," said von Heber.

"When Cerberus Cresset died, Mildmay should have died with him—more accurately, Mildmay should have died before he was able to kill Cerberus. It's a protection spell, part of the *quid pro quo* the Cabal used to get their reforms enacted. But that little box must have been the vehicle for a spell that deflected the protective spell."

"Then I don't understand," Gideon said. "Why is he . . . ?"

"There's a second tier of spells," I said. "I don't think it was supposed to work this way, since I don't think anyone ever imagined it was possible to evade the protection spell, but there are warding spells on the Mirador itself. The decoy must have been able to hold those spells off long enough for him to get out of the Mirador again—"

"Miriam said, don't waste time," Mildmay said in a gasp.

"Exactly, but it couldn't get rid of them. The spell on *Cerberus* ceased to function when he died, but the spells on the Mirador are—" I stopped, my own guilt threatening to choke me.

"All but destroyed," Gideon said.

"And that explains why Mildmay's still alive," I said, forcing myself to keep thinking, keep reasoning. "The curse can't be operating at more than a quarter of its original power. But I still don't understand what set it off."

Mildmay said something.

"What?" I said.

"The Lord Protector," he said, and I could see the effort it cost him to make the words comprehensible.

I started laughing; I couldn't help it, although von Heber and Gideon both looked rather alarmed. "I'm sorry," I said. "I'm sorry. It's just that—oh, Stephen will hate this—he's become a metonymy."

"What on earth do you mean?" Gideon said.

I took a deep breath; I could see it now, clear as day. "The assorted thaumaturgic cataclysms have resulted in the Mirador's warding spells being focused on the Lord Protector. I don't know when it would have happened or if we would have noticed if anyone had thought to look. There are lots of things about the Cabal's spells that we don't understand, and since Stephen is annemer . . . So, at the moment and for thaumaturgic purposes, Stephen *is* the Mirador."

Both Gideon and von Heber were silent, rapt in contemplation of the thing's marvelous idiocy.

"What are you going to do?" said the practical Bernard.

"We can't lift the curse," I said. "That would take a full assemblage of the Curia, and even if we had them here, they wouldn't do it. But maybe . . ."

"Maybe what?" said Gideon.

"Maybe we could put Miriam's spell back together. I understand what she did, I think, and I . . . oh."

"What's the matter?" von Heber said. "You've gone white as a sheet."

"The interdict," Gideon said.

"I can't do magic anyway," I said. "I'm useless."

"Tell us what to do," Gideon said. "We are both competent."

"It's not that. It's going to take a Cabaline—"

"Miriam wasn't," Mildmay said, panting.

"No, but . . ." I didn't know how to explain what I saw, the writhing snarling blackness around him. "There's no leverage otherwise."

Gideon and von Heber looked at each other. "Thaddeus," Gideon said thoughtfully. "Peter, Ferdinand, Victoria, Chloë, Gethruda. I suppose Chloë *might* do it."

Somewhere in the middle of his list, the answer hit me. I said in a thin, distant voice, "No. He'll die while you're arguing with them. We have to use the other way."

"*What* other way?" Gideon said.

"I . . ."

Mildmay spasmed again, swearing viciously; I caught a glimpse of his face, white and contorted in a snarl of pain, the scar like a bolt of lightning. I said in a rush, "You can use me."

"I beg your pardon?" said von Heber.

"But we just established that the interdict—" Gideon began.

I cut him off; I had to get the words out before my fear closed off my throat. "It's what Malkar did. If Robert could use it, I'm sure you can. The interdict's on me, not on my magic."

"That made about as much sense as a mud pie," said Bernard.

But Gideon and von Heber both understood. I looked away from the horror and pity in their faces and said, "We'll need a token."

Gideon said, "But shouldn't we try—"

"We don't have time." I could see the briars getting thicker and blacker and more vicious. "Please. Don't argue with me."

"What kind of token?" von Heber said prosaically.

I looked again at Mildmay, the lashing briars around him, the tornado colors clouding the air. "Glass would be best, but wood would do in a pinch. No clay and no stone. And it needs to be something small enough to carry."

Von Heber and Gideon began rummaging through their pockets.

"Oh, powers," said Bernard in disgust. He stalked away into the maze of little rooms. After a moment, we heard the sound of breaking glass, and Bernard returned with a triangular shard from one of the windows. "You'll want to do something about the edges."

"Thank you," von Heber said, and I took the shard.

"Do you understand what needs to be done?" I said to von Heber and Gideon.

"You want to use that piece of glass as an umbrella," Gideon said. "Do you really think it will work?"

"I don't know. But . . . None of the others will help him. You know that."

"Yes," Gideon said reluctantly. "But I have to ask: do you *really* want to do this? Do you know what it's going to do to you?"

"I have an educated guess," I said, and I knew the smile on my face was ghastly. *"Do it."*

Gideon looked sidelong at von Heber, who shook his head. "My understanding of Cabaline magic hardly rates the use of the label 'theoretical.' I understand what he wants, but I don't have the faintest idea how to do it."

"I'm not sure I do, either," Gideon said, "but I have committed myself to this foolhardy venture. Felix, I think it might help if you were touching him."

"Oh," I said. "All right." I knelt again, my left hand carefully cradling the shard of glass. I braced myself and reached through the briars to touch Mildmay's shoulder. He was rigid as a board; I said over my shoulder to Gideon, "Hurry!"

Gideon muttered something under his breath that I thought was a prayer. I felt his touch against my mind. Unlike Robert and Malkar, he was gentle, trying not to hurt me. I forced myself to hold still, not to fight; I had to shut my eyes against the shadows and the colors and the monsters. But this time I had chosen it, and I embraced my madness willingly.

Mildmay

The pain was like dragons chewing on my bones. I couldn't scream, because there were all them hocuses upstairs, and I was trying not to thrash out from under Felix's hand, but, Kethe, it seemed like being dead would be easier and quicker and maybe the best thing anyway.

And, I mean, I deserved it. I'd killed Cerberus Cresset. I could see him again now, his self-important face, his tattooed hands clutching at the knife in his chest. I could see he was hurt and surprised and not ready. And it was my fault. Maybe he'd deserved to die and maybe he hadn't, but I was the one had done it. And he wasn't the only one. The rest of them were there, too, standing around me, Cornell Teverius and Griselda Kilkenny and Bartimus Cawley and Lucastus the Weaver and all the others. I guessed they were hoping to see me die, and I hoped they'd feel like they'd got their money's worth out of it, because it seemed to me like I was going to die any minute now, and whatever crazy thing the hocuses were trying was just not gonna take. My heart was beating too fast, way too fast, and the cramps and the spasms had me all knotted up like a pretzel, and now I couldn't've screamed anyway, because everything in my chest had turned into lead, and the weight was going to crush my ribs, and that was going to be the end of Mildmay the Fox right there.

And then the pain faded and was gone. Just like that. I mean, I ached all over like somebody'd been beating me with sticks, but that was okay. I just kind of lay there, staring at the ceiling and being amazed that I wasn't dead, and then Mavortian said, "Well, it seems as if we don't need to worry about sharp edges."

I sat up and twisted around. Felix was still kneeling next to me, his left hand palm up. I could see the eye tattooed on his palm through the piece of glass he was holding, but it was all bubbly and wavy and weird. That was a piece of glass something pretty fucking nasty had happened to.

Felix said, very carefully, like he had to double-check every word to make sure it came out in Marathine, "You'll want to keep this on your person."

"Like Miriam's box," I said. "Okay."

"It has a . . . radius of influence, but I don't know how wide it is."

"Let's not find out then," I said. I held out my hand. After a second, he sort of woke up and tipped the glass into my palm. It was a little warmer than it should've been. Kethe. Hocus stuff. But I shoved it in my pocket, because I didn't particularly want to die, whether I deserved it or not, and I really didn't want to do it that way.

"Can you walk?" Mavortian said. "Because I think it might be for the best if we went back to the River Horse, quietly, now, before anyone becomes—"

"Unbecomingly curious," Mr. Thraxios said. "Felix and I should go back up and display ourselves to Thaddeus lest he come looking." He looked down at Felix and said, "He will, you know."

"Yes," Felix said. He squeezed his eyes shut for a second and then got up.

He looked worse than I felt, and I got to my feet in a hurry because I knew I had to say it, and I didn't want to do it from the floor. "Thanks," I said. "I mean"—and I looked from him to Mr. Thraxios—"I would've understood if you'd let me die. So . . . thanks."

Mr. Thraxios kind of waved it away. Felix shook his head, like he was trying to clear it, and said, "Be careful. There are still thorns."

"Okay," I said. I couldn't help giving Mr. Thraxios a look, because wherever Felix's head was at, it didn't look like it was no nice place to be. Mr. Thraxios gave me a nod, and I figured I'd have to take that for *I'll look after him,* because he was already dragging Felix toward the door, and I didn't know how to say none of what was bothering me.

We waited a couple minutes after they'd gone, and then left ourselves, sauntering down the stairs like there wasn't nothing wrong in the world, except that I wasn't letting go of the banister, and Mavortian and Bernard kept giving me these looks like they thought I was going to burst into flames or something. But it was good enough to get us by the soldiers, and that was good enough for me.

Felix

They were all staring at us as we came back into the workroom, bright unblinking eyes like hunting owls'.

Figure of speech, I said to myself, and the room was *not* full of bird-headed monsters. Just Stephen and Shannon and six Cabalines who hated me. For a weak, craven moment, I wished the throbbing darkness in my head would swallow me again, so that I would not have to understand why I was hated.

"Well?" Vicky said.

I could only be thankful that Gideon knew how to answer her, that he remembered our quickly fabricated lies and had at his fingertips the information we had allegedly disappeared in order to acquire. He crossed the room to the others, talking about the phases of the moon and the energies of the earth. I stepped back and sat down against the wall, welcoming the feel of the cold stones through my shirt.

"And what of the Fressandran and his entourage?"

"Messire von Heber seemed dubious as to the esteem in which he might be held. He and his thugs have gone back to their hotel."

I bit back a protest. Whether Mildmay was or was not a thug, I would do neither him nor myself any good by defending him now. Even as it was, both Shannon and Thaddeus were giving me suspicious looks, as if they could read in my face that Gideon was lying.

"He must have been tremendously thorough," Shannon said. "You've been gone such a long time."

"Messire von Heber is a most learned wizard," Gideon said stiffly.

"I can't imagine he had much to teach *you*. And what about Felix? Was he your practice dummy?"

"Shannon," Stephen growled, as I felt my whole face burn. Shannon couldn't have indicated more clearly that he thought me worthless and irrelevant if he'd hired the chorus of the Opéra Ophide. "Can this wait?"

"Of course," Shannon said; I did not like the way he and Gideon were glaring at each other.

"Thank you," Stephen said with heavy irony. He looked around, the scowl on his face almost comfortingly familiar. "I suppose you'll all have to hear this sooner or later, so it makes sense to say it just the once."

I had always been amazed at the contrast between Stephen's formal speeches as Lord Protector and his habitual terse and graceless discourse. There had been a very cruel engraving that had circulated when he first succeeded to the Protectorate, comparing him to a bear that had been taught to waltz. Like most caricatures, this one's cruelty lay in its deadly accuracy.

Stephen took a deep breath. "Envoys from Vusantine are on their way here."

"*Here?*" Vicky and Ferdinand Emarthius protested in chorus.

"Here. Giancarlo scryed to them from Sauvage. He sent Parsanthia Ward back to let me know while he recovered from the two-week migraine."

"But why *here?*" Vicky said.

"Because," said Stephen through his teeth, "the wizards of the Coeurterre don't want to go to Mélusine."

The silence darkened the room to indigo. Gideon walked across the room to stand beside me; I looked up at him gratefully, but he was watching the other wizards.

Vicky said, "Stephen, what do you think—"

"I think we've got the Kekropians licking their chops on our doorstep. Given my choice, I'd rather be in bed with the Tibernians."

"A noble sentiment," Shannon said, sneering at me.

"Dammit, Shannon, will you shut up?" Shannon looked away from Stephen's anger with a muttered apology.

"Lord Stephen," Chloë Wicker said, "I know that we have had little progress to report to you, but we have—"

"Oh, it's not *your* fault," Stephen said. "I'm not displeased . . . that is, I think you all have done tremendously well. The Tibernians aren't taking over from *you*."

"Then what *are* they doing?" Thaddeus said. I could see red spikes of anger all around him; he would never have spoken to Stephen in that way if he hadn't been infuriated, although I did not know what had angered him.

Stephen preferred honest intransigence to sycophancy. He said, "Money. They are providing money, so that we can rebuild. In return, we are letting the Coeurterre examine the damage."

"We're *what?*" Vicky said.

"It was the best Giancarlo could do," Stephen said, matching her glare for glare. "I'm not going to bankrupt the Protectorate for this, and I am *not* going crawling to Elvenner Packer for a loan."

"You'd rather go crawling to Aeneas Antipater?"

"Yes."

Shannon nervously, tactfully, cleared his throat. Stephen looked up at the watching Cabalines, none of them members of the Curia, and growled at Vicky, "Let's talk about this later."

ᔕᘛ

As we returned to the Chimera Among the Roses, I could feel myself eroding. I had weighed the cost of saving Mildmay's life and accepted it freely, but that did not make the slow crumbling into darkness any easier to bear. I stood by the window in the private parlor, staring blindly into the hotel's back courtyard, gray and drowning in rain. Stephen and Vicky had gone, pointedly, for a walk. The wizards were arguing thaumaturgy in the front parlor, which the hotelkeeper had surrendered without a murmur of protest. He was trailing gold clouds of glory at the mere idea of having the Lord Protector of Marathat gracing his establishment, and he would have given up far more than his public parlor to keep that honor.

I heard voices and turned, but I did not have a chance to escape before the door opened and Shannon came in, followed by his guard lieutenant. Shannon's eyes were as brilliant as beacon fires, and the colors around the lieutenant were coruscating gold and rose. I knew why they had chosen the private parlor, and I wanted, more than anything else, to run. But I stood there, frozen, while Shannon's brilliant eyes looked me up and down, his unforgiving anger burning around him. I could feel him sorting and discarding, looking for the words that would wound me most. Once, I would have been able to strike first and harder—Shannon did not think well on his feet—but now I just stood dumbly, waiting for my annihilation.

The lieutenant looked between us anxiously and said, "My lord, should I—"

"Don't be silly," Shannon said, and his gaze caught mine. I looked down and away; I couldn't meet his eyes. "Felix was just leaving to find his Kekropian, weren't you, Felix?"

He didn't need knife-edged words. He did it all with the tone of his voice—that casual, contemptuous familiarity that didn't even care enough to be annoyed. I meant nothing to him. Nothing at all.

"Yes, my lord," I said in a bare mumble and fled the room, my shoulders hunched against Shannon's mocking laughter.

I stumbled up the stairs to the dubious sanctuary of the bed that was dubiously mine. As I went, I saw the shadows writhing and blooming; I knew that Shannon had, at long last, hurt me more cruelly than I had hurt him.

And my longed-for illusion of security was shattered to pieces before I even got through the bedroom door. Gideon was on his knees by the far bed, throwing things into a bag.

"What?" I said, stopping where I was with one hand still on the doorknob. "What's wrong?"

"Those envoys from Vusantine," Gideon said.

"Oh," I said. It was getting harder to hear him; my ears were filling with the roars and booming of the monsters.

"They're going to want to talk to you."

The thought made me want to sit down where I was and howl. "But I've already told the Curia everything I know!"

"Not like that," Gideon said grimly. "I think we need to get out of town."

"What? But we—"

"*You* broke the Virtu, Messire Harrowgate. *You* were the instrument of the Bastion wreaking havoc on the Mirador. I don't believe anyone coming here from Tibernia is going to care very much for elaborate explanations of why those things aren't your fault."

"Oh," I said. I felt like he'd punched me. "But I don't—"

"No, don't worry. I'm not staying, either."

"You haven't done anything wrong."

"I'm Kekropian. Don't you think that's enough?"

"But, Gideon, they won't—"

"Felix," he said, deliberately and slowly, "they are going to be looking for scapegoats. You're going to be their first choice. But they are also going to be looking very much askance at anyone who came from the Bastion in the last year, and there are certain . . . let us merely say that I do not want to discuss my past with our learned colleagues from the Coeurterre. Is that all right with you?"

"Gideon, I didn't mean—"

"Come on." He stood up, slung the bag over one shoulder, and walked past me out the door.

I couldn't move; I couldn't think. My head was filling with darkness; the pain was beginning to unroll itself behind my eyes. And I could hear things, terrible things, whispering and whimpering to themselves in the corners.

A hand closed around my wrist like a vise. I looked up into greenness, sharp like daggers. *"Come on,"* Gideon said and dragged me without ceremony down the stairs.

Mildmay

So we made it back to the River Horse, and I fell on the bed and slept like a dead thing for I don't know, maybe two hours, maybe three, and then Bernard was thumping on my door, and I felt like he'd been thumping on me the whole time I'd been asleep. Kethe, I ached, and when I say I crawled out of bed, that's exactly what I mean. It took me two tries to get upright again, and I was hating every minute of it.

"What?" I said at Bernard, hanging on the doorframe to keep myself from hitting the floor again.

"New problem. We're leaving town."

"Oh, for fuck's sake. What is it *this* time?"

"Do I *look* like I know?" He didn't. He looked mad enough to spit nails. "All I know is, your nutcase brother and that Kekropian fellow are downstairs, and they talked to Mavortian, and he says we're leaving today, before they close the city gates. Pack your things and let's hoof it."

I didn't have much in the way of "things," so I made it downstairs before Bernard, even taking the stairs in this sort of horrible slow wobble. And like he'd said, Mavortian and Felix and Mr. Thraxios were all sitting in the lobby. Mavortian and Mr. Thraxios looked about ready to start chewing their fingernails. I didn't blame Bernard for calling Felix a nutcase. He looked at me when I went over to them, but I don't know what he was seeing. I don't think it was me.

"What's going on?" I said, sort of generally.

Mavortian looked at Mr. Thraxios, who said, "The reason the Lord Protector appeared in Hermione today is that an embassy from Vusantine is riding to meet him here."

"Okay," I said, "but—"

Mavortian said, "Messire Thraxios believes—rightly in my opinion—that both the Cabalines and the envoys are going to be looking for someone convenient to blame."

"Oh," I said and looked at Felix, who was staring down at his hands.

"Exactly," said Mavortian. " 'Oh.' "

"Foreign wizards are also likely to be regarded with suspicion," Mr. Thraxios said, "and I can only imagine that you would prefer *not* to attract the attention of anyone involved with the Mirador."

"Bull's-eye," I said. "So we're bailing?"

They both looked blank.

"Clearing out."

"Yes," Mavortian said.

"Where to?"

They looked blanker.

"We hadn't quite," Mr. Thraxios began at the same time Mavortian said, "It's a difficult matter to—" They both broke off and nobody got a sentence finished.

"You gotta pick a direction before we go anyplace," I said.

"Do you have a suggestion?" Mavortian said, like he wanted to hear me admit I didn't.

"Sure," I said. "St. Millefleur."

Him and Mr. Thraxios looked at each other. I don't think Felix even heard us. "Why St. Millefleur?" Mr. Thraxios said.

Powers and saints, I thought, but Bernard still hadn't showed up, so I said, "If anybody wants us bad enough to try and follow us, they'll probably figure we're heading back for Mélusine, with savers on east—along of you being Kekropian—or maybe up to Igensbeck. But we ain't got no reason to go south."

"Which is a good enough reason to try it," Mr. Thraxios said. He was giving me a funny sort of look that I couldn't quite figure out.

"And it's a big city. Bigger'n Hermione. Good for hiding, shit like that."

"How far is it?" Mavortian said.

"Depends. How're we going?"

They looked at each other, and I thought, Oh, fuck me sideways, because you could tell they hadn't even thought about that part.

"I imagine," Mavortian said, "that taking the stagecoach would be as good as leaving a letter."

"Yeah," I said. "We're gonna make an easy group to remember."

"There's nothing that says we have to go together," Bernard said from the stairs. I turned around, not being real fond of having Bernard behind me.

"Bernard," Mavortian said.

I couldn't read the look in Bernard's eyes, but I knew it was aimed at Mavortian. "There isn't," Bernard said, almost through his teeth.

"I'm going with Felix," I said, because I didn't want to watch yet another fucking fight between the two of them. "You guys do what you want."

And then they were all looking at me like I'd started barking or something. "He saved my life," I said. "And I don't know, but it looks like it fucked him up pretty bad. I owe him."

"Indeed," Mavortian said, in that way he had. "Well, contrary to Bernard's opinion, I believe there are a number of reasons why we should stay together."

Yeah, and I know what they are, I thought, but I didn't want to get into that, not with needing to clear out before anybody over at the Chimera Among the Roses noticed they had a couple of hocuses missing.

Mr. Thraxios was thinking the same, because he said, "Then let us go."

I'd been worried about Felix, but he got up when the other two hocuses did, and he followed us all just fine, out of the hotel and down to the river and across the Linlowing Bridge heading south. Nobody gave us a second look, and I got to say, I was glad to be gone.

Felix

In my dream, I am walking through the Mirador, down in the dusty halls where no one goes. I am trying to find the stairs to the Queen Madeleine Garden, except that in my dream the stairs start in Malkar's workroom, instead of from the New Hall. I don't want to go to Malkar's workroom, and I know there's another staircase somewhere, but I don't know where exactly, so I am wandering in miserable circles. Malkar's door is open, laughing at me.

Iosephinus Pompey looks at me out of a mirror and says, "There are no gardens in the Mirador. Only graveyards."

And then I am standing in the Queen Madeleine Garden, and I see that Iosephinus is right; no roses grow here now, only tombstones and mausoleums. The fountain in the middle is dry and black. It is the Boneprince, the nightmare cemetery of the Lower City, and if I stay here I will die.

I climb to the Crown of Nails; I look toward Horn Gate, the city of Mélusine writhing beneath my feet like a black, rutting beast. Horn Gate is closed, and now I know, with perfect singing certainty, that the garden, the true garden, is behind it. I struggle to open the gate, my hands throbbing and aching and the bright blood dripping from my palms. Behind me, beneath me, the whole Mirador is laughing in Malkar's voice.

The bolts screech and shriek; the gate judders open, barely far enough for me to squeeze through. I find myself again in the garden with the black, twisted trees. I remember the yellow-eyed man, who said I could be cured.

"Where am I?" I say aloud, to the trees, to the grass, to the white paths. "Please, I have to know."

In Troia, the Daughter of the Morning. In the Gardens of Nephele, where peace flows like water. Where you can be healed.

I cannot see the speaker; I do not know the voice. But I know it is not Malkar, and I know it is speaking the truth.

❧

I wake staring up at the moon, sailing serene and untouched above this sphere of troubles. I remember my dream; I remember the voice. I have to find the Gardens of Nephele; I have to find Troia. I cannot lie still any longer, when somewhere to the east are twisted trees with beautiful white flowers and people who look like me, who will help me.

I crawl to my feet. There are monsters sleeping around me. I do not disturb them. I can find my own way.

I start east across the dull winter grass. But I have barely gone fifty feet when I hear someone coming after me. I turn, quickly. It is one of the monsters, the fox-headed man whose eyes are silver with grief.

"Where're you going?" he says when he has come up to me.

"The Gardens of Nephele," I say. "Troia. East."

"Right now?"

"I have to. They can help me."

"Okay, but who's 'they'? How do you know them?"

"I dreamed it." I start walking again, but he catches my arm. "*Please.*" I pull away from him. "I have to go."

"You can't go haring off in the middle of the night by yourself. You'll end up dead in a ditch by sunrise. Come back and wait for morning, okay?"

"But they won't let me go. They won't listen."

"Yes, they will. And I'll go with you, I promise. But not tonight."

I think I can trust him. I am tired and lonely and scared; I *want* to trust him. I follow him back to where the other monsters are still sleeping, and I lie down to wait for the sun.

Chapter 9

Mildmay

Decad and a half after I stopped Felix from walking off into the blue all on his own, we landed in this little town called Yehergod that was also a duchy. I never did get a grip on how the Empire parceled itself out, and whether the dukes in the south really answered to the Emperor, and what the Bastion had to do with any of the rest of it. Basically it didn't matter, because nobody was our friend anyway, and if you want pointless, just think about Mavortian and Bernard, arguing and arguing and arguing about whether we should go straight east, or dip kind of south, or dip kind of north, or go all the way south to the coast, or what. It got clearer and clearer to me, listening to them and watching Gideon's face getting pinched and gray, that what we were doing was stupid. And not just a little stupid, neither, but the kind of stupid where somebody ought to smack you upside the head for your own good, because you're too dumb to bring yourself in out of the rain.

Which I guess means I got to try and explain why we were doing it anyway.

Mostly it was Felix. I mean, when I'd seen him wandering off in the middle of the night and bolted after him, I hadn't missed what was going on. I don't think I ever managed to explain it so Mavortian and Gideon understood, and it was worse than useless asking Felix, because all *he*'d say was, "I dreamed it." But what he meant was there wasn't no way to stop him from going. I mean, I guess we could have tied him up and carried him to St. Millefleur and locked him in an attic or something, but otherwise . . . I don't even know if he knew there was the whole Empire of Kekropia between him and where he wanted to go, but I knew he didn't care. I'd figured it was about the best I could do to get him to wait for morning.

And then I'd told the others, and they hadn't believed it, even though they knew what he was talking about, which was more than I had. But Mavortian said he couldn't have dreamed *that,* and Gideon talked about how far away Troia was and how we'd never make it across Kekropia, and Bernard just sort of sneered, and finally, I said, "Look. You can't stop him from going, and I'm going with him. Nobody's got to come with us, but we don't got to stay with you, either."

Mavortian saw that I meant it, and I think what happened was he was bound and determined not to let Felix out of his sight. And maybe he figured Felix would get tired, or I was making shit up, or he could jigger things later or something. He was always thinking about his options, was Mavortian. So he said, Okay, we'll all go. And of course Bernard said that was the stupidest damn thing he'd ever heard in his life, and Gideon said he didn't care *what* the rest of us did, he wasn't going back into the Empire, and I thought he was the only one of the five of us who had his head screwed on right way 'round.

Bernard caved—Bernard *always* caved—and then it was just Mavortian and Gideon going at it like a pair of tomcats, and it turned out that Mavortian thought we really needed Gideon along, because we had to keep the Bastion from catching on that they had a Cabaline hocus wandering around like a sheep in their backyard, and apparently the only way to do that for sure was to have a Eusebian hocus sort of finessing the spells the Bastion used to keep an eye on the magic floating around the Empire. Gideon thought as how the Bastion's spells wouldn't pick up on Felix, along of him being crazy and not able to work magic, but Mavortian kept after him, and he finally gave in and admitted that he was just guessing. "Oddly enough," he said, all snarky and mad, "the problem has never arisen before." Mavortian said that wasn't good enough. I didn't know—I mean, it wasn't nothing like what the Mirador did, which I did know some about—but I frankly knew fuck-all about the Bastion, and if Mavortian said we needed Gideon, then I figured I had to believe him. I didn't want to get caught by nobody and especially not no Eusebian hocuses.

But Gideon kept saying he was sorry, but he wouldn't go. He had all sorts of reasons why none of us should go, and I could tell he was really scared, because of the way he wasn't looking at Felix. He never tried to argue that Felix didn't know what he was talking about or nothing like that, he just kept saying we couldn't cross the Empire, and we'd be strung up in a day and a half if we tried, and we should go south to St. Millefleur and maybe see if we could find some books that would let him and Mavortian figure out what kind of magic the Gardens of Nephele used and maybe they could do something for Felix that way. I think that idea was pretty lame and both Gideon and Mavortian knew it, but I ain't qualified to judge.

So they went back and forth for a while, until I guess Mavortian figured that he couldn't sweet-talk Gideon around, and then he worked a neat little piece of blackmail that tied Gideon up with a big red bow. Either Gideon helped us, Mavortian said, or Bernard would drag him to the nearest town and denounce him as a Eusebian.

And Bernard would do it. I don't know for certain if Mavortian was bluffing or not—I don't think he was—but I know solid that if he'd told Bernard to do that, Bernard would have. Gideon knew it, too. He was kind of standing there, like he was still looking for a loophole, and Mavortian got him on the backswing, with this nasty little smile on his face that I for one could have done without. He said as how Gideon shouldn't think he could go back on the deal once we were in Kekropia, because there'd be nothing easier than telling the Kekropians he was a *defector* from the Bastion, and we all knew what would happen to him then. I didn't, but I could tell from his face that Gideon did.

And it made me mad, watching Mavortian put the screws to a guy who didn't owe him nothing, so then me and Mavortian fought for a while, but he kept saying we had to have Gideon, and finally he said, "If you truly want to help your brother, and if you truly believe that he has had this fantastic dream, then believe me when I tell you that without Gideon, we are doomed to fail."

And he meant it. I didn't know if it was true, but I could tell Mavortian believed what he was saying, that he wasn't pulling this shit just because he could. And the fact of the matter was, if he said Gideon was the only guy could keep Felix safe, then I wanted Gideon along. And I couldn't help remembering that when it had been me in a bind, with the Mirador's curse trying to knot me up like a ball of yarn, Gideon's idea had been to just stand there and let me die. And whether I could see his point of view or not, that's a nasty sort of thing to remember about somebody when they ain't giving you something you want.

So I did the only thing I could square it with myself to do, which was to go over and ask Felix if he was sure about this idea. Even when I got his attention, he wouldn't say nothing except that same old song about having a dream and having to go east, but he was absolutely sure he had to do it. And if we were drawing up sides, and it kind of looked like we were, then I was on Felix's side.

And the long and the short of it is, we went east. Got across the border no sweat. I knew how the smugglers did it, and Bernard must have spent half his life oiling across borders without nobody the wiser, he was so good at it. And I got to hand it to Gideon, once Mavortian'd put the screws to him, he went ahead and did the best by us he could. I mean, he wasn't talking to nobody, and I know he wasn't sleeping much, but he was doing what Mavortian wanted, and he wasn't bitching about it neither. Unlike Bernard.

I figured out somewhere in that first decad that a lot of that was Felix. Gideon never said nothing—I mean, he wasn't talking to us, and it wasn't like there was any point in trying to tell Felix—but I saw the way he looked at Felix and the way it hurt him when Felix flinched back from him the way he did from everybody. I ain't much with the brains, but I can see what's right in front of me, even if I can't make sense of it. Gideon was in love with Felix, and I figured that made him crazier than Felix on the worst day Felix ever had. I didn't say nothing neither—because, I mean, it wouldn't help—and after I felt like I could trust Gideon not to, you know, take advantage of Felix or something, I even mostly quit worrying about it. I had plenty of other shit on my mind.

As much as I could understand what Mavortian thought he was doing, his idea was to sort of slide along the northern border of the duchies, where we were kind of at the edge of where the Bastion could see us, but not far enough south that the dukes were much more than puffed-up mayors. One thing for sure, the Duke of Yehergod was strictly small potatoes. No ducal palace in Yehergod, and the militia was made up of the blacksmith, the miller, the hotelkeeper, and as many farmboys as they could round up in any given month. The duke was the town banker, and the only way you could tell him apart from the rest of the crowd in the bar was the gold rings in his ears.

So we figured we were safe, and we kept on figuring we were safe until about the septad-night, when we suddenly found out we weren't safe at all.

And now I got to explain how it is that I was still awake at the septad-night, which in turn is the only reason me and Felix got out of Yehergod without about three pounds of iron apiece on our wrists. See, when they backed the curse off me in Hermione, it wasn't what you might call a howling success. I mean, sure, I wasn't dead, and I wasn't having those fucking cramps, and believe me, I was grateful. But things got weird. I can't put it no better than that. Colors got funny, like there were too many of them packed in behind your basic blue or green or whatever. Sometimes I almost thought I could see the colors around people that Felix was always yammering about. And my hearing got sharper, to the point that Mavortian and Bernard yelling at each other was actually painful. I mean, it was a pain and I was used to that, but now it *hurt*. And I couldn't sleep.

That was the kicker. That was the absolute bitchkitty Queen of Swords. I'm a light sleeper at the best of times, and I don't need a lot of sleep, but now I wasn't sleeping at all. I mean, maybe an hour a night, maybe two. And my dreams were fucking awful. It was like Cerberus Cresset had set up an appointment with the inside of my head, so that every time I went to sleep, there he was, his hands clutching my knife in his chest, his eyes opening wider and wider and his mouth stuck in this prissy little circle, like he died not yet believing that somebody like me could do that to somebody like him. So I'd get to sleep around about the tenth hour of the night, and I'd thrash things through with my old pal Cerberus, and then I'd wake up and it wouldn't quite be dawn yet. And I'd lie there and wonder if it really would have been so bad, dying of cramps. I was tired all the time now. And not just tired, worse than tired, like somebody'd hung this fucking invisible lead chain on me, and I had to drag it around everywhere I went.

So it was the septad-night in Yehergod. The town was dead as a drowned dog, and I was sitting in the room I shared with Felix—along of how basically the others had said, you're the one said you were going with him, so *you* deal—looking out the window because it was better than staring at the lump on the bed that was Felix, and he might be asleep or he might be laying there staring at me. And since we were on the top floor of the hotel and it was the tallest building in Yehergod by a good stretch, I actually had a pretty nice view of the town all asleep and peaceful, and I was sitting there trying to convince myself that looking out at all that peace was making me sleepy. And then I saw something, namely a bunch of goons in chain mail heading for the hotel. Like I said, you could put the Yehergod militia in a string shopping bag and still have room for two heads of cabbage and a parsnip. That wasn't them, and that was enough to say as how these guys were bad news.

"Fuck," I said.

Next second I was across the room. For once, Felix was asleep, so I shook him awake in a hurry and said, "Get your shoes on 'cause we got to bail."

I didn't have time to see if he was with me. I was out the door and into the next room, where Bernard woke up when I was halfway through the door and said, "What the fuck do you want?"

"There's a bunch of soldiers closing in. Time to clear out."

"Fuck. You got the freakshow?"

That was Bernard's ever so fucking tactful way of referring to Felix. "Yeah," I said.

"Then I'll manage the others. Meet at the next milestone outside of town."

"Gotcha," I said and dove back into our room, where Felix was sitting like a tailor's dummy with his eyes eating up his face.

"Come *on!*" I said, dragged his shoes out from under the bed, and shoved them on his feet. "We don't got time for this."

But he was someplace else, and we really *didn't* have time. I looked out the window and the goons were still heading for the hotel, and they were close enough they could've seen me if they looked up. I knew that the duke was downstairs in a game of Long Tiffany with the hotelkeeper and a couple merchants. They'd invited me to join them. Clearly the goons knew where to find the duke, too, and about a centime's worth of my head was wondering about who'd sold him out and why, even while the rest of me was in that cold, nasty, clear place I get to when a job's gone bad. I can't help it. It's just the way I'm made.

I yanked Felix up off the bed, and the only thing I remember for certain about the next quarter hour is the death grip I had on his wrist. We went down the back stairs loud enough to wake the dead. The hotelkeeper's door was open as we went past, with the hotelkeeper and the duke peering out wondering who was dropping trunks down the stairs, and I sort of said in passing: "Soldiers coming!" The last I saw of the Duke of Yehergod, he had pure scarlet murder on his face, and I figure he knew who the snitch was and what he was going to do about it, assuming he got the chance.

We got out into the stableyard and up onto the stable roof, and I really can't tell you how I managed that, because by then Felix was coming apart at the seams, and I was swearing at him under my breath and just about turning myself inside out dragging on his dead weight. But we got up there somehow, and over the gable, and then we slithered down into the street. I took a quick glance at the stars to figure out where the fuck east was, and then I started dragging Felix out of town. We'd gone maybe a block and a half at a dead run when things got really loud back behind us. I hoped Bernard and them were okay, but all I could do was get Felix the fuck out of the picture. Mavortian was a good liar, but that wouldn't help with the Mirador's fucking carnival tattoos.

So we booked it out of town, along their nice wide flat paved Kekropian road and headed for the milestone like Bernard had said. The Kekropians mark their miles off in fives, which is a little weird, but their milestones are the size of small ponies, and they got a bust of the Emperor on them, looking a little funny along of how the Emperor's only got about a septad and two. We slowed down once I was sure nobody was chasing us, but it turned out we'd got away clean. Nobody in the hotel had caught on that Felix was a Cabaline, and I was betting them goons in their chain mail had other fish they wanted to fry.

The moon was near full and cast enough light that I felt safe to keep walking. Like I said, the Kekropians know all about roads, so there ain't no potholes to break your ankle in or nothing like that. And I was worried about how ambitious the goons might be and how far out they might be thinking they wanted to sweep, so I made Felix keep going, even though he was in one of his really bad spells and didn't even seem to know who I was.

I got to say, straight out, that I didn't have the hang of what was wrong with him. I mean, I knew he was crazy, because any fool could see that. And I knew him being crazy had something to do with his magic and why it wasn't working right—I was just as glad of that, actually, because the thought of walking around with a crazy *and* magic-working hocus was enough to completely spook me out. But I couldn't get my head around the rest of it, even though Mavortian had tried to explain it once or twice while Gideon sat there and sneered at him. Gideon understood it better than Mavortian did, and he might've been able to lay it out so as I could follow him, but Gideon wasn't about to do me no favors, and I hadn't thought it mattered enough to go crawling to him about it.

Some days I think I'm too stupid to be let out on my own, and then there's the days that prove it.

We made it to the milestone finally—I don't know what time it was, but by then I was practically staggering anyway and didn't rightly care. So I dragged Felix off the road and behind the milestone, where we wouldn't be spotted right away by anybody who happened to be looking. I would've liked to get farther, but I couldn't see enough of what the land was like to think that was a good idea. So I just sat down where I was and said, "We're gonna wait for Mavortian and them, okay?"

Felix sat down, too, and I finally felt like I could let go of him. He didn't say nothing, but that was normal.

"I'm gonna sleep," I said. "Are you tired?"

"No."

"Then will you watch? Either for Mavortian or for goons. Either way, you wake me up as soon as you see 'em, okay?"

"Okay," he said.

I curled myself up against the milestone. I was just about to fall asleep when I realized Felix had said "Okay," like any pack-brat out of the Lower City, and I hadn't known him long, but I'd figured him out enough to know that *couldn't* be a good sign. But I was too fucking tired even for that, and I fell asleep before I'd got a grip on what I was worried about.

I came awake all at once, with a kind of a jump. I'd slept longer and heavier than I'd expected, so now it was probably the third or fourth hour of the morning and there were wagons rumbling past on the road. Felix was a little ways off, watching the road like I'd asked him to, but he whipped around as soon as I moved.

"Anything?" I said.

"No soldiers. There have been a few wagons from the west, but the drivers didn't look like they'd have been at all amenable to the suggestion of passengers."

He was talking flash, and that meant he'd made it up out of the funk he'd been in when I went to sleep. His madness was like that. Sometimes he'd be okay, and sometimes it was like he'd fallen down a well and there was no rope handy. I could never tell when he was topside if he had any idea about what was going on with him down there in the dark, and I was too much of a coward to ask, and it was this great big ugly thing we never talked about, sitting there sometimes like you could almost see it between us. So what I said was, "Fuck. Looks like they didn't get out."

"I guess," he said, sounding kind of wobbly, like maybe he wasn't as up as I'd thought, and that's when I woke up enough to take a good look at him.

"Hey, you're hurt."

"Am I?"

"Yeah. What did you do to your forehead?"

He put his hand up to touch it and looked at the dried blood that came off on his fingers like he hadn't known blood was that color. "I don't know," he said.

"I must've banged you into something last night. Fuck, I'm sorry."

"Oh, that's all right. I'm clumsy enough that you shouldn't blame yourself."

"You feeling okay? Seeing double? Head hurt much?"

"No more than usual," he said and gave me a kind of an almost smile.

"Small favors," I said, thinking we'd better be grateful for all of them we could find, and stood up. "It don't look like much, but we'd better get it cleaned up anyway. Let's find the river."

"The river?" he said, and if I hadn't had a Great Septad and a septad and six things bumping around in my head like birds in a panic, I might've heard that funny note in his voice, and I might've said something better than what I did say—or maybe there wasn't no right thing to say just then. Dunno. But what I said was, "You know, the Sim. I don't want people asking—"

"I'm not going near the Sim!" he said in this kind of shrieky little voice I'd never heard out of him before. I looked down at him, where he was still sitting next to the milestone, and Kethe, he was right back down the fucking well, only worse. He was about two inches this side of a good old-fashioned fit of hysterics.

I did the only thing I could, seeing as how what we most desperately didn't want right then was anybody noticing us special, and maybe remembering us to mention to them goons in Yehergod. Especially as it was right then that I realized one of the things we'd left behind in that hotel was Felix's gloves. So I grabbed him, scruff of the neck and one wrist, and dragged and shoved and all but carried him back off the road and down into a drainage ditch. And it was probably the standing water that really set him off.

He got about half a scream out before I slapped him, hard as I could. It was the only thing I knew to do for hysterics, and I probably don't need to say how shitty I felt when it worked. But I was scared and mad, and like I said, I had these panicking birds throwing themselves around in my head, and so I kind of hissed at him, "What the fuck is wrong with you?"

His eyes were big as bell-wheels, and he was breathing in these huge kind of sobbing gasps, but he got out, "The Sim . . . I can't. Please. Not the Sim."

"Okay," I said. "Then we won't. No big deal."

And then I felt even worse, because he was staring at me like I'd said I was going to get myself upholstered in pink chintz.

"There must be a stream or something around here. That okay?"

After a moment, he nodded.

"Okay. You done with the opera?"

He went five different shades of red, but he gulped and nodded, and I said, "Then let's get out of this fucking ditch."

We climbed out on the side away from the road and sat down to get the water and mud and stuff out of his shoes and my boots. The grass was brown and brittle, but big handfuls of it still worked okay to get the worst of the muck off our feet and trousers. I figured I wouldn't worry about my socks just yet. If we could find a stream, I could take care of them and Felix's cut at the same time. His socks were still in Yehergod along with everything else we didn't happen to be wearing, and I added that to the list of things we'd have to get somehow before we went too much farther. He already had blisters on his heels and raw patches on his toes, and I felt like even more of a shit because if I'd taken half a second to think once we'd got clear of Yehergod, I'd've realized that was a problem and done something about it. I did at least have the sense not to ask him why he hadn't told me.

We found a stream easy enough. The water was clear and cold and tasted okay, and I figured that there couldn't be nothing nastier in it than we'd already found in the drainage ditch. So I washed out my socks and took a drink, packed moss around Felix's toes and heels and got his shoes back on him, and then found that by some absolute miracle, my handkerchief was still in my waistcoat pocket. So I cleaned the blood off Felix's forehead, and the thing turned out to be more a graze than a cut. I figured it probably happened somewhere about the time I was yanking him onto the roof of the stable. It wasn't serious anyway, and I could move on to worrying about the rest of our problems.

Which were considerable. First off, we'd lost the people in our party who really knew what they were doing, and if Mavortian was right, we'd lost our protection against the Bastion noticing Felix. I figured I'd better hope Mavortian was wrong, because there wasn't a single fucking thing I could do except keep my eyes peeled for dragoons. And I'd be doing that anyway. Then there was Felix being crazy and me not being able to sleep and all the rest of it. Merciful powers, I thought, how did I get into this?

Could be worse, Milly-Fox. Could be back there in Yehergod with them goons, trying to explain how come you never noticed your brother was a hocus. No, instead I was out in the middle of nowhere with my nut-case hocus brother, neither of us knowing more about how to get across Kekropia than a pair of woolly lambs. Kethe was looking out for me about like usual.

"Need a map," I said.

Felix just looked blank.

"You still want to go east, right?"

He nodded, even though it looked like he thought I was going to whop him one for it. The longer I was around him, the more he reminded me of Devie, one of Keeper's kids who hadn't been all there. She was strong as an ox, mind you, and she wasn't crazy or nothing. But she had a bitch of a time understanding what people said to her and what they wanted her to say back. She had that look a lot, the one like she wasn't sure if she'd said the okay thing or the really not okay thing. And with Keeper, if you didn't say the okay thing, you *would* get whopped. I wondered if them hocuses had been the same way.

I said, "Then we need a map."

"How are you going to find one?"

"Fuck, *I* don't know. We need a stationer's. Or a bookseller's, maybe. So a good-sized town. And some money."

"Oh," Felix said.

"Yeah. Me, neither."

We sat there a little while in silence. I think both of us were hoping the other guy was going to come up with something. If it had been one of

Felix's good days, I'm pretty sure he would've. And, I mean, he was doing okay, considering as how he'd been doing a screaming freak-out less than an hour ago, but I could tell he wasn't really all the way with me. So finally I admitted it really was up to me, and if I got Felix caught by the Bastion, then there just wasn't going to be anybody else to blame for it.

I said, "About all we can do is keep moving east and hope we find something. And, oh Kethe, we got to do something about your hands."

Felix looked at them, backs then palms, then looked up at me.

"You don't got your gloves, do you?" I said, not 'cause I was hopeful or nothing, but just 'cause sometimes you got to ask the stupid questions.

He shook his head.

"Better find you some. But 'til then, we gotta keep 'em hidden." Gideon had said—about the only piece of information he offered, and he'd said it for Felix's sake, not for the rest of us—that once we got past the Bastion itself, it would be pretty unlikely that anybody would recognize Cabaline tattoos. But we still had to be at least a decad off from that, and the people on this side *did* recognize the tattoos, and they'd know what to do when they saw them, too. "What the fuck does the Mirador want with these damn carnival tattoos anyway?"

"It is a great honor to be named a wizard of the Mirador," Felix said, sort of dreamy-like.

"Fine. Can you just keep your hands in your pockets? Stand up and let's see if that'll work."

He stood up meek as a lamb and put his hands in his pockets. He was still pretty down, then, 'cause when he was topside he wouldn't do nothing without you argued a half hour first. And it worked okay, aside from looking a little funny 'cause of him being so tall it was hard to find stuff in the secondhand shops that fit him, and the only coat we'd found that wasn't too small must've been made for a giant or something. There was sleeve to spare.

"Okay," I said. "It'll do, but you *got* to remember not to take your hands out of your pockets, or we're both gonna be fucked. Okay?"

"Yes," he said. "I'll remember."

"Okay then." I got up and shoved my hair off my face. Between our hair and my scar and Felix's height and eyes and being obviously crazy, we were going to be about as inconspicuous as a pair of flamingos, but there wasn't a single fucking thing I could do about *that,* either. "And keep your mouth shut." He spoke Midlander okay, but his Kekropian was lousy, and either way you could have buttered bread with his flash accent, and anybody caught on to what *that* meant, and there we'd be, right back in the trouble I was about killing myself to keep us out of.

"I won't say anything," Felix said.

"Good," I said, and I don't suppose I sounded very nice about it.

We came on a road sign about the ninth hour of the day. I asked Felix to read it—he could read Kekropian just fine, he just couldn't speak it for shit—and he obliged: "Here begins the Duchy of Medeia. Long life to the Emperor Dionusius Griphos."

"Oh boy," I said.

"Yes, rather," said Felix. And he sounded, thank the powers, like himself again.

"We'd better watch our step."

"Your command of the obvious is awe-inspiring," he said. I flipped him the finger like I would anybody being that snarky, and he just grinned.

What I really wanted about then was just to bolt into the bushes and forget about this whole stupid thing, but that wasn't going to come up with no workable long-term plan. "Come on," I said. "We can't do nothing about it."

"*Anything,*" Felix said, just enough under his breath that I could pretend I hadn't heard him.

And we walked into Medeia.

It was the biggest town we'd seen since we left Hermione—although still nothing but a medium-sized anthill next to Mélusine—but what was really weird was that it was all *new*. We didn't see anything over a Great Septad old until we were right in the middle of the city, where we found old buildings being torn down so bigger ones could be put up.

"Medeia is doing well for itself," Felix said in my ear.

"Yeah," I said and wondered what there was out here in the middle of fucking nowhere for people to get rich off of.

By then we'd hit the marketplace. People were looking at us a little funny, but I'd got used to that over the past decad and a half, people staring at me and Felix like we were carnival freaks. I guess I even understand it, because, I mean, I'd never known anybody else with natural red hair until I met Felix, and so there were the two of us, side by side, and I wasn't noticing red-haired people thick on the ground in Kekropia neither. I'd always wondered where my mother's red hair came from, and never found nobody who could tell me.

And you've probably seen this coming from like a septad-mile off, but believe it or not that was the first time it hit me that there was a pretty fucking major hitch in my plans. See, what you want for pickpocketing is to be just this side of invisible. You don't want nobody to notice you, and you don't want nobody to be able to remember you an hour later, much less describe you to the Dogs. That's why Keeper'd started teaching me other things when I got my face laid open, because I was going to be worse than useless for shearing the flats. I'd gone back to pickpocketing on and off once I was grown, along of it being not nearly so surprising to see a man with a scar on his face as it is a kid with two septads, and I'd gotten good at always keeping my face kind of turned, or kind of down, or just so nobody was going to get a good head-on look at me. I'm a little shorter than average, and that helps, too.

But that had all been when my hair was black. Now it was bright fucking red, and I called Mavortian some nasty things under my breath. I dragged Felix off to one side, so as not to be standing like a pair of statues in the middle of the sidewalk, and said, "You got *any* money?"

"No one has been trusting me with the petty cash, oddly enough."

"Fuck it, I ain't joking. You got any money?"

"No."

"Fuck."

"What?"

I yanked hard on a handful of my own hair. "This."

"What?"

"Kethe!" I said and just barely remembered to keep my voice down. "Ain't you caught on yet as how your hair that color is as good as shouting?"

The look on his face was as blank as a cloud, and I realized, with his funny eyes and how tall he was and along of being a hocus, maybe he'd never learned about not being noticed in a crowd.

I took a deep breath, let it out, counted a septad. Said, "Up 'til about a month ago, I dyed my hair black."

"Oh," he said, but he still wasn't following me.

"The poor man's grope," I said, that being part of an old joke about how if you couldn't afford a Pharaohlight whore, there was still something you could do with them, and about as near as I wanted to come to saying "picking pockets," even in Marathine. He looked over my shoulder at the crowd, then back at me, and finally got it.

"I see your difficulty."

"Thanks so very fucking much. Got any *ideas?*"

"It's been . . . that is, why would I know anything about such matters?"

He was trying to pull a fast one. I mean, he was a pretty good liar, but this one must've been too raw even for him, because he was blushing. And if we hadn't been in the middle of a crowd of Kekropians giving us both the hairy eyeball, I would've gone after it. But this just wasn't the time. And after a minute, he said, "Maybe a hat?"

"No money, remember?"

"Damn," he said, instead of any of the stronger things I would've chosen. He didn't ever swear—nothing worse than "damn"—and I guessed that was what the Mirador did to people.

I shook it off, although I couldn't help a sigh. "I'll do my best. You stay here—and stay *put,* you hear me?"

"No, I thought I'd wander off, find a lynch mob, and show them my tattoos," he said, in a voice so low it was barely a whisper, but the poison in it came through clear as a bell. When he was topside, he hated me talking to him like he wasn't.

"Have fun." I didn't give him another look—'cause we could stand there arguing until sundown—just turned and sauntered off.

Well, I got us money and I didn't get arrested, which I had to chalk up as a miracle, and, I mean, I was sweating peach pits the whole time. I had the twitches something terrible by the time I went back to Felix and said, "C'mon, let's bail."

"And where are we going?" he said, like I was some idiot trying to get him to go out on a picnic in a thunderstorm.

"Thought we'd find a hotel room."

He followed me then, although I knew he was itching to find some way to make it look like his idea. I picked a medium-sized hotel with a sign about halfway along between fresh paint and bare wood. It called itself The Swan's Lover, and I knew the story it was talking about. I figured that was a good omen.

The room was cheap and clean, and the only problem was Felix wouldn't stay put in it.

"There's no reason I can't come with you."

"Are you out of your fucking mind? You got reasons all over your fucking hands!"

"But you're going to buy gloves."

"So?"

"So there's no reason I can't come. You buy gloves, I put them on, and no one's the wiser."

"Kethe! No, it's just stupid. There's no reason—"

"I'm not staying in here like a parcel left to be called for."

He meant it. I'd learned all about that particular look in his eyes. And the longer we argued, the more likely it was the shops would start closing.

"Okay, fine. You fucking well win. But when we get arrested, don't bitch at *me*."

"I won't," he said and gave me the smile that made chambermaids go weak in the knees.

"C'mon," I said, like a curse, and we went out.

Got his gloves, got a map—I found out all at once that I loved maps, and I could've stayed in the stationer's for days, but I could feel Felix itching to leave. Went back to the hotel, noticing how many people were staring at us and wondering if any of them were snitches for the Imperial dragoons. We were staying in tonight. That much I was sure of.

Felix

Mildmay spent the afternoon poring over his map. It was only when it was really too dark to read that he got up and said, "We'd better see about dinner. And a bath."

"A bath?"

"Yeah. You know. If you can't be good, be clean, my keeper used to say."

The casual reference to having been a kept-thief almost stunned me. I had to decide how to answer him, to admit to knowledge or to pretend ignorance. Blindly, desperately, I chose the lie.

"Keeper?" I said, raising my eyebrows.

"I was a kept-thief down in Britomart," he said on his way to the door. To him it was nothing important; he wasn't annoyed or embarrassed or ashamed. For a moment, I hovered on the brink of saying, "I was a kept-thief in Simside," but I could not do it.

He opened the door, said, "Don't go nowhere," and was gone, taking with him the moment when I might have confessed the truth.

He locked the door behind him, which was nearly enough to make me climb out the window. Even if I was insane, I wasn't a child, and he didn't need to treat me as if I were too stupid to take care of myself.

I sat and seethed, formulating ways to tell him just what he could do with his *don't go nowhere* and his damn key, but when he came back in, he wore the fox's head and lambent silver eyes, and my fury died in my throat. I shook my head, and he was Mildmay again, looking at me with his eyebrows quirked as he closed the door.

"You okay?"

"Yes, I'm fine." The improvement I'd felt that day, as we got farther and farther from Mavortian, had lured me into thinking there would be no further retrograde motion in the path of my madness through my personal sky. But that, I realized coldly, was nothing but self-delusion. Each time my magic was used—by Malkar, by Robert, by Gideon at my own instigation—my recovery took longer and was less and less complete. The lengthy period of quiet travel after we left Hermione had given me the opportunity to notice that I *was* recovering, but that did not mean that I was sane again, or even anywhere close. Mildmay was right not to trust me.

He had been explaining the arrangements he'd made, but I wasn't listening until the phrase "bring up the bath in an hour" caught my attention.

"Bring *up* the bath?"

His eyes were green and calm and perfectly ruthless. "You ain't going in a bathhouse where any prole can just wander in and gawk."

"But . . . what did you tell the hotelkeeper?"

"That I'd pay extra." He didn't grin because he never did, but I could see his amusement in diamond sparks around him.

"All right. As long as you're sure it's safe."

"Safer'n going around looking like a pair of tramps."

"I suppose so," I said, and I couldn't deny, either to him or to myself, that I would feel infinitely better for a bath.

A chambermaid brought the food—bread, cheese, cold meat, and beer—and squeaked with pleasure at the tip Mildmay gave her.

"I thought you wanted to be inconspicuous," I said.

"We ain't, and we ain't gonna be. So I'd rather she remembered a good tipper." He put cheese on a slice of bread and started eating.

I knew he wouldn't talk until he was done; he might not care about having been a kept-thief, but he was morbidly self-conscious about the scar on his face. I took a slice of bread for myself and watched the dark colors swirling slowly around him. I wondered what the grief was that would not leave him, but asking would mean admitting that I was still seeing colors, and I was not prepared to do that. He already knew too much about me; I would not offer him further ammunition.

There was a great deal of bustle over bringing in the bath; I retreated into a corner and watched, noting that Mildmay's strategy of paying generously for odd requests was a successful one, at least in this hotel. The maids were transparently eager to please, bringing extra towels, assuring him that the second lot of water would be ready whenever he wanted it. One of them was even trying to flirt with him, although I didn't think he realized it.

He herded them all out the door again, closed and locked it, and said, "You first."

"What?"

"You go first," he said, slowly and as distinctly as he could.

"I understood you."

"Then what?"

I tilted my head meaningfully at the door.

"Nope," said Mildmay.

"What do you mean, 'nope'?"

"We ain't splitting up."

"You can stand right outside the door."

"Oh, and nobody's gonna think *that*'s weird."

"What does that matter? You said we can't be inconspicuous."

He gave me a stony look and said, "I ain't going. You want to argue about it, it's your bathwater getting cold."

His obstinacy was all around him, granite and iron. And I wanted a bath so badly, wanted to be rid of the mud and dust and stickiness.

He is not Brother Orphelin, I said to myself. I took my clothes off, deliberately, one garment at a time, not looking at Mildmay, giving him his chance to stare his fill at the wasteland of my back.

He said nothing until I was settled in the tub, my knees practically up around my ears. Then, as I was working the soap into a lather, he said in a quiet, careful voice, "What happened?"

"Malkar."

"The guy who . . . ?"

"Yes."

It was a comfortless lie, but I could not admit that being a kept-thief, so commonplace to him, had damaged me so deeply. If I told the truth now, he would remember I had not told the truth earlier, and that would tell its own tale as clearly as my scars did. Let Malkar bear the weight of blame.

We were silent for a while as I applied soap vigorously, and then he said, "I got my face laid open in a knife fight."

I looked at him; he met my eyes steadily. "They thought it would heal okay, but it got infected. This side of my face ain't moved right since."

No wonder he would not smile. I looked away, scalding with shame. He had answered my lie with truth, my silence with honesty. I plunged my head underwater, but I did not feel cleaner when I came back up.

Mildmay

My map had told me what I needed to know.

I knew where we were, because I'd got the stationer to show me. That was Medeia, a little black square out there in the middle of a whole lot of nothing, but with two of the thick black lines that meant Imperial roads crossing right through it, and I figured that explained why Medeia was looking so new and shiny. The place we wanted to get to, the coast of Kekropia where we could find a boat to take us to Troia, was way the fuck at the other edge of the map.

I'd listened to Mavortian and Gideon arguing about where they wanted to end up, which was how I knew there was an ocean between us and Troia to begin with. Mavortian had been pushing hard for Aigisthos, and even an ignorant lowlife like me knew that was the capital of Kekropia, where the Emperor hung out. Mavortian said Aigisthos was the biggest port along the whole coast, and it was so busy nobody would even notice us.

But Gideon was dead set against it, and when you consider he felt like the whole damn trip was suicide, that had to mean something. He said caravans to the Bastion—and I'd found the big red circle like a plague boil that showed where the Bastion was—anyway, Gideon said caravans to the Bastion always left from Aigisthos, and there were Eusebians at the Emperor's court, and if there was anywhere in the east end of Kekropia where somebody was going to figure out what Felix was, Aigisthos was it. And besides, he said we were way south of Aigisthos and wouldn't do nothing but add to our travel time trying to get there. His choice was a place called Klepsydra.

I'd scanned down the coastline and found Aigisthos and Klepsydra. I'd been careful to get a map in Midlander, along of it having the same alphabet as Marathine, which Kekropian don't, and although I don't read much better than I sing, which ain't at all, I'd managed to spell out AIGISTHOS and KLEPSYDRA without asking Felix for help. I didn't want him gloating over me, and I knew he would.

As best I could tell, Klepsydra was pretty much due east of Medeia. And if the map was telling me the truth, the road we'd been following would take us there. A nice straight shot, and I wondered why it didn't make me feel better—aside from dragoons and hocuses and Kethe knew what all between us and it, I mean.

But at least it was something to aim for. We started out of Medeia first thing in the morning, before the sun was even all the way up. Stopped to rest at the first milestone, and I looked over at Felix and didn't much like what I saw.

"You okay?

"Yes." But he didn't snap it at me the way he would when he *was* okay, and I thought, Fuck. Because he was going back down the well again, and I'd been hoping I'd have the other Felix, the topside Felix, for a couple days at least. When I started walking again, he followed me, and I knew he was down the well for sure, because he was hanging back. He had long legs and a fast stride. When he was in a good spell, he'd walk alongside me or even ahead of me if he got too fed up with my pace. But when he was down, he stayed back behind me, like he thought maybe I'd forget about him if I couldn't see him. It drove Mavortian stark barking mad, the way Felix would end up like three septad-feet behind the tired old mule we'd pooled our money for, because even Mavortian allowed as how he couldn't walk all the way across Kekropia. That mule didn't have but one speed, and that was somewhere between an amble and a funeral march, and there Felix would be, trailing along behind it like a stray dog scared somebody would start chucking stones. And you couldn't make him catch up, neither. Topside or drowning, he hated to be touched, and when he was in the well, he flinched anytime somebody got in striking distance, and that just plain did not help.

So I didn't say nothing and I didn't look back. I just kept walking, heading east toward this place that Felix said was going to help him.

We landed a ride with a carter around about the septad-day. I held his horses' heads while he dealt with a stone that was giving his offside horse considerable trouble, and in return he said he'd take us to the next big town, a place called Hithe. So we sat in the back with bales and bales and bales of cloth, while the carter up front sang to his horses, and all the time I was so grateful I could have kissed him if it hadn't been for that being a really bad idea. Because it was sinking in deeper and deeper just how big Kekropia was and just how long it was going to take us to get across it. I mean, I'd known that all along, but I was only just now starting to *feel* it, like a weight on my shoulders making it hard to breathe and hard to think.

But one thing I knew whether I wanted to or not. I was going to have to start cardsharping again. Pickpocketing was just not going to work a second time. I could feel it, the way I used to be able to feel sometimes not to take a job no matter how much the guy was offering. I'd never argued with that feeling, so I didn't have proof about it, but on the other hand, I hadn't ended up in the Kennel, either, and some days that felt like proof enough. And I sure as fuck wasn't going to start arguing now. Cards were safe. I was good enough I probably wouldn't even have to cheat.

It wasn't nothing I was looking forward to, though. I mean, I actually like playing cards just as a way to pass the time, but once there's money involved it turns into a whole different thing. It's like I transform or something, like in a werewolf story. I can't even explain it, but a guy I played with once, back when I was sharping for Keeper, he said he thought I was going to kill him if that was what it took to keep him from winning, and that gets pretty close to it. And it ain't about the money. I mean, it ain't the money I *want*. It's just that if there's money riding on it . . . Well, that's why I don't play for money except when I absolutely got to, because it feels like the kind of thing that's going to kill you if you give it its head.

But sometimes you ain't got no choice, and I wasn't so high-minded as to let me and Felix starve to death just because I was looking at something I didn't want to do. I just hated the shit out of it, that was all, and it didn't help none that Felix was sitting there like he was scared I was going to smack him for breathing too loud. Don't get me wrong. He was a real prick when he was topside, and I wasn't even trying to pretend I thought that was because of his situation—which was damn nasty, to be fair about things. But that ain't what gave him that tongue like a flaying knife.

That was just how he was. But I would've put up with that all the way to Hell and back home the long way round, rather than the way he got when the madness was holding him under.

Not that I had any fucking choice about it.

Felix

I can feel Keeper's anger all around me like thunderclouds.

I didn't know he was Keeper at first, when he shook me awake in the dark, but then it all became just like the last time I had seen Keeper, the curt order to get ready to leave, the sounds of adults talking in the dark, the anger and impatience, Keeper cursing at all of us as he shoved us down the stairs, coughing and sobbing. We'd been only halfway down when the roof collapsed, and that was when Joline was pinned under a burning rafter and I'd dragged her out and she'd died in the middle of Rue Orphée. Keeper'd never made it out at all.

But now it has happened again, and this time it is Joline and the others who were lost. Keeper dragged me out alone, leaving the rest to burn. I rub the yellow and purple bruises on my wrist where his fingers had clamped like a vise, and that, too, is familiar; that is part of what Keeper is.

He has gone out. I am alone in our hotel room, light-headed with relief, able to breathe for the first time all day. I open the window for a moment, just to feel the bite of the night air against my face. I think that I will sleep, while he is gone and I know it is safe.

I lie down on the bed, stretch out as I cannot when he is here. The sheets are thin enough to be translucent, but they are clean and soft. Everything is quiet, peaceful; even my hands have stopped aching.

The desire for oblivion weighs my bones like lead, but sleep remains distant, unobtainable. I open my eyes. The single candle is still burning; the room is full of shadows, but there is no reason to be frightened. Keeper is away, and I am safe.

Except that I am not. There is something wrong, something in the air of the room that should not be there. Now I cannot keep my eyes closed; the shadows are too thick, and there is a tinge of blood in their blackness. My ears are thunderous with sounds I cannot quite hear.

I can't stay lying down; there is too much of the room I can't see. I bolt up off the bed and back into the corner nearest the candle.

Then I press my hands to my mouth to stifle a scream. I couldn't see what was wrong with the room because I was lying in it. A woman's ghost is lying on the bed, bruised, bleeding from bite marks and deep scratches, her eyes black, mindless pits of agony and terror. Her legs are spread, stiff and awkward, and her body is being slammed against the mattress in a fast, brutal rhythm. She is being raped, and I cannot see her rapist—her murderer, for I know she did not live through this. She died on this bed, died with some man's breath hot on her face, his semen poisoning her body.

And I cannot see him.

I wonder if I will be able to see him when he has finished with the woman. I wonder if he will look like Malkar. I don't even realize I have moved until I am out in the corridor. Keeper said I mustn't leave the room, but I can't go back in there. I can't. Nothing Keeper can do to me can be worse than what's happening in there, on that bed I could not sleep on.

But Keeper will be furious. I remember what he did to Fenella when she disobeyed him. I remember how Joline and I held each other afterward, crying, both of us shaking as if we were fevered. I am shaking now.

I can't go back into that room; Keeper will punish me if I stay out here. I can't face the ghost; I can't face Keeper. I wish that I could simply disappear, vanish from this blood-soaked stage like the Necromancer in a pantomime.

And then I realize that I can. There is no one here to stop me or to bear tales. It is dark out; Keeper will not come looking for me in the dark. I have never been that important to him. I can find the Sunling from my dreams, and he will help me.

My shivering lessens. I proceed cautiously down the stairs. The desk clerk is deep in conversation with a young man with the head of a cat, and does not notice me when I leave.

I know where I want to go. I start walking.

Mildmay

There wasn't nobody in Hithe could play Long Tiffany to keep up with me, although a couple of the local goons fancied themselves pretty hot shit. I was careful not to win every game, on account of not wanting somebody laying for me and Felix on the way out of town tomorrow, but I won enough to give us some breathing space the next few days.

Nobody at the table was hard-core enough to want to make a night of it. So round about the septad-night, me and my winnings went upstairs.

Our door was open.

Felix wasn't there.

It felt like somebody'd hollowed me out and replaced all my insides with ice water. It was a minute before I could even start to make sense of what I was seeing.

The bed was all rumpled, but there weren't no signs of a brawl or nothing like that. Felix's shoes and socks were on the floor beside the bed, but that didn't mean nothing. He could keep himself decent, but when he was down the well, little things like shoes and combing his hair didn't happen without I took a hand. And if somebody'd grabbed Felix, they would've found out he was a Cabaline by now, and I would've heard about it. Boy would I ever.

So it looked like Felix probably left on his own two feet and without nobody else to put the idea in his head. Kethe. What the fuck had gotten into him?

But as soon as I asked, I knew the answer, because there was only about one thing in Felix's head these days, and if he'd lit out on his own it was an absolute sure thing that he was heading east.

I said some things, between my teeth and lavish on the details, while I got together Felix's socks, shoes, and coat—which he'd *also* bailed without—and bundled them up, tying the whole thing together with his shoelaces. Then I dropped the bundle out the window. It would get dirty, but that was better than having the desk clerk wondering why I was taking my clothes out for a walk. I would've gone out the same way myself, except that there was no way in Hell I was going to get Felix up that wall, and if I was going to be seen coming in, I'd better be seen leaving.

I figured I'd better lay some groundwork, in case I was bringing Felix back in a state, so I told the desk clerk I was going to go get my brother before he decided to make a night of it, and since that didn't faze him, I figured Felix must have snuck out somehow without him noticing. I went out, circled the building and got my bundle, then went back to the street and headed east. I didn't know how much of a head start he might have but I was betting it wouldn't do him much good regardless.

Hithe had rolled itself up for the night, and I was glad of it. Fewer people out, fewer people to see Felix and wonder what the fuck was wrong with him. He'd been wearing his gloves when I left, and I hadn't seen them anywhere in the room. I was praying that meant he still had them on.

Shouldn't've left him, Milly-Fox. And I knew I shouldn't've, but I still didn't see what else I could've done. I sure as fuck couldn't take him with me. Cardplayers are about the most superstitious guys out there, and they wouldn't have to know he was a hocus or that he was nuts to think I was trying to hex them by bringing him along. One look at his spooky skew eyes and they wouldn't touch any deck of cards I'd had my hands on. And me sitting up there in the room with him wouldn't do nothing for nobody, including the hotel manager.

I have these dreams sometimes where I'm on a job for Keeper, and I'm supposed to have a map and I don't, and I'm supposed to have learned the night patrol's timing and I haven't, and I'm supposed to meet somebody so they'll let me in and I'm late. And I can't remember what it is exactly Keeper wants, and everybody I ask says something different. The kind of dream where you wake up and lay there for a quarter hour before you can believe none of it was real and you ain't going to be stuck in that particular circle of Hell for the rest of your life. Traveling with Felix was turning out to be just like that, only it wasn't a dream.

I headed east pretty steady, casting out north and south every so often because I knew his sense of direction was no good even when he was topside, and I was betting he'd get himself lost pretty quick. It occurred to me after a while that it'd be funny if he'd not even got going the right way to start with, so I was looking for him east and he was going west. Fucking hilarious, Milly-Fox.

But before I really got into the second-guessing—and there ain't no way to fuck yourself up faster—I heard somebody fall over something up ahead of me. I gave myself good odds it was Felix and waited 'til he came to the next streetlamp to be sure.

It was him, all bones and red hair. I covered the ground between us faster than I'd ever covered a comparable stretch in my life, swung him around by his shoulder, and slammed him up against the wall.

"What the fuck are you doing?" I said, just barely remembering not to shout, and it was only when I saw how wide his eyes were and felt how bad he was shaking that I realized how pissed off I was and how scared, and how stupidly fucking glad I was to see that he was okay—still in one piece, I mean, because otherwise he was looking fairly well fucked over.

"Felix?"

And he said in this tiny, tiny whisper, "Please don't hurt me."

Kethe. I can't even describe what that felt like. I mean, if I could've crawled into a hole and had somebody wall me up like an anchorite right then and there, I would've done it. Not even paused for breath. But there wasn't no hole handy, and I don't suppose it would've helped Felix any if there had been.

He was still shaking, and he was about to start crying—I could see it coming, and it wasn't nothing I wanted to deal with out there in the middle of Hithe. And I was feeling like a total asshole anyway.

I eased up my grip on him—didn't let go because it seemed like when he was down the well he could only hear me when I was touching him—and said, "I'm not gonna hurt you. Promise. But what are you doing?"

He shook his head in a way I'd learned to know and hate. It didn't mean he didn't want to answer—that was how Mavortian always took it, him and his endless questions about fucking Beaumont Livy, and, powers, but it pissed him off. It just meant Felix couldn't get to the answer, like the words weren't there for the thing he needed to say.

"Were you going east? To this garden you're after?"

He nodded, and I thought he was grateful.

"Do you know it's the middle of the night?"

I hadn't meant that to come out quite as snarky as the look on his face said it did. But he nodded again and swallowed hard.

"Good. You're doing good." And I felt like even more of an asshole, seeing how much he lit up just 'cause I said something nice to him. "But what set you off?"

He swallowed again, and I could see how hard he was working to keep his shit at least sort of together. And he managed to get out, "In the room."

"In the room? What?"

But he couldn't say it. He was too scared. I knew some of that was me, but I thought some of it wasn't. Something had happened.

"Did somebody hurt you?" I said, so fast and hard that I wound him up all over again.

"Hey, it's okay," I said, and he gulped and rubbed at his eyes. "I ain't mad at you, I promise. But if somebody hurt you, I'm gonna do macramé with his finger bones. Is that what happened? Did somebody hurt you?"

He shook his head, and I racked my brain for another idea. "Did somebody come in the room at all? Say something to you?"

He shook his head to each question, and his spooky eyes were all wide and staring at me like he was scared to death of me and trusted me completely all at the same time. Kind of like how I felt about Keeper as a kid.

I tried again. "Did you see something?" And this time he nodded.

Kethe, I thought. Fucking marvelous. I didn't really want to be out here all night playing Guess-how-many-bats-in-Felix's-belltower. I said, "Can you tell me what you saw?"

I felt the breath he took through my hold on his shoulders. And his face set into no expression at all, and he said, "A ghost."

"Sacred *fuck*. What was it doing?"

He didn't say nothing for a moment. "You believe me?"

" 'Course. You saw that thing in Hermione, didn't you? And I been in the Boneprince. I know about ghosts."

He stared at me. I remembered Mavortian saying as how the Mirador didn't believe in ghosts—which, I mean, how fucking dumb do you have to be? "You can tell me," I said. "It's okay."

"It was a woman. She was being . . . raped. But the . . . I couldn't . . . *he* wasn't visible."

I couldn't say nothing for a moment, and then I said, "Kethe. No wonder you bailed. But you could've come and found me."

He looked down, and I felt his shoulders tense. "You said not to leave the room."

There wasn't no way to answer that, and I didn't try. I said, "Can you come back, do you think?"

"Will you be there?"

"Yeah. I ain't going nowhere."

"You won't get mad if I . . ."

"I won't get mad. Promise."

"All right," he said and gave me this shaky smile that just about ripped my heart into little shreds. He was trying so damn hard, and the only guy he had looking out for him was me. That was fucked up and wrong and stupid.

"Here," I said and picked up my bundle from where I'd dropped it. "I brought your shoes."

"Oh," he said, and I knew he hadn't noticed he wasn't wearing them.

"C'mon, sit down and put 'em on. We need to get back."

I undid my bundle, and put his shoelaces back in while he put on his socks and coat. He put on his shoes one by one as I handed them to him, and then we walked back to the hotel together, not talking, and went up to bed. Felix kind of hesitated before he lay down, but when I asked him if he was still seeing the ghost, he shook his head.

Felix

I try to run from the yellow-eyed man in my dreams. I remember that he is Malkar. But I can't get away from him. I could never run fast enough to escape Malkar, could never be strong enough to defeat him. When I cannot run anymore, I stop and wait for Malkar to catch me and hurt me and use me as a weapon against everything I love.

The yellow-eyed man stands facing me, and says, "Why do you run from me? I thought you understood that I mean you no harm."

I stare at him. "Who are you? Are you . . ." But I cannot say Malkar's name.

"I told you. I am Diokletian of the House Aiantis, Celebrant Terrestrial of the Nephelian Covenant."

His words mean nothing to me, and I cannot remember being told his identity before. But I do remember that, if he is not Malkar, he belongs to the gardens, and surely that means I can trust him.

"Why are you so frightened? Has someone hurt you?"

I nod, remembering Malkar, remembering Keeper. "I'm trying to come to you, but it's hard."

"I will do anything I can to help you, although there is little enough one can do in dreams."

"Thank you," I say, but there is nothing I can imagine that he can do.

The dream is shifting around us, although I do not know if it is my doing or his. We are standing now on a tiled floor beneath the tremendous vault of a dome. As color washes in, I realize that this must be his dream, for I have never seen this place before. The dome becomes bluer and bluer until it is the dazzling cerulean of the summer sky. The tiles are yellow and white and blue; the columns are white marble. Between them, I can see the breathing emerald lushness of the gardens in all directions.

"I thought you would like this," the yellow-eyed man says, and I think he is laughing a little, not unkindly, at my awe. "This is the Omphalos, the center of the Gardens."

"It is beautiful."

"Do you find it calming? Many people do."

"Yes. Yes, it is restful." I can feel my mind, like a cramped muscle, relaxing out of its tight, painful knot.

"Then could I ask you some questions?"

I look at him but see nothing of Malkar in his face, only anxiety and curiosity. "All right," I say. "I will try to answer."

"If you have the answer within you, the dream will find it. That is why I am asking now instead of waiting until you have reached this place in the waking world. Now. You said your name is Felix?"

"Yes. Felix Harrowgate."

"And you are a wizard of the Mirador?"

"Yes."

"How did you come there?"

"Malkar brought me."

"Malkar?"

"My master."

I am afraid he will ask questions about Malkar, but he is on the track of something else. "Where did you come from?"

Arabel, I almost say, but the dream demands the truth of the spirit, not of the letter. And I know where I come from; I have always known, although I have tried not to. "Pharaohlight."

"Where is Pharaohlight?"

"It is a district of Mélusine, the . . . the city of the Mirador."

He seems incredulous or angry or both. "Mélusine? How did you come to be in *Mélusine*?"

"I . . . I was born there."

"But you are Troian!" And he demands like a whip crack: "Who were your parents? What were their houses?"

"My mother's name was Methony. That's all I know."

I flinch a little, expecting to have made him angrier, but he seems thunderstruck.

"Methony?"

"She was called Methony Feucoronne," I offer. "She died when I was eleven."

The yellow-eyed man is framing another question, but mention of the Fire has brought it upon me, crackling and roaring in its greed. The Omphalos goes up like paper, and I lose the yellow-eyed man in the strangling smoke. I run through the burning gardens, blind and suffocating, until I wake up crying.

5⁄2

"You okay?" says a voice.

For a moment, I don't know where I am or who is with me, but the voice continues, "That sounded like one fuck of a bad dream," and I realize it is my brother Mildmay.

"The Fire," I say, although I know there was more to the dream than that: something about the gardens and the yellow-eyed man. He told me his name was Diokletian, but everything else slips away like water.

"Yeah," says Mildmay. "That'll do it." He isn't shocked or alarmed or pitying, and I wonder for a moment before I fall asleep again what *his* dreams are like. I wonder if they are worse than mine.

Chapter 10

Mildmay

There ain't much to be said about walking across Kekropia aside from the boredom of it. We stayed in seedy little hotels, and I played cards with guys who shouldn't've been let out alone, and saw more buffalo up close than I'd ever felt the need for. And then there was me not sleeping and Felix being crazy and us both always being afraid—me that the Bastion was going to find us, him . . . I didn't know *what* had his tail in a knot. Oh, he was frightened to death of me when he was down the well, which was mostly, but that wasn't all of it. Sometimes, out in the middle of nowhere between one ugly little town and the next, I'd realize he wasn't behind me and turn around, and there he'd be, sunk down in the middle of the road and rocking back and forth in this way that completely spooked me out. And I'd have to go back and drag him to his feet and yell at him to start walking again, and all the time he'd be kind of huddled away from me like he thought I was the Tallowman or something. That starts getting on your nerves something fierce about the third time it happens.

And when he was topside—which was less than I would've liked—he pretended like that other stuff never happened at all. He was older than me and a hocus and educated and he talked flash, and he made like that was all there was to it, and it was him doing me the favor, being out here in the middle of absolutely fucking *nothing*, with the sky like some kind of monster, just waiting 'til you weren't watching to lean down and swallow you whole.

So we walked—hitched rides when we could—and the Empire crawled away underneath us like a turtle in no particular hurry. The worst was the two or three days where we could see this ugly blot on the horizon to the north, like a thundercloud that'd left the party to go sulk. Felix said it had to be the Bastion.

He was topside most of the time for that couple of days, although he was acting even crazier than normal, muttering under his breath and watching the Bastion sidelong, like he thought it might move if he didn't keep an eye on it. I had a nightmare the second night about that happening, that we looked at the horizon and the blot was gone, and then we looked back at the road and it was right in front of us and the gate was opening like a hungry mouth to suck us in. There was a lot of running after that, and every time we thought we were safe, we'd turn around and there it'd be, waiting for us. I was about as much use as wet paper the next day, but we did finally begin to get ahead of it, and then to leave it behind, and I ain't never been so glad to see the back of anything in my life.

After that, there weren't no more landmarks, and we just headed east as best we could. I had my map and the road and the sun to keep us from getting lost, and I guess we did okay, although I got to say, of the two, I'd rather be dipped in barbecue sauce and thrown to the gators than walk across the Grasslands again. People looked at our red hair like they thought it was catching, and I caught five different chambermaids making hex signs where they thought I wouldn't see. If I'd been on my own, I would've asked what they meant by it, but with Felix to look after, I didn't want to risk pissing anybody off. I mean, I can take care of myself, but he was about as helpless as a newborn kitten, and some of them hotelkeepers I thought would've been glad to drown him like one.

And after a while—I don't know quite how long, seeing as how I lost track of the date somewhere between one armpit of a town and the next—we got far enough east that all the signs started being in Kekropian instead of just the ones the Empire put up, and people quit looking at us quite so much like we were a pair of three-headed dogs with each head uglier than the last—at least in the big towns. Instead, they started expecting that we would understand Kekropian a whole lot better than we did. Kethe, that was nasty, trying to explain in a language you don't got a good grip on that you *don't* got a good grip on it, to somebody who obviously don't believe you and ain't going to believe you even if you go on explaining 'til the end of the world. But I figured that was a sign Felix could take off those fucking gloves, and I reminded myself to be grateful for small favors.

And, Kethe, I'll remember to my dying day the first time I saw a redhead that wasn't me and wasn't Felix and wasn't Madame Scott with her henna. It was a gal maybe an indiction or two younger than me, with long curly red hair like Felix's—except for Felix's hair looking like a briar bush that day, I mean—and big yellow eyes, as yellow as a cat's. She was pretty, I guess, if you got a taste for spooky eyes. Dunno what she was doing out there—little town called Ekube, without much to recommend it beyond a local beer that was the most amazing stuff I'd ever had in my life—and since she disappeared about as soon as she laid eyes on us, I ain't ever going to know. But I got a better idea after that of what my mother must've looked like.

So we kept going east and my Kekropian got better in a hurry and I learned two variants of Long Tiffany I'd never seen before. Me and Felix worked out this half-assed sort of system, so if something in our room freaked him out, he'd have a place to go that was safe and where he knew I wouldn't be mad at him. It was a hard game to run, even aside from him being crazy, because we had to find a new place almost every day, and it had to be somewhere he'd remember in a panic and somewhere that people wouldn't come along and start wondering what the fuck he was up to. Mostly we ended up agreeing on the roof, and then I spent the whole damn evening praying to Kethe and St. Eliot against fire. It wasn't good enough, and I knew it, but it was all I could do. I couldn't stay with him, I couldn't take him with me, and I sure as fuck couldn't ask no Kekropian chambermaid to babysit.

And mostly it worked out, although I didn't deserve it to. There were three or four times I came back and he wasn't in our room, but he was always on the roof like he was supposed to be, even if it did take me an hour to talk him down—and there was that one time we both spent the whole night up there.

But that was okay, and I was dealing with the cardsharping pretty good, even if I did hate it so much I dreamed about it when I wasn't dreaming about Cerberus Cresset, when I was sleeping at all, which wasn't much, although that piece of glass was still holding off the cramps, and things weren't great, but they were going more or less okay, and I felt like maybe I had things sort of under control.

And then we came to the crossroads.

Now, the first problem was that crossroads not being on my map. I'd been wondering kind of on and off for days whether I should buy a second map, seeing as how we'd come so far east, and then telling myself that I'd better not waste the money. So I stood and cussed myself out a bit, and then I got over that and moved on to the next problem, which was that the signpost wasn't there. Oh, I could see where it *had* been, no problem, but somebody must've decided they didn't like it where it was and not yet figured out where they'd like it better because it just purely was not there.

My guess, of course, was that we just wanted to keep following the road east, but there had been some bad moments the past couple decads that had taught me you didn't assume that kind of thing about roads in Kekropia. So I was still standing there, wondering what to do, when the third problem showed up.

And that was a bunch of Imperial dragoons.

Kethe was still looking out for me a little. The land had been getting hillier, and I was glad of it, because, powers and saints, I was sick to death of nothing but flat—but you could still see people on horseback coming a long way off, so there was plenty of time for me to grab Felix and hustle him off the road. I'd been listening to all the gossip I came in earshot of, and my Kekropian had got good enough that I knew these dragoons were probably headed south to try and keep the peace in a place called Lunness Point, where the people were habitually kind of rowdy.

Well, we won't take their road, I said to myself. And then Felix got up from behind the bushes I'd picked as a hiding place and started walking away as cool as you please.

I stared after him for a second, just absolutely unable to believe my eyes. And then I said to myself, Here's number four, and threw myself after him.

I didn't catch him at once, not because I couldn't've, but because if we were going to have a fight, I wanted it to be where we wouldn't have an audience. So we were out of sight of the crossroads, Felix heading southeast like he knew right where he was going, when I finally came up even with him and said, "What the fuck do you think you're doing?"

"I hear them," he said, like it was an answer.

"What? Hear *who?*"

"The crying people," he said in the same half-witted way he said, *I dreamed it,* that made me want to shake him 'til he rattled.

And what really pissed me off—aside from being lost and having them dragoons breathing down my neck, I mean—was that the past two or three days Felix hadn't hardly been acting nuts at all. And he'd seemed pretty solid with it, not like the days when I could see in his eyes how he was balanced on the edge of the well with nothing but sheer cussedness holding him up. This time he'd really seemed sort of okay, and I guess I'd relaxed a little, and that's the best way to be sure something bites you on the ass.

What I wanted to do was club him over the head and drag him back to the road. But, the way my luck was running, that'd mean walking right back into those damn dragoons. And I didn't think I was going to have any better luck getting Felix to let go of this new idea than I'd had with the old one. I thought of him setting off on his own in the middle of the night to look for these "crying people" and felt cold all over.

I couldn't talk sense to him when he was like this, and that left me with two choices. Either I made him do what I wanted or I did what *he* wanted.

"Fuck me for a half-wit dog," I said between my teeth and followed Felix.

❧

I trailed along after Felix all fucking afternoon. We hit this kind of goat track after a while—and if you ask how I know it was goats, it was because they was standing around laughing at us the whole way. So we followed that—or, Felix followed the path, and I followed Felix—and after a while it turned into an actual road, although not flash enough for paving stones, and I saw the occasional barn or farmhouse away off on in the distance. And it still seemed like Felix knew where he was going.

Finally, when it started getting dark, I caught up with him and said, "Felix?"

He turned to look at me, and that was a good sign. After a second, he even said, "Yes?"

"It's getting late," I said. "You figured out where we're going yet?"

He pointed. All I saw was yet more damn grass.

"How far?"

He gave me this look like my eyes'd rolled back in my head and I'd started speaking in tongues.

"Are we close? Or do we got to hike two more days?"

I guess it came out nastier than I meant, because he turned red and didn't answer me. And I was pretty close to the point where I didn't care if I sounded nasty or not.

"Are we close? Yes or no?"

There was a pause that told me the answer even before he shook his head. We weren't close.

I took a deep breath, counted a septad, then counted another because the first one didn't take. Then I said, "Okay. We'd better find somewhere to sleep, and we got to do something about food."

"Oh," he said, so quiet I couldn't even hear him.

"I know. You hadn't thought of that."

If he'd been all the way topside, I would've got torn into strips for mouthing off like that. But he could feel the cold crazy water around his feet—I could see it in the way his eyes were—and he didn't say nothing.

It was starting to scare me a little, how easy I could read his face and what he did and didn't say. That ain't the same as being able to handle him, and I wasn't even pretending I had any kind of a grip on what he might do when he was topside, but I was getting to where I knew his madness like it was an old friend. And if the water and the rope and the narrow stone sides of the well was just my own way of thinking about it, I didn't think he'd've disagreed with me if I'd been fool enough to mention it, which I wasn't. I knew how deep water gave him the creeping, crawling, screaming horrors, even if I didn't have the least idea why and wasn't going to ask.

I looked around and tried to think. I knew we didn't want to go waltzing up to a farmhouse, because even if they didn't think we were necromancers or ghouls or whatever the fuck it was the people in the Grasslands thought we were, we were still pretty damn suspicious-looking strangers, and what was I going to say when they asked me where we were headed? So that wasn't no bright idea.

On the other hand, it wasn't like I'd been prepared for this jaunt into the middle of fuck-all nowhere. So what we had to eat was a couple winter apples I had in my coat pocket, and they weren't going to get us very far. If Felix hadn't been the way he was, I would've said, Fuck it, let *him* starve, and lit out on my own. But I couldn't ditch him now. It would be as good as murder.

Which kind of left us with stealing, and I wasn't feeling none too happy with that, neither, because burgling farmhouses was *way* outside my line of work, and I was having these terrible visions of getting caught red-handed with a cheese or something. And then all them questions—who are you? where are you going?—start up again, only with a nastier tone of voice and probably the wrong end of a pitchfork, too.

I pushed the heels of my hands against my eyes. I felt like that story Keeper had dreamed up for Phoskis way back when was coming true. I *was* losing my nerve. I'd been losing it for months like a sandbag with a slow leak, going back to Ginevra's death—or maybe even before that, maybe even all the way back to the Boneprince and that terrible voice in the dark saying as how Brinvillier Strych wasn't able to make the party.

There's this game they play in Gilgamesh. I used to be pretty good at it. You got this kind of tower built out of little sticks, and the game is you remove sticks until the tower falls down, and the more sticks you got in front of you when it finally goes, the higher your score. I felt like I was one of them towers, and that night in the Boneprince was when somebody pulled out the first stick—the one that wouldn't matter at all if they didn't go on to pull out more sticks and more and more—and now it was Kethe knows how many sticks later, and I was starting to topple.

And then Felix said in this little, scared, whispery voice, "Mildmay? Are you all right?"

Can't fall apart now, Milly-Fox. You got responsibilities.

"I'm okay," I said, and for once I was glad of my scar because it meant I didn't have to try and fake a smile.

I knew what I had to do. I felt the way I'd felt back in Brumaire, heading for the Anchorite's Knitting, knowing it was the wrong thing to do, but just not seeing that I had any options. Kethe knew how much longer we were going to be wandering around out here. We had to eat, and I wasn't no nature boy like Sir Ursulan in the stories, to make snares for rabbits out of my own hair. If we were going to get food, it was going to have to be from somebody else. And I'd got this thing in my mind, like a splinter buried so deep you can't dig it out, about not letting nobody see Felix and not giving nobody a chance to ask questions. I ain't a good liar anyway, and I knew there wasn't no story I could come up with that wasn't going to look as much like a lie as if I'd gone ahead and labeled it. But if I could get into somebody's larder and back out again without nobody the wiser . . . I had some money still, and I figured I could leave it on a shelf or something and it wouldn't be quite so much like stealing.

Going moral on me, Milly-Fox? Keeper asked in my head, in that particular drawling voice she used to let you know as how she hadn't thought you were sissy enough or stupid enough to get hung up on something like this. She'd used it on me when she'd told me she was going to start training me to kill people, and I'd never quite lost the sting of it, like salt on raw skin. And even though I'd seen her do it to other kids and even though I'd left her, just knowing that was what she'd say and how she'd say it was *still* enough to make me do stuff I knew better than to touch.

But another thing I learned from Keeper was even when you were doing something stupid, you had to do it right. So I caught Felix and made him look me in the eyes and said, "Okay. Here's what's gonna happen. I'm gonna go over there"—I pointed at the nearest farmhouse—"and find us some food. You're gonna stay right here 'til I get back, and if anybody but me comes snooping around, you're gonna hide. You got that?"

He nodded.

"Tell it back," I said, like I was Keeper and he was some half-bright kid I was sending on a job.

"You're going to find food." He pointed at the farmhouse. "I'm going to stay here and hide if I see anybody."

Not the world's best plan, but I didn't figure I was going to come up with nothing better. "Right," I said. "Good. You okay with that?"

He nodded and gave me that smile that he only got when he was about halfway down the well and I said something nice to him.

"Okay," I said, and then I set out to do what I thought at the time and subsequently learned for sure was the stupidest damn thing I'd ever done in my life.

Felix

I waited for hours, and he didn't come back. The sun set; the stars came out. I saw a man come out of the farmhouse and saddle a horse and ride away very fast. But he went the other direction, not toward me, and there was no one else.

Something had gone wrong. Mildmay had fallen down a well or been gored by a bull. Or been captured. He had told me to wait, but if he was hurt or trapped, I had to do something. There was no one else.

I picked up the valise that held our clean clothes and started toward the farmhouse. It wasn't a long walk.

I learned more about farm animals and equipment in the next half hour than I had ever wanted to know, but I did not find Mildmay. I was afraid that they had him in the house. There was still a candle burning in one of the upper rooms, and I could not imagine that I could get into the house unnoticed, much less get Mildmay and myself out.

I identified and avoided the henhouse; Mildmay would not be in there, and I remembered enough from my childhood in the Lower City to know just how difficult my life could become if I alarmed the hens. My circuitous path brought me up to the side of the house farthest from my starting point, and there I found the doors to a root cellar, with the shaft of a hoe shoved through their handles as a crudely improvised lock.

Here at last was the sign of a prisoner. I slid the hoe out of the door handles and opened the left-hand door as quietly as I could. The musty pungency of root vegetables rose to meet me. I descended the stairs cautiously, wishing more than ever for my witchlights, for if Mildmay was down here, they had left him without so much as a candle, and—mindful of that light in the farmhouse window that indicated someone was awake and listening—I did not dare call out.

I felt my way from step to step, my right hand maintaining a death grip on the banister. When I finally reached the cellar floor, I took a hesitant step away from the stairs, wondering if it was safe to say Mildmay's name very softly. But before I could make any kind of a noise, I was flat on my stomach on the floor, my assailant's weight pinning me down, one of his hands over my mouth, the other trapping my wrist in such a way that if I moved, something was going to break. I could hear my heart clamoring in my chest.

"I can kill you before you have time to blink," Mildmay's voice said in my ear, in Midlander, low and flat and hideously truthful. "And don't think I won't. Now tell me how long I got."

His hand released my mouth, and I gasped sideways against the floor, "Mildmay, it's me, Felix!"

"Felix?" All at once, his weight and hands were gone, and the relief was like cool air after the heat of a furnace. I sat up and gingerly flexed my wrist. "What are you *doing?*"

"I thought you had to be in trouble, so I came." I stood up, since nothing seemed damaged, although I was a little short of breath. Now that I knew where he was, I could see shreds and wisps of color against the dark, but I could not read them. "You *are* in trouble, right?"

"Oh, fuck, yeah," he said, with something that might almost have been a laugh. "C'mon, let's bail, and I'll tell you the whole fucking fairy tale later. If we hang around much longer, we're both liable to get lynched."

Mildmay stopped only long enough to close the cellar doors and stick the hoe back through the handles, then led me swiftly and unhesitatingly away from the farm buildings. We must have gone a mile and a half before he stopped and said, "You want a turnip?"

"A what?"

"Turnip. I was planning on throwing 'em at the sheriff's men, but, you know, at least they're something to eat."

I accepted the hard, bulbous object he offered, and asked, "What happened?"

"I got caught," he said, and I didn't have to see him to know that he had shrugged. "Now which way to your crying people?"

"What? You . . . but I—"

"You still want to find 'em, right?"

"Well, yes, but—"

"I got in a real nasty jam on account of them," he said, his voice as flat and hostile as it had been in the root cellar before he'd known who I was, "so don't go telling me that now they ain't important. Which way?"

The question was as hard as a slap. "That way," I said. "Away from the moon."

"Okay, then. Eat your damn turnip." He started walking, and I followed him. I ate the turnip without enjoyment; although I longed to lob it into the darkness and be done with it, I knew he would never forgive me if I did.

It wasn't until the sun rose that I got any idea of what Mildmay meant by "a real nasty jam." But the first daylight, even as it brought the red and orange and shamed magenta into full clarity around him, also showed me that he was sporting a magnificent black eye. And the stiff, cautious way he was moving suggested that there were other bruises beneath his shirt.

Then he raised one hand to push his hair out of his eyes, and my breath caught in my throat. His wrist was raw with scabbing welts. "What *happened?*" I said.

"Huh? Oh. Well, 'course they tied me up."

"Those should be washed out. And the bloodstains on your cuff."

He gave me a look, indecipherable as all Mildmay's looks were. "Okay," he said, and we turned aside to find a stream.

It didn't take long, and I remembered that we were nearing the ocean. Mildmay stripped out of his shirt without protest, and I saw the angry red and black and purple bruises along his side.

"Are your ribs all right?"

He craned his head to see them, then prodded his side experimentally. "They ain't broke," he said, then made a strange, twisted grimace that I recognized after a moment as a wince. "This 'un might be cracked."

"I don't think we have anything to strap them with," I said, looking futilely in our single valise.

"Oh, it don't need nothing like that. Just don't make me laugh for a day or two."

I decided that was mostly a joke and smiled at him.

After stretching cautiously, he turned and knelt by the stream to wash his wrists, the left being just as torn and bruised as the right.

I watched him, trying to decide if he was lying about how badly he was hurt, and suddenly, like throwing open a pair of shutters, I saw the muscles of his back moving beneath his skin, the strength of his shoulders, the long-fingered grace of his hands. I had always known that Mildmay, despite being a good half foot shorter than I, was as muscular and agile as an acrobat, but now I saw that he was beautiful.

Longing and fear hit me together like a lightning bolt, and I said hastily, "You said you'd tell me what happened."

"Powers, I guess I did." He pushed his hair away from his face again, but now I saw both grace and weariness in the movement.

"You don't have to. I mean, if . . ."

"I got worse stories," he said, and while he cannibalized our last clean handkerchief for bandages, he proceeded to give me a brutally unvarnished account of the night.

"It was my own damn fault," he said. He did not look at me as he spoke, but his voice was perfectly clear and steady, and he seemed to be making a particular effort not to let his words slur as badly as they usually did. "I knew it was a bad idea, and I did it anyway, and I guess I got what I paid for.

"I went in like I owned the place—they didn't lock their kitchen door.

There wasn't nobody around, so I found the larder and started checking out their supplies."

His face was getting redder and redder, and I saw that his casual tone was a deception. He had not been pleased with himself even before disaster struck.

"Dunno why I didn't hear her coming—I'm slipping, I guess—but all at once there was this scream from a lady with a powerful set of lungs, and I was on my way out the door when I met these five goons on their way in. They wouldn't let me try and explain. They just jumped me. I had money I would've given 'em, but I ain't rightly sure they'd've took it. They was yelling things about monsters and heathens and decent women. I think they thought I was planning on raping her. Which I wasn't. So one of 'em says as how he's going for the sheriff, and the rest of 'em chucked me in that damn root cellar, where I sat and cussed 'til you came and let me out."

He turned to look at me; I could see shame coiling round and round in the depths of his eyes, but his gaze was steady as he said, "I'm sorry if I hurt you."

"You didn't," I said, a prompt lie and safe, since I didn't think he would be able to see bruises through my tattoos. There was something he wasn't telling me, probably something else the "goons" had said that rankled even more deeply than the rest of it, but if he didn't want to tell me, I had no right to ask. I felt guilty enough for prying the story out of him in the first place.

"Give me a hand?" he said after a moment. He'd rendered the handkerchief neatly into strips, but even he was not quite dextrous enough to wrap them properly one-handed.

"Of course," I said, feeling my face flood with color, and moved over to follow his careful, patient instructions about how to get the most use out of what we had. He smelled of sweat and dirt, as I did, and also, faintly and lingeringly, of the root cellar. There were old, thin scars on his hands, and I remembered he'd said the scar on his face came from a knife fight. His palms were callused, and I could feel the strength and heat of his hands even as he held them still for me to work. I imagined what they would feel like in the softness of a caress, and bent my head hastily so that Mildmay would not see the tangle of desire and terror twisting my face.

He said, "What happened to your hands?"

I thought for a panicky moment he meant the bruises I had denied, but I looked at my fingers and saw the lumped wrongness of them. "My fingers were broken," I said, and now that he had drawn my attention to them, I could feel the stiffness, like the echo of pain. "When M—when the Mirador burned. Gideon set a healing spell on them, but I'm afraid it didn't take very well. There." And my hands jerked back from him as if he were burning. "That's the best I can do."

"Thanks." He pulled his shirt out of the stream, wrung it out, and swapped it for the clean shirt in our valise. We had had to compromise between what would fit him and what would fit me, so that extra shirt hung on him like a tent, whereas it left an inch and a half of my wrists showing at the cuffs.

He stood up, stretched again, warily, and said, "Let's go."

The crying people pleaded and sobbed, and I started toward them.

Mildmay

About sunset, Felix finally stopped walking. I came up the last of the hill to stand beside him and said, "You done stopped for a reason?"

"We're here."

"Where?"

"Nera," Felix said.

"What?"

"This was anciently the city of Nera." He wasn't talking to me; he sounded like somebody reciting a poem, and his eyes were wide and dreaming and stark barking mad. "It was the summer palace of the last great Emperor of Lucrèce. Until the Sunlings came."

"The Sunlings? But I thought they were just, you know, in stories."

For a minute I thought he wasn't going to answer me at all, but then he said, "Where did you think those stories came from?"

If he'd been topside, he would've sent that question straight through me like a skewer. But he didn't mean nothing nasty by it now. The way he was looking, I wasn't even sure he knew he'd said it.

"The Sunlings came," he went on. "They landed in their fierce, sharp-nosed boats, and they came up to the city in their shining armor, and they destroyed it."

"How . . . how d'you know?"

"They told me," he said and pointed down into the valley.

"*They?*" I asked, and I swear my voice had gone up an octave and a half.

But he just nodded like he was surprised I had to ask, and said, "The crying people."

"Sacred bleeding fuck," I said, because, I mean, it's one thing to know your crazy hocus brother sees ghosts, and a whole different thing when you find out they're telling him bedtime stories.

I don't think he even heard me. He just went on staring at that valley, with this look on his face kind of like a statue—you know what I mean, almost blank but with this little hint of a frown. I couldn't even guess at what he was thinking, and I wasn't all that sure I wanted to. Powers, he was spooking me out something fierce.

And then he said, "We have to help them. They want a maze."

"Okay," I said because I'd gone right out the other end of where it looked like any kind of use in saying this whole thing was nuts. "How're we gonna do that?"

He was in some kind of state I'd never seen before. Because I knew he was down the well—there wasn't nothing looked like *him* in his eyes, if that makes any sense—but he didn't seem scared. Not of me, not of the ghosts—it was like he'd found some place where the fear couldn't get at him. He said, "Someone told me once about mazes made by dancing. Could we do that?"

"Um. Did they tell you how?"

"No," he said like a kid admitting they ain't washed behind their ears.

"Then that ain't much good." And then I couldn't help it. My fucking curiosity reared up and made me ask, "What do they want a maze for?"

"One of their goddesses, the goddess of the underworld, was worshipped with mazes and labyrinths. If they want to come to her realm, the realm of the dead, they must trace a maze. And the Sunlings destroyed their maze with the rest of the city."

"You mean they worshipped Cade-Cholera?"

"No, of course not," he said and was himself for a second. Then he went all dreamy again. "She is the goddess of death, despair, stagnation, abandoned places. They say she is the only god who will protect them now, but they cannot reach her without a maze."

"Spooky," I said under my breath, meaning the goddess. But I was remembering the Boneprince and the dream I'd had about it and the way I'd felt when I was sitting on the Road of Marble making a crown of trumps. There wasn't nothing more I could do for the kept-thieves. I didn't know how to lay them, and, Kethe, I might never make it back to Mélusine even to give them another crown. But Felix was looking at the same sort of thing here, and he did know what to do. And he was going to do it. I could see it in the way he was looking at the valley. Where ordinary people—even ordinary crazy people—would've run screaming, he was going to do what these people needed so they could rest. And, I mean, he was my brother and everything, but I think that was where I figured out he was worth it, even if he was a pain and a half when he was down the well and a real prick when he wasn't. Because he was going to help these people who needed help, even though they'd been dead for Kethe knows how long and had seriously fucked up our already fucked-up lives besides.

But I still had to look after him. "Look," I said. "It's getting on for night, and we can't make no mazes in the dark. Sleep on it. Maybe we'll think of something."

He nodded and turned away, but even as we were going back down the hill—along of me not wanting to spend the night right on top of a bunch of ghosts—I saw him looking back, like his crying people were calling his name.

ᔓᔕ

Our big problem of course was food, namely us not having none. And seeing as how it was way early in the spring, there wasn't much just laying around. I'd discovered one of the times he was topside that Felix knew most everything about plants, and I got so damn desperate that night that I finally just uprooted this thing with a long stem and kind of wheat-looking stuff at the top and shoved it at him.

He looked at it like maybe it would bite him, and I said, "Can we eat it?"

I thought for a moment it wasn't going to do no good, and, Kethe, I just about sat down and cried. Then he pinched the bridge of his nose, like he was really trying to pull himself together, and gave the thing this glassy-eyed frown that was seriously spooky. And after a long, long pause, he said, "I think so."

"You *think* so?" I said, and he flinched back from me like now he thought *I* was going to bite him. And I got to admit, I kind of felt like it.

But I stopped and counted a septad and said, quiet and nice-like, "D'you know what it is?"

He nodded.

"Is it poisonous?"

He shook his head.

"Okay, then," I said, stripped the grains off the stalk, and ate them. I ain't got nothing nice to say about the way they tasted, but most anything'll beat starving to death, and whatever that stuff was, there was a lot of it around. I even got Felix to eat some, although it took some pretty basic bullying.

We were good for water, at least, and the stalks of the stuff that wasn't quite wheat ended up being useful as bedding. I made Felix promise he wouldn't go talk to the crying people until daylight, got him settled, got myself settled, looked up, and saw about a million and a half stars.

"Sir Ursulan here I come," I said, and I don't know how it happened, but then I fell asleep.

Felix

I dream of a burning city. My throat is raw with smoke, and shapes come and go in the lurid darkness like the salamanders who are said to live in volcanoes. At first I think I am in Mélusine, trapped in the Fire of 2263, but the buildings do not look right, and when someone rises out of the darkness and clutches my arm, he has red hair like mine and glaring yellow eyes. This is not Mélusine, but in the dream I know it is my home.

The red-haired man drags me after him down a narrow alley and out into the Forum Imperatoris Quirini X; to the stench of burning is added the stench of death. I struggle against his grip as he drags me toward the terrible ramparts of bodies, headless and limp like the massacred dolls of a cruel child. But the invader is stronger than I am, and all I can do is curse him.

As we near the steps of the palace, I can hear women screaming. I see foreign men crouching on the steps, struggling bare limbs visible between the ugly masses of their bodies. I realize what is happening and look away, fighting not to vomit. My captor notices and laughs.

We have come to the great golden sun inlaid in the marble paving of the forum at the foot of the palace stairs. The invaders have erected a crude framework of spears; between them hangs a man I have never seen up close before but know to be the Emperor, Virenus. I know his face from the likeness in our household shrine. There is a spearhead protruding from his stomach and a black shining seepage of blood down his groin and legs to a vile puddle, which is slowly eclipsing the sun.

My captor drags me to a halt before the Emperor and barks something in his harsh, cruel language. I try again to free myself from him, but his grip is like granite, and he is much bigger than I. I have no more chance against him than a fly does against the web of a spider.

The Emperor raises his head. For a moment, we look at each other, not as Emperor and subject, but as two human beings afraid and in pain. My captor barks something. The Emperor spits at him, then screams with pain. The invader's grip tightens on my arm, and he drags me away, leaving the Emperor screaming at the sky.

We are walking on blood. I am coughing and gagging; my captor seems not even to notice the stench. He jerks me to a halt. He is looking over my shoulder. I turn my head just in time to see the sword before it bites into my neck.

I am screaming. I can hear myself screaming, but I cannot stop. I can still taste smoke, still feel the imprint of the invader's fingers on my upper arm. I am dead, I am dead, but I cannot stop screaming.

I feel the weight and heat of hands on my shoulders, shaking me; I hear a voice, but I can't understand it. I try to bring my hands up to free myself, but I can't seem to move. My arms, my legs, my throbbing head . . . with the force of panic, I open my eyes. There is just enough light in the sky that I can see the red hair of the man shaking me, and my paralysis breaks.

I flail away from him, falling over my own legs in my effort to get to my feet. I catch myself against the ground, find my balance, and run. But I have barely gone a dozen steps when a weight crashes into my back, slamming me to the ground and knocking all the breath out of my body. I know it is the red-haired invader, and I try to throw him off, but my lungs are like stone, and he pins me easily.

For a moment, brief as an eye-blink, I am in a dank stone room, naked, and the weight pinning me down belongs to the man I hate most in the world. And then I am back in the dawnlight, facedown in dew-cool grass, and I can hear the short, panting breath of the man holding me, and his voice, cursing in a slurred mutter, in Marathine.

"Who am I?" I sob into the grass.

"The worst fucking shit-for-brains pain in the ass I've ever been saddled with. What the fuck is *wrong* with you?"

"Who am I? Please, just tell me who I am!"

There is a long pause, as fragile as blown glass, and then he says, in a small, deeply worried voice, "Felix, are you okay?"

"Felix? Is that my name?"

"Yeah. Felix Harrowgate. You're a hoc—a wizard. In the Mirador. You're my half brother." And in an even smaller voice, "I'm Mildmay."

"Oh!" I say and burst into tears.

"Hey." His weight is gone, and then there are hands helping me sit up; there is an arm around my shoulders, but I lean away from it, and it is gone. "It's okay. That must've been some nightmare, I guess. I'm sorry I yelled. But you're okay. Sun's coming up and everything."

I am so grateful to be alive, so grateful that he is not the man I fear and hate. I cry until my eyes are swollen and raw. He sits nearby, as patient as earth, until I have myself under some sort of control again, and can dry my face and steady my breathing.

"D'you wanna talk about it at all?"

I look at him cautiously and see the fox-headed man, whom I know and trust. "It was Nera," I say. "The burning city and the bodies and the Emperor and . . . and they killed me."

"Kethe. Was it . . . I mean, are they pissed 'cause we ain't helping 'em fast enough? Making that maze like you said?"

"No," I say, shaking my head to dispel the cloudiness of dreaming. "No, it's not like that."

"Okay," he says dubiously. Then, "Oh, fuck." He stands up, looking at the sky.

I look, too, and see the clouds massing like armies on the western horizon.

Mildmay

We'd been lucky with the weather, not getting rained on above maybe three or four times, and I figure I should've been expecting my luck to run out. Which, I mean, sure, okay, gotta have rain, I know that. But it was like with Vey in the Boneprince—it couldn't've picked a worser time.

I got Felix back to our half-assed sort of camp, and I got him to eat some more of them nasty wheat-type things that was all we had in the way of food. But both of us kept looking at the sky like it was a clock and we were afraid we'd be late—which I guess ain't so far off. If we were going to do anything, it had to be before that storm hit us. And maybe it was the storm, or maybe it was wanting to get the fuck away from this freakshow place, or maybe it was just the way Felix was looking at me, like he knew I had all the answers soon as I cared to tell him, but all at once I had an idea.

"We could do it with the grass!"

Felix gave me this worried look.

"Oh, come on. Like gardening, right? We just pull up the grass where we want the maze to be. That'd work, wouldn't it?"

It took him a long time to answer me, like he had to translate what I said into some other language he wasn't very good at, and then translate back what he wanted to say. I got to admit, if I'd thought there was any way in Hell I could've pulled it off, I'd've hit him over the head and dragged him away from Nera as fast as I could. It was doing something to him. At first I'd thought it was maybe okay, because it seemed like it was helping him keep himself together and kind of clearer-headed than he mostly was when he was down the well. But that dream he'd had—Kethe, I think about all I want is never to see nothing like that again in my whole damn life. And nothing that could do that to him was okay. I didn't care how nasty these people had died or how long they'd been trapped out here in the grass. They still weren't folks I'd've wanted to turn my back on—if I could've seen 'em, that is, which of course I couldn't.

And after a while, Felix got done with whatever it was he had to do in his head to get the words out, and said, "I think that would work."

"Okay," I said. "Let's get going."

"There's a place . . ." He got up, turned back to the hill we'd gone up the night before, and started walking. I grabbed our bag, kicked our jury-rigged bedding around a little, because if there *was* somebody out here, I didn't want to meet 'em, and hightailed it after Felix.

He went straight up the hill and down the other side like he was walking through Richard's Park on his way to the Cheaps. I went after him, keeping a sharp lookout even though I'd never seen a ghost in my life and didn't really expect I was going to start now. And it wasn't as much like the Boneprince as I'd been ready for. I didn't feel like somebody was watching me—although I kind of think that might've been because they were all watching Felix—and there really just wasn't nothing to show this wasn't an ordinary valley like septads of others all over this part of the country. I mean, if I hadn't been with Felix, I'd never've known what I was walking on top of. And while that's spooky its own self once you start thinking about it, it still ain't a patch on the Boneprince.

So we walked for a while, and I saw a couple of rocks that were maybe a little too regular to be natural, but nothing I was sure of, and then in this one particular spot that didn't look no different to me than any of the rest of it, Felix stopped and said, "Here."

I didn't say "Where?" both because I knew what he meant and because I didn't want to get tangled up in cheap cross talk like a pair of pantomime clowns. But, powers, it was just a patch of ground like every other patch of ground in this fucking valley. Except for maybe having more nettles than average, but I wasn't surprised at that one little bit.

"Okay." I looked at our piece of ground. It was flat—it had that much going for it anyway. I looked at Felix and found him looking at me like a lost puppy again. "What?" I said.

"I don't know how to design a maze."

"Ain't your crying friends told you what they want?"

"Just that they need a maze."

"Well, fuck," I said and couldn't help my head turning to see what that damn storm was up to. It kind of sneered back at me, but it was headed our way all right. I looked back at Felix. "They say anything about how big they need this maze to be?"

He shook his head.

"Right." I didn't know nothing about the rules for ghosts, but I did know all about the curtain-mazes at the Trials of Heth-Eskaladen. "Is where you're standing where they want the center?"

He nodded.

I yanked out the grass in a circle around him, making him move so I could get the stuff under his feet and scratching a big X in the dirt. I made my circle big enough for a living person because I figured I'd better not count on something smaller being any use to them. Then I knelt down and used some of the grass I'd just pulled out to diagram a maze. Felix watched like I was the hocus instead of him. I didn't make it big, and I didn't make it complicated—one path with two dead ends was all—but it still took me longer than I liked to get it laid out. Then I made Felix put his gloves on, since he didn't seem like he was in any state to recognize a nettle without it stung him, and we both started pulling grass for all we were worth. And all the time them clouds were sneaking up on us, getting bigger and blacker and uglier as they came.

My guess is it was about the septad-day when we got done, but I really couldn't tell, what with them big black clouds hanging over us like cult preachers shouting eternal damnation and the crawling fires of Hell. We'd both kind of ended up hunching our shoulders against them, because they really did look like they were just going to fall on us and squash us flat.

But finally we got the maze to where you could see that was what it was, and I straightened up and stretched until my spine popped—powers, my ribs hurt—and said to Felix, "What now?"

He looked up from his crouch, his eyes wide like a startled cat's, and I knew he didn't have the first fucking clue who I was. I realized after a second I was holding my breath waiting for him to start screaming or something, but he didn't. He just stared, but I could see he was tensed to run.

"Felix," I said. "Felix!"

He rocked back a little on his heels, like I'd hit him, but he blinked and frowned at me, and I knew he'd come back a little closer to where I was at.

"It's done," I said, slow and careful, like I was talking to Devie and trying to get her to understand before Keeper got pissed off. "What should we do?"

There was that pause again, where he was trying to work out what I'd said and what he needed to say back. "Move," he said. He stood up and walked out of the maze. I followed him, and I got to admit, since there wasn't nobody around to care if I was tough or not, I was moving at a pretty good clip.

He stopped about a septad-foot back from the edge of our stupid little maze and stood watching it like he was waiting for the curtain to go up at the Cockatrice.

What else could I do? I stood and waited with him.

Now you got to understand, first to last, I didn't see nothing. I mean, the grass was tossing around, but there was a storm coming, and you wouldn't expect nothing different. I mention it because Felix *did* see something. Like I said, whatever it was, I couldn't see it, but I believe it was there. And I got good reason.

We hadn't been standing there but maybe a quarter of an hour when it commenced to rain. I said some things under my breath, but there wasn't no shelter anyways, so there wasn't no point in trying to get Felix to move. And within a couple minutes, we were both soaked to the skin, and I might as well just get past it. I stood there, my shoulders all hunched, and every so often I'd push my hair out of my face again and try and clear the rain out of my eyes. Felix just stood and watched. He didn't seem to notice the rain. He sure as fuck didn't care.

So we stood there and stood there, and I guess every ghost in Nera was going past us, only I couldn't see them. And I got wetter and colder and started wondering kind of not quite idly about the Winter Fever, and we were still standing there like we were waiting to put down roots.

And all at once, Felix started for the maze.

There was this long moment where I was just gaping at him, stupid as a sheep, so he was halfway to the maze entrance before I flung myself after him, and he practically had his foot across the threshold when I caught him.

"What're you *doing?*" I yelled over the rain, and tried to drag him back. I wasn't expecting no trouble, because he was taller than me but way skinny, and besides I'd got used to him doing what he was told.

But this time he twisted against my grip, throwing himself forward at the maze, and I realized after a second that he was swearing at me in about the thickest Simside cant I'd ever heard in my life.

What the *fuck?* I thought. The only thing I was sure of was I wasn't letting him go in that maze we'd made for dead people, so there was an ugly couple minutes where we proved he didn't know as much about brawling as I did, and, Kethe, we ended up with me sitting on him again. I'd got his wrists, and he was screaming up into the rain, "They said I could come! They said they'd let me come!" And the way he sounded, you'd've thought we grew up together.

I just fucking did not know what to do. I mean, I purely had no idea. I knew I couldn't let him get into that maze because anywhere those people wanted to take him was no place he should be going, and my understanding was he'd end up dead. But I didn't know how to *deal* with him, how to get him to quiet down and not make me hurt him. Because I *was* hurting him, I knew it, but there just wasn't no other way. And he was screaming and fighting like I wouldn't've thought he could—no science to speak of, but good distance on pure fury—and I had to wonder if this had been down at the bottom of the well the whole time, like the Vraaken Bear chained in that cave in one of the stories about Brunhilde.

The only thing I had going for me was I knew how to use my weight. And finally I got scared and desperate enough to use a couple tricks I'd learned from this friend of Keeper's, and Felix lay still, panting, but glaring like murder was too good for me. I just hung on, kind of dazed from him having clipped me across the ear but good before I got the hold I wanted—but more I guess just from . . . I don't know, but I'd never imagined him being like this. And where the fuck had that Simside cant come from? It was like all this time I'd been standing on a trapdoor over an alligator pit, and I'd never known the trap was there, much less the gators. And now here I was down in the water and the gators were hungry. Kethe, he was giving me the bright blue horrors.

And he wouldn't say nothing. I tried asking him stuff, like where it was his crying people were going to let him go, but his jaw was set, and he just lay there, every muscle tensed up and his weird eyes like bonecutters. I knew how much he didn't like to be touched, and I knew the longer we stayed like this, the worse he was going to hate me. But I couldn't let him go into the maze. Maybe nothing would've happened, maybe his crying people were lying to him—but maybe he would've fallen down stone dead or disappeared or something. I didn't know, and I was scared stiff I might have to find out. So I hung on to him like grim spooked-out death, no matter how much it made him hate me.

I don't know how long we stayed like that—it felt like fucking *forever*, and the only good thing was I'd ended up with my back to the maze and didn't have to watch all that nothing. Felix just laid there and hated me and waited for me to fuck up. Even when I wasn't looking right at him, I could feel it. And let me tell you, that ain't no nice feeling. And oh, yeah, it was still raining like it was going into the business full-time. I just hung on and prayed I wouldn't fuck up and get Felix killed.

And finally it was over. It was kind of like that, too—no fireworks or trumpets or nothing, just Felix went limp and shut his eyes. It was a while before I felt like I could be sure he wasn't faking, but when I let go, he just went on laying there, and I guess maybe he was crying. Hard to tell with the rain, and he wasn't making no noise about it.

I stood and looked at him for a while, and the rain finally allowed as how it had to slack off some, and he still hadn't moved. I turned around and looked at the maze, and I still couldn't tell anything had happened except a bunch of rain. I went over and messed up the pattern as best I could, yanking out a lot more grass, and when I was done you could still tell it was *something,* but I didn't think anybody'd be able to figure out it was a maze. And I was going to have to hope that was good enough.

I went back over to where Felix was laying. He looked as wet and limp and miserable as the ghost of a drowned cat. "C'mon," I said, because I hadn't forgot about getting the fuck away from here. "Time to go."

It wasn't so much that I was expecting that to work as that I didn't know what else to try. So I just about swallowed my tongue when it *did* work. Felix got up good as gold and stood waiting for me to tell him what to do, just like normal. He wasn't meeting my eyes, but I couldn't blame him for that, and anyway that was normal, too.

I picked up our one bag, as soaking wet as everything else, so I felt like I was carrying a leaky goldfish bowl. "Okay," I said and took my best stab at where east was. "Let's go."

And he followed me like this whole freakshow thing had never happened. Except that it had, and looking back at him, head-down and dragging, I didn't think we were going to be able to forget it.

Felix

I follow Keeper.

My head is full of blackness and thunder, and I can smell the Sim all around me, the ever-present, unspoken threat that Keeper wears like an iron crown.

We are walking and walking. I look back for Joline, but I can't see her. Keeper won't let me wait for her. He keeps telling me to hurry up, to keep walking. I will do anything to keep him from touching me, and my every step is a betrayal of Joline.

I know she was there in the grass. The crying people said they would help me find her, that it would be easy once I had walked their maze. They said we could sleep together, Joline and I, sleep and not fear. And I could feel her there, waiting for me, at the center of the maze.

But there was a black shape, and it would not let me go to her. I fought it, but I could not defeat it, and I could hear Joline crying. She was lonely, as I was. We used to make up stories that we were really brother and sister, really the long-lost heirs of Cymellune. But all my pretending was lost with her, once in the smoke of the Rue Orphée and now again in the grass of Nera. I have nothing left but Keeper, who was waiting for me when the blackness had gone.

Everything is gray and heavy, and the shadows are getting thicker at the edges of my sight. I stay close to Keeper; even he is better than the monsters waiting in the shadows. Keeper can only hurt me.

But the shadows keep advancing, especially on my right side, my bad side. When I turn my head, they retreat, but I know that then they are advancing on the left, and there is only so long that I can bear that knowledge before I have to turn my head back the other way, and the shadows on my right giggle and start advancing again. Only my yellow eye can ward them off; the blue eye, the half-blind one, is no threat to them, and they know it.

Keeper's voice, like a cannon: "What is it now? Looking for work as a pendulum?"

I jerk my head front again; he is standing, hands on hips, waiting for an answer.

"The shadows," I say.

"Shadows?"

I know I cannot avert his anger, but the old stupid hope, that if I can just explain well enough, he won't hurt me, impels a burst of futile speech. "They're creeping up when I can't look at them properly."

"What the fuck are you talking about?"

"You know," I say, because Keeper does know. Keeper knows all my secrets. "My right eye, the bad one. It can't keep the shadows back."

"Oh fuck me sideways 'til I cry. And what're the shadows gonna do when they catch you?"

Derisive anger, like the cut of a whip. "I don't know," I say, looking down at my hands. "Something bad."

"*Something bad*. Powers! Look, you come walk here by me, and if the shadows grab you, I'll fight 'em off. Okay?"

I look up at him.

"I promise," he says with heavy patience, "I won't lay a finger on you. Okay? Would you move your ass, for the love of all the fucking powers?"

If he gets any angrier, he will get out his nun's scourge. And maybe he is right; maybe the shadows are as frightened of him as I am. Reluctantly, ready to dodge out of reach, I walk toward him.

"*Thank* you," he says; I expect to be cuffed across the back of the head, but he looks at me for a moment, darkly, then places himself on my right and starts walking.

I don't want him there; I don't want him there so much I can barely keep from screaming. But the shadows cannot get to me past him, and if I keep walking, maybe I won't make him angry. Maybe he won't hurt me.

The land is drowning in purple and red when we come to a little cluster of houses. Keeper stops short of them, gives me a long, smoldering look that makes me back away from him, and says, "If I tell you to stay right here, will you stay?"

I gulp and nod. I cannot find my way back to Joline now, and the only shred of comfort I have is that the monsters are frightened of Keeper and will not advance on me when he is near.

"Don't lie to me, now."

"I'm not, I swear. I'll stay right here."

"Okay. Then I'm gonna go see if I can get some food and maybe figure out where the fuck we are. Here—sit where you won't be in nobody's way and *don't move*."

I sit down where he tells me and wait. He walks away, trailing clouds of iron-black and old-blood red. I sit and wait. The monsters sit behind me and wait, too; I can hear their breathing.

And then Keeper is back again, motioning me to my feet. "Come on already. They sold me food, but they don't want no red-haired strangers hanging around, and I ain't keen on staying. And at least they told me where the nearest place with boats is. Come *on*."

I go, seeing iron and old-blood streamers reaching out to tangle around my legs, twine around my fingers and wrists.

We walk and walk, and it gets darker and darker. But the clouds roll back, and eventually there is a moon. The monsters cringe from the moonlight, and I can breathe more easily. Keeper shares out the food as we walk. The ground changes under our feet, going from grass, to rock, to a hard, uneven, sharp-edged jumble of stones. I stumble and catch my balance, stumble and catch my balance, stumble and fall, wrenching my ankle and landing heavily on my shoulder. I yelp.

"Felix! Are you okay?" Keeper comes back across the rocks to help me, and now I am more frightened, because that must mean he has a use for me.

"I'm fine," I say hastily, scrambling up and almost falling again. "Really."

"Okay, okay. Let's keep moving then." And he starts ahead; he never places a foot wrong that I can tell. My shoulder and ankle are throbbing, but I do not want him to know.

And then I come over a slight rise, toiling still in Keeper's wake, and find him standing stock-still, staring out . . . staring out at the sea. I stand, too, staring. It is dark and brilliant and terrifying, vaster than anything I have ever imagined, and I sink down to my knees, my hands pressed against my mouth, my eyes wide and burning. I have feared the monsters behind me, when it was the monster before me that I should have dreaded.

Beside me, thoughtfully, Keeper says, "Well, fuck."

Chapter 11

Mildmay

The woman at the farmhouse gave me the hairy eyeball up one side and down the other, 'til I wondered why she didn't just slam the door in my face and get it over with, but then she said, like every word was costing her money, "The folk *you*'ll be wanting are down to the cove," and gave me directions. Which I'd followed, best I could in the dark and with Felix acting the mooncalf all over the place.

I was just about floored by seeing the ocean. I'd heard about oceans in stories, but I'd never really been able to get my head around the idea. It made the Sim look like a kid's toy, and a cheap one besides. I gawked like a flat for probably a septad-minute—least it felt that way—before I got myself together. And then I had to get Felix up off the ground, but by then I'd managed to put that woman's directions together with what I was looking at, and could start working my way down toward the cove she'd told me about.

I was kind of puzzling the whole way about what she could've meant by "the folk *you'll* be wanting." I hadn't liked to ask her, since she'd looked maybe an inch this side of siccing the farm dogs on me, and, I mean, it didn't *matter,* as long as she'd sent me where I could find a boat. But it was like a mosquito whining in my ear, and I couldn't quite shake it.

After a little, I realized there was a light ahead of us, like a fire. I could see the glow, although not the actual fire, and I followed it, figuring that even if these people didn't have a boat themselves, they might be able to point me to somebody who did. And I was fucking well tired of stumbling around in the dark. Felix followed me, and it crossed my mind that there was something to be grateful for, since if I'd lost him out there, I might never've found him again.

We came round a big jutting rock, and there was the fire and people sitting around it. I made for it like a homing pigeon. We were still some ways out when one of the guys by the fire shouted something—not in no hostile way or nothing. I mean, I didn't understand a word of it, but he sounded friendly.

I stopped where I was and called back in my best Kekropian, "Excuse me, but I'm looking for a ship headed to Troia."

The four guys sitting there all jumped like they'd been bit and said some things in that language I didn't know, and then the one who'd shouted got up and came closer. I felt my jaw drop.

"As I am a child of Ocean," he said in Kekropian. "You aren't Piotr."

"No," I said, grabbing after my wits. "Sorry."

"Come closer, you and your friend."

"Brother," I said, purely on reflex, and came into the firelight with Felix tagging along not quite in grabbing distance.

The guy standing there was probably past his Great Septad. His hair was going gray, and he had wrinkles like trenches around his eyes. But the reason we were gaping at each other like a pair of half-wit dogs was his hair was as red as mine—where it hadn't gone gray, I mean—but he wasn't no tall, skinny Troian type, either. He was shorter than me and considerably broader in the beam. But at least now I knew what the woman at the farmhouse had been talking about. She'd thought I was one of these guys, whoever they were.

"What . . ." this red-haired guy started, then changed his mind. "Are you Troian?"

"Nope," I said.

"And you aren't Merrovin."

"If that's what y'all are, that's another nope."

"What are you?"

"Needing a boat going east."

His eyebrows went up, but he let me get away with it. "Come then," he said, and waved us toward the fire. "Sit down and tell me of your 'needing.' For I am Dmitri, captain of the *Morskaiakrov,* and we are bound for Haigisikhora, the finest port in all Troia."

We sailed for Haigisikhora a couple days later on what Ilia told me was the eighteenth of Byzioz. I'd never heard of Byzioz, so that wasn't as helpful as you might think, but I was guessing it was somewhere around the middle of Pluviôse.

From what I could tell, the *Morskaiakrov* was into smuggling and piracy and most anything that might turn a profit. Frankly, I didn't give a rat's ass what they did so long as it didn't involve pitching me and Felix over the side, and we really weren't even worth the effort. They could've left us where they found us and I wouldn't've blamed 'em, but they figured, what with us having red hair and not being Troians, we had to be some sort of distant kin, and their gods seemed to have a down on people who abandoned their relatives. And nobody ever liked to say, but they could see Felix was nuttier than a box of squirrels, and I think they thought it was unlucky if you didn't help crazy people.

They called themselves Merrows. It was a good thing they all spoke Kekropian because I'd've hated to try and learn the language they spoke in a hurry. They thought my Kekropian was funny enough.

They were most of 'em built like Dmitri. And they had these pale, pale gray eyes, like the color of water—which is to say no color at all. Spooky. And they didn't have the Troian bones like Felix did. Their faces were square and snub-nosed, and they had these wide stubby-fingered hands that looked kind of almost like paws. I can't say if that's what all Merrows look like, because the crew of the *Morskaiakrov* were all cousins or something. They had a great time explaining it to me a couple nights out and falling around laughing when I got tangled up in it.

They laughed at me a lot once they were sure I could pull my weight—and Felix's—and I figured that was okay. I mean, it didn't hurt me none, and it was way better than them picking on Felix, which they could've. And when they saw I could take it and wasn't going to get all bent out of shape about it, a lot of the mean went out of what they said. And anyway, Ilia was nice from the get-go, and Dmitri cussed me up one side and down the other, but not in no personal way.

Everybody on the *Morskaiakrov* had like three or four jobs, which was why they were okay with me working our passage, even though they didn't hardly have nowhere to put us. Ilia was the cook, along with a bunch of other things, and he was absolutely glad of me, because when I scrubbed a potato, I didn't fuck around with it. And I ain't no flashie chef or nothing, but I can cook.

So basically I did whatever anybody needed done during the day, and I learned a lot about splicing rope and mending sails and shit like that. And of course I was riding herd on Felix, and they were all real clear on how that wasn't no soft job.

Felix was way worse, and I knew it was because of Nera. He didn't talk to me no more—hardly talked at all except for whispering to himself in the spookiest way you can think of. He scared the daylights out of me, no kidding. After I got him on board the *Morskaiakrov,* I was frightened to go near him for like two, three days—not to mention ashamed.

I hadn't realized getting him onto the *Morskaiakrov* was going to be a problem. I mean, I knew how he felt about deep water, but I also knew he knew we had to cross the ocean to get to this garden of his, because we'd talked about it when he was topside. And it wasn't like I was asking him to go swimming or nothing.

So I'd worked out this deal with Dmitri—fastest damn talking I'd ever done in my whole life—and turned and said, "C'mon, Felix, let's go," and he was sitting there staring at me with this look on his face like a cat with its ears laid back.

"What?" I said. "What is it?"

But he wouldn't say nothing, and he wouldn't fucking budge, and the Merrows were all watching like a row of cats themselves, and I could feel my patience splitting down the middle like rotten cloth. It was just too much, that one little thing more than I could handle.

If I say I lost my temper, that gives you the wrong idea. And that wouldn't've been so bad, if I'd yelled at him or even smacked him one. I mean, it wouldn't have been what you might call *okay,* but there wasn't no way in Hell that face-off was going to come out okay. But it didn't have to be so fucking awful.

What happened was, I hit the cold place inside my head, the place where I'd been when I killed people for a living, the place especially where I'd ended up when a job looked like it was going bad. I can't describe it so it makes sense. It's really cold and really clear and nothing in the world matters except not fucking up the job—in this case, getting my damn brother on board this ship because it was what he'd said he wanted. And I did it. But afterward, it made me feel crawly and sick inside, like I'd felt in that farmhouse pantry getting ready to steal stuff and knowing that these people, who weren't no rich flashie bastards, were going to go hungry because of me. Only this was even worse. Because he was my brother and I knew none of this was his fault and I knew just how fucked up his head was.

But right then I was in that perfect cold place where it didn't matter, none of it. I wanted him on that fucking ship, and I was done arguing. It took me maybe half a minute to get him where I wanted him and me with a good grip on his poor stiff fingers. And two seconds later he was screaming. It was simple as that.

I guess I can say for myself that I didn't actually break them, although there was a moment where I thought about it because I was betting he'd pass out. I didn't do it, and that's something a little more okay than the rest of it. The trip out to the *Morskaiakrov* was just plain nasty. I had my grip on Felix's fingers, and he was panting. But he wasn't scared. I'd got myself on his right side, because with that eye being bad, it'd be that much more trouble for him to try and fight. And he sat there the whole way with his head turned so he could see me, and, Kethe, the look in his eyes—I wouldn't've been surprised if he'd pulled his lips back and snarled like a dog, because he purely did look ready to bite. And to this day I don't know how we would've got him up onto the *Morskaiakrov*'s deck if it hadn't been that when the rowboat bumped the ship, he looked away from me and I guess realized for the first time that there was nothing between him and a fuck of a lot of water excepting some planks. He turned like five different shades of white, and then he did faint, and me and Yevgeni manhandled him up the side.

Dmitri was standing there, watching, and he said, dry as salt, "You said this man is your brother?"

I don't blush as easy as Felix, but I felt myself go brick-red. Because right about then I came out of my cold snap and it hit me—the way it always did, later—just how I'd gone about getting the job done.

And how the fuck did I explain any of it to Dmitri and the rest of the *Morskaiakrov*'s crew, because they were all there now, standing and staring with their pale witchy eyes, waiting to hear what I'd say.

I said, "He ain't quite right in the head," and they all snorted and giggled because of course they done figured that bit out for their own selves. I was feeling worse and worse and stupider and stupider, but I kept going: "He's been hurt in his mind. That's why we're trying to find this Nephele place, to see if the people there can help him."

"The celebrants of Nephele are very wise," said an older guy with big streaks of gray in the red. He hadn't been on the beach, and I didn't know his name. "But what happened to your brother, to hurt him in his mind?"

"I don't know. I ain't a hocus."

Dmitri and the older guy kind of looked at each other, and I dragged out from somewhere the polite Kekropian word for "wizard."

If anything, their look got more squiggle-eyed, and Dmitri said, "Is your brother a wizard?"

Kethe, here it was. The question I'd been praying against for what felt like forever. And I didn't know what to say. I didn't know how these guys felt about hocuses. I didn't know if they knew the Mirador's tattoos when they saw them, or if they even knew what the Mirador was. And I ain't a good liar. I just ain't. And besides, the thing about committing yourself to a lie is that mostly you end up in twice the trouble, 'cause truth is like a whirlwind and you can't keep it in a box.

So I kind of stood there, not knowing what to say and wondering if I should just jump overboard now and save us all the bother. And after a minute, Dmitri said, "Vasili is our weather-witch."

Which I wasn't sure actually helped any, but it meant they'd already got their answer. "Yeah," I said. "But I ain't. I'm just annemer."

They kind of digested it for a minute, and I remembered and said in a hurry, "He can't work magic or nothing." I'd said it too fast and had to repeat myself, but they definitely looked happier about the whole thing after that.

And they were real nice about cramming us into their sleeping quarters. Dmitri asked if I thought a door with a lock would be a good idea, and I allowed as how it might, and so he moved all his shit out of his cabin—that being the only door with a lock on the whole ship—and I could lock Felix in there when I couldn't keep an eye on him and not have to worry. At least not as much.

And mostly, I got to admit, I was too tired to worry. The more I carried around that piece of glass, the more it seemed like I wasn't never going to sleep again. And I thought it was getting worse. I hadn't been sure, crossing Kekropia, because, you know, the more you think about not being able to sleep, the more you lay there with your eyes open. But now I was going two, three nights in a row with no sleep at all. And then the fourth night I'd sleep like a dead thing for maybe four hours, and then be wide-awake again. I didn't miss the irony of the fact that the best sleep I'd had in decads was the night we spent at Nera, and I was guessing that hadn't been natural, neither.

I would've liked to ask Felix about it, but that wasn't going to happen. Once he quit being too pissed off to see straight, he just went scared. I couldn't tell if it was me or the ocean or the Merrows or what, but getting any sense out of him would've been like squeezing blood out of a stone. And like I said, I couldn't hardly look at him for remembering the shitty thing I'd done. So I made sure he was eating and taking care of himself okay, and other than that I just left him alone. He didn't cause no trouble.

Felix

The room is small and dark and smells of salt water and excrement and rot. It pitches and tosses, and I know that I am on the ocean. Keeper comes in at intervals, but he does not seem interested in me; I am grateful. I miss my fox-headed brother. Keeper has killed him, as he killed Joline and Leo and Rhais and Pammy, and my brother's bones lie bleaching in the grass of Nera.

I want to kill Keeper, but I am so frightened of him. I know I cannot kill him; he will hurt me or throw me in the terrible ocean and laugh as I drown.

But I can't get rid of the anger. It circles endlessly around the room like a bat made of old umbrellas, crawling into the corners when Keeper comes in, but always sailing out again as soon as he locks the door behind him. It attacked me at Nera and again on the beach, enveloping Keeper and erasing him as it flung itself at me. I can't remember what happened after it wrapped its musty, peppery wings around me; I hope I did not hurt any of the small bearlike monsters, for they are not to blame. I watch the anger circling and hope that it will not engulf me again.

I think it is getting bigger.

Mildmay

The thing I liked best about the Merrows was how they were all absolutely gone on stories. That's what they did when they weren't climbing around in the rigging like a bunch of smart-ass squirrels—they told stories, first one guy, then another, and I listened with my ears flapping. 'Cause I'm a story hound in the worst way myself, and these were all new to me.

I heard about the star-crossed love of Quenivar and Marden, the voyage of the *Seawrack,* Ilpherio's quest for the Singing Stone, the feud of Yventhai and Kharmelian, and like a double septad more. I can't even remember all the names. Seemed like the Merrows had been collecting stories from everybody they ran into since forever. And I listened and listened as they went round the crew, and everybody told a story, and somewhere around the start of the third decad, Yevgeni looked over at me and said, "Hey, Scarface, you tell us a story?"

And they all perked up like they were waiting for me to make a fool out of myself again, but I said, "Sure, if you want."

They sat there looking like they'd been hit upside the head with a dead fish for a minute, then Ilia burst out laughing and said, "Come, then, and tell us a story from your Marathat," rolling the "r" out to make it sound silly.

"Okay," I said. I'd kind of been half-hoping they'd ask me and half-praying they wouldn't for a good decad and a half, so I had a story all saddled up and ready to go. I told them about Julien Tinderbox, the fox, and the second daughter of Time. Last time I'd told this story, I hadn't known how hocuses sounded, but now all I had to do was listen to Felix in my head, and I knew how to make Julien Tinderbox and all the other flash people talk. And I made the vixen Grief sound like me.

I ain't going to pretend it was the best story they'd ever heard or nothing, but it was okay, and they were all happy because it was one they'd never heard before. And I think that was when they finally quit with the teasing. I mean, they still called me "Scarface" and everything, but I didn't feel quite so much like a dartboard.

And they were nice guys. I didn't fit in with them and we all knew it, but even when they were teasing pretty bad, they never shut me out, and they could've, easy. Things could've been way worse, and I reminded myself to be grateful for what I had. Small favors.

It was still tough, though, and the nights were the worst. I hadn't liked to tell them about the whole not-sleeping thing, along of *really* not wanting to discuss the Mirador's curse. So when it was time for bed, I went into Dmitri's cabin that I was sharing with Felix and locked the door and waited for morning.

Mostly Felix acted like I wasn't there, but, powers, I made any sudden move, and he'd be staring at me like I was a snake or something. He wasn't sleeping much, neither. So we'd sit there and not do nothing and not say nothing, and sometimes he'd fall asleep and sometimes I would, but mostly it was just us sitting.

That's the sort of situation where you end up doing a lot more thinking than you wanted. And what happened to me was I got way fucking homesick. I sat there in that cramped little room and remembered Mélusine. I thought about the Cheaps and my rooms in Midwinter and the courtyard of Min-Terris's. I wondered how Cardenio was doing, and I worked out all these long speeches to tell him I was sorry I'd acted like an asshole the last time I saw him. I mean, they were like five times longer than anything I'd ever actually *say*. But they helped. And I kind of prayed—although Kethe ain't much on answering prayers and I mostly don't figure nobody else cares—that Margot was okay, and her little Badgers, and anybody who might have got in the way when the Dogs came calling.

And I thought about Ginevra. I'd been doing better with that, between Mavortian and Felix and the rest of the excitement. I mean, it hadn't ever exactly *stopped,* if you get me, but it hadn't been front and center all the fucking time and it hadn't hurt quite so fucking much. But now my head was full of her—her face, her voice, her perfume, the way she looked when she was pissed off, the way her face changed when she laughed. Some of it was going cloudy, but that just made it worse. Keeper laughed at me in my head for being so torn up over this girl I couldn't even remember right. Keeper'd always kind of sneered at me for being soft and a sissy, and I figured she'd been on to something after all. Wallowing in it, Milly-Fox, I told myself. Quit feeling sorry for yourself. But that didn't get Ginevra out of my head. Didn't seem like nothing ever would.

Felix

I wake up thinking I have been buried alive. I am in a dark, enclosed space that reeks of decay, and for a moment I cannot think of anything it can be save a mausoleum. Then I feel the world sway beneath me and realize it is worse: I am on a ship.

I lie still, trying to breathe shallowly in order not to vomit, and struggle to remember how I came here, to this non-place that cannot be mapped or marked or known. I remember Nera; I remember the maze and the dead people and the rain. But after that everything is darkness, with only lightning flashes of pain and fear. And now this room like a coffin.

I remember waking up like this once before, in the Mirador with the corpse and the snake nearby. I remember talking to a ghost boy in a maze—no, not a maze, a crypt. The maze was in Nera, itself a necropolis, and now I am awake and alone in a tomb.

I mean a ship cabin.

I get up, discovering that I have to keep my head bowed in order not to brain myself on the ceiling. The stench seems worse now that I am standing up, or perhaps it's merely that I'm using more air. I am afraid to move, afraid of falling into the ocean, or walking into the embrace of a corpse, afraid that there is something waiting for me in this reeking darkness.

I don't know how long I stand there, afraid to move but unwilling to lie down again, to become like a corpse myself. Presently there are glowing lines in the darkness, the outlines of a door. I realize that someone is approaching my tomb with a lantern.

I sit on the bed, a position that looks less foolish than standing with my head tilted like a parrot, and watch the door, hoping that the monster will be kind.

The door opens with a flood of lamplight. I bring one hand up to shield my dazzled eyes, and the monster says, "Felix. You're awake."

No, not a monster. A ghost. The ghost of my fox-headed brother. "Where are we?" I say, hoping he can tell me which circle of the underworld I have been sorted into.

He sets the lantern on its bracket before he answers me. "We're on the—" And I cannot understand either the name of the ship or the name of the place he says we are going. But I do understand the rest: "Ilia says the folks there'll be able to tell us how to get to this garden-thing you're after."

"Oh. Am I dead?"

"Are you *what?*"

"Dead. Am I . . . dead?"

"No. Why d'you think . . . oh, never mind. You ain't dead."

"Oh." I cannot decide if this is good or bad and so settle for, "Thank you."

"Sure." The colors around him are cautious, exasperated—still dark with grief, although he is dead now and surely his grief should be ended—but chased through with bright sparks of amusement. I am afraid to ask what it is I've said that he finds funny.

He sits down on the other narrow shelflike bed and tilts his head at me. "You okay?"

"Me?"

"You been a little weird lately."

It comes with being dead. But I do not say it. He says I am not dead, and I believe him. "I'm all right," I say, but it is a feeble and obvious lie.

"Okay," he says, and I can tell that all he means is that he's not going to push me. "Since you're 'all right,' d'you want to come up on deck for a little?"

"Out of the smell?" I say before I can stop myself.

"Yeah. We won't go near the rails or nothing. Just be polite to the Merrows, okay?"

I would promise anything if it would get me out of this fetid tomb. I give my assent eagerly, and he says, "Okay. Come on, then. It's a nice starry night, and you can tell me all their names."

I follow the ghost of my fox-headed brother. The passageway is as cramped and dark and reeking as the cabin, but we come swiftly to a ladder that leads us up into clear, crisp, salt-laden air. The stars are like jewels, seeming almost within reach, and I lose myself gladly in staring at them. After a moment, I remember that the ghost asked about their names, and I begin to tell him.

I have to pause for breath, for a corrective against dizziness, after I have told him the names of all the stars in Geneviève's Crown, and a voice says in Kekropian from the darkness, "We call that one the Mortar."

"Oh," says the ghost, "hey, Vasili."

A shape emerges into the light of my ghost-brother's lantern. I cannot tell if it is ghost or monster; it is a strange, dark presence, thick with clouds and smelling of rain.

"Vasili's the weather-witch," the ghost tells me and then says to the other, "Felix is feeling better."

"That is good to hear."

"It won't last," I say. "The storm is coming."

They both stare at me. I drop my gaze, my face heating.

"Yeah, well, maybe 'better' was a little strong," the ghost says after a moment.

"Your brother struggles," says the other, the weather-witch. "Do not blame him for that."

"Oh, I don't." The ghost sounds weary. "I just . . . I don't know."

"I'm sorry," I say, my voice a choked whisper.

"Oh, Kethe, no. Powers, I'm such a fuck-up." The ghost touches my arm gently, and I look up at him. The colors around him are darker now, deeper. "Felix, it's okay. It ain't your fault."

The weather-witch asks, "How long has he been this way?"

"I don't know. Don't think he knows either."

There is a silence; I look up at the stars, serene and brilliant and out of reach. I can remember standing, looking at them, somewhere else, in some other time, but they have never been as clear to me as they are now.

The ghost says, "He's getting worse."

"We will reach Haigisikhora soon," the weather-witch says. "The celebrants of the Gardens are both wise and learned. They will help."

"Thanks, Vasili," the ghost says.

"For what? I have done nothing."

"Yeah. You didn't run screaming."

"There is nothing here to flee from," the weather-witch says gently. "Neither in you nor in him."

The ghost snorts, but does not answer.

"In any event," the weather-witch says, "he was right about one thing. There's a storm coming."

"A bad one?"

"Could be. It's early to tell."

"Well, better get you below regardless," the ghost says to me. "Come on, then."

Obediently, I start back down the ladder. I have shamed my ghost-brother; from the way he and the weather-witch speak, I know it is not the first time. He stays behind me down the passageway, follows me into the cabin, and locks the door behind him.

"If there's a storm coming, you better sleep now." He is always brusque, but I hear an edge of contempt, of impatience in his voice.

"I'm sorry," I say again, sitting down.

"It ain't your fault."

"But I . . ."

"I shouldn't've said what I did. I'm just tired." He sighs and runs one hand across his muzzle. "The curse, you know."

I remember the vicious thorns and nod.

"Go to sleep, Felix," he says, taking off his boots and lying down on the other bed. "Once we're at the Gardens and you're better, we can take an afternoon and say we're sorry to each other 'til it evens out. Let it go 'til then. I'm sorry and you're sorry and there ain't a damn thing we can do about it." He rolls over to face the wall; he is done talking to me.

I lie down and watch the black anger flapping slowly across the ceiling. It feels the storm coming, too. It is waiting.

Mildmay

We'd had some storms, the first two decads of the *Morskaiakrov*'s voyage. Ilia'd said as how we were coming up on the worst of the storm season, and once they'd done with their business in Haigisikhora, they'd be putting in at Yaga, their home island—wherever the fuck that was—and staying a month or three. So I figured me and Felix were lucky we'd reached the ocean when we had, and I tried to remember to be grateful for that, too.

It was the second or third day of the third decad since we'd left Kekropia, and everybody said we should be sighting Troia in the next day or so. That made me feel way better, because it meant I'd be that much closer to handing Felix over to people who could help him. I felt like something inside me had unkinked just a little, and I was still feeling that way when I went up on deck in the morning and saw the big black smudge of cloud on the horizon.

It was just like fucking Nera all over again. I looked at Fiodor, the nearest guy to me, and I didn't have to ask. He said, "Yes, Vasili has been up all night working the weather. But Dmitri has cut things perhaps too fine, and there is only so much Vasili can do. It is hard to swerve Ocean and Sky from their deepest desires."

"Right," I said. "Can I help?"

I could, of course, and I spent I don't know how many hours doing this, that, and the other thing while Dmitri tried to outrace the storm. I got to confess I never did understand above half of what it was that went on with the ropes in that ship, but the Merrows were all real good about saying exactly what they wanted, and I didn't do nothing wrong. But the *Morskaiakrov* just wasn't fast enough, and you didn't need to know nothing about ships to see it. Them black clouds were crawling up our ass, and we weren't even close enough to see Troia yet.

At some point I went down to help Ilia with the gallons and gallons of hot tea that everybody needed, because the wind was getting harder and colder and meaner every time you had to stand up in it, and I asked him straight out, "Are we fucked?"

"Maybe," he said. "She is a stout ship, our *Morskaiakrov,* and Dmitri is a canny captain. We may yet elude Sky's anger. But I admit I would not place any large bets on it."

"Thanks," I said, and I was turning to get the tea urn to take on deck when Ilia said, "Mildmay."

I looked around fast, because they none of them hardly ever used my name. He said, "If she sinks . . . there is room for only one extra in the longboat."

"Kethe." Everything inside my chest squeezed up like a fist.

"I'm sorry," he said. "Truly. It should not have mattered."

"No, 'course not. You weren't planning on getting caught in this bitch of a storm."

"Dmitri says that we will do as you wish. If you want your brother to have that place, we will do our best, although many of us are frightened of him. But we will not blame you if you wish that place for yourself. You would be welcome to come back to Yaga with us."

And be pointed out as the guy who'd let his brother die to save his own skin? "Thanks," I said. "But you can tell Dmitri that if it comes to that, you pack food or something in that space."

Ilia's eyebrows went up, and I wished that didn't make me wonder what he thought of me. "Are you sure?"

"I won't leave him. And you'd never get him in the boat without me." That maybe wasn't strictly true, but I'd got Dmitri's measure. He wasn't no bad guy, but the second time Felix had a screaming fit because of all the water, Dmitri would dump him over the side. And I ain't saying he'd be wrong, neither. He had his crew to look out for, and if Felix capsized them, they were all going to be in a world of trouble.

"If you change your mind—"

"I know, I know. And thanks." And I grabbed the urn and went back up on deck.

The storm hit us around about sunset. And when I say hit, I ain't kidding. It was like getting clocked with a sledgehammer, and I swear by all the powers and saints it was raining straight sideways. The waves were more like cliffs, and you could feel the smack of the *Morskaiakrov* coming down again all the way up at the top of your skull. And it was pitch-black and the wind was howling so loud you couldn't hear nothing unless somebody yelled right straight into your ear.

But I heard it just fine when the ship started groaning. It was a terrible noise, and I didn't have to be no sailor to guess what it meant. I'd been helping Ilia pack the stores, and I looked up at him, and he nodded back at me. I kind of lurched my way over to him and yelled, "Y'all go on. Don't worry about us."

He gave me a look, but it wasn't the sort of thing anybody'd be inclined to argue about with the ship clearly getting ready to come apart around our ears. He made a flapping gesture—*go on to your brother*—and since there wasn't nothing else neither of us could say, I shook his hand and went.

Now, if you'd asked, I'd have to admit I didn't have nothing even resembling a plan. I wasn't keen on dying, and it was really fucking annoying to get Felix this close to this damn fucking place he'd been nagging my head off about for what felt like half my life, and then let him drown. I mean, it was just such a stupid waste. But how I was going to get him to land when I didn't know quite where land was? Not a clue. All I could do was keep moving forward and hope for the best, and the next thing forward from where I was standing was to get Felix out of Dmitri's cabin, because if he was still locked in there when the ship sank, he *would* drown, no two ways about it.

So I got to the door and unlocked it and opened it, and then I was on the floor with Felix's fingers digging into my neck. The only light I had was from the lantern I'd been carrying, and that was now three feet back down the passageway, so I couldn't see but hints of his face, but that was enough to pick out the bared teeth and the way his eyes were showing white all the way around. And I didn't need to see him at all to know he was trying to kill me.

I couldn't think what had set him off, but it was only about a half-centime worth of my head that even cared. We thrashed back and forth, and I was praying the lantern wasn't setting the ship on fire and praying I wouldn't break Felix's fingers and praying he didn't know just where the big arteries in the neck were or was at least too far gone to think of them. And he really didn't know much about fighting, because I went for the cheap, quick, and dirty way out and he didn't know enough to block my thigh with his. A hard enough kick in the balls will take the fight out of just about anybody—least anybody male—and he went limp as the decad's washing, and I was glad I couldn't hear the noises he was making, because I was sure they were awful, and I felt like the world's worst prick without that.

You ain't leaving him here to drown, Milly-Fox. You can say that much for yourself.

I rolled him off me and started to get up, and something jabbed into my thigh. I knew what it was even before I reached into my pocket, but I was still thinking stupidly, Oh fuck, oh, Kethe, no, please, when I brought my hand out again and opened it and saw my palm was bleeding and there was a septad bits of glass, all of 'em with razor-sharp edges, and that was all that was left of the spell Felix had made Gideon do in Hermione to keep off the Mirador's curse.

"Oh fuck me sideways 'til I cry," I said, just because it was all too much and there wasn't nothing else I *could* say. Then since I wasn't a hocus and didn't know and couldn't ask the only hocus that happened to be handy, I wrapped the bits of glass in my handkerchief and stuck 'em back in my pocket. Because, I mean, my guess was the virtue'd gone out of that piece of glass when it broke, but I didn't *know* that, and if there was even half a chance I was wrong, I wasn't going to waste it.

Then I staggered upright—the *Morskaiakrov* was pitching worse than ever—and grabbed the lantern. Which turned out not to be broken after all. Small favors, I thought, although it felt more like a bad joke, and dragged Felix to his feet. His face was whitish green, and he was still gasping like a landed fish, so I figured he wouldn't be interested enough in me to put up a fight for a while yet. I started back down the passage for the ladder with a fine fuck-you-all to our bag and everything in it.

And that's when the *Morskaiakrov* shuddered and lurched like a foundering horse, and I knew she was going down. I knew it, the same way I knew water was wet and I couldn't breathe it. I didn't know if the Merrows got off the *Morskaiakrov* okay before it sank, and I ain't got the least little idea how *we* got off. I mean, you could tell me giant pelicans flew down and grabbed us, and I'd believe you. I remember having to coldcock

Felix somewhere in the middle of it all, but how I figured out a hatch cover would float, and how I got it ripped free of the ship, I will just never know. Some of that was the curse waking up, I think, because when I caught up with myself again, I felt pretty damn weird.

Of course, I was also in the ocean, without my boots and with one arm across this hatch cover I didn't remember making friends with and the other arm trying to keep Felix's head out of the water. Which was enough to make anybody feel weird, especially seeing as how it was just about as black as pitch and still trying to rain sideways.

But there was more to it than that, and I only wished I could believe I was imagining it. But when you're up to your neck in seawater in the middle of a storm and you feel *hot,* you know there's something wrong with you, and it ain't small potatoes, neither. And there was this weird, deep feeling, sort of dull and sparky all at the same time, running along the bones in my arms and legs. So between the cussing and the praying, there wasn't much going on in my head in the way of actual thought. But that was okay, I guess, since there wasn't nothing I could do but wait out the storm and hope we were both alive at the end of it.

I can't tell you how long it lasted, neither. My time sense had stripped its gears, so I don't know if it was hours feeling like minutes or minutes feeling like hours. Either way it was putrid, especially since I could never figure how long it had been since I'd checked to see if Felix was breathing. And since he felt way colder than me, along of me being, like I said, too fucking hot, I couldn't quit worrying about it. So I kept feeling for his pulse or craning around—and getting a faceful of salt water, likely as not—to try and feel or hear or see if he was breathing. I must've looked crazy myself, only of course there wasn't nobody around to notice. But I kept thinking about me dragging a cold, stiff, blue-faced corpse to land, and it was just more than I could handle.

And it turned out to be a good thing I was doing my sheepdog-with-one-lamb routine, because it meant that when he started to come 'round again, I knew about it. There wasn't nothing I could *do,* mind. I just hung on to him and the hatch cover and basically prayed he wouldn't wake up in the same mood he'd been in when I knocked him out.

I felt it when Felix came 'round for real. He went stiff as a board, and I thought, Oh fuck, and there wasn't time for nothing more because all at once it was like hanging on to a wolverine that really feels it's got better places to be. He was snarling and clawing, and I think he tried to bite me.

And all I could do was hang on and hope he tired himself out before I lost my grip.

And there I did get lucky, although it was a pretty near-run thing. But he didn't have much staying power, no matter how pissed off he was. And I kind of think there was something still working up top, because there was this moment where I realized he'd quit fighting to get away from me and was fighting to wrap himself around me like a vine or something. Whatever it was that made him scared of deep water, it wasn't nothing little.

So I fought him back to a grip that wouldn't strangle me—and, powers, that's hard in the dark and the water and with somebody who can't understand what you're saying and ain't listening if he could. But it was then that I realized the storm was dying down, because if he'd tried any of them stunts when we first went into the water, I'm pretty sure we both would've drowned.

So I hung on, with both my shoulders wanting to cramp and that nasty feeling like somebody was striking lucifers along my bones getting worse and worse, and Felix like this iron weight and his breath sobbing in my ear, and I waited and the sky got lighter and the rain calmed down and the ocean smoothed out some more, and then the sun pushed its way out of the clouds and I just about cried. Because there was east, and the horizon line was kind of dim and humped, and that had to be Troia. I really didn't think we could make it, but we were close enough that dying now would look like giving up.

"Keeper didn't raise no quitters," I said, and I could even hear myself say it. And then I started kicking me and Felix and the hatch cover toward land.

But that was a no-starter, as I figured out in about a minute. Because Felix wasn't being no help at all. I yelled at him to kick instead of trying to break my collarbones, but if he even heard me, he couldn't do nothing about it. I could feel it in his body. He'd got locked up in his own fear, like he'd been turned to stone right where he was. And I couldn't do a damn thing with him like that. I kept going under, and I could feel my grip on the hatch cover sliding out from my palms toward my fingertips. I couldn't do it. If I was going to keep us both from drowning, I couldn't carry him no longer.

I stopped kicking. I got my grip back on the hatch cover. And then I hung there and thought about my breathing and about sending the good air out to my muscles, the way Keeper'd taught me when I had two septads and one. And after a minute—and I didn't dare take longer—I was able to say,

"Felix," and have it come out loud and clear, but not angry or frightened or none of the other things I was feeling. "Felix, can you hear me?"

He didn't say nothing, and I hadn't thought he would. I went on, keeping my voice nice and even, like I was talking to Devie again. "Felix, we're almost to land, and I can get us there, but I need you to get off me. Okay? You can hang on to the hatch cover. There's plenty of room, and you can see it's floating just fine. You don't have to swim or nothing, and I promise you won't drown, but you got to hang on to the hatch cover instead of me. Okay? Come on, Felix, it's safe as houses. Just move one hand. Just put it on the hatch cover." I kept talking, saying the same things over and over, praying that wherever Felix was inside his head, he could hear me and he was still somewhere he could be talked back from. At first I thought it wasn't going to work, and we were just going to be stuck here until I couldn't hang on no more and we both went down, but I kept talking, like I used to do with Devie, not getting angry or impatient, but not giving up, neither.

And after a chunk of time that can't have been as long as it felt like, Felix's hands kind of twitched a little, not actually moving but like they were kind of thinking about it. I kept talking, like I was a music box or something, because if I got excited, it would just throw him off. A little longer, and he started doing what I was telling him to. I mean, Kethe, he wasn't moving no faster than a turtle, but he was moving. One hand went out to the hatch cover and clamped on to it.

We stuck there for a second, and the arm still hooked over my shoulder dug in like he was afraid I was going to buck him off. I said, "That's great, Felix, that's just exactly right. But you got to get the other hand out there, too, and then I can duck under you, and it'll all be okay. It'll be okay, I promise, but you got to do it."

And he did it. He flung his right arm out and grabbed on to the hatch cover, and before he could change his mind about it, I dropped out from under him and came up as neat as you please just beside him. It ain't a trick I could've pulled more than once just then, and I kind of hung there for a minute myself, thinking about my breathing and about not cramping while the strength came back into my legs. Then I got my bearings and started kicking us toward Troia.

And, powers, that went on for about a million septads and a half. The land wasn't getting no closer and I wondered if it was a mirage like in the stories of Mark Polaris. So I just kicked and kicked and tried not to watch the land not getting closer and tried not to think about the hot, raspy feeling in my legs and tried not to think about what would happen if the curse started cramping me up again before we reached land. Felix wasn't helping or nothing, but he wasn't in my way, neither, and I figured that was the best I could hope for.

And then when I couldn't stand it no more and looked up, the land was closer, so I could actually see the green hills rising up behind the beach and this rickety wooden staircase that said maybe people used this beach and maybe we were going to be okay after all.

And that's when the cramps started. Just little ones, more like twitches in my fingers and toes, but I knew their big brothers wouldn't want to miss out on the fun, and they'd be along in a minute.

"Kick, you useless fuck!" I snarled at Felix, and for a wonder, he did. And I kicked, while the cramps got bigger and harder and my head started to pound, and the land came closer and closer. Just when I could reach the bottom with my feet, a big cramp got me. I lost Felix and the hatch cover and most of my air, and, Kethe, I was so fucking mad and scared that I clawed my way straight back out of it. I felt something go way fucking wrong in my leg, the kind of wrong there ain't no ifs about, and right then I didn't even care. I got my feet under me and grabbed Felix from where he was floundering and just dragged him straight up out of the water, swearing at him like a whole boatload of Simside dockworkers, calling him a motherfucker and shit-brained cocksucker and I don't know what all, anything to get him to move, to carry own his weight, to keep us both from going facedown in the surf and drowning less than ten feet from the land I'd fucking near killed myself to reach. And I could see on his face that he heard me and he understood me, and I wanted to scream because I knew he was never going to forget me yelling at him like this and he was never going to forgive it, neither, but I couldn't care. My right leg was dead. I couldn't feel it, and I only knew it was taking any of my weight because I wasn't quite falling down. And there was another big cramp coming, and I knew we had to get onto the beach before it got me. We had to, and so I yelled terrible things at my brother, some things Keeper'd called me one time, and I'd sworn, crying to myself in a corner, that I'd never say them to nobody else, no matter what. And here I was, saying them to Felix, who didn't even deserve them, just because it was that or let us both drown.

And then, somehow, we were out of the water, and my right leg couldn't take it, and I was going down, dragging Felix with me, and that was the last I knew for a good long while.

Chapter 12

Mildmay

I knew I was dreaming, but it didn't help.

There was this thing Keeper used to threaten us with—though far as I know she never actually used it on nobody—this old cooling well in a warehouse she owned down in Queensdock. You couldn't use it for keeping things cool no more, along of it having sprung a leak so there was always a couple inches of water in the bottom, but it was just the right size to shut a kid in. Like I said, she never did it, but she could've and we all knew it.

So in my dream, I'm shut in that old cooling well, and I'm pounding on the trap, begging to be let out, and there's people up top—I can hear 'em arguing over what to do with me. Every once in a while they shout a question at me, so I know they know I'm there. But they won't let me out.

And they're asking the weirdest fucking questions. They want to know why there's a death curse on me and why it hasn't killed me yet and what school of magic it's from and how I got here—wherever the fuck "here" is—and why I was with this other guy and on and on and on. And I'm trying to tell them—explain about Felix and Miriam and Cerberus Cresset and the Mirador—only I feel like I'm talking the wrong language or something. I sure as fuck ain't giving the right answers, 'cause, every time, there's this long, long pause, and then another fucking question. And I'm still begging them to let me out and the trap ain't budging.

And like I said, I knew I was dreaming, but it wasn't no good. I couldn't wake myself up. I could feel my body, but it was just this heavy *thing,* like a lead doorstop, like the trap of the cooling well, and I could only hope I was still breathing, 'cause from the way I felt, I wasn't. And, oh yeah, it hurt. It was like there were hornets swarming inside my bones—all of 'em, but most especially my right leg. There was something wrong there, something fucked to Hell and back, and I guess there was part of me that didn't even want to wake up and have to deal with this new, horrible thing that'd be waiting for me when I opened my eyes.

After a while, the dream did that thing dreams do where everything changes while you ain't looking, and I was back dreaming about Ginevra. And the people with all the questions had bailed. Which was good. In the dream, Ginevra was mad at me, and we were fighting about something, although I never did figure out what. But that actually felt familiar, because there'd been a lot of times Ginevra'd been mad at me and I hadn't had the first idea what I'd done. I tried to pretend I wasn't dreaming, that I'd just had a nightmare about her dying and the Mirador burning and all the rest of it, but the whole time my leg was hurting like nothing on earth, and I knew I was lying to myself. But even so, and even with Ginevra yelling like a banshee, it was better than being awake.

And then I thought, What about Felix?

I tried to bury that thought, but I'd got so used to worrying about Felix that I was already on to, I wonder if he's okay. And then I remembered the storm and the ocean and the beach, and thought, Kethe, what if he's dead?

And just like that, I was awake. I didn't know where I was or what day it was or how I'd gotten off the beach that was the last thing I remembered. Well, except my dreams, but they didn't help none.

I just lay there with my eyes closed for a while, taking stock. I was laying down, which was good, and it was on something soft, which was better. There was a comforter or something over me, which suggested somebody cared enough not to want me to freeze my ass off. So that was okay.

On the other hand, I ached all over in that kind of feverish way that means it don't matter what you do, you ain't gonna be comfortable this side of tomorrow morning and maybe not then, neither. My head was throbbing like some kind of drum, and then my right leg had gone and lapped the field. The swarm of hornets hadn't gotten no smaller, they'd just packed themselves into my hip and thigh and knee like a jar of olives. It felt like if I tried to bend my knee at all, the whole thing would just squish to bits like rotten fruit, and then the hornets could get out and sting me to death. Oh powers, I was fucked and fucked bad.

There was a noise, out there somewhere beyond what I knew, a kind of little rustling noise, like somebody shifting position. I didn't let my body tense up, but inside I froze solid. And then I thought, Well, fuck. Whoever that is, I ain't getting away from them nohow.

I opened my eyes.

And the bad news was, I didn't recognize a damn thing. It was a nice room—white walls, big window, a rug on the floor, a table with a chair, and two armchairs—but there wasn't a familiar thing in it. And I ain't talking like I was expecting to see my own couch or nothing. But, I mean, even the quilt on the bed had a pattern I'd never seen before, and the rug on the floor didn't even look real, it was that pretty. It hadn't been made on no factory loom, that was for sure.

And then there was the kid. He was sitting in the armchair near the door, like he wanted to be sure he could get away in a hurry. He had red hair and yellow eyes, and he was wearing this dark, quilted coat with a high, tight collar, which made him look white as flour. He was younger than me. I guessed him at two septads and three or thereabouts. He wasn't looking at me. He was staring out the window, so I could see the way his hair was braided into a knot at the base of his skull, like a woman's. He was wearing diamonds in his ears, just little chips, but enough to show this kid either had money or had somebody that liked to give him presents. And even in profile he looked like a clockwork toy that'd been wound up too tight. This was already less than good.

I waited a while, but he hadn't noticed me wake up, and he looked like he was settling down for a good hard stare, and so finally I just said, "Where am I?"

Powers, he jumped like a foot and a half. Wound *way* too tight. Looked at head-on, he had a narrow, pointy little face and a soft, little mouth. He would've made a pretty girl.

"Wh-what?" he said, and I didn't blame him. Aside from him not expecting it and my scar fucking up my Kekropian, my voice was hoarse and thick and fucking ugly as a mud pie. So I said it again, slower and trying hard for clear, and he said, "Oh," in this prissy little voice, and then, in Midlander, "You are in the Gardens of Nephele."

"Well, fuck," I said in Midlander, "we got here after all," and he jumped again and turned bright, blotchy carnation pink.

Watch your language, Milly-Fox. Keeper, and I could half feel the stinging cuff across the back of my head.

"Sorry," I said. "I ain't awake yet. What's your name?"

He drew himself up and compressed his lips and said in this nasty little voice like it should mean something to me and make me feel like a worm, "I am Khrysogonos of the House Ptolemais, Acolyte of the Nephelian Covenant."

So what crawled up your ass and died? I thought, but I didn't say it. I was holding a lousy hand here, and I knew it. I just said, "I'm Mildmay. No house or nothing." Let's pretend we're all normal and friendly. You can get quite a ways with that game if both sides are willing to play.

But this kid was having none of it. "I know what you are," he said in that same prissy, uptight little voice. "You are a murderer."

"Oh for fuck's sake," I said in Marathine. "Let's go on and call cow manure shit."

"What?" he said. "What language is that?"

He sounded like he was really confused, and I was betting on my two minute's acquaintance with him that this kid wasn't a good liar. So I felt a little better. At least I had *something*.

"Marathine," I said. There was a black second where I thought I just wasn't going to be able to stop myself from translating for him, but I bit my tongue hard, and said, "It's a proverb."

"Oh," he said, kind of blank, like he'd thought other languages didn't have proverbs or I wouldn't know any or something. Then he shook it off and said, "You murdered for money," just like a terrier after a rat. Powers, I thought, we got a prick here and no mistake.

"Yeah," I said. "So?"

I don't think he'd been expecting me to admit it, but I remembered all those questions in my dreams, and it didn't take no genius to figure out where they'd come from. And, I mean, I ain't proud of having been what I was or done what I did, but I ain't going to lie about it.

He got kind of fish-faced for a second. Then he got up, said, "We should have let you die," and swept himself out, slamming the door behind him hard enough to rattle the glass in the window.

"Oh fuck me sideways," I said. My voice wasn't all that steady, but it was still steadier than I felt. Welcome to the Gardens of Nephele, Milly-Fox, Keeper said. Solve all your problems, right? And her laugh, like acid and broken glass, chased around my head until I finally fell back asleep.

I woke up again when the door opened, and I didn't remember my dreams, which I figured was a mercy. Small fucking favors.

"It is I," said the prick, grand as a king.

"You again."

"I am assigned to your care."

"I thought you were gonna let me die."

"It is against our covenant. Personal feelings do not enter into it."

"I'm touched," I said, and he gave me a funny look like he didn't know what to do with sarcasm when he heard it. "How long've I been here?"

"A week."

Flashie calendar. Figured. "Fuck," I said.

"You nearly died," he said, like I'd said something nasty about his mother. "The *Celebrant Lunar* had to treat you personally."

"Nice of him."

"*She* is the Arkhon of the Gardens." Way more important than a shit-eating rat like me, was what he meant.

"Uh-huh. So what's wrong with me?"

I used my fuck-with-me-and-I'll-kill-you knife-fighter's voice. Keeper would've smacked me. Zephyr would've rolled his eyes. The prick flinched a little, and I felt better in a mean sort of way.

He said, in a high, angry, trembly voice, "I don't have to tell you anything." Oh, a prick for sure and certain.

"Yeah, you're right. I can figure it out for myself. My leg's busted." I caught myself then, clamped down on my temper. He was just a kid, and he hated my guts. I was lucky he wasn't trying to smother me with my own damn pillow.

"You are crippled. The Celebrant Lunar thinks you will probably be able to walk again without a cane, but it may take months."

Months. Crippled. I shut my eyes and started counting a septad. But I'd only got to five when I remembered something a hell of a lot more important.

"What about my brother?"

"Your . . . brother?"

"Yeah, my *brother*. The guy with me. The crazy redhead hocus with skew eyes. Don't you dare tell me he's dead or I'll murder *you* next."

The prick probably didn't catch the end of that, but he understood enough to scare him. Just what I needed. "He isn't dead. We are caring for him. We will heal him." And all the time kind of looking from me to the door and back again, like he was checking to see if I was going to go for him and if he could get out the door fast enough. *Very* smooth, Milly-Fox.

"Can I see him?"

"You can't even walk."

The conversation died right there, funeral, lilies, and all. I didn't figure it was any job of mine to dig it back up again, so I lay there and stared up at the ceiling and waited for him to go the fuck away.

"Are you hungry?" the prick said after a while. Guess he remembered he had a duty here.

"No."

"Do you need anything?"

"No." And I wouldn't tell you if I did, you fucking numbnuts prick.

"Then I shall leave you," he said, all grand again, and made his same exit. It was a wonder he hadn't broken the window yet.

Felix

They will not leave me alone. The owl-eyed people with their hair like fire, they are always there, staring at me, touching me. Their words drop from their mouths like stones and do not reach me. They do not seem to notice the water dripping from my hair, my clothes, my fingers. They do not understand that I have drowned and that they cannot reach me. The anger has been made stronger by drowning; it is circling and circling. I can feel its greed, its eagerness. When they touch me, it comes closer.

Mildmay

Kethe, that room was a pit. I mean, I know it wasn't really that bad, but I lay there with nothing to look at but the ceiling or the walls—or the prick when he came in—for most of a decad, and I got to where I knew and hated every crack in the fucking plaster. Although not as bad as I hated the prick.

He quit picking fights with me, and I swear to the powers and all the saints besides that I was being grateful for small favors. I mean, I didn't pick no fights with him. But when you can't get up out of bed without somebody to drag you up and then mostly carry you . . . it ain't no good time even if it's your best-ever friend giving you a hand to the water closet. And with him and me both trying to pretend the other one didn't exist, even the absolutely fucking putrid time when my knee buckled in the middle of the hall anyway, and I went down and dragged him down with me—I seriously thought sometimes that I had died on that beach, and that this was my circle of Hell.

And even with him and me ignoring the shit out of each other most of the time, and even with him nagging me to eat when I didn't give a rat's ass what he wanted and didn't want to eat, along of feeling most of the time like I'd swallowed a stone, he was practically a friend compared to my other visitors, the people who came in every couple days—celebrants, the prick said, and some of 'em were Celebrants Minor and some of 'em were Celebrants Major and I couldn't figure out what the fuck the difference was—oh, those people I just plain wanted to kill.

They came and stood over me and poked at my leg and talked to each other in this fast, heavy Kekropian with the stresses in funny places. Mostly what they did made things hurt worse, although I didn't say so because I knew if they cared at all they'd be happy about it, but after about a septad days, when nothing they were doing was making it any better, I figured I had to say *something*. Because Kethe knows they wanted me gone—and I wanted to *be* gone in the worst possible way—and it wasn't going to happen if I didn't get the fucking hornets out of my leg. So when the Celebrant Minor—skinny little gal with fat red pigtails—was done with the hornets, I screwed up my courage and said this sentence in Kekropian that I'd been practicing every time the prick wasn't in the room, "My leg is not getting any better." Good grammar and everything. Keeper probably would've passed out on the spot.

The Celebrant Minor just reared back like I'd bit her and said, "We don't work miracles. Healing takes time."

The prick translated into Midlander, because I'd never exactly got round to telling him that I understood Kekropian way better than I'd ever be able to speak it.

"I know that," I said, "but—"

"The celebrant has better things to do than listen to you whine," the prick said, and the Celebrant Minor lofted her nose in the air and stalked out. The prick followed her and slammed the door hard enough for two.

Well, that was about as dumb as kissing a gator, I thought, then I wished for the umpteenth septad time that I wasn't trapped in this fucking awful room.

After that first day, the prick wouldn't talk about Felix except to tell me he was okay and the celebrants were taking care of him and I should quit nagging. I asked him once—because I'd been having nightmares about drowned people—about the *Morskaiakrov,* if anybody knew if the crew was okay, but he just said, "Oh, smugglers," in such a snotty voice that there wasn't no point going on. And, I mean, there wasn't nothing I could do anyways. Whether they were alive or dead, me knowing wouldn't help none. But Felix was different. And the more the prick wouldn't tell me nothing, the more worried I got.

So I finally just came out one morning and said, "I want to see my brother," before he'd even got himself through the door. He stopped for a second where he was, with that stupid, blank sheep-look on his face, then came on in and shut the door. I saw he was holding a walking stick, but right then I didn't care. "I want to see him," I said, clear and slow and not shouting.

"It will not be permitted," he said.

"Why not?"

"It is the decision of the Celebrants Terrestrial. They have told me you are not to see him."

"Fuck," I said, mostly because it would make him twitch. And because I would've said it anyway, and it kept me from doing something stupid like screaming or pleading with him.

"Here," he said, a little shrill and a little shaky, and pushed the stick at me. "You need to start walking again."

The hornets just about died laughing at that one. "What?" I said.

"Walking. I thought that was what you wanted."

"I *want* to see my brother," I said through my teeth.

"No," said the prick.

"Get the fuck out of my room!" And he saw I was ready to throw that stick at him, because he went like a rabbit.

I just sat there and cussed for I don't know how long. It was better than crying and better than screaming and probably better than going and hunting down the Celebrants Terrestrial, whoever the fuck they were, and beating the shit out of them. Not that I could. I slammed my fist down on my right thigh and then just about did scream, because it was the stupidest thing I'd done since the *Morskaiakrov* went down. Kethe, it hurt. It was like there was a ball of glass shards in there somewhere about midway up, and I'd just sent the points shooting out from the bone like a firework star. I was amazed I wasn't bleeding.

But stupid or not, it did bring me back to where I could think, and after a little while longer, I worked things out to where I realized that the prick was right. I needed to start walking again. It was either that or go batfuck nuts. So I swung my legs over the side of the bed, real slow and one at a time. I sat there for a minute, with the stick ready for action out in front of me, and I felt like a sick, useless old man.

"I fucking hate this," I said and got up.

I heard myself scream—and, powers, that's a bad thing—and then I was on the floor with some new bruises, and the hornets square dancing up and down my thigh. I kind of lay there and cussed a while longer, and then I got up again. It took like an indiction and a half, but I did better, and this time when I was standing up, I stayed that way. I wasn't *enjoying* it or nothing, mind, but I was standing.

But the kicker was that I was scared to try and move. I'd never thought I was a coward, and Kethe knows I'd kept going through some pretty nasty shit when I was doing jobs for Keeper. But I just felt like I couldn't face it. Even if I didn't fall down again, I knew how much it was going to hurt, and it was like I was trying to nerve myself up to lay my hand down on a red-hot anvil. I could feel myself starting to shake, and there was a whole chorus in my head saying as how the best idea was just to get back on the bed again and lay down for a while. But I knew if I did that, I never would be able to make myself take this first step, and I furthermore knew that I'd end up, sure as fuck, having to explain myself to the prick. And I wasn't going to let him see that.

"Don't be a sissy, Milly-Fox," I said out loud, to make them whining voices shut up, and I took a step forward.

I probably should have sold tickets, because I bet it was funny to watch. Left leg fine, stick fine, right leg forward, and then my knee buckled and I was on the floor again. I wasn't swearing this time, because I'd run out of words nasty enough. I was kind of crying a little, and that made me even madder. And now, of course, if the prick walked in he'd find me laying on the floor like a drunk, and that was even worse than him finding me sitting on the bed too scared to try. I dragged myself up, cursing and panting and sobbing, and shuffled back inch by fucking inch to the bed. When I fell down on it, like a building caving in, I was sweating like I'd just fought off five or six goons. I lay there until my heart quit racing and I was breathing normal, and then I picked myself up and tried again.

By the time the prick came back that afternoon, I'd got myself all the way across to the armchair by the window, where I'd been sitting for like two hours because by the time I got there, it felt like my whole leg was made of glass and fixing to shatter. So I just sat and looked out at the piece of garden I could see through the window and loved every damn inch of it for not being plaster.

So he came in and said, "Oh," like he hadn't expected me to get that far. Then he said, "How are you feeling?"

"Fine," I said, and yes I was lying like a rug, but I wasn't about to tell him the truth.

"Good, good. Then tomorrow I'll show you the way out into the garden."

"The *garden?*" I'd been figuring they weren't going to let me out of this room until they couldn't keep me in it no more.

"Of course," he said, giving me this frown like even somebody as stupid and backward as me should've been able to figure *that* out. "You have to walk now if you want your leg to heal. And you won't bother anyone out there."

"Oh good," I said, but I know I didn't sound as snarky as I wanted to, because I was suddenly feeling like there was like twice as much light in the room or something. I mean, even with my fun new glass leg and everything, the idea of getting outside was just about enough to make me drool.

"Are you sure you're all right? You look a little pale."

"Nah, I'm fine. Little tired, maybe." Oh yeah, and my leg feels like it's liable to come to bits next time I move. But if I said anything like that, he'd take the stick back, and I wouldn't even be able to get to this armchair to look out the window.

"Don't overdo it," he said and then kind of came up short, like he'd forgot for a moment he wasn't supposed to be nice to me.

" 'Course not."

"Do you need anything? Any . . . help?"

"Nope. I'm good."

"All right," he said and left like he'd remembered he had something else he had to be doing. But I was willing to bet it was just that he'd spooked himself by treating me like a person instead of a cockroach.

I sat and looked at the garden until sundown. Then, since there wasn't nobody around to see, I crawled back to bed on my hands and one knee, dragging my bad leg like a dead dog. I barely managed to get myself under the covers before I fell asleep like I'd been sandbagged.

Felix

Hands holding me down. Pain shattering my skull. Black anger exploding everywhere, drenching everything in the colors of bruises and blood. Voices like the meaningless soughing of the wind.

I cannot free myself. There are too many hands, too much pain. I cannot fight any longer, and I shut my eyes against the colors. I don't know where I am; I don't know when this is. I don't know, if I were to open my eyes, whether I would see Malkar or Robert, the workroom in the Warren or the basement of St. Crellifer's. I am afraid to look.

After a time, the pain ebbs away; the hands are gone. I lie, as limp as threadbare linen, and try to catch hold of something, anything, in the vertiginous darkness that can tell me where I am and what is happening to me. But even when finally, desperately, I open my eyes, there is nothing familiar, nothing safe, only a small room with moonlight streaming through the window.

I roll over to face the wall and cry with pain and loneliness and grief for everyone I have lost.

Mildmay

When I had a septad and three, I went four days once without telling Keeper two of my ribs were broken. The reasons don't matter now. I mention it because that was pretty much exactly how I felt the next morning. My leg was like a bad jury-rig, and, powers, it hurt. But I knew if I let on at all, the only thing that'd happen was I wouldn't get out into the garden. And he might say I was whining again.

So I'd got up before dawn and got myself to the water closet and back, because I figured I didn't want him watching me go up and down the hall, and I was right. It was like I was dragging a big piece of jointed iron after me instead of a leg. But at least I didn't meet nobody and I didn't fall down.

So I was waiting for the prick, and, powers, *that* was a weird feeling. I sat by the window and watched the sun come up, and then I just sat and stared and waited.

He was a punctual bastard, I'll give him that much. He always came in at what I figured was the second hour of the morning—nobody'd bothered with giving the murderer a clock—and sure enough, there he was, like a piece of clockwork himself.

He wasn't stupid, neither, least not all the way down. He'd seen how bad I wanted to get out of that fucking room, and he'd figured he could use that to make me eat more, which was something he thought I should do and I thought was stupid. I guess I should've been glad he cared enough to not want me starving to death, but I didn't think it was me he cared about so much as his own hide, and all the kinds of Hell he'd be in for if he let a patient die, even a patient like me that nobody much wanted. And anyway, I'd got this stupid thing stuck in my head, this story I'd heard when I was little, about a giant who caught kids and kept 'em in cages and fed them everything they wanted. "Like a farmer fattening hogs," Nikah'd said, all bright-eyed, and it didn't matter that I knew it was dumb, that was how I felt every time the prick said anything about me not eating—like I was being kept in a cage and fattened up for slaughter.

But he stood over me 'til I'd eaten what he called a proper breakfast, and then he made this big deal of thinking it over, whether he should let me go out there today or not. I sat there and hated him, but I didn't say nothing and I didn't let it show. I hadn't been on my guard yesterday, but he wouldn't catch me out again. And he was watching, all right, watching like a hawk to see if he could get any more leverage on me. I could forgive him a lot of things, but that one still sticks in my throat like a bone.

I think he had orders, though. I'd dealt with enough flunkies and hired goons in my time to know when somebody could really make a decision or was just putting on airs, and when all was said and done, the prick was just another goon. So I didn't rise to the bait. I just sat and waited and hoped he'd strangle to death on his own fucking smugness.

And after a while, he got bored and said, "Well? Let's go then." And I got up.

I didn't fall down and I didn't scream, and since he mostly tried not to look at me, he didn't notice if I went funny colors. I probably did—I sure felt as green as spring peas—but if he didn't notice, it didn't matter, right? And once I was up, I'd kind of got the hang of not falling down again.

So the prick headed out, and I followed him as best I could. Once out the door, 'stead of turning left toward the water closet, he turned right, and I didn't even care how bad my leg hurt because by all the powers at least I was getting to go somewhere new.

All the way down to the end of the hall, and me trying not to breathe funny and not to listen to the weird step-clunk-drag I was making on the flagstones, and there was a leaded-glass door with herons and irises worked into it, and the prick said, "This door is never locked. It leads only into the Three Serenities Garden, which has no other gate. You may come out here whenever you wish." He opened the door and waited.

I suddenly had like a Great Septad and six questions I wanted answers to, but I wasn't asking him. I pretended like he wasn't there and dragged myself out into the Three Serenities Garden. I heard the door slam, and when I looked back, the prick had gone.

I knew if I fell down right there, I'd never get on my feet again without a rope and pulley. But there was a bench a little ways off. You can sit on that, I said to myself. It ain't nowhere near as far as that fucking beach was, and you got there all right. Come on, you fucking sissy. And I dragged myself over to the bench, every step like walking on swords, and then I just sat there and thought about my breathing and didn't pass out.

And after a while the pain backed off some, and I could actually take a look around.

I wasn't in the mood to admire anything Troian, so when I say that the Three Serenities was the most beautiful place I'd ever seen, you can maybe understand that I really mean it. It was still pretty early in the spring—like maybe the middle of Germinal if I had to guess—but things were starting to bud, and the trees had this sort of green misty look to them, and, powers, the grass! I mean, the gardeners at Richard's Park do a bang-up job and everything, but the grass here was like they'd laid down velvet. I was so amazed staring at it that I finally hitched myself over to the very end of the bench and leaned sideways so far I damn near fell off, and I could just brush my fingers against the blades, and it was just as fucking soft as it looked.

The rest of it I can't describe so good, 'cause I ain't got the right kind of words. I mean, I know there was something about the way the paths went in and out around the trees, and the way the flower beds were arranged, but I don't know what to call stuff like that. But it was like, I don't know, cold water in the middle of Thermidor, and I felt better just sitting there looking at it all than I'd felt in I don't even know how long.

It was a while before I could make myself get up again, and I know I wouldn't have done it if I hadn't been twitchy about the prick catching me just sitting there. Because I knew what he'd say, and I didn't want to hear it.

The first few days, I just walked up and back about a septad-foot along the path in front of that bench. When it got too bad, I'd lurch sideways off the path and fall down on the bench and wait until the hornets settled down again, and then I'd get up and take it from the top. And then around sundown, I'd haul myself back to my room, so I could be waiting for the prick when he came and not be too sweaty or pale or breathing hard. To be honest, it wasn't the sort of life I'd've wished on a dog, but at least I was so tired I wasn't having trouble falling asleep, and I was mostly not even dreaming. And although I started waking up with leg cramps, at least I knew how to work them out without screaming the place down. But it still wasn't nothing I'd've wished on a dog I hated.

I thought for a while I was the only person who ever used the Three Serenities. I figured everybody'd been told there was a murderer wandering around and had decided they'd just go somewhere else. And I couldn't blame 'em. But then, the fourth or fifth day, I'd got out there and was sitting on that damn bench waiting until I was brave enough to get up again, and the door opened, and this guy came out.

At first I thought he was Felix, and my heart tried to crawl up into my throat. But he wasn't, which I'd basically known anyway, except for being stupid. He was older than me by some, but not by a whole bunch, and he was Troian, so he was tall and skinny with the red hair back in a knot and the spooky yellow eyes. And he was sick. He was moving real slow, like it was almost more than he could do to keep standing up, and he had this big white woolly shawl wrapped around him like an old granny. And his face was bone-white, with red along his cheeks like he was wearing rouge, only I knew damn well he wasn't. I knew a consumptive when I saw one. I was absolutely fucking amazed that they let him out alone.

He kind of came up short a little when he saw me, but after a second he came on again and said, "Hello," to me in Kekropian—which I guessed I had to start calling Troian, because probably it was their language first.

I said hello back, figuring he just had better manners than anybody else I'd met, but when he was in front of me he stopped and turned and said, "I don't know you, do I? Are you a new acolyte?"

Oh Kethe, this had to be the only guy in the Gardens who hadn't been told. I said, "No, I'm a . . . I guess I'm a patient."

"I'm sorry," he said, "I didn't quite . . ."

Fucking Kekropian and its fucking consonants. "I'm a patient," I said, loud and careful and spacing the words out good.

"Ah," he said. "Like me. I beg your pardon."

"No, it's me. It ai—it's not your fault."

"You're very kind," he said and gave me the first honest-to-goodness smile I'd gotten since I woke up in that fucking bread box of a room. "What's your name? I'm Thamuris."

Oh powers, here we go. "Mildmay," I said.

"Ah." But he couldn't have recognized my name or nothing, because he went on, polite as a preacher, "I am pleased to meet you."

"Likewise."

"Do you often come to the Three Serenities?"

"I'm s'posed to walk here. For my leg."

"I'm sorry. I didn't quite . . ."

I said it again, and he nodded to show he'd got it. "And what is wrong with your leg? May I . . ."

"Sure," I said and moved over so there was room for him to share the bench. He settled himself down careful, like he was afraid he'd break, and I said, "I don't know exactly. There was a curse on me, and it f . . . it messed my leg up pretty bad."

"A curse?" he said, and I nodded to show him he'd heard me right. "But how in the blessed names of the Tetrarchs did you get cursed in this day and age? I thought that had gone out with Kekropian bonnets."

"I'm not Troian."

"So what barbaric part of the world *do* you hail from?"

"Marathat. I'm from Mélusine."

"Mélusine. The Blind City. I've read of her in books. So in Mélusine they still cast curses?"

"Yeah," I said. I didn't much want to get into it, and he just said, "Huh," like it was weird but not real interesting. And after a minute he got up, and gave me a funny little nod, and kind of floated off like he'd forgot all about me. I was fine with that. 'Nother minute, and I was up and walking myself, and I'd mostly forgot about him.

But after that I kept seeing him. He'd come drifting by my bench, or, once I got brave enough to get out of arm's reach of the bench, we'd pass each other on the paths, or I'd go by him under one tree or another. He'd be sitting there bolt upright with his eyes shut, so I guessed he was meditating, and I didn't bother him. I didn't want to make small talk anyways. It was enough for me that he didn't hate me. And I guessed nobody ever talked to him, neither, 'cause he never seemed to catch on about who I was. Which, you know, was fine with me. I had enough other shit on my mind.

My leg wasn't getting better. I was getting better at dealing with it, so I could move a little faster and I wasn't falling down no more. But the pain wasn't going away, and it wasn't getting smaller, and I'd taken enough damage in my time to know that wasn't right. And besides everybody else thought I should be getting better, too. And I wasn't.

I didn't know what to do. I wanted to tell somebody, but I'd tried that once, and I wasn't stupid enough to kiss the same gator twice. And I was kind of afraid they'd tell me this *was* better, that my leg was as good as it was going to get. And every time I thought about the prick saying that, my chest got so tight I couldn't breathe. So, I mean, yeah, I completely funked it, but I got to say there wasn't nobody trying to call me on it, neither. The celebrants had quit stopping by, and me and the prick were ignoring each other so hard it's a wonder we didn't run into each other. The only thing I was saying to him these days was, "How's my brother?" And all he was saying to me was, "Fine. He's fine." I'd been right to think he was a bad liar. He was even worse than me.

So I was worried about half out of my mind about Felix, and I didn't want to think about my leg. I didn't much want to think about Felix either, but I couldn't help that. I kept walking in the Three Serenities because it beat sitting in that fucking room and because I could drive myself into the ground and that meant I would sleep. I'd got to where sleep was the only escape I had. I knew that was bad, too, but there was a limit to how much shit I could care about at once.

So I'd kind of forgotten the walking was supposed to be making my leg better until Thamuris scared the living daylights out of me one afternoon. I don't even know where my mind was, but he said all of a sudden, "Does your leg still hurt?" and I jumped a foot.

"Kethe! Yes—" And then I caught up with myself and said, "It ai—it's not so bad."

"Come here."

I'd figured they had him on some pretty heavy-duty laudanum or something—or he was just naturally kind of cloudy—but the look he gave me was like a dissecting knife. He meant what he said, and he knew what he was talking about and he was pissed at something and I didn't want it to be me.

So I went limping across the grass to where he was sitting. He tilted his head back to look at me, and said, "Sit down."

"I'm gonna be a powerful long time getting back up."

I don't know if he understood me or not. He just said, "*Sit.*"

I sat.

"Now just hold still," he said, "and tell me if I hurt you." Which was the first time anybody in the Gardens had bothered with that part.

I sat still, and he touched my forehead, then the dip between my collarbones. He took my wrist to feel for my pulse, and then he laid his hand on my right hip. You got to understand, there wasn't nothing sexy about it. I don't know if Thamuris was straight or molly or if he even cared, but I knew that wasn't what he was after—even if anybody in the Gardens would've made a pass at me anyway, which most likely not.

He moved his hand down my right leg, just barely brushing my trousers. He was about a handswidth above my knee when that ball of glass spikes all at once started spinning around, and I made a noise. Couldn't help it.

Thamuris jerked his hand away, and the pain backed off some, although I still felt like I ought to see little bits of glass poking up through my trousers.

"Who has charge of you?" he said—well, more barked, I guess. Powers, he was pissed.

"Khrysogonos. I mean—"

"Is he one of the Celebrants Major? I'm afraid I don't know them all."

"No, he said he was an acolyte. I—"

"Not him. The celebrant. The one who is in *charge*."

"I don't know. I mostly seen Celebrants Major and Celebrants Minor, and I don't know all their names . . ."

He said a phrase Dmitri'd been fond of, only with a lot better diction and attention to the stress pattern. "I must talk to the Arkhon," he said, got up like it wasn't no effort to him, and marched off, not drifting at all, leaving me stranded like a barge run aground on a sandbar.

I tried a couple times to get up, but it was late, and whatever he'd done, it'd woken up the hornets in a big way. After the try where I did get my knee to bend, but then realized that them big black spots in front of my eyes meant I was fixing to pass out, I gave up and waited for the prick to come find me. At least he'd find me conscious.

The sun set and I sat there and got chilly. I managed to drag myself around so I could get a glimpse of the door through the trees, and even that was about more excitement than my leg could stand.

"Kethe, I hate this," I said, because there was nobody to hear me, and I wondered if Thamuris was really going to try and raise hell with the lady who ran the Gardens, and whether it would make things worse or not.

And then, finally, the door opened, and I saw a lantern. I thought, Thank the powers, and then I heard voices and thought, Oh, mother*fuck*. Because anybody besides the prick out here tonight was not somebody I wanted to meet.

The voices got closer, winding around on them artful little paths, and I started to be able to make out words.

A guy said, "So where *is* your murderer, Khrys? Do you suppose he's run away?"

The prick said, "I'm sure he's out here."

"Since he couldn't have gone anywhere else," a girl said, and there was a nasty little chorus of sniggers. I wondered if I could crawl into the bushes before they spotted me, and just how sorry I'd end up being if I spent the night outdoors.

"That's right—Khrys has the corridor key," the first guy said, and I sure wasn't no fan of the prick, but I was liking this guy even less. "I wouldn't have thought they'd let you have that, Khrys."

Everybody sniggered again, and I guessed there was a mean little private joke in there somewhere.

The prick said, stiff as a board, "I am pleased that they trust me to do my duties well," and I heard the sound of four or five people falling about laughing.

"You *are* a treat, Khrys," the guy said. "You know this assignment had nothing to do with trust, right?" I could see their lanternlight, but they'd stopped just out of sight around a bend in the path.

"What do you mean?" the prick said, and I couldn't help wincing for him. If he walked into traps like that, airheaded as a cloud, it was no wonder he was a prick.

"Blessed Tetrarchs! Do you mean you accepted that assignment and you didn't *know?*"

"Didn't know what?"

"Khrys, my lambkin," said a different girl. "This one wasn't about trust. It was about finding some poor fool to do the dirty work."

"You know Arkhilokhos's been out for your blood," said a third girl.

"I'm sure I don't know what you're talking about," the prick said, but it was that high, trembly voice that wouldn't've fooled a deaf idiot. "I was chosen because I speak Midlander, and—"

"So do I," said the guy. "So does Menelaos, and Kanake, and Laodamia. Sorry, Khrys. I'm afraid you're special."

"But just think of the experience!" said the second girl. "I've never met a murderer!"

I thought, Oh sweetheart, trust me, you ain't missing much.

"He must tell you *wonderful* stories," said the first girl. "Does he, Khrys? Does he tell you about the people he's killed?"

"No."

"Well, have you *asked?*" said the guy, and, powers, I wanted to smack him.

"No," said the prick.

"Well, where's the fun in that?" said the first girl. "I would at least have *asked*."

And here I'd thought there was nothing good to say about the prick.

"You couldn't, Myrrha darling," said the guy. "You don't speak Midlander—and the murderer doesn't speak Troian, does he, Khrys?"

"Not very much," the prick said, which showed how much he knew.

"What a pity," said the third girl. "I'm sure he'd be a fascinating conversationalist."

They laughed at that, and the girl called Myrrha said, "I heard Eranitos saying he was no better than an animal."

"He certainly looks like one with that horrid scar," the third girl said.

"Kharis!" cried the guy. "I didn't know you'd already seen him. Cheater! How'd you—"

But I couldn't stand it no more. They think you're dumb, I said to myself. Just go ahead and play dumb and get out of this. I called out in my most Marathine-accented Midlander, with the vowels dragged out so it sounded like I'd never been outside Lyonesse in my life, "Mr. Khrysogonos? That you?"

For a second, I thought they'd all fallen down a well, and I would've been grateful for it. Then the prick came round the corner, all in a hurry like there was somebody he was trying to get away from. "What are you doing out here?" he said. "Why haven't you come in?"

"I been sitting," I said, and then the rest of 'em came into view. Three girls and a guy, all tall, skinny redheads about the same age as the prick. One of the girls had the lantern, so there was enough light for me to see their faces and the way they were staring at me. All at once I felt like I didn't have no clothes on.

"So this is the murderer," the guy said in Kekropian—Troian, I mean. He was good-looking, and the set of his mouth said he knew it. I didn't like him no better for having seen him.

Deadpan's easy for me. It's making my face move that's the hard part. So I just sat there and pretended I couldn't understand them and didn't have the least little idea of what was going on.

"This is Mildmay," the prick said, still stiff as a board.

I ain't much for cat and mouse, but the opening was more than I could resist. "Are these friends of yours, Mr. Khrysogonos?"

The guy understood Midlander, like he'd said. He snorted, while the girls just looked blank and greedy. I thought the prick was going to bust. But, powers, he knew the drill and he stuck to it. "They are some of my fellow acolytes," and I'll be damned if he didn't introduce them. "Astyanax, Potidaia, Myrrha, and Kharis."

"Pleased," I said, mostly to see what this fellow Astyanax would do with it.

"I am most charmed to make your acquaintance," all smooth and pleased with himself. "Please forgive my companions—they don't speak your language."

Neither do you, asshole, I thought. " 'Course," I said.

"It's getting very late," the prick said in Troian, too fast and too loud, like he was trying to head something off before it got rolling. "Don't you think—"

"Not yet, Khrys," Astyanax said. "There's a question I want to ask . . . Mildmay first." And, powers and blessed saints, I hated the way he said my name.

I knew this wasn't going nowhere good. But there was literally nothing I could do about it, and it was way obvious that the prick didn't have no idea how to shut this guy up. So there was this nasty little pause, and Astyanax said in Midlander, all bright, social interest, "How many people have you killed?"

I was ready for it, at least. I let the question sit there a moment, let him know I was on to his game, then I said, "I done lost count," and smiled at him.

I don't smile, 'cept at people who deserve it. And myself in the mirror sometimes, just so I don't forget. It's an ugly, ugly expression, 'cause the left side of my face don't hardly move, and the whole thing ends up looking like a half-dead sneer. And I don't imagine the lanternlight helped. Astyanax and his gals kind of leaned away from me, and the prick said, "It's *very* late. Let me help you up."

He really didn't want a fight. He yanked me up out of the grass like I was half his size and said, real firm and loud, "I have to get my patient to bed. Good night." And he set off like his tail feathers were on fire, dragging me along after him. Astyanax and the girls just stood there and watched us go, and I thought, like a rain cloud, I ain't shut of this.

Felix

The door opens.

I am in the corner by the window, huddled between the foot of the bed and the wall, where the owl-eyed people can't drag me out. They have come in two or three times today, little groups of them, and stared at me, sharing stone words among themselves. But they have not approached me. I have barricaded myself in with a chair so that the anger cannot reach me. It is too big to squeeze itself into corners or under pieces of furniture. It flaps sullenly around the room, waiting for me to weaken, to give in, to make a mistake. It knows it will have me in the end. Salt water drips and pools around me.

An owl-eyed man enters the room alone and closes the door behind him. The anger orbits him, smelling for vulnerabilities. I do not move. The colors around this man are strange, not like the others'—red and black, but also great, trembling outbursts of gold. They make me dizzy.

He stands for a moment, looking at me as the others did, then crosses to the room's second chair and sits down. He says something, small iron words; the anger lets out a derisive screech, hurting my ears, and begins to coast restlessly across the ceiling. I do not move.

We stay like that for a long time. I wish I could relax, sleep, but that is what the anger wants. That would let it in. I sit and watch the anger; I do not think it can attack anyone except me, but I may be wrong. Occasionally the owl-eyed man will say something, and a rampart of small, hard words piles up in front of his feet. I wish he would leave, but I cannot speak. I have not been able to speak since I drowned.

Smaller angers begin to gather in the corners of the room and under the bed. Night is coming. And still the owl-eyed man will not leave. The anger is stronger at night; the smaller angers feed it. I do not want the owl-eyed man to be hurt, but there is nothing I can do, nothing except stay where I am, my hands locked around my knees so that the anger cannot use me.

I nearly cry with relief when he finally gets up, but then he crosses the room toward me, and my muscles tense so violently that for a moment I can't breathe.

I want to warn him to stay away, to scream and curse, to drive him out of the room. But the salt water filled my mouth and drowned me, and it is all I can do now not to let the anger fill the emptiness the water scoured out.

The owl-eyed man sits down on the bed. The anger is flapping around his head, shrieking; I am shaking with the effort of not surrendering to it. The owl-eyed man is speaking, building a wall of words between himself and me; the anger is making figure eights around us both, watching for its chance.

I cannot speak; I know that if I make any move toward the owl-eyed man, I will let the anger in. And I know that it will get in anyway. It is stronger than I am; it always has been. There is no way out, no end, no peace. I rock forward slightly and slam my head back against the wall, again and again, trying to kill the anger, to deaden my own raw nerves, my hurting mind. Again and again, until there are hands, too many hands, and the anger falls in on me and I am gone.

Mildmay

I kept walking in the Three Serenities. Thamuris muttered horrible things about the Celebrant Lunar but wouldn't tell me why, and I figured she hadn't listened to him. Maybe I'd been right about the laudanum. The prick was still the prick, but at least he didn't bring no more tour groups to gawk at me. And he still wouldn't say nothing about Felix except, "Fine," and even when I couldn't stand it no more and said, "I fucking well know you're lying," he turned a double septad different shades of red, but he didn't change his story, and I couldn't make him.

Then we hit a cold snap, the way you do sometimes in early spring, and, Kethe, it was like my entire leg was made of glass and razor blades. I got out of bed one morning and found myself on the floor. Just like that. I mean, I didn't even have time to realize I was going down, just there I was on the floor with my leg singing grand opera and a whole new crop of bruises starting up along my hip and forearm. I managed to get myself back onto the bed before the prick came in, but it was a fucking near-run thing, and I really think it was only hearing his footsteps in the hall that let me do it.

"It's the weather," he said, before he'd even closed the door behind him, and I bit down hard on my lower lip and didn't say to him what Felix had said to me once, Your command of the obvious is awe-inspiring.

"The celebrants say you shouldn't go out. Your leg isn't ready for it, and you might slip. So stay put." He smacked the breakfast tray down on the table like it might wander off, and left. I swear I felt the door slamming in my leg. I listened to his footsteps, listened to the hall door slam, and then said through my teeth, "All right, Milly-Fox, you big sissy," and got up again.

This time I stayed up, got to the table, sat down more or less under control, and just about puked at the thought of trying to eat. But I had something I wanted to do, and it wasn't stay in here all day, either. I choked down what I could, although everything tasted like glue and ashes, and then I got up again—and I wasn't enjoying it no more for the practice—and went over to the door.

I listened for a moment, purely from habit—I knew they'd made sure to give the murderer a hallway all to himself—then opened the door.

I reminded myself that I still wasn't doing anything wrong, and stood there and thought about my breathing until I believed it and had furthermore remembered that I didn't give a rat's ass anyway.

"They got you whipped, Milly-Fox," I said to myself, and turned left.

I had to take it in stages, with the water closet as my first goal, then a windowsill wide enough I could sit on it for a while, and then the door at the end of the hall. By the time I got there, my leg felt like a red-hot wire running through a pile of old masonry, but I told it to shut up—and I ain't saying nothing about how I felt when I realized I'd said it out loud—and took a good careful stare at the lock.

Even with the leg, I felt a little bit like my luck had turned. They kept it in nice shape and everything, but it was old, made for the kind of key you could use to knock out a burglar. I'd been afraid Troian locks would be seriously hot shit, all weird and fancy, but this one was practically screaming to be picked. Find something to use as a lock pick and I could get out of this jail and go find Felix.

But for now I knew I was going to be lucky to get back to the room without ending up on the floor. "Later," I said to the lock and started back down the hall.

It took me like indictions, but I was still upright when I came back through my door. I made it to the chair by the window and basically fell into it, and then I sat there for a long time thinking about my breathing and about not crying and not puking and not passing out. After a while I felt like I could open my eyes again, and then I sat there and looked out at the Three Serenities and worried about Felix and my leg and most anything else that crossed my mind. It ain't no good way to pass the time, which I guess explains why I was actually glad to hear the hall door open sometime in the early afternoon.

Feet came briskly down the hall, and I was just thinking, Funny, that don't *sound* like—when somebody knocked at my door, which the prick never did.

Powers. For a moment I couldn't even think what to do. Then I remembered and croaked out, "Come in," in Troian like a crow somebody'd trained to talk.

The door opened. It was the good-looking guy from the Three Serenities. I might have known. "Astyanax," I said.

It unnerved him, which was good. He said, "Good afternoon," in Midlander, but it came out sounding way more like a kid and way less snotty than he'd wanted. He shut the door and took the other armchair, buying himself time and probably hoping I'd say something stupid and give him the upper hand. I sat and watched him and didn't say nothing.

He had his fair share of brass. Once he was settled, he said, perfectly cool, "I have been sent to ask you a few questions."

"Okay," I said. "Who sent you?"

"I beg your pardon?"

I said it again.

"The Celebrants Terrestrial. I am empowered to use any means necessary to get answers."

"Most folks start by asking."

I got under his skin with that one. Well, it's always annoying when you make a threat, and the guy on the other end of it don't seem to care, so I can't blame him for that. He got a little red along the cheekbones and snapped out, "We need to know more about the Mirador."

"Why don't you ask Felix?"

If I'd pinked him the first time, this time I'd gotten in a real cut. I'd mostly been fishing for information, but if it pissed him off, too, I was okay with that.

"Our reasons are no concern of yours," he said, and I knew what that meant. Any questions they asked Felix, they were just getting that stare back, the one that said there wasn't nobody home, and even if there was, they weren't answering the door. Felix wasn't "fine," which, I mean, I'd already known, but now I had some actual proof. Well, I had a snotty-voiced sidestep, but it was good enough for me.

After a moment, Astyanax figured out I wasn't going to lob him one, and said, all tight and angry, "What do you know about the Mirador?"

I kind of shrugged. "Not much."

He gave me the hairy eyeball, but he wasn't very good at it. And he could hex me blue, and I still wouldn't care.

"What do you *want?*"

It wasn't a real question, but I didn't care about that, neither. "See my brother."

"What?"

"I want to see my brother."

"Oh, I'm sure you do. Do you think we're idiots?"

"What?"

"We know what you did to him."

"What I . . . *what?*"

"What you did to him," he said, like he thought I was so stupid I hadn't understood him the first time.

"I didn't do *nothing* to him!"

"Oh really? And the bruises were caused by what? Falling out of bed?"

"It was a shipwreck! Things got a little rough."

"Yes, of course." But he didn't believe me, and I knew I couldn't convince him—anybody—not without Felix . . . and then I remembered crawling onto the beach, dragging Felix, swearing at him, the look on his face, and it hit me that by now Felix might think I was a monster just like the Troians did.

I kept myself together—didn't want this smug asshole watching while I lost it. Just took a breath and put it aside. And waited for Astyanax to make the next move.

"Tell me about the Mirador," he said through his teeth.

"And what do I get out of it?"

"Surely you want to help your brother." I wanted to belt him across the face for that, for the nasty sneer and the snotty tone, but it wouldn't help, and I'd fall down if I tried.

"I want to see him first, so I know I *am* helping."

He was done with it right then: stood up, said, "I don't know why I expected any better from a common murderer," and left. He slammed the door almost as hard as the prick did.

❧

They double-teamed me that night, him and the prick. And they were mad as two wet cats in a sack about it, and that was some comfort.

I was laying in bed when they came in. Not sleeping—don't be stupid. Just laying there staring up at the ceiling and worrying about Felix until it felt like my head was going to split.

I heard the hall door open, and thought, Oh fuck what now? Two sets of footsteps, the door opened, and this huge ball of witchlight, a sort of nasty crimson-pink color that I don't think was an accident, sprang up in the middle of the ceiling like a chandelier. Astyanax said, "You thought you'd gotten rid of me, didn't you?"

"A guy can dream," I said. I didn't turn my head. I wasn't going to give him the satisfaction of even looking at him.

The prick said, "You *must* answer the celebrants' questions."

"Or what? You'll kill me? Throw me out on my ear?"

"I thought you were worried about your brother," the prick said, and something in his voice told me he didn't know what the celebrants thought I'd done, and Astyanax hadn't told him.

"I don't say nothing 'til I've seen him. That's my price."

"You're my witness, Khrysogonos," Astyanax said, and I did turn my head then, at the tight triumph in his voice. "I have been empowered to use any means necessary, and you can't deny he's being intransigent."

"But, Astyanax, shouldn't we . . ."

And that fucker Astyanax cast a spell on me.

It hurt in a completely different way than my leg. I imagine that spell is what being pressed to death feels like, and I'm here to say it ain't the way you want to go. I lay there and couldn't hardly breathe, and I could hear Astyanax asking questions and my voice kind of gasping out answers, and I couldn't do nothing about it—couldn't keep the words back, couldn't take a real breath, couldn't fucking move. My head had kind of fallen back to center—along of the weight, I think, but I ain't rightly sure—so I just had to lay there and stare at the ceiling, and feel the tears rolling down my cheekbones from the sheer stupid pain of it.

He was asking about how come Felix had gone mad. I wanted to tell him I didn't fucking know—that *nobody* knew—but the spell smashed me flat, and I heard myself say, "Virtu."

"Virtue?" Astyanax said.

"Virtu. Big globe-thing in the Mirador. Hocus-stuff."

"And what does it have to do with Felix going mad?"

"Broke it," I said, and, Kethe, even a dumb annemer like me knew there was more to it than that, but Astyanax didn't give me time to say so.

"Of course!" he said. "Destruction, the release of energy—it all makes sense."

"Wait!" I said, because there was more to it than that, and I did want them to help Felix, and they needed all the facts.

"You can tell me more about the Virtu?" he said, and the damn spell squashed a "no" out of me, 'cause I couldn't. I didn't know fuck-all about the Virtu.

"I thought not. No wonder you were trying to bluff. Come on, Khrysogonos. Diokletian's waiting."

"I should . . . should . . ."

"Oh by the Tetrarchs, you are a fool! All right, stay with your murderer. But don't expect you can come whining around for the credit later."

"Of course not," the prick said in a mutter.

Astyanax lifted his spell. I didn't want to give him anything, but I couldn't do nothing about the way I was breathing. "Thank you," he said, in that snotty mocking way that I pretty much wanted to kill him for. "You have been very helpful."

"Fuck off," I said.

"As you wish," he said and left. He didn't slam the door this time, but closed it perfectly politely, mild as a lamb. Yeah, he was all milk and honey once he'd got what he wanted.

I lay there and panted like I'd been on the wrong end of a five-on-one fight, and my eyes blurred and stung.

"I'm sorry," a voice said from near the door. "I'm so sorry. He shouldn't have done that."

I turned my head. He was standing there all hunched up in the corner, with his eyes as big as bell-wheels. "Why didn't you stop him, then?" I said.

"I can't. I'm not a wizard."

"Oh. No wonder they made you look after me."

"Yes," said Khrysogonos.

Felix

The creatures around me have terrible heads, snouted and slavering, their eyes gleaming lurid yellow, and horrid, batlike wings that trail the floor behind them with a ghastly ticking sound as their talons brush the stones. I cannot block my ears; I cannot move, and the anger beating its wings about my ears cannot find its way in. They drag me up off the bed, half carry, half drag me out of the room. I have never been out of this room, not since I drowned, and I don't want to go. It isn't safe. But the monsters don't care what I want, any more than they care about the salt water steaming against their clothes. They are too hot, unnaturally hot—or perhaps it is just that I am so dreadfully cold.

They bring me to a room, clean, well lit, but with a table in the middle, a table with straps. I remember that I drowned before, drowned in darkness, and I remember the table. The snake and the corpse and the gray pig: I see them around the table, faint ghosts, smirking at me.

I want to run, but I can't even twitch my fingers. I can't turn my head away, and I am afraid to shut my eyes. The monsters lift me onto the table, tug my limbs straight, fasten the straps. I shut my eyes as tears run down toward my ears. I am doomed, doomed. Malkar will hurt me; Lorenzo will hurt me; Keeper will rise from the sea, and he will kill me at last. There are fingers on my temples, burning me; I can feel the fire catching in the bones of my skull, raging against the salt water, coursing down my spine, my arms, my legs, gathering like red-hot coals in the knuckles of my fingers. I open my eyes and I see nothing; there is nothing left, nothing but molten darkness. I am gone.

ഽ

I woke up aching, but on the whole, I felt well: peaceful, relaxed, cheerful. There was sunlight streaming through the window, and I stared at it for a ridiculously long time before I realized what it meant; I wasn't in the Mirador.

I sat up. The furnishings of the room were elegant, well polished, spotlessly clean, but they were in no style I recognized. They certainly weren't Marathine. I looked down at myself and discovered I was wearing a linen nightshirt I had no memory of ever seeing before in my life—and it fit me, which was even stranger.

Where was I? I got up, padded across the stone floor to the window, and found myself looking out at a breathtakingly beautiful garden, everything green and glorious with the coming of spring.

Spring? But it was the middle of Bous.

No, that was clearly wrong. I sat down in the armchair by the window, put my head in my hands, and immediately came bolt upright again. My hair was nearly two feet shorter than it should have been. I spun in a frantic circle, but there were no mirrors in this charming, peaceful, unfamiliar room.

Something's wrong, I thought, and offered myself a mental round of applause for stating the obvious. Work backwards. Clearly, there was some kind of a gap in my memory, so what was the last thing I remembered?

I sat down again, slowly, because that question seemed to be unexpectedly difficult. I remembered quite clearly the soirée in the Hall of the Chimeras, the fight with Shannon, my shameful trip to the Arcane, Malkar . . .

I made a noise—a groan, a sob, a laugh. Well, whatever had happened, at least I knew who was to blame.

And then another window opened. Malkar's workroom, the taste of phoenix, the pentagram, the chains . . . Malkar's spell, the pain, the guilt, the Virtu . . .

I closed my eyes and saw the Virtu shattering. And I knew what had happened; I knew where my memory had gone.

I didn't want to know the rest. I sprang out of the chair again, as if I could somehow leave those dim, wispy memories behind, and found myself face-to-face with a tall red-haired man just in the act of entering the room.

We both started back with nearly identical yelps, and he said, in Midlander, "I beg your pardon. I thought you would still be asleep."

"No, I . . ." But I was staring at him—gawking—and could not find my wits to finish the sentence. He was a Sunling; he had to be. I had never seen anyone else with naturally red hair before, and his eyes were—

No. That wasn't true. I knew someone with red hair. I shut my eyes, one hand going up to my temple. Fox-red hair, green eyes, lurid scar, voice like Keeper's . . . but who was he, and how did I know him?

"Are you all right?" said the red-haired man.

"What? Oh! Yes, I'm fine. Just . . . everything's a little strange."

"That's only to be expected. You were badly hurt, and from what we can tell, you must have been . . . confused for a very long time—maybe more than a year."

"It was Bous when I left," I said, and my voice sounded odd and faraway.

"You are in Troia," the red-haired man said, kindly and briskly. "This is the Gardens of Nephele, and I am Diokletian of the House Aiantis, Celebrant Terrestrial of the Nephelian Covenant."

"Troia?" I said. "But I don't . . . how did I get here?"

And then I knew who the red-haired man was, the one with the scar. My brother, Mildmay, my fox, who'd guided and guarded me all the way across Kekropia.

"My brother!" I said, cutting Diokletian off before he could answer my previous question. "Where is he?"

"Your brother?"

"My brother Mildmay? Is he here? Did he drown?"

"No, he is here," Diokletian said cautiously, as if he were afraid I might attack him. "We are minding him. Do you wish to see him?"

I don't even know him. But I didn't say it. I had the feeling that the people here must have had more than their fair share of my acting crazy. I thought of what the journey to this place must have been like for Mildmay, of the weird, jumbled impressions I had of him and the horrible, fragmented versions of myself he must have witnessed. "Not . . . not yet. I don't think I'm ready."

"That's perfectly all right. There's no need to rush."

"How long have I been here?"

"About a month and a half."

"That long?"

"You were very ill," he said.

"Yes, I understand that. I just . . . I don't even know the date."

"In our calendar, it is the second day of Heraklios—the height of spring."

"What year?"

"Our calendar will mean nothing to you."

"No, of course not. Silly me."

"How do you feel?" he said.

"Rather sore, actually, but otherwise all right."

"No headaches? No difficulty seeing?"

"No, nothing like that."

"Good. I was not sure our success would be complete. We were not—and still are not—entirely sure what we were dealing with. What *happened* to you?"

"It's rather difficult to explain," I said, while my mind went into a state of sheer frozen panic. How much did these people know? How much had they learned from me when I was mad? From Mildmay? Did they know the whole truth? I could feel myself curdling with shame merely at the thought.

"Please," Diokletian said, with a wry, charming, inviting smile. "Try me."

When in doubt, play for time. "How much do you know? Was I . . . ?"

"You were never coherent enough to be asked, and your brother was of very little help."

"He's annemer. And—I beg your pardon—but are there any actual *clothes* I could wear?"

"Oh, yes, of course. I'm sorry; I didn't even think. Here." He opened a carved wooden chest tucked into the corner of the room behind the door and passed me clothes like the ones he himself was wearing: linen underthings, an unbleached linen shirt with no collar, dark, narrow trousers, a dark, quilted coat, dark wool stockings, and a pair of black-leather shoes with silver buckles. I reminded myself that by now there could be no doubt that the entire population of the Gardens of Nephele had either seen or heard about the scars on my back, and contented myself with changing as quickly as possible.

"A comb?" I said. "A mirror?"

"Here." He brought those out of the chest, too, and I was able to get my first good look at myself. I'd been braced for a nasty shock, but it was still appalling. At a rough guess, I put myself at fifteen pounds underweight, with great hollows under the cheekbones, and the dark stigmata of sleeplessness all around my eyes. I had always been pale; I was hoping it was the coat's high collar and dark purplish black color that was making me look bleached. And my hair—not quite shoulder length, and the last time it had been cut it must have been with pruning shears. And . . . I looked again, but there was no way around it: strands of *white,* at my left temple and the right side of my forehead.

It took me a moment to realize that Diokletian had picked up the thread of his answer to my question: "We could see the damage for ourselves, of course, and your brother did tell us that it was something to do with an artifact in your Mirador called the Virtu. Is that right?"

"Yes. Yes, it's a power-channeler, rather like a loom. Very old."

"And you broke it?"

I could tell by his voice that he didn't know about Malkar, and the sunlight seemed brighter and more glorious. "It broke," I corrected him with aplomb.

"Oh, I see," he said; he sounded relieved. "From what your brother said . . ."

"My brother is annemer," I said, sacrificing Mildmay's character in the service of my lie. "And not . . ." I only remembered the appalling voice, myself, but Diokletian had no difficulty in completing that sentence to his own satisfaction.

"Yes, of course. So, there was some kind of accident?"

"We were worried that the Virtu was becoming unstable," I said, extemporizing freely. "It is nearly two hundred years old, and the spells that went into its creation have been lost. The Lord Protector asked me to examine it, and . . ." A little artful amnesia was probably all right here; Diokletian wasn't to know that the circumstances of the Virtu's breaking were etched into my mind like acid into an engraving plate. "I don't really remember what happened next. I remember that it hurt."

"Indeed it must have. When we realized the extent of the damage . . . to be truthful, we were surprised the trauma hadn't killed you outright."

"I'm obstinate," I said and tried a smile on him.

He blinked and smiled back, his color a little heightened. Apparently I wasn't quite enough of a staring death's-head for that to fail; I felt better.

"There's just one more thing," I said, since I didn't especially want to hear all about what these people thought had happened to me; I wasn't entirely sure I'd be able to maintain my lie. "I know I'm being a dreadful nuisance—"

"Not at all. I'm just delighted that you're so . . ." He broke off, and I couldn't help being amused at his palpable search for a suitably inexpressive word. "So well. What can I do for you?"

"Earrings," I said. "I see that your people wear them." He had a single pair: small, heavy gold rings with teardrop pearls hanging from them. "I want to find out if my holes have closed. Plain gold rings, four pairs, not too large, if I can borrow them from somebody, or if there's a shop nearby."

He looked a little taken aback, but pulled himself together with creditable speed and said he'd see what he could do. He swept out. As soon as I was sure he was gone, I called witchlight; as quick and easy as blinking, it was there on my palm, a green chrysanthemum the size of a watch fob.

My magic was back; there was no pain, no difficulty, no failure. It was mine again, and I fought back the impulse to create some wild pyrotechnic of joy, just because I could. Instead, I sat down to do some serious thinking. I'd bought myself some time; I'd better make use of it.

Diokletian returned a little under an hour later, triumphantly bearing four pairs of plain gold rings, which he'd borrowed, he said, from two Celebrants Major, an acolyte, and a Celebrant Terrestrial with whom he was good friends. I gathered that Troians did not practice multiple piercings and wondered if they'd ever seen a Norvenan woman, and what they'd made of her if they had. I noted the peculiar ranks—celebrants? acolytes?—for future inquiry. Diokletian assured me anxiously that the rings had been cleaned with alcohol, and I gave him another smile.

I had figured my chances were about fifty-fifty with the holes, but they were all still open. I felt more myself with the earrings in; the dim kaleidoscope of the past year seemed farther away and less important. "Thank you," I said.

"My pleasure," he said, and bobbed his head.

There was a pause, a strange little hitch, and I said, "What now?"

"I beg your pardon?"

"Is there something I ought to be doing? I feel strange, just staying in here."

"Are you feeling all right?"

"I feel fine. I'm not made of glass."

"Well, the other Celebrants Terrestrial are very eager to meet you, and I'm under strict instructions to take you to see the Celebrant Lunar as soon as you're able. But . . ."

"But?"

"There's something I have to ask you first."

"What is it?"

"Was your mother really named Methony?"

"How did you know that?" I felt hollow, suddenly as thin and fragile as paper.

"You told me," he said, and he sounded confused. "In a dream."

"In a *dream?* You've got to be kidding."

"No, no, it's how I found you. I was trying to revive the practice of oneiromancy, to reawaken the Khloïdanikos, the Dream of the Garden. I assure you, the Celebrant Lunar has already torn me to bits for it. But that's how I found you: you were in the dream. And later you told me your mother's name. Was it true?"

"Yes," I said, although I made no attempt to hide my exasperation and annoyance. "What about it?"

"I . . . I knew her."

"Oh."

After a moment, Diokletian offered, "You are quite extraordinarily like her—even more so now."

"Than when I was stark mad? Thank you ever so much."

"I didn't mean that. Just . . . I did know her. I . . . I held you when you were an infant."

After a moment I realized my jaw was sagging. "But . . . how . . ."

"You weren't born in Mélusine, although that's what you told me. You were born here. She ran away, taking you with her, when you were four months old."

"Why?"

He shook his head. "Who ever knew why Methony did anything? Do you remember her at all?"

"I was only four when she—" *sold me to Keeper.* I stopped, regrouped. Answer the question asked, idiot. "I remember her eyes and her voice. I remember her singing." And gossiping with the other girls and quarreling with Madame Poluphemie and picking the pockets of a dead-drunk trick.

"She liked to sing," he said, his face softly nostalgic.

"So if I was born here," I said, "who was my father?"

Diokletian came back to the present with a nearly audible snap. "I must take you to the Celebrant Lunar. She has invited you for lunch."

And he strode out of the room as if his shoe heels were catching on fire. Nothing loath, I followed him.

The Celebrant Lunar was named Xanthippe, and I forgot the name of her house as soon as she said it. She was sixty years old. Her hair was entirely white, although thick and vibrant, her eyes the clear colorless yellow of sunlight; the rings on her swollen-knuckled hands were silver set with amethyst, and I noticed that although she moved with extreme slowness—fighting an unending, losing war against arthritis, which the old herbals in the Mirador called the bone-winter—the gems of her rings betrayed not the slightest quiver in her hands.

She asked me no questions about my madness, my brother, or anything else thorny over an extended, leisurely, and remarkably pleasant lunch, instead telling me old stories of Troia and wanting to know about the history of the Mirador and Marathat. We got into a rather involved discussion of calendrical systems, and she actually clapped her hands with glee, like a child, when I told her that the wizards' calendar of Mélusine reckoned dates from the founding of Cymellune of the Waters.

When the neat, quiet child who served us had poured tea and departed again, Xanthippe said, "And what would you like to do now?"

"I beg your pardon?"

"Do you intend to rush immediately back to your homeland? Or would you like to stay and study in the Gardens?"

"May I?"

"We should be pleased to have you."

"Because of Methony?"

"Damn Diokletian for a fool," she said without heat. "No. Nothing to do with Methony. Don't imagine that we can't see how powerful you are—and my Terrestrials are all as pleased as dogs with two tails about healing you. You might have to put up with being stared at a bit, but you can be assured your welcome would be warm. And from what you have said of your school of magic, I think there is much you could learn here—and much we could learn from you."

"Then I would be delighted to stay," I said, and she beamed at me over the strong, dark Troian tea that tasted to me of sunlight and clarity.

Mildmay

The prick was awful quiet the next half decad or so. I didn't mind. I didn't mind nothing so long as Astyanax didn't come back. The weather got warmer, then colder. I went out to the Three Serenities when I could and just stayed by the window staring out at it when I couldn't. Some days I heard Thamuris go past, and once or twice he even knocked on the door to say hello, but he was so sick, and on the laudanum to boot, and we didn't have nothing to say to each other. I was mostly just as glad the days he didn't stop.

The prick started jumping like a scalded cat when I asked after Felix, and after three or four days of it, I got sick of it and said, "Okay. Just cough it up and get done with it."

"What?"

But he was a shitty liar, just like me. "You know. Come on. Has Felix gotten worse or something?"

"No. They . . ." And then, in a tiny voice like he wanted to say it without me actually hearing him, "They healed him."

"They *healed* him? And you were keeping the surprise for my birthday?"

"I didn't know how . . . I didn't want . . ."

"Can I see him?"

Big silence, like a drowning well.

"What?" I said. "They healed him, right? That's what you said. He's okay, isn't he?"

"Yes, yes, he's fine. It's just . . ."

"What?"

"He doesn't want to see you," the prick said in a tiny, tiny voice and just about ran out of the room, slamming the door with his usual bang. I think I rattled right along with the window.

Felix

I took to the library of the Gardens, as if it were a second home. Though the archivists there spoke even less Midlander than I did Troian, we shared the language of books, and could have quite remarkably long and satisfying conversations that, if transcribed, would probably have looked like nothing more than a catalogue of books on particular branches of magic. They sought out books that would help me with my Troian; in return, and to their patent delight, I agreed to look at their small collection of books in Midlander and write up catalogue entries for them. I was the first visitor to the Gardens in over a century who had both a scholar's grasp of Midlander and a practical familiarity with it.

And thus it was, on the third day, that I found myself faced with a leather-bound volume, rather battered and having suffered at least one inundation of salt water, the title page of which read *De Doctrina Labyrinthorum*.

As was common for Midlander codices of this one's apparent age, the author's name was not given in the front—it would be at the end, a symbolic signature attesting to the document's truth—and so I was deeply bewildered to find the author's name in my head as clearly as if I had read it off the page: Ephreal Sand.

I had never been particularly interested in the theory of labyrinths—leave that to the architectural wizards, dull sticks that they were—and I had certainly never read any Midlander works on the subject. I had never seen *De Doctrina Labyrinthorum* before in my life; I was perfectly sure of that—as sure as I was that the author's name was Ephreal Sand.

I must have read a reference to it somewhere, I reasoned uneasily, but I couldn't remember doing that, either. Perhaps I'm wrong. Perhaps I just made up the name "Ephreal Sand." There was an easy way to check that, although I found myself reluctant to do so. I didn't want to look; I was afraid of what I would find.

"This is *stupid,*" I said, just under my breath, and turned savagely to the back of the book. And there it was, in plain, clear letters, unmistakable: EPHREAL SAND.

I stared at it for a span of time that felt like an hour, but was probably no more than a minute, then carefully, gently, shut the book. And then I sat there and stared at the front cover, trying to imagine how in the world I had heard of Ephreal Sand.

It wasn't something Malkar had told me; he had even less patience with architectural thaumaturgy than I did. It wasn't anything I had come across in my own studies. None of the Cabalines I had worked with in the Mirador were interested in labyrinths. I could feel my fingers going cold, because I did know—or, at least, I knew why I didn't know.

I shoved back my chair with violent suddenness and fled the library for the bright sunshine of the gardens.

For the next few days I worked around the *De Doctrina Labyrinthorum,* throwing myself into the study of Troian, the cataloguing of the other Midlander books, in order to avoid it. It sat on the desk in my carrel, mute, reproaching, and I told myself it was just another book, an obscure treatise on an obscure subject. But every time I looked at it, I felt the muscles of my shoulders and neck tensing. There was no one I could ask about it, no one here who would know any more than I did, and I was afraid that I would betray myself with my questions.

But on the fourth day, I could stand it no longer. I did not wish to admit that I was afraid of a mere book. After breakfast, I walked into the library, sat down at my desk, and defiantly, savagely, opened the book to a random page and stared at the text.

It was a melodramatic gesture, and one from which I expected nothing save the severance of the hold the book seemed to have over me. But my eye was caught by a word three-quarters of the way down the recto: *Nera*.

For a moment, my vision went black, and there was the stench of burning and blood in my nostrils. Then my eyes cleared and I was staring at *De Doctrina Labyrinthorum* again, my heart racing and my fingers clenched against the tabletop as if I were in danger of falling.

"Not now," I heard myself say, in a whisper. "Not now. I can't . . ." I closed the book, shoved it to the back of the desk, and opened an alchemical text from Ithaka. Cowardly, yes, that I would grant, but my cowardice hurt no one but myself. And that pain I could deal with.

Mildmay

He didn't want to see me. Stupid, useless shithead that I am, I hadn't thought of that. I'd thought if his head was cleared up, he'd know I wasn't no monster. But I sat there by the window, and I thought of how I'd treated him all across Kekropia, how I'd bullied him and yelled at him and hit him. I remembered the way I'd gotten him on the *Morskaiakrov*, and I thought, Maybe his memory's perfectly good. Maybe he's right.

But that thought—I couldn't stand it. I couldn't stay still with it hanging around my neck, like the albatross in one of Ilia's stories. I got to apologize, I thought. I got to tell him I'm sorry, tell him what it was like. And if he can't forgive me, I won't blame him, I'll just ask him to help me get the fuck away from here. And maybe he'll do that. I mean, it is kind of because of me that he got here without being dead. It's better than nothing.

And anything was better than sitting here with that thing bumping around behind my eyes like a wasp. I got up and dragged my stupid, aching self out the door and down the hall to the right, to where there was a portrait hanging on the wall.

I can't read Troian, so I can't tell you who the old goat was. I can say I didn't much care for him, and it wasn't no penance to take him down and turn him to face the wall. What I wanted was the wire holding him up, because it was heavy and stiff, and if I couldn't get through the hall door with it, I'd just wait until the prick brought my dinner and saw open my wrists with the table knife, because it would be all I was fit for.

Step-clunk-drag, step-clunk-drag, all the fucking way back down the fucking hall to the door. I got there without having to rest, which I decided was a win for me. Then I stopped, kind of leaned myself against the door, and started fooling around with my piece of wire, bending it into shape, testing it in the door, bending it a little different, trying again. Any real cracksman, say Sempronias Teach or Barthilde Coster, would've been just howling, watching me fuck around, but I got there in the end. The lock made this big, hollow, clicking sound, and I opened the door.

Now, of course, I didn't have the first fucking clue where I was going, just that I had to find Felix, and I was betting he hadn't been stuffed in no backwater cul-de-sac like I had. And I didn't have no feel for the geography of this place, neither. But in a weird sort of way, I'd been trained for this, and aside from the fact that it was daylight and I was a crip, it wasn't no different than doing a job for Keeper.

That's what I kept telling myself.

And I did pretty good. Nobody spotted me, although I had a close call or three. I got to the main drag—and powers more redheaded people than I'd ever even imagined—and actually for a while things were really easy, because they'd been hiding me so hard that most people in the Gardens couldn't know what their pet murderer looked like, and I figured I could risk pretending I was just another patient as long as I kept my head down. That was okay, because I sure didn't feel like leaving my feet to do whatever the fuck they wanted on all this marble. There were guys there as short as me, and I figured they probably had some Merrow blood. That was for sure my story if anybody asked.

But nobody did. Nobody looked at me twice. I worked my way down a flight of wide, slick, shallow marble stairs that was like being chewed to death by mice. I got out onto a kind of porch—I know that ain't the right word, 'cause it was too big and grand to be a porch, but I don't know what I ought to be calling it. I stood there, looking out at the gardens, and I could see now why the place was called the Gardens of Nephele, because there seriously wasn't anything else in view, and I thought, I am fucking never going to find Felix in this mess.

And that's when I heard his voice. Kethe's kind of coincidence, the kind you'd be better off without.

I knew it was him—there couldn't be another guy in this place talking Midlander with a flash Marathine accent, and besides, I recognized his voice—and I was about to start forward or wave or something when I got a good look at him.

There was another flight of steps here, these a little less nasty. He was standing at the bottom, with a crowd of redheaded people around him, and I swear by all the powers and saints if it hadn't been for his voice I wouldn't have known him. I mean, he was still skew-eyed, and his hair was about as wild as I remembered it, but he wasn't the same guy. Even the nasty-tongued Felix I'd got used to in Kekropia, that wasn't nothing but a bad imitation of what this guy was. I could feel the charisma baking off him from where I stood, even if I hadn't been able to see it in all them Troians staring at him. No wonder he didn't want to see me. Guy like him wouldn't have no use for a guy like me.

Oh Kethe, I thought, I can't. I backed away, got inside without him seeing me, and headed back to my room, hurting so much inside that I didn't even realize how bad my leg was until I got back to my hallway, and jiggered the lock again, and was just turning away from it—murderer locked in, all safe and sound—when my leg went.

Simple as that and I was on the floor. Hard. Though at least I'd twisted so I came down on my left side. Small fucking favors. I figured it was the stairs had done it, not that it mattered, and I knew, cane or no cane, there was no way I was standing up again. So I started crawling. My head was aching, my ribs were aching, my left hip was throbbing—and my right leg, dragging along behind me like a ball and chain . . . I wished it would just go ahead and fucking fall off, and then I could lie here and bleed to death and not have to worry about the prick or Felix or nobody. But it wouldn't. It just kept dragging back there, and before I'd gone a septad-foot, I was cursing it under my breath, all the nastiest things I could think of, because it was either that or start screaming, and screaming wouldn't get me back into bed where I could rest.

I crawled and crawled, and after about an indiction, somebody said, "Um."

Kethe, I just about died on the spot. My head jerked up, I jarred my bad leg, and my left hand shot out from under me, so I ended up sprawled across the hallway, staring up at the prick, who was standing in the doorway of my room, staring back at me.

"Oh fuck me sideways 'til I cry," I said and started laughing. And from there it turned into hysterics—I heard it coming and couldn't stop it, there was just too much, and every time I tried, I saw Felix again, standing down there at the bottom of them steps like he hadn't ever been crouched in the middle of a road in Kekropia like a frightened kid, and like he wouldn't know me to spit on me, and I just lost it. Once, for all, for good. I was sort of crying and screaming at the same time, because it hurt too much, all of it, and there was a voice saying, "Mildmay? Mildmay, come on. Let me help." And there was something cool and wet against my face, and I started being able to breathe again, and there were hands helping me up, and somebody basically carrying me, because my right leg had gone right out the other side of not-working, and I couldn't feel nothing except the glass shards in my thigh, and then, oh Kethe, blessed relief, I was laying down, and it wasn't on the floor.

And after a while, I pulled myself together again, and there was the prick standing by the bed looking down at me.

"Are you all right?"

And I couldn't do it no more. I couldn't lie. "I'm in *pain,* you stupid prick!"

"What happened?"

"Fuck, it don't matter."

"What happened to your leg?"

"Nothing."

"But you . . ."

"It's just like this."

"You mean, all the time?"

"What the fuck do you think I mean?"

"But hasn't it gotten better?"

"No," I said. Pure defeat. It was over now.

"You should have said."

I stared at him for what felt like a month before I could find any words at all. "I don't fucking believe this. I did, and you said not to whine at the celebrants. Remember?"

"Oh. But I didn't . . ."

"Didn't what? Didn't mean it?"

"I didn't know."

"Well, not if you never fucking asked. Oh, it don't matter. Just leave me be."

"But where did you go?"

"I was looking for Felix, but he don't want me either. Khrysogonos?"

"What?"

"Would you please go the fuck away?"

"But you—"

I caught his wrist, probably harder than I needed to, but my control was gone. "*Go the fuck away.*"

"All right," he said. I let go of him and he went. The door slammed, and I was safe, alone.

I was afraid to roll over, because of my leg, so I just lay there and pretended I didn't care about none of it until I fell asleep. I was a monster. It was what I deserved.

Felix

The world was drenched with sunlight. Ianthe, the Celebrant Major who had been assigned to improve my grasp of spoken Troian, had come and dragged me out of the library, announcing that I needed a picnic more than I needed to ruin my eyes with those dusty old books. I left *De Doctrina Labyrinthorum* behind gladly.

I had been spending a good deal of time with those who spoke Midlander—Ianthe herself, Diokletian, a pair of acolytes named Astyanax and Laodamia—but Ianthe felt (she told me) that the best way for my Troian to improve was for me to interact with those who spoke no Midlander at all. So when she and I and the picnic basket emerged from the Nephelion, there was a small group of celebrants waiting for us, who between them spoke maybe ten words of Midlander all told.

We had a splendid afternoon. I discovered, with the eager help of two of the young men in the party, that flirting took very little in the way of fluency. They taught me the names of every plant within sight, and I had a long, impassioned discussion with a middle-aged herbalist over an herb I called pathkeep and he called cloudbane, both of us making up for the deficiencies in my Troian with vigorous gestures. Ianthe sat and watched, laughing, and only twice took pity on us and intervened to sort things out.

As the sun was setting, we collected ourselves and our belongings and walked back to the Nephelion. The two charming young men invited me to come have a drink with them, but I didn't feel I wanted to venture beyond flirting yet, and declined.

I returned to my room to find an acolyte standing in the hall outside my door.

I had been introduced to him—I remembered that he spoke good Midlander, which felt at the moment very much like a miracle—but it took me a moment to dredge up his name. "Khrysogonos?" I said. "What can I do for you?"

His arms were folded, and there was a mulish set to his weak chin. "Why won't you see him?"

"I beg your pardon?"

"Why won't you see your brother?"

"And this is your business because?"

"It's killing him."

"What?"

He was red-faced and near tears, but he got it out. "You won't see him, and it's killing him."

"What—no. Wait. Come in. Sit down. Now, maybe it's just because I'm extraordinarily stupid, but I don't understand what you're trying to tell me."

He sat very stiffly on the edge of one of the armchairs and said, "Don't you care about him at all?"

"What?"

"The first thing he did when he woke up was to ask if you were all right. And then he asked to see you. The celebrants had told me you couldn't see him, and I told him that, but he kept asking and asking, and I thought maybe when they healed you, it would be all right, but then Diokletian said you didn't want to see him, and I had to tell him so, and he's not eating and he's driving himself too hard, and I know he's a murderer but even so he must love you so much, and don't you *owe* it to him?"

The outburst over, he sat and stared at me, his eyes wide and his face white; I'd never seen anyone so clearly appalled by his own words before.

"I didn't know he wanted to see me," I said slowly.

"What?"

"No one told me. Diokletian asked me if I wanted to see him, and I said I wasn't ready, but he didn't tell me he—Mildmay—was asking. I assumed he knew how I was and that everything was all right."

"It's not. Truly, it's not."

I stood up; I felt nearly incandescent with anger and fear and guilt. "Then I'll come see him right now."

Mildmay

I came awake out of a nightmare—something about Ginevra and the *Morskaiakrov,* I ain't too clear on the details—and a voice said, "Are you all right? You look like Death's been using you as a boot scraper."

For a second everything stopped. I mean, absolutely dead stopped. Then my heart started banging in my chest in this stupid way, and I turned my head, and the guy sitting in the armchair by the window gave me a little wave.

"Felix? Is that you?" Up close, it was even harder to believe. I mean, I'd thought I'd known him pretty good, but I'd really only known the deep-down crazies, not who he was at all.

"Last time I checked," he said, and that at least sounded like Felix.

"Then you don't think I'm a monster?"

"I don't what?"

Kethe, my stupid mouth. "Sorry. Nothing. Just a nightmare. But why wouldn't you see me?"

"Believe it or not, I didn't know *you* wanted to see *me*. I wasn't . . . ready."

"Okay," I said. "I mean, I get that."

"Good." He got up. "Now, I need to go talk to some people about why it didn't occur to them to *tell* me that you wanted an audience"—and I did recognize that smile, the self-mocking one—"but then I'll come back. Promise." And his smile widened into a real one, the five-alarm smile that I remembered from his good days in Kekropia.

Everything in me—heart, lungs, stomach, powers I don't know, maybe my liver and kidneys, too—rolled over at once. He was still on my side. It was okay.

He came over by the bed, staring down at me. I could see the swollen knuckles of his fingers and the Mirador's bright tattoos, along of how just at the moment I didn't want to look him in the eye. He said, "You look like you could do with some real rest. Would you like me to ward your dreams?"

"Ward?"

"It keeps the nightmares off. At least for a while."

"Powers," I said. "Yeah. That would help."

"Here. Lie back down."

He straightened the covers, like it really mattered to him that I was comfortable. "Here," he said. Light as a butterfly, his fingertips traced a pattern across my forehead, and a thick blanket of sleep rolled over me. I didn't even hear him leave.

Felix

I knew Mildmay never smiled, but the way the darkness had left his face was almost as good. It made me feel that perhaps whatever had happened to him here was not irrecuperable, that I had not woken up to the situation too late.

I had to stop outside his door, brace myself on my forearms against the wall, and count my breaths for a long time. My black rages were seductive, but I knew they would not help. Not now.

He had not let me see how scared he was; it was only the lifting of tension that had shown me it was there to begin with. And he had asked me if I thought he was a monster. From that question, I could begin to guess at the reason I had heard nothing of his condition, and I did not like my guesses. I had not wanted to see him, in my vanity and pride, but I had made that decision assuming that he was being kept informed.

And I had paid for it. It had flashed through my mind hideously when I first looked at him that I was looking at the very ghost I hadn't thought I could face, the ghost of myself in my madness—a thought that was as unsettling as it was unfair. I remembered thinking, only this morning, that my cowardice hurt no one but myself. That idea had been proved wrong with a vengeance, and I knew that whatever Mildmay had suffered, I was to blame for it.

But I did not carry that blame alone. I pushed myself off the wall, let myself through the locked door again—Malkar had loved lock spells, and I knew scores of them—and went looking for Diokletian. I had asked after my brother, and he hadn't told me what I should have known.

Peripherally, I noticed people scattering out of my way as I searched, but I truly did not care. I found Diokletian in his room, making notes on one of his cases in the hospice.

"Diokletian," I said.

"Perhaps this isn't the case in Marathat," he said, "but in Troia most people knock . . ." And then he turned all the way around and saw my face. "Blessed Tetrarchs! What's wrong?"

"Why didn't you tell me?"

"Tell you what?" His bewilderment seemed real.

"That my brother wanted to talk to me."

If anything, he seemed more baffled. "I didn't think you'd care."

"Didn't think I'd *care?* What kind of monster do you take me for?" Mildmay's word: I deserved it more than he did.

"Monster? After what he did to you?"

I stared at him for a long moment before I said, carefully, "What, exactly, did he do to me?"

"You don't remember. We were afraid some memory loss would accompany the healing."

"Never mind that. What are you accusing him of?"

"You were so frightened."

"Frightened?"

"When you came here. You were terrified of us, of everyone with red hair. And the bruises. He beat you, Felix. I think he must have been beating you regularly for weeks, if not months. And the Tetrarchs only know what else he might have done. You were in his power, as helpless as a kitten, and—"

"Stop that," I said, in a flat, hard voice that didn't sound like mine. I remembered being frightened. But I also remembered, blackly, who I had been frightened of: a man who had been dead for over fifteen years.

"You don't have to defend him any longer," Diokletian said gently. "It's all right. We're your friends here—"

"I said, stop that! I don't know how this stupid idea got into your head, but it isn't true. He didn't hurt me. He didn't beat me. And why didn't you *ask* him?"

"He would only have lied. He *did* lie."

I shut my eyes and took a deep breath. "No," I said, levelly, calmly. "He didn't."

"You don't see him clearly," Diokletian said, with a sad forbearance that made me want to throttle him. "It does you great credit. But truly, do you think a common hired murderer deserves this kind of loyalty?"

"Why not, from a prostitute?"

His breath hitched in as if I'd hit him.

"You didn't know that, did you? You didn't know what I was before I became a wizard. I am afraid that if we're drawing up sides, I'm down in the gutter. With him. Good night."

I favored him with a stiff little bow and walked out.

Shortly after dawn, I went back to Mildmay's room. He was awake, frowning at the ceiling as if it held the answer to something that was puzzling him.

"Good morning," I said.

" 'Morning." He didn't look at me or even move.

I came over to the bed. "How are you?"

"Better, I guess."

"Don't get too enthusiastic. You might sprain something."

"It don't matter."

"*What* doesn't matter?"

"Any of it. I'm still a crip, ain't I? They can't fix that for me."

"Wait." I sat down on the bed, being careful not to sit on his legs. "What? What's this crippled business?"

"They didn't tell you that, neither." He didn't believe me. What was worse was that it sounded like he didn't care. The moment of warmth between us was over; he had had too long to think, too many weeks with no one to talk to.

"No, they didn't tell me. So you'll have to."

"You don't remember."

"I don't remember much of the past year of my life. That's what being crazy does." I stopped, reined in my tongue. "No, I don't remember. Cough it up."

"D'you remember there being a curse on me?"

I had a sudden flash, frighteningly vivid, of his aura, green and black, looped and twined with black and crimson brambles. "Yes. I remember."

"D'you remember the *Morskaiakrov*?"

The ship. "Neither well nor fondly, but yes."

"It sank," he said, and gave me a flat green look. "You remember that?"

"Yes." Patience, I told myself. Patience. He'd earned that from me, if nothing else.

"When I was dragging your sorry ass to land," and his eyes were bright with tears. Rage, I realized after a second. Despite the flat voice and expressionless face, he was furious. Furious with me, probably. "I went into convulsions. D'you want to see what happened to my leg?"

"Do you think I should?"

He sat up then, fast as a cat. For a second, I thought he was going to strangle me, but he stopped himself. He shut his eyes for a moment and then said, "Yeah. Maybe you ought."

He leaned over the side of the bed and brought up a cane, a big, ugly thing that would have worked well to beat back savage beasts. He stood up, and my throat tightened as I saw how hard it was for him. He paused, as if this was something he had to steel himself to do, then limped slowly across to the chair by the window. He sat down. "And I ain't putting on the dog, neither," he said, as if I'd voiced a protest.

I wanted to. I remembered the way he had moved, all that grace and power, perfectly controlled. Gone now, to be replaced by this ugly, awkward lurch that it hurt to watch. He would not accept my sympathy; he probably wouldn't even believe I meant it. I said, neutrally, "Have they treated you badly?"

"Oh, no, everything's just fucking peachy."

"They thought you—"

"I know what they thought. And I did, so it's fine."

"No, you didn't."

"I did. I did hit you. I yelled at you. I said things to you that nobody . . . I said things I oughtn't've. And I'm sorry."

"No," I said, struggling to find something to say that he would hear, that he would accept. "What they thought, that—"

Someone knocked on the door.

Mildmay's head came up, the startled wariness of the movement making his resemblance to a fox nearly uncanny. After a moment, he said, "Come in," in Midlander.

A moment after that, the door opened, and the acolyte Khrysogonos came in.

"Sacred fuck, you knocked," said Mildmay, and Khrysogonos blushed brick-red.

"Mildmay," Khrysogonos said. "Are you busy?" Mildmay's eyebrows went up, and I thought for a moment that Khrysogonos was going to bolt back out the door. So politeness was new here. "Felix?"

"We were just talking," I said. "What is it?"

"The . . . the Celebrant Lunar is here, with Diokletian and Theophanos," another Celebrant Terrestrial whom I had met and not much cared for. "They wish—"

Xanthippe appeared in the doorway, Diokletian and Theophanos behind her, and said, "We wish to learn the truth."

Mildmay didn't say a word. He sat there, silent as a stone, and his silence denied the goodwill that the celebrants were trying to bring into the room.

"Mildmay," Xanthippe said, and I admired her for it, "we are sorry—"

"For what?" In a voice like black frost, and I didn't know about the others, but I almost wished he had stayed silent.

But Xanthippe was made of sterner stuff than that. "We misjudged you."

"No," Mildmay said.

The celebrants looked at me, as if for help, but I didn't have any to offer. I couldn't read Mildmay's face either.

Diokletian said, "Felix told me—"

"It don't fucking well matter. You saw me plain. I ain't denying it."

Xanthippe asked Theophanos a question in Troian; I couldn't follow it, but Mildmay said, "No, ma'am."

All four of them were staring at him now, Khrysogonos and Theophanos going the color of cheese curds. Xanthippe said, "How did you learn Troian?"

"I ain't *stupid,* ma'am. I can't talk right, but there ain't nothing wrong with my ears."

"Blessed Tetrarchs," Diokletian said in a whisper.

"And so," Xanthippe said, and I could feel the hair standing up on the back of my neck with the quietness of her tone, "we come to something I was told by Thamuris of the House Pandionis, Celebrant Celestial of the Euryganeic Covenant. He is ill and not of our covenant, and I trusted my own celebrants before him. But now I think perhaps I should reconsider. Mildmay, does your leg still hurt?"

For a moment it seemed as if he would burst out laughing, but he controlled himself and said only, "Yeah. It does, some."

"Some?"

"Okay, a lot."

"And have you told anyone about this?"

"I tried. They wouldn't listen."

This time, whatever Xanthippe said was blistering, and it sent Theophanos out of the room at a dead run. I thought I saw a glint of appreciation in Mildmay's eyes.

"It will take some time for the Circle to be cleansed and readied, but we have erred, and our mistakes shall be remedied. I shall consider more expressive means of atonement later."

"Please," Mildmay said. "I—"

"Celebrant Lunar?" Khrysogonos said in a thin, unhappy voice.

Xanthippe and Diokletian turned to look at him. "Acolyte?" said Xanthippe.

"You should expel me right now. Or put me back to washing floors with the novices."

"I beg your pardon?"

"He was my charge and I failed him." It was said all of a piece, the way a man might cough up something that was choking him.

"Stop it!" Mildmay said, preempting whatever Khrysogonos might have gone on to say. "Please. His head was down, fingers knotted in his hair. "I don't want nobody's guilt. I . . . I ain't worth it."

Xanthippe opened her mouth, and I shook my head at her emphatically. She raised her eyebrows at me; I nodded, and jerked my head toward the door. She rounded up Diokletian and Khrysogonos with a glance, and herded them out in front of her. The door shut behind them with a faint click.

I sat on Mildmay's bed and waited. After a time, without moving, he said, "Felix?" as if he expected I would be gone.

"Right here."

"How'd you get rid of them?"

"I glared at them," I said, and he laughed a little.

"Are you all right?" I said.

"Yeah, sure. I'm fine."

"Will you be offended if I say I think you're lying?"

"I might."

"I didn't betray you knowingly."

"I know."

All at once, I saw what I had to do if I wanted him to trust me again; I saw what he needed from me. For a moment, I didn't think I could give it, even to him, but I looked at the pain in every line of his body, remembered the man who'd handed me a turnip in a cold Kekropian field, and said, "I need to tell you something."

"What?" He didn't care.

But I did, and I realized that I cared enough for both of us. "Everything, I guess. Everything I lied to you about."

He looked up a little at that, as if he thought I was making fun of him.

"No," I said, "I mean it. I've never told anyone, but . . . will you listen?"

"Yeah," he said, and sat up straight again. "I'll listen."

For a moment, I couldn't even start. There were so many lies, all of them precious, all of them necessary. Then I just opened my mouth and let the words come out: "I was sold to a thief-keeper in Simside when I was four. He was a monster. When one of us did something that made him angry, he . . . he'd take you and drag you down to the Sim and hold you under until he decided you were sorry enough to suit him. *He*'s responsible for my back. He used a nun's scourge on us when we weren't quite bad enough for the river."

"Powers," Mildmay said.

"He died in the Fire of 2263, and I was so glad . . ." I came to a complete halt for a moment, but I had to go on. "In Kekropia, when I was . . . when I wasn't myself, I thought you were him."

"Oh fuck," Mildmay said. "Oh Kethe, no wonder you were scared of me. I am so sorry."

"No, you shouldn't be. You didn't know. I didn't tell you."

His head was up and his absinthe-green eyes were wide. "But, powers, I mean, I can imagine . . . oh, sacred bleeding fuck, you should've *told* me."

"I couldn't. Let me get a little farther with this story, and you'll see why." I managed to smile at him, although it didn't feel convincing, even to me. "As I said, my Keeper died in the Fire. He'd always done some pimping on the side—not the hard trade, just some lamprey-work and the occasional ten-year-old virgin. But word got around that he'd gone up in smoke, and the wolves from Pharaohlight started circling. And there we were, a herd of little ewe lambs. Ripe to be sheared and sold. I ended up in a brothel called the Shining Tiger, and that's where Malkar found me."

"Malkar. That's the guy—"

"Hang on," I said and nearly choked. That was the Lower City reemerging like a kraken from the depths. Malkar had schooled my voice obsessively, rooting out every last inflection, idiom, and turn of phrase. I couldn't let it come back now. I took a deep breath and said evenly, "Let me tell it in order."

He nodded; he could see I was upset, although he didn't yet know why. But he would. I looked away, because I didn't want to watch that stone face; if he reacted, I didn't want to see it.

"Malkar bought me from Lorenzo. It's not legal, but procurers in Pharaohlight do it all the time. You probably know that. I was fourteen. For the next six years, I belonged to Malkar, body and soul, in the most absolute, abject way you can imagine. He was my teacher, my lover, my torturer . . . I loved him, and I feared him. I wanted to kill him, and I worshipped him. Hopelessly."

"Like a keeper," Mildmay said.

"Yes, a little. No. More than a little. He was another version of Keeper. He took me out of the city, to a country estate near Arabel. I didn't leave it for three years, while he taught me everything I needed to know to pass myself off as a gentleman in the Mirador. And he taught me a story that didn't have Pharaohlight or Simside in it anywhere, that I was from Caloxa, a nobleman's child. He bound me to him with spells—and yes, that is heresy—and then he . . . he taught me I could never tell *anyone* the truth. I won't tell you what he did to me when I slipped, but . . . it was effective. And when I was seventeen, he brought me to the Mirador and got me initiated as a Cabaline wizard."

I glanced up; Mildmay's face was impassive, but his eyes were on me, and they were bright with interest. No matter how dreadfully, crawlingly naked this made me feel, no matter that I was shivering, even now, with the memory of Malkar's punishments and threats: it was working.

I said, "I think now that he was planning to break the Virtu even then. I think somehow his spells on me must have done something to the Cabaline oaths—even though I broke away from him when I was twenty. But it must have left him a loophole, because, you see, that's how he broke the Virtu."

"Sorry. What?"

"That's how he broke the Virtu." I could feel my chest and throat tightening, and my voice came out thin and unsteady.

"You don't got to tell me if you don't want," Mildmay said, with a cautious gentleness that I did not deserve. "I mean, you ain't obliged."

I looked him in the eyes then. I had to. I said, "No, I think I have to tell someone. The whole truth. Because I'll never tell anyone else, and . . . and I don't want to be made of lies anymore. Let me say it."

"Okay," he said. "I won't tell nobody. I swear it."

"Thank you. I know." I took a deep breath, shut my eyes, and concentrated on making my words come out slowly, evenly, clearly, and without the least hint of the Lower City in the vowels. "Malkar broke the Virtu by means of a spell that he cast on me. It let him use me, use my magic, which is stronger than his. And the way he worked the spell was . . ." I couldn't say it. I couldn't get the words out. I was staring at my tattoos now, the brilliant gold-edged vines tangling across the backs of my hands.

"Felix?" I heard Mildmay get up, heard him limp across to the bed. He sat down beside me, on my left side, and did not touch me; I flinched a little, inside, with how well he understood me. "Felix, you okay?"

"I just have to say it. I have to get it out." I reached out with my left hand, and after a moment, hesitating, he took it. His hand was square and warm and strong; I gripped it hard and said, my voice barely a whisper, "He raped me."

"He . . ."

"*He raped me*. He raped me and used me to break the Virtu and drove me mad and sacrificed me to Stephen and—" My breath hitched painfully, and I could feel my shoulders hunching, fearing punishment, but I couldn't keep the words silent anymore, the words I had kept locked in the lowest, darkest regions of my mind for years, since Malkar first half seduced, half raped me in that filthy upper room in the Shining Tiger. I said, "And I hate him."

"No fucking wonder," Mildmay said, and I felt tears spill over my eyelids, tears of relief and pain, for I had said it and not died. Mildmay had heard me and did not find me abhorrent. I let go of his hand, rubbed my face, and looked at him. The face was stone, still, but the green eyes held neither condemnation nor anger.

"It's okay," he said. "I mean, can't do nothing about it, but . . ."

"It's okay," I said, using the word deliberately.

His face brightened in its nonsmiling way, and he said, "Yeah. Still brothers, right?"

"Yes," I said. "Still brothers."

The celebrants had returned and taken him away. They would not let me go with him, for reasons that he seemed to understand better than I did. I was left with Xanthippe, who watched me fidget around the room for a bit and then said gently, "When they are ready, we will observe the proceedings. I assure you, I will not let him come to harm a second time."

"Thank you," I said, and bit back the bitter words that wanted to follow. I had no right to say them.

Still brothers? he had asked me, and I had agreed, knowing that it was what he needed, knowing also that I wanted it, although I was not entirely sure what it meant, either to him or to me. I did not remember us *being* brothers, except for strange, isolated glimpses of his protective care. I knew that he had treated me as a brother almost from the moment we met, but I had no idea why. I did not know him—although I trusted him without reservations or second thoughts.

And he trusted me. That was what he meant by "brothers," I thought: trust. *He trusted me.* It was a cruel and bitter irony; every trust that had ever been placed in me, I had betrayed, including his.

I was also painfully aware that he had no one else. Xanthippe was mortified, infuriated by the celebrants' mistake and determined to correct it, but her feelings ran no deeper than that, and I doubted that the other celebrants felt any differently—if they even cared as much as she did. They did not understand him, any more than they would have understood me if I had told them the truth. Mildmay had understood. I snorted as it occurred to me that if he had no one else, then neither did I.

"Felix?"

"Nothing." To get away from the barbed circles of my own thoughts, I asked, "What are they going to do? What went wrong?"

"We won't know for certain until the Celebrants Terrestrial have finished their initial examination. Thamuris said the curse wasn't properly lifted, and I fear that may prove to be true." She paused and added hesitantly, as if unsure how I would take it, "It was a wicked thing."

For a moment, I was not certain of my own reaction. The orthodox Cabaline still within me protested that he would not have incurred the curse if he had not killed a wizard, that it was not supposed to do what it had done, that it had never been intended to be activated: the Cabal and every Curia that had sat thereafter had assumed that the mere existence of that curse, and the fact that it had been made extremely public, would prevent its ever being tested.

But that was naïve and specious logic. True, the curse had not been designed to prolong its action on the body in the way that the concatenation of circumstances around Mildmay had caused it to do, but it had been designed to be both lethal and excruciating. And we had had that curse, that weapon, for nearly two hundred years. If we had truly not meant to use it, we would have dismantled it.

The fact remained that he had killed Cerberus Cresset, presumably at the behest of the heretic Miriam. Why, when I had forgotten so much else, did I remember every miserable detail of that conversation in Hermione? Mildmay's harsh breathing, the sweat on his face, the labored, slurred sounds of his words: I remembered it as if it had happened only an hour ago. At least Cerberus had died quickly.

"Yes," I said. "It was. It is. It is also heresy, a fact that I intend to point out to my learned colleagues when I return to Mélusine. The man he . . . killed—the man was a witchfinder, a burner of heretics."

"I don't think I understand," Xanthippe said after a moment, still sounding as if she thought I was likely to turn and savage her.

"No. Nor should you. The history of Mélusine is like a massacre in a lunatic asylum, patients and warders turning on each other, turning on themselves, turn and turn about. Mildmay is as much a victim of that as . . ." As I am. "As anyone."

"It is hard to think of a murderer as a victim."

"Of course it is," I said wearily, and we fell silent again.

Presently an acolyte, one I didn't know, tapped on the door to let us know that the Celebrants Terrestrial were ready. I followed Xanthippe out of the room, determined that this time I would not let Mildmay down. I would not leave him.

Mildmay

Next time I woke up, the hornets were gone. I was laying in my bed, everything familiar, and I was kind of achy, but there wasn't no horrible throbbing pain the way there had been. I opened my eyes and saw Felix sitting by the window, frowning over a book.

"So I guess it worked," I said.

He jumped a little, but closed his book and smiled at me like he still really meant it. "Xanthippe says you will heal properly now."

"Good," I said, and because I didn't want to talk about me, "Whatcha reading?"

"Oh, a book," he said, too carelessly.

I sat up, pushed my hair off my face, and waited.

He colored a little. "I don't know why it bothers me. You've never heard of it, have you? *De Doctrina Labyrinthorum*?"

"*Labyrinthorum?*"

"Labyrinths." And when I just looked at him, "Mazes."

"Oh. Nope. But, I mean, I ain't much with the book learning."

"No, I just wondered if I'd . . . if I'd said anything about it. Before."

"Not that I heard."

"It really doesn't matter," he said and dropped the book on the floor like it had pissed him off. "I'll figure it out eventually. I wanted to be sure you were all right."

"I think I am," I said. "I ain't keen to go for a walk just yet, mind, but I think I'm okay." I could feel myself starting to blush, but I said it anyway, "Thanks."

"Don't thank me until I've done something to be grateful for," he said dryly. "I am not under any illusions as to my culpability in this debacle. I failed you."

"Kethe. Don't . . ."

"Don't what? Don't treat you like a person instead of an object? Don't acknowledge that you have been shamefully misused and betrayed?"

"Please." My face felt like it was on fire. "It don't matter."

"*Yes, it does*. I know that, even if you don't." He stopped. I could see the temper in him, and all at once he looked more like the guy I'd known in Kekropia than he had done. I remembered him screaming at me in the rain, him trying his damnedest to kill me on the *Morskaiakrov,* and I felt kind of a chill. That's part of him, too, Milly-Fox, and don't you forget it.

He stood up, came over to the bed, and knelt down, all stiff like he'd swallowed a poker. He looked me in the eye, and his face was still temperish and pale, like he was getting ready to throw a tantrum, and he said, all tight and angry, "I am sorry."

I could see that this was some really big deal to him, that he would *never* have said it if he didn't sincerely feel like he had to, so I just said back, "Thanks."

And he nodded and got up again and said, "You should sleep. Xanthippe said that was the fastest way for you to heal right now." And then, almost shyly, "May I ward your dreams again?"

Which I figured was the closest he was going to get to saying he cared about me, and that was okay. "Thanks," I said again. "I'd . . . I'd be glad of it."

He smiled, and I lay back down. His fingers brushed across my forehead, and sleep came, simple and warm.

I heard him say, or maybe I just dreamed it, "Sleep well, little brother."

P9-DDX-601

CAMBRIDGE STUDIES IN LINGUISTICS

English Phonology and Phonological Theory

Synchronic and Diachronic Studies

In this series

1. DAVID CRYSTAL: *Prosodic systems and intonation in English*
2. PIETER A. M. SEUREN: *Operators and nucleus*
3. RODNEY D. HUDDLESTON: *The sentence in written English*
4. JOHN M. ANDERSON: *The grammar of case*
5. M. L. SAMUELS: *Linguistic evolution*
6. P. H. MATTHEWS: *Inflectional morphology*
7. GILLIAN BROWN: *Phonological rules and dialect variation*
8. BRIAN NEWTON: *The generative interpretation of dialect*
9. R. M. W. DIXON: *The Dyirbal language of North Queensland*
10. BRUCE L. DERWING: *Transformational grammar as a theory of language acquisition**
11. MELISSA BOWERMAN: *Early syntactic development**
12. W. SIDNEY ALLEN: *Accent and rhythm*
13. PETER TRUDGILL: *The social differentiation of English in Norwich*
14. ROGER LASS and JOHN M. ANDERSON: *Old English phonology*
15. RUTH M. KEMPSON: *Presupposition and the delimitation of semantics*
16. JAMES R. HURFORD: *The linguistic theory of numerals*

* Issued in hard covers and paperback.

ENGLISH PHONOLOGY AND PHONOLOGICAL THEORY

SYNCHRONIC AND DIACHRONIC STUDIES

ROGER LASS

Department of Linguistics
University of Edinburgh

CAMBRIDGE UNIVERSITY PRESS

CAMBRIDGE

LONDON · NEW YORK · MELBOURNE

Published by the Syndics of the Cambridge University Press
The Pitt Building, Trumpington Street, Cambridge CB2 1RP
Bentley House, 200 Euston Road, London NW1 2DB
32 East 57th Street, New York, NY 10022, USA
296 Beaconsfield Parade, Middle Park, Melbourne 3206, Australia

Library of Congress catalogue card number: 76-650

ISBN: 0 521 21039 9

First published 1976

Printed in Great Britain at the
University Printing House, Cambridge
(Euan Phillips, University Printer)

For Jaime

Contents

Dem einzelnen Wissenschaftler ist die Tradition, in der er steht, nur selten geläufig, d. h. auch sein wissenschaftliches Selbstverständnis ist keineswegs klar und explizit. Bestimmte Argumentationsweisen und Begriffsunterschiedungen gehören einfach zu den Voraussetzungen, die er mehr oder weniger unbewußt gelernt hat, als er in die Wissenschaft eingeführt wurde. Diese Voraussetzungen sind zweifellos wirksam in seiner Tätigkeit; manchmal bekommen sie den Charakter dogmatischer Grundüberzeugungen. Genau in diesem Sinne ist eine bestimmte Tradition dann eher ein Prokrustesbett für die Weiterentwicklung der Wissenschaft. Alte, angeblich bewährte Verfahren und Begriffe werden nicht mehr in Frage gestellt; sie entfalten gleichsam in den Überlegungen des Wissenschaftlers ihre Eigendynamik. Seine Probleme ergeben sich bereits aus diesen Verfahren und Begriffen und nicht mehr in einer ursprünglichen Konfrontation mit Eigenerfahrungen; neue Fragestellungen kommen gar nicht mehr auf oder werden von vornherein zurückgewiesen unter Berufung auf die überlieferten Anschauungen.

Dieter Wunderlich, *Grundlagen der Linguistik* (1974)

We must beware of solving, or dissolving, factual problems linguistically; that is, by the all too simple method of refusing to talk about them. On the contrary, we must be pluralists, at least to start with: we should first emphasize the difficulties, even if they look insoluble... If we can then reduce or eliminate some entities by way of scientific reduction, let us do so by all means, and be proud of the gain in understanding.

Sir Karl Popper, *Objective Knowledge* (1973)

Preface

All sciences[1] periodically congeal. That is, they develop a (Kuhnian) 'paradigm' in its most restrictive form, and become orthodoxies. When this happens, what Niels Bohr (1958: 65) has called 'the never-ending struggle for harmony between content and form' is partly resolved in favour of 'form': the paradigm triumphs, and the free-ranging theoretical speculation that marked the pre-paradigm stage is subordinated to the concerns of 'normal science'.[2] To some extent this effectively discourages basic metatheoretical research (since the metatheory is by this time 'given'); and it also restricts the range of data available to investigation in general. For since the metatheory sets up *a priori* definitions of what questions are intelligible, it therefore defines, at least indirectly, what data is 'interesting'.[3]

One of the commonest forms that this recurrent congealing takes is reductivism. What for earlier generations were 'mysteries' (or at least deep and interesting complexities demanding explication) are, by the newly enlightened, seen as 'nothing-but' something simpler. The proponents of this kind of reductivism characteristically take it as more than mere demythologizing: it is in some sense 'explanatory'.[4] But it often turns out – as I think it has in current linguistic theory – that many of the 'explanations' are either simple refusals to talk about certain issues, or what we might

[1] Or other intellectual disciplines. I use 'science' here in the (broad) sense of *Wissenschaft*; I doubt whether linguistics is a 'science' in the sense of the English word. Cf. the sketch for an argument to this effect in ch. 1, § 10 below, and the fuller discussion in the *Epilogue*.

[2] For 'paradigms' and 'normal science' see Kuhn (1962) and the papers by Kuhn, Watkins, Toulmin and Popper in Lakatos & Musgrave (1970). The triumph of 'normal science' is apparently a good thing for Kuhn; not so for other philosophers of science. The collection of papers cited immediately above is a very instructive confrontation of 'Kuhnians' and 'Popperians' on this and other issues.

[3] See especially chapters 2, 4 and 7 below.

[4] Cf. the attitudes embodied in much 'ordinary language' philosophy, Freudian *Sexualtheorie*, behaviourist psychology, and current generative linguistics toward the profound difficulties that exercised the immediately preceding generations. Freud's all-or-nothing view of the sexual aetiology of neurosis is a classic example. There is now a growing anti-reductivist sentiment in biology: cf. the essays in Koestler & Smythies (1969).

call 'higher taxonomy'. Under this last heading (essentially reduction of mystery by means of the naming fallacy) I would include for instance the Chomsky & Halle theory of markedness (cf. Lass 1972, Lass & Anderson 1975: appendix IV for discussion), and the taxonomy of linguistic change in terms of 'optimization' (Kiparsky 1965, 1968, King 1969).

This general pattern of taxonomic reductivism is nicely illustrated by aspects of the history of linguistic theory since Bloomfield. A programmatically behaviourist science, strongly influenced by Vienna Circle positivism, which dealt with nothing-but behavioural output, shunned anything remotely 'mental', and utilized only taxonomic operations of segmentation and classification, was transformed by the 'Chomskyan revolution'. It was transformed (judging by the early literature) into a mentalistic, deductive, anti-positivist, explanatory theoretical science: certainly a programmatically anti-behaviourist one. The general sense was one of 'liberation': freedom from biuniqueness, from surfacism, and the like. And this 'new' linguistics has of course become in its turn congealed and reductivist, classically dogmatic. Language change, for instance, is now nothing-but rule addition, rule change, or 'optimization'; there are two and only two 'theoretically significant' levels in phonology; there are only binary features, and only universal articulatory ones at that (cf. ch. 7 below), and so on.[1]

This is not to say that there aren't welcome signs of reaction against this fossilization. I do not picture myself as a lone voice crying in the wilderness, rather as a minor John the Baptist in very good company. But it does seem as if, in the two areas that concern me most (historical linguistics and phonology), things are moving more slowly than in syntax or semantics.[2] This book, then, is my own contribution to the ongoing

[1] I don't mean to say that this kind of paradigm-fossilization ever can (or should?) be avoided; only that it should be recognized when it happens, and treated as a serious but curable form of philosophical pathology. The polemical tone I take from time to time should therefore not be interpreted as *ad hominem* even when I mention names, nor as apportioning 'blame'.

[2] The 'orthodoxy' in phonology is embodied in Chomsky & Halle (1968); and in historical linguistics in Kiparsky (1965, 1968), and King (1969). Some of the most important challenges seem to be: the revival of 'functionalist' notions by Kisseberth (1970a); the elevation of paradigmatic considerations and analogy to independent theoretical status (Harris 1970, Kiparsky 1971, 1972); and the attack on the idea of 'homogeneity' by Weinreich *et al.* (1968). More fundamental challenges to the theory can be found in the work of Wang and his associates on lexical diffusion (cf. Chen 1972); the reconsiderations of the feature framework by Ladefoged (1971) and Maran (1971); and the attack on extrinsic ordering by Koutsoudas and others (Koutsoudas 1971, Koutsoudas *et al.* 1972).

discussion, not in any sense a 'revolutionary' document (though it may in part be a reactionary one).

The studies collected here grow out of frustration with certain blind alleys in current 'standard' theory. They are best taken as preliminaries to theory, essays in the focussing of dissatisfactions, and attempts to clarify important points that have gotten buried under a mass of misleading and dogmatic argumentation. I would not of course be displeased if some genuine contributions to linguistic theory, the theory of English phonology, or the history of English came out of these papers: but the main emphasis is on ground-clearing, and I will be happy if I have accomplished a little of that.

These essays are, despite their disparate topics, not unrelated: they are tied together by two threads related to Bohr's polarity of 'content' and 'form'. To quote him again (1958:65), 'no content can be grasped without a formal frame, and...any form, however successful it has hitherto proved, may be found to be too narrow to comprehend new experience'. Much of the trouble with current theory seems to derive from the two problems of artificially constrained formalism, and a restricted data base.

To clarify these two 'threads': they are (a) the failure of certain 'canonical' claims in linguistic theory to account for important synchronic and historical facts about English (and other languages); and (b) the advantages (and consequences) of using a wider than normal data base, and of applying to it (among other things) certain traditional but now rather neglected procedures like comparative reconstruction.

These threads intertwine. The difficulties caused by reductivism are in general obvious: but they become clearer when the resulting theories are confronted with a wider range of data. I will therefore be dealing here with more of English than linguists usually look at; English phonological studies, at least most theoretical ones, have in the past largely been restricted to an excessively narrow (and typologically misleading) range of dialects. From a reading of the historical literature, for example, one could be forgiven for thinking that the historical development of English has been a single-minded march toward RP or Kenyon–Knott American English: Scots, Northern and North-Midland English, and many other dialects with their own individual structures and histories have been relegated to footnotes or ignored.[1]

[1] A minor case in point is the statement one finds over and over again in handbooks and histories that Old English and some dialects of Middle English had front rounded vowels, but that these are now 'lost'. To take Britain only, this is by and large true for the South; but not only have some of the ME ones remained in Scotland and the North

There is another concern here which in a sense overrides the others: and this is the question of what kind of discipline linguistics is, and what kind of 'knowledge' its procedures yield. Many linguists confidently take it to be an 'empirical science'; others, myself included, are not so sure. Epistemological questions of this kind are bound to arise from any close consideration of theory in relation to data, especially when historical argument is involved. So in a sense this book may appear to fall between two incompatible stools: in many places I am concerned with refining the strictly empirical basis of phonological discussion, while in others I cast doubts on the empirical basis of the discipline in general. This is not to be taken as confusion, but rather as an attempt to separate two different kinds of linguistics, and to establish the kinds of argument relevant to each. In any case this should not be too much of a problem for the reader: I have tried to separate the two kinds of discussion as far as possible.

Three of the chapters below (2, 4, 7) have appeared previously, in one form or another, in 'informal' publication: chapter 2 as Lass (1969), 4 as Lass (1973a), and 7 as Lass (1973c). But they have been drastically revised, in some cases virtually beyond recognition, and are very different from (and I hope better than) their trial runs. The original sources are in any case often hard to come by, and the papers are relevant to the general argument of the book.

Before closing this already overlong preface, I must acknowledge with pleasure my debt to those colleagues who have taken the trouble to read all or part of the material collected here, and to discuss it and related matters at length. I therefore thank the following, both for positive suggestions and for saving me from error (the remaining mistakes are of course my own): Gillian Brown, John Anderson, James R. Hurford, John Ohala, Mary Vaiana Taylor, John Taylor, Charles Bird, Geoff Pullum, Terry Moore, La Raw Maran, and Fred Householder. I am also grateful to Sidney Allen and Bob Le Page for their careful reading of the manuscript for Cambridge University Press, and for many valuable suggestions. And finally I thank my wife Jaime for her patience and encouragement during the writing of this book, and for keeping me fed while I did nothing particular to deserve it.

Edinburgh R.L.
July 1975

of England; new ones have arisen. The same is true in Northern Ireland. Thus many dialects of Scots have [y] and [ø:] from ME /ø:/, others have [y] from ME /u:/, and in Northumberland we find [ø:] for ME /ɔ:/ (cf. Lass 1972).

Part I

VOWEL CONTRASTS AND THEIR DEPLOYMENT IN ENGLISH: 'LENGTH' AND 'SYSTEM'

Scientific research in many domains of knowledge has indeed time and again proved the necessity of abandoning or remoulding points of view which, because of their fruitfulness and apparently unrestricted applicability, were regarded as indispensable for rational explanation. Although such developments have been initiated by special studies, they entail a general lesson of importance for the problem of the unity of knowledge. In fact, the widening of the conceptual framework not only has served to restore order within the respective branches of knowledge, but has also disclosed analogies...with respect to analysis and synthesis of experience in apparently separated domains of knowledge, suggesting the possibility of an ever more embracing objective description.

Niels Bohr, *Atomic Science and Human Knowledge* (1958)

I *On the 'two kinds of vowels' in English*

1. Introductory: the problem

Linguists have been arguing about the structure of the English vowel system for just about as long as they have been concerned with the theory of synchronic description. It has been clear to observers since at least the sixteenth century (e.g. Hart 1569) that many dialects of English have – phonetically – three types of vocalic nuclei: 'short', 'long' and 'diphthongal'. But phonologically things are not so simple. There seem to be two basic questions: (a) how many primitive nuclear types does English have at a more abstract level? and (b) how are these to be characterized?

There have, recently, been two main kinds of answers. One, that of the British descriptive tradition stemming from Daniel Jones (though others have espoused it as well) is that there are as many underlying ('phonemic') types as there are surface types. The other, typified by the 'simple' vs. 'complex' analysis of Trager & Smith (1951), and more recently by the quite different (though related) 'lax' vs. 'tense' analysis of Chomsky & Halle (1968), is that there are only two basic types – regardless of differences in phonetic realization that may suggest more.

In order to get to the major point of this chapter, I must dispose of a minor one: the problem – as outlined above – of dichotomy vs. trichotomy. That is, I want to show that phonologically speaking there is very little evidence in favour of more than two systemic primitives, and a good deal against it. My major point, which I will devote most of this chapter to, is that while the system is clearly dichotomous, none of the dichotomies that have been proposed are adequate. Of the two major choices, the Trager & Smith 'simple'/'complex' and the Chomsky & Halle 'lax'/'tense', the former has considerably more to recommend it; though not in the Trager & Smith form, nor in the particular way this is interpreted for phonetic representations by Chomsky & Halle. I will show further that the 'lax'/'tense' dichotomy, with its complex apparatus of rules to epenthesize postvocalic 'glides', etc., fails on at least three major points: (a) it is not even observationally adequate, in that its terms and consequences are not publicly verifiable; (b) it fails to capture a number of real generalizations, and encourages the formulation of erroneous ones; and (c) it is burdened with a good deal of *ad hoc* and unnecessary machinery, which makes it impossible to account naturally for a wide range of English dialects. I will outline the Trager & Smith proposals in §2, the Chomsky & Halle ones in §3, and then go on to argue for my own quite different one.

But first let us look at the general type of data that has called forth the various analyses. We can begin by noting that whatever the arguments may be for having more than two primitive vowel types, there is no doubt that linguists of all persuasions would admit that there must be at least two. That is, there is minimally a dichotomy such that we can identify two basic types, on the basis of their phonological and phonetic properties. One class of this dichotomy contains the nuclei of *bit*, *bet*, *bat*, *put*, *pot*, *but*; and the other those of *meet*, *mate*, *boot*, *boat*, *bought*, *father*, *suit* (if different from *boot*), *bite*, *doubt*, *quoit*.[1] Let us provisionally call these two classes respectively (A) and (B). The phonetic realizations may be exemplified by forms from three fairly representative (though rather differently organized) vowel systems: New York City, RP, and a slightly 'standardized' North-Eastern English, Bridlington in the East Riding of Yorkshire. I cite these in (1) below in a detailed narrow transcription, to avoid as much 'phonological' prejudice as possible (the data is taken from three typical informants: the New York system is my own).

So English (phonetic) vowel systems like these can have either two or three contrasting nuclear types: short monophthongs vs. diphthongs (NYC), or short monophthongs vs. long monophthongs vs. diphthongs (RP, Br). I know of none with only short and long monophthongs – though I will consider one that comes close in §7. Observe that group (A) is all short monophthongs, and (B) is either all diphthongs or a mixture of diphthongs and long vowels. As we can see from (1), a given lexical class can be either long monophthongal or diphthongal, depending on dialect, if it is included in (B): cf. *meet*, *bought*, *boat*.

[1] This refers to (relatively) 'standard' dialect types, e.g. RP and the like in Britain, most U.S. dialects, and 'Anglicized' Scots. Scots proper is excluded, as its vowel system is not dichotomous (cf. Aitken 1962, Lass 1974b, and ch. 2, §1 below); as are (for the moment) the more typically regional English dialects. The latter are often in fact typologically similar to RP, but their histories have been so divergent that lexical comparison would be confusing at this point. This is especially true since the words representing vowel classes in (1) are cover symbols for etymological categories: *bit* is ME /i/, *boat* is ME /ǭ/, *quoit* is ME /oi/, and so on.

(I)

(A)	NYC	RP	Br	(B)	NYC	RP	Br
bit	ι̨	ι	ι	meet	ι̨i	į:	ę̈ι
bet	ε̣	ε̣	ε	mate	ε̣ι	ęι	ę̟:
bat	æ	æ̣	a	boot	ɤ̈ω	ų:	ų̟̈:
put	ɤ̈	ω	ų	boat	əω	öω	ǫ:
pot	ä	ɒ	ɔ	bought	ǫə	ɔ̣:	ɔ:
but	ə	ʌ̈	ɤ	father	ɑ̟ə	a:	a:
				suit	ɤ̈ω	ιu	ų̟̈:
				bite	äι	äι	aι
				doubt	æω	äω	aω
				quoit	ǫι	ɔι	ɔι

Given data like this, it is not self-evident that a dichotomous analysis is adequate, at least for dialects like RP or Bridlington. The difference in phonetic typology (diphthongs only in some dialects, both diphthongs and long vowels in set (B) for others) is unimportant to some linguists (Trager & Smith, Chomsky & Halle); to others, the long vowel/diphthong distinction is important enough to necessitate a third primitive type (Jones 1950, 1956; Gimson 1965 in explicitly 'phonemic' terms).[1] The disagreement here is really over whether this difference is to be handled at the classificatory level, or whether it is in some (loose) sense 'allophonic' or 'realizational' (I omit analyses that posit a fourth class – triphthongs like [aiə] in *fire* – since these most likely derive from diphthongs followed by underlying /r/).

The question then is whether in dialects like RP and Bridlington class (B) is to be taken as phonologically homogeneous. Do long vowels and diphthongs represent different primitive types? For instance, should *meet*, *boot* in RP have a different kind of phonological representation from *mate*, *boat*? And should these latter two (but not *meet*, *boot*) be classed with *bite*? Similarly, for Bridlington, should *meet* go with *bite*, while *mate*, *boat* are in a different class?

I think we can show that it is an overdifferentiation to extend the difference in phonetic types in (B) to a principle of higher-level classification.

[1] It has been suggested to me (by Gillian Brown) that it is not quite fair to say that the Jonesian tradition really claims that there are 'three primitive types'. Gimson (1965, 86ff.) for instance distinguishes between long 'relatively pure' and long 'diphthongal...with prominent first element', which can be read as suggesting a basic short/long dichotomy, with two late realization types. In this case I suppose I should say that the claim here is for two-and-a-half primitives. But the three-way distinction is certainly made in the 'systemic' notation; and as long as a notation does in fact have systemic reference, it seems to me that a claim for primitivity is being made

Phonologically (or to be more precise but less fashionable, phonologically and morphophonemically) one must argue for a dichotomy in which all members of (B), regardless of their surface realizations, form a set opposed as a whole to (A). We will see later, in the light of my proposals about the lexical form of the English vowel system, just why the long vowel/diphthong contrast is so trivial.

The two arguments for dichotomy are well-known and rather simple; but I restate them here just to set up a clear motivation for the two-class assumption. Besides, one of them is the basis of the Chomsky & Halle proposals we will be looking at below. The first one, the purely phonological, is based on distribution; most significantly the nuclei of (B) can appear in word-final position under accent, while those of (A) are excluded: thus *bee, bay, boo, boy*, etc. but *[bɩ], *[bɛ], *[bæ], *[bɷ], and so on.[1]

The second argument, the morphophonemic, is of course the now famous one from paradigmatic alternations. That is, English shows a large number of fairly regular alternation sets, in which one term is a member of (A) and the other of (B); but where monophthongal and diphthongal members of (B) are not distinguished from each other in any way.[2] Thus, to take a few typical forms from the three dialects in (1):

(2)

	(A)				(B)		
	NYC	RP	Br		NYC	RP	Br
div*i*nity	ɩ̝	ɩ	ɩ	div*i*ne	ɑ̟ɩ	äɩ	aɩ
ser*e*nity	ɛ̣	ɛ̣	ɛ	ser*e*ne	ɩ̝i	ɩ̣̝:	ë̝ɩ
ins*a*nity	æ	æ̣	a	ins*a*ne	ɛ̣ɩ	e̝ɩ	e̝:
c*o*nical	ä	ɒ	ɔ	c*o*ne	əɷ	öɷ	o̝:

(The [ɑ̟ɩ] in NYC is automatic before voiced segments.)

There are a sufficient number of these alternations, together with similar phenomena related to stress-placement (cf. §9 below) to support a claim that (B) is a unitary morphophonemic class. And the historical origins of

[1] Leaving aside occasional oddities like some New York speakers' [ˌəɷvə ˈhɩ] 'over here', [ˌəɷvə ˈd̪ɛ̣] 'over there', and much British [t^hä] 'ta'. The New York forms never represent speakers' norms, and *ta* is an isolated (and in this respect deviant) lexical item. A further criterion for distinguishing between the two sets is occurrence before /ŋ/: only set (A) occurs here (and not all of it), except in onomatopoetic forms like *boing*. But this is far less significant than the other environment.

[2] This argument is of course the basis of the Chomsky & Halle account of English vowel phonology, which we will consider later on in detail. The seeds of it are in Harris's remarks on English morphophonemics (1960: §14. 223).

the two classes are transparent: (A) is ME 'short' vowels, and (B) is ME 'long' vowels and diphthongs.

It is arguable whether this kind of data supports a 'derivational' solution, where say *divine* and *divinity* have the same lexical nucleus, and the surface divergences are the result of synchronic rules. This notion is the foundation of the Chomsky & Halle proposals, which I discuss in detail below. My own feeling is that the empirical support for such a claim is minimal (cf. Ohala 1973). But my argument here, though it is directed against the Chomsky & Halle account of the English vowel system, is not cast in terms of an attack on 'derivational phonology' as such (see Derwing 1973: ch. 4, for a nice one). Rather I am concerned only with the correct primitives for characterizing the English vowel system at some reasonably abstract level. Therefore (with one exception: §6) I am prepared to argue my case largely within the framework of generative phonology; and I will accept the possibility that paradigms like those in (2) can reasonably be generated by synchronic rule-sequences of any degree of length or complexity.

2. The Trager & Smith analysis

It seems clear that trichotomous analyses are too closely tied to unimportant surface details to be truly 'phonological' (though this does not excuse us from making detailed and accurate phonetic observations: see §4 below). So we are left with dichotomies. And I think that there are two proposals of this type that merit particularly serious considerations: Trager & Smith (1951), and Chomsky & Halle (1968: henceforth *SPE*). I will consider both of these in some detail, as they form a necessary background to my own proposals.

Operating within the methodological and theoretical framework of 'American structuralist' phonemics, Trager & Smith construct an elegant analysis based almost entirely on the classic 'taxonomic' phonemic criteria: distribution (complementation and commutability) and 'phonetic similarity', as well as the overall metacriteria of 'simplicity' and 'symmetry'. The details of their analytical procedure are familiar, and don't concern us here; but their results do.

Essentially Trager & Smith propose that all vocalic nuclei in English are phonologically either 'simple' or 'complex'. The simple nuclei consist of vowels alone, and the complex ones are sequences of vowel plus 'glide' or 'semivowel'. They recognize three of these glides: a fronting glide /y/, a backing glide /w/, and a centring glide /h/. Phonetically, /y/ is realized as a nonsyllabic vowel in the [i–e] range, /w/ as one in the [u–o] range, and /h/ as something in the general vicinity of [ə], or (after nonhigh vowels) as length. The glides are further taken as postvocalic instantiations of the initials of *you*, *woo*, *hue*, respectively, thus eliminating a set of extra elements from the system. We will see later that Chomsky & Halle have retained two thirds of this analysis in their system (/y/ and /w/), but have accounted for the phenomena grouped by Trager & Smith under 'postvocalic /h/' in a rather different way.

Trager & Smith were apparently not aware of the existence of vowels like [iː] in English ('Nowhere do we find a completely static tense long vowel of the type of...[i]'; p. 15): so their system is restricted to dialects that don't have such segments. But to take one that fits their set-up: the New York forms in (1) would be phonemicized this way:

(3)

bit	i	meet	iy
bet	e	mate	ey
bat	æ	boot	uw
put	u	boat	əw
pot	a	bought	ɔh
but	ə	father	ah
		suit	uw
		bite	ay
		doubt	æw
		quoit	ɔy

This is perfectly consistent with the phonological and morphophonemic facts discussed in §1: the dichotomization is the right one. We will see later that a somewhat similar analysis can handle dialects with steady-state long vowels as well.

The Trager & Smith system also embodies an attempt to define an 'overall pattern' that will (hopefully) characterize all the dialects of English; hence it has important theoretical implications outside the range of any one analysis. In the end they come up with a symmetrical nine-vowel system, each member of which may combine with one of the offglides /y w h/. And each dialect combines different elements from this overall inventory, which is thus effectively a kind of pan-English diasystem. The inventory is:

(4)

i	ɨ	u
e	ə	o
æ	a	ɔ

There are three heights, and three front/back dimensions, and each element has a delimited range of phonetic exponents. Thus the New York system above 'selects' /æ/ as the first element in the nucleus of *doubt*, but /a/ for that of *bite*; whereas RP selects /a/ for both. And while New York has phonemic /ə/ in *but*, Bridlington (I imagine) would have /u/, though this would raise problems with *put* (but Trager & Smith were apparently not acquainted with systems of this type).

Many significant dialect differentia are thus handled by Trager & Smith at the level of inventory; differentia of the type that Chomsky & Halle would handle by having different rules operate on the same underlying representations.

3. The Chomsky & Halle analysis

Perhaps the most widely accepted theory of the structure of the English vowel system today is the elaborate and ingenious one that Chomsky & Halle have developed in *SPE*. This account is not exactly equivalent to earlier ones, since it is programmatically 'non-taxonomic', and is not concerned with surface inventories in any detail (though as we will see it is in a way quite 'phonemic'). That is, in line with orthodox generative metatheory, it explicitly denies the theoretical status of phoneme inventories arrived at by analysis of surface contrasts, the validity of commutation-tests, etc. (The arguments are of course familiar: cf. especially Chomsky 1964, Householder 1965, Chomsky & Halle 1965).

As is well known, the foundation of this particular account of English vocalic phonology is a set of arguments based on (presumed) derivational processes which generate paradigms like those in (2) above: and perhaps its most striking feature is that none of the surface nuclei in group (B) are lexically represented in their phonetic forms. The phonetic representations are the result of complex chains of derivation critically dependent on lexical or post-lexical specification of vowels as [+tense].

I will outline – with some comment – the basic *SPE* theory, especially insofar as it deals with the lexical representations of English vowels. To begin with, the underlying inventory of English must be taken to be a subset of the 'universal' vowel inventory, which is characterized (cf. *SPE*: ch. VII) in terms of five binary features: [±high, ±low, ±back, ±round, ±tense]. The first four define basic articulatory configurations, and the last is, as we will see, not a 'proper' feature but a contentless dichotomizing operator. In terms of position and lip-attitude, the universal inventory is:

(5)

	−back		+back	
+high	i	ü	ɨ	u
−high −low	e	ö	ʌ	o
+low	æ	œ	a	ɔ
	−round	+round	−round	+round

With the addition of [±tense], we have 24 vowel types: /i ī e ē/, etc. (In the discussion that follows, I will in general use the *SPE* symbols when I am directly discussing Chomsky & Halle's claims; otherwise, e.g. in citing English data, etc., I will use those of the IPA. I will further assume that this 'universal' system is reasonable; but see ch. 4 below.)

These vowels represent the contrastive lexical types available to any language; but the features defining them are 'phonetic' as well as (merely) classificatory. Therefore the symbols used for lexical representation are (properly) available for phonetic transcriptions of utterances as well as for phonological representations of varying depths. Thus *SPE* gives the stressed nuclei of the forms in (2) this way:[1]

(6)

(A)		(B)	
div*i*nity	i	div*i*ne	āy
ser*e*nity	e	ser*e*ne	īy
ins*a*nity	æ	ins*a*ne	ēy
c*o*nical	a	c*o*ne	ōw

The surface realizations of (B), as well as the [a] in (A), are derived from quite different underlying forms by a series of rules that I will sketch out below. Whatever problems there may be with the 'reality' of the derivations, etc., it is possible to handle the phenomena within the *SPE* theory, but (a) without the tense/lax distinction, and (b) utilizing other possibilities that Chomsky & Halle themselves admit at other points in the theory. And this will enable us to achieve a much more satisfactory

[1] Considering Chomsky & Halle's general attitude toward 'impressionistic phonetics' (cf. ch. 7 below, § 1), it is hard to tell how a statement that the stressed nucleus of *divine* 'is [āy]' is to be taken. Since they continually cite forms 'in their dialect' as primary data, one would assume that the 'tense' [ā] in [āy] and the 'lax' [æ] in [æw] (e.g. in *profound*) are supposed to have some auditory correlates that correspond specifically to 'tenseness' and 'laxness'. But I have no idea what they might be. I will not press the point here: but we will see later (§4) that there is reason to doubt that these are really observation statements in the usual sense. The 'perceived tenseness' is really a bit disingenuous, i.e. it is derived from *a priori* phonological judgements, not from any kind of intersubjective reality. See also the discussion in the Appendix to this chapter.

account even of the *SPE* dialect, as well as covering dialects that *SPE* could account for only with difficulty.

Essentially the morphophonemic alternations of (2), as well as others like *profound/profundity*, are derived via the differential treatment of underlying tense and lax vowels by phonological rules. If a vowel is tense, and is not subject to any rules laxing it, it is input to a series of rules to be described below, including 'diphthongization' and 'vowel shift'. If it is laxed, then it surfaces ultimately in its post-laxing form, or with certain further modifications. Contrariwise, of course, an underlying lax vowel, if subject to a tensing rule, will surface the way its tense lexical congener does. Thus both *divinity* and *divine* have lexical nuclear /ī/; this is laxed in the antepenult of *divinity*, but in *divine* undergoes diphthongization to [īy], vowel shift (a) to [ēy], vowel shift (b) to [ǣy], and finally backness adjustment to [āy]. Without going into great detail, the vowel-shift complex consists of the following rules.

(i) Diphthongization. A homorganic 'glide' [y] or [w] is inserted after a tense vowel.

(ii) Vowel shift (a) and (b). Any tense vowel agreeing in backness and rounding (i.e. excluding lexical /ā/ and /œ̄/)[1] is input to these two rules. The first reverses the value for [high] on nonlow vowels, and the second reverses the value for [low] on nonhigh vowels.

(iii) Backness adjustment. A low tense vowel that emerges from (ii) reverses its value for [back].

(See the discussion in *SPE*: ch. IV.) These rules are presumed to operate on all forms of the general type included in group (B) in (1), as well as some others; but with special modifications in the case of *father*, *bought*, *suit*, which I exclude for now. These rules are originally established for the paradigmatic alternations, but are then extended by the 'free ride' principle to nonalternating forms with the proper nuclei, in the usual way. Thus the group (B) items below will have the following surface and underlying (lexical) nuclei:

(7)

	Surface	Lexical
meet	īy	ē
mate	ēy	ǣ
boot	ūw	ō
boat	ōw	ɔ̄
bite	āy	ī
doubt	æw	ū
quoit	ɔ̄y	œ̄

[1] *Father* has underlying /ā/ and *quoit* has /œ̄/.

(Since the /ǣ/ in *quoit* is [−back, +round], it does not undergo vowel shift; after diphthongization, the only rule that applies is backness adjustment.) So the forms in (7) will have the following (simplified) derivations (I omit the rule laxing [ǣ] in [ǣw], and some other minor processes):

(8)

Input	mēt	mǣt	bōt	bɔ̄t	bīt	dūt	kʷǣt
Diphthongization	ēy	ǣy	ōw	ɔ̄w	īy	ūw	ǣy
Vowel shift (a)	īy	—	ūw	—	ēy	ōw	—
Vowel shift (b)	—	ēy	—	ōw	ǣy	ɔ̄w	—
Backness adjustment	—	—	—	—	āy	ǣw	ɔ̄y
Output	mīyt	mēyt	būwt	bōwt	bāyt	dǣwt	kʷɔ̄yt

There are certain complications in deriving the phonetic representation of the nucleus of *suit*, etc. (*SPE* [yūw] from lexical /ɨ/) that are not directly relevant here. But what is relevant is a problem that arises in *father* and certain other forms. Now the vowel shift rule acts only on vowels agreeing in backness and rounding; thus /ǣ/ fails to undergo it. But what about /ā/? If this receives a homorganic glide, it becomes [āw], and this causes some trouble (*SPE*: 205):

For example, *father* and *Chicago* do not become phonetic *[fāwðər], *[šəkāwgōw], respectively; rather [ā] receives a centering glide of some sort, or a feature of extra length (with various dialectal differences that do not concern us here).[1]

That is, *father* and *Chicago* end up with a stressed nucleus that *SPE* represents as [āʌ].

Similar problems arise in other forms with surface [āʌ] (from underlying /æ/), and [ɔ̄ʌ] (from underlying /ā/ and /ū/). So there must be a way of getting phonetic clusters ending in [ʌ] from prephonetic sequences ending in [w]. The answer Chomsky & Halle arrive at is based on a previous argument (p. 203) to the effect that nuclear (not postvocalic) [ʌ] is to be derived from lexical /u/, e.g. in *but*. This is accomplished by adjusting the vowel shift rule so that certain lax vowels (including /u/)

[1] Two points: (a) these 'various dialectal differences' should be a matter of concern, precisely in case an analysis can be proposed that accounts for all of them under a single generalizing formula. And (b) if such a generalization is possible in one framework but not in another, this is an argument against the one that can't do it. I assume that a unitary analysis is more highly valued the more dialectal divergence within a language it can handle 'naturally'. Thus the 'other' dialects have a distinct bearing on the plausibility of an analysis of any one.

are subject to it. Thus /u/ becomes [o]. Then there is an additional rule of rounding adjustment, which (among other things) turns [o] to [ʌ]. So certain postvocalic [w] have to be converted to [u] before vowel shift, so that these [u] can undergo the rules described above.

The necessary transition is effected by a rule of 'glide vocalization', which 'makes the glide [w] vocalic when it follows [ā] or [ū] but not... other vowels' (p. 208). Other conditions on the rule are not relevant here. The rule itself is (p. 208, rule (74)):

(9) $$\begin{bmatrix} -\text{cons} \\ +\text{back} \end{bmatrix} \rightarrow [+\text{voc}] \; / \; \begin{bmatrix} \alpha \text{ round} \\ \alpha \text{ high} \\ \text{V} \end{bmatrix} \text{ —}$$

Thus we find the following initial stages in the derivations of *father*, *laud* (p. 206), *maudlin* (p. 208), *spa* (p. 215):

(10)	*father*	*laud*	*maudlin*	*spa*
	fāðVr	lād	mūdlin	spæ
	fāwðVr	lāwd	mūwdlin	spæw
	fāuðVr	lāud	mūudlin	spæu

Father, for instance, next becomes [fāoðVr] by vowel shift, and then [fāʌðVr] by rounding adjustment. Within the chosen framework, the arguments leading to these underlying forms, and the rules producing the various stages, seem to be well-motivated; but 'diphthongization' and 'glide vocalization' raise some serious questions. Let us note for now only three interesting pairs of sequences that occur in (10): [āw āu], [æw æu], and [ūw ūu]. These as we will see are the foundation upon which – with the help of some evidence and a rather different sort of argumentation – we can construct a more satisfactory proposal.

4. On the non-reality of postvocalic '[y w]'

What exactly does glide vocalization do? Its primary purpose seems to be to turn certain postvocalic [w] into [u] so that they can be acted on by the other ('independently motivated') rules and yield correct phonetic representations. But why are these [w] there in the first place? Apparently, because the diphthongization rule puts them there. But why does it? And the answer to this, I think, shows that glide vocalization is a pseudo-solution to a pseudo-problem. The postvocalic 'glides' in *SPE* are engendered by one of the more persistent *pseudodoxia epidemica* of recent English phonological studies: the curious notion that the second elements of English diphthongs are nonvowels.

Let us consider Chomsky & Halle's motivation for the crucial diphthongization rule (*SPE*: 183):

It is a well-known fact that English tense vowels are diphthongized or have offglides. For the nonback vowels [ī] and [ē], the glide is [y] (that is, high, nonback, nonround); for the back vowels [ū] and [ō], it is [w] (that is, high, back, round). Generalizing these *phonetic observations* [emphasis mine: RL] somewhat, let us simply give a rule of diphthongization to the effect that after *any* tense vowel, a high glide is inserted which agrees in backness with the vowel in question, and is, furthermore, nonround if nonback and round if back...

I emphasize the phrase 'phonetic observations' in the above quotation: because whatever the *SPE* analysis is based on, it's not 'phonetic observation' in the usual sense of this term. What Chomsky & Halle appear to 'observe', as far as I can tell, is Trager & Smith PHONEMIC representations. That is, what is involved here is a critical misconception about the nature of diphthongs; as we will see, a theoretical, not observational one in the strict sense, and one fostered by the American tradition in general. This colours what (I'm afraid) Chomsky & Halle take to be 'observations', but are in fact already 'phonemicizations' of a very specific type.[1]

There are two critical issues here: the major one of the 'glides', and the related one of 'tenseness'. I will deal with the 'tense' vowels first. Let us observe initially that there is a troublesome circularity in the passage above. First of all, 'tense' [ī ē] (which presumably represent the vowel types [i e]) never appear in the *SPE* dialect WITHOUT their glides. Second, the first element in the nucleus of say *meet* is never – at least in my experience of dialects of the type that the *SPE* analysis is based on – anything like [i], but something much more like [ɩ]. *SPE*, however, gives this nucleus as [īy]. If this is really, as I'm sure it must be, [ɩi], then there is no tense vowel phonetically; the macron over the [ī] must be a purely

[1] This is not to say that I believe in 'pure Baconian' observation; indeed, the whole question of what constitutes an 'observation statement' as opposed to a 'theoretical statement' is a complicated one, and it may be that no hard-and-fast distinction is possible. Any given 'observation' may in fact be merely a relegation to the status of 'background knowledge' or an 'extension of the sense' of certain theoretical claims: a shift in the locus of a theory rather than a 'perception'. Observation in any case is at least partly 'conventional', not the impression of 'reality' on a *tabula rasa* (see the discussion of this problem in Lakatos 1970, especially 108ff.). But, to return to 'convention', there are certainly publicly agreed-on canons of observations in phonetics, and I suspect that these are transgressed here. More on this below.

phonological – not phonetic – 'observation'. The vowel is in fact as 'lax' as the [æ] in [æw]. The only way we can identify it as 'tense' is by knowing *a priori* that it belongs to a lexical category designated as 'tense', i.e. that it derives from underlying /ē/ via vowel shift, etc. (Or, more to the point, I suspect, that *meet* historically has ME /ē/.) It is recognized, further, as tense by its 'glide', i.e. 'tense' = 'having a glide'. The statement that 'English tense vowels are diphthongized or have offglides' seems to mean simply that English vowels that are diphthongized or have offglides are diphthongized or have offglides.

I conclude that [+tense] is not a specification (like [+high]) that is verifiable in phonetic outputs. It must be a purely abstract 'diacritical' operator at a prephonetic level, which is projected onto phonetic representations by hindsight. Whether 'tenseness' is in fact a feature at all, in English or any other language, seems dubious (cf. the discussion in the appendix to this chapter). Certainly, given the *SPE* definition (324–5), which is anyhow parametric rather than polarizing, as a proper classificatory feature should be, there is no way of transcribing it, or even of recognizing it except proprioceptively. The only kind of test I can think of that would in fact make it specifiable and support their claim for it would be something like electromyography: if the increased muscular effort, etc., that they say characterize it exist, then there should be some instrumental verification.[1] Certainly Chomsky & Halle cite no such evidence, either for English or for any other language (the impressionistic descriptions they cite are obscure, and in any case irrelevant to English: the cineradiographic descriptions they cite on p. 325 are not to the point, since they depend on antecedent definitions of what is being looked at). I might add further that many of the vowel types which appear to be 'lax' by definition, like [ɛ] (= 'lax' [e]) appear in dialects of English with the standard stigmata of phonological 'tenseness', like length: there are certainly dialects with contrasting long and short [ɛ].

Let us return to the 'phonetic observation' of [y w] as postvocalic segments. First, note the distinction Chomsky & Halle make between vowels that are 'diphthongized' and those that have 'offglides'. Judging from their discussion, I presume that this means vowels plus [y w] as opposed to vowels plus [ʌ], etc. (Only the former type, we recall, are produced by the rule of diphthongization.) The distinction seems to be between what we might call 'true diphthongs' and vowel clusters. That

[1] For a model of the empirical testing of a feature by experimental techniques, see Ohala & Ohala (1972).

is, diphthongs with high nonsyllabics are a different kind of phonological animal from those with nonhigh ones. This is a venerable error; the other, that therefore the high nonsyllabics are nonvocalic, is more recent (specifically American), and equally unfounded. The first was discussed by Sweet nearly a century ago (1877: §§205–6):

Of the diphthongs in which the glide follows the vowel..., the most frequent are varieties of what might be called the (ai) and (au) types, as in 'h*i*gh' and 'h*ow*'. It has accordingly been laid down that in all diphthongs the movement must, as in these...be in the direction of narrowing, and that 'none others are genuine'.

Again, it has been assumed from the spelling *ai* and *au* that the second element of these typical diphthongs must necessarily be (i) and (u), whereas the fact is that they usually stop at some lower position.

Until these prejudices are got rid of, no one can attempt the very difficult task of analysing diphthongs into their elements.

(This misapprehension is not, by the way, endemic among American PHONETICIANS – only linguists. See for instance the discussion of diphthongs in Heffner 1950: §4.15. I will return below to the origins of the phonologists' error.)

Sweet further remarks on an interesting and relevant perceptual problem: that nonsyllabic vowels, under certain conditions, can sound higher than they actually are. He notes that 'Glides after front vowels which have an upward movement, and glides after back vowels which have a forward and upward, or simply forward movement, have the effect of [i]' (1877: §207.4). Thus a sequence [œe] may sound superficially like [œi], etc. But the point is, of course, that a properly trained observer will discriminate the two. And further, since both nonsyllabic [i] and [e], in this case, are possible, it is clear that a speaker's neuromuscular programme can discriminate the two, and tell him to make one just as easily as the other (in fact, it can tell him to make any other vowel in this context as well, as we will see).

It is easy to extend this perceptual difficulty further, I suppose, and 'hear' [j] (*SPE* [y]) after the nuclear vowel of *bite* or *beet*, and [w] in *doubt* or *boat*; but presumably linguists (especially phonologists) shouldn't be that naïve. And in this connexion it is particularly interesting that the 'observation' of [y w] – assuming that these mean IPA [j w], and are, further, distinct from [i̯ u̯] respectively – is simply not borne out by the observations of good field phoneticians. It is instructive that Trager & Smith, whose study of American English is based on superbly detailed and sophisticated phonetic observations, found no postvocalic 'glides' closer than [i u], and in general found them more like [ɪ ʊ] or even [e o] (1951: §§1.1–1.22).

Given these facts, we must now ask why these postvocalic segments should have been identified as allophones of the same phonemes that occur in the initial positions of *you*, *woo*. For Trager & Smith, the answer was obvious: the 'onglides' in these latter forms have (respectively) 'front vowel timbre' and 'back vowel timbre' (§1.32), and the initial of *woo* is rounded. And these segments vary with the height of succeeding vowels in much the same way as the postvocalic 'glides' vary with the height of preceding ones. And even though the 'onglides' before high vowels are [i̭^] and [ṷ^] ('raised' high vowels, i.e. nonvowel approximants), and these don't occur postvocalically, it is still true that say [i̭^ –] in *ye* and [– i̭] in *bee* are in complementary distribution. So they can be assigned to the same phoneme.

Two strands of argument have to be disentangled here. One is the claim that the initials of *woo* and *you* are nonvocalic, which is well supported; though the claim that they belong to some special category 'glide' is not. And the second is that if these segments are nonvowels, then the things that come after vowels, which (in some dialects anyhow) are similar must be nonvowels too. This second claim brings us back to complementary distribution again.

Now the grounds for taking initial '[y w]' as nonvocalic – or more strongly, as consonantal – are very good indeed. There are both phonetic and (morpho)phonological arguments, some of the most important of which are:

(i) Their 'marginal' syllable locus (post-pause or /C/, pre-/V/) is *par excellence* a consonantal position.

(ii) In many dialects, these segments are much more tightly occluded than in the forms Trager & Smith cite. In much Scots, for instance, the initial of *woo* is a labiodental or bilabial approximant, or even a weak fricative, with little if any velarization; and the initial of *you* is often a fricative [j]. Further, the 'voiceless *w*' in *what*, etc., is often [ɸ]. In addition, the segments that appear postvocalically in diphthongs are nothing like this: they are vowels of the [ɪ e] type in *bite*, and of the [u ʉ ÿ] type in *doubt*. Certainly it would be hard (without strong phonological evidence) to justify [ʋ] or [β] and [ÿ] being allophones of one phoneme. (This may of course be irrelevant: Scots might be simply a 'different language' in this regard.)

(iii) In most dialects of English, the element following the initial voiceless obstruent in *cute*, *quit*, etc. is voiceless; and in no case do high vowels devoice here, e.g. in *keep*, *coop*.

(iv) The only other 'normally' voiced segments that show a strong tendency to devoice in the same environments are /r l/, e.g. in *creep*, *clean*, *croup*, *clue*. Nasals do not appear here; but in a similar environment, after voiceless fricatives, '/y w/' devoice, as do /r l/, but nasals do not: *fume*, *sweep*, *free*, *sleep*, with voiceless second segments ([fj̊u:m], etc.), but voiced second segments in *snoop*, *sneak*, *smooth*, *smear*.[1]

(v) The definite and indefinite articles take their preconsonantal forms before these segments: *a year*, *a war* where *a* is [ə], *the year*, *the war*, where *the* is [ðə] (cf. Gimson 1965: 207 on the last two points, and Lass & Anderson 1975: 'Preliminaries').

In this light, it seems most reasonable to classify these segments as 'liquids', i.e. as the respectively palatal and labiovelar congeners of /r l/. (A similar suggestion has been made for Russian /j/ and /j w/ in other languages by Fergusson 1962.)[2] But dosn't this miss a generalization? It is neater if these segments belong to the same class as postvocalic [i u], etc. Otherwise, we have a 'defective distribution': /y w/ can appear only before vowels. The best answer, I think, is 'so what?' Certainly English [ŋ] is restricted to postvocalic position, and [h] to prevocalic. (Of course Trager & Smith get out of this one by having /h/ appear postvocalically as well, but this is a fiddle; and Chomsky & Halle derive it from /x/, which also appears preconsonantally, as in *right* < /rixt/; though it doesn't appear postvocalically unless an obstruent follows.)

There appears to me to be nothing wrong with defective distributions: within limits. They are a fact about natural languages, and we will have them as long as languages continue to change. (Though to be sure, generative phonology can often arrest the processes of change, as it were, by postponing restructuring until the last possible minute.) The present distribution of /h/ in English is a good example of this. [h] was once an allophone of /x/, which appeared in all positions; in early OE it was deleted intervocalically, and later on (except in Scots and a scatter of other dialects) it vanished before consonants. Now it remains (in those

[1] Not all dialects devoice /r l/ and '/y w/' after voiceless stops. To be strictly accurate, this generalization holds only, as far as I know, for those dialects that aspirate prevocalic /p t k/. The devoicing is then an assimilation to the voicelessness of the post-occlusive [h], not that of the stop. Those dialects that have unaspirated initial /p t k/ usually have fully voiced /r l/, etc. following them.

[2] Cf. also the discussion and references in Fischer-Jørgensen (1975: 228).

dialects that have it at all) only initially (cf. Vachek 1964: ch. 2). The case with the two 'glides' is the same, more or less: in OE they were consonantal segments which could appear both before and after vowels, so that (still considering them to be 'glides') there was a genuine /VV/ vs. /VG/ contrast. But in ME they were subject to a rule of postvocalic vocalization, and became high vowels; the subsequent development of English has isolated them (see Lass & Anderson 1975: ch. VI for details).

In other words, while the distributional arguments for the identification of say the initials and finals of *woo*, *ye* (*SPE* [wūw], [yīy]) have some force, the phonetic evidence and phonological arguments seem to me to be stronger. At least I would prefer to assign the initials to a class like 'liquid', and the finals to 'vowel'; since any 'generalization' we might lose in this way is in any case only a distributional one, and the explanatory yield of taking the finals as vowels seems quite high. In this case, unfortunately, *tertium non datur*: it is impossible to interpret the initials as vowels, as the arguments above suggest. So if the finals are in fact vowels, then the two sets of segments cannot belong to the same class.

In partial summary: it seems clear that any 'observation' of postvocalic nonvowel 'glides' in English is already a phonemicization, and an arguable one at that. There are no phonetic grounds for assuming that 'high' postvocalic approximants (which are often mid anyhow) are anything but vowels; and therefore no grounds for taking 'centring glides' (i.e. vowels like [ə]) to belong to some different class; and certainly these cannot by any stretch of the imagination be called nonvocalic.[1] The only justification for having two phonologically distinct complex nucleus types, and therefore incorporating into the grammar elaborate machinery to get rid of one of them, is a conjunction of the analytical prejudice so neatly anatomized by Sweet with an internalization of Trager & Smith's own analytical prejudice. This conjunction is apparently then projected into the realm of 'phonetic observation', and the results of this are fed back into the phonological analysis.

Interestingly enough, one of the results of *SPE*'s phonemicizing the

[1] Of course Trager & Smith took postvocalic [ə] as an allophone of /h/; but they were not (particularly) conconcerned with phonetic specifiability at the classificatory level. Chomsky & Halle, however, claim to be after 'naturalness' and 'optimality' of interlevel mapping, so they are not immune to criticism from this angle.

complementary initial and postvocalic 'glides' together is the creation of another complementation, this time on the feature level: in postvocalic position in phonetic representations. Note that the following two types of phonetic complex nuclei, and these only, are allowed by *SPE*:

(11) [īy]-type [āʌ]-type

$$\begin{bmatrix} -\text{cons} \\ +\text{voc} \end{bmatrix} \begin{bmatrix} -\text{cons} \\ -\text{voc} \\ +\text{high} \end{bmatrix} \qquad \begin{bmatrix} -\text{cons} \\ +\text{voc} \end{bmatrix} \begin{bmatrix} -\text{cons} \\ +\text{voc} \\ -\text{high} \end{bmatrix}$$

That is, since 'glides' are $\begin{bmatrix} -\text{cons} \\ -\text{voc} \end{bmatrix}$, but vowels are $\begin{bmatrix} -\text{cons} \\ +\text{voc} \end{bmatrix}$, the feature-specifications [+voc] and [+high] are in complementary distribution in postvocalic nonconsonants. This is the consequence of identifying prevocalic and postvocalic 'glides' as both nonvowels, and the attendant 'two-kinds-of-diphthongs' assumption.

I have already suggested that complementary distribution itself is not a terribly important criterion: there is always the case of [h] and [ŋ] (even though here one might invoke 'phonetic similarity': but are [j] and [ɩ] all that similar?) I think though that on the basis of the preceding discussion, the situation in (11) does indeed suggest the loss of a real generalization, not the spurious one that is produced by taking say a prevocalic [w] and a postvocalic [u] to belong to the same underlying unit. In that case there are both phonetic and phonological counter-arguments; in this one, dissolution of the apparent complementation between [+voc] and [+high] works the other way, both phonetically and phonologically, as we will see. Clearly both [+voc] and [+high] should be allowed to appear together in a postvocalic segment that is also [−cons].

But it is interesting that even this complementation does not occur – necessarily – at prephonetic stages of derivation. There (cf. (10)) we can have sequences with postvocalic high VOWELS as well, e.g. [āu æu ūu]. These however, for Chomsky & Halle, are of no 'theoretical interest': the stages where they appear are not 'significant levels', i.e. they are neither 'systematic phonetic' nor 'systematic phonemic'. What appears in 'intermediate' derivational stages does not – apparently – have ANY necessary relation to phonetic output, except the possibility of being turned into it by 'natural' or 'motivated' rules. Actually, however, what appears here IS both interesting and important: it is the key to the proper representation of English vowel contrasts.

5. On accounting for dialects with long vowels

Note that the difference between nuclei of the types [aw] and [au] – which seems to be nonexistent in English – is 'distinctive' in the *SPE* theory. A pair of morphemes can potentially at least be distinguished only by the feature that distinguishes [w] and [u]. And any rule effecting a change of one to the other alters not only a classificatory feature, but one near the top of the hierarchy, a 'major class feature'; and changes like this have no phonetic motivation in English (though they have had in the past, and do in other languages: cf. Brown 1970).

Now if we accept that there is no justification for postvocalic 'glides', since the nuclear types /VG/ and /VV/ do not contrast in English, as only the second type exists; and if the opposition [+tense]/[−tense] is (at least for English) circular and phonetically meaningless (cf. §4 and the appendix to this chapter), where does this leave us? After all, both 'glides' and 'tenseness' were introduced for a reason. I now contend that if we get rid of these two dubious factors, we are not worse off than before, but better; because it is perfectly possible to handle the phenomena that Chomsky & Halle consider central to English vocalic phonology without resort to either of them. And further, without any rule of 'diphthongization' in their sense, and without any 'vocalization'. In addition, the analysis that results from this purging operation will permit us to handle a wide spectrum of dialect types in a simple and natural way, which would not be possible within the *SPE* framework proper.

We can approach this by considering the widespread dialects that have a number of monophthongal long vowels in the forms of group (B) in (1). How do we represent a long vowel? *SPE* doesn't tell us specifically how to do this (except that they assume that 'tenseness' can somehow be realized as length). But in some of the derivations they give we can see the elements of a natural answer. First of all, what is meant by a representation like [e:]? Presumably the symbol [:] means 'an extra mora of length', i.e. the articulation of an [e] carried over without interruption into another temporal unit beyond 'its own'. Thus [e:] is another way of writing [ee], under the assumption that – *ceteris paribus* – the space between two brackets normally filled by one symbol represents, for a given language, the time-span appropriate to a single mora for some segment type.

If this is so, then a representation like [ee] is paralleled in some *SPE* derivations by one like [æu]: the only difference being that in the latter case the two vowels in sequence are not identical. But even the possibility of (positionally) identical vowels in sequence is provided for in representations like [ūu]. So I suggest that a reasonable 'systematic phonetic' representation for a steady-state ('monophthongal') long vowel is a sequence of two identical vowels. Recall also that Chomsky & Halle specifically note that in *father*, etc., some dialects show 'a feature of extra length': so they would have to account for phonetic representations like [ɑ:] in some way. I claim that this 'feature' is in fact not a feature but a segment. Under this interpretation both long vowels and diphthongs have the structure /VV/, as opposed to short vowels, which are /V/. The dichotomy in English – even at the phonetic level – is then /V/ vs. /VV/: the difference between long vowels and diphthongs is simply a matter of identity or nonidentity of nuclear constituents. Thus long vowels are /V_iV_i/, and diphthongs are /V_iV_j/, where 'i', 'j' are any potentially distinctive feature specifications. (See §8 below.)

I will now examine the consequences of this view for a derivation in a dialect with long vowels, and then go on to the *SPE* dialect. We must determine whether this analysis has more to recommend it than phonetic accuracy (not that this is so bad). Let us take a dialect that has [i:] in *meet* and [e:] in *mate*, a quite common type in the North of England. How do we generate these forms, assuming that [VV] is equivalent to [V:]? Let us attempt this within the *SPE* tense/lax framework. If we begin with underlying /mēt/, /mǣt/, we can get this far with the orthodox rules:

(12)			
	Input	mēt	mǣt
	Diphthongization	mēyt	mǣyt
	Vowel shift (a)	mīyt	—
	Vowel shift (b)	—	mēyt

Then we need two additional rules: an extension of glide vocalization to turn [īy] to [īi], and [ēy] to [ēi]; and a rule to assimilate the second element in [ēi] to the first. So the derivation continues:

(13)			
	Output of (12)	mīyt	mēyt
	Vocalization	mīit	mēit
	Height assimilation	—	mēet

At this point we probably have to deal with the second elements of the diphthongs. If 'lax' [i e] = (IPA) [ɩ ɛ], then the clusters [īi] and [ēe] will surface as *[iɩ], *[eɛ], respectively. So we need a rule of tenseness assimilation; the second vowels in the clusters will take on the tenseness values of the first ones. The derivation finishes this way:

(14)	Output of (13)	mīit	mēet
	Tenseness assimilation	mīīt	mēēt

The output forms are equivalent then to [mi:t], [me:t].

At this point we ought to start looking for some other way of deriving long vowels. It seems clear that the feature [+tense], rather than being a source of insight, is an embarrassment; and I have already shown that there is no evidence for [y w]. The way out seems fairly clear: instead of restricting vowel clusters to phonetic (or at least post-lexical) representations, let us extend them to the lexical level. Since the surface representations of (B) are – for all dialects – vowel clusters anyhow, we can bypass the whole diphthongization/vocalization complex, and derive the phonetic forms directly from an underlying representation that is itself phonetically plausible.

So let us represent all the group (B) forms in the lexicon, not with single vowels marked [+tense], but with geminate vowels. Thus *meet*, *mate*, will be respectively /meet/, /mææt/ rather than /mēt/, /mǣt/. We could then revise the vowel shift rule so that it applied to clusters only, not to single vowels with a diacritic specification. So instead of the *SPE* vowel shift, which I give below as (15a), we would have (15b):[1]

(15) (a) *SPE vowel shift*

$$\begin{bmatrix}\gamma\ \text{back}\\ \gamma\ \text{round}\end{bmatrix} \rightarrow \left\{\begin{array}{l}[-\alpha\ \text{high}]\ /\ \left[\begin{bmatrix}\overline{\quad\quad}\\ \alpha\ \text{high}\\ -\text{low}\end{bmatrix}\right]\\[2em] [-\beta\ \text{low}]\ /\ \left[\begin{bmatrix}\overline{\quad\quad}\\ \beta\ \text{low}\\ -\text{high}\end{bmatrix}\right]\end{array}\right\}\ /\ \begin{bmatrix}\overline{\quad\quad}\\ +\text{tense}\\ +\text{stress}\end{bmatrix}$$

(b) *Revised vowel shift*

$$\text{(i) SD: } \underset{1}{\begin{bmatrix}\alpha\ \text{high}\\ -\text{low}\\ +\text{stress}\end{bmatrix}} \underset{2}{\begin{bmatrix}\alpha\ \text{high}\\ -\text{low}\end{bmatrix}} \quad \text{SC: } \underset{1}{[-\alpha\ \text{high}]}\ \underset{2}{[-\alpha\ \text{high}]}$$

$$\text{(ii) SD: } \underset{1}{\begin{bmatrix}\beta\ \text{low}\\ -\text{high}\\ +\text{stress}\end{bmatrix}} \underset{2}{\begin{bmatrix}\beta\ \text{low}\\ -\text{high}\end{bmatrix}} \quad \text{SC: } \underset{1}{[-\beta\ \text{low}]}\ \underset{2}{[-\beta\ \text{low}]}$$

$$\text{Condition on (i, ii): 1, 2} = \begin{bmatrix}\gamma\ \text{back}\\ \gamma\ \text{round}\end{bmatrix}$$

[1] I take the preliminary version of the rule (*SPE*: 190) for convenience. The full version (243) could be handled the same way.

This at least would be the general format. I will return to some matters of formalism below.

In the revised framework, the derivations of *meet*, *mate* in the dialect under consideration would be:

(16)			
	Input	meet	mææt
	Vowel shift (i)	miit	—
	Vowel shift (ii)	—	meet
	Output	miit	meet
		(= [mi:t]	= [me:t])

Compare (12–14). Instead of at least four rules in the derivation of each form (five in *mate*), we need only one: and the phonetic representations come out the same. But the nonattested [Vy] stage doesn't appear, and consequently we don't need a special rule of 'vocalization' to get rid of it. (I assume that the fewer of such 'rescue rules' (Zwicky 1973) we have, the better the grammar is.) And there is no need for 'diphthongization' either, because the effect of this (a two-segment nucleus) is given in the lexicon. And further, the dubious 'tenseness' is not needed, because the well-motivated configuration /VV/ of the nuclei triggers the rules affecting them.[1] I would think that any 'loss of value' incurred by the more extensive specification of (15b) is offset by the elimination of other rules, and the consequent shortening of the derivation (aside from the phonetic considerations I have been emphasizing throughout).

Now what if we used the same underlying representations as in (16) for the *SPE* dialect, where the phonetic representations of the forms are something like [mɩit], [meɩt]? (I assume that these are reasonable interpretations of what [mīyt], [mēyt] must mean, once we reject postvocalic 'glides' and 'tenseness'). There are certainly a number of ways to handle this, none of them any more *ad hoc* than *SPE*'s 'diphthongization' and subsequent 'glide vocalization' (which latter, *pace* Chomsky & Halle, ALL their forms must go through to yield the correct phonetic output). For instance, all postvocalic vowels except those after [a ɔ] could be raised to [+high] at an appropriate point, thus giving [ei] in *mate*, but keeping [aʌ] in *father*, [ɔʌ] in *laud*, etc. Or, more in line with what I suspect the phonetic facts actually are, these nuclei could be represented at

[1] We might possibly also need some other way to specify contrasts like [ɛ] vs. [e:] 'long and short of the same vowel'. This could be done by low-level rules that map /i e/ into [ɩ ɛ], if such a mapping is needed: but the notion 'corresponding pair' of vowels is dubious for English. (See the discussion in the appendix to this chapter.) In any case, there is nothing (except the *SPE* feature system) that prevents /ɩ/ and /ɛ/ from being primitive lexical types.

the systematic phonetic level as [aa] and [ɔɔ], with a low-level phonetic rule reducing nonhigh vowels to [ə] after other vowels. And so on.

I might note here that we COULD make a less radical departure from *SPE* by having tense monophthongs in the lexicon, and having a 'diphthongization' rule that inserts high vowels after other vowels marked [+tense]. But this will raise other difficulties, since as we will see there is no particular motivation for having the epenthesized segments be [+high], but good evidence that they should be the same as the preceding ones. In this case we would gain nothing; we might as well have the clusters in the lexicon.

Before going any further, I should note that a vowel-cluster framework poses no particular formal problems. Any process that can be handled under the 'lax'/'tense' system can be equally well handled under the 'single'/'double' one. If for instance /V/ is equivalent to /V̆/, and /VV/ to /V̄/, there is a very natural way of handling *SPE*'s processes of 'tensing' and 'laxing'. Any rule of 'tensing' is vowel epenthesis, and any 'laxing' is a deletion. Thus, schematically:

(17)	*SPE*	*Two-vowel system*
	V → [+tense]/ —— Q	∅ → V/V —— Q
	V → [−tense]/ —— Q	V → ∅ /V —— Q

As far as I can tell, the cluster analysis can handle all the rule types that the other can; and furthermore, it can capture directly, as we will see, relationships and typological differentia that are only indirectly statable (if at all) in the *SPE* framework.

6. The *SPE* vowel shift in a /V/ vs. /VV/ grammar

The revision of the vowel shift rule in (15b) is inadequate, as a little consideration will show. That is, while it will account perfectly well for the results of vowel shift in *meet*, *mate*, *boot*, *boat*, it will not work for *bite*, *about*. These latter forms require – for correct output – that the first and second vowels remain distinct throughout the shift. Otherwise /ii/ in *bite* will go to [ee] and then [ææ], and /uu/ in *about* will go to [oo] and then to [ɔɔ]; backness adjustment will then convert these respectively to [aa], [ææ], so that *bite* will have the same nucleus as *father*.

The simplest way to block this, while still keeping within the RULE framework of *SPE*, is to prohibit vowel shift from applying to both elements of a divocalic nucleus just in case they are both LEXICALLY [+high]. That is, we impose a derivational constraint that says:[1]

(18)
If a nucleus is lexically of the form [+high] [+high], both stages of vowel shift apply to its leftmost member only.[2]

If we allow this, the derivations for *meet*, *mate*, *boot*, *boat*, *bite*, *about* are quite straightforward. All we need is a rule (for the *SPE* dialect and similar ones) to raise the nonsyllabics in *mate*, *boat* to [+high]. Under this analysis, it is the PRESENCE of this one rule of postvocalic raising – rather than the ABSENCE of the complex of rules required for generating steady-state long vowels in (12–14), that distinguishes this dialect from one with long vowels in these forms.

This is another piece of support, in a sense, for my proposal. For it is certainly historically proper that a dialect with [ei] in *mate* and [ou] in *boat*, say, should show an extra rule in comparison with one that has [e:] and [o:]. The former dialects are innovatory here: these diphthongs are a late development (as in fact Chomsky & Halle note in their discussion of the history of the English vowel system: ch. VI, §5, on the orthoëpic testimony of Batchelor). It seems to me an error to take an innovating American dialect as a 'norm', and characterize a conservative British one with long vowels as having an 'extra' rule. The correct statement, if grammars can in any sense 'recapitulate history', is the reverse.

[1] On the general motivation for derivational constraints see Kisseberth (1969). There is an extensive literature on the subject, much of it summed up in Dinnsen (1972).

[2] Even without a derivational constraint, this could be handled by a 'readjustment' rule like this:

$$\begin{bmatrix} \text{V} \\ +\text{high} \end{bmatrix} \rightarrow [-\text{Vowel shift}] \;/\; \begin{bmatrix} \text{V} \\ +\text{high} \end{bmatrix} \;\rule{1em}{0.4pt}$$

This would certainly have the desired effect. But there are (at least on historical grounds) reasons for preferring the constraint, which treats the divocalic high clusters as aberrant units. (In any case, the rule above is probably notationally equivalent to the constraint.) I prefer the unitary treatment, however, because of the exceptionality of the high vowels in the historical vowel shift (cf. chapter 2 below), and because I object in principle to rules introducing 'minus rule' features (cf. Lass 1973b).

A derivational constraint of the kind I propose could be accused of being purely *ad hoc*; but this is not necessarily bad. *Ad hoc* formulations are clearly necessary, though they should be restricted to those aspects of a language that are irreducibly idiosyncratic. The constraint directly reflects disorder in an 'optimal' structure due to a historical cause; so it is 'justified' in the sense that it is simply a piece of reporting. Thus, if there is a synchronic vowel shift, and if the /VV/ analysis is justifiable, then we need a constraint to block diphthongization; and this constraint reflects the embedding in the synchronic grammar of the structure of its historical origins (cf. ch. 2, §§3–4 below).

The two-vowel analogue to the derivations shown above in (9) will be (19) below; I omit *quoit*, to which I return shortly:

(19)

	meet	*mate*	*boot*	*boat*	*bite*	*doubt*
Input	ee	ææ	oo	ɔɔ	ii	uu
Vowel shift (i)	ii	—	uu	—	ei	ou
Vowel shift (ii)	—	ee	—	oo	æi	ɔu
Backness adjustment	—	—	—	—	ai	æu
Nonsyllabic raising	—	ei	—	ou	—	—
Output	ii	ei	uu	ou	ai	æu

(Some late rule can change [ii] to [ɩi] and [uu] to [ʊu] if need be, and shift the other final [i u] to [ɩ ʊ].)

So much for the general equivalence of my proposals to those of *SPE*, and the possible advantages of my analysis even within a generative account. I turn now to one serious argument that can be levelled against my proposals from the *SPE* point of view: my analysis cannot handle the derivation of [ɔi] in *quoit* naturally, if I begin with my equivalent to *SPE*'s /ǣ/, which is of course /ææ/. At least we would need a very odd rule to raise the second member from low to high, and then to unround it. And this would have no motivation whatever within the general derivational set-up: it would be totally *ad hoc*.

I agree: and at this point change tack a bit. Up to now I have been (aside from a few incidental remarks), conducting the PHONOLOGICAL part of this discussion within the bounds of the *SPE* model, and assuming tacitly that their goals are the right ones. I cannot accept this here, however: I claim rather that the inability of my system to generate [ɔi] naturally from /ææ/ is not an argument against it, but one in its favour. I take it that the more tightly constrained an analysis is, the 'richer' and more 'highly valued' it is. There may be something to a theory that can derive [æu] in *profound* and [ʌ] in *profundity* from the same lexical source; but if that analysis can be extended so that a representation like /ææ/ for the source of [ɔi] can be given a free ride on the rules established for the other case, then it should be penalized, not rewarded.

The reason for this is simple. The arguments that Chomsky & Halle use to get say /ū/ in *profound*, and ultimately in *doubt*, are based initially on paradigmatic alternations. These alternations are the primary reason for having any rules at all. That is, 'optimization' or some such principle should lead the child to extend the derivation of [æu] in *profound* to the nonalternating case of *doubt* (if children are really that clever, which seems unlikely). At any rate, if phonological analyses are to be 'justified' in the orthodox way, with reference to language acquisition, this is the direction of such an attempt. But [ɔi] is the one nucleus in group (B) that participates in NO alternations at all. At least I don't see any reason to take e.g. *point/punctual*, *joint/juncture* and the like to be 'synchronically related'. Unless of course we're writing a grammar, not for a normal English-speaking child, but for an etymologist. In which case we could derive *right*, *regular*, *rectum* from underlying /regt-/, and *cow*, *beef* and *bovine* from /gʷō-/, etc. The point is that an analysis which excludes [ɔi] from the 'regular' morphophonemics of English shows a proper appreciation of its 'peripheral' status (in the Praguian sense: cf. Vachek 1964). That is, it is not a native nucleus, it participates in no alternations, its functional load is low compared to the other group (B) vowels, etc. Therefore it should not be given a free ride on the rules that govern 'real' alternations, but should be entered in the lexicon as /ɔi/.

This does of course wreck the symmetry of the underlying system: let us refer to Chomsky & Halle's motivating arguments for the choice of /ǣ/ in the first place (*SPE*: 191–2):

> Notice...that we have no vowel-glide sequences in the lexicon...since [æw] and [āy] derive from /ū/ and /ī/, respectively. Hence the lexical redundancy rules will be much simpler if we can represent [ɔ̄y], too, as a monophthong V* on the lexical level. The optimal solution would be to take V* as some vowel which fills a gap in the phonological system and which is converted to phonetic [ɔ̄y] by independently motivated rules. In fact, this optimal solution can be obtained in this case.

Of course it CAN: but the argument, 'if [ɔ̄y] can be /ǣ/, then the vowel shift will cover it' reminds me a bit of the argument type 'if my aunt had wheels she'd be a bicycle'. There is a limit to how far we can allow metacriteria to dictate the form of what are after all supposed to be 'psychologically real' entities.[1] It seems to me that the cost of following *SPE* here is too great, and the whole effort misdirected. Because the truth of the matter is, not that [ɔi] 'fills a gap in the phonological system', but that it is more like an excrescence on it. The excessive power of the

[1] Again, I am taking a point of view 'within the paradigm', for the sake of argument. I am not convinced, however, that any formal argument can be said to have any bearing on 'psychological reality'; I suspect that such extrapolation is a category mistake (cf. Botha & Winckler 1973: ch. 4 on the methodological shakiness of this type of extrapolation). Finally, I am not convinced that 'psychological reality' is a particularly interesting or relevant goal for linguistic theory; at the moment, it does not even seem to be an intelligible one.

theory here creates a monolith (where '*tout se tient*') out of a system that is clearly a good deal less orderly: as is in fact to be expected in a natural language.

7. Some dialect evidence for vowel-clustering

I have proposed so far that since (a) there is no justification for 'vowel-glide' sequences in English, and (b) *SPE* admits vowel clusters at some derivational stages anyway (including nonhigh nonsyllabics in phonetic representations), we should represent all group (B) nuclei in the lexicon with two vowels. And this should apply *a fortiori* to [ɔi], which here would be the only 'true' diphthong; though the distinction is pretty trivial if all the other (B) nuclei are vowel clusters anyhow. I want to explore in this section some further evidence bearing on this proposal, specifically the dialect distributions of certain nuclear types.

I suggested earlier (p. 12n) that one good argument for a particular analysis might be the range of cognate dialect types it accounts for under the same rubric. The more of the variety of English dialects a given proposal can naturally subsume, the better (*ceteris paribus*) an account of English phonology-as-a-whole it is. Recall Sweet's comment cited earlier (§4) on the notion that 'genuine' diphthongs are those where the movement is in the direction of 'narrowing'. In many dialects of English these are of course the commonest; but in many others there is a wealth of diphthongal nuclei whose second elements are either (a) opener than the first (even to the extent of being fully open), or (b) of the same height as the (nonhigh) first one. And these types occur even in words of the *meet*, *mate*, *boot*, *boat* classes. Further, while many of these dialects show diphthongs of the 'narrowing' type as well, they also have monophthongal long vowels, and the combination of non-narrowing diphthongs and long vowels outweighs the 'normal' narrowing type.

Here are two fairly typical examples. In Haddon-on-the-Wall, Northumberland (SED network area 1. 8)[1] we find: [ɩø] in *boot*, [øə] in *foal*, [ea] in *spade*; [i:] in *sheep*, *do*, [u:] in *about*, [a:] in *saw*, and [ø:] in *snow*. The narrowing diphthongs are [ɔɩ] in *boil*, [ɛ̤̈ɩ] in *white*, [ɩu:] in

[1] Data from Orton & Halliday (1962). SED = Survey of English Dialects. I cite the actual forms recorded by the SED, rather than representatives of the categories in (1), because these dialects have had such divergent historical developments that comparison with the 'standard' types would be unhelpful. On the general history of the North Midland dialects see Hedevind (1967) and chapter 3 below; for detail on the North, Orton (1933).

suit, and [ɔɷ] in *grow*. Another type can be exemplified by Dentdale (Yorkshire, W.R.: Hedevind 1967). Here we have [ię] in *beat* (distinct from *beet*, which has [əi]), [ea] again in *spade*, and [ua] in *smoke*, as well as long [e:] in *bait*, [ɔ:] in *all*, [a:] in *know*. The narrowing diphthongs are the above-mentioned [əi], plus [aɩ] in *white*, [ɔɩ] in *boil*, [ɩu] in *new*, and [aɷ] in *about*; and there are a few forms with [əu], like *coop*, *pull*.

All of this only goes to show that both long vowels and diphthongs with nonhigh second elements are quite 'normal' for English; even when the elements are as far apart as [u] and [a]. Clearly this argues for both elements of diphthongs being taken as vowels: otherwise we need a vastly extended range of 'vocalization' rules, to give us input to an equally large set of lowering rules.

As a final example of a dialect type where a vowel cluster treatment seems infinitely preferable to a tense vowel/diphthongization one, consider Harwood, Lancs. (SED area 5. 12). Here the only 'true' diphthong is the reflex of ME /oi/. Otherwise – using the forms in (1) as examples of the etymological categories – the vocalic nuclei are:[1]

(20)

(A)		(B)	
bit	ɩ	beet	i:
bet	ɛ	mate	e:
bat	a	boot	ʏ:
pot	ɒ	boat	o:
but	ɷ	bought	ɔ:
		suit	ʏ:
		bite	a:
		doubt	ɛ:
		quoit	ɛɩ

A vowel cluster analysis of a dialect like this has considerable synchronic and historical advantages. Synchronically, they are obvious: there is only one item in the whole inventory that looks even remotely like something in an *SPE*-type dialect, with at least highish second elements in group (B). The conversion from *SPE* underlying representations would be laborious and unmotivated; and yet the same cluster analysis that could handle these nuclei naturally could also derive all the *SPE* forms; and

[1] *Father* is omitted, as in these dialects it usually belongs to the *bat* or *mate* classes. The other source of long low vowels that we find e.g. in RP – lengthening of ME /a/ before voiceless fricatives and certain /NC/ clusters, is not operative here (cf. ch. 4 below): though there are generally [a:]-type vowels before (historical) /r/. But I omit these, as I am not sure whether there is a synchronic postvocalic /r/ here, and in any case I am interested only in 'autonomous' segments.

derive them with an increase in phonetic accuracy and a decrease in unmotivated stages, as I showed above.

Historically, an analysis that posits double vowels at least as far back as ENE will clarify, among other things, the odd nuclei in *bite* and *about*; these derive from [ai] and [ɛu] respectively, which in turn go back to ME /ii/ and /uu/. Forms like these are very widespread, and the processes involved are simple. In each case we have assimilation of the second element to the first, a very common form of 'monophthongization' (more on this in the next section). And similarly, the [ʏ:] in *suit* derives from mutual assimilation of [iu]: the first element takes on the rounding of the second and the second the frontness of the first. The [ʏ:] in *boot* is simpler, as there has been nothing except centralization here: this is from ME /yy/, which is in turn from /øø/ from earlier /oo/ (cf. Lass 1972, and chapters 2 and 3 below). It seems clear that it would be inordinately wasteful and obtuse to handle this history in *SPE* terms, with rules operating on tense vowels, etc. And conversely, the history as well as the synchrony of other dialects can easily be accommodated in the vowel-cluster framework.

I conclude that there is good reason for taking the underlying dichotomy in all dialects of English that have one (i.e. except Scots: cf. ch. 2, § 1 below) as being of the form /V/ vs. /VV/, where /V/ is 'short monophthong' and /VV/ is 'long vowel or diphthong'. The only difference between the latter two types is the identity or non-identity of the nuclear constituents.

8. Some remarks on 'moricness' and sound change

There is of course nothing radically new about bimoric interpretations of long vowels. There was a time when they were quite popular, and they are now undergoing something of a revival.[1] The problem is not – in principle – the justification of a major theoretical departure, but an

[1] For bimoric analyses of the historical development of English vowels, see especially Vachek (1959), and for Old English Wagner (1969), Anderson (1971). For a more detailed treatment, with special attention to Old English phonology in general and the developments in later periods, see Lass & Anderson (1975). Synchronic /VV/ analyses have also been proposed for West Greenlandic (Rischel 1974), and (in part) for Lithuanian (Kenstowicz 1970) and Estonian (Lehiste 1970). It has also been suggested that 'length' in general may be universally a clustering phenomenon by Woo (1972). She deals largely with the claim that all 'contour' tones are phonologically sequences of steady-state tones, each bound to an individual sonorant segment; but she also makes some interesting remarks on diphthongization and similar phenomena, somewhat along the lines suggested here (cf. especially ch. 2).

exploration of the consequences of a reasonably established notion for an area where it has not been rigorously applied.

From a historical point of view, one of the great difficulties with the *SPE* analysis is that there is no natural relationship between 'tense' vowels and diphthongs. In the synchronic grammar, or in the formalism used for the statement of historical changes, the relation is achieved by notation: it is the specification [+tense] that triggers the diphthongization rule. We have already seen the kind of synchronic trouble that causes. If we extend this analysis, as *SPE* does, into the historical realm, we find considerable difficulty in accounting for the well-known congruity of diphthongs and long vowels in any reasonable way. We cannot explain why (except for the notation) the two types of segments should be 'related', or why the class (B) of nuclei, under divergent historical developments, gives EITHER long vowels or diphthongs or both. The problem is that the relation in the *SPE* framework is unidirectional.

SPE begins, as far as I can see, with an assertion. That is, with a very few exceptions they assume that diphthongs have at some level 'tense' syllabics, i.e. that 'true' diphthongs (which as we have seen are not a real category anyway) are in some sense 'augmented' tense vowels. And we can add to this the idea that for some reason tense vowels are 'likely' to diphthongize, and hence that a diphthong is a reasonable historical development of a tense vowel. This is of course, to use the current shibboleth, 'taxonomic' rather than 'explanatory'; the fact itself seems true enough, but all we have done, in essence, is given the fact a name, rather than attributing it to anything demonstrably 'intrinsic' (despite the attempts in this direction in *SPE* and Jakobson & Halle 1964).

Even if, however, we take as valid the rather dubious notion that the 'articulatory effort' supposedly associated with tenseness is a reasonable explanation for diphthongization ('glide-formation'), we are at a total loss to explain the equally common inverse development: the 'monophthongization' of diphthongs. If 'tense' vowels so often diphthongize, why should diphthongs equally often monophthongize to 'tense' (i.e. long) vowels? That is, if /V̄/ → /V̄G/ is 'natural', the theory gives no such qualification to the equally common mirror-image change (in fact, apparently, it counter-predicts it). We might note in this connection that in the early stages of the English Vowel Shift, while ME /ī ū/ diphthongize, /ai au/ monophthongize to long vowels. Phenomena like this are easily found in the histories of most language families.

But if we get rid of 'tenseness' and 'glides', the relation becomes fully natural in both directions: a diphthong is simply a dissimilated long vowel, and a long vowel is an assimilated diphthong (in this 'developmental' relation, that is). If we think along these lines, we can then develop a rather simple formal typology for all rules involving vowel clusters; and we can relate them in a natural way to certain frequently observed and traditionally well-accepted and well-documented types of sound change.

Let us assume that the essential contrast in languages that have 'two kinds of vowels' is monomoric vs. bimoric nuclei. And that vowel clusters can be handled in rules like any other clusters, i.e. they can function as wholes, or their members can be separately treated in various ways.[1] Among the single-element processes are progressive and regressive assimilations and dissimilations, and deletion of segments; among the whole-cluster processes are 'raising of long vowels', 'retraction of long vowels', etc. We can thus set out – schematically – the most important types of processes affecting bimoric nuclei, including the development of such clusters from single vowels ('lengthening' and 'diphthongization' of 'short vowels'), and the reduction of bimoric nuclei to monomoric ('shortening'). As far as I can tell, there are only five basic rule types involved, which seem to cover all synchronic and diachronic processes affecting these nuclei: assimilation, dissimilation, epenthesis, deletion, and feature-change covering two segments.

In the schema (21) below, each type is labelled with its traditional name. The formalism is to be interpreted as follows: 'F_i' is any feature by which a pair of contiguous vowels may differ, and 'α' $\neq$ 'β'.

(21) *Rule-types involving bimoric nuclei*

a. *Raising, lowering, fronting, retraction of long vowel*

$$\text{SD:}\ \underset{1}{\begin{bmatrix} \text{V} \\ \alpha \text{F}_i \end{bmatrix}} \underset{2}{\begin{bmatrix} \text{V} \\ \alpha \text{F}_i \end{bmatrix}} \qquad \text{SC:}\ \underset{1}{[\beta \text{F}_i]}\ \underset{2}{[\beta \text{F}_i]}$$

b. *Diphthongization of long vowel*

$$\text{SD:}\ \underset{1}{\begin{bmatrix} \text{V} \\ \alpha \text{F}_i \end{bmatrix}} \underset{2}{\begin{bmatrix} \text{V} \\ \alpha \text{F}_i \end{bmatrix}} \qquad \text{SC:}\ \begin{Bmatrix} \text{(i)} \quad \underset{1}{\phantom{[\beta \text{F}_i]}} \quad \underset{2}{[\beta \text{F}_i]} \\ \text{(ii)} \quad \underset{1}{[\beta \text{F}_i]} \quad \underset{2}{\phantom{[\beta \text{F}_i]}} \end{Bmatrix}$$

[1] Presumably triphthongs would be handled by the same kind of formalism; but phonologically at least they are as far as I know rather rare. For some remarks on how they might be treated, see Lass & Anderson (1975: chs. III, VI).

c. *Monophthongization of diphthong*

$$\text{SD: } \underset{1}{\begin{bmatrix} V \\ \alpha F_i \end{bmatrix}} \underset{2}{\begin{bmatrix} V \\ \beta F_i \end{bmatrix}} \qquad \text{SC: } \left\{ \begin{array}{lll} \text{(i)} & 1 & \underset{2}{[\alpha F_i]} \\ \text{(ii)} & \underset{1}{[\beta F_i]} & 2 \end{array} \right\}$$

d. *Lengthening of short vowel*

$$\text{SD: } \underset{1}{[V]} \qquad \text{SC: } 1 \quad 1$$

e. *Diphthongization of short vowel*

$$\text{SD: } \underset{1}{\begin{bmatrix} V \\ \alpha F_i \end{bmatrix}} \qquad \text{SC: } 1 \quad \underset{2}{[\beta F_i]}$$

f. *Shortening of long vowel*

$$\text{SD: } \underset{1}{\begin{bmatrix} V \\ \alpha F_i \end{bmatrix}} \underset{2}{\begin{bmatrix} V \\ \alpha F_i \end{bmatrix}} \qquad \text{SC: } 1 \quad \emptyset$$

9. A final argument: the 'strong'/'weak' cluster distinction

The last piece of evidence I want to invoke in favour of the /VV/ analysis is again synchronic. This concerns the relation of certain syllable types in English to the placement of stress. Early on in their exposition, Chomsky & Halle discuss the importance of what they call 'weak' and 'strong' syllable-final configurations for the operation of their stress rules.

Although the stress rules undergo a great deal of modification in the course of the argument, the simple form given early in chapter III of *SPE* will suffice to illustrate the point. Chomsky & Halle provide (p. 70) the following prose gloss of the essentials of their main stress rule (rule (19)):

(22) Assign main stress to

(i) the penultimate vowel if the last vowel in the string under consideration is nontense and is followed by no more than a single consonant;

(ii) the last vowel in the string...if this vowel is tense or is followed by more than one consonant.[1]

[1] As Chomsky & Halle note, these definitions require some extension, particularly in the case of /VCr/ clusters that behave as if they were weak, and /VCl/ clusters that seem to be strong (*SPE*: 70, 83, 103–4). But this is probably not a matter of segmental specification, as they claim, but rather of the assignment of syllable boundaries in obstruent + liquid clusters (cf. Anderson & Jones 1974a and n. 2, p. 35: also Allen 1973a: 137–41, 210–22).

The question is: why should these two types of sequences,

$$\text{(i)} \begin{bmatrix} \text{V} \\ -\text{tense} \end{bmatrix} \text{C}_0^1 \quad \text{and} \quad \text{(ii)} \begin{bmatrix} \text{V} \\ +\text{tense} \end{bmatrix} \text{C}_0 \quad \text{or} \quad \text{VC}_2$$

be different in their phonological behaviour? Or, more to the point, why should the latter two pattern together as a single type, as against the other? Merely to call the first type 'weak' and the second type 'strong', while it makes the correct distinction, does not explain anything. This would be not so bad if the patterning-together were inexplicable, but this is not the case; there is an explanation which *SPE*'s choice of primitives obscures.

As Chomsky & Halle note, the rule sketched out above in (22) is virtually identical to 'the rule governing stress distribution in Latin' (p. 79, note 15). Leaving aside the implicit assumption that Latin had a tense/lax distinction,[1] this is of course true: the two types of 'strong cluster' in English correspond to two types of 'long' or 'heavy' syllables in Latin. That is, in Latin, a syllable with a nuclear long vowel or diphthong is for certain purposes equivalent to a syllable containing a short vowel plus /CC/, and both are opposed to syllables containing a short vowel plus not more than one consonant which are 'short' or 'light'.[2] Similar groupings of syllable types obtain in Greek (though with differences of detail: Allen 1973a: 207ff.), and in Sanskrit, where /V̄/, /VCC/, and /VC#/ (as well as nasalized vowels) make a syllable heavy (*guru*), while /V/, /VC/ are light (*laghu*). Cf. Allen (1953: 85–7).

The same kind of pairing of /V̄/ and /VCC/ occurs – more relevant to my concerns here, perhaps – in Old Germanic prosody. In the Germanic alliterative line, the 'lift' (*Hebung*) is normally occupied by a long or heavy syllable: either one with a nuclear long vowel or diphthong, or a

[1] For arguments that this was in fact the Latin dichotomy see Allen (1973a).

[2] To be more precise: according to traditional syllabifications, a syllable is light if it is open and has a nuclear short vowel, and heavy if it is either open or closed but has a nuclear long vowel or diphthong, and also heavy if it contains a short vowel and is closed. The general convention is that given /V̆CV/, the division is /V̆.CV/, so that the first syllable is open (i.e. light); given /V̆CCV/, the division is /V̆C.CV/, so that the first syllable is closed (i.e. heavy). Thus (to take examples from Allen 1973a: 129), *făcĭlĕ* is /CV̆.CV̆.CV̆/ (all light), *dēpōnō* is /CV̄.CV̄.CV̄/ (all heavy), and *cŏntĭngĭt* is /CV̆C.CV̆C.CV̆C/ (all heavy). Final /VC/ may also be heavy (Allen 130–1); this I suspect is to be explained in terms of the frequent consonantal function of word boundaries (Lass 1971, Lass & Anderson 1975: ch. v). Some /V̆CCV/ sequences, however, can be interpreted as /V̆.CCV/: particularly if the /CC/ sequence is stop + liquid: thus *pătris* may be either /CV̆.CCVC/ or /CV̆C.CVC/ (cf. Allen 1965: 89; Allen 1973a: 69–71). There are complications involving morphological structure as well (Allen 1973a: 140–1); but this is the general picture.

short vowel plus /CC/ (cf. Pope 1966; Lehmann 1956: 76; Hulbert 1935: 229; Gordon 1957: §§29, 176–7).

The interesting problem is why this grouping or equivalence should be so 'natural'. In the *SPE* framework, the naturalness is merely the result of a correct observation, and a pair of generalizing names; but in the framework I propose here, it can be explained. At least the secondary phenomenon, the grouping of /V̄C/ and /VCC/ under one heading, can be; the relevance of these clusters to the English stress rules appears to be idiosyncratic.[1]

The explanation, like many others that have to do with 'syllable quantity', seems to be essentially numerical.[2] A strong cluster, very simply, has more 'pieces' than a weak one. More accurately, the 'strength' of a syllable depends on the number of segments in it which are (a) postvocalic, and (b) pre-marginal, in a rather special but not unreasonable sense. That is, mere counting of pieces cannot be the whole answer, since a strong cluster /VV/ has the same number of segments as a weak cluster /VC/. If the definition of 'strength' is principled, there must be a way of accounting for the difference. The answer is that the 'strength metric', if we can call it that, has as its domain strictly the NUCLEUS of the syllable. The metric may be expressed by a series of operations like this:

(23)

(i) Scan the input string and determine syllable boundaries.[3] The domain of the procedure is a single bounded syllable. Within a pair of boundaries, disregard the RIGHTMOST NONVOWEL segment.

[1] If the theory of syllabic structure proposed by Allen (1973a), where syllable 'release' and 'arrest' are defined in physiological terms, is correct, then this is less idiosyncratic than it seems. But for now I will keep to a rather more abstract frame of reference.

[2] Cf. the discussion of the West Germanic gemination in Lass & Anderson (1975: Appendix II). Numerical considerations are probably also involved in phenomena like 'resolution' in Germanic (and other) verse, where under certain conditions /V̆CV̆/ can be metrically equivalent to /V̄C/ or /V̆CC/. This essentially numerical 'resolution' principle is relevant not only to metrics, but in some cases to morphology. Thus in Old English, neuter *a*-stem nouns take nom./acc. plural affixes only if their stems are light: *scip/scipu* 'ship', *hof/hofu* 'dwelling', with plural endings but *word* 'word', *hors* 'horse', *dēor* 'animal', *wīf* 'woman' with no endings. Further, the nom. sg. of *ō*-stem feminines have an ending if they are light and none if they are heavy: *faru* 'journey', *lufu* 'love' vs. *lār* 'learning', *lēah* 'lea', *wund* 'wound'. The same is true in the *i*-stems: *wine* 'friend' vs. *dǣl* 'part', *ent* 'giant'; and in the so-called 'athematic' nouns: *studu* 'post' vs.' *bōc* 'book', *turf* 'turf'. (Cf. Lass & Anderson 1975: 269; on the various historical causes of these alternations see Campbell 1959: ch. VII, especially §§345–6.)

[3] This will probably have to be done differently in different languages. For a preliminary theory, see Anderson & Jones (1974a).

(ii) Count the number of segments remaining after the leftmost vowel. This value is S (= 'strength').

(iii) If $S > 0$, the syllable is 'strong'; if $S = 0$, it is 'weak'.

Let us see how this works for the four crucial syllable types /VC/, /V/, /VCC/, /VV/. The results of applying the procedure (23) are as follows:

(24)

(a) /VC/. (i) gives /V/; (ii) therefore $S = 0$. (iii) /VC/ is weak.
(b) /V/. (i) gives /V/; (ii) therefore $S = 0$. (iii) /V/ is weak.
(c) /VV/. (i) gives /VV/; (ii) therefore $S = 1$. (iii) /VV/ is strong.
(d) /VCC/. (i) gives /VC/; (ii) therefore $S = 1$. (iii) /VCC/ is strong.

The determinant of syllabic 'strength' in this sense is simply the number of segments between the first /V/ and the rightmost nonvowel. The /VV/ analysis for long vowels seems to provide a reasonable way of computing this, and explaining why two (apparently) disparate syllable types are so frequently grouped together.[1]

10. A weak conclusion

I think it can fairly be said that a geminate vowel analysis is a viable alternative to any other dichotomy that has been proposed. One might now ask whether it is in fact THE correct one; but I do not think one should. I am certainly not, in this case, making any ontological claims: I am proposing what is essentially a 'metaphysical' explanation in the sense in which philosophical systems can propose non-ontological metaphysical theories about the world. In the distinction made by Walsh (1963: 66), it is possible for a theorist to be 'saying how things must be taken if we are to make sense of them, not professing to inform us about what there is in the world'.

So I am not making any truth claims, either testable (in the empirical sense) or even, strictly, non-testable. It seems to me that given the nature of theories about unobservables, and certain general properties

[1] The notion of a canonical 'number of pieces' for certain syllable types also furnishes an explanation for phenomena like 'compensatory lengthening'. If under certain conditions a language tends to preserve numerically-based syllable structures, the loss of a segment in a long stem will promote gemination of some other. Thus pre-OE */gans/ > OE *gōs* /goos/; and for another way of handling this, by lengthening consonants after loss of a preceding nasal, cf. ON *rekkr* 'warrior', *drekka* 'drink' vs. OE *rinc, drincan*. The same principle probably underlies the gemination of consonants after short vowels that took place in Swedish as part of the loss of phonemic vowel length, where heavy syllables were generalized to all stressed positions. See the discussion of Swedish quantity in the Appendix to this chapter, and Bergman (1973: 45–7).

of theoretical argument, such claims (at least at the moment, and in the local context of linguistics) are probably not intelligible. But whether or not they are, it is at least clear that they are not empirical: there seems to me to be no reasonable and convincing way to test a claim that the underlying representations of English vowels are 'really' anything: such claims have no empirical consequences.

This does not, of course (as the quotation from Walsh above may suggest), reduce proposals about underlying forms and similar unobservables to vacuity, nor does it make their discussion empty. On the contrary, even if one cannot take 'truth claims' about such artifacts seriously, one can construct better solutions to certain problems using some kinds than using others. This is precisely what I have tried to do here, and what I will try to do later on in chapter 3, where I will take up the geminate vowel hypothesis again. That is: to test the relevance for a certain kind of problem-situation of a certain kind of proposal: not to 'prove the truth' of such a proposal. (Indeed, it is unlikely that in linguistic argument one can ever 'prove' anything, since all interesting arguments are 'nondemonstrative', i.e. formally invalid: cf. Botha & Winckler 1973: ch. 2. The question of 'absolute truth' is in any case rather simple-minded and irrelevant to intellectual discourse in general: cf. ch. 3, §4 below, and the *Epilogue*.)

The real empirical issues touched on in this chapter have in fact been rather shallow ones, i.e. related for the most part to questions of observation and the psychology of transcription. In the current primitive state of 'explanatory' linguistics, I think this is more or less the way things are bound to be: the empirical issues are fairly superficial, and the metaphysical or philosophical ones (which are more interesting anyway) are quite profound.

This attitude is clearly at variance with what seems to be the orthodox one these days, e.g. the claims of 'mentalist' linguists that considerations of 'psychological reality' and the like have empirical status. On careful consideration, however, it appears that such claims are at the moment so inflated (with respect to their testability) as to be generally empty (aside from reflecting what seems to be a hangover from the Positivist tradition, a need to have some kind of direct nexus between descriptive statements and a 'reality' outside). I see no particular reason for such a simple nexus to exist, and establishing it is so far beyond our present capabilities in any case, that it is not even a very interesting area of speculation.

To clarify (perhaps), the preceding discussion is, like most contemporary linguistic discussion (regardless of what its producers say about what they do) a study in the PHILOSOPHY of linguistic description, with empirical considerations brought in as points of departure and peripheral correctives. This may seem merely contentious: my arguments are, to be sure, of the type that many linguists choose to call 'empirical' or 'scientific'. And the reader is free to treat them as such if he likes: I suspect it will make very little difference in the end, at least as far as the descriptive and explanatory merits of my proposals are concerned. But the issue of philosophy vs. science is an important one, which I will leave here, but return to in detail in the *Epilogue*. In the meantime, I will only say that calling an argument or claim 'metaphysical' or 'philosophical' does not in my eyes devalue it, nor does calling it 'scientific' necessarily constitute a form of praise. And in any case, my arguments can be taken in isolation from their background; they stand or fall, more or less, on their own merits, regardless of what kind of discourse I happen to think I'm conducting.

Appendix: On defining pseudo-features: some characteristic arguments for 'tenseness'

I

I suggested in the preceding chapter that the claims made for 'tenseness' as a vowel-feature in English are circular and contentless; and that in any case an analysis of the English vowel system can do very well without it. I would like to consider this in more detail than was appropriate in the body of the chapter. And more importantly, I want to suggest that the classic arguments for the existence of the feature (in any language) are suspect: that there seems to be no particular evidence either for the utility or the reality of such a feature.

Now what does it mean to say that a feature is not 'real'? A simple statement of belief ('I don't believe there is a feature [tense]') is irresponsible: it is neither empirical nor metaphysical (in the rational sense of the latter term: see the *Epilogue*). I suggested above in §4 that at least for English, the *SPE* treatment is methodologically dubious, in two ways: (a) tenseness is not identified independently, but only inferred from an EFFECT it purportedly has on vowels (the 'glides' that follow tense ones); so that it can be identified only *a posteriori* no the basis of a prior (historically based) partitioning of the lexicon. And (b), which is related: there is no empirical (instrumental, perceptual) evidence given for the feature. (On the quality of what is supposed to be 'evidence', see below.) Or at least Chomsky & Halle posit the feature with no attempt to specify what would constitute a test for recognizing it (much less a disconfirmation procedure).

This does not in itself cast doubt on the feature: only on the *SPE* arguments. But I will try to show here that these same problems crop up even in more careful analyses, which attempt to specify some kind of recognition procedures. There are three major difficulties:

(i) Even the few apparently 'empirical' tests for recognizing the feature fail, either through being hopelessly subjective, or through logical incoherence, since

(ii) most of these are based on the presumed 'effects' of tenseness. And all of these 'effects' are independent variables, parameters that require independent notation in any case, so that

(iii) attribution of them to 'tenseness' is a mere assertion: it becomes an *ad hoc* classificatory device for a set of properties that may or may not have any 'natural' relation. Certainly the case for the relation being natural, and therefore demanding a 'common cause', is not made.

Further, there is a serious difficulty in that because of the clinal rather than purely disjunctive nature of the feature, the classic definitions are based largely on the notion 'corresponding (pair of) tense and lax vowels'. But

(iv) the notion 'corresponding' is undefined, and in many (most?) cases where it is invoked, it cannot be justified except through the prior assumptions that one of a given pair of vowels is in fact tense and the other lax, and that it is precisely tenseness or laxness that is the primary differentiator of the pair. So that

(v) any differences said to be produced by tenseness are referred to pretheoretical assumptions, and are thus neither empirical nor rationally arguable, merely empty.[1]

Let me begin this discussion with an anecdote, which though inconclusive in the extreme, nevertheless suggests something about the nature of the problem. I once had a discussion with an American colleague of mine,[2] in which he was trying to define for me a certain vowel quality. He used an imitation-label

[1] Obviously no demonstration that existing arguments are flawed 'disproves' the feature itself. As William Wang has appositely remarked (1969: 21; cf. Chen 1972: 465), 'We cannot prove that the platypus does not lay eggs with photographs of a platypus NOT laying eggs.' But it is clearly up to the champions of the oviparous platypus to produce some eggs (as of course they have); at the very least I am claiming in what follows that the champions of tenseness have not been so successful.

[2] American not only by birth (which I am too, and which is irrelevant), but in terms of training and metalanguage. My training, as is obvious, is essentially 'British': the tradition I was trained in, and in which I work as a descriptive phonetician and teach as a university lecturer is the one that students are normally trained in in major British universities. This obviously colours my phonological thinking.

technique which ran (as I recall) more or less like this: 'Make the vowel in *book* and tense it.' There was (obviously) an immediate failure of communication: I couldn't think of anything to do with the vowel to produce the desired effect, except to alter the horizontal or vertical position, or the duration, or the degree of lip-rounding. That is, I did not know how to produce 'tenseness', since it corresponded to no articulatory parameter that I could control, or that I was aware of having seen reliably described as controllable.

So there was, at the very least, a failure of metalanguage: and there were two possible reasons for it. One possibility was that the different traditions we were trained in blocked effective communication, since the parameter involved was one that my tradition did not recognize. The other was that there was NO parameter involved, but rather a case of The Emperor's New Feature. The fact that my colleague was himself not able to produce the vowel in question effectively ended the discussion, and left me with my doubts intact.

So far I have offered nothing but one ineffectual (and possible pointless) anecdote in evidence. But my suspicion that there was no parameter other than the traditional locational and quantitative ones involved in any English vowel system (at least) was reinforced by a textbook description I came across later, which seemed to me a model of misleading proprioceptive definition; but one whose misleadingness and muddled argument brought a number of important points into focus, including perhaps the problem that lay at the basis of the discussion mentioned above. The passage in question is from a widely used textbook (Schane 1973), and so is doubly woıth examining, as it gives some clue to the means by which errors are perpetuated.

In the course of an exposition designed to 'prove' that only three vowel heights are necessary for phonological description, Schane says (13): '...there are articulatory differences between the so-called tense and lax vowels. Tense vowels are produced with greater muscular tension, they are maintained longer, and the articulatory organs deviate more from the rest position... (The differences in muscular tension can be verified by pressing the fingers against the throat while uttering tense and lax vowels.) From a perceptual point of view, tense vowels are more distinct.'

I tried Schane's 'verification'. Taking the 'tense' vowel of *beat* and the 'lax' one of *bit* (his examples), I tried 'pressing the fingers against the throat' while uttering them. After a little experimentation, I found two parts of the 'throat' where I could indeed feel something (other than vocal band vibration): the anterior belly of the digastricus, directly under the mandible, and an area right above and slightly posterior to the thyroid cartilage. If I pronounced [i] and [ɩ] (corresponding to *beat* and *bit*), I could feel something of a 'difference': but ONLY WHEN PASSING FROM ONE VOWEL TO THE OTHER: there was no particular difference between the vowels themselves. Obviously, what I felt was simply the movement of the tongue from a close front position to a half-close retracted one – certainly not a difference in 'tension'. I got almost exactly the same kind of effect by passing from one 'tense' vowel ([i]) to another ([e]) – as might be expected. And if I placed my fingers in position, and then pronounced [ɩ] or [ə], I felt very little: again, not very surprising, since in these vowels there is very little movement of the tongue from what seems to be its 'rest' position: or at least very little of the type of movement that one gets in going from [i] to [ɩ]. After some further testing, I found that the effect that Schane calls 'differences in muscular tension' could be demonstrated with any pair of vowels where the second was either (a) opener, or (b) less peripheral than the first: I tried it with pairs like [e]:[ɛ], [u]:[ɷ], [ɨ]:[ə], [ɔ]:[ɒ], etc.

This may seem like a lot of time to spend on a rather crude proprioceptive exercise; but it did help to convince me that the 'differences in...tension' which can be 'verified' in this way are simply the expectable differences in tongue position caused by moving from one vowel to another IN A PARTICULAR DIRECTION. They have nothing to do with 'tension', but with the muscular movements defining two independent parameters, height and peripherality.[1]

On one level, of course, this 'verification' procedure is simply logically empty: this is due primarily to the notion 'rest position' (see further §2 below). If this is (cf. *SPE*: 300) roughly [e̜], then of course [i] will be further from it than [ɩ], [u] will be further than [ɷ], and so on. In any given vowel pair which is so set up that one member is closer and/or more peripheral than the other, the first one will 'deviate' more: simply because of the space in which the contrast is defined. That is, if [i]:[ɩ] are a pair (by definition), then they will have as a pair the properties that belong to such antecedently defined pairs. Whether they are in fact 'a pair' is a problem I will return to in §2; but without some evidence, all we have is a tautology.

But before considering the notion 'pair' in more general terms, let us see what the arguments (other than historical) might be for pairing in English. The idea that the nuclei of *beat*:*bit*, *bait*:*bet*, etc. are 'pairs' can only be based on a rather tortuous 'deep' phonological argument, which presupposes both tenseness and a particular analysis of the English vowel system and vocalic phonology (as I pointed out in ch. 1). That is, IF underlying /ī/ and /i/ are related as tense: lax; AND IF *beat* has surface [īy] and *bit* has [i]; AND IF *SPE* [īy] means something other than [ɩi] (cf. §4 above); AND IF *divine* and *divinity* share the lexical nucleus /ī/: then and only then are [i] and [ɩ] 'the same' except for some one feature specification. But this is not a phonetic argument, and Schane's description is not a phonetic description.

Schane's points about 'distinctness' and 'duration' seem to be equally empty. In what way is the nucleus of *beat* 'more distinct' than that of *bit*? Certainly it is longer: but only if you hold it longer. One can perfectly easily produce [i] and [ɩː] (and many Scots dialects have [i] in *beat* and [ɩː] in *beer*, for example). Or is 'distinctness' some independent property? If so, I have yet to see it convincingly defined, in such a way that it is relevant to the particular contrast involved here.

[1] Most other proprioceptive descriptions of 'tense' articulations are just as unverifiable, e.g. Chomsky & Halle's remark (*SPE*: 324) that 'in nontense sounds the entire gesture is executed in a somewhat superficial manner'. Sievers's comments which they quote with approval (324–5), about the 'Verschiedenheit der Articulationsweise' are equally empty, as far as I can tell.

2

The circularity and empirical dubiousness of Schane's discussion (like that in *SPE*: 324–6) is in part a legacy of the now classic paper on 'tenseness and laxness' by Jakobson & Halle (1964), and of the discussion in Jakobson *et al.* (1951). In these earlier analyses, the same strategy seems to appear: we select a vocalic opposition that we 'know' is 'really' tense: lax, and then look at the 'superficial reflexes' of the distinction.[1] And we come up with peripherality for tense vowels vs. nonperipherality for lax ones, length for tense vowels vs. shortness for lax ones, or tense vowels closer than the 'corresponding' lax ones.

According to Jakobson *et al.* (1951: 36), 'in a tense vowel the sum of the deviations of its formants from the neutral position is greater than that of the corresponding lax vowel'. Thus we have two notions that require explication: 'neutral position', and 'corresponding'. We will see that both of these are doubtful at best. Let us approach this by way of an example: Jakobson *et al.* (37) give as a 'corresponding pair' the vowels in French *saute* ('tense' /ọ/) and *sotte* ('lax' /o/). And they give formant values for a native speaker which show that in fact /ọ/ has a greater deviation than /o/. But this begs two questions: or rather 'neutral position' begs one, and the pairing of these two vowels begs another.

First, the neutral position. Jakobson *et al.* (18) define this as 'the position for producing a very open [æ]'. I am not convinced that this is particularly 'neutral': any more, for instance, than a very open [ɜ] or [ʌ]. I am not convinced, either, that there is any such thing as a 'universal' neutral position. It seems at least as reasonable that the neutral position for any language should in fact be related to its general 'articulatory basis' (Honikman 1964). That is, 'the gross oral posture and mechanics, both internal and external, requisite as a framework for the...merging of the isolated sounds into that harmonious, cognizable whole which constitutes the established pronunciation of a language' (Honikman 1964: 73). Certainly the whole muscular setting of the speech apparatus varies immensely from language to language; as do, for instance, 'hesitation vowels', which might also be a source of information about a truly linguistic 'neutral position'. Thus most dialects of English have [ə], while Scots generally has [e], and German and French often have [œ̈] or [ɵ] (cf. Honikman's comments on the articulatory setting for French, especially the role played by lip-rounding). Certainly a good deal

[1] This is a typical Jakobsonian reductivist strategy, like the reduction of rounding, retroflexion, and pharyngealization to 'flatness' (Jakobson *et al.* 1951; §§2.422, 2.4236). The supposedly common feature 'underlying' these disparate articulations (or which the articulations 'implement') is clearly an EFFECT, not a 'cause'. It seems perverse to claim that retroflexion and lip-rounding are merely physical exponents of flatness; the obvious solution is that flatness is the result of a number of configurations that produce acoustically similar articulator shapes. (This is not an argument against flatness, or against acoustic features, or even against the primacy – in certain cases – of acoustic features: cf. ch. 7, §§5–7 below.)

more research is needed before we can confidently claim a universal neutral position.[1]

But let us accept the neutral position as [æ̞]. There is still no need for tenseness. And this is because the differences between the vowels that Jakobson *et al.* use as examples are clearly differences in position, length, or both: there is no 'publicly' verifiable sense in which the pairs they give 'correspond' except for one feature (I will return to this problem in §3 below). Thus the vowels of *saute* and *sotte* (in the dialects of French I am familiar with) are different in a very simple 'spatial' way: *saute* has [o], and *sotte* has a rather advanced and weakly rounded [ɔ] (often a markedly centralized [ɔ̈]). In terms of the vowel space, [o] is certainly 'further' from [æ̞] than [ɔ̈]: so there is no reason to be surprised at the formant values, which are simply reflexes of the different cavity shapes that these articulations produce. But by the same token there is no reason to assign any ADDITIONAL cause to the differences. In order to justify an extra parameter like tenseness, one must first of all in any case admit that the differences in the spectra are due to differences in configuration; then in addition one must claim that despite this, there is some other, 'hidden' feature that produces the configurational differences, i.e. that they are not independent variables. But this is clearly otiose, since no one has yet, to my knowledge, demonstrated a pair of vowels that in fact differ only in tenseness: the primary (measurable) differences involved are always in quality and/or length.

In the absence of any morphophonemic or phonological evidence that these two vowels are in some way 'related' (see below), there is further no justification for taking them as a 'corresponding pair': except if, as Jakobson *et al.* do, one uses a notation where they are the same except for a diacritic signifying the feature that has been defined in advance as distinguishing them (i.e. /o̩/ vs. /o/). Without this unsupported auxiliary assumption, [o] and [ɔ̈] are simply two members of the French vowel system – not a 'pair'.

3

But what would constitute an argument for pairing? This brings me to my final point: the slipperiness (and in many cases, I suspect, the emptiness) of the notion 'corresponding pair of vowels'. I suggest that just because a language happens to have both short and long (phonemic) vowels, this does not mean that its vowel system is organized in 'correlated pairs'. This kind of symmetry, while attractive to linguists (myself included) and perhaps common

[1] It is interesting that the neutral position in *SPE* is much closer than that given by Jakobson *et al.*: Chomsky & Halle say that it is about [ę] (300). There is no discussion of why it has shifted so far up, which tends to make one suspicious that it is an analytical convenience rather than a fact about languages. Actually, Chomsky & Halle need an essentially 'front' and 'mid' neutral position, because the features [high, low, back] are defined in terms of deviation from just such a position (*SPE*: 304–5). If instead of [back] they used [front] as the 'deviated' horizontal dimension, the neutral position would presumably have to be [ɤ̞].

enough, is not in principle the only way of organizing a dichotomous system. Schematically, there seem to be two basic ways in which such systems can be organized. Taking two vowel sets *A*, *B* as the poles of the dichotomy, we can say:

(i) Let $A = \{a_1, a_2, \ldots a_n\}$, and let $B = \{b_1, b_2, \ldots b_n\}$. And let there be a unique function *f* that determines the relationship between any $a_i \in A$ and any $b_i \in B$. This is a dichotomous system composed of 'corresponding pairs', where every pair (a_i, b_i) implements the same opposition as every pair (a_j, b_j).

OR

(ii) Let $A = \{a_1, a_2, \ldots a_n\}$, and let $B = \{b_1, b_2, \ldots b_n\}$. Let there be NO function determining the relation of pairs (a_i, b_i). Then no pairs (a_i, b_i), (a_j, b_j) can be said to implement the same opposition, or to 'correspond'. The only opposition (in the formal sense) is between *A* and *B*, and there are no 'corresponding pairs': *A* and *B* are opposed only as wholes.

In a system of type (i), all oppositions between members of *A* and corresponding members of *B* may be privative (the function *f* can be used to define this); in a system of type (ii), since there are no genuine 'correspondences', all oppositions are equipollent.

The types (i, ii) above are the two 'uniform' types of dichotomous systems. There are of course, for systems in general, at least two other possibilities: (iii) systems which are 'heteromorphic', i.e. which are partly of type (i) and partly of type (ii); and (iv), systems which are non-dichotomous.[1] We might call systems of type (i) 'pair-based', and those of type (ii) 'set-based'. There is no reason (other than *a priori* assumptions about the structure of vowel systems) to prefer one to the other. Pairing, like strict (transitive) binarity, is an arguable assumption (cf. ch. 7, §4.3 below).

It seems to me that there are two situations in which, given a system with short and long vowels, it is reasonable to posit a type (i) organization: these are (a) where the vowels in question are qualitatively identical and differ only in length; and (b) where two vowels, one short and one long, appear in an alternation where it can be shown independently that length is the basic parameter involved.[2]

[1] It is unfortunately rather easy to force a type (iv) system into a type (i) mould by simply taking a dichotomizing feature, suitably defined, and dividing the members between its two values. I think this is what Jakobson *et al.* did with French [o] : [ɔ̃] and various other pairs. The *SPE* analysis of the English vowel system is another case in point: note that in my vowel-cluster analysis of English I did not invoke the notion 'pair': all I suggested was a set-based (type (ii)) opposition of /V/ : /VV/.

[2] There are other possible criteria for pairing. One, for instance, is 'equivalence' in terms of the position of a vowel within its own particular subsystem (long or short). Thus if the closest long front vowel in a system is [i:], and the closest short one is [ɪ], this could establish them as a pair on the basis of their occupying corresponding (in this case 'extreme') positions in the two systems (cf. Allen 1959: 245; Allen 1973a: 133). I

The first situation can be exemplified by Mangalore Kannaḍa, which has a vowel system like this:[1]

(1)

```
i:  i      u  u:
e:  e      o  o:
      ɐ: ɐ
```

It seems quite reasonable to interpret this as a 'five-vowel system plus length' – at least on purely phonetic grounds: the vowels line up nicely in the vowel space, and no special assumptions or Procrustean strategies are involved.

The second situation can be exemplified by at least some pairs in Swedish. Because of a vowel shift (cf. ch. 2, §6 below), and various other historical complications, such as lengthening and shortening before and after the shift, not all the Swedish vowels fall into obvious pairs.[2] But there are a good number that do, and these are instructive. Consider the vowel pairs [i:]:[i], [y:]:[y], [ẹ:]:[ɛ], [ø:]:[œ], [o:]:[ɔ], [ɑ:]:[a] (as in, respectively, *vit*: *visst* 'white: certainly', *dyr*: *dygn* 'dear: 24 hours', *egen*: *efter* 'own: after', *söt*: *kött* 'sweet: meat', *åka*: *åtta* 'to travel: eight', *glas*: *glass* 'glass: ice cream').

Are these in fact pairs? Certainly they all realize independent phonemes; and the identity in quality of the long and short close vowels suggests that pairing is a reasonable mechanism to suspect. But one should ask for more evidence before the assumption that [ẹ:]:[ɛ] or [ɑ:]:[a] are pairs is accepted. Arguments from pre-assumed symmetry (with fine realization handled by 'phonetic detail rules') are not, to my mind, acceptable. And there is such evidence: I will discuss it briefly, just to point out what seem to me the minimal requirements for an ARGUMENT (not an assertion) that vowel pairing exists. I will discuss another language with a rather similar vowel system below, to show how the arguments can fail.

In Swedish, vocalic and consonantal length are in complementary distribution. All (primary) stressed syllables are 'long'; they consist of either a long vowel plus a short consonant (and/or boundary), or of a short vowel plus a long consonant (or cluster). Of the vowels mentioned above, then, only [i: y: ø:, ẹ: o: ɑ:] appear before short consonants or finally, and only [i y œ ɛ ɔ a]

suppose this falls between my two criteria: the crudely phonetic one and the crudely phonological one. But I would not be prepared to accept this alone as an independent criterion: in the case of nonidentity of articulation I would require some phonological evidence, of the type illustrated below. (Allen in fact provides this for Latin: 1973a: 133.) I would think that given phonological evidence, the invocation of equivalent points in contrasting subsystems is unnecessary; without such evidence, it is not compelling.

[1] The values given represent 'phonemic norms', based on environments where processes like vowel harmony do not interfere. In any case, vowel harmony affects only /ɐ/ (which is [ə] before /i u/); the only other significant allophonic variations, again involving short vowels, are that /i e u/ are [ɩ ɛ ɷ] before nasals, and /e/ is [ɛ] before sibilants. I am grateful to Dr S. K. Aithal for the data on which this analysis is based.

[2] On the complications of Swedish vowel morphophonemics see Hammarberg (1970).

appear before long consonants or clusters.[1] This still does not establish anything more than an $A:B$ (type (ii)) relationship: two complementary sets opposed as wholes. We need more evidence before we can match members of one set with those of the other.

This evidence is morphophonemic. To take one example, Swedish has two noun genders, 'common' and 'neuter'; and adjectives (if they are 'indefinite' singular) agree in gender with the nouns they modify. In order to form an indefinite neuter singular from a common-gender stem, a /t/ is suffixed: e.g. *varm* 'warm, common', *varmt* 'id., neuter', respectively [varm], [varmt]. In this example, and in others of similar structure, the suffixing has no effect on the vowel (as is the case also with disyllabic initial-stressed adjectives like *mogen*: *moget* 'ripe', and those ending in long dental obstruents in common gender, like *glatt* 'smooth' [glat:], which do not change in neuter).

But if the adjective has a root structure ending in /V:C/, the suffixation produces an 'overlong' sequence */V:CC/: the stem vowel is then shortened. This is especially clear in regular dental-final stems (in /-t/ or /-d/), where the result of neuter formation is a form ending phonetically in a long [t:]. Thus, for the adjectives *vit* 'white', *het* 'hot', *söt* 'sweet', *våt* 'wet', *glad* 'glad':

(2)	Common		Neuter	
	Underlying	Phonetic	Underlying	Phonetic
	/vi:t/	[vi:t]	/vi:t+t/	[vit:]
	/he:t/	[hẹ:t]	/he:t+t/	[hɛt:]
	/sø:t/	[sø:t]	/sø:t+t/	[sœt:]
	/vo:t/	[vo:t]	/vo:t+t/	[vɔt:]
	/glɑ:d/	[glɑ:d]	/glɑ:d+t/	[glat:]

This seems to show clearly that true 'pairs' (a type (i) relationship) are involved – even with [ɑ:] and [a]. If a long vowel is shortened (and we know on the grounds of distribution that [-C:] is a 'short' environment), it does not simply lose length: we do not get *[søt:], *[vot:], etc. If the vowel is nonhigh, we get a qualitative difference as well; and we can now reasonably say that [ɑ:]:[a], [ø:]:[œ], [ẹ:]:[ɛ], etc. are 'corresponding pairs'. And we can, if we wish, refer the qualitative differences to some low-level realizational generalization, i.e. that nonhigh short vowels are one height lower than corresponding long ones, and that for low vowels the relationship long: short is realized additionally as back: front. There is clear structural support (both in terms of distribution and of 'process') for these claims.

But now consider another (related) language, which also has both long and short vowels, and which also has a number of similar short: long pairs:

[1] The transcriptions of Swedish forms that follow are somewhat simplified, but this does not affect the points at issue. The close vowels [i: y:] usually have a fricative offglide [j], and [ẹ:] is normally [ẹ:ə]; other details, like aspiration and the dentality of the coronals, will also be omitted. For a discussion of Swedish quantity from a phonological point of view, see Lass (1974b) and the references there; for a detailed phonetic account, with measurements of duration, see Lindblom & Rapp (1973).

modern Standard German. This is a language in which a tense/lax dichotomy is assumed by many scholars; and where, even if the dichotomy is interpreted as long/short (or anything else), the notion 'corresponding pair' is taken pretty much for granted. Thus Chomsky & Halle (*SPE*: 324): 'we find examples of tense vs. nontense sounds in modern German, for instance, where this feature plays a differentiating role in pairs such as *ihre*, "her", versus *irre*, "err"; *Huhne*, "chicken", versus *Hunne*, "Hun"; *Düne*, "dune", versus *dünne*, "thin"; *wen*, "whom", versus *wenn*, "if"; *wohne*, "reside", versus *Wonne*, "joy"; *Haken*, "hook", versus *hacken*, "hack".' The nuclei of these pairs (in modern Standard North German) are respectively [i:]:[ɩ], [u:]:[ɷ], [y:]:[ʏ], [e̞:]:[ɛ], [o:]:[ɔ], and [ɑ̟:]:[ä].[1] What is the justification for a pairing where tenseness (or any other single feature) is responsible for the differences? Surely these pairs are on the face of it not really close enough so that they can be (phonetically) interpreted as differing only by one feature: the short vowels are not at the same height as the 'corresponding' long ones, and [ɩ ʏ ɷ] are less peripheral as well than [i: y: u:]; and [ä] and [ɑ̟:], while of the same height, differ in backness. One would think that some kind of argument (other than what is historically obvious) should be given.

But, as I said, the pairedness of these vowels is generally taken for granted, more or less as a matter of tradition (regardless of whether length or tenseness is made responsible). To take just a scatter of sources besides *SPE*, this particular pairing is presented without supporting argument by Moulton (1947), Heike (1961), Ross (1967b), Wurzel (1970) and Erben (1972: 33). It has even led to the oft-repeated pseudo-generalization that the long vowels are 'closer' than the corresponding short ones (and thus to the erection of 'open' vs. 'close' as a dichotomy: cf. Philipp 1970: 23–4). And this leads (if we take the long vowels to be tense) to the 'observation' that tense vowels tend to be closer and/or more peripheral than lax ones.[2] This is clearly a case of discovering exactly what you put there in the first place.

The idea of 'pairs' in German, however, seems to be a red herring. There are no phonological or morphophonemic alternations that could clearly establish e.g. [i:]:[ɩ] as a pair: since length in German is not constrained by syllable structure the way it is in Swedish. There is in fact one piece of evidence that seems to suggest non-pairing. In certain instances, long vowels are shortened under weak (non-primary) stress: but when they shorten, they do

[1] The system partially represented in these transcriptions is based on those of a number of North German informants; I am especially grateful to Otto Wustrack and Rolf Koeppel for their time and patience. (Virtually the same transcription is used by Philipp 1970.)

[2] This creates problems with dialects that have the marginal phonemic contrast of /ɛ/ : /ɛ:/ (e.g. in *Betten* : *bäten*). If /ɛ/ is taken as the 'short' counterpart of /e:/, then the generalization fails for /ɛ:/; if /ɛ/ : /ɛ:/ are taken as a pair (which no one seems to do, but which is at least phonetically reasonable), then the set of relations /ɩ/ : /i:/, etc. has an unaccountable gap. But the 'marginality' of /ɛ:/ (which for most speakers merges with /e:/ in all but the most exaggeratedly careful speech styles) allows us to omit it from the central system, and sidestep the problem (which is in any case a pseudo-problem). On the status of /ɛ:/ see Moulton (1947: note 3) and the discussion in Philipp (1970: 22–4).

NOT take on the quality of the (supposed) 'corresponding' short vowel. They merely lose length, but retain their original quality. Thus, to take one example, the preposition *über* is ['y:bə] in isolation, and in *übersetzen* ['y:bəzɛtsn̩] 'carry over'. But with reduced stress, in *übersetzen* [ybə'zɛtsn̩] 'translate', we do not get *[ʏbə-]: the vowel retains its close peripheral articulation (see further Philipp 1970: 120–1). This would seem to suggest that [y:] and [ʏ] are independent, members of two contrasting sets, but not of a pair (again, regardless of their historical relationship).

There is certainly evidence in German for a type (ii) bipartition of the vowel system (like the (A):(B) one I suggested earlier for English). And in this division, further, the long vowels and diphthongs behave as a set, just as in English: e.g. long vowels or diphthongs only may appear in final stressed open syllables, etc. But there is no particular evidence for pairwise oppositions between individual members of the two sets.

4

Finally, then, I see nothing in either the typical data used to support the notion of vocalic tenseness, or the argumentative strategies by which the data is handled, that would tend to make me believe either (a) that in general the 'pairs' used to illustrate the distinction are really pairs that are identical except for some one feature; or (b) that the feature supposed to characterize the general domain of 'tense' vowels is indeed a single feature. There is nothing in either the data or the arguments to suggest a 'hidden' generalizing parameter underlying the disparate observable ones. I see no reason why some vowel systems (like German and English) cannot be based on large dichotomies without cross-category pairing, while others (like French) are simply networks of qualitative oppositions, with no dichotomizing features. And for those systems that (like Kannaḍa) have a genuine pairing relationship, I see no evidence for anything underlying the pairs except the length that they show. Whatever the merits or demerits of the cluster-analysis I proposed for English, this is certainly independent of the tenseness issue, which seems to be merely a distraction.

I do not intend, by casting doubts on the typical arguments for tenseness, to restrict all phonological argument to observables. Certainly the tenor of my discussion of the English vowel system makes this clear. But I do think it important to distinguish phonetic arguments from arguments about explanatory abstractions, and to separate observational reports (of whatever quality) from pure assumptions. That is, we should keep to some kind of publicly verifiable criteria when we are discussing what is presumably the phonetic basis of an explanatory abstraction.

The characteristic arguments for vocalic tenseness seem in general to be little more than reifications of a somewhat dubious intuition (certainly not one widely shared among phoneticians). And this reification simply adds an undetectable and otiose parameter to the set of measurable and useful ones, and (circularly) reduces an arbitrarily chosen set of observables to a hidden 'generalization'. Certainly nearly all the discussion of tenseness that involves actual measurement begins by assuming tenseness, and then measures something else which is presumed to derive from it.

Until there is some more compelling evidence for THE FEATURE ITSELF than proprioceptive intuitions and circular argument from supposed effects; and until there is some genuine evidence, in each relevant case, that 'corresponding pairs' of vowels are indeed pairs, I would prefer to assume that if two vowels differ in height and/or peripherality, then position is what distinguishes them; and if two vowels differ in length, then length is what distinguishes them. And if two vowels differ in both quality and length, it is the job of a thorough phonological analysis of the language in question to decide what kind of structure they are members of. This last decision is certainly not to be left to 'universal' feature inventories.[1]

[1] For an equally sceptical but rather differently oriented approach to the general problem of 'tenseness' (both in terms of 'articulatory basis' and phonological/phonetic characterization) see Lebrun (1970). This paper contains an excellent critical survey of the literature, as well as some additional arguments (mainly phonetic) against positing a feature of 'tension' on the grounds of its (presumed) effects. Lebrun has an especially interesting discussion (122–3) of EMG measurements of segments (mainly consonants) presumed to be 'tense': the one obvious type of empirical evidence relating to the feature as usually defined proves to be not very useful in establishing it. There is however a small measure of support in the work (on vowels) of MacNeilage & Scholes (1964), which shows greater bioelectrical activity in [i e u] than in [ɩ ɛ ω] (cf. Lebrun: 124): but this does not support the usual pairwise tense/lax distinction, since the EMG evidence suggests that [ɔ] is 'tense' and [o] is 'lax'.

2 *Rules, metarules, and the shape of the Great Vowel Shift*[1]

1. Preliminaries: On 'sound shifts'

This chapter was provoked in the first place by a quite specific problem: the order of the initial stages of the Great Vowel Shift, and their relation to the shift as a whole. But this turned out to have extensive theoretical ramifications; and though it is still central, most of the chapter is really an attempt to justify some general theoretical proposals that arise out of the original problem. I will argue here for two currently rather unfashionable notions: (a) that phonological systems *per se* (i.e. structured inventories of segments in opposition) are necessary primitives in phonological theory; and (b) that we need some rather new kinds of formal mechanisms, which seem at first to be less 'rigorous' than the generally accepted ones. Point (b) grows out of a conviction, which I will try to support in detail, that the current machinery for handling phonological change is seriously inadequate, and partly based on erroneous principles. This is particularly true of the emphasis in current theory on 'rules' and 'rule-addition' in the usual sense, and the attendant restrictive formalism. The evidence, as the title suggests, will be drawn primarily from the English ('Great') Vowel Shift; though I will also consider similar events in the histories of German and Swedish.

It is still an open question in historical linguistics just what you have to do to 'explain' a sound change. That is, once you have stated the rules for it, and explored the relevance of metatheoretical concerns like 'simplicity', 'naturalness', etc., is the job finished? Or is there still a

[1] This is a much revised and expanded version of Lass (1969). Since that rather crude and preliminary paper appeared, I have profited from discussions with John Anderson, Gillian Brown, Bengt Sigurd, and Alvar Ellegård, among others. But I owe an outstanding debt to Richard Carter, for calling his 1967 paper to my attention, and discussing an early draft of this study with me in great detail. I must also acknowledge an indirect debt to Robin Lakoff, whose paper at the 1969 UCLA conference on Historical Linguistics in the Perspective of Transformational Grammar (now R. Lakoff 1972) encouraged me to continue thinking along the lines of greater abstractness than current formalism allows.

need to explain (or, more modestly, to describe) the larger structure of the change, i.e. its relation to the whole system that it operates in? I suggest that there is, and that even a reasonably adequate description (let alone anything 'explanatory') will often depend on just this sort of consideration. The basic question, as we will see, is this: are rules enough? I will try to answer this by considering, in specific cases, the consequences of assuming that they are.

Let me begin with a general reflection on the way historical linguists think. I suspect that if one were to ask a randomly chosen group of them to name some 'major sound changes' in the history of Germanic, there would be virtual unanimity on at least a few: e.g. Grimm's Law, the High German Consonant Shift, the English Great Vowel Shift. Certainly the first two have been recognized since Grimm's time as significant events. These all have certain things in common: notably, they are 'global' operations on large phonological subsystems (all nonsibilant obstruents in Grimm's Law, all long vowels and diphthongs in the Great Vowel Shift). These events are large-scale transformations: they have left the languages they affected very different from what they were before, either in inventory (Grimm's Law, the High German Consonant Shift), or in morphophonemic complexity (the Great Vowel Shift).

Now consider changes like these vis-à-vis one like the Anglo-Frisian Brightening (*Aufhellung*), where Proto-West Germanic */ɑ/ fronted and raised to [æ] in certain contexts (cf. Lass & Anderson 1975: ch. II). In current diachronic phonological theory, there is no way of (formally) distinguishing the two types, except – trivially – by the number of segments involved; i.e. a change specifying 'all low vowels' (which the language in question happens to have one of) affects fewer segments than one specifying 'all long vowels and diphthongs' (which the language has many of). But both are instances merely of 'rule-addition'. Or to be more accurate, the Anglo-Frisian Brightening is the addition of one rule, and Grimm's Law and the Great Vowel Shift are the cumulative results of a series of rule-additions. But there is no formal sense in which something like Grimm's Law can be identified as a 'unitary' phenomenon: to give it a name is simply to recognize after the fact that a sequence of rule-additions had such a massive effect (and is so useful in comparative study) that we can informally use 'Grimm's Law' as a mnemonic.

Now I do not mean to deny that Grimm's Law involved the 'addition of rules' to the grammar of pre-Germanic IE, any more than I would deny that the Anglo-Frisian Brightening was a rule added to the grammars of certain West Germanic dialects. There is no doubt that the local mechanisms by which the individual changes in Grimm's Law came about are identical (formally) to the mechanism involved in the Anglo-Frisian Brightening. But I think there is more to it than this. There is a sense in which there is 'some such thing' as Grimm's Law, over and above a *post facto* taxonomization by linguists of a group of historical events. The subsumption of these events (and no others) under one rubric is not an accident, but a genuine identification of 'something real'.

I suggest that calling both types 'rule-addition' is (even observationally) inadequate. A proper theory of historical phonology should be able to give us a differential specification of those objects that correspond to the intuitive notion 'major sound change'. The theory should, that is, provide some formal justification for setting off certain blocks of rules in the history of a language from others; and it should be able to do this even if they fail to be identifiable in terms of the usual signs of 'relatedness', e.g. adjacency in sequence, collapsibility by abbreviatory notations, and so on.[1]

Some kind of recognition procedure like this, which transcends simplistically formal criteria, is badly needed; for many of the processes that linguists unhesitatingly recognize as unitary phenomena[2] are spread out over long periods of real time (like the Great Vowel Shift), with various extraneous changes intervening between the sub-units. And further, because there are certain events which have not generally been considered unitary, but could usefully and insightfully be if we developed the theory in the right direction.

The problem is, of course, that with many sequences of historical change, it's only when they're over that we recognize them as having been unitary. But this after-the-fact identity is nonetheless compelling. We feel constrained to say, not that events A, B, C occurred and we can conveniently call them 'the X'; but rather that 'the X' occurred, and the stages in it were A, B, C. This is not a trivial distinction.

Given our identification (whatever it's worth) of such an 'X', we have

[1] Note that the amount of purely formal 'generalization' that can be extracted from Grimm's Law is negligeable: cf. Lass (1969, 1974a) and Lass & Anderson (1975: ch. v).

[2] Unanimous acceptance by reputable scholars is not an unreasonable indication that something exists: at least as a heuristic. See e.g. Pike's use of this in the vexing matter of establishing the existence of 'segments' (1945: 42–55). At least one should be slow to consider everything that doesn't fit the currently fashionable mould as mass delusion.

two choices: either its 'X-ness' or unity is an illusion, an epiphenomenal and accidental result of our analysis of a series of in principle unrelated (or unrelatable) incidents; or it's not. And if it's not, then we must probably adopt something like the notion 'final cause'. The rule-additions are 'effects' prior in time to their 'cause', which is the completed change that we recognize the rules as having contributed to. And at the same time this 'cause' is statable as an antecedently existing condition which determines that the particular rules we find (and no others) should have arisen. I frankly do not see any way out of an ultimately finalistic view of at least some kinds of linguistic change.[1]

Let me give a fairly simple preliminary example of a sound change with an inapparent structure, which can insightfully be brought to the surface by finalistic considerations. One way of characterizing certain events in the history of Scots is to say that in the seventeenth century, two rules were added to the grammar that had the following effects:

(1)

(a) Long vowels and diphthongs[2] shorten everywhere except before /r v ð z #/.

(b) The nonhigh short vowels /e a o/ and the diphthong /ai/ lengthen before /r v ð z #/.

(These two changes have recently been christened 'Aitken's Law' by Vaiana 1972, after the classic description by A. J. Aitken 1962. For further discussion see Lass 1973b, 1974b.)

At first it looks as if we simply have two rules – with opposite effects – operating in the same environment. But when we look at the SYSTEMIC RESULTS of the two changes, we find that they have effected a total transformation of the structure and organization of the vowel system. Before the operation of Aitken's Law, Scots (like all other dialects of English) had a lexically dichotomous vowel system: long vs. short. After Aitken's Law, there was no longer phonemic length, but only predictable phonetic length: all vowels (including diphthongs) were lexically short, with length occurring only in surface forms before /r v ð z #/. Thus instead

[1] I have the consolation here of being in no worse company than that of Sapir, whose notion of 'drift' must surely be taken in this sense, though he never explicitly said so (Sapir 1921: chs. VII–VIII). See also R. Lakoff (1972), and for a detailed discussion of the issues involved in finalistic explanation, Lass (1974b).

[2] By 'shortening' of the diphthongs I do not mean 'monophthongization', but rather 'temporal compression' of a bimoric nucleus into a complex ('gliding') monomoric one, which contrasts with short vowels not in moric structure but in lack of steady-state articulation. See Lass (1974b: 339, n. 9).

of a dichotomy, we now have a single underlying system, with a low-level lengthening rule: the organization has been transformed from a typical 'West Germanic' one (with largely free quantity) to a 'Scandinavian' type (with predictable quantity).[1]

To see the precise effect of this, consider the reflexes in a Scots dialect (Central Fife) of the etymological categories used as diagnostics for the English vowel dichotomy in ch. 1 above. Here is a representation of the categories in the display (1) (ch. 1, §1) for this dialect:[2]

(2)

(A)		(B)	
bit	ɛ̈	meet	i
bet	ę	mate	ẹ
bat	ä	boot	ÿ
put	ÿ	boat	o
pot	ɔ	bought	ɔ
but	ʌ	suit	ÿ
		bite	ɛ̈ɩ
		doubt	ÿ
		quoit	ɔɩ

The distribution of length can be illustrated with one vowel from each set (that is, unique to each set: the historical processes involved in Aitken's Law, as well as certain others, have obviously made the notion 'set' meaningless): thus for /ä/ we get [ɑː] in *far, have, has*; and for /i/ we get [iː] in *fear, sleeve, breathe, sneeze, bee*. The diphthongs also have long alternants: /ɛ̈ɩ/ is [ɑ·e] in *fire, five, fly*, etc., and /ɔɩ/ is [ɔ·e] in *Moir, boy*. These length alternations lead to a very characteristic Scots phenomenon: apparent 'minimal pairs' for length involving stems in final /d/ vs.

[1] But the result in Scots is not a generalization of 'long' syllables to all positions: rather a total predictability of vowel length when it does occur. All vowels are now short except before /r v ð z #/; and all vowels except the reflexes of ME /i u/ (which did not lengthen under (1 b)) are long here. Thus although all length is predictable, there is a sense in which all shortness is not: regardless of the qualities of the reflexes (e.g. ME /i/ in various dialects may have values like [ɩ ɛ̈ ɛ] and ME /u/ may be [ɤ̈ ʌ ə]), two vowels will always be illegally short in the long environments. Thus in central Fife (cf. Lass 1974b) there is short [ɛ̈] < ME /i/ in *fir, give, his*, and short [ʌ] < ME /u/ in *fur, love, buzz*.

[2] I have omitted *father*, as it contains the lengthener /ð/. It is obvious in any case that this system is much smaller than the typical English one, since ME /ū ǭ ẹu/ have fallen together. The identity of *pot* and *bought* is due, not to merger, but to the fact that ME /o/ did not diphthongize before /x/ in the North (cf. Lass & Anderson 1975: ch. VI). There is however an extra segment in the inventory, which does not appear in the chart: a diphthong of the [ʌü] type, mainly from ON /au/, which as far as I know occurs only in short environments, as in *loup* 'leap' < ON *hlaupa*. See Lass (1974b) for further discussion of systems of this kind, and of some varying geographical patterns in the implementation of Aitken's Law.

weak preterites of vowel-final verbs: *tide* [tɛ̈ɪd] vs. *tied* [tɑ·ed], *greed* [grid] vs. *agreed* [əgri:d], etc. (i.e. underlying /–Vd/ vs. /–V#d/).

So these two simple rules have led to a massive typological change, from a dichotomous to a nondichotomous vowel system. Another way, therefore, of looking at Aitken's Law is to say that rather than there being simply an addition of two rules, there was a radical restructuring of the vowel system, IN A CERTAIN DIRECTION (the loss of phonemic length). In this case, rather than the rules (1a–b) being primary, they are the AGENTS of the restructuring. The restructuring itself is definable then as both the after-effect of the rules, and their motivation in the first place. The implication of this will become clearer as I proceed.

Eventually I want to claim that there are extensive classes of sound change[1] which involve 'generalizations' if you will larger than those statable either as single rules or as schemata. And further, that these generalizations are 'real' ones, justifiable by testing as reliable as any we can get in historical matters. These generalizations are at least as real as, and possibly more so than, alternative ones, based on different metatheoretical notions.

To sum up the difficulties I will attempt to deal with: there are serious problems in the way we currently deal with large-scale phonological change, and the way we formalize our intuitions about the groups of events that constitute such changes. Crucially, as our tools for formal description have become more precise and powerful, we have lost, rather than gained, in our ability to express certain 'significant generalizations';[2] generalizations which were easy to handle in pre-generative frameworks, and which even now we can manage quite nicely in prose. I will be concerned with one of them here: 'sound shifts'. The now canonical framework for describing phonological change, stemming from Halle (1964), Kiparsky (1965, 1968), Chomsky & Halle (*SPE*), and many others (and now erected into a pedagogical orthodoxy in King 1969) is inadequate. It incorporates a crippling and unnecessary formalist reductivism; and I will try to propose at least a preliminary alternative.[3]

[1] There is no need to restrict this to phonological change: certainly the same kind of things happen in morphology and syntax (cf. the loss of case-endings in IE). I am just using a rather simple and tractable type of example.

[2] Not everybody's 'significant generalization' is everybody else's. But I trust that what I see as one is no more wildly eccentric than what others may see as one.

[3] For criticism of the 'standard' theory of historical change from a quite different point of view (attacking quite different failures) see Weinreich, Labov & Herzog (1968). For other types of criticism, see Chen (1972), and Anttila (1974a, 1975).

2. The ordering paradox in the Great Vowel Shift

I will focus here on some problems in the staging of events in the English Great Vowel Shift (henceforth GVS). This is one series of historical changes that scholars of all theoretical persuasions unanimously recognize as 'something that happened'. I will try to show that this unity is not merely imposed by hindsight.

By way of introduction, let us consider some major descriptions and interpretations of the GVS, beginning with Jespersen's classic account of the whole process. The overall picture he gives is this (1909: 231):

(3)

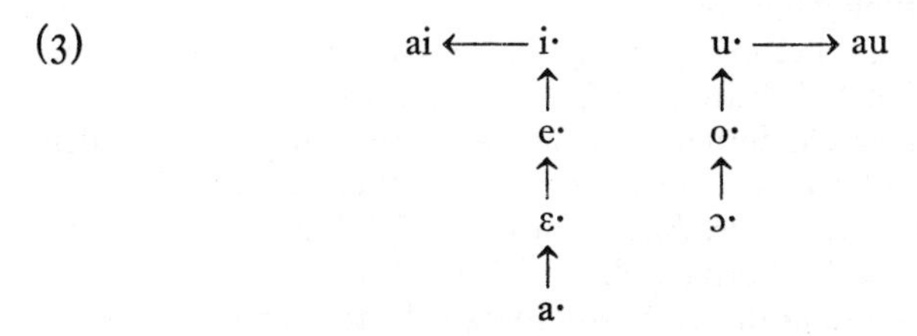

This schema is interpreted as follows (231–2):

> The great vowel-shift consists in a general raising of all long vowels with the exception of the two high vowels /i·/ and /u·/ which could not be raised further without becoming consonants and which were diphthongized into /ei, ou/, later [ai, au]...
>
> the changes of the single vowels cannot be considered separately; they are all evidently parts of one great linguistic movement, which affected all words containing a long vowel in ME.

(On Jespersen's use of slants and square brackets see below, ch. 4, §2.)

This conception is unitary and monolithic. There was a system-wide tendency toward raising, and since at one end of the continuum this was phonetically impossible, the high vowels as it were 'did the next best thing' and diphthongized. (We will see later that in a somewhat different sense this is really the case.)

But despite his conviction of the unity of the GVS, Jespersen considered that the two crucial events – diphthongization of the high vowels and raising of the mid vowels – were temporally ordered. He felt that the evidence suggested that diphthongization came first:

> after /i·/ and /u·/ had been diphthongized, there was nothing to hinder /e·/ and /o·/ from moving upwards and becoming /i·/ and /u·/; where /u·/ subsisted, /o·/ was not allowed to move upwards (232).

The last remark is directed against the ordering of the two changes proposed by Luick (1898: 78). Because of the existence of NE dialects where ME /ū/ remains undiphthongized, Luick claimed that the raising of the mid vowels must have been the trigger for the whole process. His entire conception of the GVS hinges on this. I quote here from his final formulation (1964: 554, 559–60):

Die frühesten Vorgänge der neuen Epoche sind zugleich die weitreichendsten; sie ergreifen entweder unmittelbar oder in ihren Folgenwirkungen sämtliche bisher geltenden langen Vokale und einen Teil der Diphthonge. Aber alle diese Veränderungen gehen auf drei Impulse zurück, von denen in der Gemeinsprache nur zwei Geltung kamen.

Der erste Impuls setzte bei me. ẹ̄ und ọ̄ ein, in Wörtern wie *see*, *too* und bewirkte, daß sie zu den Vokalextremen [*ī*, *ū*] vorrückten...

Während durch die geschilderten Vorgänge neue [*ī*] und [*ū*] entstanden, wurden die schon seit alter Zeit bestehenden umsgestaltet: me. *ī* und *ǒu*, d.i. [*ū*], in Wörtern wie *by*, *ride*, *now*, *house* wurden in Diphthonge des Typus [*ai*, *au*] oder nahe verwandte Formen übergeführt...

Aus der Übereinstimmung dieser Verbreitungsgebiete gibt sich, daß ein innerer Zusammenhang zwischen diese Wandlungen bestand und daß diejenige von ẹ̄ und ọ̄ das Primäre war...

Jespersen and Luick agree on one fundamental point: the shift is a single event, with an inner coherence. Only the motive forces in the two accounts differ. For Jespersen, the controlling mechanism is diphthongization: all the other events are predictable from it (though he would not have put it that way) by a kind of drag chain relation. For Luick, on the other hand, there is a push chain started by the raising of the mid vowels; the low vowels raise later by a drag chain like that posited by Jespersen for the high-mid relation. But their emphases also differ: for Luick the notion of *enchaînement* or entailment is basic; for Jespersen, it is the shape of the whole change, and not the interrelations, that counts. I will show that these two conceptions can be drawn together in a natural way, and that both Luick and Jespersen – though in rather different ways – were right about the structure of the GVS.

Given a cluster of innovations like the GVS, which appears to have some kind of internal structure, one could ask a number of different kinds of basic questions about it. For instance:

(a) Why did it happen in the first place? (Let us call this THE INCEPTION PROBLEM.)

(b) Given the fact that it did happen, and that one change or the other (diphthongization or raising) began it, why should the rest of the changes have been the particular ones they were? E.g. why was vowel raising (at least in the early stages) apparently iterative, but not diphthongization? (This is THE OVERALL-SHAPE PROBLEM.)

(c) Given the *fait accompli*, where did it start, and what sequence did the events in the cluster occur in? (This is THE ORDER PROBLEM.)

Question (a) was not apparently of particular interest in this earlier period of GVS scholarship; though as we will see it was – at least briefly – later on.[1] An answer to (b) was hinted at, rather informally, in the chainlike mechanisms suggested by both Luick and Jespersen; though it was, to both of them, clearly less interesting than (c), which absorbed most of their efforts.

We will see now that recent attempts to answer (b) have in a sense presupposed an answer to (a); and further, that we can't give an intelligible answer even to the apparently 'factual' question (c) without doing something about (b). Actually, of course, (b) and (c) are not two independent questions: the order problem and the overall-shape problem are the same. I will not attempt here to deal with (a) at all: at the moment I do not know what would constitute an answer, other than a statement of the bald fact that it happened. But in a way this is the least interesting question of the three, in that the correct mode for solving 'absolute origination' problems like this is apparently unknown (even though 'causal' answers of certain types are quite reasonable: see Lass 1974a, 1974b). At any rate, it seems to me that there are (in general) deductive solutions to overall-shape problems, but no such approach to the question of why shapes should change at all in the first place.[2]

To return to the central question, (c): what was the order of the two initial stages? Did diphthongization precede vowel raising, or vice versa? Jespersen shows, I think quite conclusively, that we cannot tell from

[1] In a way this is unfair: there were overall 'causal' explanations like those notably of Horn & Lehnert (1952: now echoed by Samuels 1972). But I find this one impossible to understand for the most part, and what I do understand seems to rest on undocumentable claims about the influence of stress, etc. The explanation I will propose here, however, is not causal; it is rather an attempt to clarify how the GVS began, and why it subsequently took the particular course it did.

[2] Not that there are no hypotheses (even well-founded ones) on the general mechanisms that bring about certain kinds of change (e.g. sociolinguistic ones). But these are not of the same logical type, since they are generally not predictive. Further, the basic inception problem is not answered by any kind of 'contact' hypothesis, since it is perfectly possible for a language to resist influence. Finally, the domain of explanatory hypotheses like these is external, and I still think the case has yet to be made for total permeability of the core structure and dynamism of a language to sociolinguistic influences.

historical evidence: the first good phonetic witness, John Hart (1569) shows both changes well established. So any answer must be largely based on theoretical argument, since there seems to be no compelling (external) evidence. At least not from the relevant period; though I will show that there is some very useful evidence from a later one, which may insist on a solution rather different from either Jespersen's or Luick's – though in principle more like the latter's.

But before we consider this in detail, let us take a look at one later account of the GVS: the essentially Praguian one of Martinet (1955). This represents, I think, a considerable advance in the use of theoretical argument in cases of this kind. Martinet here utilizes the well developed formal theory of the structure and dynamics of oppositional systems which stems from the earlier work of Trubetzkoy and others: he has at his disposal, that is, a fairly explicit metalanguage for talking about large-scale (or other) sound changes in terms of systems-as-wholes.[1]

I will introduce this analysis with a brief description of some of the main characteristics of what can (loosely) be called 'Praguian' explanations of sound changes. These tend, by and large, to be 'homeopathic' or 'therapeutic': a phonological system has some kind of entelechy, a condition of well-formedness defined on it *qua* system, and it tends to 'try and re-establish' this condition, an 'equilibrium' if you will, if it has been 'disturbed' for some reason or another. Sound change – or the evolutionary history of languages in general – is thus 'dialectical' in a Hegelian sense: every dissolution of the pre-established equilibrium prompts a re-equilibration, and the re-equilibrations do not cycle back to the antecedent condition proper, but to another, similar, 'point of rest'. (In terms of general evolutionary theory, the forces prompting re-equilibrations are 'immanent', but the defining conditions for particular equilibria are 'configurational'. For this distinction see Simpson 1964.)

Thus it is an immanent property of vowel systems that they tend toward 'symmetry', in the sense of valuing highly 'correlations' or matched pairs with respect to certain features (see Trubetzkoy 1969, III. 3–4). Or, systems have internal 'economies', constraints which among other things lead to the loss of items of low functional yield (Vachek 1964 on the loss of systemically 'peripheral' phonemes in English). It is the first of these points that has been most influential in Prague-oriented commentary on the GVS. For instance, some writers

[1] Strictly speaking, Jespersen does invoke a notion of 'system', but it is not a very clear or precise one.

(e.g. Vachek 1959) have claimed that certain late OE and early ME sound changes affecting vocalic quantity acted to disturb the original (OE) correlations of vowel-pairs by length, and that this was the initiating condition. This in fact is Martinet's point of departure.

He begins with a basic claim, that English has had for a long time a tendency toward *isochronie*, 'l'état qui résulte de l'élimination du trait phonologique de quantité vocalique' (1955: 248). This tendency has been as it were part of the defining equilibrium (along with the favouring of matched pairs of vowels), and the pivotal factor in a dialectical process which subsumes the GVS. Because of certain sound changes in late OE and early ME (notably vowel-shortening before consonant clusters, lengthening before other clusters, and lengthening with attendant quality change in open syllables) it gradually came about that the 'modalité anglaise de l'isochronie' (251) became the dominant principle of vocalic organization. That is, these changes had the effect of making quantity – for the most part – a function of environment alone, so that length had a low functional yield for lexical distinctiveness. Instead, the distinctive parameters became quality (open vs. close) and nuclear type (vowel vs. diphthong).[1]

So in ME vowels began to pair by quality: but certain uneven distributions (brought on especially by the quality changes that accompanied open-syllable lengthening) left the two high vowel sets, back and front, once more paired by length. Martinet suggests the following late ME vowel system (253):

(4)

ī	ĭ		ŭ	ū
	ẹ		ọ	
	ę		ǫ	
		a		

The only pairs whose distinctiveness at this point is still non-isochronic are /ī/–/i/ and /ū/–/u/. But since the grammar as a whole is still characterized by isochrony, there must be an adjustment to bring the 'aberrant' high vowels into congruity with the rest of the system:

L'exception à l'isochronie que représente le maintien des paires /ī/–/ĭ/ et /ū/–/ŭ/ doit naturellement tendre à s'éliminer, car l'expérience phonologique montre qu'une opposition quantitative se maintient mal lorsqu'elle se limite à deux paires. La liquidation de ces deux paires se produit par diphtongaison des longues, ce qui élimine une quantité devenue insolite pour un tel degré de

[1] As the argument in ch. 1 above suggests, this typological change probably never occurred: English is still a 'moric' language, with a /V/ vs. /VV/ structure. The details are not at issue here, however, only the principles underlying the argument.

fermeture: [ī], impossible dans le cadre de l'isochronie, passera à [ɪi̯], c'est à dire que /ī/ se resoudra phonologiquement en /i+i/, et que la réalisation phonétique se calquera sur cette interpretation (253).

Later in the shift, due to this and other factors which it is not necessary to go into here, a new length distinction developed among the mid and low vowels, and the long mid vowels moved up into the 'deux cases vides' (255) that were left by the diphthongization of /ī ū/. Following this, the low vowels raised, and /ā/, which 'pouvait avoir une légère tendance à pousser vers l'avant' fronted, and its space at the back was filled by the reflex of /au/.[1]

Essentially then the history of the GVS is one of continuous flux, with typological subchanges one after another creating unstable conditions, either in the form of opposition types of low functional yield, or *cases vides* which had to be filled by other vowels. The lesson of the shift, says Martinet, is that it illustrates 'le fait que les langages, ou mieux leurs usagers, ne sont jamais guidés par une aversion ou une préférence pour tel ou tel type articulatoire, mais par ce que tel ou tel type articulatoire représente de préjudiciable ou d'avantageux pour l'économie de la langue à un moment précis de son histoire' (256).

Whatever objections in detail one might have to this account, whatever objections one might have as to the PARTICULAR principles invoked for purposes of explanation, there is no doubt that this is a theoretically sophisticated view, and a considerable advance over earlier attempts at least in the sense that it provides a more powerful (and perhaps potentially explanatory) framework for description. And nowhere is this clearer than in Martinet's conception of the locus for an explanation. The GVS is to be explained in terms of processes which affect, in some way, the system AS A WHOLE: it is not a mere succession of local events whose unity is the product of hindsight. The theory itself gives us *a priori* terms for explanation. So that every individual change that was part of the process was brought about, not only as a 'consequence' (in some sense) of a preceding change, but specifically as a consequence of that change having disturbed a pre-existing state of well-formedness, defined on the entire vowel system as a structure.

Martinet thus claims in effect that the entailment of one change by another can be deduced from some abstract condition which transcends

[1] ME /a/ was in fact already front: cf. ch. 4 below. The drag chain involving /au/ also worked rather differently, as this nucleus came – ultimately – to replace the lower mid back vowel /ǭ/ (= /ɔɔ/) in *law*, etc.

the changes themselves: and which is in an ill-defined but important sense 'characteristic' of the grammar of English. We will see that it is necessary to revive this notion in order to account satisfactorily for the shape of the GVS: in particular, to resolve the order problem. And we will see also that this same notion will enable us to explain the shapes of certain other vowel shifts, and will suggest further that the order problem is not a matter of real time sequence, or even abstract, 'descriptive' order, but something quite different.

Since the advent of generative phonology, the GVS has been taken up again; and the standard treatment (that in *SPE*) has followed Jespersen's account of the order of the first two stages, rather than Luick's. The reason for this will become clear shortly. Chomsky & Halle begin, as Jespersen did, from the testimony of John Hart (1569). The early stages of the GVS are established on the basis of Hart's deviation from the (putative) late ME vowel system.

Leaving aside the ME diphthongs (which pose some special difficulties not relevant here), the relation between the ME long (*SPE*'s 'tense') vowels and Hart's are as follows (*SPE*: 252–66):[1]

(5)

$$\begin{array}{ccc} \textit{ME} & & \textit{Hart} \\ \begin{Bmatrix} \bar{\text{i}} \\ \bar{\text{e}} \\ \bar{\text{æ}} \end{Bmatrix} & \rightarrow & \begin{Bmatrix} \text{ei} \\ \bar{\text{i}} \\ \bar{\text{e}} \end{Bmatrix} \end{array} \qquad \begin{array}{ccc} \textit{ME} & & \textit{Hart} \\ \begin{Bmatrix} \bar{\text{u}} \\ \bar{\text{o}} \\ \bar{\text{ɔ}} \\ \bar{\text{a}} \end{Bmatrix} & \rightarrow & \begin{Bmatrix} \text{ou} \\ \bar{\text{u}} \\ \bar{\text{o}} \\ \bar{\text{a}} \end{Bmatrix} \end{array}$$

In a schematization like (3), the GVS at this stage looks like this:

(6)

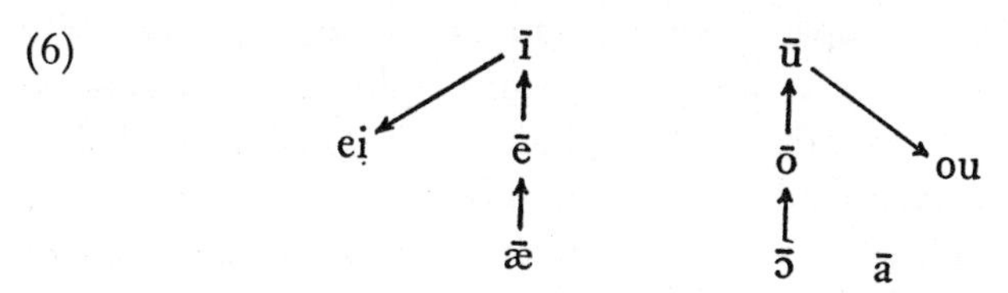

[1] Following the arguments in ch. 1, I use [ei ou] etc. for *SPE*'s [ey ow]. In *SPE*, further, the symbol [a] is used for [ɑ]. The ME vowels /ǣ ɔ̄/ are the traditional /ę̄ ǭ/ (Jespersen's /ɛ· ɔ·/). In addition, *SPE* assumes (incorrectly: cf. ch. 4 below) a three-height vowel system for ME instead of the usual four-height one. But these are matters of detail, not principle, and are not really relevant HERE. Note also that in this chapter I will use single-symbol representations for long vowels, e.g. /ē/, etc., as these are more convenient and more familiar than /ee/ and the like. For the most part this will not obscure anything, since in many cases the vowel clusters behave as units: the history of OE and ME /ii ee oo/ is not the same as that of /i e o/. Later on in this book (chs. 3, 4, 5), where the phonetic quality of individual vowels is more strictly relevant, I will use IPA rather than 'philological' notations.

At this point it doesn't matter particularly whether we look at (6) historically, as a mapping in real time from one vowel system to another, or synchronically, as a derivation of Hart's surface vowels from an underlying system like that of late ME. In any case, we need the same rules to get from one inventory to the other. *SPE* gives them as follows (I show only the results, as the formalism is not at issue):

(7) a. *High vowel diphthongization*

ī → īi, ū → ūu

b. *Vowel shift*

ī → ē, ē → ī

ū → ō, ō → ū

c. *Vowel raising*

ǣ → ē, ɔ̄ → ō

Rule (7b), like its supposed synchronic analogue in NE (cf. ch. 1, §3 above) is an alpha-switching rule, which reverses the height coefficients on nonlow vowels. Since it is specified only for 'tense' nuclei, it also affects the [ī ū] in the diphthongs [īi ūu], producing [ēi ōu], which become [ei ou] by a later rule of 'laxing'. The raising rule (7c) applies only to vowels that agree in backness and rounding, and so excludes the supposedly back /ā/.

Synchronically, then, if we take Hart's underlying vowel system to be like the late ME one, there are three rules, ordered as in (7); and historically speaking, these are presumably reflexes of rules that arose (in this order) at three or fewer times in the period between late ME and Hart. And it is these three rules, not apparently related to each other, nor necessarily directly adjacent either historically or synchronically, nor as far as we can tell anything but adventitious, that produced the GVS. But scholars have unhesitatingly identified the GVS as having an 'inner coherence'.

With this in mind, let us return to Luick's claim about the order of events. From now on, by 'order' I mean sequence in real time; I am not concerned with the structure (if any) of Hart's synchronic grammar. For all we know, whatever happened historically, a grammar containing (7a–c) might be (though I doubt it) 'optimal' for a post-GVS child, on the basis of his parents' output. Historically, however, we are not concerned with 'optimality', but with how the innovations got there. And as far as I can see, the *SPE* formulation (and the theory it is based on) cannot handle Luick's order: even if it should turn out to be correct. This as we will see is crucial.

Recall that according to Luick the 'impulse' of the GVS was the raising of the long mid vowels /ē ō/. This set up a push chain, 'forcing' the high vowels to diphthongize. Now in a theory which insists on strictly linear rule-application, this could not have happened. For it turns out that either diphthongization and raising occurred simultaneously (which because of the structure of the rules is formally impossible for an *SPE*-type grammar), or raising must have come second. For clearly if raising came first, it would collapse /ē ō/ with /ī ū/ respectively; and then we would need some procedure to disentangle those [ī] and [ū] that are from raised /ē/ and /ō/ from those that aren't, and to block the operation of diphthongization for the first lot. If the rules go in Luick's order, then, we must mark 'original' /ē ō/ with some purely *ad hoc* feature like [−diphthongization], so that the [ī ū] they become do not meet the SD of the diphthongization rule. Or, failing this, we must impose a derivational constraint like the one I suggested in ch. 1, §6, which in the synchronic grammar prevents both elements of /ii/ and /uu/ from shifting. But the *SPE* theory doesn't allow the latter, and the former is so clearly *ad hoc* and lacking in simplicity that it should be a last resort. So it looks as if within the framework of standard theory Jespersen must have been right and Luick must have been wrong.

3. Some data: and a partial solution to the order problem

It turns out that there is relevant evidence which shows that the Jespersen/*SPE* order cannot be correct. As Richard Carter has pointed out in an important paper (1967), there are some curious developments in modern Northern British dialects (which Luick observed but did not exploit fully) that virtually force a decision on us. Consider for instance the typical developments of ME /ī ū ō/ in four dialects (this data is similar to Carter's but more detailed and less geographically restricted):[1]

(8) (a) Lowick, Northumberland (SED area 1. 1)

ME	*NE*
ī	ɛ̈ɩ
ū	u:
ō	i:

[1] English data from Orton & Halliday (1962); SED = Survey of English Dialects. The Berwickshire data is from Wettstein (1942), and the Buchan from Dieth (1932). The parenthesized length sign and the diphthong alternants in the Scots forms are of course reflexions of the loss of phonemic length (cf. §1 above).

(b) Threlkeld, Cumberland (SED area 2. 4)

ME	*NE*
ī	aɩ
ū	u:
ō	ɩə

(c) Chirnside, Berwickshire

ME	*NE*
ī	əi ~ ɒe
ū	u(:)
ō	ë(:)

(d) Buchan, Aberdeenshire

ME	*NE*
ī	əi ~ ɑ·e
ū	u(:)
ō	i(:)

We can sum up these facts, and some related ones, as follows:

(a) There are no English dialects with undiphthongized ME /ī/.[1]

(b) There are many dialects like those shown above in (8), which have undiphthongized ME /ū/, normally represented by [u(:)].

(c) In general, those NE dialects which show the 'expected' reflex of ME /ū/ (i.e. a nucleus of the [aɷ] type or something similar) have a high back vowel or upgliding back diphthong for the reflex of ME /ō/. (But see ch. 3 below.)

(d) But those dialects which have [u(:)] for ME /ū/ have a FRONT nucleus for ME /ō/: either a monophthong (like [i:]) or a diphthong with a front syllabic (like [ɩə]).

Now dialects meeting the criteria (b) and (d) above, like those shown in (8), are precisely those whose ancestors lay within an area where an important ME sound change took place. In this area (roughly the whole of 'Northern' ME), /ō/ was fronted in the fourteenth century to /ø̄/. (This was later raised in England to /ȳ/, and in Scots to /ȳ/ in certain environments: this accounts for the NE reflexes of the types shown in (8).) The effect of this change is to produce a vowel system with a 'gap' in the back series:

[1] Where NE dialects show [i:] for ME /ī/, this is either lexically sporadic (e.g. in *life* in Penrith, Cumberland: Reaney 1927: 52) or historically conditioned. Thus NE [i:] can derive in certain cases from Old Northumbrian *-eġ-* in *died*, *eye* (see the maps in Kolb 1966: 237–53). Even in these dialects, however, there are diphthongs in all other positions. So the generalization that no NE dialect has undiphthongized ME /ī/ still holds.

(9)

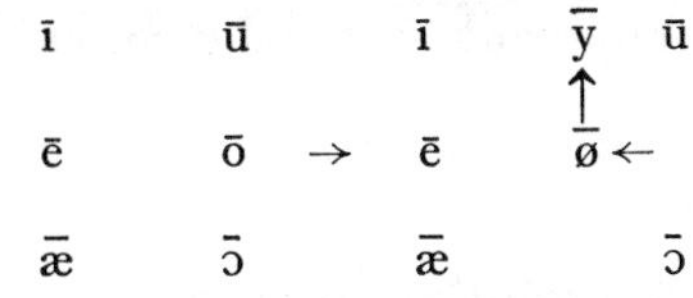

ī	ū		ī	ȳ	ū
				↑	
ē	ō	→	ē	ø̄ ←	
ǣ	ɔ̄		ǣ		ɔ̄
(a) (Pre-14th-c.)			(b) (Input to GVS)		

(For details see Jordan 1934, §54, Lass 1972; and for Scots, Aitken 1962, Lass 1973b, 1974b. I use the *SPE* version of the vowel system again here for convenience, but cf. p. 63, note 1 above.

To the facts covered under the headings (a–d) above, we can now add:

(e) There are no NE dialects with consistent unraised ME /ē/.[1]

According to Carter, facts like those set out in (a–e) suggest a special type of relationship between diphthongization and raising: that the raising of the ME mid vowels was a NECESSARY CONDITION for the diphthongization of the high vowels. Where a mid vowel has failed to raise (because it was not there at the time of the GVS), there is no diphthongization of the high vowel one above. (Of course when /ø̄/ from /ō/ goes to /ȳ/ it does raise; but there's no vowel above it, only an empty slot, and it doesn't raise in the series where it originally belonged.) So the condition on diphthongization must be:

(10)

High vowels will not diphthongize unless the mid vowel immediately below in the same series (front, back) raises.

Carter then interprets the dialect evidence as support for Luick's claim that mid vowel raising is in some way central to the GVS: but in rather different terms from Luick's. The relation between diphthongization and raising is not necessarily one of ordering or (temporal) priority, but of IMPLICATION. What really happened in ME, according to Carter, was not the addition of a set of rules like (7a–c), but rather an abstract schema, with certain consequences. A schema that can be interpreted, as Carter puts it, as a general instruction to the grammar, like this:

(11) $\bar{V} \rightarrow [+\text{raise}]$

The consequences of this higher-order schema are the various rules that implement the GVS. I will now attempt to extend Carter's in-

[1] There is an apparent counterexample in Northern English and Southern (Border) Scots dialects with [ɛi] and the like in *see, bee,* etc. But this is due to a later change (parallel to the first diphthongization in the GVS in type), involving lowering of the first mora of a bimoric nucleus. For a discussion of this change (and the related one of /ū/ to [ʌu]) in the Borders see Vaiana (1972).

sight, and develop a framework that will incorporate such schemata in a reasonable way.

4. Further steps in the solution: metarules

Carter's schema (11) is a partial solution to this problem: how do we express a holistic intuition (in this case firmly based on dialect evidence) about large-scale sound changes? And the difficulty with phonological theory at the moment is that though it is primarily designed to permit the expression of abstract relationships, it is in some cases formally too concrete to do it. Certainly notions like a rather crude sort of *Zusammenhang* can be captured: rules that are collapsible by braces, or by variables, are 'related'. But what we cannot formulate with any precision is overall, 'global' relatedness.

Some progress has been made in this direction with the development (notably by Kisseberth) of the idea that rules may enter into 'functional conspiracies' (Kisseberth 1970a, b). That is, sets of rules that seem formally unrelated but ultimately have similar effects can be seen as unified in functional terms, i.e. with reference to their operation in the whole grammar.

With the GVS our problem, as suggested by the Luick–Jespersen disagreement and Carter's schema, is one of defining an 'impulse'. How did the GVS begin? If we assume that it is a unitary, 'conspiratorial' process, how can we formalize it? In particular, how can we locate the impulse as raising, and yet keep this separate, in a sense, from the rules that effect it? That is, if there is anything in the idea that, however we ultimately formulate things, there is an impulse at work such that local events in a cluster can be deduced from it, and some of these events can be deduced in turn from others, then we must find a way to state these relationships. The basic notion we're after seems to be something like a hierarchy of 'causes' of decreasing centrality, branching as it were from a single root. The overall claim which I will try to document is that shifts like the GVS have an internal structure: they are a set of dependencies.

For instance: if, as Luick implies, and Carter claims explicitly, the raising of mid vowels entails the diphthongization of high vowels, then we have to be able to state the notion 'entails' in our notation in some way. (Otherwise our formalism will prevent us from making predictions.) Clearly, in cases like the GVS, it will be necessary to include, for explanatory purposes, notions like 'phonological space' and 'chain'. In other words, things like inventories and paradigms, etc., may have to be given more than the epiphenomenal status they now have in standard theory (cf. Shopen 1970, Harris 1970, Lass & Anderson 1975: ch. VI on paradigms). I will return to these matters later.

For now let us say only that it may be necessary to posit 'taxonomic' inventories or inventory-like structures which are available to the grammar as such, with 'spatial' dimensions (like vowel height) specified in them. Such inventory representations would act as 'grids' against which the trajectories of rule-effects could be plotted; and conspiracies etc. could be seen as acting in accordance with well-formedness conditions defined by these inventories. Phonology, that is, should become more paradigmatic and less syntagmatic: or at least the paradigmatic side (in terms of systemic positions, not just features) must be revived. We are suffering, in short, from a loss of the central notion 'system of oppositions'. What I have adumbrated here, and will discuss in detail below, is not as much of a departure from certain aspects of current theory as it may seem: we will see that proposals of this sort are more or less in line with the apparently acceptable notion of 'output conditions', which while not statable with the same precision say as transformations proper, may in many cases serve in a more abstract way to 'filter' ill-formed surface (or deep) structures (cf. Ross 1967a, Perlmutter 1971).

But now to my proposal. I will begin by asking just how 'precise' a phonological rule has to be. Let's say that a language has two rules, which have the following effects:

(12)

$$\text{(a)}\quad \begin{Bmatrix} \text{e} \\ \text{o} \end{Bmatrix} \rightarrow \begin{Bmatrix} \varepsilon \\ \text{ɔ} \end{Bmatrix}$$

$$\text{(b)}\quad \begin{Bmatrix} \text{i} \\ \text{u} \end{Bmatrix} \rightarrow \begin{Bmatrix} \text{e} \\ \text{o} \end{Bmatrix}$$

Such sets of rules are fairly common: cf. the ME 'lengthening in open syllables' (Lass 1969, 1974b). Using for the moment the features suggested by Wang (1968) for handling four-height vowel systems, we can state the rules (12a–b) as (13a–b):

(13)

$$\text{(a)}\quad \begin{bmatrix} \text{V} \\ +\text{high} \\ +\text{mid} \end{bmatrix} \rightarrow [-\text{high}]$$

$$\text{(b)}\quad \begin{bmatrix} \text{V} \\ +\text{high} \\ -\text{mid} \end{bmatrix} \rightarrow [+\text{mid}]$$

Now these rules – using any system of height features – do not collapse. But there is clearly a generalization here, which is that 'nonlow vowels lower one height'. I maintain that it is perverse to deny the existence of processes like 'lowering by one height', and that accordingly there should be rules of the form:

(14) $$\begin{bmatrix} \text{V} \\ +\text{height}^{n} \end{bmatrix} \rightarrow [+\text{height}^{n-1}]$$

This is obviously what (13) is all about, and the insight should not be lost to save exclusively binary rules. That is, there are processes which can be 'captured' with binarily specified, individual rules, but which are undergeneralized if so expressed. (Using the parameter 'strength' rather than height, one could for instance see rules like (14) for the 'soft mutation' in Welsh or for stop-lenition in Danish.) It may very well be that the rules actually operating in the grammar, for the language in (12), would be (13a–b); but these rules can be reasonably taken as derivative reflections of a schema like (14). This schema is a general condition DEFINED ON the grammar, but IMPLEMENTED IN the grammar by the (particular) rules (13). A schema like (14) I will now call a METARULE.[1]

Let us take higher-order, 'abstract' rules then as a reasonable possibility. We note that there are cases where the relation between some pair of rules must be stated, not as a matter of order or sequence, but of implication. We must capture relations like that between raising and diphthongization in the GVS, where as far as I can see neither 'order' nor 'simultaneity', strictly speaking, are involved. The only thing, at any rate, that we have evidence for is COVARIATION: i.e. some rule or schema X implies (has as its deductive consequence) some rule or rules Y. (Cf. the discussion of synchronic covariation in Weinreich, Labov & Herzog 1968.)

So that in addition to statements of the logical form 'If *x*, then *y*', where the variables *x*, *y* are feature-specifications, we need statements of the same form where *x*, *y* are rules – even sequences of rules – or schemata. Thus we might express the relation between mid vowel raising and high vowel diphthongization in the GVS like this:[2]

[1] The term is not my own. The first use I am aware of is in Ross (1966) for the 'tree pruning' convention (which is in fact a higher-order, abstract rule like what I propose here). For an independent and somewhat different use of the term, but one still within the general scope of my definition, see Kim (1970).

[2] In accordance with ch. 1 above, I assume that 'diphthongization' of a long vowel can reasonably be treated as dissimilation of a bimoric nucleus. It could of course go the other way: instead of /ii/ becoming /ei/ it could become /ie/. So it would be possible to

(15)

If: SD: $\underset{1}{V}\ \underset{2}{V}$ SC: $\underset{1}{[+\text{raise}]}\ \underset{2}{[+\text{raise}]}$

Then: SD: $\underset{1}{\begin{bmatrix}V\\+\text{high}\end{bmatrix}}\underset{2}{\begin{bmatrix}V\\+\text{high}\end{bmatrix}}$ SC: $1 \rightarrow [-\text{high}],\ 2$

There is one basic question that I have not approached: why should there be this implication? The trivial answer is that if there weren't, the mid vowels would collapse with the high ones, and this is not what happened. But I think the fact that it did not is important: it defines a particular and easily recognizable kind of sound shift, in which a further condition applies: that the number of systemic oppositions not be reduced by the shift (cf. Grimm's Law, and the discussion in Lass 1974a). A shift like the GVS must have an output condition: NO COLLAPSE.[1] This is defined on the oppositional system as a whole. We can then reformulate (15) this way:

(16) a. *Metarule:* $\underset{1}{V}\ \underset{2}{V} \rightarrow \underset{1}{[+\text{raise}]}\ \underset{2}{[+\text{raise}]}$

b. *Condition:* No collapse if (a)[2]

c. *Implication:* If ~ (b), then:[3]

$$\underset{1}{\begin{bmatrix}V\\+\text{high}\end{bmatrix}}\underset{2}{\begin{bmatrix}V\\+\text{high}\end{bmatrix}} \rightarrow \underset{1}{[-\text{high}]}\quad 2$$

generalize this, e.g. by having the SD be a sequence /V_i V_j/, where i = j, and the SC simply 'i ≠ j'. But I limit myself here to the attested English facts: the final, more general version will look quite different.

[1] No-collapse shifts of course are only one particular variety of massive change; there are probably at least as many vowel shifts that do not have chain-like structures, and which do result in collapse, often in massive merger. Thus in some dialects of Yiddish that I am familiar with, MHG /u uo y ye i/ all collapse in /ɩ/ : /mɩs/ 'must', /bɩx/ 'book', /ʃtɩk/ 'piece', /bɩxer/ 'books', /kɩnd/ 'child' (NHG *muß, Buch, Stück, Bücher, Kind*). Further, MHG /ū ȳ/ collapse in /oi/ : /hoiz/ 'house', /moizer/ 'mice' (NHG *Haus, Mäuser*); and MHG /ō ø̄ ei/ collapse in /ei/ : /teit/ 'death', /ʃein/ 'beautiful', /veis/ 'I know' (NHG *Tod, schön, weiß*).

[2] In the later stages of the GVS there is collapsing of some categories in some dialects. Thus ME /ę̄/ and /ẹ̄/ in *sea* : *see, beat* : *beet* in most of the South of England. But this happens quite late (not firmly until the eighteenth century); and it is not part of the 'original design' of the GVS, which is a covarying chain (cf. ch. 3 below). Other dialects collapse later in still other ways: in some Scots, for instance, ME /ę̄ ẹ̄ ọ̄/ in *beat, beet, boot* collapse in [i(:)].

[3] Observe, by the way, that the uniqueness of high vowels in this analysis – which is empirically motivated – is the origin of the derivational constraint suggested in ch. 1, §6. This constraint restricts (synchronic) vowel shift of high vowels to the first members only of lexical divocalic clusters both of whose members are high. So if there is a

Note that there is no NECESSARY contradiction between (16) and the *SPE* rules for John Hart's synchronic grammar. Given (16) as the precipitating metarule, those rules are (perhaps) perfectly reasonable implementations of the instruction-set (16).[1] The metarule is an attempt to capture the difference – to my mind an essential one – between the rules that a dialect happens to have and the (historical) reason it has them. Or, more precisely, the reason why those rules have the forms and effects – especially the latter – that they do. That is, the rules and their ordering in Hart's dialect, or in a diachronic 'plain-story' account of the GVS, do not in themselves tell us why dialects with undiphthongized ME /ū/ have front reflexes of ME /ō/. The schema (16) is at least an attempt in that direction.

This is an important distinction, since it limits and makes precise the domain of my proposal. I am not saying that metarules, for instance, are ACQUIRED by children; they are EVENTS in the history of a language that precipitate system-wide changes. The output that children use for acquisition, on the other hand, is of course directly generated by the rules in their parents' grammars that implement metarules. (Or, if the locus of the metarule is the child's grammar, then the output is determined directly by the implementing rules.)

In partial conclusion: it looks as if the significant empirical notion 'vowel shift' is lost if we persist in thinking of sound change only in terms of 'rule-addition'. There seem to be coherent processes of language change that demand a more abstract formulation than is proper to phonological rules in the strict sense. And in this case it seems that an important and regular kind of dialect differentiation is explicable only in terms of metaconditions on rules operating on whole systems: not in terms of the rules themselves.

In the next section I will attempt to support the claims I have made so far by looking at a superficially quite different vowel shift, which nonetheless turns out to be governed by the same condition; and in the one after that, I will consider still another, which in a different way will support the conclusions I have reached so far.

synchronic vowel shift in English, it is expectable for it to have a constraint of this type. And if there isn't one (which seems likely), we still need the implication in the metarule anyhow for historical reasons.

[1] That is, if we leave aside the question of whether alpha-switching rules are ever 'reasonable'. I incline toward the view of Stockwell (1966) that they are a most implausible type of rule to be involved in historical change. But see the admirably thorough discussion in Wolfe (1972).

5. Supporting evidence: the High German Vowel Shift

I have claimed that we need a new kind of phonological statement, solely on the basis of the GVS. But is this the only case of its kind? It would help if we could find other instances where similar implicational relations seem to hold. I am not claiming, of course, that there is anything 'universal' about a schema like (16): only that it is possible, and in some cases necessary. In this section I will attempt to show how the same kind of schema holds for what is at first glance a quite different sort of vowel shift: though still a West Germanic one. I refer to the set of disparate and widely spaced innovations which I will call, collectively, the High German Vowel Shift (HGVS). These events are not generally treated as a unit in the handbooks, but we will see that there is a good reason why at least one group of them should be. The following exposition adheres closely to the standard accounts, e.g. Wright (1907), Prokosch (1916), Kirk (1923), von Kienle (1969).

The long vowel and diphthong system of pre-eighth-century Old High German seems to have been like this:

(17)	ī		ū
	ē		ō
			ā
	ai	au	eu

(As I have done previously, I will represent long vowels for convenience as /V̄/; but the nature of some of the changes strongly suggests a cluster analysis like that given for English in chapter 1 above.)

The HGVS can be analysed as consisting of three main stages, or perhaps more accurately, two stages with a 'bridge' period between whose main effect is to add new vowels to the inventory. These three stages correspond (roughly) to the 'transitions-from' pre-OHG to OHG, OHG to MHG, and MHG to 'Early Modern' German (*Frühneuhochdeutsch*). I will describe each stage briefly, and then sum up the ways in which the whole thing corresponds to the GVS. I will then show how a schema like (16) is applicable at least to the later stages: again through consideration of divergent dialectal reflexes.

The first stage, which is complete by about the end of the eighth century,[1] is as follows.

[1] With regard to the orthographic manifestation of these changes, the following account is oversimplified. Thus I assume that the diphthongization of /ē ō/ is a single process: but the spellings showed up at different times, and in fact suggest a number of

(a) High and low vowels remain; but all the other members of the long vowel and diphthong system change, as follows:

(b) *Mid vowel diphthongization.* /ē ō/ diphthongize and raise their first elements, ending up as /ie uo/ respectively (probably via /ea oa/: von Kienle 1969, §§23–4, Kirk 1923, §26). Thus WG **hēr* 'here' > OHG *hier*, WG **fōt* 'foot' > OHG *fuoȥ*.

(c) *Mid diphthong raising.* /eu/ goes to /iu/ in certain contexts, e.g. before /x/: WG **leuxtjan* 'illuminate' > OHG *liuhten*. Otherwise /eu/ > /io/.

(d) *Low diphthong raising and monophthongization.* /ai/ and /au/ split, as follows: /ai/ > /ē/ before /r x w/ and finally; otherwise /ai/ > /ei/. Thus Go. *maiza* 'famous' = OHG *mēro*, Go. *stains* 'stone' = OHG *stein*. The other /a-/ diphthong, /au/, becomes /ō/ before /x/, dentals, and finally, otherwise /ou/. Thus Go. *dauþus* 'death' = OHG *tōd*, Go. *augō* 'eye' = OHG *ouga*. The effect of these changes is a drag chain: the monophthongal reflexes of /ai au/ move into the front and back mid positions vacated by the diphthongization of /ē ō/ (cf. (a) above).

The whole series of changes can be schematized like this:

(18)

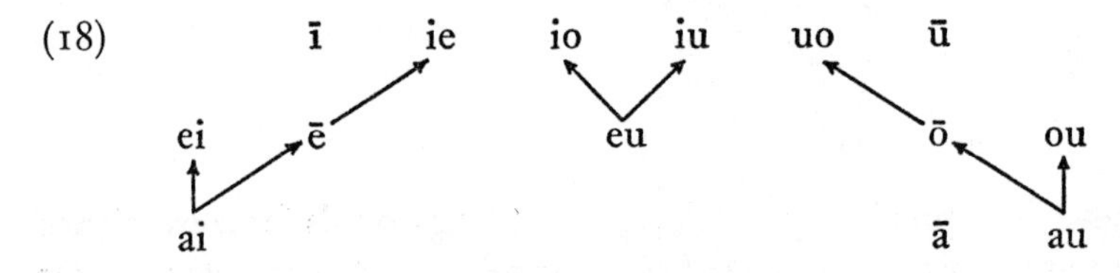

The general outlines are clear: mid vowels, whether single (in this case 'long monophthongal') or in diphthongs, raise one height; they then diphthongize if they were monophthongal. Low vowels in diphthongs raise, but the backness value of the second member dominates (cf. the developments of ME /ai au/ in *day*, *law*). Monophthongal /ā/ does not change, and neither do the high vowels. At the end of this we have the following inventory:

(19)

ī	ie	io	iu	uo	ū
ē	ei			ou	ō
					ā

intervening stages. For instance /ē/ appears as *e* in Frankish and Alemannic until the eighth century, when it becomes *ea*; in the ninth century we get *ia* spellings throughout OHG, and *ie* by 850 or so. A similar progression through the dialects shows up with /ō/ (von Kienle 1969, §§22–3). But the FACT of diphthongization is all that concerns me here: see further p. 77, n. 1.

The next stage is complicated by the operation of *i*-umlaut, which adds a number of new vowels and diphthongs, so that the total inventory affected by the final stage is increased. Basically, back vowels front without change of roundness before a suffixal /i j/. The umlauts of the long vowels and diphthongs are as follows:[1]

(20)

ū → ȳ	uo → ye
ō → ø̄	ou → øu
ā → ǣ	

During the final stages of the HGVS, these new nuclei will undergo changes (roughly) corresponding to those affecting their unmutated congeners. Thus it is irrelevant whether or not the umlaut is synchronically recoverable at any particular stage of MHG (cf. King 1969: ch. 4). If [ȳ ø̄], etc. are derived vowels, then the shift I am about to discuss is synchronically ordered after umlaut; if the lexicon has already been restructured, there is no problem. After the umlaut, then, we have this inventory:

(21)

ī	ie	ȳ	ye	uo	ū
ē	ei	ø̄	øu	ou	ō
ǣ					ā

The third stage consists of the following main changes:

(a) *High diphthong monophthongization.* /ie/ > /ī/, /uo/ > /ū/, /ye/ > /ȳ/. MHG *tief* 'deep' > NHG *tief* (where *ie* = [i:]), *fuoȥ*, 'foot' > *Fuß*, *füeȥe* 'feet' > *Füße*.

(b) *High vowel diphthongization.* /ī/ > /ai/, /ū/ > /au/, /y/ > /oy/ (or perhaps better, th. final reflexes are /ae ao ɔø/: see the discussion in Philipp 1970: ch. 1). Thus MHG *bīssen* 'bite > *beißen*, *hūs* 'house' > *Haus*, *liute* (*iu* = [y]) 'people' > *Leute*.

(c) *Diphthong lowering and backness switch.* /ei/ > /ai/, /ou/ > /au/. MHG *stein* 'stone' (*ei* = [ei]) > NHG *Stein*, *boum* 'tree' > *Baum*. Backness Switch affects /øu/, which becomes /oy/, merging with /oy/ from /ȳ/, e.g. *böume* 'trees' > *Bäume*. Diagrammatically, then:

(22)

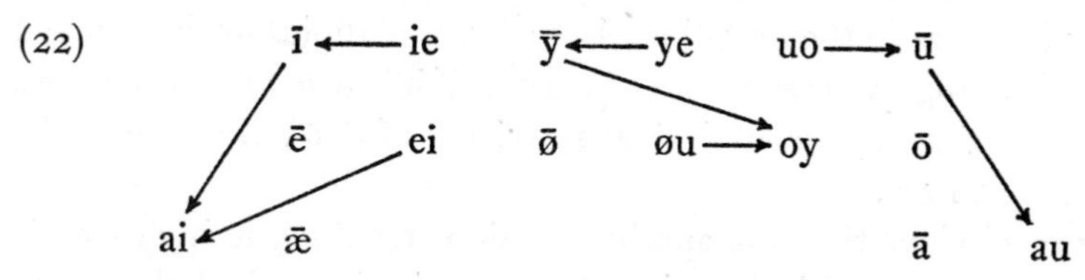

[1] In what follows I use IPA [y ø] for traditional 'Germanistic' [ü ö], to avoid confusion with dialect material cited elsewhere in this book, where [¨] is a diacritic for centralization.

Note that the mid vowels /ē ø̄ ō/ and the low /ā/ are unaffected. For convenience, the whole set of processes can be summed up in tabular form:

(23)

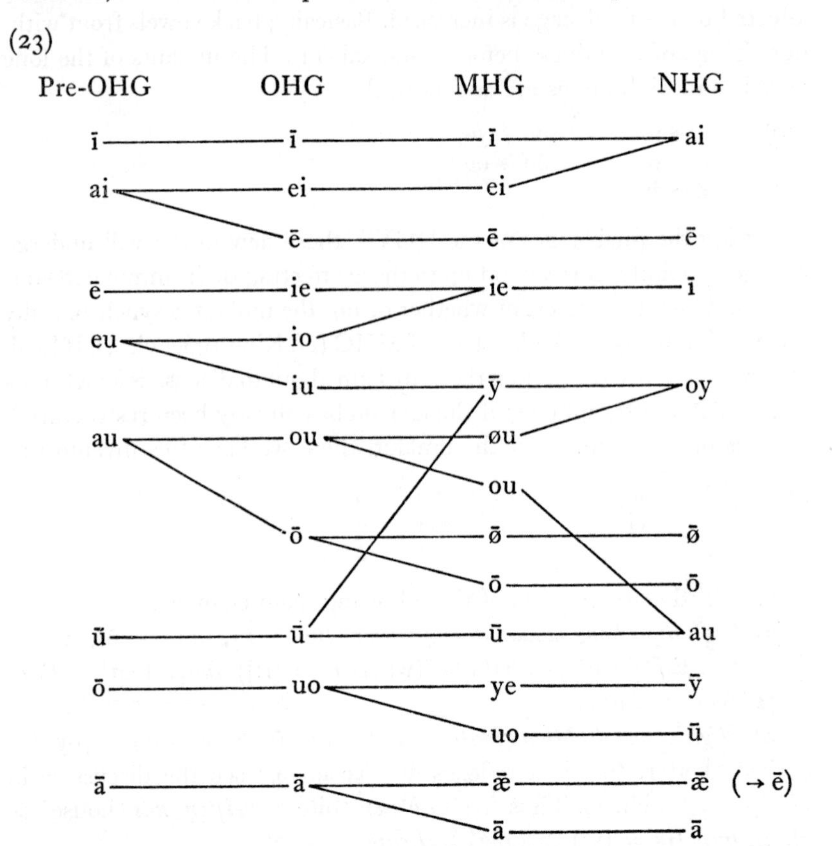

The complexity of a display like (23) tends to obscure the outlines: is this really similar to the GVS? The wide temporal spread of the changes is a source of confusion; but a careful examination shows us two familiar processes operating in the last phase, after having had, as it were, the stage set for them in the first. That is, high vowel diphthongization and mid vowel raising. At least we have the latter if it is true that the changes /ie/ > /ī/, /uo/ > /ū/ are equivalent to raising of /ē ō/. And this is the case, as we will see.

It seems obvious that monophthongizations resulting in high vowels that do not collapse with the original ones, as in those cited above, are functionally equivalent to 'direct' raisings. If this is so, and if the implicational set-up I suggested earlier were to hold also for the HGVS (i.e.

that it is a 'no-collapse' shift), then we could make a testable prediction. That is, if there is some dialect where /ie uo/ have not monophthongized, then that dialect should have high monophthongs for MHG /ī ū/. And such dialects do in fact exist. Consider the reflexes of the four relevant segments in the modern descendants of the Alemannic dialects. First, High Alemannic (*Schwyzertüütsch*), specifically the dialects of Zürich and Bern (*Züritüütsch, Bärndütsch*). These show the following developments of MHG /ī ū ie uo/ (Keller 1961: 32, 40–2, 91–3):

(24)	MHG	NHG
	ī	i:
	ū	u:
	ie	iə
	uo	uə

And now the slightly different but analogous case of Low Alemannic, i.e. Northern Alsatian (Keller 1961: 119–20):

(25)	MHG	NHG
	ī	i
	ū	y
	ie	iə
	uo	yə

(There has been a later fronting of MHG /ū/ and of /u/ in diphthongs, and there is thus no high back vowel: but the essential shape is the same.)

The situation in German is thus exactly analogous to that in English; only here it is clearer, because the implication holds for both front and back vowels. The primitives in this operation are the same: a mid vowel 'displaced' from its proper series has no effect on a high vowel, but one that remains does. Even though the first elements of pre-OHG /ē ō/ raise, the resulting /ie uo/ are still distinct from /ī ū/ by virtue of their nonsyllabics, and do not cause high vowel diphthongization until they 'get back in line' as it were by monophthongizing. The sequence is:[1]

[1] Some scholars claim that the relation between the two changes is in fact chronological, and that the diphthongization of /ī ū/ not only preceded the monophthongization of /ie uo/, contrary to what I have claimed, but that the two changes began in different dialects. Thus Prokosch (1916: 143). But his account is based entirely on the appearance of orthographical representations in texts of the Bohemian and Saxon Chancelleries. So what he says may indeed be true of the SPELLINGS associated with these segments; but there is no real evidence that it is true of the segmental changes themselves. In fact, if it is the developments in Alemannic are inexplicable. This simply points out, as far as I can see, the danger of using orthographical evidence for dating sound changes; spellings can never give us more than a date when people happen to

(26)

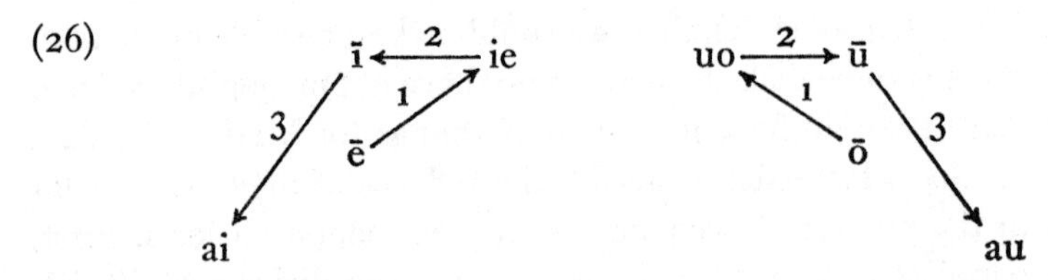

Of course the relation (2, 3) is implicational, not (necessarily) sequential. The order of integers represents a CAUSAL rather than a temporal chain. A pair of changes like /ie/ > /ī/ and /ī/ > /ai/ undoubtedly represents a long series of mutual adjustments over time (i.e. chains of this type are in the strict sense 'co-varying'). But the implication of the metarule provides in advance for just this mutuality.

The two apparently rather different West Germanic vowel shifts we have looked at show a strikingly similar mechanism at work: an implicational relationship between the diphthongization of high vowels and the raising of mid vowels immediately below them. In German, diphthongized mid vowels fail to monophthongize to high vowels in some dialects, and these are the ones that show original high vowels that have not diphthongized. This corresponds exactly to the English situation, where those dialects in which ME /ō/ had fronted, and was therefore not present to raise in the back series in the GVS, also show unshifted /ū/. The primary differences between the German and English shifts, then, are first the way the relevant mid vowels 'get out of the channel', and second how many of them do it. So the schema (16), in a general way, seems to characterize for both cases the major internal relations between the various changes that make up the shifts.

6. Non-diphthongizing vowel shifts: the North Germanic pattern as evidence for a general implicational schema

I have been suggesting not only that metarules are involved in certain types of sound change, but that systems are too. They are in fact the domains on which (at least certain) metarules are defined. In this section I will consider some more evidence for this, and illustrate a rather different kind of vowel shift that nonetheless still shows the dominant role of abstract conditions defined on 'spatially' organized vowel inventories.

notice them. As far as the HGVS goes, I would claim that there is no (non-orthographical) counterevidence to the implicational sequence I have proposed; and that this is preferable to orthography-based sequences like Prokosch's because it makes sense of dialectal divergences as well.

This will lead to a reformulation of (16) in what appears to be a maximally general way. It will turn out, I think, that while (16) was a step in the right direction, it was over-specific: the basic principles are still more abstract and general.

Let us look at the vowel shifts in Swedish and Norwegian. Beginning about the fourteenth century, these dialects underwent a shift of the long back monophthongs. In Swedish, which I will take as my main example, the shift has been described this way (Wessén 1955: 55):

Till sin klang torde de ha varit väsentligen likartade som långa och som korta. Ex.: *făra, grāta*; *sŏfa, sōl*; *hŭnder, hūs*...Emellertid har uttalet av desser vokaler i svenskan starkt förändrats, då de varit långa: *ā* har blivit *å*, *ō*...har blivit slutet *o*-ljud...och *ū* har blivit främre slutet *u*-ljud...Förändringarna ha icke skett samtidigt: först har *ā* förändrats, senare *ō* och sist *ū*.[1]

This quite traditional view is of course problematical because of the particular theory of sound change it espouses; and, outside of Sweden, I suspect, it is misleading because of its rather inaccurate interpretation of the Modern Swedish vowels, which is keyed to the orthography rather than the pronunciation. But both these difficulties raise some interesting points.

First for the theory: it is clear that Wessén's claim that the changes went in sequence from low to high is meta-empirical: i.e., while it is based in part on spelling evidence, the strongest determinant is the notion that non-merging chains must always go in temporal sequence, not in implicational networks. Thus he says that '*ā* har under medeltiden antaget ett alltmera slutet uttal, skjutits bakåt och slutligen blivit labialiserat' (1955, 55).[2] This implies, I suppose, that /ā/ was a low central vowel, perhaps [ɐ:] and that this shifted up and then back, so, that when it reached [o:] it pushed /ō/ up to /ū/. (It seems more probable, though, aside from anything else, that in the usual Scandinavian manner /a/ was [a] and /ā/ was [ɑ:].) This account further implies a stage [ɔ:] for /ā/, which seems unlikely: since the shift operated, as far as we know, in a vertically three-term system, the points at which distinctiveness was critical for the long vowels must have been [ɑ o u], i.e. the type [ɔ], if it existed, 'belonged' to short /o/, as in Modern Swedish.

[1] 'The long and the short vowels were probably the same in articulation...The pronunciation of the long ones, however, was greatly changed in Swedish: *ā* became *å*, *ō*...became a close *o*-sound...and *ū* became a close front *u*-sound...These changes did not occur simultaneously: first *ā* shifted, then *ō*, and finally *ū*' [my translation: RL].

[2] '*ā* gradually became closer and closer, was shifted back, and finally became labialized' [my translation: RL].

The essential point is that since orthographical and phonological change do not proceed at the same pace, and since changes can, as I have shown, have relations other than precedence, there seems no compelling evidence for anything but a covarying chain. That is, an implicational consequence of a metarule, but here restricted to the back vowels.

The Modern Swedish vowels, whose nature Wessén's terminology somewhat obscures, are of particular interest in explicating what seems actually to have happened. Mainly, the reflex of OSw. /ō/ is not really a 'close *o*-sound', but rather, if anything, an 'open *u*-sound', i.e. a high vowel. (The range I have most often heard is roughly [u̜ː] to [o̜ː].)[1] Further, the sound written *å* is higher mid, usually [o̜ː] or even [oː]; and the 'front close *u*-sound' requires special comment. This is an extremely interesting vowel, because it enters into a very rare type of opposition.[2] As Malmberg points out (1971a, b), it has roughly the tongue position of [ø], but is distinguished from both [ø] and [y] by the TYPE of lip-rounding. Malmberg, who uses the symbol [ɯ] for it, writes as follows (1971b, 258):

> Ce qui distingue le type [ɯ] du type [y]–[ø]–[œ] est une DIFFÉRENCE DE LABIALISATION. Si les [y]–[ø] se distinguent des [i]–[e] par un AVANCEMENT DES LÈVRES – ayant pour résultat un allongement du résonateur buccal et une certaine diminution de son ouverture – on dirait que c'est par une CONTRACTION DES LÈVRES que [ɯ] s'oppose a [y] et [o]. L'effet acoustique de cette contraction est...une diminution encore plus grande de la fréquence propre du résonateur buccal... [Emphasis Malmberg's: RL.]

This is further supported by both articulatory and spectrographic data. Earlier Swedish scholars had distinguished, quite usefully, I think, this special lip-attitude as *inrundning* 'in-rounding', as against the *utrundning* 'out-rounding' of [y ø].[3] At any rate, this vowel, the reflex of OSw. /ū/, is front, in contrast to /u/, and 'in-rounded', in contrast to /y ø/.

Given this, we can see that the Swedish back vowel shift is a push-

[1] The confusion here may be due to the fact that in at least some Swedish dialects, it is apparently the case that '[uː]' is really a close [o]-type vowel with an abnormally tight lip-rounding, i.e. a degree of stricture appropriate for the next height up (cf. Sweet 1877: 153). But it sounds like a high vowel, and if it has the rounding appropriate to high tongue position it can be taken as systemically high.

[2] It is often transcribed [ʉ] in modern treatments of Swedish, but this is not to be confused with IPA [ʉ].

[3] Chomsky & Halle (*SPE*: 315) suggest that this vowel be distinguished from [y ø] by the specification [+covered], i.e. it has a greater degree of laryngeal elevation and pharyngeal tension. But even if these effects exist, Malmberg's evidence seems conclusive for locating the distinctiveness in lip-attitude.

chain whose end result is rather different from that of the West Germanic chains in phonetic implementation, but identical in principle. Fronting and in-rounding looks like a way of following out an implication of systemic raising, and avoiding collapse. We can see how this strategy works by looking at the whole system which defines the domain for the shift. The long vowel system of Old Swedish at the time of the shift was probably of this type:

(27)

ī	ȳ	¦	ū
ē	ø̄	¦	ō
ǣ		¦	ɑ̄

So if a nonlow vowel fronts, and is not to collapse with any existing categories, it may not become /i e y ø/. It must therefore make use of some feature other than (ordinary) rounding to maintain distinctiveness. Thus (using the nonce-symbol [ë] to avoid confusion with IPA [ɯ] and [ʉ]):

(28)

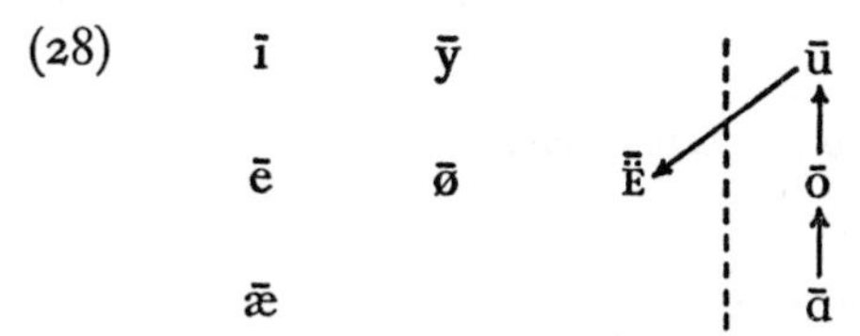

(Typical forms showing the changes are OSw. *gās* 'goose', *gōd* 'good', *hūs* 'house', Modern /goːs/, /guːd/, /hëːs/.)

In Norwegian, the results of the shift are more or less the same for the reflexes of old long /ɑ̄ ō/; but /ū/, instead of fronting all the way, centralized to /ʉː/.[1] Thus the form of the shift here is:

(29)

ī	ȳ	¦	ʉ̄ ←	¦ —	ū
		¦		¦	↑
ē	ø̄	¦		¦	ō
		¦		¦	↑
ǣ		¦		¦	ɑ̄

(For articulatory descriptions see Popperwell 1963: 25–30.)

I doubt if it is possible to give a satisfactory answer to the question of why Norwegian and Swedish show such different vowel-shift patterns

[1] I mark length in the modern vowels only for historical convenience; both Swedish and Norwegian have lost phonemic length, and all quantity is environmentally predictable. See the discussion in ch. 1, §9 above, and ch. 1, Appendix; also Lass & Anderson (1975: ch. v), and Lass (1974b).

from English and German; or why they differ from each other in the way that they do.[1] But even failing any answer other than 'language-specific idiosyncrasy', there is still an obvious theoretical moral to be drawn. If we take all the material we have looked at together, it seems that we have four instances of one general type: a raising-induced covarying chain. If we look beyond the idiosyncratic details of the individual shifts – length of time involved, rules intervening between one stage and the next, the specific modalities of change affecting the high vowels – we find one common factor. And this is that if a metarule comes into play, specifying raising and no-collapse, the operation for high vowels is getting out of the way of the mid vowels without merging with any other elements in the system.

I shall call this operation DEFLECTION. It can be defined 'aetiologically' as a 'functional', system-induced strategy for coping with covarying chains under a no-collapse constraint. So we can now reformulate (16) in a much more general way, as an overall characterization of Germanic vowel shifts:[2]

(30) *Germanic vowel shift schema*

(a) *Metarule:* $\bar{V} \rightarrow$ [raise]

(b) *Condition:* No collapse if (a)

(c) *Implication:* If $\sim$ (b), then: $\begin{bmatrix} V \\ +\text{high} \end{bmatrix} \rightarrow$ [deflect]

(Note that (30) is not, like (16), restricted to long vowels; there are short-vowel chains as well in Germanic, one of which is described below in ch. 4, §4.)

I assume that certain universal constraints will operate here: e.g. that the instruction [raise] is so defined that it is incompatible with the specifications [−cons, +high]. And I also assume that the implementa-

[1] Haudricourt & Juilland (1949: 105–7) give a similar interpretation of the Swedish vowel shift, with emphasis on the avoidance of collapse through covariation, and the creation of a new vowel from /ū/. But their characterization of the modern reflex is incorrect: they take it as close ('*fermée*') and central ('*une mixte arrondie*': 106). This analysis is clearly more appropriate for Norwegian. But the principle certainly holds: and Haudricourt & Juilland illustrate it further with examples from Greek, Portuguese, and French (the French example is the implicational relationship between the raising of /ọ/ to /u/ and the fronting of /u/ to /y/). For discussion of (synchronic) covariation of a related type in English, see Labov (1972) and Trudgill (1974: 117–20).

[2] For Germanic vowel shifts in general, but excluding for instance the Icelandic one, which is a totally different affair (cf. Benediktsson 1959), and the Yiddish changes mentioned earlier.

tion of [deflect] is language-specific. Thus the schema (30) is all that a 'meta-grammar' of Germanic vowel shifts contains; the rest is up to the languages involved.

It is important to note also that the domain of (30), in effect, must be SYSTEMIC: it refers to configurations in phonological space, not to individual segments or to features on them. That is, the specification [+high] in (30c) is operative only if the space immediately below the high vowel in question contains a mid vowel. The metarule and its implication thus presuppose a two-dimensional structural description. The condition (30b) can only be negated if the configuration (31a) below appears; if (31b) appears, then condition (30b) is tautological, and the high vowel doesn't have to do anything:

$$(31) \qquad \begin{array}{c} [+\text{high}] \\ \begin{bmatrix} -\text{high} \\ -\text{low} \end{bmatrix} \\ \text{(a)} \end{array} \qquad\qquad \begin{array}{c} [+\text{high}] \\ [\qquad] \\ \\ \text{(b)} \end{array}$$

The domain of (30), that is, can be defined as a series (front, back, or central) with the top two positions occupied. And the schema itself can be taken as a set of instructions like these:

(32)
(a) Read the metarule.
(b) Does configuration (31a) exist?
(c) If yes, consult language-specific option for [deflect].
(d) Formulate rules accordingly, and implement (a).

If this is reasonable, it suggests further that shifts of the type (30) are typically non-iterative, which seems to be the case. Later historical events may involve further movement, however: thus in English sixteenth-century [ei] in *bite*, etc. becomes [ɛi], [æi], [ai] in most dialects, and goes as far as [ɑi] or [ɒi] in some. But the initial shifts appear to be singulary: they are the product of what Luick called *Impulse*, and what I have tried to define more carefully and called metarules. And the possibility of formulating metarules becomes itself a partial definition of the notion 'sound shift': which is what I was after in the first place.

7. Some conclusions

The approach I have taken here is a retreat from what I consider to be excessive 'concreteness'. But it is clearly only a very preliminary way of getting at some basic problems in the description of large-scale phonological change. Whatever the defects of the particular proposals, the direction still seems to me a fruitful one. It is not of course an attempt to get rid of phonological rules in the usual sense, but rather to add a dimension that seems to be lacking in current historical phonology, to the detriment of its explanatory (and even descriptive) power.

There are two main conclusions to be drawn from this study (aside from whatever clarification of the GVS, etc. may have resulted): (a) that phonological systems as STRUCTURED INVENTORIES OF SEGMENTS, SPATIALLY ARRANGED, must be taken into account in the description of language change; and (b) that there are higher-order, abstract rules, different in type from actual phonological rules, which have an important part to play in precipitating historical change. And these are in fact often necessary in order to explain change at all. This is especially clear in cases like the Germanic vowel shifts, where the metarules have deducible consequences, i.e. they serve to 'predict' (or 'retrodict') certain classes of historical events.

I conclude with some brief and speculative remarks on the relation of my putative metarules to 'grammars' (in the usual sense of the term), and their effects on grammars formulated by post-metarule 'generations' of speakers. (I assume for the moment the plausibility of current 'mentalist'/'rationalist' theories of language change and acquisition, though with great reservations: cf. ch. I above, *passim.*) First of all, metarules are not, in the usual way, 'added to' grammars. They are EVENTS in linguistic history whose nature is induced from their effects: the rules they cause to be added, and the effects of these rules on the overall systems. The closest (synchronic) analogue, as I said earlier, is something like an output condition or derivational constraint. Metarules in fact may best be described as diachronic redundancy rules, with pan-systemic domains.

Such metarules do not of course 'appear' in derivations, or the rule-sequences in grammars, nor do they act in the same specific and 'local' sense as grammar-internal redundancy rules. They are themselves short-lived, since they are events in real time, not structures; they are in no sense part of a speaker's 'competence', but are metaconditions defining (temporarily) the possible forms of certain artifacts of that competence. The artifacts may of course persist for considerable lengths of time; if the *SPE* vowel shift is really a fact about English phonology, or if the

Swedish vowel shift has a synchronic analogue (cf. Hammarberg 1970), then they certainly do.

I think we can visualize the working of metarules in this way. Let a metarule arise (however it does), and act on a grammar G_i, giving rise to a rule or set of rules which implement its instructions. And let the output of G_i serve as 'primary linguistic data' for the generation acquiring language from the speakers characterized by G_i. The grammar G_j of this second generation will incorporate the results of the implementation of the metarule (with whatever changes the processes of 'optimization' require) – but not the metarule. Its job is done when the first implementation strategies have developed. It will have served its purpose by causing G_i to produce the machinery which can be taken over by G_j. The difference between G_i, G_j with respect to some metarule M will be this: G_i will have M as a condition on its output, plus the rule-sequence $\{R_1, \ldots R_n\}$ defined by the implementation of M; whereas G_j will have only $\{R_1, \ldots R_n\}$ as defined by M, but not M. The addition of M as a condition on G_i will then be defined as 'the sound change M'; while the sequence $\{R_1, \ldots R_n\}$ in both G_i, G_j will be 'the reflex of M'. (I am not of course claiming that 'generation' and 'G_i, G_j' are to be taken in a simplistic, immediate-succession sense; nor am I claiming that all change is immediate in its effects, with no time-lags caused by diffusion, etc.)

If the above is taken as the substance of my proposals, then the implications are these: in order to describe certain kinds of massive, 'global' change in an empirically correct and intuitively satisfying way, we must revise our conception of the role played by 'rules' (*sensu stricto*) in the initiation of change. We should view many (perhaps all) global operations on language systems over time not as the addition of rules to grammars, but as the operation of higher-order, abstract metarules on these grammars: metarules whose consequences happen to be – in many cases – rules of the type made familiar by current research in generative grammar.

Rules, then, are in many cases derivative phenomena, developed as a result of a grammar's having to cope with certain kinds of large-scale, abstract 'instructions'. To take rules themselves as primary, as both the agents and vehicles of change, is to misvalue them, and to attribute originating force to them which is not properly theirs. To put it another way, rules are in many cases merely the particular, local devices that grammars use to implement metarules.

3 *The Great Vowel Shift and its aftermath in the North Midlands: more evidence for the vowel-cluster hypothesis*

1. An apparent 'violation' of the vowel shift metarule

This chapter attempts to bring together two themes raised earlier; it is also a case study in the use of theoretical notions as heuristics in reconstruction. The theoretical point is important: as a historical linguist I am naturally very much interested in the protocols for conducting arguments in the absence of direct evidence, and the development of inferential strategies for exposing 'concealed' histories.

The two earlier themes are: (a) the chain-like structure of the GVS, particularly its character as a covarying 'no-collapse' chain (ch. 2, §4); and (b) the notion that both 'long vowels' and 'diphthongs' in English should be treated phonologically as vowel clusters. The investigation here may bear some incidental fruits: the clarification of the rather complex and not much explored vocalic histories of certain English dialects.

In particular, I will show that certain dialects with apparently 'deviant' GVS reflexes actually give us a clear picture of the original shape of the process – perhaps even a clearer one than the more familiar 'standard' Southern or the basically similar Northern ones. These reflexes provide both a clear picture of the no-collapse condition on the original shift, and a measure of support for the vowel-cluster hypothesis.

Let me begin however with a brief recapitulation of some of the arguments in chapter 2, but with more detail on the GVS as a whole. The late ME input to the shift (except in the North) was probably a long vowel/diphthong system of this type:[1]

[1] In chapter 2, I used the *SPE* version of the ME vowel system for convenience, since I was largely concerned with their claims (cf. p. 63, n. 1). Here I return to a more traditional (and I think correct) version. Very little of this is controversial, except for the location of ME /a:/ as a front vowel: for some justification see chapter 4 below, Appendix. Here /e:o:/ are the traditional /ẹ̄ ọ̄/ and /ɛ:ɔ:/ are /ę̄ ǭ/. For the sake of

(1)

i:			u:		
e:		eu	o:	oi	
ɛ:		ɛu	ɔ:		ɔu
a:	ai	au			

The GVS is a system-wide chain: the long nonhigh vowels raise, the high vowels diphthongize, and some of the diphthongs raise their first elements like the corresponding long vowels, while others monophthongize and fill the slots vacated by the raised mid vowels (e.g. /eu/ > /iu/, /au/ > /ɔ:/: on the latter see ch. 5 below, §1). The earlier stages seem to have involved no mergers; but some categories merged later on, different ones in different dialects. In Southern British English and its descendants (in general), there were mergers of /ɛ:/ and /e:/ (*beat*, *beet*), /ai/ and /a:/ (*day*, *same*), and /ɔu/ and /ɔ:/ (*grown*, *bone*). If we exclude for the moment both the mergers and the developments of the diphthongs, the bare bones of the early shift (THE GVS proper) can be represented this way:

(2)

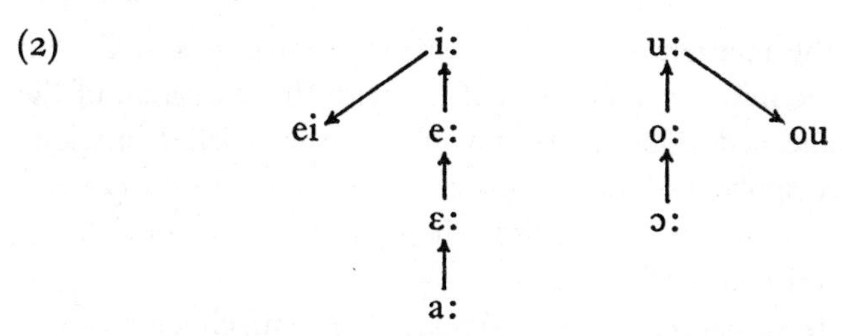

The values /ei ou/ for ME /i: u:/ were reached by the sixteenth century (e.g. in Hart 1569); the raising of /a:/ was later, as Hart does not show it, though there is evidence for it later in the same century, in Bellot (1580) and Bullokar (1580), where a value like [æ:] or [ɛ:] is indicated (see the discussion in Wolfe 1972: 37–44).[1]

As far as the mergers of /ɛ:/ and /e:/, and /ai/ and /a:/ are concerned, these are later still: /ɛ:/ and /e:/ are still separate in Coles (1674), but

identification, the old etymological categories are represented by the following modern items: /i:/ *bite*, /e:/ *beet*, /ɛ:/ *beat*, /a:/ *same*, /u:/ *house*, /o:/ *boot*, /ɔ:/ *bone*, /ai/ *day*, /eu/ *new*, /ɛu/ *dew*, /au/ *law*, /ɔu/ *grown*, /oi/ *boil*.

[1] This discussion follows the careful and detailed summary of the early grammarians given by Wolfe (1972: ch. III). For works not cited in my bibliography, i.e. which I have not consulted personally but for which I follow Wolfe, see her references. Wolfe's book is by far the most linguistically sophisticated treatment of these sources available (albeit less detailed – and eccentric – than Dobson 1957). It must be remembered that I am dealing here only with the 'standard' developments, i.e. those in dialects ancestral to RP, etc. Indeed, most of the early orthoëpists are explicitly concerned with the educated London standard of their times. (On 'standard' English in this period, see Dobson 1959.)

show some (context-sensitive) merger in Cooper (1687), especially before /r/ (Wolfe 1972: 84–7, 91–107). There is still vacillation here as late as the work of Thomas Tuite (1726), between merged and non-merged forms: ME /e:/ is always /i:/, but ME /ɛ:/ may be either /i:/ or /e:/. By the time of Douglas (c. 1740), the merger is complete (except of course for the famous *break*, *great*, and a few others like *pear*, *wear*, which still have /e:/. Cf. Wolfe: 103–5).

The merger of /ai/ and /a:/ is extremely complex and variable: to give an idea of it I quote Wolfe's account (p. 106):

> Hart and Bellot both show a merger of ME *ai* and *ē* as monophthongal [ē] or [ɛ̄], and Gil [1619: RL] and Butler [1633: RL] describe this as a current non-standard pronunciation of which they disapprove. Robinson [1617: RL] shows optional monophthongization of ME *ai* to merge with...*ā*, and the coalescence of ME *ai*, *ā* is shown by the later grammarians...though many of the writers such as Wallis [1653: RL] and Wilkins [1668: RL] still describe a diphthongal pronunciation for ME *ai*.

In other words, the mergers that characterize the current situation in general postdate the mid-seventeenth century, with the exception of the clearly more advanced developments shown a century earlier in whatever dialects Hart spoke and Bellot observed. So the schema (2) is a reasonable representation of the earliest shape of the completed long-vowel shift in its no-merger form.[1]

So much for these earlier events. My argument in chapter 2 was based essentially on an interesting set of implications, which seemed to support two claims: (a) that the original GVS was a no-collapse chain, and (b) that the initial 'impulse' was the raising of the mid vowels, not the diphthongization of the high ones. The implication, to recapitulate, is this: if a dialect has undiphthongized ME /u:/ (e.g. [u:] in *house*), it has a front nucleus for ME /o:/ (e.g. [i:] in *boot*). The reason for this is that in pre-GVS Northern ME, there was a context-free shift of /o:/ to /ø:/ (with later raising to /y:/) which left a gap in the system that was input to the shift. (The back vowel series here was /u: ɔ:/, with no /o:/ to raise and 'displace' /u:/.) Thus the prediction: if ME /u:/ is undiphthongized, ME /o:/ is front.

But this implication is irreflexive: a fact which I did not mention earlier, as it was not relevant to that argument. The inverse, that if ME

[1] Some writers (e.g. Stockwell 1966) have claimed that the initial shift of /i: u:/ did not involve lowering, but centralization: thus they went to /ɨi/ and /ʉu/ respectively. Wolfe's discussion (1972: esp. 107–8) seems to dispose of this idea.

/o:/ is front, ME /u:/ is undiphthongized, does not hold. There are in fact dialects with nuclei like [ɩə ɩu ʏ:] for ME /o:/, but [aɷ ʌɷ əɷ] for ME /u:/ (though none with consistent [u:] for both ME /u: o:/). Dialects of this type are found in the North Midlands (basically parts of Yorkshire, Lancashire, Cheshire, etc.: for discussion and maps see Wakelin 1972: ch. 5).[1] The exact reasons for this state of affairs – historically – are obscure: but it seems to have something to do with the NML being a 'transition area' over which innovations have travelled freely (and still do) in both directions, from the North and from the South. Though the dialects, despite their bewildering profusion of both Northern and Southern characters, are still basically Northern.[2] It seems that in general, some of the more orderly processes of change that we find at the extremes of the country have been interrupted or short-circuited by continual interdialectal diffusion, so that we get the peculiar situation of the NML being at once innovating with respect to the North and the South, as well as conservative with respect to both. It certainly seems clear, however, that diphthongized ME /u:/ is not an original part of the GVS here, but a late importation.[3]

[1] In the SED *Basic Materials* for the North (Orton & Halliday 1962), the following areas show a diphthongal ME /u:/ ([əu ʌɷ aɷ] or late monophthongal derivatives like [ɛ: a:]) and a front ME /o:/ ([ɩa ɩu ʏ:]): Coniston, Lancs (5.1), Yealand, Lancs (5.3), Harwood, Lancs (5.12), Bickerstaffe, Lancs (5.13), Melsonby, Yorks (6.1), Muker, Yorks (6.6), and Bedale, Yorks (6.8).

[2] Even though Northern and Southern features coexist in the NML, and thus mark it as 'transitional', its basic Northern character still shows through. Thus we find short [a] for ME /a/ in the Southern lengthening environments (before /f θ s ns/: cf. ch. 4 below); [ɷ] for ME /u/; monophthongal nuclei like [e:] for ME /ai/, rather than Southern [eɩ]; and non-merger of ME /ɔu/ and /ɔ:/. The only clear Southern features are rounding of OE /ɑ:/ in *bone*, etc., and diphthongs for ME /u:/ (cf. Wakelin 1972, map on p. 87, and ch. 4 below, Appendix). Among the uniquely NML features are non-merger of ME /e:/ and /ɛ:/, and separation of /ai/ and /a:/, which I return to below. Non-aspiration of /p t k/ may also be (weakly) criterial for the NML; certainly it is commoner here than in the North and the South (though it is very frequent in Scotland). Cf. the phonetic notes on the SED areas in Orton & Halliday (1962: 11–39).

[3] The peculiar position of the Midlands in general as a kind of no-man's-land between the North and the South was noticeable at least as early as the fourteenth century. In a famous passage from his *Polychronicon* (1327: text in Mossé 1950: 289), Ranulph Higden says (1. lix): 'De praedicta quoque lingua Saxonica tripartita, quae in paucis adhuc agrestibus vix remansit, orientales cum occiduis tamquam sub eodem coeli climati plus consonant in sermone quam boreales cum austrinis. Inde est Mercii sive Mediterranei Angli, tanquam participiantes naturam extremorum, collaterales linguas arcticam et antarcticam melius intellegunt quam ad invicem se intellegunt iam extremi.' In John of Trevisa's rendition of the last sentence (1385: *ibid.*), the Mercians 'þat buþ men of myddel Engelond, as hyt were parteners of þe endes, undurstondeþ betre þe syde longages, Norþeron and Souþeron, þan Norþeron and Souþeron undurstondeþ eyþer oþer.'

These dialects are interesting in other ways: they show a much more complex and differentiated development of the ME long vowel/diphthong system than either the South or the North. And these developments do not seem at first to be insightfully describable in terms of a chain: the vowels appear to wander about in the vowel space in unaccountable ways. We will see, however, that these wanderings can be referred easily to an initial stage that shows the chain at its clearest, as in (2): the peculiarities arise later. And these very peculiarities turn out to be simpler and more reasonable than they look, if they are interpreted in the light of the proposals I made earlier about the role of vowel clusters in English.

2. The GVS in Dentdale, Yorkshire (W.R.)

For an example, let us take the dialect of Dentdale, in the West Riding of Yorkshire, as described by Hedevind (1967). The reflexes of the ME long vowels and diphthongs show up as follows (I include RP and a typical Northern dialect – Lowick, Northumberland, SED area 1. 1 – for comparison):[1]

(3)

ME	*Example*	*Dent*	*Lowick*	*RP*
i:	white V. 10. 7	aɩ	ɛ̨̈ɩ	aɩ
e:	sheep III. 6. 1	əɩ	i:	i:
ɛ:	wheat II. 5. 1	ię	i:	i:
a:	spade I. 7. 6	ea	iə	eɩ
u:	about VII. 7. 8	aɷ	u:	aɷ
o:	boots VI. 14. 23	ɩu	ɩɤ	u:
ɔ:	foal III. 4. 1	ua	ø:	öɷ
ai	tail III. 2. 2	ę:	e:	eɩ
au	saw- I. 7. 17	a:	a:	ɔ:
ɛu/eu	suit VI. 14. 21	ɩu	ɩu	ɩu
ɔu	grow IX. 3. 9	aɷ	ɔ̣ɷ	öɷ
oi	boil V. 8. 6	ɔɩ	ɔ̣ɩ	ɔɩ

(The 'pseudomorphic' character of NML is quite clear from these forms, which are fairly typical of a wide range of dialects.)

[1] I give typical items from the SED questionnaire to represent the etymological categories. ME /a:/ is /a/ lengthened in open syllables, and ME /ɔ:/ is /o/ in the same environment, to facilitate North/South comparisons: since ME /ɔ:/ in the South represents OE /ɑ:/, but not in the North; and ME /a:/ in the North represents OE /ɑ:/ but not in the South (see ch. 4, Appendix). I collapse /ɛu eu/ under one heading, since these have merged in all NE dialects.

In Dent, the shifts of ME /i: u:/ are the same as in the South, as is the relatively minimal change of /ɛu eu/. The reflex of '/o:/' (actually of course of /y:/ < /ø:/) is typically Northern. But virtually nothing else in this system seems to display the character we have come to expect; nor do the Northern and Southern mergers take place: though others do, like that of /ɔu/ and /u:/. In particular, ME /ɔ:/ has not raised to /o:/, but seems to have 'skipped a step', and at least one of its elements is now high. Nor has /e:/ (apparently) raised to /i:/. And /au/ has not filled the vacated /ɔ:/ position, which is empty in Dent but filled in RP.[1] Among the expected mergers – at least from the Southern point of view – /ɛ:/ and /e:/ remain separate, as do /a:/ and /ai/.

As I said earlier, there is little superficial resemblance here to the Southern and Northern chain shifts: but this is in fact due largely to later developments. We can probably say this with some confidence, because it is reasonable to assume that the GVS (even with the Northern exception for /u:/) was pretty uniform throughout Britain, at least until the late sixteenth century. We can make this assumption partly on the basis of configuration, and partly on probabilities. That is: even these rather bizarre NML reflexes show great congruities IN PATTERN to Hart, e.g. in the non-merger of ME /ɛ: e:/ and /ai a:/. Clearly, however the vowels got to the places they did, the original design is manifest here. There is nothing in Dent, in fact, to suggest any differences in development up to at least the point represented by Hart. Further, to take probabilities into account: it would be odd indeed if both the 'syde longages' (Northern and Southern: cf. p. 89, n. 3) were to show evidence of identical developments that failed to affect 'Myddel Engelond', from the earliest stages of the GVS. There could not have been three separate vowel shifts, with the two not in contact identical. It is thus the later developments that represent innovations in the NML; and here is where things get interesting.

We can thus suggest that up to about the sixteenth century, the GVS developments in Dentdale were like those of (4). (That is, Dent was essentially a Northern dialect with unshifted /u:/; and it had no /o:/, but rather /y:/ from /ø:/ from /o:/. The circled segments in (4) are new ones created by the shift.) It seems clear that since /ai/ did not merge with /a:/, the former nucleus remained unchanged;

[1] In RP, /ɔ:/ is occupied by the reflexes of ME /au/, and also those of short /o/ before /r/ (see ch. 5 below). In Dent, ME /or/ is usually [ɒʴ ~ ɒ:ʴ], with some older speakers still having [ɔɾ ~ ɔr] (Hedevind 1967: §4: 39).

and we will see later that /o:/ is a quite reasonable stage on the way to /ua/ from /ɔ:/. The merger of /ɛu eu/ is also late, as it is everywhere.

(4)

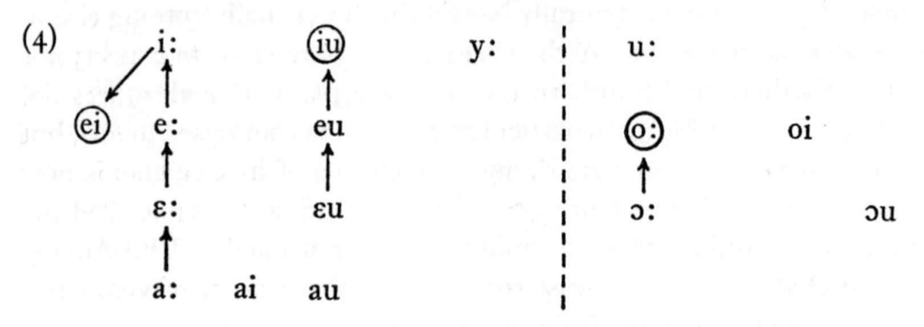

At this period, then, we can assume that the total inventory in Dentdale was:

(5)

	i:		iu	y:	¦	u:		
ei	e:		eu		¦	o:	oi	
	ɛ:				¦			ɔu
		ai	au		¦			

(The low /a:/ is recreated at a later stage by monophthongization of /au/.)

3. A speculative history of the Dentdale vowel system

One of the most striking features of Dentdale and similar dialects is the large number of diphthongs of the 'non-narrowing' type (cf. ch. 1, §7), i.e. diphthongs whose second elements are mid or low, and whose first are closer, like [ea ua ię]. And it is here (as I suggested in chapter 1) that the consequences of not analysing these nuclei and their ancestors as vowel clusters become very clear. That is, any other analysis will force us to posit, at some point in the history, an unmotivated typological break, where original 'long' or 'tense' or 'complex' nuclei turn into vowel clusters.

The simplest case is if long vowels are vowel + length, i.e. /V/ + /:/. Here, developments like /ɔ:/ to /ua/ are simply unmotivated. If we assumed a vowel plus /y w h/ analysis, as Stockwell (1961) does, then /ɔ:/ would be /oh/, where /h/ is realized as [ə] or something of the sort. Here we would have to account – again arbitrarily – for the 'vocalization' of this consonantal offglide; since there is certainly no warrant in this framework for taking an open peripheral vowel like [a] as an allophone of /h/. And if we began with a 'tense' /ɔ̄/, we would (if we assumed the

SPE 'norms' for tense vowels) have a stage /ɔ̄w/, with subsequent vocalization of /w/, and then a host of later vowel changes.[1]

Actually the vowel changes themselves are perfectly acceptable: this is after all what the GVS is about. But the initial stage, the typological change from /V:/ or /Vh/ or /V̄/, is still unmotivated. (And in the nature of things, since both 'consonantal' offglides and 'tenseness' are analytical artifacts rather than even potential observables, this stage is unsupportable in principle from any empirical evidence. See further ch. 1.)

A somewhat more realistic line is taken by Hedevind, who seems (at least implicitly) to believe that long vowels can in some sense be taken as bimoric (though he confuses the issue by adding 'tenseness' as well). Thus he suggests that when ME /a:/ reached the stage /ɛ:/ in the GVS, 'the diphthongization that set in' at this point 'resulted in the NW in a differentiation to [eɛ], i.e. a raising and tensening of the first element and a slackening of the second' (§5: 28). The 'first element' must mean that /ɛ:/ has two elements, i.e. is /ɛɛ/, and 'differentiation' suggests the idea of diphthongization by dissimilation (ch. 1, §8). He argues, correctly I think, that the development to [ea] must have come about through some such process, and not through the development of a central 'offglide' (Luick's *Abstumpfung*, 1964: §495).

Hedevind suggests that, considering the presence of 'obsolescent' [ɩa] in forms of this category in Dent, plus older records of this pronunciation, the development must have been like this:

(6) a: → æ: → ɛ: → eɛ → iɛ → ɩa → ea

(It is certainly true that all the stages in this development except [eɛ] are documentable somewhere in the North or NML of England: a point I will return to later.)

Let us however try to achieve a clearer picture, without the typological break between /ɛ:/ and /eɛ/ (even if this is – at least for Hedevind – mainly notational). I will operate on the hypothesis that both long vowels and diphthongs are vowel clusters, so that /a:/ is /aa/, and therefore structurally parallel to /ea/, etc. We can now reinterpret the Dent input to the GVS (cf. (5)) this way:

(7)

ii			yy	¦	uu		
ee		eu		¦		oi	
ɛɛ		ɛu		¦	ɔɔ		ɔu
aa	ai	au		¦			

[1] Actually /ɔ̄w/ with 'glide vocalization' would get us into trouble, since the output would be /ɔu/, which would merge with ME /ɔu/; and clearly this happens later.

The changes illustrated in (4), the first stages of the GVS, are then:

(8)

ii	ee	εε	aa	eu	εu	ɔɔ
↓	↓	↓	↓	↓	↓	↓
ei	ii	ee	εε	iu	eu	oo

It is at this point that the new developments, those which are characteristically NML, supervene. And these can now be interpreted in terms of INDEPENDENT TRAJECTORIES IN THE VOWEL SPACE for the individual members of the vowel clusters. The change, for instance, from '/a:/' to /ea/ is now no longer a typological shift, followed by a series of vowel changes, but simply:[1]

(9) aa → εε → eε → iε → ea

This is the necessary background to an attempt to characterize in a fairly simple way the whole set of Dent reflexes of the ME input system (7). In what follows, I will make a number of assumptions, both about what constitute well formed changes, and about what constitute well formed outputs for changes; and these require some discussion. If they are methodologically ill-founded, the reconstruction will be empty.

First, on the general matter of permissible changes. It is clearly necessary to invoke some kind of constraints on what can change into what, and how; since any reconstruction where intermediate stages are totally unconstrained is not vulnerable to any judgement. The problem of course is how to discover (or invent) and 'justify' such constraints. Obviously, it is undesirable to 'weaken' a theory arbitrarily, by imposing constraints for their own sake; so we should if possible discover some empirical (or quasi-empirical) source for them.

The most obvious source of constraints on vowel changes in a domain like this one, where we are treading on relatively unknown ground, is the universe of better-known changes (as far as one is aware of it). And in addition, the division in this universe between frequently and infrequently attested changes. We can adopt a very simple heuristic: let us say that in a given instance we have a diachronic correspondence /X/ : /Y/, and a set $P = \{p_1, p_2, \ldots p_n\}$ of possible paths between /X/ and /Y/. What we do then is rank (as far as we can) the members of P in de-

[1] It might seem that a direct progression /aa/ → /εa/ → /ea/ is simpler: but if the arguments supporting the essential identity of the early stages of the GVS in all dialects hold, then Dent must have had /aa/ → /εε/; and the reflexes of /aa/ in Dent and neighbouring areas insist on a stage /ia/ at some point. The simplest line of development does not necessarily square with the evidence: cf. the absurd history of ME /a/ sketched out in ch. 4 below.

creasing order of probability (relative to the observed probabilities of the path-types in the universe of discourse). If we can achieve a ranking like this – however informal, however (necessarily) limited by our own experience, and the available data – then we can make a methodological decision.[1] This is simply that, given a choice of paths, and given no compelling evidence for one or the other, we take the most probable (i.e. best attested) one. Our heuristic tells us that this is in fact the one that was taken.[2]

So on the basis of my own experience of vowel changes, and especially in English, I would want to characterize what is generally permissible (i.e. without extra evidence) as follows:

(a) Changes of vowel-height are in general restricted to one step at a time, unless there is convincing evidence to the contrary. I.e. unless we are pretty sure on independent grounds that it happened, /ɛ/ → /i/ is not well-formed, but /ɛ/ → /e/ is.[3]

(b) Direct front-to-back shifts, with no central vowel intervening, are well-formed (cf. the Germanic *i*-umlaut).

(c) But there are three cases where large-scale shifts of articulation are to be expected: identity-assimilation (e.g. /au/ → /aa/), mutual assimilation (e.g. /ai/ → /ee/), and mutual dissimilation (e.g. /yy/ → /iu/).

It is clear that (a–c) will constrain the possible set of independent trajectories for the members of vowel clusters fairly tightly. But we still need some more constraints, of a slightly different kind, to cope with the rather complex problems that can arise. Before I attempt to reconstruct the whole Dent development, then, I will illustrate both the problems and the procedures with a specific example: the development of ME /ɔ:/ (= /ɔɔ/) to /ua/. This is the only one I will deal with in detail; the

[1] The ranking is in practice not statistical, but merely impressionistic. Since we lack tables of sound change grouped by frequency of given types, we generally make such 'naturalness' decisions on the basis of how many examples of one type we know as against how many of another type. This is the best we can do right now; but it does not vitiate the ideal procedure. At the moment, of course, it is really what Abercrombie (1963) very properly calls a 'pseudo-procedure': but unlike the ones he rightly castigates, I think this is (a) useful, and (b) quite possible, at least for smallish areas.

[2] This is the sort of strategy that insists that the correspondence Latin /p/: Germanic /f/: Celtic zero (e.g. L. *porcus*: OE *fearh*: OIr. *orc*) cannot derive from an IE zero-initial, with labial epenthesis in non-Celtic dialects. Similarly, given a pair of rules like Verner's Law and the Germanic *Verschärfung*, it requires more evidence to justify the latter than the former: we EXPECT Verner's Law. See the discussion in Lass & Anderson (1975: ch. v).

[3] There are a few well-attested cases of 'bypassing', e.g. where ME /i/ lowers to /ɛ/ but /e/ remains /e/ in Scots: cf. ch. 4, §4 and ch. 5 below.

rest of the results can be checked against the available material quite simply, as we will see.

First of all, let us note that dialects like this pose difficulties of a rather special sort. We must rely on our heuristics much more than in other cases, e.g. the development of London Standard. The out-of-the-way 'provincial' dialects were never the centre of orthoëpic attention; they were rarely described by early writers in any detail, and most of what we do know about them from direct description is due largely to incidental comments.[1] So we lack, for these dialects, the careful descriptions and analyses that we have for London vowel systems in the crucial period: the sixteenth to eighteenth centuries. Because of this, in trying to establish the histories of dialects outside of the South, we must rely heavily on a combination of comparative procedures and theoretical considerations, both of which can be epistemologically tricky: in other words, we must reconstruct, since we are rarely able to chronicle (see further §4 below). And because reconstruction is so central, we must have, I think, some tighter and more specific constraints than I have so far suggested.

Most important: if, in the absence of direct testimony for intermediate stages, we have to construct a history of a particular vocalic nucleus, we must utilize not only the general constraints I gave above, which concern only progression from one vowel to another; we must constrain WHICH vowels appear as the results of changes as well. We must control not only processes but outputs. So in addition to the first three criteria given above, which I give below in a compressed form as (i), we ought to have another, which I give below as (ii). In constructing a history, then, we should take pains to ensure that:

(i) the individual changes are 'natural', i.e. attested cross-linguistically (and if possible, in English); and

(ii) the intermediate stages, between the input and the observable output, are also natural: specifically that they too are attested in some language (and if possible, in English).[2]

[1] E.g. Hart (1569: 33) on the Scots' 'abuse' of the 'auncient' sound of *u*: he remarks that they, like the French, confound 'the soundes of i and u togither: which you may perceyue in shaping thereof, if you take away the inner part of your tongue, from the vpper teeth or Gummes, then shall you sound the u, right, or in sounding of the French and Scottish u, holding still your tongue to the vpper teeth or gums, and opening your lippes somewhat, you shall perceyue the right sounde of i.' This is as far as I know the first dependable description of [y] in Scots.

[2] The reason for this criterion is that I am concerned here with sound changes, not synchronic derivations. There are no strong constraints on what can appear as an

The rider 'and if possible, in English' reflects a requirement of language-specific naturalness: we should be able to identify all changes – in the perspective of the known history – as 'possible changes in English'. And even more important, we should be able to identify all outputs as 'possible nuclei in English'. (This suggests that I assume there has been no change in phonological typology since at least Middle English times; and in fact I see – overall – no very strong indications that there has been.)

It is possible, further, to suggest a much stronger version of (ii): that all the nuclei we reconstruct be attested in some dialect of English as reflexes OF THE SAME ETYMOLOGICAL CATEGORY. This makes the idea ot language-specific naturalness even more binding: since now we have another constraining notion to work with, that of 'possible development for a given etymological category in English'. This may seem at first an absurdly strong kind of constraint: but we will see that it may be of some theoretical interest.

To see how my suggested criteria can help to determine a reconstructed path, let us first survey the present-day reflexes of ME /ɔɔ/ in the North and NML. The SED material (s.v. *foal* III. 4. 1 < OE *fŏla*) yields the following main developments (each exemplified by one area where it occurs):

(10)	*NE reflex*	*SED area*
	øː	Lowick, Nb. (1. 1)
	œː	Embleton, Nb. (1. 2)
	øə	Haddon-on-the-Wall, Nb. (1. 8)
	u̜·ə	Stavely, We. (4. 4)
	ɷa	Threlkeld, Cb. (2. 4)
	ɷə	Haltwhistle, Nb. (1. 7)
	ɷ̈ə	Wark, Nb. (1. 5)
	ọə	Allendale, Nb. (1. 9)
	oː	Marshside, Lancs. (5. 10)
	o̜ː	Eccleston, Lancs. (5. 11)
	ɔɩ	Thistleton, Lancs. (5. 7)
	ɔə	Helmsley, Yorks. (6. 10)
	ɒɩ	Ribchester, Lancs. (5. 8)

If all these derive from /ɔɔ/, which became /oo/ in the (presumably) 'universal' first phase of the GVS, there is certainly plenty of evidence

'interlevel' unobservable in a synchronic grammar; but the product of a sound change should be a potential observable, i.e. it is subject, even in the absence of direct testimony, to the typological constraints that we assume should hold for the language at a superficial level.

for the independence of the two members of the cluster. The first /ɔ/ has reflexes covering a range including [ɔ o ɷ u ø œ], and the second has a range including [o ə ɩ ø œ]. This suggests the size of the set of possible combinations we have at our disposal: and this, remember, is for only a limited area of the country. And this range, large as it is, still constrains the total set of available combinations. Even under the strong form of (ii) above, we still have considerable latitude: much more, in fact, than we really need in this instance.

With the data in (10) before us, we can construct a development that begins like this:

(11) (a) ɔɔ
↓↓
(b) oo
↓↓
(c) uə

Stages (a, b) are attested by history and orthoëpic evidence; stage (c) is amply attested in the dialects. (That is, I assume that since there is a limit to the fineness of specification we can recover, [ɷ] can be taken as at least roughly equivalent to [u]). And further, the transition from (b) to (c) meets the one-step-at-a-time constraint proposed earlier, as well as the language-specific naturalness condition: the shift of /o/ to /u/ is already part of the GVS, and changes like /o/ to /ə/ are attested in values like Allendale's [o̩ə] < /oo/, and in values like [əɷ] < ENE /ou/ < ME /uu/ in Scots, Canadian, and some U.S. dialects.[1] The problem is how to get from /ə/ to [a], since we have Dent [ua] beside the [ɷə] types.

A simple progression that would meet all my conditions would be:

(12) ə → ɜ → ɐ → a

Now this one is not attested, but somewhat similar ones are: e.g. the change of [ʌ] < ME /u/ to [ä] (perhaps via [ɐ]) in London and elsewhere in the South. Certainly the range of variation in Southern English, where the 'diaphone' /ʌ/ covers a territory including [ʌ ʌ̤̈ ä a] suggests that this is a reasonable development (cf. Gimson 1965: 103). Now since the attested reflexes here imply a skipping of the half-open slot [ɜ] on the way from [ə] to the low advanced-central [ä] (unless [ʌ̤̈] can be considered 'a kind of [ɜ]'), we might posit something similar for the Dent

[1] At least this is so if we assume that they derive directly from the early GVS stage /ou/. Some [əɷ] of course derive by later changes from [aɷ] or [ɐɷ]: see e.g. Labov's study of the centralization of low vowels on Martha's Vineyard (1963).

change. That is, bypassing of [ɜ] on the way from [ə] to [ɐ], so we get a hypothetical stage *[uɐ] between [uə] and [ua]. If we want, then, to restrict the size of possible shifts of articulation – even at the cost of introducing unattested intermediary stages in the history – we can complete the schema (11) this way:

(13)

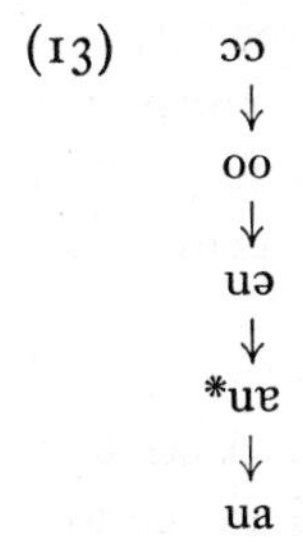

(The unattested reflex-type is starred; I will continue this practice below.)

We can now tentatively reconstruct the development of the whole Dentdale vowel system, from the ME input (7) to the present (with the rest of the arguments implicit):

(14)

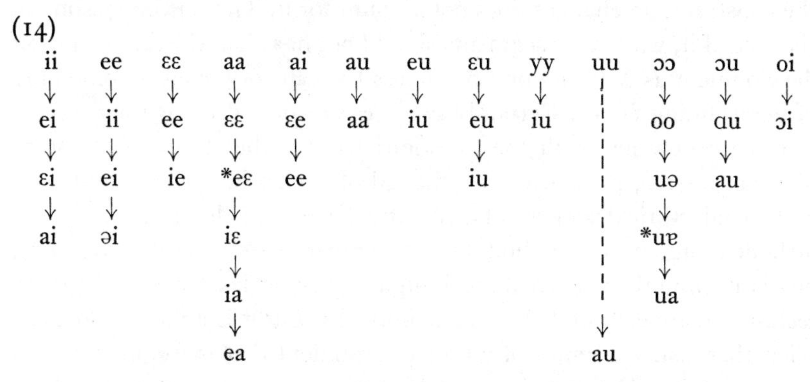

(The broken arrow for /uu/ represents the probable direct borrowing from the South. Note that the fact that two or more changes are in the same horizontal row does not imply temporal simultaneity: the idea is simply to suggest what happened, not when. The network of chronological relations is a separate problem, which I will not investigate here.)

4. On the status of 'speculative histories'

Considering the constraints I proposed above, the results here are rather interesting. If we take the constraint on change-types as unbreakable, then it produces two outputs which fail the language-specific naturalness condition: the starred *[eɛ] and *[uɐ], which are not attested anywhere in English, as far as I know. But of the outputs which are well-formed, ALL meet the strong form of criterion (ii) in §3: they all occur somewhere in English as reflexes of the same etymological category. Thus, to take the odder ones, [ɛe] for ME /ai/ occurs in some forms of RP (Jones 1950: §162); [ei] for ME /ɛɛ/ shows up as [ẹɩ] (which is as close as makes no difference) in Muker, Yorks (area 6. 6); and [ɑu] for ME /ɔu/ occurs in Allendale, Nb. (area 1. 9). All the rest seem pretty clearcut and non-controversial.

So it looks as if – despite the problem represented by the two starred outputs (which in any case are not wildly out of line) – the basic strategy is fairly sound. It is particularly interesting that a close adherence to a set of constraints on change-TYPE will in fact cause a reconstruction to come close to meeting the strong condition on etymological CATEGORIES. This clearly needs more extensive testing: but it does suggest that there may be something of theoretical interest in the etymologically defined notion 'well-formed reflex'. If this is so, it requires some explanation; the constraint on changes does not account for it. There is no reason, on the face of it, why other segments should not have had the same kinds of development as ME /aa/ or /ɔɔ/, unless the category itself is some kind of determining factor. Certainly this area is worth investigating.

We are now left with the question: what is the status of a history like that in (14), produced with the aid of such a battery of conditions and metahistorical constraints? What I have been doing is surely not orthodox comparative method (though comparative evidence is involved); nor is it any other 'normal' technique either, at least insofar as these techniques are expounded in the handbooks. But it is a rather more explicit than usual instance of a type of argument that is frequently used in a more implicit way (e.g. by Hedevind on a smaller scale). It is 'legitimate', I suppose, in that it's done; but what exactly does it give us? Can (14) or any similar object be interpreted as a 'real' history, or is it merely an artifact of the heuristics? And finally, is it an 'empirical hypothesis' about the history of this dialect?

To take the last question first, the answer is a flat 'no'. The proposals made here are not 'empirical' for the simple reason that they are not in principle testable, and cannot be decisively refuted. And they are not testable for peculiarly HISTORICAL reasons (unlike hypotheses about underlying representations, which are generally untestable for rather different ones). That is, they are untestable because the data that would constitute a test is missing: if it weren't, there would be no need for reconstruction. This is the reconstructive historian's dilemma: the only reason to reconstruct something is that the thing you want has irretrievably vanished (it is pointless to say that IF a Dentdale orthoëpist were suddenly to come to light, we would have a test: this is not testability-in-principle). But despite this lack of testability, reconstructions are valuable.

Any reconstruction, it seems to me, is (a) pleasing and interesting once you have it, and (b) fills in gaps in such a way as to fulfil the historian's explanatory mandate, which is to tell us how things got the way they did. Inferential gap-filling of this kind is one of the historian's primary functions, and one which is irreducibly metaphysical. There are no 'justifications' (in any strong sense) for reconstruction, and surely no (general) refutations.[1] But a historian who does not reconstruct is merely a chronicler; to be interesting, he has to take risks.

These risks are built in: I doubt that hypotheses of an interesting degree of abstraction in historical linguistics (or any other historical discipline) can ever be empirical. The incursion of history into a field of investigation makes it, in Scriven's phrase (1959), an 'irregular subject': the usual empirical modes of argument no longer hold.[2] This means that the knowledge we gain from historical investigation is of a special and provisional type, more provisional even than other types of knowledge

[1] This is not to say that much of the trust we put in techniques like comparative method is not based on justifications: it is. But they are rather simpler: if we take a test case, for example, with a known antecedent, and find that by applying the techniques we get something very like the antecedent, we have a check on our procedure. And if we have successes this way, it increases our confidence in the results in those (more important) cases where the antecedent is unknown (which is what we developed the technique for in the first place). But this does not make the techniques themselves 'empirical': the unknown antecedents are precisely the cases where no test is possible. See the discussion of the problem in Lass (forthcoming).

[2] This is true of historical hypotheses in the (otherwise) empirical sciences as well: e.g. evolutionary theory, which is certainly not 'empirical' in the usual sense, though it is explanatory (cf. Scriven 1959, Popper 1973: ch. 7). Even experimental support of evolutionary hypotheses is indirect in the same way that the justification of comparative method is. The most interesting post-Darwinian innovations, for instance, like the massive theoretical structure erected by Waddington, with its brilliant (and highly explanatory) notions of 'chreods' and 'genetic assimilation' are as far as I can tell rationally metaphysical, not empirical (cf. Waddington 1957, 1969). The most important notions are simply not testable. See further my *Epilogue* below. It seems likely that all empirical sciences have a metaphysical component, anyhow; even positivism in its strongest form is based on a metaphysical commitment. Cf. the discussion in Harré (1972).

derived from empirical testing or 'nondemonstrative inference' (Botha & Winckler 1973).

But this does not mean that historical argumentation, any more than any other non-empirical kind, is useless or nonproductive. If we accept that the heuristics and argumentative strategies are fundamentally rational, and if we are willing to forego 'certainty' in the quest for increasing (partial) understanding, then we have something.[1] In the local test case I have produced here, we have possibly gained some insight into the history of a particular dialect, and into the type of evolution that English vowel systems undergo. And this insight is 'explanatory' without being in any real sense 'empirical'. Historical linguistics should not arrogate to itself an empirical, 'scientific' status that it has no legitimate claim to; but on the other hand, if it follows its own proper paths, it has nothing to apologize for.

[1] The pursuit of certainty (either in empirical or metaphysical domains) is in any case the pursuit of an illusion. If we eliminate, in any given instance, a false theory, we may be that much closer to the truth: but there is no guarantee that we will ever reach it, nor that we could possibly tell even if we did. The concept of 'truth' must rather play the part of a 'regulatory idea' (Popper 1973: ch. 1). It is possible to have 'growth' or 'progress' in knowledge without engaging in a 'quest for certainty' (Popper 1973: 37).

Part II

EXPANDING THE DATA-BASE: THE YIELD OF COMPARATIVE METHOD

History is not an account of facts but of relations that are inferred to have existed between supposed facts. It is not at all easy to make a crucial observation as to what a particular fact is, or to discriminate between facts and inferences. The 'facts' of historical scholarship are often simply useful hypotheses that in turn relate, by rough rules of inference, a variety of secondary 'facts' to each other. The most insightful accounts of historical events turn out to be intricate webs of suppositions and inferences removed at many steps from the citable data on which the conclusions ultimately rest.

R. P. Stockwell, 'Mirrors in the history of English pronunciation' (1968)

4 *What kind of vowel was Middle English /a/, and what really happened to it?*[1]

1. The problem

The first question in the title is prompted by a rather surprising fact: at this late date in the history of diachronic English studies the characterization of ME /a/ is still unsettled. Was it a low back vowel, or a low front vowel? Both of these contradictory views have been held and argued for since the nineteenth century, and we seem no closer to a solution than when the discussion began. I will try to show here that it is possible, given the application of well-tried traditional procedures to a large body of data that has not been properly utilized, to come up with a principled and unambiguous solution.

I assume further that it is self-evident that such a solution is worth having: in the case of a vowel that has undergone a number of important changes in its history, we must locate it somewhere definite in the vowel space, so that we know where it started, and how it got wherever it did get. The second question in the title is suggested by the materials that provide an answer to the first: ME /a/ got a lot more places than most traditional (and modern) 'histories of English' would lead us to suspect. We will find that the answer to this question is both complex and interesting.

Given the excellence of English as a field of historical investigation, and the immense amount of talent that has been brought to bear on the matter (the authorities I will cite here are a virtual *Who's Who* of historical English studies), why has ME /a/ not been adequately (and non-controversially) characterized? I think there are two main factors involved: (a) reliance on ambiguous orthoëpic testimony under the misapprehension that it is in fact clear, and (b) neglect of the most important single source of evidence. (A third factor, which has made some

[1] This chapter is a revised and expanded version of Lass (1973a), with numerous inaccuracies corrected. The appendix is completely new. I am grateful to J. A. Kemp and John Wells for comments.

contribution, is the interference of metatheory.) I shall look at all of these as I proceed.

Let us first consider why the characterization of ME /a/ is so important. This is mainly because it arises from a very complex set of developments in earlier stages of the language, and participates in equally complex ones later on. And the entire history of the West Germanic short low vowel */a/ – the beginning of it all – in English will vary according to our conception of the shape of the vowel system at any given point. For instance, following the handbook accounts, the earlier part of this history can be represented as follows:

(1)

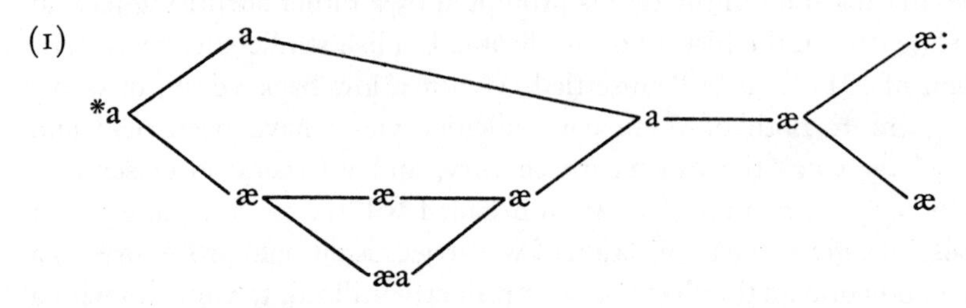

The first branching is the so-called 'Anglo-Frisian Brightening'; the second is 'Breaking' and 'Velar Umlaut'; the first coalescence is the late OE monophthongization of *ea* (= [æa]); the second is the merger of *a* and *æ* in many ME dialects; the next development is the change of ME /a/ to [æ] in the seventeenth century; and the final branching is the lengthening of ENE /æ/ before /f θ s/ and other segments (see below, §5) in the late seventeenth century. (I will go into the later part of this development in detail below.)

Now obviously these developments will be interpreted differently depending on the kind of system one sees them as happening in. For instance, just to take the late ME and early NE parts of the history, which will be our concern here, the following characterizations of the late ME short vowel system are current in the literature:[1]

(2)

i	u	i	u	i	u
e	o	e	o	e	o
	a		a		a
(a)		(b)		(c)	

[1] Throughout this chapter symbols in [ ] have their IPA values; symbols in / / have systemic reference only, i.e. /a/ doesn't (necessarily) mean [a], but rather the etymological category under discussion. Unless otherwise specified, symbols in a systemic display like (2) are equivalent to those in / /.

System (2a), phonetically interpreted, would have /a/ = [ɑ]; this is the view of Jespersen (1909: 1), Ekwall (1956), Jones (1950), Gimson (1965),[1] and Chomsky & Halle (1968). It is probably also, though with some unclarity, that of Luick (1964), Wright & Wright (1924) and Horn (1909). System (2c), where /a/ = [a], is assumed by Zachrisson (1913), Dobson (1957), and Danielsson (1963). System (2b), if phonetically interpreted, would mean, I presume, that /a/ = [ɐ]; but a figure of this type, as usually proposed (e.g. Mossé 1947, Martinet 1955) normally represents a set of correlations or 'pure oppositions', where /a/ has in Trubetzkoyan terms a '*maximale Öffnungs-*' or '*Schallfüllegrad*', but no (particular or necessary) front/back location. While such a characterization may be adequate on the most abstract phonological level, it will not do for history or typology: an open vowel must have its opening somewhere.

The need for localization becomes especially pressing if we consider a change like the development of [æ]. Virtually everyone agrees that whatever ME /a/ was, it became, probably during the seventeenth century (though some, e.g. Davies 1934, Wyld 1956, date it to the fifteenth, on rather slim evidence) a vowel of the type [æ]. At least this general character (closer than [a], opener than [ɛ]) seems a reasonable value for Wallis's 'à exile' (1653) and Cooper's 'a lingual' (1687). So if ME /a/ was [ɑ], then this development involved fronting and raising; if it was [a], then it only raised. A decision becomes even more crucial when we consider a dialect with [a] for ME /a/: if the original was back, then there has been a sound change; if the original was front, nothing at all has happened. Surely we must have principled answers to questions like whether or not a sound change has taken place, and if it has, where.

Let us turn to some of the traditional accounts of ME /a/ and its developments. The following are quite typical of the less detailed overall statements we find:

Dem me. *a* entspricht heute in der südenglischen Gemeinsprache *æ*, während im Nordenglischen altes *a* bewahrt ist...Die südenglischen Palatalisierung beginnt im 16. Jahrh.... (Horn 1909: §40.)

Er [ME *a*: RL] wurde auf einem großen Teil des Sprachgebietes, vielleicht

[1] Jones (1950: 69) gives a specimen of reconstructed Chaucerian 'pronunciation', showing [a] in *fast, that,* [a:] in *hate*, and [ɑ] in *all, small.* Gimson (1965: §6.25) gives [ɑ] for OE /a/ and [a] for ME /a/. Neither Jones nor Gimson give any evidence or argument in support of these values. (See the Appendix to this chapter for a discussion of what such arguments – which cannot be based on the kind of evidence I use below for ME /a/ – might look like.)

auf dem ganzen, in die Reihe der Palatallaute vorgeschoben und zu einem æ-Laut, low-front-wide oder low-front-narrow, umgebildet. (Luick 1964: §536.)

ME *a*...became *æ* about the end of the sixteenth century, but in the northern and nearly all of the midland dialects it has remained down to the present day... (Wright & Wright 1924: §62.)

(We will see later that Luick was wrong about the extent of the change to [æ]; the Wrights, though closer to the truth, were still too conservative.)

None of these is really satisfactory. Horn is ambiguous, because it is not clear what he meant by *Palatalisierung*. If he meant only raising, then /a/ was [a]; if he meant fronting, then it was [ɑ]. Luick is clearer: I presume we can take *vorgeschoben* literally, in which case /a/ was [ɑ]. But he gives no evidence. The Wrights are problematical, because their characterization of the NE dialect reflexes, judging from other remarks in the same work, is wrong; as is Horn's, if he meant that ME /a/ was [ɑ], and that this quality ('altes *a*') is what remains in the North.

The difficulty with many of these earlier writers (and some later ones) is that they either could not or did not distinguish [a]-type from [ɑ]-type vowels. This is probably the case with the Wrights, since their symbol *a* is the short version of the long *ā* in 'Standard' *ask*, *bath*, *path* (§15). This latter vowel must surely be something like [ɑ:], or in its advanced forms [ɑ̟:] or [ɐ:]; so that *a* must be [ɑ] or [ɑ̟] or [ɐ]. At least this holds if what they meant by 'Standard' was something like RP, rather than a 'regional' standard (e.g. Joseph Wright's own Yorkshire: cf. Jones 1956 on RP '[ɑ:]' and Gimson 1965 on '/ɑ:/').

But there is certainly no evidence for vowels of a distinctly back (or even fully central) quality as reflexes of isolative ME /a/ in any Northern English dialects (the quite different Scots situation will be treated in §4 below). The same confusion is (surprisingly) apparent in Sweet, who gives the symbol (a) as representing a back vowel, and says (1891: §674) that it occurs in (Standard) NE only long, as in *father*, *farther*, *alms*, but that 'short (a) occurs...in many English dialects, as in the Yorkshire *man*'. This is certainly not correct if (a) = [ɑ] or anything similar.

I bring Sweet in here because of his great influence, and because Joseph Wright elsewhere uses his classifications. It is interesting in this connexion to look at Wright's grammar of his own Yorkshire dialect (1892), where he says that his vowel in words like *hand*, *back*, *staff* is 'mid-back-wide', and that it is 'like the *a* in German Mann, but with the tongue slightly more advanced' (§4). Clearly Wright's own ear was in this case better than Sweet's, and he gives his vowel a correct perceptual description, while following Sweet in assigning it an erroneous location. The main point is that 'back' for Wright (as well apparently as for Sweet) included anything in the [a]–[ɑ] range.

As Dobson points out (1957: §59), the fact that Sweet (and later Wyld) did not distinguish [a] and [ɑ] led to the general assumption (in this field at least) that [æ] was the lowest front vowel, and that therefore anything opener than [æ] can be 'a kind of' [ɑ]. This confusion has been revived now as a matter of principle by Chomsky & Halle, following the lead of Jakobson, Fant & Halle (1951). The notion that [æ] and [ɑ] are the only distinct nonround low vowels has now been incorporated into the putative 'universal' feature framework (cf. ch. 1 above: §3).

2. Some characteristic arguments for the location of ME /a/

Traditionally (and quite properly), the starting point for investigations of ME vowel-quality, especially if one is interested in developments during the early stages of the GVS, is the earliest available phonetic descriptions. So one works backwards (to characterize ME /a/) and forwards (to characterize later developments) from the sixteenth-century orthoëpists: especially John Hart, who most scholars agree is a crucially important – and accurate – witness. But on closer examination it turns out that Hart's evidence (for this vowel anyhow) is totally ambiguous.

In describing the five 'auncient' vowel sounds, Hart (1569: 30) says of this one:

The first, with wyde opening the mouth, as when a man yauneth: and is figured a.

Hart, like the Icelandic First Grammarian and other early writers, did not seem to be able to distinguish front/back position as an independent parameter. As his general descriptions make clear, he distinguished only closeness/openness, and (for non-open vowels) lip-rounding. As far as I can see, all we can tell about the vowel 'figured a' from Hart's description is that it is open: but we can't tell if it's front or back, round or unround. The most we can say is that if it's front it's unround, and if it's back it could be either unround [ɑ] or round [ɒ] (though the latter is unlikely for historical reasons). It is not surprising then that the ambiguity of this description has led to the two separate and contradictory views mentioned in §1: that ME /a/ was front, and that it was back.

What is surprising is that this description has been accepted by so many historians as unambiguous.

Of the two interpretations, the back one seems to be older, and can be exemplified by Jespersen (1909: 1). I will quote his argument at some length, because it raises a number of important issues. (Note that in the passage below, /a/ = [ɑ]: cf. §3.31. Jespersen uses letters in slants for earlier pronunciations, and letters in square brackets for modern ones.) He begins (§8.52) by saying that 'in the 16th c. the back sound' for ME /a/ or early ENE /a/ 'is very clearly described by H 1569'. Later he says that there was a 'general change of early /a/ to [æ], by which short back /a/ disappeared from the language' (§8.63). He continues:

To the theory here adopted that ME had /a/ it has been objected that it is unnatural to assume a change and a rechange in OE *sæt* with front /æ/ > ME *sat* with back /a/ > Mod *sat* with front [æ], and that it would be more natural to assume a preservation of the unchanged OE vowel through all periods, only disguised by the Frenchified spelling *a*. But it must be remembered that we are not concerned with this sound only, but with the descendants of OE *a* (*crab*), *ea* (*shadow, half*), *ā* (*hallow*), *ēa* (*chapman*), of Scandinavian *a* (*hap*) and of French *a* (*act*). There is no trace of any difference between these sounds in ME or early or late ModE, and if we assume ME /sæt/, we must assume /æ/ in all the other cases as well. This *a* always goes together with long *a* in *name*, *able*, etc. Hart's careful analysis 1569 indicates the back quality of short *a*.

A few comments are in order. First of all, the argument from parallelism with long /ā/ is circular, because it depends entirely on the assumption that short /a/ was back. As we will see shortly, this is precisely the argument that Dobson uses for FRONT articulation of /a/. Second, we will see that there is very good evidence for an extensive pattern of 'change' and 're-change' in the evolution of this vowel: but not precisely of the type that Jespersen proposed.

In the same section (8.3) Jespersen gives one further argument for back articulation: 'the change to [ɔ] (a back round, not a front round vowel) after *w*'. This has no force, however, since /w/ in most dialects of English has velar coarticulation, so that even if /a/ were front it could reasonably be retracted.

A good representative of the opposing view is Danielsson, who treats this matter in a careful study of Hart's phonology (1963: 79). Danielsson realizes, as Jespersen apparently did not, that from the actual description itself 'we can only conclude that Hart used a low...vowel' (he also says that it was 'lax', but I can't tell what that means here, and that it was unround, which is likely). But, he argues, since Hart says later in his treatise that the Germans use a 'broader' sound than the English, 'this must mean that the German "broader" (retracted or back) variety of *a* did not exist in English'. And further, 'we may thus be entitled to the conclusion that Hart's *a* was a front...vowel, probably identical with PresE [a]'. Unfortunately, however, we have no real way of knowing whether Hart did in fact mean retracted or back by 'broader'; so the whole argument really rests on one interpretation, at the distance of four centuries, of Hart's impressionistic term. This is not very much help.

Danielsson does not suggest a value for ME /a/ itself; but other scholars who apparently believe Hart to have had a front vowel posit a back vowel in the preceding stage. Thus Ekwall (1956: §26) makes a clear distinction between a back [ɑ] which he writes [a] and a front [a] which he writes [à], and correctly identifies the modern Northern vowel as the latter. And he seems to take [a] as a reasonable stage between [ɑ] and [æ]:

> Spätme. *a* wurde wahrscheinlich [a] gesprochen, und diese Aussprache ist auch für das 16. Jahrh. vorauszusetzen...Die Stufe [a] wird von dem übergang zu [ɔ] nach *w*...vorausgesetzt;...Die Stufe [æ] wird unzweideutig erst von Wallis 1653 bezeugt; als Zwischenstufe zwischen [a] und [æ] ist das noch im Nordenglischen gebräuchliche [à] vorauszusetzen.

Note that Ekwall repeats Jespersen's argument from [ɔ] after /w/, and while suggesting [a] as a transition stage between [ɑ] and [æ], gives no direct evidence for the back vowel stage.

Dobson (1957: II, §59) also interprets ENE /a/ as front, and extends this back to ME as well. Dobson's claims rest on rather shaky grounds, though he does argue his position in some detail, as Jespersen did. Basically he asserts that late ME /a/ must have been a front vowel because ME long /ā/ behaves in the GVS as if IT were one. And since the primary source of ME /ā/ (in the South at least) is earlier short /a/ lengthened in open syllables, ME /a/ must have been a front vowel too. This is apparently based on the assumption that open-syllable lengthening does not involve quality change as well; but this can hardly be maintained, since it is clear that when the ME high vowels /i u/ lengthen they become respectively /ẹ̄ ọ̄/ (e.g. *evil*, *wood*), and when /e o/ lengthen they become /ę̄ ǭ/ (*bear*, *nose*). (See further Lass 1969, 1974b.)

In any case, since at least two out of the five ME short vowels definitely, and two more probably, change quality when they lengthen, the fact that ME /ā/ is a front vowel, which Dobson asserts but does not support, cannot be used to justify a front analysis for /a/. It might be said in this connexion anyhow that identical articulation for short and long open vowels is not the usual situation in Germanic.[1] The only other significant case I know of for [a] as the value of late ME /a/ is made by Zachrisson (1913: 123), largely on the basis of French orthoëpical testimony.

As far as I can tell, then, the tradition, when it is explicit enough to be interpreted clearly, is unanimous in assuming that late ME and early, pre-Wallis ENE /a/ was a low vowel, and split as to whether it was back or front. And it is clear that evidence for a value of the general type [æ] first appears in the mid-seventeenth century.

The most recent large-scale work to come to grips with the problem is *SPE*. This represents, with respect to our problem, a regression to the inaccurate (or at least under-discriminating) phonetics of Wright and Sweet. That is, Chomsky & Halle do not distinguish [a] from [ɑ], but assert as a matter of principle, in setting up a feature inventory, that there are only two distinct nonround low vowels, one back and one front, which they write [a] and [æ].[2] This is unfortunate, because, as we will see, the restriction of the possible nonround low vowels to only these two forces on us a grossly oversimplified and false interpretation of the historical (and synchronic) evidence. I will assume from here on – and the material in the following sections will make clear, if it's necessary, just what my grounds are – that low front but lower than [æ] vowels must be taken as independent, distinct from both [æ] and [ɑ]. This distinction is part of the necessary machinery for characterizing both the typology of Modern English dialects, and the historical development of the language.

Chomsky & Halle say that 'Late Middle English is commonly assumed to have possessed' the 'simple vowels' /i e u o a/ (lax) and /ī ē ǣ ū ō ɔ̄ ā/

[1] Though it seems to be true in many dialects of German. The more usual situation is exemplified by Swedish and Norwegian, where the short open vowel is front and the long one is back. This is also, true, by and large, of short open vs. long open vowels in most dialects of English, e.g. in *back* vs. *far*. The opposite, short back and long front, is found in Dutch. (See the Appendix, however, for a further discussion of Dobson's claims.)

[2] It may be true that no language in fact has phonemic /a æ ɑ/ at a given time; but there is certainly a typological difference between a language whose openest front vowel is [æ] and one whose openest is [a]. We will see later how important this is in English. (Chomsky & Halle also deny the existence of phonemic central vowels, which raises a problem for dialects like mine, with contrastive [æ], [ä], and [ɑ] – in *marrow, sorrow, morrow* respectively.) The conflation of [a] and [æ] is in principle just as bad as the Jakobsonian conflation of pharyngealization, rounding, and retroflexion under [+flat] (Jakobson, Fant & Halle 1951): just because two things aren't distinctive doesn't mean they're the same.

(tense), where 'tense' vs. 'lax' is parallel to the traditional 'long' vs. 'short'[1] (*SPE*: 252). From their chart of feature values (176), the assignments are clear: /æ/ is [−back, +low], /a/ and /ɔ/ are [+back, +low], and the latter two are respectively [−round] and [+round]. This involves a claim that the maximal high/low contrasts in the late ME vowel system (or any other) are /i/ vs. /æ/ (or /œ/, which does not concern us here), and /u/ vs. /a ɔ/. And since there are only two features available for height, no language may have more than three contrastive values for this parameter (cf. Ladefoged 1971: 76 on four-height systems). We might note here also that Chomsky & Halle's claim that the 'common' assumption is that ME /a/ was back is not correct: this is an assumption of the way their metatheory interprets low vowels, not of the scholarly tradition.

On the basis of their assumptions about vowel heights, and certain notions about 'optimal' vowel systems (which I will return to briefly later on), Chomsky & Halle can interpret Hart's description of *a* quite unambiguously: 'we shall therefore regard [a] as low, back, nonround' (260). The sole warrant for 'therefore', it should be noted, is the description by Hart cited earlier, plus the assumption that [a] and [ɑ] are universally nondistinct.

As they point out later (266), Wallis's classification of his 'à exile' as in *Sam* among the 'palatal' vowels (*palatinae*) means that it must be front, i.e. [æ]. And this characterization, together with the feature specifications of the vowels shown above, and the assumption that Hart's underlying system was the same as the late ME one, means that the rule for producing [æ] must be a simple fronting (their rule (31)):

(3) $$\begin{bmatrix} +\text{low} \\ -\text{round} \end{bmatrix} \rightarrow [-\text{back}] \;/\; \underline{\quad\quad} \begin{Bmatrix} \# \\ [+\text{cons}] \\ [+\text{voc}] \end{Bmatrix}$$

The following discussion will show how oversimplified this is, and how many important historically-based dialect differentia it allows us to sweep under the rug.

Before continuing, it might be well to note that while I am ostensibly concerned with 'Middle English /a/', I have concentrated up to now on the sixteenth-century vowel. This is due (a) to the (probably correct) assumption of most scholars that there was no significant change in this vowel from say the fourteenth century to Hart; and (b) the related fact

[1] On the pseudo-feature [±tense] see ch. 1 above.

that since Hart is the first really good witness we have, characterization of the ME system effectively begins with him. I take it that in practice, when we reconstruct the ME short vowels, we do so largely on the assumption that the system remained stable at least through Hart's time; and that it is precisely Hart's detailed attention to the long vowels that brings out the skewing of the long and short vowel systems that was produced by the GVS.

3. The determining evidence and its implications

It seems that nearly all of the 'standard' accounts of ME /a/, whatever articulation they assume, are based primarily on chains of argumentation that begin with Hart, and subsidiary considerations having to do with such matters as 'parallel' behaviour in the GVS, later sound changes, etc. Further, for many scholars the 'conservative' Northern pronunciations are brought into the picture, often (as we will see clearly now) misinterpreted as back vowels. And since Hart's description of 1569 is ambiguous, most of the arguments are based entirely on theoretical considerations. The prime example of this is the chain of reasoning we can extract from writers like Chomsky & Halle, and earlier (implicitly) from the Wrights: if there are no (distinct) nonround low vowels except [ɑ æ], then the fact that Wallis's 'à exile' was (a) an innovation and (b) obviously front, means that Hart's *a* was back. (I am not objecting to reasoning of this sort; it is just that there are better ways to go about solving this particular problem, which give surer answers.)

I turn now to my primary claim, that these issues are resolvable by means of available but neglected evidence. The one source of information that might really help, and by far the most vital source in a reconstructive venture like this, is the one that has not been systematically employed: the actual set of reflexes of ME /a/ in a wide range of modern dialects. And not just the restricted (and typologically rather deviant) set represented by RP and (some) American dialects. This latter set has traditionally been the sole foundation of descriptions of 'English', both historical and synchronic, and the other material has generally been neglected (except by Luick and a few other earlier scholars, who had far less material at their disposal than we have). In other words, English historical phonology, one of the most highly developed subfields within historical linguistics generally, has made virtually no use of perhaps the most important, longest established, and best validated tool of the discipline: comparative method. And there is enough material available now to do this reasonably well.

In this section I will present a preliminary comparative study; the results will, I think, get us as close as we can get to an adequate characterization of ME /a/, in addition to opening up some interesting aspects of its subsequent history. I begin with some remarks relevant to a typology of NE dialects according to a clear (and relatively datable) dividing line: the presence or absence of lengthening of ME /a/ (with or without quality change) before /f s θ/. This innovation can be fairly well fixed in the mid-to-late seventeenth century: certainly after the change of /a/ to [æ] witnessed by Wallis in 1653. The first good testimony seems to be Cooper (1687). Of the vowel 'a lingual' he says (1687: ch. 1, §3; Sundby 1953: 4):

A is formed by the middle of the Tongue a little rais'd to the hollow of the Palate. In these *can*, *pass by*, *a* is short; in *cast*, *past* for *passed*, it is long.

If Cooper's evidence is accepted, then we may take any dialect with lengthening as having developed it relatively late; and we can also probably take any qualitative change associated with the lengthened vowel as later still. The evidence certainly does seem to permit this treatment; though there are some difficulties that I will discuss later.

I will sketch out the comparative material as follows: the data will be drawn from the Survey of English Dialects (SED) *Basic Material* volumes, produced at Leeds under the direction of Harold Orton. From this material I have collated the reflexes of ME /a/ in two contexts: the 'isolative' development, exemplified by (*tom*) *cat*, item III. 18. 8, and the development before /f s θ/ etc., exemplified by *last*, item VII. 2. 2. (The item numbers are those of the Leeds questionnaire.) In the tables that follow, the number preceding each county is its SED reference number; and numbers in parentheses after a county name indicate those areas within it in the SED network where the given vowel occurs. If there are no numbers after a county name, all network areas may be taken as showing the same reflex.[1]

[1] Where no response was available for (*tom*) *cat*, I used (*tabby*) *cat* III. 13. 9. Where there was no response for either (a very small set of instances) I used *bat* IV. 7. 7 to keep the postvocalic context the same. Because of the small number of missing responses I have collated these without comment under *cat*. The point here is an overall survey of a typical environment for a typical reflex, not an account of the intradialectal variability that is bound to exist. I assume inherent variability as a matter of course, but I also assume that in elicitations of the SED type, what is most likely to emerge is a 'canonical' pronunciation; and this I take to be of prime theoretical interest in an investigation like this.

This material is by no means exhaustive; it is merely what seems to me, on the basis of what is available, to be both representative and suitable for a preliminary examination. And this chapter is after all only that. The actual amount of data in the Leeds volumes is so great that it would be counter-productive to attempt to hand-sort it: comparative work on this scale should be done by computer. This initial overview therefore stands subject to correction and refinement; but I think the results are in principle accurate and revealing.

The volumes of the SED I have drawn on are: for the North (N), Orton & Halliday (1962); for the West Midlands (WML), Orton & Barry (1969); for the East Midlands and East Anglia (EML), Orton & Tilling (1969); and for the Southern Counties (S), Orton & Wakelin (1967). The criteria for classification are given in the headings of the tables that follow.

TABLE 1. *Group A–1. Open vowel in* cat. *No lengthening before /f s θ/*

		cat	*last*
N	1. Northumberland	a	a
	2. Cumberland	a	a
	3. Durham	a	a
	4. Westmorland	a	a
	5. Lancashire (exc. 12)	a	a
	6. Yorkshire (exc. 21, 23)	a	a
	7. Cheshire	a	a
WML	8. Derbyshire	a	a
	11. Shropshire (2)	a	a
	12. Staffordshire	a	a
	16. Worcestershire (1)	a	a
EML	9. Nottinghamshire	a	a
	10. Lincolnshire (exc. 10, 14, 15)	a	a
	13. Leicestershire (exc. 6, 8)	a	a
	14. Rutland	a	a

TABLE 2. *Group A–2. Higher than open vowel in* cat. *No lengthening before /f s θ/*

		cat	*last*
N	6. Yorkshire (21)	æ	æ
WML	15. Herefordshire (5)	æ	æ
	23. Monmouthshire (1)	æ	æ

TABLE 3. *Group B–1. Open vowel in* cat. *Lengthening only before* /f s θ/

		cat	*last*
N	5. Lancashire (12)	a	a:
WML	11. Shropshire (1, 4, 6, 8, 11)	a	a:
	15. Herefordshire (7)	a	a:
	17. Warwickshire (2, 7)	a	a:
	23. Monmouthshire (5)	a	a:
	24. Gloucestershire (4–7)	a	a:
	25. Oxfordshire (1–3)	a	a:
	Oxfordshire (4)	ä	ä:
EML	10. Lincolnshire (14)	a	a:
	13. Leicestershire (6, 8)	a	a:
	18. Northamptonshire	a	a:
	26. Buckinghamshire	a	a:
	27. Bedfordshire (exc. 2)	a	a:
S	31. Somerset (9, 11)	a	a:
	32. Wiltshire (1, 6)	a	a:
	36. Cornwall (1, 3)	a	a:
	37. Devon (1–7, 9–11)	a	a:
	38. Dorset (1, 2, 5)	a	a:
	39. Hampshire (1, 2, 4, 5)	a	a:

TABLE 4. *Group B–2. Higher than open vowel in* cat. *Lengthening only before* /f s θ/

		cat	*last*
WML	15. Herefordshire (6)	æ	æ:
	16. Worcestershire (4, 5)	æ	æ:
	24. Gloucestershire (1, 3)	æ	æ:
S	31. Somerset (1–4, 13)	æ	æ:
	33. Berkshire (1)	æ	æ:
	36. Cornwall (7)	æ	æ:

TABLE 5. *Group C–1. Lengthening and quality change before* /f s θ/. *Long vowel front, opener than short vowel*

		cat	*last*
WML	11. Shropshire (7, 10)	æ	a:
	15. Herefordshire (1–4)	æ	a:
	16. Worcestershire (3, 6)	æ	a:
	23. Monmouthshire (2, 3, 6)	æ	a:
	24. Gloucestershire (2)	æ	a:
	25. Oxfordshire (6)	ạ	a:

TABLE 5 (*cont.*)

		cat	*last*
WML	10. Lincolnshire (15)	æ	a:
	19. Huntingdonshire (1)	ạ	a:
	Huntingdonshire (2)	æ	a:
EML	20 Cambridgeshire (1)	æ	ạ:
	21. Norfolk (2)	æ	a:
	Norfolk (10)	æ̣	æ:
	22. Suffolk	æ	a:
	27. Bedfordshire (2)	ạ	a:
	29. Essex (1, 3, 5, 8, 9)	æ	a:
	28. Hertfordshire (1)	ạ	a:
S	31. Somerset (5)	æ̣	a:
	Somerset (6)	æ	æ̣:
	Somerset (7, 9)	æ	a:
	Somerset (12)	a	a:
	33. Berkshire (5)	æ·	a:
	36. Cornwall (6)	æ	a:
	38. Dorset (4)	ạ	a:
	39. Hampshire (3)	æ	a:
	40. Sussex (2, 5)	æ̣	æ:
	Sussex (3)	ɛ	æ:

TABLE 6. *Group C–2. Lengthening and quality change before* /f s θ/. *Long vowel front, closer than short vowel*

		cat	*last*
WML	11. Shropshire (9)	a	æ:
S	32. Wiltshire (2, 4, 5, 8, 9)	a	æ:
	33. Berkshire (2)	æ	ɛ:
	36. Cornwall (2)	a	e:
	Cornwall (5)	æ	e:
	Cornwall (4)	a	æ:
	37. Devon (8)	a	e:
	38. Dorset (3)	a	ạ:
	39. Hampshire (6)	a	æ:
	40. Sussex (6)	æ	ɛ:

This material provides some interesting conclusions. First, consider the distribution and nature of the reflexes of ME /a/ shown in Tables 1–7. Out of 39 counties, a total of 314 network areas, only one (Oxfordshire 25. 4) shows anything other than a fully front vowel for the isolative reflex. (And in the light of the rest this can probably be taken as an

TABLE 7. *Group C–3. Lengthening and quality change before /f s θ/. Long vowel retracted or back*

		cat	last
WML	16. Worcestershire (2, 7)	a	ɑ:
EML	20. Cambridgeshire (2)	ạ	ä:
	21. Norfolk (1, 3, 6)	ɛ̨	ɑ:
	Norfolk (4, 12)	æ	ɑ:
	Norfolk (11, 13)	æ̣	ɑ:
	Norfolk (9)	æ̣	ɑ̈:
	28. Hertfordshire (2)	ạ	ä:
	29. Essex (2, 6, 10, 14)	æ	ä:
	Essex (4, 13)	æ	a̠:
	Essex (11)	æ̣	ɑ:
	Essex (7, 12, 15)	ɛə	ɑ:
S	30. Middlesex	æ	ɑ:
	32. Wiltshire (3, 7)	a	a̠:
	33. Berkshire (3)	æ	æ̠:
	Berkshire (4)	æ	a̠:
	34. Surrey (1)	æ	ɑ:
	Surrey (2)	ɛ	ɑ̟:
	Surrey (4)	ɛ	ɑ:
	Surrey (3)	æ	ɑ̟:
	Surrey (5)	ɛ̨	ɑ̟:
	35. Kent (1, 4, 5)	ɛ	ɑ:
	Kent (2, 7)	æ	ɑ:
	Kent (6)	ɛ̨	ɑ:
	Kent (3)	æ̣	æ̠ˑ
	39. Hampshire (7)	æ	ɑ:
	40. Sussex (1, 4)	æ	ɑ̟:

TABLE 8. *Group D. Anomalous or ambiguous distributions, on basis of sample*

		cat	last
N	6. Yorkshire (33)	æ	a
	Isle of Man (1)	æ̣ˑ	æ̨ˑ
	Isle of Man (2)	æ̣	æᵊ
WML	17. Warwickshire (1)	æ	a
	28. Hertfordshire (3)	æ:	ɑ:

informant's idiosyncrasy.) Of the total, 210 (about $\frac{2}{3}$) show a vowel of the [a] type, while 104 (about $\frac{1}{3}$) show a closer vowel. I therefore conclude that there is no evidence that ME /a/ was ever a back vowel in any dialect in England; and that we must reconstruct for the ME short vowel system one of the type (2c), i.e.

(4)
```
i   u
e   o
a
```

(Actually, the short mid vowels are half-open: see ch. 5 below.)

A secondary conclusion is that the distribution of the closer vowels ([æ], [ɛ], etc.) suggests, as does the historical record, that the raising of ME /a/ is an innovation;[1] so is the presence of back vowels in dialects with lengthening. The comparative picture nicely confirms Wallis's testimony of [æ] with no lengthening and Cooper's later account of [æ] plus lengthening. I will return to these points later, and work them into a typology and history of the main NE dialect types.

4. The Scots evidence

Before we can finally accept the reconstruction of ME /a/ as a front vowel, we must look at one more kind of evidence. I said above that while it is the case that English dialects do not show back vowel reflexes of isolative ME /a/, this is not entirely true of Scots. For there are some Scots dialects – notably those of the Southern Border Counties (e.g. S. Berwickshire, Roxburghshire) – which do in fact have back vowels in words like *cat*. It remains to be seen whether dialects like these tend to support or disconfirm my reconstruction.

Let us take a characteristic dialect of this type, that of the Chirnside (Berwickshire) area, as described by Wettstein (1942). Here the reflex of ME /a/ in all positions (except for special developments before /x/, /l/, etc.) is a low rounded back vowel, [ɒ(:)] (the historical length distinctions have been lost here, as generally in Scotland: see Aitken 1962, Lass, 1974b, and ch. 2, §1 above). This back vowel takes on a special significance, however, if we consider it in relation to the reflexes of the other ME short vowels:

[1] It is possible that the [ɛ]-type vowels in Essex and the SE may reflect earlier (late OE) developments, i.e. the well-known merger of OE *æ* with *e* rather than *a* in these areas. But since the closer vowels occur also in OE *a*-words (e.g. *cat* < *catt*, not just *bat* < *bæt*), this is a point of necessary indeterminacy. That is, the fact that *cat* and *bat* have the same vowel may be due either to early merger, precipitated by the non-phonemicity of [æ] in OE ('Loss of Anglo-Frisian Brightening': cf. Lass & Anderson 1975: ch. II); or it may be due (as I will assume later on) to a raising after the late OE merger.

(5)

ME	Chirnside
i	ɛ
e	a
u	ʌ
o	o
a	ɒ

In a quite typical Scots fashion, the reflex of ME /i/ is a mid vowel; but the larger picture is rather different. In the Central Scots dialects (e.g. Fife, the Lothians, etc.), ME /i/ is also a mid vowel, usually of the type [ɛ] or [ɛ̈]; but it is always OPENER than the reflex of ME /e/, which is usually [e]. Thus in Edinburgh [łet] 'let', [bɛ̈t] 'bit'. The same phenomenon occurs also in the North, e.g. Caithness, where in some dialects the typical reflexes of ME /i/ and /e/ are respectively [ɛ] and [ɛ̝].[1] But the Chirnside dialect shows a different pattern. Rather than it being the case that ME /i/ 'bypasses' /e/, there has been a chain shift: ME /i/ has gone (probably via /e/) to /ɛ/, and the original /e/ has gone to /ɛ/ and then to low /a/, while the low /a/ has become a back vowel.

Now since, as far as I know, the only dialects that consistently have low back vowels for ME /a/ are also those where in addition (a) ME /i/ is mid, and (b) ME /e/ is at least as low as [æ] (e.g. Morebattle, Roxburghshire: Zai 1942),[2] it would seem that a fully back isolative reflex of ME /a/ is the predictable result of a lowering shift of the front vowels, producing a push chain that forces /a/ to retract. Thus we seem to have the following steps: first /i/ lowers to /e/, causing /e/ to go to /ɛ/; then /ɛ/ lowers, setting up a second chain. This development can be schematized as follows:

(6)

Pre-shift	Shift I	Shift II
i		
	↓	
e	e	
	↓	↓
	ɛ	ɛ
		↓
a	a	a → ɒ

[1] Edinburgh forms cited from my own observations; Caithness from materials collected by J. Y. Mather of the Linguistic Survey of Scotland, Edinburgh, to whom thanks are due for permission to quote, and for general assistance on matters concerning Scots dialects.

[2] For earlier stages of Roxburghshire dialects, see the admirable account in Murray (1873). On the whole historical development in this area, the most recent and complete account is Vaiana (1972), which takes into consideration the materials collected by the Linguistic Survey of Scotland.

The important thing to note, then, is the special historical development of those dialects with back vowels for ME /a/, as compared with those (Scots) ones with bypassing of /e/ but no lowering. The implications that hold seem to be these:

(a) If ME /i/ is mid, then ME /e/ may be either mid or low.
(b) If ME /i/ is mid, but ME /e/ is not low, then ME /a/ is not back.
(c) If ME /i/ is mid and ME /e/ is low, then ME /a/ is back.

I conclude that [ɑ] or [ɒ] in *cat*, etc. in Southern Scots does not support a back value for ME /a/, but is counterevidence. Those dialects with back reflexes of ME /a/ are additional support for the claim that ME /a/ was [a]; the back vowels arise only through an innovatory chain shift.

5. A sketch of the history of ME /a/ in England

If we look again at Tables 1–7, we can begin to plot the evolutionary trajectory of this vowel. The relevant facts, in summary, are:

(i) No dialect in England shows a back vowel for 'isolative' ME /a/.

(ii) All show a front vowel, usually either of the [a] or the [æ] type, though a few show vowels of the [ɛ] type (including a diphthong [ɛə]).

(iii) Judging from the historical record, [æ] for ME /a/ is a late (seventeenth-century) innovation.

(iv) Those English dialects that have a back vowel (or better, a nonfront vowel) in any ME /a/ words have it in the 'combinative' environment, i.e. before /f s θ/.

(v) In these cases the nonfront vowel has lengthened.[1]

(vi) Some dialects have length before /f s θ/, but no change of quality, i.e. they have patterns like [a ~ a:] or [æ ~ æ:].

[1] It is worth noting that the fact that a dialect is of the TYPE that has [ɑ:] in *last* doesn't mean necessarily that it will have [ɑ:] in ALL forms that (apparently) meet the SD for lengthening. The developments are actually more complex, and (in detail) less regular than they seem to be initially. Thus the environment that I have been calling 'before /f s θ/' actually also includes (e.g. for RP and similar dialects) /ns/ (*chance, dance*), /nt/ (*plant, slant*), /mpl/ (*example, sample*), and in some cases /ð/ (*rather*: but not *gather*), /nd/ (*demand, command*). The nasal environments may be a special case: i.e. from French nasalized vowels rather than ENE /æ/. Thus we do not get [ɑ:] in native forms like *ant, hand, stand* (except in some Scots). Further, there has been a certain amount of lexical selectivity operating (as *rather* vs. *gather* suggests), since we have contrasting pairs in RP like the following (the first members have [æ] and the second have [ɑ:]): *gas* : *pass*, *tassel* : *castle*, *rant* : *plant*, *cancel* : *chancel*, *ample* : *sample*. (I owe the above forms to John Wells.) It is also worth noting that there is vacillation, even in RP, between [æ] and [ɑ:] in certain forms: notably *plastic, lather, transfer* (Gimson 1965: 106).

(vii) Both lengthening and retraction postdate the development of [æ], if the Wallis–Cooper sequence is reliable. And retraction postdates lengthening, judging from the fact that Cooper shows only length.

(viii) A scatter of (Southern) dialects show lengthening before /f s θ/ with raising rather than retraction; i.e. they show vowels like [ɛ:] or [e:] in *last*. These are (distributionally) a rather minor and localized group, and rather difficult to interpret historically. I will deal with them later.

These distributions, and the conclusions reached in §§3–4, suggest that at least the following processes, or something like them, have been involved (in various dialects) in the post-ME history of /a/:

TABLE 9. *The major events in the history of ME /a/ in the post-ME* period

i. Raising I. /a/ → [æ].
ii. Lengthening. ME /a/ (whether or not it has raised) is lengthened before /f s θ/. The outputs are thus [a:] or [æ:].
iii. Lowering I. [æ:] → [a:].
iv. Retraction. [a:] → [ɑ:].
v. Lowering II. [æ] → [a].
vi. Raising II. [æ] → [ɛ].
vii. Raising III. [æ:] → [ɛ:].
viii. Raising IV. [ɛ:] → [e:].

(The processes (v)–(viii) will be discussed below.)

Observe that in the comment at the end of Table 9 I have referred to 'processes', and in the heading to 'events', not 'rules'. This is deliberate: I am not convinced that there are very many 'rules' (in the usual sense) that accomplish changes as large as [a] to [ɑ]. Such apparent 'rules', at least historically, are often merely interpretations of two chronological poles of a cline, not actual 'quantum jumps', which I doubt are often that large. Certainly in this particular case the range of values for lengthened ME /a/ bears this out: an inspection of Tables 1–7 reveals a spread covering [æ: ạ: a: a̲: ä: ɑ̈: ɑ̟: ɑ:]. That is, there has been a process of lowering, lengthening, and retraction going on for some considerable time.

As in most sound-changes so-called, the end points can be taken in a sense as the right- and left-hand sides of a rule, stated (perhaps) in binary features. But the intermediate stages, here anyway, are more subtly graded. The classical arguments against 'gradual' sound change (e.g. those summarized in King 1969: ch. 5) are often not borne out by the kind of evidence actually available from studies of sound change observed in progress (e.g. Labov 1963), or from studies against the background of synchronic variability (e.g. Labov 1966, Trudgill 1974). It is always possible that apparent gross articulatory shifts are not historical events, but artifacts of diachronic study, which arise largely through the lack of documented intermediate stages. Certainly, given correspondences that suggest large-scale changes, it should require more evidence to allow us to interpret them as unitary changes than as gradual 'drifts' of articulation.[1]

We can now begin our historical sketch by setting up a somewhat more elaborate typology than that in Tables 1–7. The main aim here is to segregate the dialects according to what historical processes from the list in Table 9 they have undergone. This will in general be self-evident; the only serious problem will be the dialects in Table 6: those with [æ: ɛ: e:] in *last*, and anything from [a] to [ɛ] in *cat*. These seem to fall into several rather different types, whose relationships to the others are at least on the surface uncertain. This difficulty will become clearer if we construct a preliminary typological grouping according to whether dialects have or have not undergone the change to [æ] (Table 10).

We can now return to dialects with [ɛ:] etc. in *last*. The material in Table 6 shows a bewildering number of types, which seem to crosscut the classification in Table 10, and whose histories for that reason are difficult to disentangle. There are dialects with [ɛ ~ æ:], dialects with [a ~ æ:], and dialects with [a ~ e:]. Obviously all of these have undergone lengthening; the question is what other processes have occurred, and in what order. I do not think there is a fully determinate solution, but I can offer some suggestions that may enable us to fit these dialects coherently into the whole pattern.

First of all, it is clear that the raising of the lengthened vowel is inde-

[1] Cf. the remarks on 'probability' of change as a determinant of reconstructed paths in ch. 3, §3 above; also Andersen (1972). This is of course not to say that singulary shifts do not occur: merely that they are (relatively) rare, and require more support than drifts. This is especially true when drifts are strongly suggested – as here – by the evidence. But certainly the 'bypass' shift of ME /i/ in Scots, and the shifts of certain short vowels in U.S. English (cf. ch. 5 below) are clear examples. Further, many changes that appear to be direct articulatory shifts are actually better interpreted not as 'changes', but as SUBSTITUTIONS (i.e. dialect borrowings). The Northumbrian shift of [ø:] to [o:] in ME /ɔ:/ words (cf. Orton 1933) may be an example; the (pseudo) change of /e/ to /o/ in Scots (*hame* → *home*, *windae* → *window*, etc.) surely is. In this light, the one-step-at-a-time constraint in ch. 3, §3 above might better be taken as a constraint on the OUTLINES of sound changes.

TABLE 10

Group I. Dialects without [æ]
  Ia. No lengthening, no quality change: [a] in *cat, last.*
  Ib. Lengthening only: [a] in *cat,* [a:] in *last.*

Group II. Dialects with [æ]
  IIa. Raising I; no lengthening, no quality change: [æ] in *cat, last.*
  IIb. Raising I; Lengthening: [æ] in *cat,* [æ:] in *last.*
  IIc. Raising I; Lengthening; Lowering I: [æ] in *cat,* [a:] in *last.*
  IId. Raising I; Lengthening; Lowering I; Retraction: [æ] in *cat,* [ɑ:] in *last.*

(The symbols here represent general vowel types, not detailed articulatory specifications: thus '[ɑ:]' = [ä: ɑ̟: ɑ:], etc.)

pendent of the raising (beyond [æ]) of the short one: thus most of the [ɛ]-dialects belong to the group with retracted or back long vowel (Table 7). And further, there are [a]-dialects in the group with raised long vowels. It is also clear, I think, that the raising to [ɛ:] and [e:] implies a stage [æ:], since this is the openest vowel found in the group where the long vowel is closer than the short one. This leaves us with two alternative historical sequences.

(i) Dialects with the [a ~ æ:] or [a ~ e:] patterns derive from the historical type [a ~ a:], with raising only of the long vowels.

(ii) All these dialects derive from the historical type [æ ~ æ:], with lowering of [æ] in some cases, raising in others, and no change in the rest.

The alternative (i) would make the histories of these dialects virtually disjoint from those of the others, i.e. make them reasonable representatives of neither Group I nor Group II (Table 10). Alternative (ii) would integrate them into the pattern, in that now all dialects with any modification of the long vowel whatever would be in essence Group II or something similar, i.e. the more radically innovating ones. The lowering of the short vowel and the raising of the long ones would account for the skewing we get, and would do so at a point in time after the overall division into types I and II.

We are now faced with the problem that given the evidence, there doesn't seem to be any strong principled reason for valuing one solution more highly than the other, except the one given above: i.e. the (metatheoretical) decision that rule-sharing among cognate dialects is to be more highly valued than largely disjoint histories. Or, to put it another way, that we want to make divergences occur as late in a historical sequence as possible (the idea that genetic trees branch more densely the lower down you get). I have a sneaking intuitive suspicion that this is a well founded decision, but I'm not at all sure what 'highly valued' really means here. There is however no doubt that such purely methodological valuations are proper or at least useful constraints on reconstruction (cf. ch. 3, §§3–4 above).

It all amounts to this: either these dialects are historically [æ ~ æ:] types with later modifications of [æ:] upwards and [æ] either up or down; or they are [a ~ a:] dialects with later changes of both vowels by raising only. The total distributional evidence, and what we have of a historical record, seem to me to suggest that when we have patterns of length plus quality-difference, the answer is that even [a:] may derive via a sequence [a] → [æ] → [æ:] → [a:]; and if this is the case it is not unduly surprising for short [æ] from earlier [a] to revert to its original open articulation also. And anyhow this certainly happened when the Anglo-Frisian Brightening undid itself in late OE (cf. (1) above). So I will assume that these Southern dialects are essentially variants of type IIb in Table 10, sharing the same initial histories plus a set of innovations (Lowering II, etc. in Table 9).

We can now revise Table 10, and incorporate the problematical dialects, along with those that fit into types IIc, IId, but have [ɛ] in *cat*. The revised typology is given in Table 11:

TABLE 11

A. The major dialect groups

Group I. Dialects without [æ]

- Ia. No lengthening or quality change: [a] in *cat, last.*
- Ib. Lengthening only: [a] in *cat,* [a:] in *last.*

Group II. Dialects with [æ]

- IIa. Raising I only: [æ] in *cat, last.*
- IIb. Raising I; Lengthening: [æ] in *cat,* [æ:] in *last.*
- IIc. Raising I; Lengthening; Lowering I: [æ] in *cat,* [a:] in *last.*
- IId. Raising I; Lengthening; Lowering I; Retraction: [æ] in *cat,* [ɑ:] in *last.*

B. The minor dialect groups

Group III. Dialects with [ɛ]

- IIIa. IIb plus Raising II: [ɛ] in *cat,* [æ:] in *last.*
- IIIb. IId plus Raising II: [ɛ] in *cat,* [ɑ:] in *last.*

Group IV. Dialects with long vowel closer than short

- IVa. IIb plus Lowering II: [a] in *cat,* [æ:] in *last.*
- IVb. IIb plus Raising III: [æ] in *cat,* [ɛ:] in *last.*
- IVc. IIb plus Raising III, Raising IV: [æ] in *cat,* [e:] in *last.*
- IVd. IIb plus Lowering II, Raising III, IV: [a] in *cat,* [e:] in *last.*

This typology can be illustrated historically with some sample derivations, as follows.

TABLE 12

	Ia		Ib		IIa		IIb		IIc		IId	
ME	kat	last	kat	last	kat	last	kat	last	kat	last	kat	last
(1)	—	—	—	—	æ	æ	æ	æ	æ	æ	æ	æ
(2)	—	—	—	a:	—	—	—	æ:	—	æ:	—	æ:
(3)	—	—	—	—	—	—	—	—	—	a:	—	a:
(4)	—	—	—	—	—	—	—	—	—	—	—	ɑ:
(5)	—	—	—	—	—	—	—	—	—	—	—	—
(6)	—	—	—	—	—	—	—	—	—	—	—	—
(7)	—	—	—	—	—	—	—	—	—	—	—	—
(8)	—	—	—	—	—	—	—	—	—	—	—	—
NE	a	a	a	a:	æ	æ	æ	æ:	æ	a:	æ	ɑ:

	IIIa		IIIb		IVa		IVb		IVc		IVd	
ME	kat	last	kat	last	kat	last	kat	last	kat	last	kat	last
(1)	æ	æ	æ	æ	æ	æ	æ	æ	æ	æ	æ	æ
(2)	—	æ:	—	æ:	—	æ:	—	æ:	—	æ:	—	æ:
(3)	—	—	—	a:	—	—	—	—	—	—	—	—
(4)	—	—	—	ɑ:	—	—	—	—	—	—	—	—
(5)	—	—	—	—	a	—	—	—	—	—	a	—
(6)	ɛ	—	ɛ	—	—	—	—	—	—	—	—	—
(7)	—	—	—	—	—	—	—	ɛ:	—	ɛ:	—	ɛ:
(8)	—	—	—	—	—	—	—	—	—	e:	—	e:
NE	ɛ	æ:	ɛ	ɑ:	a	æ:	æ	ɛ:	æ	e:	a	e:

KEY (cf. Table 9): (1) Raising I; (2) Lengthening; (3) Lowering I; (4) Retraction; (5) Lowering II; (6) Raising II; (7) Raising III; (8) Raising IV.

The 'derivations' in Table 12 are of course strictly diachronic; they are accounts of event-sequences in real time, not properties of the synchronic grammars of these dialects. Indeed, it seems doubtful whether dialects like these have any 'depth' of rules in forms of these categories. Or, indeed, if a sequence like that for IId or IVb could ever appear in a speaker's (not a linguist's) grammar. But this is not really relevant to my essentially typological and historical concerns here.

6. Conclusion: A word about 'optimal' vowel systems

The preceding discussion centres around a substantive claim: that in the light of comparative evidence there is no warrant for assuming that ME /a/ was ever – at any level – a back vowel. (This may not be true of OE /a/; see the Appendix following.) ME /a/ must be reconstructed as fully open and fully front.

The typological differentia of the NE dialects, as displayed in the tables, further suggest that – in terms of what we might call a 'dia-systemic' or 'overall' vowel inventory for English – the history of the vowel system must be considered in relation to a grid that has at least the following independent vowel types in the mid-to-low range:

(7) e
ɛ
æ
a ɑ ɒ

Such a system is the minimal one necessary for (a) describing adequately the range of the NE reflexes of ME /a/, and (b) charting the trajectories along which the NE vowel system developed. There is certainly no reason to believe for instance that [a] and [æ] or [a] and [ɑ] are non-distinct vowel types; or for that matter that [e] and [ɛ] are distinct by some feature like 'tenseness', since they both appear in long and short vowel systems (cf. ch. 1), and as the nonsyllabics and syllabics of diphthongs (cf. ch. 3). And further, the fact that we cannot justify on comparative grounds the reconstruction of a system with a low back vowel for any dialect argues strongly against the current notion (e.g. in *SPE*) that in some way backness is 'optimal' or 'unmarked' for low vowels, i.e. that the 'simplest' five-vowel system is of the type (2a) shown earlier in this chapter.

It certainly seems to be the case that the minimal vowel system in a natural language will have at least one high vowel and one low one; but whether the low one is front or back (or central) is a language-specific option (for a further critique of markedness and similar notions cf. Lass 1972). At the very least there seems to be no doubt that the only short vowel system reconstructible for ME has one short open vowel, and that is front.

Appendix: Some remarks on ME /ā/ and OE /a/ and /ā/

1. The position of ME /ā/

I think we have now reached a reasonable decision about ME /a/; reasonable, that is, given the nature of the evidence, and the epistemological difficulties that beset historical-comparative argumentation in general (cf. ch. 3, §4 above). I want now to see what we can do about filling in the picture of the low vowels in pre-ME times, as well as characterizing the long congener of ME /a/. This discussion will be of interest both in what it can do and what it fails to do: in particular, the areas of indeterminacy that show up should be of some theoretical interest (perhaps an *impasse* can be as useful in its own way as a conclusion, by raising the question of whether certain problems are in principle soluble at a given stage in the development of a theory).

Let us begin with ME /ā/. The location of everything else in the ME long vowel system that served as input to the GVS seems fairly clear: that is, we had a four-height system whose top three spaces were occupied in the way traditionally represented as (1a) below; reasonable phonetic values are given in (1b):

(1)	ī	ū	i:	u:
	ē̩	ō̩	e:	o:
	ę̄	ǭ	ɛ:	ɔ:
	(a)		(b)	

In early ME, the short mid vowels were apparently 'close' /e o/ (Luick 1964: §378); they lowered later to /ɛ ɔ/, so that at the time of the vowel shift the system as a whole was more or less like this (with /a/ in, but no /ā/):

(2)	i:	i	u	u:
	e:			o:
	ɛ:	ɛ	ɔ	ɔ:
		a		

There are two main kinds of arguments that bear on the location of ME /ā/: those from the GVS itself, and those from considerations of 'symmetry'. The first are probably the soundest, and run more or less this way. When /ā/ shifted, it did so in a chain with the front vowels, i.e. apparently displacing /ɛ:/ which in turn displaced /e:/ (the two vowels /ɛ:/ and /e:/ later merged in the 'standard' dialects: cf. ch. 3, §1 above). Thus the long low vowel did not participate in a back vowel raising chain, as it did in Swedish and Norwegian (cf. ch. 2). Aside from orthoëpic evidence for this (cf. Jespersen 1909, Kökeritz 1953), the comparative evidence is unambiguous, certainly, for the frontness of the reflexes of /ā/. So we can probably take the long low vowel as /a:/, giving the system:

(3)

i:	i	u	u:
e:			o:
ɛ:	ɛ	ɔ	ɔ:
a:	a		

(It seems likely that /i u/ were [ɩ ɷ], but this is relatively unimportant in terms of the general pattern in which the vowel space is filled.)

We can add one further argument: in §2 of the main body of this chapter I said that Dobson's claim for a front ME /a/ on the basis of congruity with ME /ā/ was weak, because of the lack of convincing evidence in either direction, which led to circularity. But now that we have established with reasonable certainty that /a/ was front, we have a clear point of departure for such symmetry arguments (we no longer have to argue from *ignotus* to *ignotior*).

The evidence for ME /a/ seems fairly sound; and we are pretty sure that /a/ was not affected in the early stages of the GVS by any major articulation-changing rules. We can now invoke the symmetry argument also from lengthening in open syllables, which Dobson misused. It is clear that ME /i u/ lowered when they lengthened, and that /e o/ did also (if they were still half-close at the time, which seems likely). If this is the case, if lengthening in open syllables included a lowering metarule (cf. Lass 1969), then it is clear that /a/ could not lower when it lengthened, but must either have retracted or stayed where it was. And there are no mergers that suggest it might have raised. Since the comparative evidence is unambiguous for a front value at the time of the vowel shift, the open-syllable behaviour plus the vowel shift arguments suggest that (3) is the correct picture, and that Dobson's claims can be taken as valid: though not on his own evidence.

2. The low vowels in Old English: long /ā/

With the ME system fairly well justified, let us turn to the OE input to it. In particular, what were the OE low vowels /a/ and /ā/ like? The fact that ME /ā/ seems to have been [a:] is of considerable importance here, because of the complex developments of OE /ā/.

As is well known, there is an '*ǭ/ā*' isogloss that separates – roughly – the 'North' from the 'South' in Britain. According to the handbooks, OE /ā/ became ME /ɔ:/ in the South beginning about 1100 (cf. Jordan 1934: §44), but remained /ā/ in the North. (I am using the 'philological' notations /ā/, etc. to indicate vowels of uncertain position: /ɔ:/ represents a commitment.) Because of the vowel shift and other evidence, there is little doubt that ME 'long open *o*' was [ɔ:]. And, as we saw above, ME /ā/ was [a:]. (Even though the sources for ME /a:/ are different in the North and the South – /a/ lengthened in open syllables in the latter, OE /ā/ in the former – the post-GVS developments suggest that the two vowels were the same. Thus mid front vowels in Scots *hame* 'home' < OE *hām*, Southern *same* < ME *sāme* < OE *săma*.)

Clearly then we have two choices for OE /ā/: [a:] or [ɑ:]. The consequences of the choices seem to be these:

(a) OE /ā/ = [ɑ:]. In this case, it raised and rounded in the South, presumably to [ɒ:] and then [ɔ:]. (There is no reason to assume raising first and then rounding, i.e. a stage [ʌ:].) In the North it merely fronted.

(b) OE /ā/ = [a:]. In this case, it retracted and rounded and raised in the South, and remained unchanged in the North. The evolution in the South would be [a:] → [ɑ:] → [ɒ:] → [ɔ:].

We might try and decide which of these is 'simpler', as a guide to choosing one. We note that in (*b*) there is a three-stage development in the South, but no change in the North; in (a) we have only two stages in the South, but one in the North. Both (a) and (b) have three changes, but in (b) one dialect remains constant. Which is more 'highly valued'? In the absence of direct evidence, I think there is no answer: do three changes count more heavily if they are spread over two dialects than if they are concentrated in one?

A choice – which will in any case not be made on the strongest of grounds – will require other criteria. One of them might be some notion of 'expectability' or (language-specific) 'naturalness': given an unconditioned change of a low vowel in English, which do we expect, fronting (as in (a)) or retraction (as in (b))? And further, unconditioned fronting in the North, or unconditioned retraction in the South?

We can start off by looking at the most typical cases of retraction of low vowels in English. One historical case has been dealt with already: the change of /a:/ to [ɑ:] before /f s θ/. I know of no other certain historical examples, but synchronic ones are fairly common. Thus in much American English there are alternations of [a] (or [ä]) with [ɑ:] or [ɑə], as in *lock* ~ *log*, *box* ~ *bogs*, *cot* ~ *cod*, etc. (cf. ch. 5 below). This lengthening and retraction also occur before /r/, e.g. in *car*, *heart*. Further, these same dialects (and some British ones) show alternations of [aɪ] and [ɑɪ], e.g. in *bite* ~ *bide*, *bite* ~ *buy*. In both cases, overall systemic considerations suggest retraction before voiced consonants and finally, rather than fronting. Similarly, many Scots dialects show [ɛ̈ɪ] ~ [ɑe] or something similar, with the latter before /r v z ð #/ only (cf. ch. 2, § 1 and Lass 1974 b.) These may also show [a] ~ [ɑ:], with the lengthened and back vowel in the same environments. But just about all the well-motivated examples of retraction I can think of are context-sensitive; and further, most of the contexts crucially involve the specification [+voice] (whatever else may be going on). So it seems on the face of it that context-free retraction is not a particularly 'natural' type of rule for English.

Unconditioned fronting, however, is another matter, especially in the North. Thus we have, to begin with, the fronting of ME /o:/ to /ø:/ in the fourteenth century (cf. ch. 2 above, and Lass 1972 and 1974b). And further, we have the fronting of /u/ in Scots, where after the loss of phonemic length in the seventeenth century, the /u/ from unshifted ME /u:/ collapsed in many dialects with the /y/ from earlier /y:/ from /ø:/. Thus in these dialects we get [y] or [ÿ] in both *loose* and *louse* (cf. further Lass 1972). These examples relate, unfortunately, only to nonlow vowels: the one most likely case of fronting of a low vowel, the 'Anglo-Frisian Brightening', cannot yet be invoked because we haven't reached a decision on whether it was a fronting and raising of early OE /ɑ/ or a raising only of early OE /a/. I will deal with this in the next section.

But, given this rather sketchy argument from a general typology of English sound change, we can assume – however diffidently – that OE /ā/ was a back vowel [ɑ:].

3. The low vowels in Old English, continued: short /a/

We now come, in our survey of English low vowels, to OE short /a/. Was it [a] or [ɑ]? This again is difficult, but we can at least look at the types of arguments that might be useful. First of all, when we are dealing with characterizations extending this far back in time, where a stage (i.e. ME) with its own special properties has intervened between the stage we want and the modern dialects, we have to use a wider pattern of comparative evidence. And when we do, it suggests, overall, that it is (relatively) 'natural' in Germanic for short low vowels to be front (e.g. standard Danish, Swedish, Norwegian, Icelandic, German). But once again, given the time-lapse, and further, given entities as notoriously unstable as vowels, such a general pattern is not even as good as the one we got within English for ME /a/.

If we look back at OE itself, there is some phonological evidence that suggests a back value. That is, there are processes in which /a/ is apparently a member of a class consisting of /u o/ and the velar fricative /x/ – all unambiguously back segments – as well as /r l/, which may have been [ʀ ɫ] (Lass & Anderson 1975: ch. III). These processes are both rules of diphthongization, where front vowels develop an epenthetic [-u] before: (a) /rC lC x/; and (b) consonant plus /u o a/. Process (a) is 'Breaking', and (b) is 'Velar Umlaut'. Typical examples of (a) are (WS) *earm* 'arm' < **ærm*, *seolf* 'self' < **self*, *feoh* 'cattle' < **fex*; examples of (b) are *heofon* 'heaven' < **hefon*, *meodu* 'mead' < **medu*. (The graph *ea* = [æɑ], and *eo* = [eo].) The surface representations derive from prephonetic (or historical) [æu eu] by a process of intradiphthongal harmony (Lass & Anderson 1975: ch. III).

This evidence, however, is also problematical. For there are cases where a fully front [a] may behave phonologically more like a back than a front vowel. Thus in Swedish /k g/ palatalize to [ç j] before front vowels in general, but not before [a]: *gift* [jift] 'marriage', *kött* [çœt:] 'meat', but *katt* [kat:] 'cat', *gammal* [gam:al] 'old'. Thus [a] behaves, with respect to palatalization, like back [ɑ:] (cf. *kal* [kɑ:l] 'bald', *garn* [gɑ:ɳ] 'yarn'). This COULD of course be handled in a synchronic grammar by assuming low-level fronting of underlying /ɑ/, ordered after palatalization; but this possibility may be simply an artifact of theories that allow extrinsic ordering in synchronic derivations (cf. Koutsoudas, Sanders & Noll 1972).

So it looks as if we may have a general indeterminacy-in-principle, which cannot be argued around, and is therefore not evidentially useful: i.e. it may be the case that low-front, in general, is not necessarily equivalent to front pure and simple, with respect to backness assimilation (cf. OE breaking, etc.) or frontness assimilation (cf. Swedish palatalization). We could conceive, that is, that different languages might cut the vowel space differently, so that in some [a] goes with the front vowels, and in others with the back vowels. The two types of languages would then be organized like this:

(4)

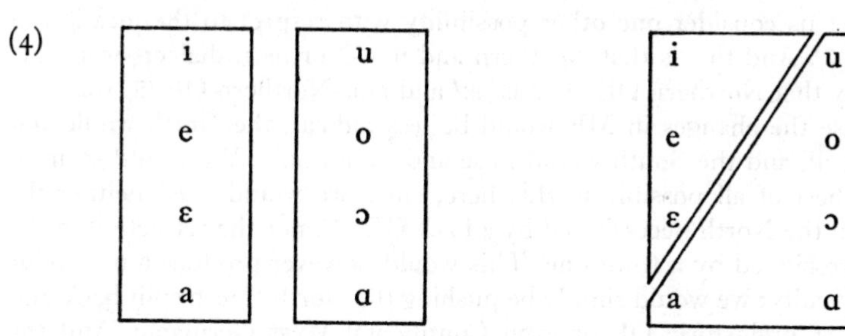

If this is the case, if low vowels which are nonback (including central ones?) carry a free option, then arguments from allophony are inconclusive. We cannot use evidence from class-grouping with back vowels to assign backness to a low vowel; though we can use evidence from class-grouping with front vowels to assign frontness.

The only other useful line of argument, as far as I can see, is to look at the rest of what is fairly well established about the OE vowel system, and see if that suggests anything. It is generally assumed that OE had (at least phonetically) a pair of low front vowels [æ] and [æ:] (the former from WG */a/ via 'Anglo-Frisian Brightening', the latter from various sources in various dialects, including WG */ā/ and the *i*-umlaut of */ai/). For a dialect like say West Saxon, we generally assume a system like (5) below (including the /ɑ:/ established in §2, but without the short low vowel):

(5)

i:	i	y:	y	u	u:
e:	e	ø:	ø	o	o:
æ:	æ				
					ɑ:

On the basis of (5), one might be inclined to argue that short /a/ was back, since even superficially contrastive [æ a] in the same system is rare in Germanic: the typical case where both these types exist would be one like an English dialect with [æ] in *cat* and [a:] in *last*, (with regard to quality, not length) or vice versa. A front series with both short [a] and [æ] is a little too 'crowded' to be readily accepted in the absence of strong evidence. So it would be reasonable to suggest that short /a/ was back, and that the whole system was:

(6)

i:	i	y:	y	u	u:
e:	e	ø:	ø	o	o:
æ:	æ				
				ɑ	ɑ:

In this case, OE /ɑ/ fronted to ME /a/ in all dialects, Northern and Southern, and /ɑ:/ fronted only in the North.

4. A final confusion: was there only one OE /ā/?

Finally, let us consider one other possibility with respect to the location of OE long /ā/. And this is that Northern and non-Northern dialects were different. Say that Northern OE /ā/ was /a:/ and non-Northern OE /ā/ was /ɑ:/. In this case the changes in ME would be less radical: the North would not change at all, and the South would raise and round only. We would seem to have the best of all possible worlds here, since we would need neither the fronting in the North necessitated by a back OE /ā/, nor the retraction in the South necessitated by a front one. This would however produce a methodological difficulty: we would simply be pushing the North/South split back into early OE or prehistoric OE or even Continental West Germanic. And the further back we go, the more tenuous the evidence becomes. I conclude that it is not useful to attempt to date the North/South split of the long low vowels any earlier than the twelfth century, when the evidence for it first appears; we can fairly safely assume the same backness value for OE /ā/ in all the dialects, and locate the innovations in ME. Similarly, we can locate the fronting of OE /ɑ/ in ME also, or at least in very late OE: probably at the time that we first get evidence for the merger of *æ* and *a* in *a* in some dialects.

The histories of the low vowels in OE and early ME can now be summed up as follows:

(7)

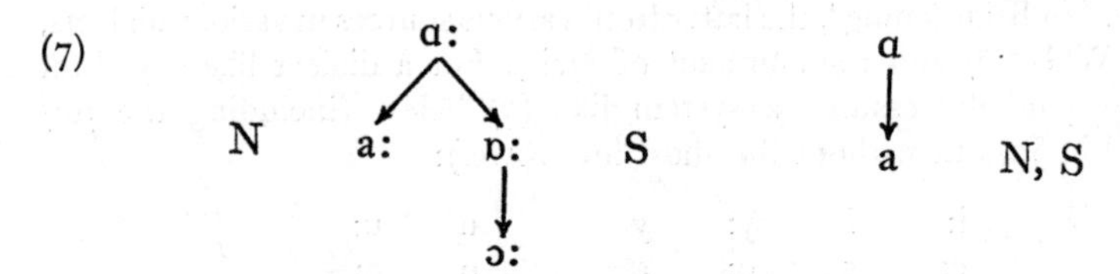

ME /a/ is subject to the various changes described in the body of this chapter, and Northern /a:/ raises in the GVS, as does Southern /ɔ:/. The main difference in the overall developments in the latter two categories (aside from phonetic detail) will then involve the distribution of vowels in lexical sets. Thus in the North words with OE /ā/ and words with ME /ā/ from /a/ lengthened will have the same vowel, and the only source of ME /ɔ:/ will be lengthening of short /o/; while in the South words with OE /ā/ will have the same vowel as words with ME /ɔ:/ from /o/, and OE /ā/ and /a/ lengthened will not be the same. So (with typical values):

(8)

North			South		
OE ā }	home }	[e:]	OE ā }	home }	[ou]
ME ā }	same }		ME ǭ }	smoke }	
ME ǭ	smoke	[uə]	ME ā	same	[ei]

5 *Middle English /ɔ/ in New York City English*

1. Split and merger patterns

Contextually determined changes of vowel quantity have occurred a number of times in the history of English.[1] These processes, together with numerous (both related and unrelated) qualitative changes, have led to exceedingly complex historical trajectories for many vowels, with numerous splits and mergers in a given history. A further result of this has been that a given vowel quality in a given dialect may have quite diverse historical origins. A familiar example is the evolution of OE /e/, /e:/, and /æ:/ in RP and similar dialects:

(1)

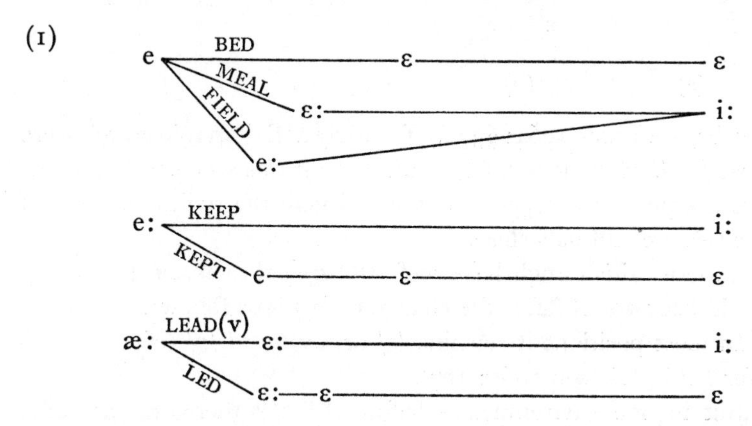

(The symbols for the NE categories are conventional, based on the Jonesian analysis of RP; Jones 1950, 1956.)

Thus NE /ε/ can derive from OE /e/, OE /e:/ shortened before /CC/ clusters (*kept*), and OE /æ:/ shortened in the same environment (*led*); while /i:/ can come from OE /e/ lengthened to /ε:/ in open syllables and then raised to /i:/ in the GVS (*meal*), OE /e/ lengthened before

[1] For discussion of some of these changes in the light of the overall history of English vocalism, see Lass & Anderson (1975: Appendix 2), and Lass (1974b).

homorganic sonorant + voiced stop clusters to /e:/ and raised to /i:/ in the GVS (*field*), or /æ:/ via /ɛ:/ raised in the GVS to /i:/ (*lead*).

The earlier examples of complex histories like these have been worked out in detail in the handbooks; but some later ones – especially those whose elucidation requires the use of interdialectal comparison – have not been much (if at all) discussed. This chapter is an attempt to clarify one of these: the sequence leading to the characteristic reflexes of the ME short mid back vowel in New York City English. I will approach this here through a comparison with the rather simpler developments in RP and related Southern British dialects. We will see that there is a wealth of historical innovation involved, which as far as I know has not been adequately treated in the literature.

A few comments on the earlier history of this vowel will help to set the stage. Early ME (until c. 1100) had a short vowel system like (2a) below; during the twelfth century, it changed into something like (2b):[1]

(2)				
	i	u	i	u
	e	o		
			ɛ	ɔ
	a		a	
	(a)		(b)	

(For details, see Luick 1964: §378.) The early ME short mid vowels were half-close /e o/, which lowered to /ɛ ɔ/. At least this seems to have been the case everywhere except in Scotland, where the typical reflexes of these vowels are still half-close.

In Southern British English (henceforth SBE), the subsequent history of the mid back vowel (after the change to /ɔ/) is as follows.

(i) In most positions it remains /ɔ/ or lowers to /ɒ/ (cf. the range given for RP in Gimson 1965: 107).

(ii) But in one environment – before /f θ s/ – there was at some point (probably mid seventeenth century) a lengthening, e.g. in *soft*, *cloth*, *loss*. These forms now have – for speakers who retain the lengthening – /ɔ:/.

Thus there is now a distinction between /ɔ:/ from lengthened ME /ɔ/ and /ɒ/ from the isolative development: and because of other factors, to be mentioned below, this distinction is now phonemic. In general, the reflex of lengthened ME /ɔ/ is (a) long, and (b) closer than that of the

[1] On the location of ME /a/ and its subsequent history, see ch. 4 above.

unlengthened vowel.[1] This lengthened form is now archaic; it is characteristic of older speakers, of what Gimson (108) calls 'conservative' RP. For most younger speakers it is being – or has been – replaced before /f θ s/ by /ɒ/.

We will confine ourselves for the moment to this rather archaic form of RP (or, more generally, SBE), because it is here that an important merger shows up, which accounts for the phonemicity of /ɔ:/. That is, /ɔ:/ is also the ISOLATIVE reflex of the ME diphthong /au/, e.g. in *law*, *bought*, *all*. There has then been a merger of lengthened ME /ɔ/ with the isolative reflexes of /au/, giving this pattern:

(3)

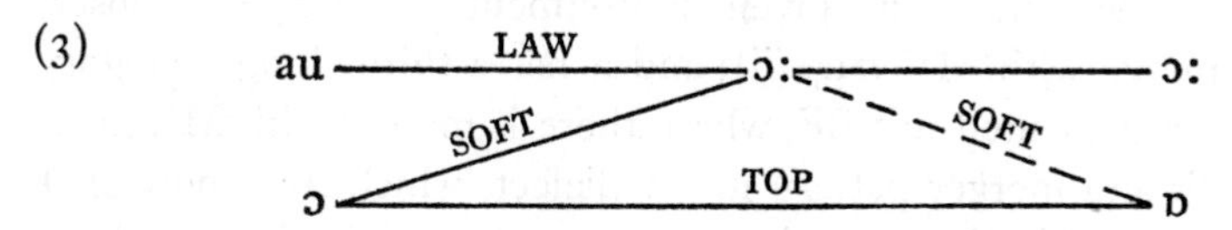

(The broken line for *soft* represents the later 'de-merger' I spoke of above.)[2]

In the U.S., however, there is evidence for a much more complex development. In my own dialect, which may be taken as representative of New York City (and many other non-New England, non-Southern, East Coast dialects), ME /ɔ/ has the following reflexes.

(i) [ä] before voiceless stops and /n/: *top*, *pot*, *fox*, *con*.

(ii) [ɔə] before voiceless fricatives and /ŋ/:[3] *soft*, *cloth*, *loss*, *song*. This

[1] In the precise form /ɒ/ : /ɔ:/, this distinction is rather more conventional than (strictly) accurate: the most usual RP value for /ɔ:/ really approaches [o:] (Gimson 1965: 109). The /ɒ/ : /ɔ:/ opposition is actually more complicated – perceptually – than I am making it out to be for historical purposes. But as long as both length and quality are taken into account in the notation, the picture is not really falsified (see further Gimson 109–10).

[2] Gillian Brown informs me that some ME /au/ words, where there is a following /l/, have now also 'demerged': e.g. *salt*. Here young speakers have consistent /ɒ/. In one environment, though, where there was also lengthening (probably in ME), there has been no shortening; and this is before /r/. Thus *shot* and *short* are never true homophones, as far as I know. I will not attempt to explain the redevelopment of short vowels in those forms that now have them; but I suspect that long and short nuclei must have coexisted before /f θ s/ for a long time, and that an existing variant is simply acquiring prestige and being re-generalized.

[3] There are a few exceptions here, where ME /ɔ/ is [ä] before /ŋ/: e.g. *thong*, *tongs*. This is in fact the value that 'naturally' goes with orthographic *-ong* (from non-ME sources), as in *prong*, *gong*, (*ping*)-*pong*, (*King*) *Kong*, Chinese names like *Fong*, *Wong*, and others like *Dong* (with the luminous nose). The [äŋ] in *schlong* 'male organ' is from Yiddish /ʃlaŋ/ (also the verb *schlong* 'to defeat epically'); *dong*, *wong*, also slang terms for the male organ, with [äŋ], probably derive from distortions of *schlong* ('euphemistic'?).

is also the reflex of ME /au/ in *law*, *bought*, *all*, and of ME /ɔr/ in *course*, *torn*, *for*.

(iii) [ɑə] before voiced stops and /m/: *cob*, *cod*, *cog*, *Tom*.[1] This is also the reflex of ME /ar/: *cart*, *far*. (One exception to the pattern is [ɑə] in *John*.)

If we take /ɔə ɑə/ as reasonably derived from earlier /ɔ: ɑ:/ (my dialect has no monophthongal long vowels), then aside from the quality differences, this dialect is typologically different from SBE primarily by virtue of there being a third reflex of ME /ɔ/, category (iii) above. That is, it is similar to SBE in having some reflexes of ME /ɔ/ which are short and open (i), and some which – in a given environment – are long and closer, and which merge with ME /au/ (ii); and it has a third 'long' category which is not represented in SBE, where there is merger with ME /ar/.[2]

So the split and merger pattern in my dialect, which from now on I will call NYC, is this (I am leaving out a number of the intermediary stages, which I will introduce later, when the evidence is a little clearer):

(4)

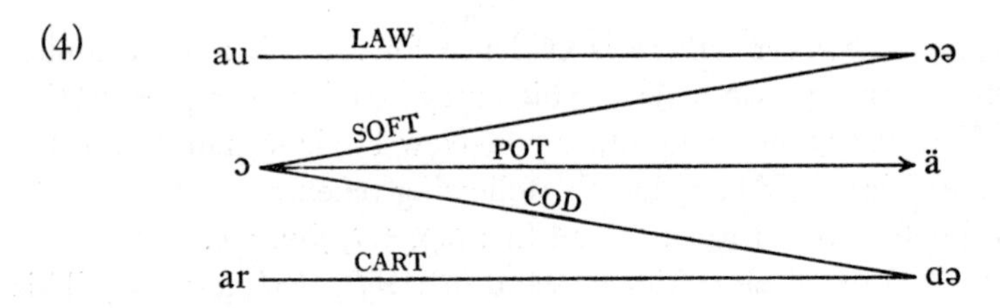

2. The history

The NYC dialect, then, in addition to the unrounding, lowering and fronting of ME /ɔ/ which typifies a large part of the U.S., must have had at least two lengthenings in its history: an early one, parallel to that in SBE, before /f θ s/, while /ɔ/ was still a nonlow rounded vowel; and a later one, before /b d g/, when it was unround and low. The differences between NYC and SBE, which will lead us to a reconstruction of the history, can be tabulated in a reasonably clear manner. Let us call ME /au/ (I), ME /ɔ/ before /f θ s/ (II), ME /ɔ/ before /b d g/ (III), and ME /ɔ/ elsewhere (IV). The four categories will then look like this:

[1] I find the differential developments before the three nasals incomprehensible.

[2] My dialect also has /ɑə/ in many cases where SBE has /ɑ:/, besides ME /ar/: thus *father*, *drama*, *calm*, from various historical sources. But notably no /ɑə/ from lengthened ME /a/, e.g. in *half*, *path*, *last*. Here I have [æ̝̈:], which is the normal lengthened form of /æ/ < ME /a/ before certain classes of segments (mainly either voiced or continuant).

(5)	I		II		III		IV	
	NYC	SBE	NYC	SBE	NYC	SBE	NYC	SBE
	ɔə	ɔ:	ɔə	ɔ:	ɑə	ɒ	ä	ɒ

(In SBE there is a slight length increment before voiced stops; but this is not large enough to affect category-assignment, i.e. there is no /ɒ:/ alongside /ɒ/ and /ɔ:/.)

We can use these distributions, along with what we know about the history from other sources, to construct at least a tentative picture of the series of innovations that brought them about, during the post-ME period. A probable characterization and order is as follows:

(i) ME /e o/ → /ɛ ɔ/ (Lowering I.) All dialects except Scots.[1]

(ii) ME /au/ → /ɔ:/ (Monophthongization.) All dialects.[2]

(iii) /ɔ/ → /ɔ:/ before /f θ s/ (Lengthening I.) SBE, some U.S. dialects.

(iv) /ɔ/ → /ɒ/ (Lowering II.) Much SBE, especially RP and ancestors of NYC (see below).

(v) /ɒ/ → /ɑ/ (Unrounding.) U.S. only.[3] The most likely date for this is late seventeenth–early eighteenth century, as it defines in large part a 'Transatlantic' isogloss.

(vi) /ɑ/ → /ɑ:/ before /b d g/ (Lengthening II.) NYC only.

(vii) /ɑ/ → /ä/ (Fronting.) U.S. only.[4]

(viii) /ɑ:/ → /ɑə/, /ɔ:/ → /ɔə/ (Diphthongization.) NYC only.

[1] Most Scots dialects have [e]-type reflexes of ME /e/, but [ɛ]-types for ME /i/. There has been a lowering of /i/ which 'bypassed' the half-close position without merger; to use a term of Allen's (personal communication), a 'leap-frogging'. Cf. ch. 4, §4 above.

[2] Strictly speaking, not all dialects show THIS monophthongization: the North-East of England typically has [a:] (e.g. Northumberland and Durham: cf. Orton & Halliday 1962: s.v. *saw* – I. vii. 17). We also find [a:] in the North Midlands: cf. ch. 3 above.

[3] There have been sporadic unroundings of ME /ɔ/, usually with lowering to [ɑ] or even fronting as well, throughout the period from c. 1400 to the present (cf. Wyld 1956: 240–2). The only 'standard' forms, however, in which the unrounded version (which merged with ME /a/) survived are *strap* (cf. the doublet *strop*) and *Gad* 'God'. But many SBE speakers do have (short) [ɑ]-variants in at least some lexical items with /ɒ/. The unrounding is much more widespread in Scotland: cf. names like *Tam*, *Rab*, etc., and spellings in earlier Scots like *aff*, *aft*, *bannet*, *gat*, *labster*, *parritch*, *pat*, *saft*, *stap*, *tap* (all from Fergusson 1851). The Scots unrounded vowels in *lang*, *sang*, etc., are not from the same source: these are original OE /ɑ/ which did not round before /ŋ/ in the North.

[4] This has gone considerably further in many U.S. dialects, i.e. all the way to [a]. In some, especially Western New York State and the Northern Midwest, there has been a chain shift, where /ä/ has become [æ] and /æ/ has become [eə]. Thus [læk] 'lock', [leək] 'lack'. There has been a bypassing of /ɛ/ here, since *peck*, etc. still have [ɛ̞].

The overall history here shows three innovations common to SBE and its descendant, NYC (i–iii); possibly a fourth (iv) is also common to both groups, i.e. it belongs to a 'Proto-SBE/NYC' period, before the split characterized by (v–viii).[1] If we take the forms *law*, *fog*, *loss*, *top* as exemplifying the possible ME inputs, we can schematize the whole history as follows.

(6) Developments in 'Common SBE/NYC'

Early ME input	lau	fog	los	top
Lowering I	—	fɔg	lɔs	tɔp
Monophthongization	lɔ:	—	—	—
Lengthening I	—	—	lɔ:s	—
Lowering II	—	fɒg	—	tɒp
ENE output	lɔ:	fɒg	lɔ:s	tɒp

(7) Post-split developments

	SBE	NYC	SBE	NYC	SBE	NYC	SBE	NYC
ENE input	lɔ:	lɔ:	fɒg	fɒg	lɔ:s	lɔ:s	tɒp	tɒp
Unrounding	—	—	—	fɑg	—	—	—	tɑp
Lengthening II	—	—	—	fɑ:g	—	—	—	—
Fronting	—	—	—	—	—	—	—	täp
Diphthongization	—	lɔə	—	fɑəg	—	lɔəs	—	—
NE output	lɔ:	lɔə	fɒg	fɑəg	lɔ:s	lɔəs	tɒp	täp

3. Implications

The primary implication is obvious: there is more history to English than we usually assume, and one way of discovering it is to ask questions about dialect-differentia and where they came from. That is, to apply comparative method on a reasonable scale WITHIN one language, and see what it turns up. Whatever its shortcomings (and there certainly are many), comparison is a very useful heuristic: it produces history, which after all is what historical linguists should be doing. History in any significant sense is not something given; it is a product of intellectual operations on the inchoate mass of forms we hunt through looking for intelligibility. Therefore, quite simply, the more operating we do, the more history we get.

As I suggested in chapter 4, comparative procedures of the type illustrated there (and again, on a smaller scale, here) suggest that there is

[1] On the basically SBE origins of the East Coast U.S. dialects, see Kurath (1928, 1964).

still a rich lode of history in English waiting to be uncovered (much of it, I think, not even suspected to exist). The process of digging this material out not only gives us more history, which is pleasant because we now have more to think about and to operate on further; it also enables us to 'solve' (insofar as historical procedures ever allow us to do this) certain problems that have been with us for a long time, but have gone stale in their unsolvedness through lack of fresh evidence to base arguments on. Certainly the location of ME /a/ (ch. 4) is a case in point.

But in addition to producing more data, and furnishing solutions to old problems, the construction of histories can raise new ones, which were not clearly problematical before the background history that throws them into relief was constructed. These can often have interesting theoretical implications; and I will close this chapter by considering one such 'new' problem.

In my dialect there is one exceedingly curious form, whose curiosity becomes apparent only when we look at the history sketched out above in (6) and (7). This is *dog*, which is /dɔəg/. Now etymologically *dog* (ME *dogge*) is in the same class as *fog* (ME *fogge*), *hog* (ME *hogg*), and *log* (ME *logge*), all of which have /ɑə/, as expected. But */dɑəg/ doesn't occur. That is, *dog*, with ME /ɔ/ before a voiced stop, seems to have 'illegally' undergone Lengthening I (along with *soft*, etc.) rather than Lengthening II, as it should have.[1] This suggests that there may be a certain indeterminacy in the early stages of innovations like this (but not that 'each word has its own history', of course).[2] That is, while in general rules are restricted by the terms of their SD's, these may be able to expand (within certain limits) to accommodate certain items lexically marked for them, so that the SC's can operate even if the SD's aren't fully met. (This seems better than a 'minor rule' of Lengthening I for *dog* only.) So in other words, a major rule can be a minor rule – or can adjust itself so that it can be used as one – for certain selected items.

[1] But notice that *song*, *long*, *wrong*, etc., also have /ɔə/, i.e. they have undergone Lengthening I too. Is it a coincidence that the only ME /ɔ/ word to have done it illegally ends in a velar?

[2] Note that I say 'word'. It may very well be the case that every NAME (at least in principle) has its own history. Certainly proper names may have wildly implausible and thoroughly non-*Lautgesetzlich* histories, almost to the point where they have no 'etymologies', properly speaking, at all. See the documentation in Lass (1973d).

Part III

ISSUES IN GENERAL THEORY: FEATURES, RULES AND CLASSES

> Whenever a theory appears to you as the only possible one, take this as a sign that you have neither understood the theory nor the problem which it was intended to solve.
>
> Sir Karl Popper, *Objective Knowledge* (1973)

6 *On the phonological characterization of* [ʔ] *and* [h][1]

1. The categorial status of the glottal stop

The 'standard' characterization of [ʔ] (*SPE*: 303) is an oblique challenge to the traditional term 'glottal stop': and, as I will show, an unjustified one. Chomsky & Halle, with no discussion, assign [ʔ] to the category 'glide', along with [h] and [j w]. This class itself is specified as [+sonorant, −consonantal, −vocalic].

This interpretation appears to derive from Jakobson, Fant & Halle (1951: 19): 'The so-called glides...like the English *h* and the "glottal catch", are distinguished from vowels in that they have either a non-harmonic source as in the case of [h] or a transient onset of the source as in [ʔ]. They are distinct from consonants in that they have no significant zeros in their spectra.' Earlier (p. 17) Jakobson *et al.* define 'zeros' as regions in spectra that show no energy output: these are due to 'the interaction of...two resonating systems in parallel which are created either by a) the opening of a supplementary passage or by b) the non-terminal location of the source'. Thus a laryngeal source (not being non-terminal) will not cause 'significant zeros', but a supralaryngeal stricture will.

The distinction is circular: the definitions of 'vowel' and 'consonant' depend respectively on harmonic source and non-terminal source. Therefore glottal strictures (as opposed to glottal harmonic sources) are neither vocalic nor consonantal, and [ʔ h] are excluded from the class 'consonant' because the definition excludes them. I will argue here that the physiological correlates, phonological behaviour,

[1] I owe some of the notions I explore in this chapter to discussions with Charles Bird: especially the idea (developed in §§2ff.) that laryngeal and supralaryngeal articulations can be fruitfully treated as separate 'gestures', independent components of single segments. But he is not responsible for what I have (or haven't) made of the idea. I have also profited from discussions with John Anderson, Gillian Brown, Tim Shopen and Fred Householder; and from detailed comments by Sidney Allen (especially on matters concerning Sanskrit).

and historical sources of segments like [ʔ] and [h] do not support the acoustic definitions: their behaviour is not quite as unique as their spectra.[1]

It seems to me an error to interpret these two segments as uniquely nonconsonantal and nonvocalic; and to group them with [j w] as *SPE* does is a worse one (though this will not be my primary concern here). But there is certainly very good motivation for classifying [ʔ] and [h] together: only the proper class is not sonorant, and does not include [j w] or any other approximants. I will argue for this position on both synchronic and historical grounds. My basic aim will be a reformulation of certain aspects of current feature-theory, with a view toward establishing non-oral (i.e. laryngeal) strictures as true consonantal 'articulations': though as ones which may be hierarchically 'inferior', in a special sense, to 'normal' oral ones.

The solution lies in departing from current conventions that assign features to segments in an unordered or loosely hierarchized set, with only one matrix for each segment. The basis of this claim will be the impossibility of writing natural rules for certain exceedingly common processes within the current framework, and the awkwardness and obtuseness of the rules one can write.

I will begin with [ʔ]. But before considering some phonological and historical arguments, we ought to look at the way this segment is made; especially since the *SPE* definitions of the category 'sonorant' and the subcategory 'glide' are physiologically based (as is the category 'consonant'). The glottal stop is amply described in the literature: the earliest reliable account I know is that of Sweet (1877: 6) who classifies it among the voiceless stops: 'When the glottis is suddenly opened or closed on a passage of breath or voice, a percussive effect is produced, analogous to that of (k) or any other "stopped" consonant.'

The standard modern phonetics texts all give similar descriptions: e.g. Pike (1943: 133; 139–40), Jones (1950: 150), Gimson (1965: 162), Malmberg (1963: 43), Abercrombie (1967: 28, 53). I will quote two descriptions here, one pedagogical and the other more theoretical, which are suggestive for the line of argument I intend to follow. The first is from Abercombie (1967: 53):

[1] It is interesting that the Jakobsonian class 'glide' does not include the approximants [j w]; these are classified as nonsyllabic vowels (Jakobson *et al.* 1951: 20). This interpretation unfortunately cannot work for English (cf. ch. 1 above); but it seems appropriate (phonologically) for certain other languages, like Lugisu (Brown 1970). At least Jakobson *et al.* do not force [j w ʔ h] into the same class.

No articulators are used in making this sound, but the vocal cords act very much in the same way as articulators to produce a complete but brief closure in the path of the air-stream, with resulting momentary compression of air behind the closure if the air-stream is egressive...as with any other stop.

(Note that this account differentiates glottal stops from others by defining 'articulators' as supralaryngeal only.)

The second passage is from Ladefoged (1971: 15–16):

A...state of the glottis which clearly contrasts with both voice and voicelessness is that during a glottal closure, where the vocal cords are held together throughout their length. From a phonological point of view it is often convenient to consider a glottal stop along with articulatory stops...But from a phonetic point of view it has to be considered as a state of the glottis, because of the combinatory restrictions: if there is a glottal closure there cannot simultaneously be voice, or voicelessness, or murmur, or laryngealization.

(Earlier on (p. 9) Ladefoged defines 'voicelessness' in a very specific way, as a configuration with 'the vocal cords...apart at the posterior end'.)

This description is important for what follows: especially its suggestion that even though a glottal stop is like an 'articulatory stop' in some ways, a problem arises because the configuration that produces it is in the same part of the vocal tract where the (non-articulatory) 'states of the glottis' are produced. But this is not in fact a real problem.

Note that even though, as Ladefoged says, the state of the glottis during [ʔ] is incompatible with either voice or voicelessness as usually defined, the same is true in part during the occlusion of any voiceless stop. That is, though it is possible to have voicing during the closure phase of a stop (with an attendant build-up of subglottal pressure), it is not possible to have 'voicelessness' – even if the glottis is open. At least it is possible, in the strict sense, to have 'physiological' voicelessness (Ladefoged's definition cited above), but not 'perceptual' voicelessness, which linguistically is what counts. During the closure of [p t k] etc., the ORAL tract is sealed, with respect to air-flow, in precisely the same way as the whole supraglottal tract is sealed during [ʔ]; the (perceived) voicelessness of a stop depends on the timing relation between RELEASE of the closure and either the onset of another closure (as in clusters like [kt]) or the onset of voice on a following voiced segment. So that in a real sense the state of the vocal tract during a glottal closure and during an oral (voiceless) stop closure is the same: there is no air-flow.[1]

Now consider Chomsky & Halle's feature 'sonorant'. They define sonorant articulations as those where 'spontaneous voicing' can occur, that is where a low rate of transglottal air-flow is sufficient to produce a pressure drop.[2] An obstruent, in this scheme, is a segment where there is sufficient constriction somewhere in the vocal tract to make a higher rate of airflow necessary in order to produce voicing. They further define the constrictions which produce nonspontaneous voicing as 'more radical than those found in the glides [y] and [w]' (*SPE*: 302). Thus stops, fricatives, affricates are nonsonorant, and vowels, nasals, liquids, and 'glides' are sonorant.

This is circular and equivocal, in the same way as the definition of Jakobson *et al.* cited above. If we arbitrarily define 'constriction' as only supraglottal, then obviously glottal constrictions fail to qualify. But if we consider that in the normal way of things we are dealing not with a glottalic egressive but with a pulmonic egressive air-stream, then a glottal closure or stricture is simply the first in a series of possible obstructions of the air-stream, since the lungs, not the glottis, are the initiators. And in this view, it is certainly true that the constriction for [ʔ] at least is 'more radical' than that for [j w]; since it prohibits any air-flow at all. This certainly does not permit 'spontaneous voicing': so that even according to the *SPE* definition, it seems clear that the glottal stop must be an obstruent.

Let us now turn to phonology. My initial comments will be restricted to English, though I will bring in one other (unrelated) language later on. Let us consider the distribution of [ʔ] in those dialects of English where it occurs elsewhere than at initial vowel onset).[3] Specifically, let us look at some cases where [ʔ] appears as a substitute for other segments.

[1] The complete lack of airflow in a glottal stop has been taken as a criterion for assigning it a unique status. Thus Firth (1948: [= Palmer 1970: 6]): 'Phonetically, the glottal stop, unreleased, is the negation of all sound whether vocalic or consonantal.' But the extent of sealing of the vocal tract can itself be taken as a criterion of 'optimal' consonantality. For Jakobson (1968: 69) the labials are 'optimal' consonants because they alone 'obstruct the entire oral cavity'. (But this depends of course on which end we start from.)

[2] Ladefoged (1971: 109–10) has shown that this is probably erroneous; but for the sake of the *SPE* arguments this does not matter. The definition of [ʔ] as a sonorant is contradictory even in their terms, as we will see.

[3] That is, I am interested only in the (segmental) phonological functions of [ʔ], not the possible 'prosodic' ones. As Firth remarks (1948 [Palmer 1970: 6]), the glottal stop can be 'the perfect minimum or terminus of the syllable', or 'just a necessary metrical

A. *New York City*. In my own dialect, a 'substitutive' [ʔ] (normally in allegro speech) occurs as follows.

(i) For /p t k/ in homorganic /NCN/ clusters, where we get forms like: ['sɛnʔn̩s] or ['sɛ̃ʔn̩s] 'sentence', ['wəŋʔŋ̍] or ['wə̃ʔŋ̍] 'one can', ['səmʔm̩] or ['sə̃ʔm̩] 'something', etc. The order of frequency is probably /t p k/.

(ii) For /t/ before a syllabic /n/: ['bəʔn̩] 'button', etc. This is in a sense a subcase of (i), as [n̩] appears only after dental obstruents. Syllabic nasals in general, in fact, are restricted to positions after a homorganic obstruent: cf. ['bəʔn̩] from ['bətn̩] above, but ['bärəm] 'bottom'.

(iii) For /t/ before word-boundary plus another consonant: ['fɤ̈ʔbɔəɫ] 'football', ['ðæʔwən] 'that one', [ˌðæʔ'kʰæt] 'that cat' and so on.

In all these cases [ʔ] is the reflex of a voiceless stop.

B. *Scots*. In many Lowland (and other) Scots dialects, [ʔ] occurs consistently as follows (data from my own observations of Lothian and Fife speakers).

(i) For /t/ intervocalically, or after vowel plus liquid or nasal with another vowel following: ['wɔʔər] 'water', ['näʔjərəɫ] 'natural', ['ɔɫʔe-geðər] 'altogether', ['enʔər] 'enter', ['kärʔrɪdʒ] 'cartridge'. Substitution for /k/ is rare, but it occurs: ['bläʔər] 'blacker'.

(ii) For /p t k/ before word-boundary. This applies in 'citation' forms or sentence-finals: [toʔ] 'top', [käʔ] 'cat', [bäʔ] 'back'; if the following word is vowel-initial: [ˌteʔ ə ˌsiʔ] 'take a seat'; or if it is consonant-initial: ['bläʔ'käʔ] 'black cat'. We also get [ʔ] for /p t k/ in compounds, where the second element begins with a consonant: ['fÿʔbɔɫ] 'football', etc. (Most commonly, a boundary intervenes: [ʔ] for /t/ is

pause or rest, a sort of measure of time'. It can also be 'a general syllable maker or marker', in fact 'all or any of these things, or just a member of the consonant system according to the language' (cf. further pp. 17–19). While I admit the possibility of varying functions or statuses for [ʔ] (or any other segment), I am not at all convinced for example that the use of [ʔ] as a marker of syllable onset is in fact 'prosodic': it may very well be segmental phonological in a very simple way. Thus dialects with obligatory [ʔ] before initial vowels may have a phonotactic structure that forbids /#V–/, but allows only /#CV–/ as a minimum initial cluster. In this case [ʔ] is a realization of /C/ (unspecified further), which contrasts with all other consonants. (The argument used by Moulton 1947 for German, that since [#ʔV–] never contrasts with [#V–], the glottal stop is not a phonemic consonant but merely a 'juncture' marker, i.e. a 'prosody', is not convincing: zero can simply be an optional realization of /C/.) This is borne out, I think, by the argument of §2 below. As a further possible support, note that in Old Germanic poetry, while consonants alliterate only with each other, ALL vowel-initials form an alliterating class. This may suggest that they are phonologically all /#CV–/, i.e. that there is no syllable type */#V–/.

most usual in e.g. *Pat says*, and much rarer in e.g. *Patsy*: though the latter does occur. Further, the vowel before the segment that becomes [ʔ] is accented in all cases that I know except one: [ho'ʔeɫ] 'hotel'.) In all these cases the order of likelihood for substitution seems to be /t k p/.

(iii) For /p t k/ before a syllabic nasal (these are always homorganic): [oʔm̩] 'open', [bʌʔn̩] 'button', [broʔŋ̩] 'broken'.

Material like this could be adduced from any number of dialects: for RP and related types see Gimson (1965: 164–5); for Cockney see Sivertson (1960: §4.14). But the two examples above will suffice for my purposes here.

In all these dialects, one thing is clear: whenever [ʔ] appears as a replacing segment, it is naturally to be derived from a more remote representation minimally specified as [+obs, −cont, −voice].[1] To put it the other way round: when, under conditions of a certain amount of potential redundancy, voiceless stops (and only these) are neutralized, they become [ʔ]. Now if [ʔ] is, as Chomsky & Halle claim, a 'glide', then this is rather peculiar: why shouldn't [w] or [j] (or even [h]) ever appear here? Note also that [ʔ] is never a variant of any of the other 'glides'.

In the *SPE* framework, this common rule of stop neutralization is extremely complex: it involves reversal of value on two features high up in the hierarchy ([+cons] → [−cons], [+obs] → [−obs]), as well as alteration of all the oral stricture features. And it also violates, in a serious, and what's worse, arbitrary way any reasonable 'naturalness condition' (Postal 1968: 53ff.). That is, the principle asserting that there is (*ceteris paribus*) a non-arbitrary and at least partially universal mapping between phonological and phonetic representations.[2]

[1] The substitution behaviour here may or may not be related to so-called 'glottal reinforcement', i.e. 'an initial glottal closure, with an oral plosive articulation occurring simultaneously with the latter part of the glottal closure, i.e. before the glottal release' (Higginbottom 1964: 129). Higginbottom's data for RP has some interesting parallels with my New York and Scots material: though whether or not the same phenomena are involved is uncertain. In any case, this is probably not relevant: as my discussion in §2 will show, the phenomenon of 'reinforcement' may not really be that, but rather something more like the 'unmarked' condition for voiceless plosives (at least in English). That is, an aspirated plosive is a lenited one, but one with glottal closure may be 'optimal'. See further Lass & Anderson (1975: ch. v).

[2] Postal (1968: 187) attempts to deal with this problem while preserving [ʔ] as a sonorant. He proposes what he calls a 'subordinate switching assumption', which operates according to 'universal marking conventions' (if I understand him correctly) as follows: if the value for consonantality on a stop is switched from '+' to '−', the 'subordinate switching' automatically changes all marked values into unmarked ones. Thus in the example he gives, if consonantality is switched on a nongrave, diffuse apical

Of course 'naturalness' in this sense is relative: it is probably impossible to say (given the current state of the theory) that any given phonological-to-phonetic mapping NECESSARILY violates it. And in fact naturalness in this sense has not yet been formally defined in any very satisfactory way. It is still a pre-theoretical and intuitive notion, like 'simplicity' (insofar as this means anything more than symbol-counting). But it seems reasonable to feel that very common rules – especially those which operate low in the phonology – are likely to be rather uncomplicated; especially in their manipulation of higher-level categories.

Observe that if we try to formulate the rule for glottal stop replacement of other segments, say in the Scots dialects discussed above, we run into difficulties. Leaving aside the problem of how to state predicted gradients of applicability in rules (see Weinreich, Labov & Herzog 1968), let's say that we have a dialect where only /t k/ are involved, and not /p/ (as in intervocalic position in example (i) above). In addition to switching the major class features, the rule will also have to specify values for stricture and tongue-body features like anteriority, coronality, backness, etc. And second, even if we do write such a rule, it will be unmotivated: if [ʔ] is a glide, then the rule is one that changes voiceless stops to glides (in fact, all to the same one) in certain environments: so why not, for instance, change velars to [h], labials to [w], and dentals to [j]? I will return to this problem in the next section, and suggest a principled solution.

2. On two-gesture representations

The substitution-behaviour of the glottal stop in English strongly suggests that it may have a relation to /p t k/ similar to that which [ə] has to the short vowels: it is the 'reduction-stop', just as [ə] is the 'reduction-

stop, all these specifications, which are 'the opposite of those defining glottal stops' will reverse. But aside from the phonetical implausibility of [ʔ] being nonconsonantal, there are more serious problems. What if the stop concerned were grave? Would this make [ʔ] nongrave in this case? If glottal stops are defined as the 'opposite' of a given set of specifications, what determines the limits of 'subordinate switching'? Especially if some of the features hierarchically below consonantality agree with those that [ʔ] is supposed to have. Further, since the articulation of a glottal stop is by definition outside the pharynx and oral cavity altogether, it cannot ever be specified positively for a feature like graveness (or *SPE*'s backness). In the Jakobsonian system, for example, since graveness is defined by a particular oral cavity shape, a specification [+grave] would have to derive from coarticulation, depending on vocalic environment. And given substitution say for /p t k/ in all vocalic contexts, the situation would be impossible. Postal's argument does not salvage the classification of [ʔ] as a sonorant.

vowel'; it is the neutralization of the /p/ : /t/ : /k/ contrast. (It is noteworthy that in *SPE*, one of the instances where the oft-repeated slogan that representations like [p] or [ə] are 'informal abbreviations' for feature complexes is not adhered to is in characterizing vowel reduction: it seems that the feature specification for [ə] is [ə]. It is in fact – given the *SPE* features – impossible to specify [ə] at any level but the n-ary phonetic, since the system allows no central vowels.)

But it is possible to specify [ʔ]. According to *SPE* (307), it is:

$$(1)\qquad \begin{bmatrix} +\text{sonorant} \\ -\text{consonantal} \\ -\text{vocalic} \\ -\text{anterior} \\ -\text{coronal} \\ -\text{high} \\ +\text{low} \\ -\text{back} \end{bmatrix}$$

(The specification [+low] – if it's not a typographical error – is rather odd: surely a segment articulated outside the oral cavity cannot involve a tongue-body feature.)

Given the specification (1), we can write a rule for changing /t/ to [ʔ]. Assuming that [ʔ] is [−cont, −voice], and that any features not mentioned in the SD of the rule are supplied by redundancy rules, we have:

$$(2)\qquad \begin{bmatrix} -\text{son} \\ +\text{ant} \\ +\text{cor} \\ -\text{cont} \\ -\text{voice} \end{bmatrix} \rightarrow \begin{bmatrix} +\text{son} \\ -\text{cons} \\ -\text{ant} \\ -\text{cor} \\ +\text{low} \end{bmatrix} \Big/ \begin{Bmatrix} \text{V} \;\_\_\_\; \text{V} \\ \_\_\_\; \# \end{Bmatrix}$$

The SC must specify at least five features. If the rule were extended for /k/ as well as /t/, it would be much worse: /k/ must go from [+back] to [−back], from [+high] to [−high], as well as [−low] to [+low]. This seems a singularly 'costly' and complex rule – as well as involving no apparent generalization. (Actually, the generalization is obvious from a common-sense point of view; only the formalism does not allow us to state it. Cf. the discussion of 'sound shifts' in ch. 2 above.)

I have already shown that in certain ways [ʔ] is similar to (the closure phase of) a postvocalic voiceless stop. There is a complete cut-off of airflow through the vocal tract: i.e. a configuration that can reasonably be called voiceless, consonantal (if we rescind the *ad hoc* restriction against glottal strictures being so called), and certainly noncontinuant. In other words, something very like the features of a voiceless stop, but MINUS SUPRALARYNGEAL ARTICULATION.

This allows us to make a fairly obvious departure from the usual mode of phonetic/phonological description. Let us say that every segment – from one point of view – can be characterized as (at least) 'bi-gestural': there are two relevant articulatory configurations, one laryngeal and the other supralaryngeal. Thus a vowel schema would be something like this:

(3) *Laryngeal gesture:* 'voice'

Supralaryngeal gesture:
- a. Open approximation to some degree *n*.
- b. Location of closest stricture at some point *p* on the front/back axis.
- c. Some lip attitude (spread, rounded, etc.).

Phonologically speaking, these two gestures apportion between themselves two kinds of linguistically relevant information – or, again, 'gestures'. These are (a) a CATEGORIAL GESTURE ('vowel', 'voiceless stop') and (b) a LOCATIONAL or DISTINCTIVE GESTURE ('back unround', 'palatal'). For most segments, these two gestures are spread over the two major articulatory loci, as in (3): but the preponderance of specifically DISTINCTIVE information is carried by the supralaryngeal gesture. In other words, we take it as 'normal' (in the statistical sense, for any language and cross-linguistically) that distinctiveness is in the main supralaryngeally specified.

Some segments, however, have what I will call SHIFTED (LOCATIONAL) GESTURES. Here both the categorial and the distinctive subcomponents are realized only laryngeally: prime examples are [ʔ] and [h]. (The motivation for a 'derivational' view of these segments, i.e. that an actual 'shift' is involved, has been suggested already for [ʔ], at least in English; the evidence for [h] will be given later.) In terms of systems of oppositions, then, [ʔ] and [h] are 'pure categorial': they represent the categories 'voiceless stop' and 'voiceless fricative', pure and simple, with no superadded locational information. Thus [ʔ] and [h] are DEFECTIVE; their matrices lack defining specification for features that are purely intra-oral, like 'coronal', 'back', and so forth. They are missing an entire component or parameter that is present in 'normal' segments.

One way of characterizing this – without doing much violence to standard theory – would be to add to the inventory a feature [± oral].

All segments with supralaryngeal articulation are [+oral]; those with only laryngeal stricture are [−oral]. (Note that [+oral] is not the complement of [+nasal]: nasality in this sense is also an 'oral' feature.)

The specification [−oral] thus implies the lack of any DISTINCTIVE oral stricture: and a feature-changing rule marking a segment [−oral] has the effect of erasing all specifications for the oral features (on feature-erasing see Lass 1974a). Thus rule (2) above, for changing /t/ to [ʔ], could be reformulated as below in (4): I now assume that [ʔ] is a non-continuant obstruent:

$$(4) \quad \begin{bmatrix} -\text{son} \\ +\text{ant} \\ +\text{cor} \\ -\text{cont} \\ -\text{voice} \end{bmatrix} \rightarrow [-\text{oral}] \; / \; \begin{Bmatrix} \text{V} \;\rule{1.5em}{0.4pt}\; \text{V} \\ \rule{1.5em}{0.4pt}\; \# \end{Bmatrix}$$

This leaves us with a segment marked only [−son, −cont, −voice], i.e a glottal stop. (Note by the way that the erasure of distinctive oral specification does not make a segment nondistinctive in the phonological sense vis-à-vis others in the same system: though of course a laryngeal may be so. That is, while [ʔ] is not distinctive in English except categorially, [h] is as distinctive as any other voiceless fricative. The laryngeals can be terms in distinctive oppositions: but they are different IN TYPE from other segments, and historically they tend more often than not to originate through shifted gestures. See further §3 below.)

The glottal stop analysis will hold for [h] as well; it is a [−oral] voiceless fricative, i.e. specified only as [−son, +cont, −voice], with no features of location. I will discuss this further in the next section.

There is, however, another way – and I think a better one – for handling these phenomena. This is in terms not of a feature changing rule with an attendant erasure convention, but in terms of a formal erasing operation, with no cover-feature. Let us represent any phonological segment, not as a single matrix, but as containing two submatrices, each specifying one of the two basic parameters: the laryngeal gesture and the oral or supralaryngeal gesture. The general format will be:

$$(5) \quad \begin{bmatrix} [\text{oral}] \\ [\text{laryngeal}] \end{bmatrix}$$

These two submatrices are formally independent: i.e. it is possible for a rule to operate on one parameter – even to the extent of deleting it –

without affecting the other. It is also possible (cf. the discussion of 'shifted' gestures above) to move a feature specification from one submatrix to the other. Thus the 'de-oralization' of a voiceless stop to [ʔ] involves the following two operations:

(6) (a) *Gesture-shift:* $\begin{bmatrix}[-\text{cont}] \\ \downarrow \\ [-\text{cont}]\end{bmatrix}$

(b) *De-oralization:* [oral] → ∅

Step (a) copies the specification [−cont] onto the laryngeal submatrix; step (b) erases the oral submatrix entirely, leaving the matrix as a whole defective, i.e. with feature specifications only in the laryngeal parameter. I will explore the consequences of this later. (Note that (6) assumes the vocal bands to be in the 'classical' voiceless position, i.e. abducted; if the glottis is closed, there is no gesture-shift, and only step (b) takes place.)

To sum up the formal aspects of this proposal so far:

(i) Any phonological/phonetic segment is represented as a two-part matrix, consisting of submatrices labelled [oral] and [laryngeal].

(ii) The notational independence of the two parameters implies that each is a possible proper domain for a phonological rule: in addition to the whole segment being such a domain.

(iii) The independence of the two gestural submatrices is not necessary for any given rule; rules operating only on oral features (e.g. [+high] → [−high]) or only on laryngeal features (e.g. [+voice] → [−voice]) may be stated in terms of the features alone, in the usual way.

Point (ii) above may seem unnecessary, since presumably rules like those in (iii) would simply leave the irrelevant submatrix unchanged. But I want to extend the notion of independence further (§4 below) to claim that submatrices as wholes can function in rules; not only in deletions, but also in rules appealing to the notions 'homorganic' and 'identical'. It might be noted that this is in a sense merely an extension of the obvious fact that entire matrices can function as units in rules, as in the two polar cases of epenthesis and deletion.

Before proceeding to a discussion of [h], it might be instructive to look at one other example of the appearance of [ʔ] where its relation to voiceless obstruents is particularly clear. In Burmese, there is good evidence for [ʔ] as a historical reflex of word-final voiceless stops; and what is more, as the end-point in a process of neutralization of stop contrasts in this environment.

Consider the following cognate forms (data from Maran 1971: 29–30. WB = 'Written Burmese', for the most part representative of an earlier stage; NB = 'North Burmese'; SB = '(Irawaddy Delta) Standard Burmese'):

(7)

WB	NB	SB	Gloss
tap	tat	taʔ	attach
tat	tat	taʔ	know
tak	tet	teʔ	climb
khyup	khyuk	chouʔ	sew
khut	khuk	khouʔ	chop
khiuk	khek	khaiʔ	fight
lac	lit	liʔ	abscond

Old Burmese had a final stop system /p t k/ and an affricate /c/ (probably [ʧ]: Maran: 38). Through a complex process that Maran calls 'depletion', these finals were reanalyzed, with a gradual loss of distinctiveness. In SB, all the supralaryngeal obstruent finals are gone, and replaced by [ʔ]. It is noteworthy that [ʔ] arises only from voiceless obstruents; it does not appear as a reflex of historical sonorant finals: WB *ran* 'evening', NB *yan*, SB *yaN* (*N* = nasality), and so on. (There is no evidence for /ʔ/ in Old Burmese or Proto-Lolo-Burmese.) Clearly this pattern is similar to what we have seen in English; and more evidence of this type, for the continuants [h ɦ], will be discussed in the next section.[1]

3. On the nature and status of [h]

If [ʔ] is the 'minimal' voiceless stop, it would seem reasonable, as I said earlier, to take [h] as its continuant congener, i.e. a de-oralized voiceless

[1] Another piece of suggestive evidence for the obstruent status of [ʔ] comes from some data discussed by Sapir (1938). In a paper on 'glottalized' continuants in certain American Indian languages (Navaho, Nootka, Kwakiutl) he suggests quite convincingly that glottalized nasals and palatal continuants, where 'the glottal closure is synchronous with the momentarily voiceless initial phase' (326) can in Navaho be traced back to original /d/ + sonorant clusters that have undergone 'contraction', or have as he says been '*d*-modified'. It is also interesting that in some Scots dialects (notably Fife), there are cases where intervocalic /d/ may become [ʔ], as in [breʔ an bʌʔər̥] 'bread and butter' (I owe this example to Margaret Anderson). These dialects also have extensive final obstruent devoicing; and we note also that the initial phase of Sapir's segments is voiceless.

fricative (and for that matter, to take [ɦ] as a de-oralized voiced fricative: though this latter is not quite so simple, as we will see). Purely synchronic evidence for this is hard to find, but there are a few suggestive phenomena in English; the historical evidence here, however, is extremely interesting, and I will devote most of this section to it.

But first some phonetic remarks. Let us take English (RP) /h/, which Gimson (1965: 175) describes as a fricative, with 'continuous noise' in the range of 500–6500 cps; though it is often also 'an anticipatory voiceless version of the following vowel'. (This latter remark means, I presume, that in addition to aperiodic noise, it shows some kind of formant structure as well.) He classifies it as a 'fortis glottal fricative' (185), but points out that since its friction is 'largely of the mouth cavity type associated with the following vowel', many linguists consider that it shares 'notable characteristics with vowel...articulations', and that it is often interpreted 'phonemically as being in complementary distribution with the second element of the long vowels...and the diphthongs' (186). This latter treatment of course reached its apogee (or nadir) in Trager & Smith (1951: cf. ch. 1 above).

This account, and others like that of Jones (1956: 201–2), make it clear that on phonetic grounds there is no reason *a priori* not to assign to [h] the categorial features at least of any other voiceless fricative.

Phonologically, and specifically synchronically, however, the case for [h] is not as good as that for [ʔ]. There seems to be very little synchronic substitution evidence available that points unambiguously to an obstruent status. The little bit that there is, though, gains some considerable force when it is considered in conjunction with the extensive historical evidence from a number of languages, which I shall get to shortly. But within English itself there are two facts of interest: one is a sporadic substitution, and the other is a matter of dialect distribution. The substitution occurs with some frequency in Scots, and involves a change of /θ/ to [h] between vowels: typical examples are [ae'hĩŋk] 'I think', and ['evrɪhĩŋ] 'everything'.

But now let us consider a phenomenon directly related to the phoneme /h/ itself: the common 'dropping of *h*'. It is well known that most British (non-Scots) dialects of English have lost their historical initial /h/ (one of the few survivals is rural East Anglia: cf. Trudgill 1974: 7, 83); and it is also the case that initial /h/ deletes frequently in all dialects (even Scots) when it is in positions of low sentence stress, e.g. in *give him, tell her*, etc.

But no other fricatives drop with the same uniformity (if at all). Why shouldn't /f s θ/ also delete? One possible suggestion, based on the ideas in the previous section, is as follows. Let us say that /f s θ/ are 'full' fricatives, i.e. 'normal' segments, where both the oral and laryngeal submatrices contain feature specifications. Then say that [h] bears the same relation to /f s θ/ that [ʔ] does to /p t k/, i.e. its oral submatrix is null: it has been deleted.

Let us take a rule deleting [h] in some position. If a rule says that [h] → ∅, we define '∅' (for a segment) as the MAXIMALLY EMPTY MATRIX, i.e. one with no specifications in either submatrix. We thus have the progression shown below:

(8) Full segment → [h] → ∅
(e.g. /θ/)

$$\begin{bmatrix}\begin{bmatrix}+\text{ant}\\+\text{cor}\\+\text{cont}\end{bmatrix}\\ [-\text{voice}]\end{bmatrix} \rightarrow \begin{bmatrix}\varnothing\\ \begin{bmatrix}+\text{cont}\\-\text{voice}\end{bmatrix}\end{bmatrix} \rightarrow \begin{bmatrix}\varnothing\\ \varnothing\end{bmatrix}$$

So [h] starts out with one strike against it: the fact that it is missing specifications in one of its submatrices. This means that it will be less resistant to deletion than a fully specified segment on the grounds (aside from anything else) of rule-simplicity. A rule that deletes [h] requires a simpler proper analysis than one that deletes a full fricative (assuming that separate submatrices may count as units in an evaluation measure), since only one submatrix need appear in the rule. And this does seem to suggest possible grounds for [h] getting lost more easily than just about anything else. (See Joos 1952 for some further examples and a not dissimilar explanation.)[1]

The suggestions above are not very satisfactory: they are based entirely on formal criteria, which may be red herrings, and in any case are not as interesting as physical or perceptual explanations. And here there is a possibility of developing an explanatory framework of this type. Observe first that [h] has probably a smaller area of occlusion than any other fricative. And second, that it is perceptually less distinct than other segments, because of its lack of a locational gesture in the oral cavity:

[1] Other grounds have of course been suggested for the instability and frequent loss of /h/ in English: notably by Vachek (1964), who claims that this is due to its low functional load and 'marginal' position in the English system of oppositions. The marginality is certainly clear; but I do not think that a very good case has yet been made for functional load as an important factor in language change (cf. King 1967).

this accounts for the ease with which it is influenced by the cavity shapes of surrounding vowels. And this in turn may suggest why it is so eminently deletable: perceptually it is in fact a voiceless anticipation of a vowel, and as such can easily merge with one if the voicing is simply extended back a bit. This all suggests that the schema (8) may have some value: it claims in effect that [h] is a reasonable 'way-station' between a fully specified obstruent (especially a fricative) and zero; and that *ceteris paribus* it will be lost more easily – in languages in general – than other segments.

Let us now turn to the historical evidence. It is a striking fact that it is rather uncommon to reconstruct */h/ as a proto-segment in languages with long histories. When we find it, we can very frequently trace it back to some other segment which has undergone lenition. This is true for example in three important language families that immediately come to mind: Indo-European, Uralic, and Dravidian. This material is interesting in itself, and gives the claims I am advancing here some support. I will examine some representative data from these three families below.

A. Indo-European. We reconstruct no PIE */h/.[1] The most important sources of /h/ in the dialects may be summed up as follows.

(i) *Armenian*. PIE */p-/: Arm. *het* 'footprint', Skr. *padám* 'id'; Arm. *hin* 'old', L. *senex* (Meillet 1964: 15–16).

(ii) *Latin*. PIE */gʹɦ/. L. *humus*, Gr. *khamaí*, OCS *zemlja*; L. *anser* 'goose' < */hānser/, G. *Gans*, Gr. *khēn* (Buck 1933: 127). Buck suggests a developmental sequence (p. 118) of '*gh* > *kh* > *χ* > *h*'.

(iii) *Greek*. PIE */s/. Gr. *heptá*, L. *septem*; Gr. *hēmi-*, L. *sēmi-*; Gr. *hépomai*, L. *sequor* (Buck 1933: 132). It is probable that PIE /s/ intervocalically also passed through a stage /h/ before deletion (Buck: 133).[2]

(iv) *Iranian*. PIE */s-/. Avestan *hanō*, L. *senex* (Meillet 1964: 95). The more complex developments in Indic will be discussed below.

[1] That is, '/h/' in the sense in which I have been talking about it, i.e. a glottal fricative with no distinctive oral articulation. This has nothing to do with the problem of the PIE 'laryngeals', which are not generally assumed to be laryngeal in my sense anyhow (and could hardly have had their presumed effects if they were: an /h/ with 'colouring' is a contradiction). Though Lehmann (1955: 108) attempts to make a case for one of his four laryngeals having [h] as a primary allophone, he admits that it may also have been pharyngeal. None of his evidence points clearly to a PIE */h/ proper, in any case. Cf. further the discussion in Polomé (1965).

[2] For a discussion of other possible sources of Greek /h/, see Buck (1933: 134–5). In line with my suggestion that /h/ from obstruent lenition is often a way-station on the path to zero, note that in Ionic /h/ was lost in Classical times ('psilosis'), and that it has been lost in Modern Greek as well.

(v) *Brythonic Celtic*. PIE */s/. The most frequent examples are initial: Welsh *haf*, Cornish *haf*, Breton *hañv* 'summer', OHG *sumar*, Skr. *samā* 'year'; W. *halen*, OCo. *haloin*, Br. *holenn* 'salt', L. *sal*, Go. *salt* (Lewis & Pedersen 1961: §24.1).[1] It is also probable that the loss of PIE */p/ in Goidelic Celtic involved a stage /h/: there are suggestive examples in both Goidelic and Brythonic. Thus Irish *én* 'bird', OCo. *hethen*, cognate to L. *penna*, OHG *federa*, etc. Possibly also OIr. *hil* 'many', cf. Gr. *polús*, Go. *filu* (discussion and more examples in Lewis & Pedersen: §29).[2]

(vi) *Germanic*. PIE */k/. E. *heart*, G. *Herz*, L. *cord-*; E. *hound*, G. *Hund*, Gr. *kúōn*, gen. *kunós*.

The Germanic material is particularly instructive, as it shows – if we take a larger group of environments – a sequence [k] → [x] → [h] → zero. All native Germanic /h/ are from PIE */k/ by Grimm's Law. We find initial /h/ in the examples above; we find [x] (or if palatalized, [ç]) before obstruents in German, e.g. *Nacht, acht, Licht* (L. *noct-, octo, lūc-*); and zero, with 'compensatory' gemination, in Swedish *natt* 'night', *åtta* 'eight'; while the English cognates here show 'compensation' in the length of the vowel. It looks as if the original fricative may be 'protected' from lenition by a contiguous obstruent: note that in Grimm's Law PIE */p t k/ do not spirantize if another obstruent precedes (E. *star*, L. *stella*, or OE *hæft* 'captive', L. *captus*). This also shows up with PIE */s/ in Greek: an obstruent prevents the change to /h/, as in *estí* 'he is', cf. Skr. *ásti*, L. *est* (for further discussion of the mechanisms involved, see Lass & Anderson 1975: cf. v).

There is other evidence in Indo-European, too, which bears out the claims that (a) [h] is one quite normal result of the weakening of a voiceless fricative, and (b) the next stage after this weakening is deletion. Thus to take one more example, in Spanish L. /h-/ went to zero, while L. /f-/ became /h/ and then zero. Modern Spanish orthography often obscures this sequence, since *h-* has been replaced in words that began with /h-/ in Latin: but this is a late spelling reform. So both *hombre* < L.

[1] Even in Irish, which retains initial */s/, Lewis & Pedersen report intrasentential lenition to /h/ (§24.1). The change of */s/ → /h/ has some exceptions in Brythonic: W. *saith* 'seven', Co. *seyth*, Br. *seiz* (= L. *septem*), etc. For more examples, see Lewis & Pedersen (§24.2). There is also some evidence for /h/ as a lenition product in intervocalic position, though it has generally (as in Greek) been lost: Irish *eo* 'salmon', gen. *iach*, Middle W. *ehawc*, MnW. *eog*, OCo. *ehoc*, Middle Br. *eheuc*, MnBr. *eok* (= L. *esox*). Cf. Lewis & Pedersen (§24.3).

[2] Lewis & Pedersen suggest that */p/ 'became at first a bilabial *f*; an echo of this is found in the development of *sp* and in the *w*-diphthong from *op* before *u*...Before *s*... and *t*... *f* became /x/; elsewhere it became *h*, which disappeared...' (§29).

homo, and *hijo* < L. *filius* now have zero initials; but as late as the sixteenth century, the *h-* in *hijo* represented a segment.[1]

(vii) *Indic*. The history here is rather complex, and I will deal only with the basic outlines of the Sanskrit developments. Most interestingly, in Sanskrit there are two glottal fricatives, a voiced [ɦ] and a voiceless [h] (the latter, *visarga*, written *ḥ* in modern transliterations). The historical sources of these segments bear out what I have been suggesting, as well as adding a third member – [ɦ] – to the already established set [ʔ h].

The main source of Sanskrit /ɦ/ is PIE palatal */g'ɦ/:[2] e.g. Skr. *híma-* 'snow' = Gr. *kheimōn*, L. *hiems*, OCS *zima*; Skr. *aṃhú-* 'narrow', *áṃhas-* 'distress' = L. *ango*, *angustus*, OCS *ązŭkŭ* 'narrow' (Burrow 1959: 72; cf. Mayrhofer 1972: §27). Another source is the 'secondary' palatalization of PIE */gɦ/ and */g^{w}ɦ/ (probably via a stage *[ʒɦ]), which often leads to morphophonemic alternation of /ɦ/ and /gɦ/: *hánti* 'he strikes' ~ *ghn-ánti* 'they strike' ~ *ghaná-* 'striker' (cf. ON *gunn-r* 'battle', OCS *goniti* 'pursue': Mayrhofer: §27).[3]

The voiceless /h/, on the other hand, arises normally from PIE final (pre-pausal) */s r/: *áśvaḥ* 'horse', *agníḥ* 'fire', L. *equus*, *ignis*; *pítaḥ* 'father, voc.' (stem *pitár-*). It is also extended to the sandhi of final /s r/ with certain following consonants (cf. the detailed discussion in Allen 1962: 57ff., 70ff.).[4]

B. Uralic. Again, no */h/ is reconstructable (cf. Collinder 1960). But [h] appears in many of the languages as a reflex of some Proto-Uralic

[1] Cf. Menéndez Pidal (1918: 101–2): '...en la antigua ortografía, más fonetica que la de hoy, se escribia ombre, onor, eredero, como aun se hace en las reimpresiones del Diccionario de Nebrija...en el siglo XVI; pero en el de Covarrubias de 1611 ya se escriben con *h* estas palabras, para imitar la ortografía latina. En la ortografía de Nebrija la *h* representaba un verdadero sonido y se empleaba sólo en vez de una *f* latina: verbi-gracia *hacer* facere, *hijo* filium...'

[2] The PIE 'voiced aspirates' were probably breathy-voiced stops (which I represent here with a stop symbol plus [ɦ]). See the discussion in Lass (1974a).

[3] There are sporadic /ɦ/ < PIE */dɦ/, e.g. *gṛha-* 'house' < **gṛdha* (cf. Go. *gards*: Mayrhofer §27), *snuh-* 'to drip' (cf. Avestan *snaod-*: Burrow 1959: 69); also < PIE */bɦ/ (cf. *grah-* 'to seize' beside Vedic *grabh-*). These are probably dialectal (including Prakrit influence), but some cases of /ɦ/ < */dɦ/ are well entrenched in the grammatical system, as e.g. 1st plur. mid ending *-mahe* (cf. Av. *-maiδe*).

[4] There are later lenitions in Indic that produce new glottal fricatives: e.g. in the Mārwāṛī dialect of Rājasthānī, Skr. /s/ becomes (voiceless) /h/, and /ɦ/ remains as /ɦ/ (Allen 1958: 123f.). It is of interest, in view of my claims about the general 'weakness' of glottal fricatives, that /h/ in Sanskrit is particularly prone to assimilation to following obstruents: it could be realised as [x ʃ ʂ s ɸ] depending on what followed (Allen 1953: 49–51).

(PU) obstruent, often with very clear evidence supporting [h] as a stage in lenition. I will cite just a few examples (all from Collinder) to illustrate typical developments in initial and intervocalic positions.

(i) *Initial.* PU */k/ weakens to [h]: Finnish *kuole-* 'die', S. Ostyak *hăt-*, Hungarian *hal-* ~ *hol-*, Yurak *haa* (50–1). PU */č/ weakens to [s] in Hungarian and to [h] in Finnish: Erza Mordvin *čova* 'thin', Hu. *sovány*, Fi. *hupa* 'soon consumed' (52). PU */š/ goes to [h] in Finnish, deletes in Hungarian: Votyak *šyr* 'mouse', Fi. *hiiri*, Hu. *egér* (61).

(ii) *Intervocalic.* Here we find more varied developments; but the most interesting is that of PU */k/, which shows not only weakening to [h] and deletion, but another form of lenition, i.e. voicing. Thus Fi. *joki* 'river', Yurak *jæha*, Yenisei Samoyed *jaha*, Ostyak *jogəñ*, Vogul *jõõ*. And if further indication is needed that we are dealing here with genuine lenition, and not just unrelated variation, consider the fact that geminates are resistant: this is another case of 'protection' by a contiguous segment (cf. PIE */s/ in Greek).[1] Thus Fi. *lykää* 'push', Vogul *lökəm-*, Hu. *lök*, all with PU */-kk-/ (78–9).

C. Dravidian. There is no reconstructable Proto-Dravidian (PD) */h/ (cf. Emeneau 1970, Zvelebil 1970). But /h/ (in most cases actually [ɦ]) has developed in a number of Dravidian dialects, from various sources. Typically it is the reflex of a PD voiceless stop, either labial, palatal, or velar.

(i) PD */p-/. In Brahmin dialects of Kannaḍa, */p-/ has become [ɦ]; in many non-Brahmin dialects (e.g. Okkaliga) it deletes. Thus Old Kannaḍa *pesar* 'name', Brahmin *hes(a)ru*, Okkaliga *yesru* (the *y-* represents a prothetic [j], automatic before mid front vowels) (Zvelebil 1970: §1.21.1.1).

(ii) PD */c-/. Here there is a three-way development, reminiscent of Uralic. Where */c-/ does not remain, it spirantizes to [s], dearticulates to [h], or deletes. So PD */cīr-/ 'nit': Kota *cīr*, Tamil *īr*, Ka. *sīru*, Pengo *hīr*, Kuvi *hīru* (Zvelebil: §1.25.1).

(iii) PD */-c-/. Similar to (ii): Ta. *mācu* 'spot, stain',[2] Ka. *māsu* 'to be stained', Kuvi *māhali* 'to be dirty' (Zvelebil: §1.25.2).

[1] On the resistance of geminates to lenition, see Lass (1971), Lass & Anderson (1975: ch. v), and the data from Telugu and Kannaḍa discussed by Raja (1969).

[2] The representation *mācu* is 'morphophonemic', i.e. it follows the Tamil orthography. Synchronically /c/ is realized as [s] intervocalically. It is also worth noting that in some Tamil dialects, /k/ is realized in this position as [h] (while in others it is [x] or [ɣ]: again [h] as a lenition product): see Zvelebil (1970: §§1.26.2.21–2).

(iv) PD */k-/. PD */kī/ 'pus': Tulu *kīvu*, Ta. *cī*, Kolami *sīm*, Manda *hīven*, Kui *hīvenji* (Zvelebil: §1.26.1).

The examples I have given so far seem to me to support the notion of submatrix deletion as a form of lenition, with glottal (i.e. dearticulated) fricatives as the stage before final deletion. I would like to propose then as a (tentative) diachronic universal, a progressive lenition schema, like this:

(9) Progressive obstruent weakening

Weakening I: feature change

[−cont] → [+cont]
or
[−voice] → [+voice]

Weakening II: matrix change

$$\begin{bmatrix}\text{[oral]}\\ \text{[laryn]}\end{bmatrix} \rightarrow \begin{bmatrix}\varnothing\\ \text{[laryn]}\end{bmatrix} \rightarrow \begin{bmatrix}\varnothing\\ \varnothing\end{bmatrix}$$

(For some detailed suggestions about lenition, and a discussion of the general theory of phonological 'strength', see Lass & Anderson 1975: ch. v.)

There seem to be no firm restrictions about (stepwise) left-to-right progression in the schema. But it seems likely that any transition like [p]→∅ has at least an intermediate stage [h]. The overall historical picture, however, based on evidence from a number of languages, suggests that major lenition processes basically go from left to right, with a null matrix as the final stage, and a half-null one (i.e. [h]) as the penultimate stage.

At any rate, if [h] may be considered a defective (because non-oral) segment, and the normal stage before zero in obstruent lenition, then there is some empirical support both for the matrix-deletion schema (9), and the entire separable-matrix idea.

4. A convention for segment-identity[1]

The formal argument in §2 can be extended in a useful way to cover certain other phenomena that standard theory does not deal with very insightfully. Consider the case of 'homorganicity'. Let us take a language like Kannaḍa, which has the noncontinuant obstruent series /p b t d ʈ ɖ c ɟ k g/, and a rule of homorganic nasal-assimilation saying that nasals agree with following stops in point of articulation. Now in order to specify a system like this in the lexicon, we need at least the features [±anterior, ±coronal, ±high, ±back]:

[1] The proposals in this section are adumbrated in tentative discussions in Lass & Anderson (1975: ch VI, Appendix II). This chapter supersedes the work of mine referred to there.

(10)

	p	t	ʈ	c	k
ant	+	+	−	−	−
cor	−	+	+	−	−
hi	−	−	−	+	+
back	−	−	−	−	+

(It is possible that [± distributed] is really needed for /t/ vs. /ʈ/, but we will not worry about that here.) The nasal assimilation rule would then be:

(11)

$$[+\text{nas}] \rightarrow \begin{bmatrix} \alpha\text{ant} \\ \beta\text{cor} \\ \gamma\text{high} \\ \delta\text{back} \end{bmatrix} / \text{——} \begin{bmatrix} +\text{obs} \\ -\text{cont} \\ \alpha\text{ant} \\ \beta\text{cor} \\ \gamma\text{high} \\ \delta\text{back} \end{bmatrix}$$

Note that we need agreeing variables for every positional feature; and in fact, we may well not have enough features in (11) to specify agreement in all relevant features for two fully specified segments: after all, there are nondistinctive ones as well like lowness, rounding, and so on, which must be taken care of somewhere. In other words, a statement of homorganicity, to be really precise, demands something like:

(12)

$$[+\text{nas}] \rightarrow \begin{bmatrix} \alpha\text{ant} \\ \beta\text{cor} \\ \vdots \\ \omega\text{F}n \end{bmatrix} / \text{——} \begin{bmatrix} +\text{obs} \\ -\text{cont} \\ \alpha\text{ant} \\ \beta\text{cor} \\ \vdots \\ \omega\text{F}n \end{bmatrix}$$

The status of 'F*n*' would depend on one's notion of just how fully specified a fully specified matrix has to be.

This is of course wildly uneconomical; but it is actually necessary if rules are to be truly 'algorithmic', i.e. if they are to require no extrinsic 'interpretation' to make them work correctly. (Of course we could add all kinds of low-level redundancy rules and interpretive conventions to make things work, but I will show that this is not necessary.) More significantly, however, the use of variables in rules like (11) misses the point: what defines 'homorganicity' is not pairwise agreement of arbitrary features, but total identity of all positional features in two (or more) matrices. There are only two relevant options: with respect to a pair of segments (x, y), either $x = y$ in articulatory specifications, or $x \neq y$. And if this is the case, then it is over-concrete and under-general to list the individual features when the rule is concerned only with THE SET OF ALL PAIRS (x, y) such that $x = y$, and nothing else. (This holds *a fortiori* for rules involving full identity, like gemination and so on. I will return to this below.)

Given the proposals in §2 above for the representation of phonological matrices as bi-parametric, there is an obvious solution. And this is to define the oral submatrix as a whole, let us say, as the domain of agreement, rather than the individual features in it. If our goal is to represent identity of complete gestures, or large subparts of them, rather than pairwise feature agreements, we can do this easily by means of an extension of the usual convention governing variables.

Let us represent agreement between submatrices by Greek-letter variables standing OUTSIDE the proper submatrix brackets. Thus the simplest case, a sequence of two wholly identical segments, would be represented this way:

(13) $$\begin{bmatrix} \alpha[\text{oral}] \\ \beta[\text{laryn}] \end{bmatrix} \begin{bmatrix} \alpha[\text{oral}] \\ \beta[\text{laryn}] \end{bmatrix}$$

Here 'α' and 'β' are variables ranging over ANY COMBINATIONS of the values '+' and '−' on any features in the inner brackets; subject to the usual convention that all values in the domain of a given pair of variables agree. Thus (13) is equivalent to:

(14) $$\begin{bmatrix} \begin{bmatrix} \alpha\text{ant} \\ \beta\text{cor} \\ \vdots \end{bmatrix} \\ \begin{bmatrix} \gamma\text{voice} \\ \vdots \end{bmatrix} \end{bmatrix} \begin{bmatrix} \begin{bmatrix} \alpha\text{ant} \\ \beta\text{cor} \\ \vdots \end{bmatrix} \\ \begin{bmatrix} \gamma\text{voice} \\ \vdots \end{bmatrix} \end{bmatrix}$$

Now to the slightly more complex case of homorganicity without total identity, as in the nasal assimilation discussed earlier. Here we can use the same format as in (13), only with all NON-AGREEING features differentially specified. Thus the sequence 'nasal + homorganic voiced stop' would be:

(15) $$\begin{bmatrix} \alpha\begin{bmatrix} \text{ORAL} \\ +\text{nas} \end{bmatrix} \\ \\ \beta[\text{LARYN}] \end{bmatrix} \begin{bmatrix} \alpha\begin{bmatrix} \text{ORAL} \\ -\text{nas} \\ -\text{cont} \end{bmatrix} \\ \beta[\text{LARYN}] \end{bmatrix}$$

(If [+nas] → [+voice] is specified in the language by lexical redundancy rules, the agreement in laryngeal features is guaranteed.)

If the laryngeal gesture is irrelevant, i.e. if the agreement is to all stops, voiced or voiceless, the sequence can be given as:

(16) $$[\alpha\begin{bmatrix}\text{ORAL}\\ +\text{nas}\end{bmatrix}]\ [\alpha\begin{bmatrix}\text{ORAL}\\ -\text{nas}\\ -\text{cont}\end{bmatrix}]$$

This formalism can be utilized directly in the statement of rules. The Kannaḍa nasal assimilation (11) can now be restated:

(17) $$[+\text{nas}] \rightarrow [\alpha[\text{ORAL}]]\ /\ \underline{\quad\quad}\ [\alpha\begin{bmatrix}\text{ORAL}\\ -\text{nas}\\ -\text{cont}\end{bmatrix}]$$

Note also that this format enables us to state generalized 'universal' schemata much more perspicuously (and correctly) than the use of pairwise variables would. Say we wanted to give – in the metatheory – a general formula for the extremely common nasal assimilation of which (17) is one specific example. But a formula allowing for all possible nasals (labiodental, uvular, etc.) and all kinds of following obstruents (or other consonants). We could then give nasal assimilation as a METARULE (cf. ch. 2 above), in a generalized form which each language utilizing it could implement according to its inventory and its own specific requirements. (This says that we expect languages to have SOME nasal assimilation rule, but not any specific one. For instance, in my dialect, nasals are obligatorily homorganic – within the morpheme – to following obstruents; except in the case of the affricates /tʃ/ and /dʒ/, where a preceding nasal generally stays alveolar.) The schema would be:

(18) Nasal assimilation metarule

$$[+\text{nas}] \rightarrow [\alpha[\text{ORAL}]]\ /\ \underline{\quad\quad}\ [\alpha\begin{bmatrix}\text{ORAL}\\ -\text{cons}\end{bmatrix}]$$

And types like consonant gemination and vowel lengthening could also be expressed as universal schemata:

(19) $$\varnothing \rightarrow \begin{bmatrix}\alpha[\text{ORAL}]\\ \beta[\text{LARYN}]\end{bmatrix}\ /\ \begin{bmatrix}\alpha[\text{ORAL}]\\ \beta[\text{LARYN}]\end{bmatrix}\underline{\quad\quad}$$

This defines the notion 'replication of a segment'; the individual instances could be defined by using binary feature specifications as limiting cases.

This is still a rather rough working proposal; but I think it deserves further consideration. It certainly has uses beyond those I have discussed here, notably in the statement of lexical redundancy rules. For further discussion of these matters see Lass & Anderson (1975, ch. VI and Appendix II).

7 *Complementary modes of description in phonology: the problem of 'natural classes'* [1]

The capacity of a thing to reveal itself in unexpected ways in the future, I attribute to the fact that the thing observed is an aspect of a reality, possessing a significance that is not exhausted by our conception of any single aspect of it. To trust that a thing we know is real is, in this sense, to feel that it has the independence and power for manifesting itself in yet unthought of ways in the future.

Michael Polanyi, *Duke Lectures* (1964), IV

1. Introductory

1.1. In current phonological theory, the notion 'natural class' is defined in two ways: intuitively and formally. Ideally the two definition-types buttress each other. As Chomsky & Halle remark (*SPE*: 335), 'the sets comprising all vowels or all stops or all continuants are more natural than randomly chosen sets composed of the same number of segment types'. This intuitive definition has as its empirical correlate 'the observation that it is the "natural" classes that are relevant to the formulation of phonological processes in the most varied languages'.

Formally, the naturalness of a class is definable in terms of the number of features its members share: to take what is probably the classic formulation, 'a set of speech sounds forms a *natural class* if fewer features are required to designate the class than to designate any individual sound in the class' (Halle 1964: 328). Thus, for instance, the class [θ ð t d s z], using the *SPE* features, can be exhaustively defined as [+ant, +cor]. But this kind of formal definition often conflicts with the intuitive notion 'natural class'. Take the class specified as [−ant, −cor]: this comprises

[1] An earlier version of this chapter appeared as Lass (1973c). Preliminary versions were given as talks at Indiana and Cambridge universities. I have profited greatly from discussion after these talks with Charles Bird, Tim Shopen, J. L. M. Trim, Erik Fudge and Terry Moore. I am also grateful to Gillian Brown, John Anderson, Jim Hurford, Frances Katamba and Margaret Nicholson for helpful comments.

palatals, velars, uvulars, pharyngeals, and all (non-retroflex) vowels. We would expect to find rules in languages invoking the first class; but certainly not the second. Both are formally 'natural' in Halle's sense, but only the first is intuitively so, i.e. it fulfils expectations based on our experience of natural-language phonology. Phonological theory must therefore have mechanisms that will enable us to distinguish these purely formal (and counterintuitive) classes from those which are both formally and intuitively satisfactory. This problem has led to various proposals, notably the theory of markedness, based on the supposed 'intrinsic content of features' (*SPE*: 400ff.; see the criticisms in Lass 1972).

Current thinking on this matter (and related ones, like rule-naturalness, 'marked' and 'unmarked' orders, evaluation measures, etc.) has tended to proceed along dogmatically monolithic 'universalist' lines. The goals of linguistic theory have become skewed – excessively, to my mind – in the direction of establishing all and only the universal properties of natural languages. And this to such an extent that concerns like typology, and the detailed differentia of languages and language families, have been rather badly neglected. Such things are not, from the strict universalist perspective, 'interesting'. There has also been an undesirable emphasis on 'reduction', of which this is a particular case: an oversimplified use of Occam's Razor which often leads to conflict with fact, or at least to the suppression of certain types of facts. I will return to this later.

1.2. I am not however deprecating universalist inquiry: the establishment of universals is surely among the primary goals of linguistic theory, even (but no more) *primus inter pares*. But an excessive universalist bias, particularly since it entails a very high level of abstraction, can have some undesirable side-effects. Not the least of these is the tendency to define all theoretical primes in a rather gross way solely in terms of a universal metatheory, without paying too much attention to how many diverse kinds of language-specific phenomena get lumped together under one universal primitive notion. This leads to a kind of macroscopic view of things which obscures numerous microscopic details: and these are often of equal interest, in the long run, to the theory. One aspect of this, which I will consider below, is an observable contempt for the 'low-level' or the 'merely phonetic' – which often serves as a virtual *cloaca maxima*.

The treatment of 'natural classes' is a good example of this. Virtually all discussions of or appeals to this notion that I know of take for granted (a) that the phonetic (and phonological) feature inventory is universal; (b) that the principles governing phonological grammars (including the so-called 'evaluation measure') are also universal; and (c) that therefore 'natural class' in both the intuitive and formal sense must be defined once and for all in the metatheory.

This last point – which though not usually stated explicitly nonetheless seems to be taken for granted – means, as far as I can tell, that the combinatorial possibilities for what features may constitute a natural class are given in advance (or should be) by the metatheory: so that there is presumably a universal (closed) set of possible natural classes, which is the same for all languages. This follows directly from the fact that a formal definition alone cannot suffice, because it generates impossible classes. And if the solution to formal difficulties like this is some transcendent notion of 'naturalness' (which is metatheoretically defined), then only appeal to some universal definition can possibly tell us whether a given formally natural class is in fact natural.

If this holds, then any class not *a priori* definable (i.e. predictable as natural) is less natural, i.e. more 'complex' or less 'highly valued' than one which is universally defined (presumably by a conjunction of 'correct' feature specifications, and interpretive conventions). And if such an 'undefinable' class, one which within the universal framework is no more natural than any other, should keep showing up repeatedly in the rules of some language over the course of time, then this class is merely an idiosyncratic property of this particular language, and therefore 'uninteresting'. Its recurrence is unmotivated; it is a peculiar fact of no theoretical significance.

I don't propose to argue here that there are no universal natural classes; but I will try to show that (at least) a universalist (i.e. *a priori*, metatheoretical) definition is too limited, and that it loses for us an excellent opportunity to explain some interesting facts about languages. And further, that this failure is also tied up with a complex of other assumptions about the nature of primes in phonology which are part of current theory, and, I think, mistaken. I will deal with this directly.

1.3. The particular claim I want to make here may be sketched out this way: that beyond possible universal classes, there may be language-specific groups of segments which figure as natural classes in a very obvious way – though in terms of the present theory, and certain of its basic assumptions, they cannot be formally defined as such. These classes are natural in particular languages, at particular points in their histories, and (often) only in relation to certain types of rules. These restrictions do not in any way, as we will see, impair the explanatory potential of these classes, once they are defined; they operate in what are, from any point of view, 'significant generalizations'.

Further, what constitutes such a class in one language (or even one dialect) for a particular rule-type, may not do so for another (even cognate) language or dialect, or even for another type of rule in the same language, or the same type of rule at a different historical period. In other words, an important factor in typological definition may be the class-selectivity of certain rules at certain times.

I will try to show, in addition, that one of the important mechanisms involved in the establishment of such classes is a language-specific interpretation of and choice of features, such that relations and contrasts that apply at the phonological level may not at the phonetic, and vice versa. That high-level 'classificatory' features may be replaced by others, whose scope and terms of definition are different, and which may be (a) universally nondistinctive, but (b) phonologically relevant. I will show, further, that in all cases these features are empirically motivated, i.e. physically definable.

1.4. By way of introduction, I will try to restate what seem to me to be some crucial assumptions about features and their role in a phonological grammar (or metagrammar), as they are currently held in what we might call the 'standard theory' of generative phonology, i.e. the model typified by *SPE*.

I. *Primacy of features.* Features, not segments, are the primes of phonological theory (which features doesn't matter at the moment).

II. *Universality of the inventory.* 'The total set of features is identical with the set of phonetic properties that can in principle be controlled in speech; they represent the phonetic capabilities of man, and, we would assume, are therefore the same for all languages' (*SPE*: 294–5). A corollary to this is that the internal structure of the feature-system will be such as to favour as 'natural' just those classes which appear consistently in rules, and to disfavour those – though formally definable as 'natural' – which do not appear.

III. *The minimalness criterion.* Despite the assertion that features represent the 'PHONETIC capabilities of man', attempts to frame systems generally attempt to capture rather the PHONOLOGICAL capabilities: i.e. to develop the smallest system capable of accounting for all the CONTRASTS in natural languages. Despite the retreat in current theory from the essentially Praguian outlook of Jakobson *et al.* (1951), this notion still remains. Thus Halle (1973: 931n) says that it is desirable *a priori* 'to restrict as much as possible the variety of features admitted into the framework'. The best universal inventory is the smallest. This can of course be taken too far, as Jakobson did with the feature [+flat] (see McCawley's comments, 1967). But reduction of the inventory is methodologically desirable (see discussion below, §§4.5, 5.8).

IV. *The two 'significant levels'.* Aside from the lexicon (which is a minimally redundant classificatory representation), there are two and only two 'theoretically significant' levels in a phonological description: a fully specified classificatory ('categorial') input to the phonological component ('systematic phonemic representation'), and the output of the rules of that component ('systematic phonetic representation'). I will return shortly to the nature of this output level.

V. *Parallelism: phonological–phonetic convertibility.* Both of the levels in (IV) are described in terms of the same set of features; or to put it a bit more weakly, the phonetic features are in some way parallel to the phonological ones, so that mappings between levels are not arbitrary. (This is true at least insofar as they are constrained by some sort of 'naturalness condition': cf. Postal 1968 for some discussion.) Very simply, a mapping is 'optimal' if it meets a condition of phonological–phonetic invariance (cf. *SPE*: 168–9), and its optimality decreases with the increase of invariance violation. So a mapping /t/ → [t] is optimal, a mapping /t/ → [s] is less optimal, though still within the bounds of a reasonable conception of categorial naturalness; and the latter is certainly more optimal and natural than a mapping /t/ → [a].

This parallelism, however, is based on a one-way extrapolation: the basis for the definition of the phonological features, in any system that purports to be 'natural' or 'explanatory' (or not just algebraic) is always strictly phonetic: acoustic in the Jakobsonian framework, articulatory in *SPE*. So even at the deepest phonological level, the correlates on the basis of which feature-specifications are assigned derive from the most superficial possible level: i.e. from the analysis of performance effects.

This 'source' level, interestingly, is not in fact accepted in general as theoretically valid: since for *SPE* at least the 'systematic phonetic' level is 'perceptual', i.e. 'mental' in their rather eccentric sense of this term, and not a matter of physical or acoustic reality at all (cf. *SPE*: 14, 25–6, 43). I will return to this directly.

VI. *Interlevel categorial constancy.* Along with the above goes an unstated, but I think no less clear assumption: and this is that the feature specifications (statements of category-membership) assigned to a given segment type are the same at all levels. Thus the matrices defining [t d] as against [k g] are always [+ant, +cor, −back] as against [−ant, −cor, +back]. Even at the level where specifications are in terms of integers rather than plus/minus values, the same constancy holds: [+cor] may be mapped into [*n* cor], but this *n* will always be one of the possible surface values assignable to the coefficient 'plus' for this feature. Any segment type, that is, belongs, at any point in a derivation, to the same class it belongs to at any other. (This is not of course to say that the class-membership of a segment can't change: e.g. if it is converted into something else. But if say some [k] becomes [s], then it is a member, from that point on, of the invariant class defining [s]-types.) The classes, as defined by their feature specifications, are apparently also theoretical primes.

1.5. Let us inquire now what the precise meaning of the 'systematic phonetic' level is, and the kinds of features and specifications it contains. It is important to note that this level is not to be equated with what we would normally call 'phonetic output': it is not physically realized, but (presumably) the programme for neuromuscular production (or the interpretation) of sentences. Chomsky & Halle offer this definition of the output of the phonological rules (14):

> a phonetic representation is actually a feature matrix in which the rows correspond to a restricted set of universal phonetic categories...and the columns to successive segments...such representations are *mentally constructed* by the speaker and the hearer and underlie their actual performance in speaking and 'understanding' [italics mine: RL].

They say further (25) that they 'take it for granted...that phonetic representations describe a perceptual reality...Notice, however, that there is nothing to suggest that these...also describe a physical or acoustic reality in any detail.'

It seems, in fact, that phonology – in principle – does not deal with the latter kind of reality at all:

it is impossible to expect (and for purposes of investigating linguistic structures, unnecessary to attain) a complete correspondence between the records of an impressionistic phonetician and what is predicted by a systematic theory that seeks to account for the perceptual facts that underlie these records (26).

I pass over the curious usage of 'facts' in this quotation with no further comment than this: I do not understand what it means.

Unfortunately, Chomsky & Halle neglect here – as elsewhere – to suggest any procedures by which we can get from this impressionistic record (which does, after all, exist) to specifications of the all-important 'perceptual facts'. What are they? How fine a set of distinctions do we have to make (or conversely, how gross a set are we permitted to make)? What can be safely disregarded in the impressionistic phonetician's record? It seems to be assumed (at least by implication) that a qualified linguist can tell automatically what categorial sets any physical or acoustic reality should be put into. In other words, that in some occult way it is self-evident which of two polar positions on a (binary) phonological scale any given point on a physical or acoustic phonetic continuum belongs to. (For further discussion of this problem see Botha 1971.)

To be fair, however, Chomsky & Halle do suggest that there is some way in which the binary input specifications (the 'systematic phonemic' representation) are ultimately converted into something approaching a detailed articulatory programme: although the relation between the final 'systematic phonetic' output and any physical or acoustic reality is still unclear:

in the representations that constitute the surface structure (the output of the syntactic rules), specified features will be marked as plus or minus; but the phonological rules, as they apply to these representations, will *gradually convert these specifications to integers*; we will not actually give the rules that effect this conversion in most cases... (65) [italics mine: RL].

(Though they do say in the same passage that 'in principle, all rules should be given'.) What is very curious indeed about the integral values they do give, is that these occur only in rules assigning stress – which in their framework is not a binary feature. The *SPE* rules assign values like [2 stress], etc., to vowels that are otherwise marked only [+high] or [+back], and so on.

The mechanics of the conversion to integers works like this:

> The notation [+stress]...serves as a 'cover symbol' for all segments with integrally marked values of stress; a rule applying to a segment containing the specification [+stress] automatically applies to all segments which contain the specification [*n* stress], for some integer *n*, and which are not otherwise excluded by the formulation of the rule.
>
> We expect that the same (or some similar) convention is needed for all features... (66)

This relies on assumption V (*Convertibility*) above: it seems that any phonological specification can be used as a cover symbol for a phonetic specification; and of course vice versa. So the convention again assumes that we know in advance how to do this; how to take any value on either level and either reduce it to binarity or expand it to n-arity. We might put it this way: for any specification [+F] for some feature 'F' at the (highest) systematic phonetic level, there is a lower-level specification [*n* F] such that *n* is one integer out of the set of possible (phonetic) scalar values for the coefficient '+' on 'F'. This feature 'F' is then obviously 'the same' feature all the way through: the increasing fineness of specification in effect merely dissolves bipolarity into a cline: but the poles must be known *a priori* for the whole thing to work.

1.6. But what about the level at which mental representations, whether their specifications are binary or n-ary, are realized as physical occurrences in real time? Is this of no significance at all for the theory, even though it is really the only source of data for the theory to work on? (It seems curious that we should spend so much time 'investigating' the properties of unobservable and constructed 'levels', and so little investigating the actual properties of the material that suggests these other levels to us.) A related question: is it possible that there is some level (even more than one) below the systematic phonetic (which latter is often only a name for inaccurate transcription anyhow: cf. ch. 1), which is (a) not even necessarily physical in the strictest sense, (b) qualitatively different (in that it is non-classificatory in the usual sense), and (c) also theoretically significant? Is it correct to say that the 'universal' and rather simple machinery I have been looking at is all there is, that there are no generalizations that cannot be expressed in the terms and categories given *a priori* by the standard theory?

I will claim in what follows that there is much more to phonological explanation than the standard theory allows, and that much of it is not appropriately described in terms of 'levels' in the usual sense. There is a domain which is theoretically of the greatest importance, but which is different from the *SPE* 'systematic' levels in at least two ways. First, in that it includes features of different kinds, some of which are universally nondistinctive, i.e. always redundant in terms of a reasonable set of classificatory features. And second, in that it impinges on the area customarily assigned to 'performance'. That is, since the 'higher' levels in standard theory are 'mental', and this one must include phenomena accessible to short-term auditory monitoring.

In the next section of this chapter, I will examine in some detail a set of phenomena that indicate to me that the whole complex of assumptions I have been discussing stands in need of serious revision. In the remaining sections, I will make some theoretical proposals concerning the necessary revisions, and look at some other data which suggests still more revisions. These revisions will lead to a discussion of some critical issues in theory formation: notably that the minimalness criterion (§1.4, III) should probably be scrapped (at least in its strong form), and that the goal of 'unique' descriptions in general is neither attainable nor particularly desirable. That is, I will suggest that – in a special sense – mutually 'contradictory' descriptions of the same phenomena should be admitted into grammars. This orgy of revisionism will finally conclude with some suggestions for a reinterpretation of the orthodox notion that sound change is (necessarily) 'grammar change' in the usual sense. I will suggest that many important changes must be interpreted as deriving from a much less abstract, much lower-level locus than is usually thought. (Note that this is the obverse of the GREATER abstractness I proposed in chapter 2.)

2. Some evidence from English

My data here is a set of processes ('sound changes') drawn from various points in the history of English, and various dialects. Some of these are major, across-the-board changes, and others are quite sporadic (i.e. not strictly *Lautgesetze*). I assume that for my purpose the extent of a rule's diffusion across the lexicon is not important: what counts is that it occurred, in however few or however many items at any time. I will examine each one relatively briefly, as the cumulative evidence, not the individual details, is my focus.

2.1. *The Old English period*

2.1.1. i-Umlaut. From earliest Germanic times there has been a tendency for mid vowels to raise before following high vowels: the first rules of this type show up in the strong verb vowel alternations induced by historical suffixal vowels. Thus OE *bere* 'I bear', vs. *bir(e)st* 'thou bearest', *bir(e)ð* 'he bears' < Gmc. */ber-ō, -isi, -iθi/. This early tendency for high front vowels and 'semivowels' (more likely fricatives at this stage) to serve as assimilatory goals is generalized in the later *i*-umlaut, in which back vowels front and short low vowels raise to mid before a following /i j/. Thus we get alternating pairs like *hāl*: *hǣlan* 'whole: heal', *mann*: *menn* 'man: men'. The rule may be (crudely)[1] stated like this:

(1) $$\begin{bmatrix} -\text{cons} \\ \left\langle \begin{matrix} +\text{low} \\ -\text{long} \end{matrix} \right\rangle \end{bmatrix} \rightarrow \begin{bmatrix} -\text{back} \\ \langle -\text{low} \rangle \end{bmatrix} / \underline{\quad} \; C_0 \begin{bmatrix} -\text{back} \\ +\text{high} \end{bmatrix}$$

2.1.2. Vowel-raising before /n/. The nonlow vowels */e o/ typically appear in OE as (orthographic) *i*, *u* before clusters of a non-labial nasal plus consonant. Thus class III strong verbs with nasal stems show *i*, *u* where nonnasal stems of the same class show *e*, *o*: *drincan*, *druncen* 'drink, drunk' vs. *helpan*, *holpen* 'help, helped, p.p.' (cf. Campbell 1959: §741, Lass & Anderson 1975: chs. I, II). Assuming that this occurs before a rule of homorganic assimilation that turns /n/ to [ŋ] before velars, we can state it this way:

(2) $$\begin{bmatrix} -\text{cons} \\ -\text{low} \end{bmatrix} \rightarrow [+\text{high}] / \underline{\quad} \begin{bmatrix} +\text{nas} \\ +\text{ant} \\ +\text{cor} \end{bmatrix} C$$

2.1.3. Vowel-raising in the Anglian smoothing. The Anglian dialects of OE underwent, early in their histories, a process generally called 'smoothing' (*Ebnung*). Here diphthongs (whether historically 'original' or from preconsonantal epenthesis or 'breaking') were monophthongized before velar obstruents, or clusters of liquid plus velar. Thus Angl. *mæht* 'might', *werc* 'work' vs. West Saxon *meaht*, *weorc* (Campbell 1959: §§222–33).

[1] The specification [−long] is of course an expository fiction. For a better version of this rule, using the vowel/cluster dichotomy, see Lass & Anderson (1975: ch. IV). The basic arguments for length as clustering are given above in chapters 1 and 3. On the umlaut in general see also Lass (1970), and Campbell (1959: §§190–204).

Some of the vowels produced by this monophthongization raised: in particular both short and long [æ] from *ea*, *ēa* (whose first elements were [æ]: Lass & Anderson: ch. III). Specifically, short [æ] raised to [e] before a velar preceded by a liquid, and long [æ:] raised to [e:] whether or not a liquid intervened. Thus Angl. *mæht* but *merg* 'marrow', *hēh* 'high' vs. *meaht*, *mearg*, *hēah*. Using [± long] again to distinguish the vowel types, the rule is:

(3)
$$\begin{bmatrix}-\text{cons}\\-\text{back}\\+\text{low}\\\langle-\text{long}\rangle\end{bmatrix} \rightarrow [-\text{low}] \,/\, \_\_ \left\langle\begin{matrix}-\text{obs}\\+\text{cor}\end{matrix}\right\rangle \begin{bmatrix}+\text{obs}\\+\text{back}\\+\text{high}\end{bmatrix}$$

Crucially, low front vowels raise in an environment which is either high and back, or a sequence of coronal plus high and back.

2.1.4. Late West Saxon smoothing. This is rather sporadic, but frequent enough to deserve notice. Here again the *ea*-diphthongs monophthongized and raised, but without any [æ] remaining unraised. The context too was more extensive than that of the smoothing: not only before velars, but after palatals as well. Thus *seh* 'he saw', *ehta* 'eight', *ēge* 'eye', *ċēs* 'he chose', *scēp* 'sheep', *ġēr* 'year', earlier *seah, eahta, ēage, ceas, scēap, ġēar* (*ġ* = [j], *ċ* = [tʃ], *sc* = [ʃ]). Similar phenomena show up as well in ninth-century Kentish (details in Campbell: §§312–14). The rule would be:

(4)
$$\begin{bmatrix}-\text{cons}\\+\text{low}\\-\text{back}\end{bmatrix} \rightarrow [-\text{low}] \,/ \left\{\begin{matrix}\begin{bmatrix}+\text{obs}\\-\text{back}\\+\text{high}\end{bmatrix} \_\_ \\ \_\_ \begin{bmatrix}+\text{obs}\\+\text{back}\\+\text{high}\end{bmatrix}\end{matrix}\right\}$$

But since [æ] doesn't appear after velars in OE, we can state both contexts in terms of a single specification [+high]; and since we then have a 'mirror-image' environment, we can use Bach's 'neighbourhood convention' (1968), and suppress the environment bar:

(5)
$$\begin{bmatrix}-\text{cons}\\+\text{low}\\-\text{back}\end{bmatrix} \rightarrow [-\text{low}] \,/ \begin{bmatrix}+\text{obs}\\+\text{high}\end{bmatrix}$$

2.1.5. *Palatal umlaut.* This unfortunately named process is not an 'umlaut' at all, but monophthongization and raising before clusters of /x/ + dental obstruent. In dialects like WS which had a diphthong *eo* (from earlier /exC/), this was monophthongized, and the resulting [e] raised to [i]. In the Anglian dialects in which all the earlier diphthongs had been 'smoothed' before velars (cf. §2.1.3), there was simply raising. Thus earlier *cneoht* 'servant', *weoht* 'creature', *seox* 'six' > *cniht, wiht, siex* (*ie* = [i], *x* = [xs]).

Since we do not know if OE had an '*ich/ach*' rule, we cannot tell if /x/ after front vowels was palatal or velar (many Gmc. languages like Yiddish and some dialects of Scots have [x] or even [χ] for /x/ after front vowels). Therefore I will state the rule using just the feature [+high]:

(6)
$$\begin{bmatrix} -\text{cons} \\ -\text{high} \\ -\text{low} \\ -\text{back} \end{bmatrix} \rightarrow [+\text{high}] \;/\; \underline{\qquad} \begin{bmatrix} +\text{obs} \\ +\text{high} \end{bmatrix} \begin{bmatrix} +\text{obs} \\ +\text{ant} \\ +\text{cor} \end{bmatrix}$$

(See further Campbell: §§304–11, Brunner 1965: §§122.1–2.) Note also that in dialects with both post-smoothing raising and palatal umlaut, the two rules together constitute a context-restricted chain shift: low front vowels go to mid and mid go to high before velars and/or palatals: i.e., nonhigh vowels go one step up in this set of contexts.

2.2. *The Middle English period*

2.2.1. *Pre-dental raising.* Beginning c. 1200, there is a strong tendency for /e/ to raise before dental obstruents, and before a dental nasal plus another consonant. Thus *briþren* 'brethren', *brist* 'breast', *linth* 'length', *stynch* 'stench' (Jordan 1934: §34). The rule is:

(7)
$$\begin{bmatrix} -\text{cons} \\ -\text{high} \\ -\text{low} \\ -\text{back} \end{bmatrix} \rightarrow [+\text{high}] \;/\; \underline{\qquad} \begin{bmatrix} +\text{cons} \\ +\text{ant} \\ +\text{cor} \\ \langle +\text{nas} \rangle \end{bmatrix} \langle +\text{cons} \rangle$$

Not many of these forms have survived in 'standard' English, but some dialects (especially in the North of England and the Scottish Borders) show extensive survivals, indicating that this was a widespread and pervasive process.[1]

[1] Standard English shows e.g. *silly* < ME *seli, cringe* < OE *crengean,* and a few others. Many forms however showing typical reflexes of ME /i/ for etymological ME /e/ have been reported in other dialects: e.g. by Orton (1933: §§55–7) for Byers Green,

2.2.2. Pre-velar raising. About the same time as the preceding, we find frequent raising of /e/ before velars: and many more of these have survived. Thus *English*, *wing*, *sick*, *string*, *mingle*, all of which have historical (OE or ON) /e/. The form of this rule must be nearly identical to (7):

(8)
$$\begin{bmatrix}-\text{cons}\\-\text{high}\\-\text{low}\\-\text{back}\end{bmatrix} \to [+\text{high}] \;/\; \underline{\qquad} \begin{bmatrix}+\text{cons}\\+\text{high}\\+\text{back}\\\langle+\text{nas}\rangle\end{bmatrix} \langle+\text{cons}\rangle$$

For dialects in which both (7) and (8) operated (cf. those described in Orton 1933, Zai 1942), we can posit an abbreviatory schema:

(9)
$$\begin{bmatrix}-\text{cons}\\-\text{high}\\-\text{low}\\-\text{back}\end{bmatrix} \to [+\text{high}] \;/\; \underline{\qquad} \begin{bmatrix}+\text{cons}\\ \left\{\begin{matrix}[+\text{back}]\\ \begin{bmatrix}+\text{ant}\\+\text{cor}\end{bmatrix}\end{matrix}\right\}\\\langle+\text{nas}\rangle\end{bmatrix} \langle+\text{cons}\rangle$$

The disjunction in the SD of this rule is of particular interest: we will return to it later on.

In some dialects, notably in the South and Midlands, there was a sporadic back-vowel parallel to (8), at least before nasal + velar, as shown in spellings and rhymes of OE /o/ with /u/ (Jordan 1934: §31 and *Anm.*). This could be incorporated in (9) by substituting the specification ⟨+back⟩ for [−back] in the vowel matrix.

2.2.3. Diphthongization before /x/. In dialects outside of the North, epenthetic high vowels developed between nonhigh vowels and a following velar (or palatal?) fricative: [i] after front vowels, and [u] after back. If there was assimilation of /x/ to [ç] after front vowels, it's a toss-up whether the epenthetic vowel should be said to agree with the consonant or the preceding vowel in backness. But because of the uncertainty raised in §2.1.5, I will assume vowel–vowel agreement. The rule is:

(10)
$$\varnothing \to \begin{bmatrix}-\text{cons}\\+\text{high}\\\alpha\text{back}\end{bmatrix} \;/\; \begin{bmatrix}-\text{cons}\\-\text{high}\\\alpha\text{back}\end{bmatrix} \underline{\qquad} \begin{bmatrix}+\text{obs}\\+\text{high}\\+\text{cont}\end{bmatrix}$$

Durham; by Hedevind (1967, §4: 17) for Dentdale, Yorkshire; by Zai (1942, §§61–2) for Morebattle, Roxburghshire, and by Wettstein (1942) for Chirnside, Berwickshire. There is some possibility that these Northern forms are not due to the ME raising, but to a later and more extensive one (cf. §2.3.2); the chronology is difficult because of the state of the early documentation. What counts, however, is not when the change occurred, but the fact that it did at all.

Examples: *heigh* 'high' < LOE *hēh*, *taughte* 'taught' < LOE *tăhte* < *tǣhte*, *plough* < OE *plōh* (see Jordan, §§97.2, 121–6, Lass & Anderson, ch. VI).

2.2.4. Diphthongization before dentals, palatals and velars. The ME records show a sporadic but widely distributed epenthesis of [i] after /e a/ before: palatal continuant obstruents, a dental nasal + palatal cluster and a velar nasal + velar cluster. Typical forms are *aische* 'ash' < OE *æsc*, *bleinte* 'blinked', pret. of *blenchen*, *seinde* 'singed', pret. of *sengen*, *leinþe* 'length' < OE *lengðu* (Jordan, §§102–3). The rule might be given as:

(11)

$$\varnothing \rightarrow \begin{bmatrix} -\text{cons} \\ +\text{high} \\ -\text{back} \end{bmatrix} \Big/ \begin{bmatrix} -\text{cons} \\ -\text{round} \\ -\text{high} \end{bmatrix} \underline{\quad} \begin{bmatrix} +\text{cons} \\ \begin{bmatrix} -\text{back} \\ +\text{high} \\ +\text{cont} \end{bmatrix} \\ \left\langle \begin{bmatrix} +\text{nas} \\ \left\{ \begin{matrix} \begin{bmatrix} +\text{ant} \\ +\text{cor} \end{bmatrix} \\ [+\text{high}] \end{matrix} \right\} \end{bmatrix} \right\rangle \end{bmatrix} \langle +\text{cons} \rangle$$

Results of this show up in modern dialects too (e.g. East Devon: Hart 1959: §57); there is also a more far-reaching modern counterpart that I will discuss later (in §2.4.1).

2.3. The early Modern English period

2.3.1. Non-vowel-shift raising of ME /a/. Many fifteenth-century sources show instances of this before dentals and palatals: e.g. *gled* < ME *glad* < OE *glæd*, *becheler* < OF *bacheler* (in dialects where we would expect *a* in these forms: Jordan §265). In the sixteenth century, well before the general change in the South of ME /a/ to [æ] (cf. ch. 4 above), we find numerous cases of *e* for expected *a*, nearly all of them before dentals and velars (see examples in Kökeritz 1953: 163–4). It is uncertain whether these *e*-spellings represent phones of the [æ] or [ɛ] types; the traditional assumption is [æ], on the grounds that a new segment would be written with the letter representing the most similar existing one, so that a raised [a] would be more like [ɛ] than [a], and a change of [a] to [æ] is more likely than one of [a] to [ɛ] (ME /a/ seems to have been [a]: see chapter 4 above). But whatever the *e* represents, it is certainly nonlow, i.e. it is raised from original ME /a/. So the rule would be:

(12)
$$\begin{bmatrix} -\text{cons} \\ -\text{back} \end{bmatrix} \rightarrow [-\text{low}] \,/\, \rule{1em}{0.4pt} \begin{bmatrix} +\text{cons} \\ \left\{ \begin{matrix} \begin{bmatrix} +\text{ant} \\ +\text{cor} \end{bmatrix} \\ [-\text{high}] \end{matrix} \right\} \end{bmatrix}$$

2.3.2. Raising of /e/ before dentals, palatals and velars. I assign this to the ENE period because that's when the most extensive spelling evidence begins to show up. It seems to be a further development of the low vowel raising (12), and perhaps also of the two ME raising rules collapsed in (9). Typical distributions and evidence can be found in the material cited from Shakespeare by Kökeritz (1953: 186ff.), and in the modern forms given by Orton (1933), Hedevind (1967), Zai (1942) and Wettstein (1942). In all these cases there is some raising before labials as well, but very little. This suggests that while there might be some case to be made for an across-the-board raising, the PREFERRED environments are the ones I have been discussing. The rule would be:

(13)
$$\begin{bmatrix} -\text{cons} \\ -\text{back} \\ -\text{high} \\ -\text{low} \end{bmatrix} \rightarrow [+\text{high}] \,/\, \rule{1em}{0.4pt} \begin{bmatrix} +\text{cons} \\ \left\{ \begin{matrix} \begin{bmatrix} +\text{ant} \\ +\text{cor} \end{bmatrix} \\ [+\text{high}] \end{matrix} \right\} \end{bmatrix}$$

Note that this is the third case (cf. (11, 12)) where the specifications [+ant, +cor] and [+high] are paired disjunctively in the environment of a rule.

2.4. *The Modern English period*

The processes to be discussed now are ones that I have personally observed in various dialects of English. I have no historical information on them, but they can be seen quite clearly to be either recurrences or continuations of some of the rules or rule-types that I have been looking at.

In the brief descriptions that follow, I will not give formal statements of the rules: because when we reach the point in time where we have directly observable phonetic data, it becomes harder to reduce it to neat binary specifications (cf. the discussion in §1.5 above). At least I find it difficult; and since these observations are being made at the n-ary, 'phonetic detail' level, and are not part of grammars of the dialects concerned, but simply impressionistic transcriptions, not even within the province of 'systematic phonetics', it is difficult to choose appropriate 'simplified' versions. I am not saying that the rules cannot be stated: but I simply do not want to get into the problem of how to state them, in the absence of a fully-developed theory of multi-valued feature coefficients, and a consensus on their use.

My main desire here is to give some reasonable data, and to avoid unanswerable questions like how high a raised [e] has to be before it's 'really' [+high], etc. I will simply assume, as phonologists do in general, that given the current state of the art, anything in the [iɩ] or [u ɷ] range is a 'high vowel', and so on.

2.4.1. Diphthongization before dentals, palatals and velars. Many U.S. dialects (Southern and Central Indiana, for example) show epenthesis of high vowels (nonsyllabic) before palatals and velars, agreeing in backness with the preceding vowel. Thus (from rural Bloomington, Monroe County, Indiana): [fɩiʃ] 'fish', [spȩɩʃɫ̩] 'special', [pʰɩig] 'pig', [bæɩg] 'bag', [sɩ͡iŋ] 'sing', [hɔɷg] 'hog', [bɷ̈uʃ] 'bush', etc. (Some speakers have epenthetic [ɩ] before [ʃ], in *bush*, etc., even after back vowels.) This diphthongization is commonest in monosyllables, and rare before /k/. These dialects also show (but less commonly) diphthongization before /n/+obstruent: [kʰæ̃ɩnt] 'can't', [lȩɩnθ] 'length', etc. The epenthetic vowel here is not the same one that appears before /n/ alone: cf. [kʰæ̃͡ən] 'can'. This looks pretty much like the same type of thing described in §2.2.4 above, though limited to less than the full array of possible contexts. (On the classification of [ʃ ʧ] as 'palatals' rather than 'palato-alveolars' or something of the sort, see below, §4.2. I will assume this classification – as I have up to now – until then, when I will attempt to justify it further.)

2.4.2. Raising of /ɛ/ before /n/. Many of the same dialects that show the diphthongization described above in §2.4.1 also show neutralization of the /ɛ/ : /ɩ/ contrast in [ɩ͡ə] before /n/: thus we get [pʰɩ͡ən] for *pen, pin*. This is not general before all nasals: [hɩ͡əm] 'him, hymn', but [hȩ͡əm] 'hem'.

2.4.3. Raising of /æ/ before the velar nasal. Some U.S. dialects of the Northern Midwest (e.g. Gary and South Bend, Indiana, Detroit, Michigan) show raising of /æ/ before [ŋ(C)] in words like *bang, hang, thank, strangle*. These will have nuclear [ɛ̃] or [ɛ͂ɩ], as opposed to [æ̈] or [æ̈ə] in *cat, bad*, etc.

2.4.4. Raising before /r/. Many American (and British) dialects have five distinct front vowels before /r/, e.g. in *mere, mirror, Mary, merry, marry*. In my own New York City dialect, the stressed nuclei of these words are respectively [ɩiə ɩ ɛ̤̈ə ɛ̝ æ]. Many other U.S. dialects (perhaps the majority), however, show a more limited set of contrasts: *mere* and *mirror* have the same nucleus, usually [ɩiə], and *Mary, merry, marry* have [ɛ̤̈ə]. There seems – historically – to have been epenthesis of a high vowel after [ɩ], and raising of [ɛ æ] in this environment. (In these dialects /r/ is an alveolar approximant, sometimes retroflex, sometimes velarized: in the latter case, the so-called 'molar *r*' described by Uldall 1958.)

In many Scots dialects (notably Central) there is a similar situation: raising of (historical) long mid vowels before /r/ (here usually [r]), so that vowels of the [i:] type appear both in *beer, here, fear* (where they are expected as the GVS reflexes of ME /e:/), and in *bear, hair, fair*, where they are not expected (these words have ME /ɛ:/). The situation with the short vowels is more like New York: *mirror, Mary, merry, marry* remain distinct. Thus the short vowels before /r/ are unaffected, but the historical half-close:half-open contrast in the long vowels has been neutralized in a high vowel.

3. The nature of the problem

3.1. If we look back at the data in §2, we find that there are three basic types of change involved: FRONTING (*i*-umlaut of the OE back vowels, §2.2.1); RAISING (*i*-umlaut of [æ], raising of /e o/, §2.1.1; raising before /n/, §2.1.2; raising in the Anglian smoothing, §2.1.3; late West Saxon smoothing, §2.1.4; palatal umlaut, §2.1.5; ME pre-dental raising, §2.2.1; ME pre-velar raising, §2.2.2; ENE raising of ME /a/, §2.3.1; ENE raising before dentals, palatals, and velars, §2.3.2; NE raising before /n/, §2.4.2; NE raising before [ŋ], §2.4.3; NE raising before /r/, §2.4.4); and HIGH VOWEL EPENTHESIS (ME diphthongization before /x/, §2.2.3; ME diphthongization before dentals, palatals, velars, §2.2.4; NE diphthongization before dentals, palatals, velars, §2.4.1).

We have now looked at sixteen processes, quite widely separated in time and space. They have involved two kinds of positional shift in vowel articulation, and one kind of nuclear modification. And in all of them the crucial environments, the agents triggering the structure changes of the rules, have been among this set: high front vowels, dental (including alveolar), palatal (including so-called 'palato-alveolar') and velar consonants. (We might also include high back vowels like [u], since these also appear as the outputs of raising and epenthesis rules.)

3.2. At the moment then we are left with a set of sixteen processes, involving considerable recurrence and similarity, and a group of segments that seem to be implicated in them. And it seems further that there is some kind of overall generalization involved: these processes are all 'assimilations' of some kind. Only when we try to state the rules so that it's clear from the statement that this is the case, we find that our intuition of generality has no formal support. In case after case, in fact, the SD's of the rules are disjunctions. That is, we cannot seem to state the rules so that they not only have the right output (which is a trivial undertaking in any case), but so that they also 'explain' in some way what is going on. The disturbing thing is that there seems to be no way, using any of the currently well-developed feature systems, and operating under the metatheoretical assumptions discussed in §1, to characterize the obviously important and 'natural' class we are dealing with. We have only a simple observation statement about our rules, and no formal backing.

3.3. We can focus the problem more clearly if we consider how the segments we are interested in are characterized in the two best developed and most widely used feature systems we have: the acoustic ('Jakobsonian') framework detailed in Jakobson *et al.* (1951: henceforth *PSA*) and the articulatory one proposed by Chomsky & Halle in *SPE*. They compare as follows:

(14) *PSA*

	Dentals	Palatals	Velars	[i]	[u]
Compact	−	+	+	−	−
Grave	−	−	+	−	+

SPE

	Dentals	Palatals	Velars	[i]	[u]
Anterior	+	−	−	−	−
Coronal	+	−	−	−	−
High	−	+	+	+	+
Back	−	−	+	−	+

As far as our rules are concerned, each of these characterizations does some things right, but both do a lot wrong too. And some are a lot wronger than others. Thus the *PSA* features correctly group dentals and [i] as a class, but allow no features in common between [i] and velars. So in this system a rule that raised vowels before dentals would be an assimilation, and one that did it before velars would be a dissimilation. The *PSA* palatals share one specification each with dentals and velars, but there is no feature shared by all the classes. And worst of all, perhaps, [i] is specified identically with the dentals, so that there is no way of capturing its far closer relationship with palatals like [j ç].

SPE, on the other hand, allows a common specification for palatals, velars, and [i]; but because the definition of 'anterior' rules out vowels, only [– back] is shared by these classes, and velars have nothing in common with dentals. But [u] is correctly grouped with the velars. So *SPE* can state pre-palatal and pre-velar raising as assimilations, but the only reasonable change before dentals would be fronting, which does not occur.

Further, if we were to consider the characterization of labials in both systems, we would find that their exclusion from the class I have been discussing is not motivated: in *PSA* labials share graveness with velars and noncompactness with dentals; in *SPE* labials are anterior, along with dentals, and share noncoronality with [i], palatals and velars.

To sum up so far: the positional classes dentals, palatals and velars, and the high front vowel [i] seem to be 'naturally' related; the evidence for this (from English) is the frequency with which they are implicated in rules, and the particular relations they show in these rules. Thus we find epenthesis of [i u] before all three consonant classes, and changes of mid vowels to high ones before them, etc. And no currently available feature inventory allows this obviously important class to be generalized; the *SPE* system, which I used in stating some of the rules, in fact defines it by disjunction.

4. A possible step in the right direction: 'second-order' features

4.1. I want to argue now, not that the *PSA* and *SPE* features are 'wrong', but that they have been misused. And the worst misuse has been in the insistence that one or the other (or any set, for that matter) is THE correct one, everywhere. That is, under the assumptions of *universality* (§ 1.4, II), *minimalness* (§ 1.4, III), *two 'significant levels'* (§ 1.4, IV), and *interlevel constancy* (§1.4, VI), neither framework as such is relevant to the kinds of rules I have been considering, nor to many other significant phonological processes. Though they are, as we will see, undoubtedly relevant to others.

The arguments to follow will be concerned with attempting to support the following basic points: (a) that the set of features available for phonological description is not necessarily coterminous with the set of lexical (or phonetic) CLASSIFICATORY features; (b) that in any case some of the supposed 'universal' features are rather dubious; (c) that because of (a) the minimalness criterion and certain associated principles should not be observed; and (d) that in general we need to change our presently rather simplistic notion of what a phonological grammar looks like. The revised version will incorporate, essentially, an unbroken continuum from the lexicon all the way to physical phonetic output, with no particular status granted either to the (universal) 'systematic' levels, or to 'competence'. This will be more fully developed in §§5–7.

4.2. To begin with, let us look for a moment not at features as primes, but at some grosser articulatory facts. First, observe that of the possible distinctive articulation places in English – labial, dental, palatal, velar, uvular and glottal – only three seem to operate as a class with respect to raising and diphthongization: dental, palatal and velar.[1] (We will see later that labials/velars can be a class for other types of rules.) Now what do these three types have in common from an articulatory point of view? In this connexion I revert to a rather old-fashioned but well-motivated taxonomy: the division of consonantal articulations into 'labial', 'lingual' and 'laryngeal' (cf. Pope 1934, and other works of that vintage). Both labials and laryngeals have two important properties in common, one basic and the other derived: (a) their occlusion is outside the oral cavity proper, as defined anteriorly by the inner surfaces of the incisors and posteriorly by the tongue-root; and (b) therefore neither, without co-articulation, can involve the tongue as active articulator.

I now propose a feature [±lingual], and define it as follows: horizontally speaking, all predentals and postvelars are [−ling], and dentals,

[1] Labials as such do not figure in any raising or similar rules, as far as I know, nor do the glottals. In those dialects with uvulars (e.g. in Northumberland) these seem to cause, as might be expected, mainly lowering and retraction, though sometimes rounding as well: thus a uvularized [ɔʁ] as the unstressed (reduced) vowel in *here* [hiɔʁ], *mother, father*, etc. Also there is the typical Tyneside [ɔ:] (with or without uvularization) in *work, shirt*, etc. (cf. Hepher 1954).

palatals and velars are [+ling] (as are high vowels, for reasons I will get to shortly). The reason for limiting [+ling] essentially to pre-uvulars is that uvulars and pharyngeals, even though the tongue is involved in them, are not made with primary activity of either the blade or body, which is crucial here.[1] So: any segment made with the blade or body of the tongue as primary active articulator – in a sense to be defined more precisely below – is [+ling].

In *SPE*, all the articulations I am calling 'lingual' involve the features anterior, coronal, high and back. One of these – [±anterior] – seems unnecessary: or at least it's unnecessary as a classificatory feature if we are a bit more careful in our decision as to what constitutes a POINT of articulation.

Let us consider the purpose of the distinction [+ant] vs. [−ant]: why do we need it, if we also have, on the horizontal plane, the distinction [+back] vs. [−back]? *SPE* needs this feature, because while [−back] specifies tongue-body retraction, [−ant] locates an OCCLUSION – not merely a stricture – regardless of what it is made with. And further, since it defines only occlusions, both back vowels and velars are [+back], while dentals are [+ant] but front vowels are [−ant]. This does admittedly claim that front vowels are 'more like' palatals, which are also [−ant, −back]; and this is true enough. But we would still like to capture the essential 'frontness' of dentals and front vowels as being similar in kind.

The *SPE* disjunction, however, is necessary, apparently, because otherwise two important classes cannot be distinctively specified: labials, which are [+ant, −cor], as against the [+ant, +cor] dentals; and palato-alveolars, which are [−ant, +cor], as against the [+ant, +cor] dentals and the [−ant, −cor] palatals and velars.

This seems to lead to a circularity: in the case of sibilants, [+ant, +cor] defines [s]-type segments, as against [ʃ]-types, which are [−ant, +cor]; and *SPE* defines as [+ant] any occlusion made anterior to [ʃ] (*SPE*: 304). Thus the segment to be defined is the definition of the feature, and you can't get at one without the other.

4.3. This equivocation is not in fact necessary: at least for English, since in this language palato-alveolars are not a true POSITIONAL class. Seg-

[1] The feature [±lingual] is used for this same class in a description of Lumasaaba by Brown (1972); and a (nonbinary) feature of 'close lingual articulation' is suggested by Allen (1973b: 105) for the notorious 'ruki' class.

ments like [ʃ ʒ tʃ dʒ] are (a) phonetically as much (truly) palatal as alveolar, and (b) phonologically the same or more so. To take the phonetic side first: [ʃ ʒ] for instance vary considerably from dialect to dialect, and even from speaker to speaker, in the backness of the coronal occlusion. Thus for some [ʃ] is indeed quite posterior to [s], while for others it is only marginally so (if at all). What is however distinctive in all these cases is tongue SHAPE, not position, in two ways. Thus in the first place [ʃ] always has the blade of the tongue domed, whereas it is hollowed for [s] (cf. Ladefoged 1971: 47–8). And in the second place, they are strongly PALATALIZED: there is definite raising of the tongue toward the hard palate (cf. O'Connor 1973: 138, 143). The palato-alveolars are hyphenated not because of an 'intermediate' position, but – properly – because of their SECONDARY ARTICULATION.

Thus the reasonable characterization for them is palatalized alveolars: i.e. [+cor, −back, +high]. This way, [ʃ ʒ] are distinct from [s z] as [+high] vs. [−high]. They are in a sense an 'overlapping' class, since they share [+cor, −back] with the alveolars, and [−back, +high] with the palatals. This is further borne out by the phonological evidence: certainly [ʃ] for instance is historically (and sometimes synchronically) the result of a palatalization: in OE it derives from /sk/, and in later periods from /sj/, just as [ʒ] derives from [zj] (cf. *issue, vision*). The same can be said of [tʃ dʒ]. The early origins are palatalized /k/ and /Ng/ in OE (cf. Lass & Anderson 1975; ch. IV), and the later are /tj/ and /dj/ (cf. *Christian, soldier*). If we eliminate [±ant], we can still, then, characterize the palato-alveolars naturally; and we retain the double affinity that their complex articulator-shapes suggest.[1]

The only remaining use, it seems, for [±ant] is to distinguish the labials from the postdental noncoronals. This can be done quite naturally by means of [±ling]; but I do not think that this feature is relevant to the classificatory level. What I would prefer here is a feature like [±labial], where the action of the lips in forming labials is positively specified, not simply left to an interpretation of [−cor]. After all, [±cor] also is a feature that specifies one particular articulator. I think

[1] The classification could of course vary from dialect to dialect. Thus in some they might be 'true' palatals (i.e. noncoronal). But phonologically they could be distinct even in this case by the specification [+strident] (or better, [+sibilant]): e.g. in one that had, like some Scots, a phonemic /ç/. They would also be distinct from alveolar sibilants by [+high]. At the most we would still need only the features [coronal, high, back] to maintain binary distinctiveness among the three significant classes of linguals: what I have been calling dentals, palatals and velars.

that in this case the algorithmic neatness of binary feature-systems leads to a fundamentally wrong conclusion: that since labials can be distinguished from dentals by a single specification OF THE SAME HIERARCHICAL RANK as that distinguishing dentals from palatals, they therefore should be. (I will return in §6 to the problem of the difference between 'can be' and 'should be' in phonology.)

That is: the most natural classification would seem to me to be one that, even at the expense of a loss of binary neatness, specifies unique segment-types uniquely. What counts for labials is their labiality, just as what counts say for pharyngeals is their pharyngeality, i.e. their retracted tongue root. Segments like these would seem to be more naturally classified by means of SINGULARY features, as indeed has been suggested by Ladefoged (1971), in a framework where 'points' of articulation are not merely the results of conjunctions of binary specifications, but are real topological points.

I will not push this here; but if we did want to save the binary framework, we could in fact do it, as I suggested, by using [±ling]. Thus we could say that labials are not opposed to dentals in the same way as dentals are to palatals, and palatals to velars. Rather it would be the case that dentals, palatals and velars are members of one class opposed as a whole to the class of all nonlinguals. They are opposed as members of bipolar, individual oppositions only to the other linguals.

So instead of having a (necessarily) linear set of binary oppositions on a continuum from labial to pharyngeal, say, we could have two disjoint classes at the same hierarchical level, each of which is (or may be) a conjunction of class-internal binary oppositions. But these binary oppositions would not hold between members of one class and those of another We could represent this as follows:

(15)

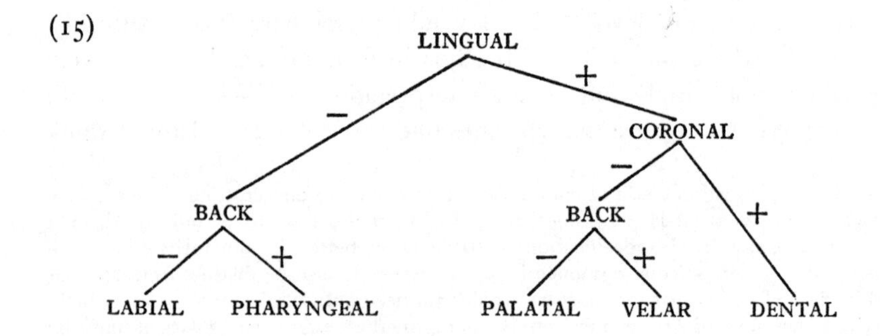

This merely goes to show that there are more ways than one to do anything, even given a specific set of formal conditions to meet. I will however leave this problem without further solution; though I will go on in the next section to suggest some further problems with [±ant]. Even if none of my classificatory solutions work, at least someone may figure out a better way. And the main point, as we will see in §4.6, is that the hierarchy (15) does hold at a certain 'level', or in a certain domain, and is useful for that reason: as long as we don't confuse it with what should be going on elsewhere.

4.4. I argued above that it seemed reasonable to reject [±ant] as a distinctive feature because it did not serve to specify a real single phonological class; and that it failed to do so because at least one of the sets of segments it tried to define by position was a secondarily-articulated class whose definitive feature was tongue shape.

But in addition to this, there is another argument against anteriority that can also shed some light on the naturalness of linguals as a class. Let us look again at how the three distinctive (non-coarticulated) lingual classes are specified in *SPE* for anteriority, coronality and highness:

(16)

	Dentals	Palatals	Velars
Anterior	+	−	−
Coronal	+	−	−
High	−	+	+

For linguals, it is then the case that anteriority and coronality agree:

(17) $[\alpha \text{ant}] \rightarrow [\alpha \text{cor}] \; / \; \overline{[+\text{ling}]}$

Further, coronality and highness predictably disagree, as do anteriority and highness:

(18) a. $[\alpha \text{cor}] \rightarrow [-\alpha \text{high}] \; / \; \overline{[+\text{ling}]}$

b. $[\alpha \text{ant}] \rightarrow [-\alpha \text{high}] \; / \; \overline{[+\text{ling}]}$

So anteriority and coronality predictably agree for linguals; and coronality and highness, and (transitively) anteriority and highness, predictably disagree. And this by definition, since of course no lingual can be simultaneously noncoronal and nonhigh, which follows from the fact that linguality is defined by the tongue as active articulator, with its target some structure on the maxillary column. The two features are functionally equivalent: [+cor] is the dental version of [+high], and [+high] is the postdental version of [+cor].

In terms of the *SPE* definitions, it is obvious why these relations should hold. Both the features coronal and high take as their reference-point the so-called 'neutral' position, i.e. (roughly) the oral-cavity configuration for a half-open vowel (front), where the blade of the tongue is at rest in the vicinity of the lower incisors, and the body shifted slightly toward the palate (but cf. the appendix to ch. 1 above). In a coronal articulation, the blade is raised above this position; in a high one, the body is raised. This means in effect that coronal articulations are the SUPRANEUTRAL ones anterior to the point at which the body of the tongue can make a comfortable occlusion, and high ones are those posterior to the point at which the blade can do so. Thus for any lingual articulation the specifications [+cor] and [+high] define respectively the non-neutral tongue position in the front and back halves of the oral cavity.

4.5. If [±ling] defines consonantal articulations made within the oral cavity proper (as in fact it does), then we can define the (for English) intuitive natural class dentals/palatals/velars as also formally natural: it is exhaustively specifiable as [+ling]. But even if this is so, we still can't characterize all the segments we need to state our rules insightfully. We have solved, as it were, the problem of the relevant consonantal environments, but not the vocalic ones, or the crucial structure changes. We have not established any relation between lingual consonants and the changes they induce.

What advantage we have achieved can be seen in a simple restatement: the earlier rule (13), with its disjunction of anterior coronals and high consonants in the SD can now be stated in such a way that the originally disjoint environments are 'generalized'; though the rest of the rule is still as obtuse as it was:

(19) $$\begin{bmatrix} -\text{cons} \\ -\text{back} \\ -\text{high} \\ -\text{low} \end{bmatrix} \rightarrow [+\text{high}] \,/\, \underline{\qquad} \begin{bmatrix} +\text{cons} \\ +\text{ling} \end{bmatrix}$$

I now return to the high vowels. If for palatals and velars, as I have suggested, [+ling] = [+high], is it possible that for vowels we could say that [+high] = [+ling]? Certainly the *SPE* definition of [+high] specifies only elevation of the tongue body, not occlusion, so this would fit. But should high vowels have some feature in common with a whole class of consonants that other vowels lack? I would say yes: for among the vowels the high ones are unique in that they alone might be said to have 'homorganic' consonants. At least in the specific sense that there are consonants that are more occluded versions of high vowels, like [j ç] in relation to [i], [w] in relation to [u]. Certainly insofar as increasing stricture leads to consonantal articulation, it is clear that equivalences like this do not exist for mid vowels (though in a different sense they might for low back vowels and pharyngeals). Obviously 'one step up' from [e] is [i], still a vowel, whereas one step up from [i] is [j]. High vowels are in this sense 'potentially consonantal', while nonhigh ones are not. So we arrive at a classification like this:

(20)

	Low V	Mid V	High V	Dental	Palatal	Velar
Lingual	−	−	+	+	+	+
Low	+	−	−	−	−	−

We can now state most of our rules as direct assimilations: nonlingual vowels become lingual before linguals (or after them), the diphthongizations insert the appropriate [+ling] vowels in environments marked the same way, and so on. We can also begin to see why some raising rules (e.g. raising of ME /a/, §2.3.1, raising of NE /æ/, §2.4.3), which do not produce truly lingual vowels, should nevertheless operate. Given a lingual environment, and a vowel [a] which changes say to [ɛ], it is clear that [ɛ] is MORE LINGUAL than [a]. In other words, we might profitably imagine a kind of 'approach gradient' to lingualness, here subject to some sort of 'one step at a time' condition. In other words, a METARULE (cf. ch. 2 above) carrying the instruction: 'approach lingual in lingual environments, but only one step at a time'. Another classic example of this is the *i*-umlaut (cf. §2.1.1), where each vowel approaches the 'goal' [i] in its own way: [u] by becoming [y], [o] by becoming [ø], [ɑ] by becoming [æ], and [æ] by becoming [e].

4.6. Now let us return to the 'level' or domain where [±ling] is relevant. The argument in §4.3 suggested that given this feature, the distinctive relationships among [±ant], [±cor] and [±high] are dissolved; it turns out that one of these features is always redundant.

This is true enough; but it is a problem only if [±ling] is taken as a DISTINCTIVE or (strictly, i.e. lexically) CLASSIFICATORY feature. This is not what I intend. If [+ling] were, for example, to 'supersede' both [+cor] and [+high], it would of course not be possible to maintain the distinctiveness of dentals and palatals; we would have, as in (15), only [±back], and this would give us:

(21)

	Labial	Dental	Palatal	Velar
Ling	−	+	+	+
Back	−	−	−	+

The point is that [±ling] is not designed to REPLACE the other features, but in a very specific way to SUPPLEMENT them.

Let us note first that [+ling] is not an *ad hoc* specification: it is definable in terms of a real physical property. We might say that – from an observational point of view – linguals are linguals whether or not there is a case for a feature [±ling]. (I will return to this shortly.) Thus its relevance or utility in any given case may be challenged, but not its basis in phonetic fact. This is in a sense a tautology, but at the definitional level we can use a few of those. I therefore take it that [+ling], like [+round], is an empirical property of segments, not merely a device to make grammars work, like the '[−next rule]' convention, or underlying /ǣ/ in English (cf. ch. 1).

But given this, how do we square it with the distinctiveness problem? And further, with the general notion (the Minimalness Assumption, §1.4, III) that the fewer features one has, the better the system? The answer is that first of all there is more of interest in phonology than distinctiveness (which is perhaps the primary lesson that generative phonology has taught us); and second, that a dogmatic adherence to the principle of reduction of primes can cause loss of insight as well as gain in 'economy'. The real question is: which is more important?

That is: [±ling] is in no sense a 'neutralizing' feature, or a conflation of distinctive oppositions, because it does not exist on the same level as the (primary) DISTINCTIVE features. It appears to do so, of course: since it subsumes both [+cor] and [+high] on consonants, and [+high] on vowels, so as to define dentals, palatals, velars, and high vowels as a natural class distinct from all other classes of segments.

The impression of neutralization is due to a property of current theory: its failure to recognize UNIVERSALLY NONDISTINCTIVE FEATURES, in the specific sense of segment-by-segment distinctiveness within phonological systems. And this is just what I am proposing. There is no 'conflation' of features involved at all, on either the classificatory or phonetic levels: I assume that if two segments are distinct, they are distinct. Rather, the invocation of [+ling] is the invocation of a property that – by definition – must be present: whatever the DISTINCTIVE features involved may happen to be.

So the specification [+ling] is not distinctive, and does not affect lexical ('phonemic') specification; but it is nonetheless PART OF THE OVERALL PHONOLOGICAL REPRESENTATION (whether or not it is ever used). I am thus suggesting that it is possible for segments – while retaining their lexical and surface-phonetic distinctiveness – to enter notwithstanding into other classificatory schemata, for purposes imposed by particular rule-types in particular languages at particular times.

I therefore distinguish features which may be distinctive for individual pairs of segments like [±high], etc. from features which are NEVER distinctive in the same sense. We could for instance handle all existing LEXICAL DISTINCTIONS (I suspect) without [±ling] (and without [±ant] too, for that matter, if palato-alveolars are not a positional class: i.e. labials would be [−cor, −high, −back]). But we cannot apparently handle all PHONOLOGICAL PROCESSES in an insightful way without it.

4.7. This proposal has the effect of increasing the number of features required for phonological representations, at some level. In addition to the (minimal) set of 'universal' distinctive classificatory features there is now a new set: let us call them SECOND-ORDER FEATURES. These are never 'distinctive' in the usual sense; but they are still 'classificatory' – in the specific sense of defining potential 'natural classes' on the basis of real properties which are nonetheless not relevant either for lexical or perceptual distinctiveness. The 'classification' involved here must be relevant only for phonological rules (both synchronic rules and sound changes), and therefore does not belong either to the lexical domain (where classification is relatively 'abstract') or to the phonetic domain (where it must be primarily perceptual). Though we might observe that a specification like [+ling] could well be 'perceptual' in the sense of muscular proprioception. (I will deal with phonetic perception in more detail in the following sections and suggest still more features.)

This does of course run counter to the present trend toward minimizing features; but this is because I am dealing with a level of representation that neither *PSA* (which was concerned with 'algebraic' distinctiveness to the point of conflating lip-rounding, retroflexion, and pharyngealization under one feature) nor *SPE* (which is concerned in a 'perceptual' sense with the 'phonetic capabilities of man') deal with.

(And anyhow, to insist on the 'cheapest' possible representation, without considering other factors, may well be an illegitimate use of Occam's Razor: that excellent principle, we recall, says that *entia non sunt multiplicanda praeter necessitatem*, not just that *entia non sunt multiplicanda*.) There is no point in minimizing entities if you end up minimizing away ones that you need for decent explanations. And this is especially the case if the entities involved are physically real ones (I will return to this point in §§5 and 7 below, and to the minimization problem in §6). We have precious few entities like this, and we ought to hold onto the ones we have.

As we will see, it is in fact necessary to make phonological representations much more complex. The main point so far is that a notion like this one of second-order features enables us to define 'natural class' at any given grammatical level, in relation to a given rule-type, for a given language at a given time. And I think we can allow ANY such features, provided only that they be empirically motivated. (I use 'empirical' here in the sense of 'publicly verifiable or identifiable by means of the senses or conventional instrumentation', not in the rather eccentric meaning it has taken on in current theory: see my remarks on the empirical status of linguistic argument in the *Epilogue*.)

4.8. A proposal like this is not designed to appeal to the hard-line universalist or to the doctrinaire reductivist, but it seems to me (since I am neither) to be reasonable. Most important, it enables us to do, certainly in the case I have been discussing, one of the things that linguistics is supposed to be all about: to explain something. That is, the class under discussion turns out to be 'natural' in both the intuitive and formal senses: as long as we go out and look for what makes it natural, rather than giving up in advance. And as long as we do not restrict ourselves to the limiting notion of immutable universal features and classes, of as small a number as possible, which in many ways is the same thing. We will see more of this in the next three sections.

What I am saying in essence is that a class like [+ling] for instance is a potential one for any language: since the feature is always there to be used. But this does not mean that it ever will be, for any particular language or any particular kind of rule. But if it is utilized, we shouldn't be surprised. It is important to realize that the claim I am making is not a retreat in the direction of the Null Hypothesis, i.e. that language behaviour is hopelessly idiosyncratic and varies without limit, and that there are no explanatory generalizations. Quite the reverse: I am saying that there are more of them than we think, but of a different kind, or of different kinds. I claim basically that if the type of behaviour we associate with natural classes occurs for some group of segments in a language, we will find (if we look hard enough, and EXPECT new classes to turn up) reasons for the group involved to be in fact quite natural.

5. Complementarity: can there be more than one modality for 'naturalness'?

5.1. If the preceding arguments point in the right direction, it seems worth exploring the possibility that class-groupings of segments in natural languages can be 'natural' in different ways, depending on what criteria a language uses for grouping; e.g., whether it groups only lexically (in terms of 'distinctive' features) or perhaps utilizes second-order classes as well (or still others, as we will see). We must constrain ourselves this far: there is no point in talking about 'naturalness' unless the notion itself remains inviolate, i.e. based on publicly identifiable properties of some kind. Every grouping that meets the behavioural criterion of being a natural class must be defined according to some 'real' (i.e. physical) property, not an *ad hoc* one invoked for the sake of making a class. So far we have considered this only in terms of articulation: where classes of segments are as classes nondistinct by position, but distinct by tongue activity, and thus require recognition of that property to define them. But given this, is there any reason why all classes should be strictly articulatory?

I will illustrate with an example, the lenition of intervocalic voiced stops in Old English. In this process, labials and velars are grouped as a leniting class, with dentals excluded: thus *hafað* 'he has' [havaθ] (lexical /habaθ/), *boga* 'arcus' [boɣa] (lexical /boga/), but *glidon* 'they glided' [glidon] not *[gliðon] (lexical /glidon/). Actually, the 'lexical' forms may be historical, not synchronic: but this does not matter here. In a paper on this lenition (Lass 1971) I gave the rule for the process in what now seems to me a quite unsatisfactory way: given a phonemic stop inventory /p b t d k g/, the only definition of the leniting class, in the current framework, is [−cor]. This works, but fails to say anything. Here is the rule (Lass 1971: 22):

(22) $$\begin{bmatrix} +\text{obs} \\ -\text{cor} \\ \alpha\text{voice} \end{bmatrix} \rightarrow [\alpha\text{cont}] \ / \ \text{V} \text{ —— } \text{V}$$

Formally, this is a 'correct' statement, since I have 'accounted for' the facts: that /b g/ lenite but /d/ fails to, and that voiceless stops also remain. The rule thus 'captures' both the positional classes involved and the relation in this environment between continuancy and voicing. But correct or not, it seems singularly uninsightful. What kind of class is 'noncoronals'? Does it really have the same status as 'coronals'?

I suppose that the attempt I have been making in this chapter so far to establish 'weaker' claims about class-naturalness in phonology could be considered (though I don't consider it so) as a retreat from a 'strong' theoretical position; but it is not a retreat in the direction of the Null Hypothesis. On reflection, however, it seems to me that the 'orthodox' notation in (22) embodies precisely such a retreat. Why should a rule like this exclude dentals? Or, perhaps more interestingly, why should it include labials and velars? If in fact these two classes are 'selected' by the rule, it would be nice if there were some (positive) principled grounds for the selection. Or at least if inclusion and exclusion could both be motivated (see below).

5.2. First of all, this is not the only point in the history of English in which labials and velars have something in common, as opposed to dentals. In the OE lenition they are the weak class; in many Modern English dialects they are the strong or resistant class in the same environment. Thus in my own dialect /t/ and /d/ are neutralized between vowels to an alveolar tap of the type [ɾ]; but there is no weakening of /b g/ and no voicing of /p k/. In many British dialects there is a similar distribution: among the voiceless stops only /t/ weakens in this position, to [tˢ] or [t̞] or [s] in some cases, to [ɹ] in others ('[t̞]' is an 'open [t]', i.e. a nonsibilant alveolar fricative).[1] The labials and velars always remain. In all these cases it is clear that the lenition can be formally stated by specifying the included class, using the *SPE* features, as [+ant, +cor, −cont].

But again, what about the obverse, in this case exclusion? From an overall descriptive point of view, I think it is just as important in a situation like this to know why something doesn't happen, as to know why it does. In a developmental sequence like the one I've been sketching here, where labials/velars are at one point a weak class, and at another a strong class, it is necessary to be able to specify them as a class: otherwise

[1] Another example, this time not in lenition: in Northumbrian dialects with both uvular [ʁ] and apical [ɹ] for /r/, it is often the case that [ʁ] appears after labials and velars, and [ɹ] elsewhere: thus [gʁɒnd] 'ground', [bʁan] 'bran', but [tɹai] 'try' (Hepher 1954: 107.)

the generalization about 'shifts' of strong and weak classes, historically, would be lost.

Because of these historical relationships, it is therefore not enough to specify only the included classes in both rules: what we really want is to capture the fact that there are two classes involved, each of which is natural in the same way, i.e. by virtue of some feature it possesses. I would insist on this even though in standard theory we are allowed to write a rule and then just accept by convention that it does not apply 'elsewhere'. The idea that if you don't write it, it doesn't happen, can be extremely misleading, and force us into specious generalizations while we lose the real ones. (For a case study, see Lass 1973b.)

5.3. Labials and velars of course are not paired as a class only in the English instances I have mentioned, but in other contexts, and in other languages. And not only in lenitions, though this seems very common (as are lenition rules, by and large). I will now look very briefly at four other exemplary instances, from two other language families, before going on to some conclusions: two are lenitions, one is a rounding rule, and one is a rule of vowel harmony.

I will begin with two incidents from the history of Korean, which Lee (1971) has pointed out as involving this class. The first is a fifteenth-century rounding, in which /ɨ/ > [u] before /m p ph k kh/. The second, which Lee calls 'i-umlaut', causes fronting of the back vowels /a ə o ɨ u/ before a following /i/: just in case there is an intervening consonant which is either a labial or a velar. Examples of the rounding are *ətɨp-* 'dark' > *ətup-*, *təɨk* 'more' > *təuk*; of the umlaut *caphi-* 'catch' > *cæphi-*, *məkhi-* 'eat' > *mekhi-*.

Now let us consider the lenition of the Proto-Uralic (PU) voiceless stops */p t k/ in two contexts in the modern Uralic dialects. The table below (after Collinder 1960: 45–51, 77–88) shows the typical reflexes of these protosegments in word-initial and intervocalic positions, in three languages: Finnish, Hungarian and Ostyak (the Finnish examples are merely to illustrate uniform non-lenition):

(23)

	Word-initial		
PU	Finnish	Hungarian	Ostyak
*p–	p	f	p
*t–	t	t	t
*k–	k	h	k

PU	Intervocalic Finnish	Hungarian	Ostyak
*–p–	p	v	w
*–t–	t	z	t
*–k–	k	k	g

5.4. We can now observe the following: in the Korean rounding, as in the OE lenition, the positional class involved is labials/velars. They both cause the rounding, and they are required to intervene between a vowel and a segment causing umlaut. In Uralic, labials/velars are the weak (leniting) class for Hungarian in initial position, and for Ostyak intervocalically. Ostyak shows no initial weakening, and Hungarian shows intervocalic weakening of labials/dentals, which I return to immediately below.

What all this shows, very simply, is the operation of different inclusion classes, preferential for different environments in different languages or dialects: and these represent choices out of the possible range of natural classes – which should, initially, be defined this way anyhow, not deductively (at least until we have looked at the evidence). One of these classes, that involved in the Hungarian intervocalic lenition, can in fact be defined by the *SPE* feature specification [+ant]; this would seem to be an argument for its inclusion in the inventory as a second-order feature (though my arguments against its distinctiveness still hold). But in the other cases, in OE, Korean, Hungarian initial and Ostyak intervocalic lenition, the 'uncapturable' class labials/velars appears. ('Uncapturable' specifically in the non-OE instances, where there is a phonemic palatal series; as well as 'uncapturable' if 'capture' = 'explain'. Cf. §6 below.)

There is an interesting difference in the problems involved in specifying this class, between OE and the other languages; for OE has no phonemic palatals, whereas the others do. Thus while [−cor] is formally sufficient to capture labials/velars 'negatively' in OE, the others require a disjunction: in a language with palatals, labials/velars can only be specified distinctively as:

(24)
$$\left[\left\{\begin{matrix}\begin{bmatrix}+\text{ant}\\-\text{cor}\end{bmatrix}\\ [-\text{back}]\end{matrix}\right\}\right]$$

(I will return to this in §6.) It seems then that in languages with palatals we have to treat labials/velars explicitly as a 'non-class'; this is the same conclusion that the *SPE* (and *PSA*) features led us to in the case of dentals/palatals/velars. The notation, in other words, tells us by convention that we are dealing with something that is mathematically not a 'class', and therefore not 'natural'. The moral of these instances (which are only a very small sample) is clear: there is something reasonable and natural about grouping labials and velars together. At least natural languages do it over and over again. Yet 'the theory', in the form of its proposed feature system and attendant metatheoretical assumptions, tells us that this cannot be a natural class, because there are no features to specify it; and we know that one of the definitions of 'unnatural' classes is that correct feature systems cannot specify them. We must define labials/velars by disjunction, not inclusion, which proves they are not the natural class they look like.

5.5. But if they are not an articulatory natural class, they certainly are, as everybody knows, an acoustic one. And the *PSA* features, now 'superseded' by *SPE*, give us an empirically motivated and positive definition, based on a particular 'tonality feature'. Labials and velars show spectra with concentrations of energy in the lower formants, i.e. they are [+grave]. We will see shortly that there is more to this feature than the mere fact that it can make certain intuitive natural classes into formal ones as well; though this is not, *ceteris paribus*, a negligeable virtue.

If we follow current theory, however, we cannot avail ourselves of the potential insight here, because of a cardinal 'meta-assumption' which governs the others discussed in §1.4. We might call this the 'assumption of monolithic rectitude'. This says that if one system is 'right', then it is right everywhere and at all levels, and all others are wrong. (This is presumably a 'strong' claim, and therefore methodologically desirable.) If linguistics is an 'empirical science', then any such assumption, of course, is out of place: there are no 'correct' theories, and no such thing as 'proof' of a position. (I am not claiming, by the way, that linguistics IS an empirical science, in the precise sense in which this term is used for instance by Popper, whose influence is clear in the above statement; see my discussion in the Epilogue. But it certainly seems that Chomsky & Halle, for instance, think that it is. In which case they have no business assuming that anything is 'correct', only that it is not yet falsified.)

But even if we retreat from a 'naïve verificationist' position, and say not that any set of features is 'correct', but that it is (at the moment) adequate, this criticism of the monolithic rectitude assumption still holds. Because it allows a temporarily adequate system to carve out more territory than it is entitled to; in fact, insists that it does so. If it turns out, say, that there are phonological rules in natural languages which involve acoustically defined classes, this is not – as Halle for instance seems to think (see §6 below) – a 'counterargument' against articulatory features. All it says is that in addition to rules involving one kind of feature, there are rules involving others. This is an important point, because the rather naïve 'black-or-white' view that I have been outlining is a serious barrier to progress.

5.6. Let us follow this methodological point a bit further. If acoustic features are required, does this mean that all phonological matrices must include not only the 'universal' (distinctive) articulatory features, and the second-order articulatory features, but also acoustic ones as well? Are these still another second-order type?

The answer to this is complicated; and my version involves a complete abandonment of the 'monolithic rectitude' assumption. Why should articulatory features only be 'basic' and 'universal'? Judging from the OE, Korean, and Uralic examples discussed above, there are a lot of things going on in natural languages that suggest that acoustic features can be just as 'distinctive' as articulatory ones (and more so, of course, in those cases where the articulatory ones are irrelevant). So it is simply not true that the *SPE* articulatory features are 'right' and the *PSA* acoustic ones 'wrong', or even that the *SPE* features are primary and the *PSA* ones 'secondary'.

Rather the two sets are COMPLEMENTARY, in the special sense in which this term has been used in quantum theory (cf. Bohr 1958 for a rather non-technical exposition). Two theoretical constructs are complementary if they are both – though apparently contradictory – applicable to different aspects of the domain under study, in such a way that no complete description is possible without both. A classic instance in physics is the problem of the nature of light: rather than being 'either' particulate 'or' wavelike, it is both: depending on what aspects of its behaviour one looks at. Thus the phenomena attributable to photons require that light be particulate, but interference-phenomena require waves. This is only a problem if one adheres to a very strong philosophical monism, i.e. if one insists *a priori* that there are unique descriptions for everything.

I think that a similar view is necessary with regard to phonological features. Very simply, they are articulatory insofar as the phenomena one is describing are articulation-based, and acoustic insofar as acoustic properties are involved. The two aspects of phonology are complementary: but in a much more obvious sense than the complementary properties of light. On sober consideration, the problem of which features are THE features reduces to a case of the blind men and the elephant: it all depends on which part you're holding on to.

5.7. Let us assume then that both articulatory and acoustic representations are legitimate and necessary, since all features of both types are uniformly co-present. And let us look at the Korean rounding now in these terms. I give the rule below in two forms, (25a) in *SPE* features, and (25b) in *PSA* features:

(25)

a. $$\begin{bmatrix}-\text{cons}\\+\text{high}\\+\text{back}\end{bmatrix} \rightarrow [+\text{round}] \,/\, \underline{\qquad} \begin{bmatrix} +\text{cons}\\ \left\{\begin{matrix}\begin{bmatrix}+\text{ant}\\-\text{cor}\end{bmatrix}\\ \begin{bmatrix}+\text{high}\\+\text{back}\end{bmatrix}\end{matrix}\right\}\end{bmatrix}$$

b. $$\begin{bmatrix}-\text{cons}\\+\text{diffuse}\\+\text{grave}\end{bmatrix} \rightarrow [+\text{flat}] \,/\, \underline{\qquad} \begin{bmatrix}+\text{cons}\\+\text{grave}\end{bmatrix}$$

(Note by the way that the *PSA* feature [$\pm$cons] is not articulatory; it is defined in acoustic terms: *PSA*, §2.22.)

In (25b) we have made the class involved natural by collapsing the disjunction. I will now attempt to show that in this case we have done something else as well, by switching to acoustic features. For instance, in (25b) the class is natural, but is the rule? It is reasonable, on articulatory grounds, for labials to produce rounding; but why velars? (Except that they're now in the same class with labials, which is not very insightful by itself.) We will find, however, that the substitution of [+flat], shall we say an acoustic 'effect', for [+round], an articulatory 'cause', is highly suggestive, and may lead to an explanation of why rules like this should exist.

Let me illustrate this by referring to a useful set of spectrograms in *PSA* (48), illustrating the acoustic properties of the oppositions grave/acute and flat/plain. These are of Turkish vowels, not Korean, but they will serve to make the general point. If we look at the spectrograms for /u/ vs. /y/, we find that in the grave segment /u/, the second formant is lower than in the acute /y/. The same holds for /o/ vs. /ø/, /ɨ/ vs. /i/, /a/ vs. /e/. If we now also compare the flat (rounded) vs. nonflat pairs /y/ : /i/, /u/ : /ɨ/, /ø/ : /e/, we find that one of the correlates of flatness is a lowered F_2 in each of the rounded members of pairs in the same acuteness/graveness series, with respect to the position of that formant in the nonflat member (there is also downshifting of F_3 in the rounded vowels).

PSA defines the features grave and flat in terms of formant relations: in particular, grave segments are defined by the locus of F_2: 'when it is closer to the first formant the phoneme is grave; when it is closer to the third and higher formants it is acute' (30). And flattening is manifested 'by a downward shift of a set of formants or even of all the formants in the spectrum' (31). And it is well known also that the secondary articulations of labialization and velarization have among their effects a marked lowering of the second formant (cf. Brosnahan & Malmberg 1971: 67).

I think the point is pretty clear now: grave consonants, like grave vowels, have low second formants, and lip-rounding causes (among other things) a drop in that formant. So (25b) can be taken as a tonality-assimilation rule: drop F_2 on a diffuse vowel before a consonant with low F_2. I will return later to a consideration of what kind of mechanism might implement a rule like this: it would seem at first more natural that a rule should specify (for a speaker) some instruction that can be directly coded into neuromuscular terms, rather than a 'secondary' instruction to bring about some acoustic effect. But this all depends on where you see rules as originating. For now, from a strictly formal point of view, the essential thing is that it is possible to restate (25b) so that it is clearly assimilatory. (Though the status of the restatement with respect to the professed goals of current theory is unclear: I don't think it is a statement about the speaker's 'competence' or 'tacit knowledge', but a descriptive generalization. I would maintain, though, that such a generalization is also 'explanatory' in a respectable way.) The new rule might look like this:[1]

(26) $$\begin{bmatrix} -\text{cons} \\ +\text{diff} \\ +\text{low } F_2 \end{bmatrix} \rightarrow [+\text{lower } F_2] \; / \; \rule{1.5em}{0.4pt} \begin{bmatrix} +\text{cons} \\ +\text{low } F_2 \end{bmatrix}$$

Something like what this rule presumably effects can be visualized by comparing the spectra for Turkish /ɨ/ and /u/ (*PSA*: 48). One thing at

[1] Another case where graveness apparently produces lip rounding rather than retraction occurs in Austrian dialects of German. Here a velarized /l/ (often later deleted) causes rounding of preceding nonlow front vowels (cf. Keller 1961: 210).

least is clear: whatever the theoretical status of this rule, there is nothing *ad hoc* about the characterization either of the environment or the change. The features certainly are rather primitive, but the basic development is of a type that is instrumentally verifiable. From the *SPE* point of view, of course, this isn't saying much, since spectrograms, like the records of 'impressionistic phoneticians', aren't 'perceptual', and have no theoretical significance, at least not in the rather hermetic world of 'mentalist' phonology (cf. §1.5 above).

6. *Procrustes redivivus*: an interlude

6.1. Now that I have given a slightly more extensive justification for the use of both articulatory and acoustic features, I must return in more detail to the question of 'proliferation' of features (cf. the initial remarks in §4.5 above). In its strongest form, the 'minimalness criterion' (§1.4, III) says in effect that given two theories, one that requires n features, and another that requires $n-m$ (where $m < n$), the second theory is better.

The consequences of this assumption come out clearly in Halle's comments on a proposal of Ladefoged's similar to mine, that we admit acoustic features into the framework for the purpose of explaining the naturalness of classes like labials/velars. Halle's objections are worth quoting (1973: 932):

L remarks that certain contrasts can be described in articulatory terms only with great difficulty. It hardly needs saying that the fact that something is difficult...is no proof of its impossibility: one need only watch...a performance of a circus acrobat.

After this methodological pronouncement, Halle says that Ladefoged's examples 'are not particularly persuasive'. He instances the grouping of labials and velars (as against dentals and palatals), and then makes the following extraordinary statement:

Dentals and palatals can be naturally characterized (as was done in *SPE*) as sounds produced with the active raising of the blade of tongue toward the roof of the mouth (coronal), in contrast to labials and velars which are produced without participation of the tongue-blade (non-coronal).

The factual error here is obvious: it is not the case that dentals and palatals are 'naturally characterized' as coronals: in palatals the active articulator is the body of the tongue, not the blade. A coronal palatal articulation would be a very retracted retroflex, not a 'palatal' in the normal sense. But what makes this comment of Halle's really startling is the fact that *SPE* correctly characterizes palatals as NON-CORONAL (304, 307). So the claim that dentals and palatals can be captured as a natural class in the *SPE* framework is – on *SPE*'s own testimony – incorrect. As I remarked above (§5.4), [−cor] can characterize labials and velars, but it cannot keep them distinct from palatals. This is why I used it for Old English, which has no phonemic palatals; but it can't be used for a language with palatals. On these grounds Ladefoged's and my proposals must be assumed to be sound.[1]

6.2. Let us however consider the case of OE again, where the voiced stop inventory is /b d g/, and /b g/ lenite but /d/ doesn't. Halle is of course correct in saying that /b g/ are [−cor]; and this doesn't involve particularly the problem of 'acrobatic' characterization (see the first quotation above). But the fact that labials/velars CAN be grouped as [−cor] does not mean that they SHOULD. A grammar which groups them as [−cor] and one which groups them as [+grave] are in fact only weakly equivalent. If the goal of classification is only some form of weak adequacy (i.e. the ability to specify natural classes SOMEHOW), then Halle's point is well taken (again, only for languages without palatals). But if a stronger kind of adequacy (approaching 'explanation' rather than just taxonomy) is required, then Halle's position is untenable, and mine and Ladefoged's is better.

That is, the invocation of a feature like graveness not only 'captures' the class /b g/, it explains it to some degree. Non-coronality, as I said above, does not; since it fails to account for the fact that vowels (or palatals) are not included. And further, the acoustic definition of graveness, as I have shown, also explains why for example lip-rounding will occur before velars as well as labials: it is the position of the second formant that is central to both features. In the *SPE* framework, if /b/ and /g/ are both [−cor], and /b/ is not even [+round] (though 'by convention' we can take rounding in labial environments as 'natural') then the

[1] Allen (personal communication) suggests that 'there are however cases where one would wish to class palatals and dentals together (as against labials and velars): thus in the Skr. retroflexion of /n/ after /ṣ/ and /r/, which is blocked if a dental or a palatal intervenes (but not a labial or velar) – the former class being termed *vighnakṛt*, i.e. "interfering".' (Cf. further Allen 1951: 939ff. [= Palmer 1970: 82ff.], Allen 1953: 66f.) This is perfectly in keeping with my proposals here: the 'close lingual articulation' of the palatals and dentals (Allen 1973b: 105) seems to be a second-order feature of the type I discussed earlier.

Korean rounding is a totally arbitrary rule, as is every instance of rounding before back consonants (or before spread labials, for that matter). This suggests that in some cases 'a performance of a circus acrobat', though impressive, may be rather a waste of effort. And this acrobat falls off his wire, anyhow.

I conclude that there are – so far – no legitimate methodological or empirical arguments for restricting the content of a feature-inventory to features of only one kind. Halle simply asserts an extreme reductivist position, with no evidential (or other) backing; i.e. his is an argument from possibilities (cf. my comments above, ch. 1, §6, on the 'if my aunt had wheels' strategy). Halle in fact makes his position explicit by saying (931) that 'the purpose of theory construction in every science is precisely to limit the number of answers one might potentially accept in response to a given question'. Surely not just this? Not to furnish good explanations even if the resulting theory can give non-unique answers? This particular kind of monism is not really a worthy goal for a serious intellectual discipline; and the more interesting practitioners of most sciences seem to do very well without such a constraint: certainly highly sophisticated sciences like physics have no trouble living with non-uniqueness. I don't think, actually, that anyone has successfully challenged Chao's brilliant demonstration of inherent non-uniqueness (1934), except by assertion or the construction of auto-immune theories. It is certainly not very hard to build enough procedural (and data-ignoring) constraints into a theory to make it perform the rather uninteresting task of yielding only unique descriptions.

I see no very strong reason to resort to acrobatic endeavours in order to fight the possibility of both complicated and complementary solutions. A willingness to live with this kind of slight apparent disorder is a healthy attitude of mind, which has been quite fruitful in the physical sciences and elsewhere. And there is certainly no need for linguists to cling to a self-limiting and sterile epistemological position like this: especially linguists who say that their philosophical orientation is non-positivist.

7. Some last speculations and a direction

7.1. The possibility of acoustic as well as articulatory explanations for sound change raises some interesting possibilities for a model of this mystery of mysteries: or at least a partial model. Let us return to the question of the mechanisms by which articulatory changes might grow out of acoustically specified rules. John Ohala (1971), in a critique of the notion 'explanatory generalization' in current phonological theory, has raised some suggestive and perhaps relevant points. He suggests, along lines similar to those I have been pursuing here, that both articulatory and acoustic evidence must be used in constructing phonological explanations, both synchronic and diachronic; and that they must be used in at once more far-ranging and more precise ways than has usually been the case.

One of his examples of an acoustic explanation is of particular interest here. It is well known, as he remarks, that 'once high vowels become distinctively nasalized, they then tend to lower' (13).[1] He instances the case of nasalized /i/ in French, which developed via the stages [ĩn] and [ĩ] to modern [ɛ̃] (e.g. in *fin* [fɛ̃] from earlier [fĩ] from [fĩn]: cf. *finir* [finiʀ]). Why should this lowering occur? Ohala suggests that the answer is in part acoustic: opening of the velopharyngeal sphincter ('nasal coupling') has a specific effect on vowel spectra. That is, the result of 'opening the velum is to raise the first formant of a vowel and thus auditorily it seems lowered' (13).

Ohala does not try to connect this specifically with the attendant articulatory change; but I think it can be done quite easily, via some consideration of the perceptual mechanisms which might be involved. Let me suggest the following speculative account of how the undoubted acoustic fact might have definite articulatory consequences. To begin with, we have the fact that at a particular point in the history of French, vowels are nasalized before nasal consonants (low vowels in the tenth century, high ones not until the twelfth: cf. Pope 1934, ch. XI). Later on, final nasal consonants are deleted, and nasalized vowels are denasalized before intervocalic nasals.

The crux is the nature of an input stimulus (say for a child acquiring the language) like [ĩ]. A child hearing the [ĩ] that the adult speaker is producing receives a rather complex input: he hears the vowel [i], the special resonance produced by nasal coupling, and the further special effect of that coupling, raising of the first formant. Thus the speaker's articulatory [ĩ] may sound like a conjunction of a lower vowel, say [ẹ], and nasalization, [~].

[1] This is a tendency, not a universal necessity. Thus in some dialects of U.S. English, nasalized vowels raise (there is a merger of /ɛ/ and /ɩ/ in [ɩə] in *hem, him* as well as *pen, pin* (cf. §2.4.2 above. The change discussed there seems to be due to linguality; this one to nasalization.)

The child takes both these facts – the nasality, and the perceived vowel which is lower than the articulated one – and puts them together in his articulatory programme. And what he comes out with, reasonably enough, is [ẽ̞]. He has preserved the nasalization, but disjoined one of its acoustic concomitants from it, and reinterpreted this as a different articulatory gesture. So he produces not only a nasalized vowel that sounds lower than its tongue position is, but a nasalized vowel that is in fact lower than his input sounds. If something like this were to continue for a while, even by very small stages, it is easy to see how we might eventually arrive at [ɛ̃].[1]

7.2. It may be possible, that is, for changes to take place through a hearer's mis-sorting of output cues. In this case, he takes two simultaneous properties of a segment, and in effect treats them as two independent parameters. It is also, I suspect, possible for something virtually the inverse of this to happen: that is, a hearer can perhaps take two acoustic cues in sequence, and collapse them.

A possible example of this may be the rounding of /ɨ/ before velars in Middle Korean, discussed above (§§5.3, 5.7). It is clear that /ɨ/ has a lower F_2 than /i/ (by virtue of its graveness) and that /u/ has a lower one than /ɨ/, since /u/ is essentially a rounded /ɨ/ (in the dialect of the author of the paper referred to above, /ɨ/ is realized as [ɯ̈]). It is further the case that there will be a lowering of the second formant in the transition to a consonant with a low second formant. There will thus be a falling F_2 transition between /ɨ/ and /p k/ which would not occur between /ɨ/ and /t c/. In other words, the transition between /ɨ/ and /k/ is '/u/-coloured', since the [+flat] /u/ is (acoustically) a [−flat] /ɨ/ with flattening. Might it then be the case that the hearer could read the dropping of the second formant back into the preceding vowel? That is, he takes two phenomena that appear in the output in temporal sequence, and reinterprets them as simultaneous properties. He extrapolates the lowered second formant back from the preconsonantal transition into the vowel whose articulation ends with it, and then adjusts the vowel (presumably through

[1] We might ask why the process stops at [ɛ̃]: why not go on to [æ̃], [ã]? I suppose that if we can ask why sound changes stop, the answer must depend on systemic factors in some cases. This may be one: perhaps [æ̃] is impossible because French has no non-nasalized [æ], whereas it does have [ɛ] and [e]. Or perhaps [æ̃] and [ã] would be perceptually too similar to the already present [ɑ̃]. Obviously this is an important question, but my argument here (such as it is) does not depend on my ability to answer it. (It is interesting, by the way, that English speakers often substitute [æ̃] for [ɛ̃] when learning or speaking French; I have even heard [ã].)

monitoring) so that it becomes the nearest grave vowel with a lower F_2 than /ɨ/, i.e. /u/.

The mention of monitoring brings up another point: must we assume that the locus of this kind of perceptual 'error' is restricted to situations in which there is at least a 'speaker' and a 'hearer'? I don't see why we need necessarily invoke any 'intergeneration' or other interpersonal transmission for the explanation of changes like this. For clearly the two poles of any act of language transmission are present by definition in any normal user of language. That is, since speakers have the capacity for short term monitoring (and correction) of their own output signals, any speaker is a kind of cybernetic network. The same effects that can be ambiguously or incorrectly interpreted on the basis of someone else's output could in principle be handled the same way by a speaker on the basis of his own output.

This is of course speculation: but I raise it just to suggest that there is no compelling reason why all change should take place in the (interpersonal) transmission of language: why can't some at least take its origin from the vicissitudes of use?

7.3. Let us note that none of the speculations immediately above (or in the rest of this chapter) are intended as a 'new theory'. They are only examples of the kind of hypotheses that might be worth looking at if we are going to develop one. My whole argument has been pointing in one direction: toward opening up the universe of phenomena available to investigation. This expansion of the relevant could have the desirable effect of enabling us to look at more things that might have consequences for linguistic theory. I propose then, as a beginning, that we take seriously some kind of expansion of the feature inventory like the one I have been discussing.

We may take the conditions defining the possible phonological features, and the rules they may enter into, as something of this kind:

(i) If a feature – regardless of its modality (e.g. acoustic, articulatory) – is an empirically verifiable property of a segment or group of segments, then it appears by definition in phonological representations.

(ii) It is therefore potentially available for defining 'natural classes' in phonological rules.

(iii) Not all features necessarily ever have a (purely) 'distinctive' function; some never do. But they are nonetheless present if they meet condition (i).

(iv) Given the universe of features, there will be rules of an appropriate type to define them; and these rules – even the ones involving in principle nondistinctive features – will occur in phonological derivations. In a model based on these conditions, the representation for a segment like /k/ might well look something like this (features in parentheses are in principle nondistinctive):

(27)
$$\begin{bmatrix} +\text{obs} & +\text{grave} \\ +\text{cons} & +\text{compact} \\ -\text{cor} & -\text{diffuse} \\ +\text{high} & -\text{flat} \\ +\text{back} & \vdots \\ -\text{cont} & \\ -\text{voice} & \\ (-\text{ant}) & \\ (+\text{ling}) & \\ \vdots & \end{bmatrix}$$

Any one of these features could be utilized by rules at any stage of derivation; the lexicon would be more complex, and we would need more redundancy rules (three sets, in fact); but the phonological rules proper would themselves be of the standard form, and there would be no more of those than in any other model. The only difference would be the presence of more features, of more types. And there would be no objection in principle to having, for instance, an acoustic and an articulatory rule adjacent in a derivation. (For instance, if the OE lenition of /b g/ mentioned earlier – rule (23) – were stated in terms of [+grave], it would be close in the synchronic ordering to other rules stated in articulatory features.)

7.4. Notice further that my proposals have definite consequences for the locus of phonological change. If I am right, if things like low-level monitoring can have an effect on production, or if perceptual 'errors' can produce change, then we can no longer accept the idea that all sound change is change in 'competence', the addition of high-level rules to grammars, whose effects leak down into performance. Rather earlier ideas, like those of Bloomfield, which assigned change to the lowest levels of phonetic output, and then had it leak up into language structure, must be revived. But again, only when appropriate. High level 'competence'-oriented change and low-level 'performance'-oriented change may also be complementary.

I find it a rather hopeful sign that complementaristic notions are beginning to creep into the literature. It seems to be at least heuristically valid to assume that if two sets of phenomena that by common consent belong to the same domain must be described in terms of two (apparently) contradictory theories, then the theories are not contradictory but complementary. This has been shown, for example, in Schane's resuscitation of the phoneme (1971). While the standard arguments (e.g. those in Chomsky 1964, Postal 1968) against the contrast-based phoneme still hold, they hold only for the specific phenomena that generative phonology wants to explain. If one looks at other things, then there are cases where well-formed explanations seem to demand the taxonomic phoneme. Far from causing any difficulty, this should be what we expect. It is time for linguists to stop engaging in Procrustean reductions, and to recognize that serious science (or any serious intellectual discipline) does not require non-complementarity or uniqueness of description.[1] Is language really so much simpler than the physical world that its study requires theories this different in kind from physical ones?

Finally, the whole line I have been pursuing is a plea for a new orientation for research in this and related areas: a less exclusive definition of 'interesting' than is fashionable, and a greater sensitivity to the lower level particular facts of particular languages. Perhaps if we succeed to some degree in allowing data at all levels to have, once again, binding consequences for theory, we can abandon models at once too universal and too monolithic. If people hear as well as speak, then perceptual facts (in the usual, not the *SPE* sense) as well as articulatory ones have a place in phonology. And if we admit this, then we must admit more kinds of features.

We certainly lose nothing if we broaden the scope of the theory and its permitted outputs so that questions bearing on formerly opaque matters are at least intelligible, or if we abandon too-strict dividing lines between 'deep' and 'superficial', and so on. We don't after all know anything yet about the form taken in the brain by information about the 'phonetic capabilities' of the users of natural languages. And it therefore seems reckless as well as counterproductive to limit our research strategies in advance by purely metatheoretical prohibitions, with no evidential backing at all.

[1] To be fair, it is not the case that complementarity is non-controversial in physics, or that uniqueness is not required (by some, at least). Certainly a number of physicists and philosophers of science have attacked the Bohr–Heisenberg 'Copenhagen interpretation' of quantum theory as obscurantist and irrational. For some comments and references see Lakatos (1970: 145–6). But the point of view is still a respectable one.

Epilogue: Linguistics as metaphysics: on the rationality of non-empirical theories

It is a commonplace in current linguistic discourse that all significant theoretical proposals, and the cornerstones of generative metatheory in particular, are 'empirical hypotheses', or have 'empirical consequences'. The case for this has been overstated, as scholars like Botha (1970, 1971) and Derwing (1973) have shown. Indeed, Botha's careful studies of linguistic methodology have suggested that there is a striking paucity of empirical content in most standard grammatical argumentation. And Derwing has even proposed (though not, I think, very convincingly) an 'empirical' alternative. But both Derwing and Botha (along with the tradition they criticize) assume without comment that the only proper goal of linguistics is to be an 'empirical science' in some strict sense of the term; i.e. that if it is not a science like physics, let's say, then it has no real claim to intellectual respectability. (Actually Botha does not go quite this far, but I think Derwing does.) Whether linguistics is such a science or not, the arguments seem to say (and this goes for arguments both for and against the 'standard' theory), it should be.

Now claims of this kind have been current in linguistic apologetics since the middle of the nineteenth century (i.e. since the post-Darwinian elevation of the natural sciences to the top of the pedestal). Certainly every (Kuhnian) 'revolution' in linguistic theory since then seems to have taken off from some prestigious model based on current notions of what constitutes 'science' (e.g. the *Junggrammatiker*, Bloomfield, Chomsky).[1] There is certainly nothing wrong with this; I don't see how it can harm any field of rational inquiry to try to be as empirical as possible. But we must not lose sight of the fact that there are other kinds of rational discourse besides (strict) empirical science, which are in their own way as intellectually respectable, and as much part of the Western critical tradition.

[1] Note especially Bloomfield's contribution to the *Encyclopedia of unified science* (1960), and his famous 'Postulates' (1926). For further discussion of this see Wunderlich (1974: 29–32).

Let us approach this rather complex matter by way of a definition: just what is an 'empirical scientific theory'? The best definition I know of is that of Sir Karl Popper, who developed a now famous 'demarcation criterion' for distinguishing between scientific and other theories. It runs more or less this way (Popper 1968a: ch. 1): scientific theories are FALSIFIABLE or REFUTABLE, whereas other kinds ('metaphysical' or 'philosophical') are not. (This is not *per se* an objection to these theories, as we will see.) But – significantly – in Popper's view no theory is ever VERIFIABLE in any positive sense: i.e. we can never be certain of the truth of a theory. What we can be certain of, what is indeed the only kind of epistemological certainty available to us, is the FALSITY of a theory. There are no 'proofs' in science (with some exceptions to be mentioned below), only disconfirmations. Thus the whole 'progress of knowledge' in any domain is an asymptotic approach to some truth (of whose existence we are axiomatically convinced) via the progressive elimination, through testing, of false theories; i.e. through an increase in 'verisimilitude', which is not the same thing as 'truth', but is related. (For instance, correct prediction is an index of verisimilitude, but not of truth; Newtonian dynamics was truthlike insofar as it made correct predictions, but Einstein's revisions were more truthlike, and so on.)

Popper defines his requirements of scientific theories this way (1968a: 40–1):

I shall not require of a scientific system that it shall be capable of being singled out, once and for all, in a positive sense; but I shall require that its logical form shall be such that it can be singled out, by means of empirical tests, in a negative sense: *it must be possible for an empirical scientific system to be refuted by experience*. [Italics Popper's: RL]

If we accept this definition (which I for one do) then all claims to have discovered 'the correct set of phonological features' or the 'correct grammar' of some language are of course empty: one hopes that examples of these unfortunate usages in print do not really represent a 'naïve verificationism', but are merely a *façon de parler* for 'the least disconfirmed set of features so far', etc. (This may be an over-generous estimate.) As Popper has suggested elsewhere (1973: ch. 1), the 'truth' or 'correctness' of a theory is merely an interim report on the progress – up to the moment of discussion – of attempts to disconfirm it.

How does current linguistic theory fail to meet Popper's conditions? As Botha has shown (specifically for phonology, our main concern here), it fails in two main ways (though there are others):

(a) through vagueness – defining basic entities in such a way that they are untestable even in principle, i.e. they have no empirical consequences;

(b) through 'blocking devices', theoretical artifices that prevent disconfirmation even in the face of contradictory empirical evidence.

The latter point is painstakingly and decisively illustrated by Botha with examples like Chomsky & Halle's claim (*SPE*: 25, n. 12) that the transformational cycle is a 'universal'; this is blocked by the rider that it may 'apply vacuously' in certain languages. Botha also examines in detail the use of artifices like exception-features or revised underlying representations which make rules work where they otherwise would fail, but which are inaccessible to any kind of empirical examination (see Botha 1971: 212–15, 220–4).

These problems are not too serious, however; a vague theory can be made accountable to experience by increasing its precision, and a theory with blocking devices can be made disconfirmable-in-fact if it is already disconfirmable-in-principle, by removing the devices. But more serious difficulties arise where the lack of disconfirmability is due not to vagueness or 'self-immunization', but to the nature of the theory itself. Are such theories of any use?

If refutability is the hallmark of scientific theories, and if the empirical content of a theory is in direct proportion to its refutability, what are we to make of the majority of theoretical proposals in linguistics (leaving aside those which Botha deals with), both synchronic and diachronic? It is quite clear that many of them are unfalsifiable for structural reasons. That is, they make claims for which no 'crucial experiment' or even reasonable testing procedure can be devised. Take for instance, to bring this home to my own concerns, my proposal for 'metarules' (ch. 2), my argument for vowel-clusters in English (ch. 1), or my reconstructions of the history of ME /a/ (ch. 4), and the evolution of the Dentdale vowel system (ch. 3). As far as I can see, the arguments I have constructed in these cases, like the *SPE* arguments for lexical /ǣ/ in English, or the synchronic vowel shift, cannot be falsified in any reasonable sense of the term: that is, by confrontation with 'experience'. And since they cannot, in the nature of scientific discourse, be fully 'verified' or 'justified', what are we to do with them? What is all the argument about?[1]

[1] This holds, as far as I can see, for nearly all arguments in generative phonology, especially those, like the ones for /ǣ/ and the synchronic vowel shift, which are based on 'homing in' (Zwicky 1974).

I return to Popper, and another important point he makes – this time about the typology of theories. He sets up (1968b: ch. 8) a threefold hierarchy of theories, according to the kinds of argumentation they involve. There are (a) 'demonstrable' theories, in the Aristotelian sense of 'knowledge by demonstration': these are the only kind that can ever be finally 'justified', but are generally not the most interesting. Indeed, as he remarks elsewhere, they are not found 'outside logic and finite arithmetic' (1973: 38).[1] There are also (b), true empirical theories, which are refutable; and there are finally (c), theories which are neither demonstrable nor refutable, but are RATIONALLY ARGUABLE. This class of theories he labels 'philosophical' or 'metaphysical'. I think that most theories in linguistics are not in fact scientific in the strict sense, but belong to category (c): linguistics is at this point largely – if not nearly exclusively – a form of philosophy or metaphysics.

This is not however necessarily a bad thing: because it does not exclude linguistics from the realm of rational (i.e. conjectural/critical) discourse. That is, even though metaphysical theories cannot be refuted, and therefore do not have genuine empirical content, they are neither vacuous nor useless. Popper's justification of theories of this type as worthwhile intellectual products is of some interest. Thus he says (1968b: 199):

> every *rational* theory, no matter whether scientific or philosophical, is rational in so far as it tries to *solve certain problems*. A theory is comprehensible and reasonable only in its relation to a given *problem-situation*, and it can be rationally discussed only by discussing this relation. [Italics Popper's: RL]

That is: the very fact that we recognize a problem, and set up SOME kind of theory, is already an accomplishment, already a rational act. Popper continues:

> Now if we look upon a theory as a proposed solution to a set of problems, then the theory immediately lends itself to critical discussion – even if it is non-empirical and irrefutable. For we can now ask questions such as, Does it solve the problem? Does it solve it better than other theories? Has it perhaps merely shifted the problem? Is the solution simple? Is it fruitful? Does it perhaps contradict other philosophical theories needed for solving other problems?
>
> Questions of this kind show that a critical discussion even of irrefutable theories may well be possible.

[1] On the Aristotelian theory of knowledge by 'demonstration' see Greene (1966: ch. 2). For detailed discussion of 'demonstrative' and 'nondemonstrative' inference in linguistics, see Botha & Winckler (1973).

It seems quite clear that most linguistic discussion – at least of larger theoretical issues – fits into this framework, rather than that of the 'crucial experiment' paradigm of strict empirical science. Certainly most attempts at 'explanation' in the literature are not attempts to achieve 'prediction' or even 'explanatory adequacy' in Chomsky's special sense, but are rather attempts to pose questions like the ones Popper cites in the passage above. Most of my arguments here – as well as the *SPE* arguments I attack in places – are precisely of this sort. That is, they do not set up a potential experimental situation which could generate a refutation: they seek instead for some kind of SUPPORT on the grounds of problem-solutions, better problem-solutions, or the recognition of new problem-situations. And they appeal also to considerations of 'fruitfulness': given two theories T_1, T_2, if T_2 encompasses more explicanda than T_1, it is more fruitful; or if it can serve as a heuristic for identifying more explicanda that hadn't been observed before, it is also fruitful, though in a rather different sense.

I think that the word *empirical* has become so prestigious that it has blinded linguists to the respectability of non-empirical theories: even to the point where they use the term in contexts where in any strict sense it is not applicable. Botha has shown this in great detail (1971: §§5.2.3.2–3, 5.4, and the definitions of 'empirical' cited from *SPE*: 182), and I will not attempt to go over this ground again. But I would like to discuss briefly another instance, which has a bearing on the problem of identifying what kind of discourse linguists really engage in.

I have suggested that the sort of nonempirical critical discussion that Popper describes is really the 'explanatory' paradigm of contemporary linguistics: not the 'empirical' kind at all (e.g. Hempel's 'covering-law' explanations, etc.: Hempel 1966). And other conceptions of 'explanation', such as the very special use of the term by Chomsky in his notion of 'explanatory adequacy', where an 'evaluation measure' algorithmically selects 'a correct description' are too eccentric and devoid of methodological support (as well as too vague) to be taken seriously.[1] If we have had in the past to reject the doctrinaire 'surfacism' of some of the post-Bloomfieldians, we are now also forced to reject the 'rationalist' positivism of current orthodoxy: especially because it makes inflated

[1] There are numerous reasons for rejecting such 'verificational' or 'justificatory' devices as evaluation measures. For some of them see Botha (1971: ch. 4), and Matthews (1972: chs. 11–14). There is some further discussion, with specific reference to 'markedness', in Lass (1972).

claims, based on serious confusions of the proper domains of empirical and philosophical discourse.

Let me illustrate this with one example. In his discussion of the distinction between 'descriptive' and 'explanatory' adequacy, Chomsky says (1965: 40):

on the one hand, the grammar can be justified on external grounds of descriptive adequacy – we may ask whether it states the facts...*correctly, whether it predicts correctly how the idealized native speaker would understand* arbitrary sentences and gives a *correct account of the basis for this achievement*; on the other hand, a grammar can be justified on internal grounds if, given an explanatory linguistic theory, it can be shown that this grammar is the highest-valued...permitted by the theory and compatible with given primary linguistic data. In the latter case, *a principled basis* is presented for the construction of this grammar, and it is *therefore justified on much deeper empirical grounds*. [Italics mine: RL]

There are some noteworthy terminological (and therefore conceptual) confusions (or at the very least, equivocations) here. First of all, the notion of 'predicting' the behaviour of a theoretical construct (the 'idealized native speaker') is surely not empirical: there is no conceivable direct test of the 'behaviour' of a deliberately constructed unobservable.[1] Second, there can be no 'correct account' of 'the basis for this achievement' in any clear way, since there is no way of ever telling that such an account is in fact 'correct': and in any case such an account is not disconfirmable by experience, since it is further removed from experiential accountability than the construct it belongs to. Third, when we come to 'explanatory adequacy', we are even further from anything remotely empirical, because the 'principled basis' for the construction of the grammar is a function of the metatheory, not of any observable or testable reality. There is no justification here on 'much deeper empirical grounds', but rather a complete abandonment of anything empirical at all.

If the point of view I have been proposing about the worth of metaphysical theories is acceptable, then there is nothing wrong with a (partially) nonempirical linguistics. But there is definitely something

[1] It is deliberate: cf. Chomsky's famous (or infamous) dictum that 'Linguistic theory is concerned primarily with an ideal speaker-listener, in a completely homogeneous speech-community, who knows its language perfectly and is unaffected by...grammatically irrelevant conditions...in applying this knowledge' (1965: 3). The purely constructed nature of this object is becoming increasingly clear through studies of language in context: cf. Weinreich, Labov & Herzog (1968).

wrong with trying to keep up the pretence that a discipline whose fundamental principles are built up in the manner just described is an empirical science. In fact, Chomsky makes a statement earlier in the same chapter which – if we take it seriously – is an effective denial of the possibility even in principle of an empirical linguistics, as well as a model of theoretical self-immunization. After some remarks on the general lack of 'reliable experimental... procedures for obtaining significant information concerning the linguistic intuition of the native speaker', he says (1965: 19):

Furthermore, there is no reason to expect that reliable operational criteria for the deeper and more important theoretical notions of linguistics (such as 'grammaticalness' or 'paraphrase') will ever be forthcoming.

This means that the most basic motivations for syntactic transformations, for instance, are irreducibly metaphysical, and not empirical at all (let alone having some 'deeper' kind of empirical support). There is no way of verifying or refuting the claim that a sentence is or is not 'grammatical', or that two sentences are or are not 'paraphrases' – except by appeal to intuition. Which is of course circular, since this is the explicandum. These notions are therefore 'theoretical' only in the rather special sense of being axiomatically transparent, i.e. something like Kant's 'synthetic *a prioris*'.

I conclude that linguistic theory is not now, and in general will not be, an empirical scientific theory. But I conclude further that it is – or can be – a nontrivial and rational metaphysical (or largely metaphysical) theory, i.e. one open to rational discussion in the light of its application to particular problem-situations.

There is, of course, on the other hand no reason why it cannot be a fundamentally empirical science, i.e. one in which metaphysical preoccupation and discussion are reduced to an absolute minimum.[1] But if this is to be done, it will involve shifting the basic emphasis away from 'insight' in the sense in which linguists normally go after it, and restricting the purview of the field to those aspects of its domain which are capable of having empirical claims made about them. This will involve an

[1] If, as Chomsky claims (1964, 1966), the roots of current theory are at least partly in the 'Cartesian' tradition, then this further suggests that we should take metaphysics seriously. After all, the foundation of the Cartesian edifice is the claim that one statement possesses 'manifest truth': *cogito, ergo sum*. And, as Descartes insisted, nothing is less refutable than that. (Whether or not the 'Cartesian' tradition that Chomsky roots himself in is really 'Cartesian' is of course a vexed question: cf. Aarsleff 1970.)

increased concern with 'classical' deductive (predictive) explanation, and the development of a much further-reaching, relatively rigorous experimentalism (cf. Ohala 1973, Derwing 1973: ch. 6ff.).

But I have been suggesting here that this shift of emphasis would be counterproductive; it would simply impose an arbitrary restriction on the size of the domain that linguistics is competent to deal with. If we reject behaviourism and positivism, surely there is nothing shameful in the titles 'metaphysician' or 'philosopher'.[1] But it is certainly possible – and, I would maintain, valuable – to allow linguistics to be metaphysical where its questions are metaphysical ones, and at the same time insist that it be empirical where it must be: there are problems worth trying to solve in both domains. We must keep the two separate, while recognizing their independent and rather different values. To refuse to recognize metaphysical questions as metaphysical is, as I think I have shown, to condemn the theory to internal confusion and terminological subterfuge; to ban them because we want to be 'scientists' is perhaps to sell our birthright for a palatable but not fully nourishing mess of pottage. Linguistics without metaphysics would be a more, not a less, trivial undertaking than a purely empirical science.

The most important point, however, is to know at all times exactly what we are doing. As Harré has said (1972: 17), 'the explicit identification of the structure and components of one's conceptual system releases one from bondage to it'.[2]

[1] Even the 'hardest' empirical science has its metaphysical components (e.g. 'structure' is a metaphysical notion: cf. further Harré 1972). 'Pure' science or 'pure' metaphysics are simply idealizations of extreme points on what is really a continuum: if empirical sciences have their metaphysical dimension, metaphysical theories are about something. Actual 'exponents' are always a mixed bag. The real difference is emphasis: what do you spend MOST of your time doing?

[2] For a much more detailed view of the problems raised in this discussion (though with reference rather to 'hermeneutics' than metaphysics) see Itkonen (1974). The issues are treated there against a much wider philosophical background.

References

Aarsleff, H. (1970). 'The history of linguistics and Professor Chomsky', *Language* 46. 570–85.

Abercrombie, D. (1963). 'Pseudo-procedures in linguistics', *Zeitschrift für Phonetik, Sprachwissenschaft und Kommunikationsforschung* 16. 9–12.

(1967). *Elements of general phonetics*. Chicago: Aldine.

Abercrombie, D., Fry, D. B., MacCarthy, P. A. D., Scott, N. C. and Trim, J. L. M. (1964). *In honour of Daniel Jones: papers contributed on the occasion of his eightieth birthday, 12 September 1961*. London: Longmans.

Agesthialingom, S. & Raja, N. K. (1969). *Dravidian linguistics (seminar papers). Proceedings of the seminar on comparative Dravidian held at the Annamalai University, Annamalainagar, January 11–14, 1968*. Annamalainagar: Annamalai University.

Aitken, A. J. (1962). 'Vowel length in modern Scots', Edinburgh: University of Edinburgh, Department of English Language.

Allen, W. Sidney (1951). 'Some prosodic aspects of retroflexion and aspiration in Sanskrit', *BSOAS* 13. 939–46. In Palmer (1970): 82–90.

(1953). *Phonetics in Ancient India*. London: Oxford University Press.

(1958). 'Some problems of palatalization in Greek', *Lingua* 7. 113–33.

(1962). *Sandhi. The theoretical, phonetic, and historical bases of word-junction in Sanskrit*. The Hague: Mouton.

(1965). *Vox Latina. A guide to the pronunciation of Classical Latin*. Cambridge: Cambridge University Press.

(1973a). *Accent and rhythm. Prosodic features of Latin and Greek: a study in theory and reconstruction*. Cambridge Studies in Linguistics, 12. Cambridge: Cambridge University Press.

(1973b). 'χθών, "ruki", and related matters: a reappraisal', *Transactions of the Philological Society* 98–126.

Andersen, H. (1972). 'Diphthongization', *Language* 48. 11–50.

Anderson, J. M. (1970). '"Ablaut" in the synchronic phonology of the Old English strong verb', *Indogermanische Forschungen* 75. 166–97.

Anderson, J. M. & Jones, C. (1974a). 'Three theses concerning phonological representations', *Journal of Linguistics* 10. 1–26.

(1974b). *Historical linguistics: Proceedings of the First International Conference on Historical Linguistics, Edinburgh, 2–7 September 1973*. 2 vols. Amsterdam: North-Holland.

Anttila, R. (1974). 'Formalization as degeneration in historical linguistics', in Anderson & Jones (1974b: 1, 1–32).

(1975). 'Was there a generative historical linguistics?', in Dahlstedt (1975: 70–92).
Bach, E. (1968). 'Two proposals concerning the simplicity metric in phonology', *Glossa* 2. 128–49.
Bach, E. & Harms, R. T. (1968). *Universals in linguistic theory.* New York: Holt, Rinehart & Winston.
Benediktsson, H. (1959). 'The vowel system of Icelandic: a survey of its history', *Word* 15. 282–312.
Bergman, G. (1973). *A short history of the Swedish language.* Lund: Berlingska Boktryckeriet.
Bloomfield, L. (1926). 'A set of postulates for a science of language', *Language* 2. 153–64.
(1960). 'The linguistic aspects of science', *International Encyclopedia of Unified Science*, vol. 1, no. 4. Chicago: University of Chicago Press.
Bohr, N. (1958). *Atomic science and human knowledge.* New York: Wiley.
Botha, R. P. (1970). *The methodological status of grammatical argumentation.* The Hague: Mouton.
(1971). *Methodological aspects of transformational generative phonology.* The Hague: Mouton.
Botha, R. P. & Winckler, W. K. (1973). *The justification of linguistic hypotheses. A study of nondemonstrative inference in transformational grammar.* The Hague: Mouton.
Brosnahan, L. F. & Malmberg, B. (1971). *Introduction to phonetics.* Cambridge: Heffer.
Brown, G. (1970). 'Syllables and redundancy rules in generative phonology', *Journal of Linguistics* 6. 1–18.
(1972). *Phonological rules and dialect variation.* Cambridge Studies in Linguistics, 7. Cambridge: Cambridge University Press.
Brunner, K. (1965). *Altenglische Grammatik, nach der Angelsächsischen Grammatik von Eduard Sievers.* 3 Aufl. Tübingen: Niemeyer.
Buck, C. D. (1933). *A comparative grammar of Greek and Latin.* Chicago: University of Chicago Press.
Burrow, T. (1959). *The Sanskrit language.* London: Faber.
Campbell, A. (1959). *Old English grammar.* Oxford: Oxford University Press.
Carter, R. J. (1967). 'Theoretical implications of the Great Vowel Shift', Unpublished MS.
Catford, J. C. (1957). 'Vowel systems of Scots dialects', *Transactions of the Philological Society* 107–17.
Chao, Y. R. (1934). 'The non-uniqueness of phonemic solutions of phonetic systems', *Bulletin of the Institute of History and Philology, Academia Sinica* 4. 363–97.
Chen, M. (1972). 'The time dimension: contribution toward a theory of sound change', *Foundations of Language* 8. 457–98.
Chomsky, N. (1964). *Current issues in linguistic theory.* The Hague: Mouton.
(1965). *Aspects of the theory of syntax.* Cambridge, Mass.: M.I.T. Press.
(1966). *Cartesian linguistics.* New York: Harper.

Chomsky, N. & Halle, M. (1965). 'Some controversial questions in phonological theory', *Journal of Linguistics* 1. 97–138.
(1968). *The sound pattern of English.* New York: Harper.
Collinder, B. (1960). *Comparative grammar of the Uralic Languages.* Stockholm: Almqvist & Wiksell.
Cooper, Christopher (1687). See Sundby, B. (1953).
Dahlstedt, K-H. (1975). *The Nordic Languages and modern linguistics,* 2. Stockholm: Almqvist & Wicksell.
Danielsson, B. (1963). *John Hart's works on English orthography and pronunciation.* II: *Phonology.* Stockholm: Almqvist & Wiksell.
Davies, C. (1934). *English pronunciation from the fifteenth to the eighteenth century.* London: Dent.
Derwing, B. L. (1973). *Transformational grammar as a theory of language acquisition.* Cambridge Studies in Linguistics, 10. Cambridge: Cambridge University Press.
Dieth, E. (1932). *A grammar of the Buchan dialect (Aberdeenshire), descriptive and historical. Vol. I: Phonology-Accidence.* Cambridge: Heffer.
Dingwall, W. O. (1971). *A survey of linguistic science.* University of Maryland: Linguistics Program.
Dinnsen, D. A. (1972). 'General constraints on phonological rules.' Bloomington: Indiana University Linguistics Club.
Dobson, E. J. (1955). 'Early Modern Standard English', *Transactions of the Philological Society* 25–54.
(1957). *English pronunciation 1500–1700.* 2nd ed. 2 vols. Oxford: Clarendon Press.
Ekwall, E. (1956). *Historische neuenglische Laut- und Formenlehre.* Berlin: De Gruyter.
Emeneau, M. B. (1970). *Dravidian comparative phonology: a sketch.* Annamalainagar: Annamalai University.
Erben, J. (1972). *Deutsche Grammatik. Ein Abriss.* Munich: Hueber.
Fergusson, C. H. (1962). Review of M. Halle, *The Sound pattern of Russian. Language* 38. 284–98.
Fergusson, R. (1851). *The works of Robert Fergusson, edited, with life of the author and an essay on his genius and writings by A. B. G.* Edinburgh: Fullarton.
Firth, J. R. (1948). 'Sounds and prosodies', *Transactions of the Philological Society* 127–52. Reprinted in Palmer (1970: 1–26).
Fischer-Jørgensen, E. (1975). *Trends in phonological theory. A historical introduction.* Copenhagen: Akademisk Forlag.
Fodor, J. & Katz, J. J. (1964). *The structure of language: readings in the philosophy of language.* Englewood Cliffs: Prentice-Hall.
Gimson, A. C. (1965). *An introduction to the pronunciation of English.* London: Arnold.
Gordon, E. V. (1957). *An introduction to Old Norse.* 2nd ed., rev. A. R. Taylor. Oxford: Clarendon Press.
Greene, M. (1966). *The knower and the known.* London: Faber.

Halle, M. (1964). 'On the bases of phonology', in Fodor & Katz (1964: 324–33).

(1973). Review of Ladefoged (1971), *Language* 49. 926–33.

Hammarberg, R. (1970). 'Umlaut and vowel shift in Swedish', *Papers in Linguistics* 3. 477–502.

Harré, R. (1972). *The philosophies of science: an introductory survey*. London: Oxford University Press.

Harris, J. (1970). 'Paradigmatic regularity and naturalness of grammars.' Paper read at the LSA meeting, 1970.

Harris, Z. S. (1960). *Structural linguistics*. Chicago: University of Chicago Press.

Hart, J. (1569). *An orthographie, conteyning the due order and reason, howe to paint thimage of mannes voice, most like to the life or nature*. Facsimile Reprint (1969). Menston: The Scolar Press.

Hart, R. C. (1959). 'The phonology of the dialect of Hemyock in East Devon.' Unpublished B.A. Thesis. Leeds: University of Leeds.

Haudricourt, A. G. & Juilland, A. G. (1949). *Essai pour une histoire structurale du phonétisme français*. Paris: Klincksieck.

Hedevind, B. (1967). *The dialect of Dentdale in the West Riding of Yorkshire*. Studia Anglistica Upsaliensia, 5. Uppsala: Appelberg.

Heffner, R-M. S. (1950). *General phonetics*. Madison: University of Wisconsin Press.

Heike, G. (1961). 'Das phonologische System des Deutschen als binäres Distinktionssystem', *Phonetica* 6. 162–76.

Hempel, C. G. (1966). *Philosophy of natural science*. Englewood Cliffs: Prentice-Hall.

Hepher, S. J. (1954). 'The phonology of the dialect of Scotswood, Newcastle-on-Tyne.' Unpublished B.A. Thesis. Leeds: University of Leeds.

Higginbottom, E. (1964). 'Glottal reinforcement in English', *Transactions of the Philological Society* 129–42.

Honikman, B. (1964). 'Articulatory settings', in Abercrombie *et al.* (1964: 73–84).

Horn, W. (1909). *Historische neuenglische Grammatik. I Teil: Lautlehre*. Strassburg: Trübner.

Horn, W. & Lehnert, M. (1954). *Laut und Leben*. 2 vols. Berlin: Deutsche Verlag der Wissenschaften.

Householder, F. W. (1965). 'On some recent claims in phonological theory', *Journal of Linguistics* 1. 13–34.

Hulbert, J. R. (1935). *Bright's Anglo-Saxon Reader, revised and enlarged*. New York: Holt.

Itkonen, E. (1974). *Linguistics and metascience*. Studia Philosophica Turkuensia, Fasc. II. Turku: Kokemäki.

Jakobson, R. (1968). *Child language, aphasia, and phonological universals*. The Hague: Mouton.

Jakobson, R., Fant, C. G. M. & Halle, M. (1951). *Preliminaries to speech analysis*. Cambridge, Mass.: M.I.T. Press.

Jakobson, R. & Halle, M. (1964). 'Tenseness and laxness', in Abercrombie *et al.* (1964: 96–101).

Jespersen, O. (1909). *A modern English grammar on historical principles. I, Sounds and spellings.* Copenhagen: Munksgaard.

Jones, D. (1950). *The pronunciation of English.* 3rd ed. Cambridge: Cambridge University Press.

(1956). *An outline of English phonetics.* 8th ed. Cambridge: Heffer.

Joos, M. (1952). 'The medieval sibilants', *Language* 28. 222–31.

Jordan, R. (1934). *Handbuch der mittelenglischen Grammatik. I Teil: Lautlehre,* rev. Ch. Mathes. Heidelberg: Winter.

Keller, R. E. (1961). *German dialects: phonology and morphology.* Manchester: Manchester University Press.

Kenstowicz, M. (1970). 'On the notation of vowel length in Lithuanian', *Papers in Linguistics* 3. 73–114.

von Kienle, R. (1969). *Historische Laut- und Formenlehre des Deutschen,* 2 Aufl. Tübingen: Niemeyer.

Kim, C-W. (1970). 'Two phonological notes: A♯ and B♭.' Bloomington: Indiana University Linguistics Club.

King, R. D. (1967). 'Functional load and sound change', *Language* 43. 831–52.

(1969). *Historical linguistics and generative grammar.* Englewood Cliffs: Prentice-Hall.

Kiparsky, P. (1965). 'Phonological change'. Unpublished Ph.D. Thesis. Cambridge, Mass.: M.I.T.

(1968). 'Linguistic universals and linguistic change', in Bach & Harms, (1968: 171–202).

(1971). 'Historical linguistics', in Dingwall (1971: 576–649).

(1972). 'Explanation in phonology', in Peters (1972: 189–227).

Kirk, A. (1923). *An introduction to the historical study of New High German.* Manchester: Manchester University Press.

Kisseberth, C. (1969). 'On the role of derivational constraints in phonology', unpublished MS.

(1970a). 'On the functional unity of phonological rules', *Linguistic Inquiry* 1. 291–306.

(1970b). 'The Tunica stress conspiracy.' Unpublished MS.

Koestler, A. & Smythies, J. R. (1969). *The Alpbach Symposium 1968. Beyond reductionism: new perspectives in the life sciences.* London: Hutchinson.

Kökeritz, H. (1953). *Shakespeare's pronunciation.* New Haven: Yale University Press.

Kolb, E. (1966). *Phonological atlas of the Northern region.* Bern: Francke.

Koutsoudas, A. (1972). 'The strict order fallacy', *Language* 48. 88–96.

Koutsoudas, A., Sanders, G. & Noll, C. (1972). 'The application of phonological rules.' Bloomington: Indiana University Linguistics Club.

Kuhn, T. S. (1962). *The structure of scientific revolutions.* Chicago: University of Chicago Press.

Kurath, H. (1928). 'The origin of the dialectal differences in spoken American English', *Modern Philology* 25. 385–95.

(1964). 'British sources of selected features of American pronunciation: problems and methods', in Abercrombie *et al.* (1964: 146–55).

Labov, W. (1963). 'The social motivation of a sound change', *Word* 19. 273–309.

(1966). *The social stratification of English in New York City*. Washington: Center for Applied Linguistics.

(1972). 'The internal evolution of linguistic rules', in Stockwell & Macaulay (1972: 101–71).

Ladefoged, P. (1971). *Preliminaries to linguistic phonetics*. Chicago: University of Chicago Press.

Lakatos, I. (1970). 'Falsification and the methodology of scientific research programs', in Lakatos & Musgrave (1970: 91–196).

Lakatos, I. & Musgrave, A. (1970). *Criticism and the growth of knowledge*. Cambridge: Cambridge University Press.

Lakoff, R. (1972). 'Another look at drift', in Stockwell & Macaulay (1972: 172–98).

Lass, R. (1969). 'On the derivative status of phonological rules: the function of metarules in sound change.' Bloomington: Indiana University Linguistics Club.

(1970). 'Palatals and umlaut in Old English', *Acta Linguistica Hafniensia* 13. 75–98.

(1971). 'Boundaries as obstruents: Old English voicing assimilation and universal strength hierarchies', *Journal of Linguistics* 7. 15–30.

(1972). 'How intrinsic is content? Markedness, sound change and "family universals"', *Edinburgh Working Papers in Linguistics* 1. 42–67.

(1973a). 'What kind of vowel was Middle English /a/, and what really happened to it?' *Work in Progress (Department of Linguistics, Edinburgh University)* 6. 60–84.

(1973b). 'A case for making phonological rules state things that don't happen', *Edinburgh Working Papers in Linguistics* 3. 10–18.

(1973c). 'On the non-universality of "natural classes", and how some of them get that way'. Bloomington: Indiana University Linguistics Club.

(1973d). Review of P. H. Reaney, *The origin of English surnames*. *Foundations of Language* 9. 392–402.

(1974a). 'Strategic design as the motivation for a sound shift: the rationale of Grimm's Law', *Acta Linguistica Hafniensia* 15. 51–66.

(1974b). 'Linguistic orthogenesis? Scots vowel quantity and the English length conspiracy', in Anderson & Jones (1974b: II, 311–52).

(forthcoming). 'Internal reconstruction and generative phonology', to appear in *Transactions of the Philological Society*.

Lass, R. & Anderson, J. M. (1975). *Old English phonology*. Cambridge Studies in Linguistics, 14. Cambridge: Cambridge University Press.

Lebrun, Y. (1970). 'On tension', in: *Linguistique contemporaine: Hommage à Eric Buyssens*. Bruxelles: Editions de l'Institut de Sociologie de l'Université Libre de Bruxelles.

Lee, B-G. (1971). 'A reconsideration of NC/MH's feature system.' Unpublished MS.

Lehiste, I. (1970). *Suprasegmentals*. Cambridge, Mass.: M.I.T. Press.

Lehmann, W. P. (1955). *Proto-Indo-European phonology*. Austin: University of Texas Press.

(1956). *The development of Germanic verse form*. Austin: University of Texas Press.

Lehmann, W. P. & Malkiel, Y. (1968). *Directions for historical linguistics: a symposium*. Austin: University of Texas Press.

Lewis, H. & Pedersen, H. (1961). *A concise comparative Celtic grammar*. Göttingen: Vandenhoek & Ruprecht.

Lindblom, B. & Rapp, K. (1973). 'Some temporal regularities of spoken Swedish', *PILUS* 21. Stockholm: Institute of Linguistics, University of Stockholm.

Luick, K. (1898). *Untersuchungen zur englischen Lautgeschichte*. Strassburg: Trübner.

(1964). *Historische Grammatik der englischen Sprache*. Reprint, 2 vols. Oxford: Blackwell.

MacNeilage, P. & Scholes, G. (1964). 'An electromyographic study of the tongue during vowel production', *Journal of Speech and Hearing Research* 7. 209–32.

Malmberg, B. (1963). *Phonetics*. New York: Dover.

(1971a). 'Distinctive features of Swedish vowels: some instrumental and structural data', in Malmberg (1971c: 249–55).

(1971b). 'Les voyelles suédoises et la notion de "fermeture vocalique', in Malmberg (1971c: 264–77).

(1971c). *Phonétique générale et romane: études en allemand, anglais, espagnol et français*. The Hague: Mouton.

Maran, L-R. (1971). *Burmese and Jingpho: a study of tonal linguistic processes*. Occasional Papers of the Wolfenden Society on Tibeto-Burman Linguistics, IV. Urbana: Center for Asian Studies.

Martinet, A. (1955). *Economie des changements phonétiques*. Bern: Francke.

Matthews, P. H. (1972). *Inflectional morphology. A theoretical study based on aspects of the Latin verb conjugation*. Cambridge Studies in Linguistics, 6. Cambridge: Cambridge University Press.

Mayrhofer, M. (1972). *A Sanskrit grammar*. Alabama Linguistic and Philological Series, 20. University, Alabama: University of Alabama Press.

McCawley, J. D. (1967). 'Le rôle d'un système de traits phonologiques dans une théorie de langage', *Langages* 8. 112–23.

Meillet, A. (1964). *Introduction à l'étude comparative des langues indo-européennes*. Alabama Linguistic and Philological Series, 3. University, Alabama: University of Alabama Press.

Menéndez Pidal, R. (1918). *Manual de grammática historica española*. 4th ed. Madrid: Suarez.

Mossé, F. (1952). *Handbook of Middle English*. Baltimore: Johns Hopkins Press.

Moulton, W. G. (1947). 'Juncture in Modern Standard German', *Language* 23. 321–43.

Murray, J. A. H. (1973). *The dialect of the southern counties of Scotland.* London: Asher.

O'Connor, J. D. (1973). *Phonetics.* Harmondsworth: Penguin.

Ohala, J. (1971). 'The role of physiological and acoustic models in explaining the direction of sound change'. Paper delivered at the First Annual All-California Linguistic Conference, Berkeley.

Ohala, J. (1973). 'On the design of phonological experiments.' Unpublished MS.

Ohala, M. & Ohala, J. (1972). 'The problem of aspiration in Hindi phonetics', *Annual Bulletin of the Research Institute of Logopedics and Phoniatrics, Faculty of Medicine, University of Tokyo* 6. 39–46.

Orton, H. (1933). *The phonology of a South Durham dialect.* London: Kegan, Paul, Trench, Trübner.

Orton, H. & Barry, M. V. (1969). *Survey of English dialects. B, Basic Material: the West Midland counties.* Leeds: Arnold.

Orton, H. & Halliday, W. (1962). *Survey of English dialects. B, Basic Material: the Northern counties and the Isle of Man.* Leeds: Arnold.

Orton, H. & Tilling, P. M. (1969). *Survey of English dialects. B, Basic Material: the East Midland counties and East Anglia.* Leeds: Arnold.

Orton, H. & Wakelin, M. (1967). *Survey of English dialects. B, Basic Material: the Southern counties.* Leeds: Arnold.

Palmer, F. R. (1970). *Prosodic analysis.* London: Oxford University Press.

Perlmutter, D. (1971). *Deep and surface structure constraints in syntax.* New York: Holt, Rinehart & Winston.

Peters, S. (1972). *Goals of linguistic theory.* Englewood Cliffs: Prentice-Hall.

Philipp, M. (1970). *Phonologie de l'allemand.* Paris: Presses Universitaires de France.

Pike, K. L. (1943). *Phonetics. A critical analysis of phonetic theory and a technic for the practical description of sounds.* Ann Arbor: University of Michigan Press.

Polomé, E. (1965). 'The laryngeal theory so far: a critical bibliographical survey', in Winter (1965: 9–78).

Pope, J. C. (1966). *The rhythm of Beowulf.* 2nd ed. New Haven: Yale University Press.

Pope, M. K. (1934). *From Latin to modern French, with special consideration of Anglo-Norman.* Manchester: Manchester University Press.

Popper, K. R. (1968a). *The logic of scientific discovery.* New York: Harper.

(1968b). *Conjectures and refutations: the growth of scientific knowledge.* New York: Harper.

(1973). *Objective knowledge: an evolutionary approach.* Oxford: Clarendon Press.

Popperwell, R. G. (1963). *The pronunciation of Norwegian.* Cambridge: Cambridge University Press.

Postal, P. M. (1968). *Aspects of phonological theory.* New York: Harper.

Prokosch, E. (1916). *The sounds and history of the German Language*. New York: Holt.

Raja, N. K. (1969). 'Post-nasal voiceless plosives in Dravidian', in Agesthialingom & Raja (1969: 75–84).

Reaney, P. H. (1927). *A grammar of the dialect of Penrith (Cumberland)*. Manchester: Manchester University Press.

Rischel, J. (1974). *Topics in West Greenlandic phonology*. Copenhagen: Akademisk Forlag.

Ross, J. R. (1966). 'A proposed rule of tree-pruning', *Mathematical Linguistics and Automatic Translation, Report No. NSF-14*, IV. 1–IV. 18. Cambridge, Mass.: Harvard Computation Laboratory.

(1967a). 'Constraints on variables in syntax.' Unpublished Ph.D. Thesis. Cambridge, Mass.: M.I.T.

(1967b). 'Der Ablaut bei den deutschen starken Verba', *Studia Grammatica* 6. 47–117.

Samuels, M. L. (1972). *Linguistic evolution*. Cambridge Studies in Linguistics, 5. Cambridge: Cambridge University Press.

Sapir, E. (1921). *Language*. New York: Harcourt, Brace.

(1938). 'Glottalized continuants in Navaho, Nootka, and Kwakiutl (with a note on Indo-European)', *Language* 14. 248–74.

Schane, S. A. (1971). 'The phoneme revisited', *Language* 47. 503–21.

Scriven, M. (1959). 'Explanation and prediction in evolutionary theory', *Science* 130. 477–82.

Shopen, T. (1970). 'Caught in the Act', Duplicated. Bloomington: Indiana University, Department of Linguistics.

Simpson, G. G. (1964). *This view of life: the world of an evolutionist*. New York: Harcourt, Brace & World.

Sivertsen, E. (1960). *Cockney phonology*. Oslo Studies in English, 8. Oslo: Oslo University Press.

Stockwell, R. P. (1961). 'The Middle English "long close" and "long open" mid vowels', *Texas Studies in Literature and Language* 2. 259–68.

(1966). 'Problems in the interpretation of the Great English vowel shift.' Unpublished MS.

Stockwell, R. P. & Macaulay, R. K. S. (1972). *Linguistic change and generative theory*. Bloomington: Indiana University Press.

Sundby, B. (1953). *Christopher Cooper's English Teacher (1687)*. Lund Studies in English, 22. Lund: Gleerup.

Sweet, H. (1877). *Handbook of phonetics*. Oxford: Clarendon Press.

(1899). *A new English grammar*, I. Oxford: Clarendon Press.

Trager, G. L. & Smith, H. L. (1951). *An outline of English Structure*. Studies in Linguistics, Occasional Papers, 3. Norman, Oklahoma: Battenburg Press.

Trubetzkoy, N. S. (1969). *Principles of phonology*. Tr. C. A. M. Baltaxe. Berkeley & Los Angles: University of California Press.

Trudgill, P. (1974). *The social differentiation of English in Norwich*. Cambridge Studies in Linguistics, 13. Cambridge: Cambridge University Press.

Uldall, E. (1958). 'American "molar" r and "flapped" t', *Revista do Laboratorio de Fonética Experimental da Facultade de Letras da Universidade de Coimbra* 4. 3–6.
Vachek, J. (1959). 'Notes on the quantitative correlation of vowels in the phonematic development of English', in *Mélanges de linguistique et de philologie, F. Mossé in Memoriam* 444–56. Paris: Didier.
(1964). 'On peripheral phonemes of Modern English', *Brno Studies in English* 4. 7–110.
Vaiana, M. E. (1972). 'A study in the dialect of the Southern counties of Scotland.' Unpublished Ph.D. Thesis. Bloomington: Indiana University.
Waddington, C. H. (1957). *The strategy of the genes*. London: Allen & Unwin.
(1969). 'The theory of evolution today', in Koestler & Smythies (1969: 357–95).
Wagner, K. H. (1969). *Generative grammatical studies in the Old English language*. Heidelberg: Groos.
Wang, W. S-Y. (1968). 'Vowel features, paired variables, and the English vowel shift', *Language* 44. 695–708.
(1969). 'Competing changes as a cause of residue', *Language* 45. 9–25.
Wallis, J. (1653). *Grammatica linguae Anglicanae*. Oxford.
Walsh, W. H. (1963). *Metaphysics*. London: Hutchinson.
Wakelin, M. (1972). *English dialects: an introduction*. London: Athlone Press.
Weinreich, U., Labov, W. & Herzog, M. (1968). 'Empirical foundations for a theory of language change', in Lehmann & Malkiel (1968: 95–195).
Wessén, E. (1955). *Svensk språkhistoria*, 2 vols. Stockholm: Filologiska Föreningen vid Stockholms Högskola.
Wettstein, P. (1942). *The phonology of a Berwickshire dialect*. Bienne: Schüler S.A.
Winter, W. (1965). *Evidence for laryngeals*. The Hague: Mouton.
Wolfe, P. M. (1972). *Linguistic change and the Great Vowel Shift in English*. Berkeley & Los Angeles: University of California Press.
Woo, N. (1972). 'Prosody and phonology'. Bloomington: Indiana University Linguistics Club.
Wright, J. (1892). *A grammar of the dialect of Windhill, in the West Riding of Yorkshire*. London: Kegan, Paul, Trench, Trübner.
(1907). *Historical German grammar. Vol. I: Phonology, word-formation, and accidence*. Oxford: Oxford University Press.
Wright, J. & Wright, E. M. (1924). *An elementary historical New English grammar*. London: Oxford University Press.
Wunderlich, D. (1974). *Grundlagen der Linguistik*. Hamburg: Rowohlt.
Wurzel, W. U. (1970). 'Studien zur deutschen Lautstruktur.' *Studia Grammatica* 8.
Wyld, H. C. (1956). *A history of modern colloquial English*, 3rd ed. Oxford: Blackwell.
Zachrisson, R. E. (1913). *Pronunciation of English vowels 1400–1700*. Göteborg: Wald-Zachrisson.

Zai, R. (1942). *The phonology of the Morebattle dialect (East Roxburghshire)*. Lucerne: Raeber.

Zvelebil, K. (1970). *Comparative Dravidian phonology*. The Hague: Mouton.

Zwicky, A. (1973). 'Taking a false step', *Working Papers in Linguistics (Ohio State University)* 14. 100–12.

(1974). 'Homing in: on arguing for remote representations', *Journal of Linguistics* 10. 55–70.

Index

For convenience, all pre-ENE etymological categories are represented in 'philological' notations, like ME *a*, *ā*, *ę̄*, *ǭ*, etc., regardless of varying treatments in the text. All text entries are conflated under single symbols: e.g. references to ME *ā*, /ā/, /a:/ will be found under '*ā*, ME', etc. Symbols in / / or [ ] will be used only where ambiguity might otherwise arise (e.g. ME *o* vs. ME /ɔ/), or for analyses of modern languages. In the alphabetization, *æ* follows *ad*, *ɛ* follows *e*, *ɔ* follows *o*, and symbols with diacritics follow those without (e.g. *ǫ* follows *o*, and long vowels follow short). The following major abbreviations will be used:

ENE Early Modern English
IE Indo-European
ME Middle English
NE New (= Modern) English
NHG New (= Modern) High German